THE BLACK KNIGHT OF AVALON CHRONICLES

Book 3

The Black Knight of Avalon

By Sunbow Pendragon

Sunbow Pendragon was born one night, because of a dream...a dream that lasted several hours and encompassed the entire series named *The Black Knight of Avalon Chronicles.*

She dreamt first of *The Ruby Phoenix*, a tale of Camelot written from a point of view unique to this author's vision. She dreamt the entire tale in one night, and rose the next day to put pencil to legal pad and write the first draft of the books, which she read nightly to her husband after his long day's work. *The Black Knight of Avalon*, a detail of the hero's childhood and rearing followed next. One by one, the story of Camelot through the Black Knight's eyes came flowing through the pencil; every night the story would be read to a most attentive man. Every day for a year, she wrote diligently and produced this tale, the first two written by hand, from then on the rest transcribed directly onto a word processor disk. She would like to thank Raymond and Inez for helping her to acquire a word processor at the very moment when she needed it.

I, Sunbow Pendragon, thank the Universe, both Goddess and God, for sustaining our family through this refining process. I would also like to express my gratitude to all those who offered inspiration. Some of those include: Terry Brooks, Marion Zimmer Bradley, Anne McCaffrey, Mary Stewart, Thomas Mallory, and many others beyond recalling the names. It is not my intent to offend by the content within; my position is that this work is divinely inspired and was transcribed as accurately as possible.

Love and Light,

Sunbow Pendragon

Table of Contents

Chapter 1

Down the dusty, dry road he traveled, the Storyteller. Some said he was an old Druid priest, trained on fabled Dragon Island long ago, others said he had only a fertile imagination and the gift of gab. Whichever explanation was truth it mattered little; for the oldster was loved, honored and cherished whenever he appeared in a village.

"The Storyteller is coming, the Storyteller is coming!" a child's voice rang out in the warm afternoon sun. The cry was taken up by other young voices and soon giggling, laughing children surrounded the old man. He smiled fondly down on their fresh, new faces and the sweets appeared from his deep pockets as if by magick. Soon, each child had a bright piece of candy in their mouth and the oldster was brought by his young escorts to a cool, shaded seat in the central courtyard under the branches of an ancient oak tree. A cold, foaming tankard was brought by the innkeeper's wife, as well as a plate of food, while the villagers put away their working tools and gathered round him. He greeted those he knew with a gentle smile and a nod as he ate slowly and carefully until the provender was consumed, then his tankard was re-filled and he made himself comfortable. Only then did he clap his hands gently to gain quiet.

"My thanks, gentle people, for the meal and drink; I offer ye this tale in return, a story of the days of King Arthur Pendragon and his Knights of the Round Table," his resonant voice rolled over them, filling their ears with a quiet thunder.

"Please, Father, can it be a story with the Black Knight in it?" an eager young voice asked.

"Ah, but all tales of Camelot contain the deeds of the Black Knight when properly told," the oldster chuckled. "But as ye have asked, I shall gladly and gratefully consent. Would ye like to hear of how the Black Knight came to be?"

"Aye, aye, aye!" answered the entire group.

"Very well then, are ye all comfortable?" he teased.

"Aye!" the children answered impatiently, while their parents smiled at their eagerness.

"Then open thy hearts and ears, sons and daughters, and remember the days of Camelot, the Kingdom of Light," the old man began, sitting back and clearing his throat. As the people listened, pictures formed in the listener's minds so skillful and practiced was the old man at telling the tales.

"In the days before Arthur took the High Throne of Britain, there lived another King of Britain. His name was Uther Pendragon; he was the father of Arthur, and a notorious wencher, even after marrying the fair Igraine of Cornwall. During his campaigns he took many a camp follower to his bed; one night his lusty eyes lit on a dancer, a beauty whose body was sinewy and cat-like. Her eyes flashed a deep, emerald green as she danced her very best for him that night, hoping to allure the King and become his favorite. He watched her dance at his fire and his desire flared. She laughed when he suggested they spend the night together, but she came to his bed anyway that night in the winter. In the morning, Uther sent her away with a bag filled with good Roman gold and she never crossed his mind again.

When the woman knew herself to be with child, she went to Avalon to beg them to rid her of the burden of an unwanted child, but the Lady of Avalon Vivaine forbade this, having seen the child's fate in the Mirror of Ceridwen. Instead, she persuaded the renegade daughter of Avalon to stay and allow the priestesses to care for her. Their agreement was that the child was to remain on Avalon, and they would foster the child after 'twas born. The woman agreed and all was well until just before the boy's first birthday. The woman left abruptly, inexplicably taking the boy-child, who she had named Aaronn, with her and disappeared for three years. Vivaine and the Druids searched in vain for those three years and had given up hope of ever finding him until one stormy night when the elementals were at play in the skies…"

"O my, that one was loud and close, eh Artos?" chuckled Sir Cai, the seneschal to the King.

"Aye, foster brother, and how it echoes even inside Camelot's strong walls," Arthur Pendragon chuckled in return, and flinching involuntarily as yet another flash of lightning was accompanied by a crash of thunder.

"Perhaps another round of warmed wine would be in order, My Lord?" Cai asked courteously.

"Aye, Sir Cai, another cup of warmed wine would be welcome," agreed the young King tiredly. Cai saw it, the weariness of the wars on his foster brother's face and went quickly to the new kitchens of the royal castle of Camelot. Wine slowly warmed over hot water and Cai dipped out the potent libation into the heated crockery serving pitcher. A pounding sounded at the scullery door, then a crash of thunder and Cai hurried to open the service portal. He saw no one at first and made to close the door as another bolt of lightning lit the night. Cai saw with a start the outline of a four or five-year old boy standing in the downpour, clutching a ragged, tattered blanket.

"Hullo boyo, where is yer mum?" he asked.

A shrug and a tear were all the answer Cai needed. He brought the filthy tot inside and put him on a chair in front of the fire. Handing the shivering lad a leftover doughnut and a cup of well-honeyed tea, he sent an apprentice to fetch the King. A note pinned to the boy's ragged tunic caught Cai's eye and he unpinned it carefully, then handed the ravenous boy another doughnut.

"What is amiss, Cai?" came Arthur's voice from behind. Cai handed him the note and Arthur read it, with difficulty because of the soggy condition the note was in.

"To Arthur Pendragon, High King of the Britons. I give to ye this child, he is Aaronn, the bastard son of Uther Pendragon. I do not need a child to feed or care for and so I leave him in yer care as he is yer brother. I have sent along proof of his father, for I wish ye to know I speak the truth."

Arthur's eyes opened wide and he quietly handed the note to Cai. The seneschal read it, whistled softly and returned the missive to Arthur, whom read it again, then tossed the note into the flames of the hearth fire.

"No one can know of this, Cai, *no* one!"

"Aye, Artos, no one will know from my lips."

"Feed him, bathe him and tuck him into a comfortable bed, Caius. Find him some decent clothes and shoes too. Ye might also count the silverware as well," he added the last as he retrieved two forks, two spoons and a small pewter plate from the folds of the boy's rages.

"Aaronn, I am Arthur Pendragon...," he began.

"The King?" the boy interrupted without warning. "Ma said to give this to you," he went on, handing Arthur a wrinkled and ragged pouch of leather. Arthur opened it and saw within a ring, a carved ruby inset in pure gold. As Arthur withdrew the ring, he saw that the ruby was cleverly carved into a dragon and knew the truth.

"Thank you, Aaronn, for this gift," the King nodded. "Ye need not steal from me. Ye are at home now and I shall be yer guardian. Ye will want for naught under my roof, so stealing will not be allowed. Do ye understand?" he asked solemnly.

"Aye, My Lord King," Aaronn lisped childishly, extracting a purse with Cai's initials on it from his trouser pocket and handing it, shame-faced, back to the seneschal.

"I sorry, Sir Cai," he said honestly and suddenly began to cry. "I want my mommy," he sobbed.

"I know, Aaronn, but she cannot take care of ye anymore. I can, and I want to," Arthur consoled the boy, patting him gingerly on his filthy head, mindful of the lice he saw clinging to the greasy strands.

"I at home now?" the boy asked through his tears and both men heard the wonder in his voice.

"Aye, Aaronn, 'tis yer home now," Arthur answered.

"I'm sleepy," the boy yawned as he almost fell wearily from the chair. "Bedtime?" he asked hopefully.

"Aye Aaronn, after a quick, hot bath," Cai answered.

"All...right," the boy yawned widely.

"Come with me, Aaronn," the seneschal said, taking the boy's grubby hand in his and guiding him to the steamy bathhouse. After a short time, Aaronn emerged clean, dry and deloused. Cai then took him to the guest quarters, dressed him in clean soft pajamas and turned him into the warm covers.

"G'night, Uncle Sir Cai," the boy murmured softly. Cai grinned lopsidedly, already liking the boy.

"Good night, Aaronn my boyo. Sleep ye sound and welcome to Camelot."

Only a soft sigh answered and Cai wisely left a mantled candle in the room. After checking the fire in the hearth, he limped from the room, closing the door softly behind him. Things were certainly going to be interesting from today forward, he thought as he returned to the great room. Once there, he summoned a matronly woman and asked her to sit with Aaronn through the night, to assure the boy's comfort.

The young boy awoke with a start late the next morning and he lay quietly in the grand bed until he remembered where he was. Rolling from the bed, he looked for his clothes but found only a quilted dressing robe. As well, there was a kindly-looking woman in the chair beside him, leaned back and breathing quietly as she slept. He pulled the robe over his pajamas, enjoying the luxury of warm, soft, clean clothing against his skin. As he sat in front of the hearth, a knock sounded on the door and the portal opened to admit Sir Cai. Aaronn's face brightened at the sight of the seneschal and the laden tray in the man's hands.

"Come Aaronn, eat yer fill. We are going to the tailor and the cobbler today to get ye some decent clothes and footwear made," the seneschal explained as he poured some fresh, warm milk into a wooden cup for the ravenous boy. Cai watched as the contents of the tray were hungrily and swiftly consumed, down to the very last crumb. Aaronn sat back then, licking his fingers before wiping them thoroughly on the fine napkin. A quiet burp erupted from the now-sated boy and with true childish glee, the lad said with a smile;

"'Scuse me, Uncle Sir Cai."

"Ye have some manners, boyo, 'tis good to see ye have been taught well," Cai complimented. "Shall we go now?"

A vigorous nodding was all the answer Cai needed and he took a small package from behind him.

"For ye lad, ye cannot wear rags to the tailor's, after all," he said brusquely to cover the humor at the expression on Aaronn's young face as he opened the parcel and found a simple shirt, trous, hose and soft slippers.

"Mine?" he chirped in wonder.

"Aye lad, all for ye," Cai answered, unable to hide his smile any longer. Aaronn ventured a quick hug around Cai's lame leg.

"Thank ye, Uncle Sir Cai," he tried to say calmly, but his excitement was obvious. The shirt and trous were slipped over the full unders that had also come with the package, and then hose and slippers before the two were off to the tailor's. Aaronn took it all in, his observant eyes watching the sights and sounds of Camelot Castle. He smiled broadly as he marched along beside Cai, hand-in-hand, clearly at home already, Cai thought. The tailor's door was open, so the pair walked in.

"Good morning, Tailor Josiah."

"Good morning, Sir Cai. Is this the King's new ward?"

"Aye and he needs a full wardrobe of sturdy clothing," Cai answered.

The tailor nodded and beckoned the boy over to the small table he used for measuring. Cai helped him up onto the platform, then prepared to take his leave. "Aaronn, I must go for now, but I shall be right back," he said, turning for the door. He was totally shocked by the lad's utter panic reaction.

"Ye leave Aaronn here?" the lad sobbed, his whole body trembling in fear.

"Just for now, Aaronn, I shall return shortly," Cai assured him. Aaronn wiped away his tears before blowing his nose loudly on the cloth Cai offered.

"Ye will come back, soon?" he snuffled.

"Of course, Aaronn, of course," Cai assured quietly. "Remember, ye are the King's own ward now. No one will ever hurt ye again."

Aaronn nodded, blew his nose again and gave Cai another quick hug before the seneschal was allowed to leave. As he stood quietly while the tailor started his measurements, Cai gave him a wink and a nod before exiting the room and heading for the kitchens. Everything there was still on schedule and some of the Knights were now sitting down to midday meal.

"Ho, Sir Gawaine!" Cai called out, seeing the huge Orkneyman.

Gawaine looked up from his plate, where he still occasionally struggled with the utensils. The first-born son of King Lot of the Orkneys had been recently knighted, despite being still officially a hostage to guarantee Orkney's compliance to the treaty of alliance and non-aggression towards Britain and the High Throne. The short civil war had been brought to an abrupt end by Arthur's bruising defeat of the forces of King Lot, King Uriens and King Caw. All three had bent the knee and sworn fealty after the treaties had been signed. It had only been three years since that day and every year since the raiders had come: Irish, Scotti, sea pirates and worst of all, the fierce Saxons united under the banner of the Coiled Serpent of Cerdic Elesing. It being late autumn, the raids had stopped when the heavy rains had begun, as usual. Now the Knights took advantage of the slack time to rest and recuperate from the long spring and summer raiding season. Many a man had been lost, as had many a horse, Cai wondered where the extra fighters and mounts would come from to re-build their ranks. He sighed heavily and gave the matter over to the Goddess, Great White Ceridwen. She would see to the matter of Arthur's kingdom, Cai thought blithely, after all She had put Arthur on the High Throne.

"Aye, Sir Cai?" the scarlet-maned warrior answered.

"How is yer arm and shoulder today?" Cai asked.

"Ah, th' gentle Lady Morgaine roobed one o' her salves on't boot a fortnight ago, an' already it ha' stooped itchin'. 'Tis a woonder," he said, smiling.

"Good, I am glad 'tis better," Cai said warmly, having grown to like the young, enthusiastic man since he had learned a modicum of manners. "And yer horse?" he asked, knowing of Gawaine's fondness for that particular animal.

Gawaine's face fell and Cai saw the tear trickle down his young but weathered face.

"We ha' t' poot 'im down last night, Sir Cai. Th' wound, 'twas rottin' an' he were sufferin' so, I joost coul' nae stan' it nae more," the Knight told Cai softly.

"I'm sorry, Sir Gawaine. The King will replace him, I am sure."

"He'll try, I've nae doubt o' tha'," the Orkneyman sighed.

Patting Gawaine on the shoulder, Cai went to his kitchen supervisor and finished briefing her on the supper preparations, then he went to retrieve Aaronn. He found the boy still standing patiently while the tailor finished the final measurements and wrote them carefully on the pattern he had drawn.

"Are ye back so soon, Sir Cai?" he asked, looking up. "Ye have a good lad here; he stood so quietly and so patiently while ye were away. I wish all children were as well behaved," Josiah sighed heavily.

"We go now?" asked Aaronn eagerly as Cai assisted him down from the platform.

"Ye have not 'borrowed' anything from the Master Josiah, aye?" Cai asked quietly into Aaronn's ear. The boy's face fell somewhat, he produced and returned to the tailor two pairs of scissors and a box of silver sewing pins.

"Remember what the King told ye about taking things?" Cai reprimanded softly.

"I sorry, Master Jo-si-ah," Aaronn stumbled over the name, apologizing earnestly. "No more stealing!" he childishly vowed.

"Good boy, Aaronn," the tailor complimented, secretly admiring the lad's stealth, for he had watched him constantly. "Stealing is very bad, like lying. If ye keep that up then no one will trust ye."

Aaronn's face reflected his regret and the tailor embraced the boy to show him there were no hard feelings.

"Ye still sew clothes for Aaronn?" the boy asked hesitantly as he fingered a bolt of soft, black cloth.

"Of course, Aaronn," the tailor laughed. "Do ye like that cloth?"

"So soft and warm," Aaronn answered wistfully. "I like."

The two older men laughed out loud at that and the tailor handed Aaronn another set of ready-made clothing. "Here, take these as a present from me."

"Thank ye," Aaronn said, feeling the sturdy fiber and smiling brightly.

Ye gods and goddesses, Cai thought, the boy looks just like Artos did at the same age. The knowledge made him shiver inwardly and he prayed no one among Arthur's enemies saw the resemblance.

"Uncle Sir Cai, I'm hungry. Can we eat now?" Aaronn asked hopefully, still unused to having food for the asking.

"Of course Aaronn, if ye are hungry," chuckled Cai, for it had only been a scant hour and a half since the boy had broken his fast. The two went down to the kitchens and Cai heaped a plate full of roasted beef, cheese, bread, hard-boiled eggs and a salad made of the last of the domestic greens salvaged that day from the now miserable-looking garden plot that had been Cai's pride all summer. Aaronn easily polished off that plateful, leaving only the empty dish and spoon behind.

"Are ye full now, boyo?" Cai asked. "Would ye like some more?"

"More?" the astonished Aaronn asked in return. "I can have more?"

"Of course, 'till ye are full, lad," Cai chuckled.

Aaronn held out his plate and Cai half-filled it, then watched in admiration as the lad finished this plate as well, then drank a full cup of milk with a wedge of berry pie. A quiet burp and an equally quiet, "'Scuse me," followed the meal.

"All done now, Aaronn?" asked Cai.

"Aye, Uncle Sir Cai," answered the now-sated lad. "What now?" he asked expectantly.

"Ye have asked a good question, Aaronn. I have supper to attend, and ye would likely to be bored if ye stay here in the kitchen," speculated Cai, wondering what to do.

"Perhaps I can be of service, brother Cai," ventured a contralto, feminine voice.

"Lady Morgaine, truly ye are Goddess-sent today!" Cai exclaimed. "May I introduce Aaronn, the King's new ward?"

"Hullo, Aaronn," answered the priestess. "My name is Morgaine," she introduced herself to the dark-haired lad at Cai's side.

Aaronn eyed her suspiciously. "Ye come from Avalon, do ye know my mommy?" he asked slowly.

"Nay, Aaronn. I do not know yer mommy," Morgaine answered. "I am the King's sister."

"O!" Aaronn answered, longing in his voice. "I have no sisters or brothers."

"Would ye like to play with some other children?" Morgaine asked, kneeling down to his eye level.

"Could I?" Aaronn asked wistfully, looking at Cai for permission.

"Of course boyo, go and play for a while, and remember this morning's lesson," Cai reminded gently.

"No more stealing!" Aaronn stated firmly in his childish tenor.

"Good boy, Aaronn," Cai said, giving him a pat on the head. "Now, go with the Lady Morgaine and I shall see ye later."

Aaronn nodded, gave the seneschal an impulsive hug and kiss on the cheek as he knelt there with him, then he took Morgaine's hand and left the busy kitchen with a final wave to the seneschal. Cai smiled after him, already fond of the boy, returned the wave and turned back to his work.

"Gwenna, start a big batch of doughnuts for the morning, would ye?" he asked one of his assistants. "Make sure they have plenty of those good, plump raisins in them too!" he went on. The woman nodded, grinned and turned to the task while Cai concentrated on the cake he was decorating.

Meanwhile, Morgaine and Aaronn walked together to the children's school. Most of those gathered here were orphans and fosterlings from the petty king's lands and all knew Morgaine from her storytelling, they clustered around her excitedly asking for more stories.

One young girl saw Aaronn and she asked, "Who is that?"

"Yvette, 'tis Aaronn, he is the King's own ward, come to live at Camelot," Morgaine told her.

"This home now!" Aaronn blurted stiffly, unused to dealing with other children. Morgaine's eyes opened wide at the emotion in the boy's voice.

"Aye, Aaronn, 'tis what the King said," Morgaine said calmly and watched Aaronn relax again.

"Wanna play?" Yvette asked the lad and he hesitated, glancing at Morgaine. She read the expression on Aaronn's face and the priestess realized the boy desperately wanted to play and that he wanted her to stay.

"Go on, boyo, I shall stay as long as ye need me," she said softly.

The lad beamed a radiant smile and ran off with the other children. They taught him all the games willingly and the group played for over two hours without incident. Finally, the bell sounded for dismissal and the other children ran off to their quarters where their caretakers waited to bathe and dress them for supper. Aaronn watched them run off together, laughing and giggling and turned to Morgaine with a forlorn face.

"I go too?" he asked, tears forming in his green eyes.

"Today, ye are with me, Aaronn," she told him and held out her arms to the boy. Aaronn rushed to her and the Avalon priestess let him bury his tearful face in her shoulder.

"I miss my mommy," he whispered through the tears.

"I know, Aaronn, but she cannot be with ye anymore. We are yer family now," Morgaine crooned, hoping to soothe the boy's fears.

"Why?" he sobbed. "She not love me?"

"Aaronn, I am certain yer mother cares for ye greatly, otherwise she would not have brought ye here for fostering. Ye are home, Aaronn, and Ceridwen is thy Mother now," Morgaine said to the now-quiet boy. He shed a few more tears, then dried his eyes on Morgaine's sleeve and blew his nose on the cloth Cai had given him.

"We go to supper now?" he asked at last.

Morgaine laughed and hugged him close. "Of course Aaronn and after ye clean up, we will go to table."

Aaronn nodded as a slight smiled tugged at the corners of his mouth. The two returned to Aaronn's quarters, Morgaine following Aaronn who found the room without hesitation; she waited outside while Aaronn quickly stripped, cleaned up and pulled on his gifts from the tailor. He emerged a short time later, dressed and freshly washed.

"Ye remembered to wash, Aaronn!" she exclaimed, patting him on the head. "Good boy!"

He beamed and took Morgaine's hand as they walked down to the dining hall. The children's table was closest to the kitchens and the supper was just being brought out as they arrived. Morgaine sat beside Aaronn and helped him load his plate, then stayed his hand when the boy, unaccustomed to group dining, began to eat before Arthur gave the blessing.

"Great Mother-Father God, Omega and Alpha, grant Thy blessing on this food and upon all those who partake of it. Thank ye, Mother Ceridwen, for Thy Blessing upon Thy people and Thy land. Blessed be all Life," the young King intoned.

"So mote it be," answered the company, then the meal was served. Large bowls were set out and thick pease porridge, seasoned heavily with garlic, basilica, oregano, thyme and bay leaves was ladled in. Hearty wheat bread, made from coarsely ground flour, accompanied the soup along with slices of various cheeses and cups of milk were made available to those who wished it.

"Good news, My King and Companions, we have finally finished the first batches of cheese, even now the wheels are aging in the cold cellar. 'Tis one thing less that we will have to barter for," Cai cheerily announced.

"How long 'till they are done?" asked the King.

"At least four months, My Lord," Cai answered.

"No sooner than that?" asked Sir Tristan.

"Sorry, Tristan, but 'twill take that long to mellow them enough for consumption," Cai answered.

"We are all looking forward to the blessed day," Arthur quipped dryly. A ragged chuckle went around the Company and they fell back to eating the homey, delicious fare. When the meal was finished, Arthur turned to Morgaine.

"Will ye sing for us while we eat the cake Cai made for dessert; something soft and sweet, before we go off to bed?" he asked of Morgaine, hoping she would be agreeable

"Of course, my brother," Morgaine laughed softly as she turned to Aaronn. "Will ye be all right without me beside ye?" she asked.

"Aaronn sleep here tonight?" he asked quietly, indicating the dining hall.

"Of course not, ye will sleep in yer room," Morgaine told him, wondering about his former life.

"Good, these benches are hard," Aaronn answered, stuffing a piece of cake neatly into his mouth and chewing contentedly. Morgaine's harp was brought and the Company settled back in their seats and prepared to enjoy the woman's singing. After about half an hour into Morgaine's performance, Aaronn joined the rest of the youngsters in huge yawns.

"Come Aaronn, time for bed." murmured Cai's voice into the sleepy lad's ear.

"Nay, want to wait for sister Morgaine," the boy protested sleepily.

"Yer almost asleep where ye sit boyo, now come along with me," Cai stated firmly, but gently and took the boy's hand into his own.

"All…right," Aaronn agreed reluctantly.

"Good lad, ye will have many an opportunity to hear Morgaine's singing," Cai told him.

"Hope…so, she is pretty," Aaronn answered. Cai got him back to his room, helped him undress and clean up then tucked the coverlet around him.

"G'night, Uncle Cai," Aaronn murmured sleepily, giving the man a gentle and affectionate hug around the neck before settling into a comfortable sleeping position. Cai smiled and sat beside him on the bed, waiting until the rhythm of his breathing steadied and quieted, assuring Cai that the boy was truly asleep. The seneschal banked the fire and checked the night candle, glanced at the sleeping lad; then slipped noiselessly from the room, closing the door behind him with a barely audible click.

Returning to the kitchen, Cai gave the instructions to the night cook and retired to his own chambers. He had only begun the supply requisition lists when Morgaine entered the room and closed the door meaningfully behind her.

"How did Uther's bastard son come to be here?" she asked, point-blank.

"Whoever do ye mean?" Cai replied innocently.

"Caius Ectorius, 'tis I, Morgaine of Avalon," she replied, just a bit irritated. "I cared for Artos for a little while before the Merlin took him away. I know what young Pendragon seed looks like."

"'Tis Artos ye need to ask, he ordered me not to discuss Aaronn with anyone. I could not...," Cai protested.

"I am a priestess of the Mother, Cai, I know how to keep secrets," Morgaine laughed.

Cai looked at her, then shook his head. "Ye will have to ask Artos," he replied, stubbornly keeping to his word.

"He is right to trust ye so," Morgaine said approvingly. "Forgive my prying."

"Nonsense," Cai snorted, relieved that she had dropped the subject. "Ye are only asking the wrong person the right questions."

They both laughed outright at that and embraced warmly, wishing each other a good sleep and pleasant dreams. Cai went to bed while Morgaine went directly to Arthur's quarters and knocked.

"Aye?" he answered.

"'Tis Morgaine, Artos. I need to see ye, right now," she told him quietly through the door. She heard footsteps and the click of a lock before the door swung open to admit her. She entered, closed and locked the door, then turned to the young King. He was older now, visibly and his once sunny-blonde hair had darkened to honey-gold by the years spent under mail and helm. His deep blue eyes were bloodshot and red-rimmed from exhaustion, his once boyish physique had broadened and bulked from the many battles he had fought in the last three years.

"What is it, sister? I am losing sleep," he asked, shortly.

"When did Uther Pendragon's bastard son come to Camelot?" she asked bluntly in return. He blinked and then smiled.

"I should have known ye would be the first one to figure it out, sister," he chuckled ruefully. "He was left outside my scullery door last night, during that lightning and thunder storm, a note and token pinned to the filthy rags he wore," Arthur told her, showing her the ring.

"He has the Sight, ye know," she told him. "He should go to the Druids."

"I agree and as soon as he is mentally and physically ready, I shall send him there. 'Till then, however, he is in desperate need of a bit of stability in his life," Arthur said with a sigh.

"Agreed," Morgaine nodded. "Shall I work with him?"

"He needs the company of other children for a while, I think. He seems to speak well enough for his age, but I am sure he does not read or write. School will be good for him, aye?" Arthur asked thoughtfully.

"Aye, a beginning must be made in his education, both formal and social. Goddess only knows what he has been through for the last three years," Morgaine agreed. "He played very nicely with the other children in the school today."

"Good, then he can start in a few days. 'Till then, would ye look after him for me?"

"Of course, my royal brother, I should be only too happy to do so. He is a bright boy and eager to learn," Morgaine laughed. "He showed me the way back to his room from the schoolyard by memory this afternoon," she told Arthur.

"After only one day?" he exclaimed, surprised. "He does have a good memory."

"Aye, it should be very helpful to him later," Morgaine commented and experienced a brief flash of Sight, a short series of pictures of Aaronn as an adult, dressed in black and aboard a black steed.

"Are ye well, sister?" Arthur asked.

"The Sight...aye, I am well, brother," Morgaine faltered.

"What saw ye?" the young King asked in a hushed voice as he assisted her into a chair.

"'Twas Aaronn, all grown up and riding a black steed, dressed all in black." The two stared at each other for a long moment before Morgaine wondered aloud; "What has the Goddess sent ye, Arthur Pendragon?"

"Only time will tell, sister," Arthur answered, wonder in his tone. "The Goddess' wisdom cannot be questioned, only observed and enacted, as Vivaine has so often told me."

"Aye," was all that Morgaine could answer as she rose and went to the door. "Good night, brother mine."

"Sleep ye sound, sister," he answered, closing the door behind her.

Chapter 2

Aaronn slept sound and dreamlessly, waking easily just after dawn. He lay there, feeling relaxed and comfortable for the first time he could remember in his young life. Being with his mother had been all hard work and bad food; never knowing where or when they would sleep from night to night, never having enough to eat, always stealing and always on the move. Now, he could eat what he wanted, be safe while sleeping and feel the love that the people around him gave so generously. A knock came on his door and Morgaine's pleasant voice came through.

"Good morning Aaronn, are ye awake?"

"Aye, sister Morgaine," the boy answered, "I awake."

She entered, carrying a laden tray and a basket of neatly folded clothes. "These are for ye, from the tailor, Aaronn. And the cobbler has also finished yer shoes," she told him, holding out the appropriate-sized boots for him.

"For me?" the boy breathed as he looked at them in awe. He had never had such footwear before.

"Of course, they are just yer size. Now put on yer clothes and new boots, then we can have breakfast," Morgaine informed him, laughing a bit at the wonder on the lad's face.

The boy delightedly dressed in the new, heavy trous, dyed a practical brown and a bright blue shirt, and then pulled on the hose and new boots. He clomped around the room several times, glorying in the sound the made on the oaken floor.

"I like my new boots!" he declared at length. "They fit good!"

"I am glad. Shall we eat now?" Morgaine chuckled as Aaronn bolted for the table, tucked the napkin under his chin and watched in anticipation as Morgaine quickly blessed the meal and loaded a plate for him. Aaronn ate hungrily and asked for more, Morgaine gave him another serving of the scrambled eggs, sliced fried ham and toast with blackberry jam, with a large cup of fresh milk. When the plate was completely clean and the cup's contents drained, Morgaine put everything back on the tray and turned back to Aaronn.

"Tell me, boyo, what ye would like to do today?" she asked.

"I choose?" he asked.

"Aye."

"We go to see the horses? I love horses," Aaronn requested.

"Very well, the stables 'tis," Morgaine agreed.

Hand in hand, the two went to the stables, which were still mostly in the process of construction. Fifty horses occupied the finished wing and they stood quietly according to their training while Aaronn solemnly stroked and patted each of the huge warsteeds. Each animal was subject to Aaronn's attentions, even Arthur's snow-white stallion, Ceincaled. All of them seemed to enjoy the youngster's presence and several whickered when Aaronn and Morgaine finally exited the stables.

After seeing the horses, Aaronn wanted to play, so Morgaine took him to the school. The other children welcomed him and as it was a period of recess, they played until the teacher called them to return to their studies.

"May Aaronn join the class? He has had no formal training," Morgaine requested.

"Have too!" Aaronn protested. "See? One, two, three, four, five, six, seven, eight, nine, ten," he recited proudly. "A, b, c, d, e, f, g,…'"

"Very good, Aaronn, ye know yer numbers and letters very well," the teacher complimented with a smile.

"Thank ye," Aaronn answered, face beaming.

The two women smiled at each other and Aaronn was accepted into the school. Morgaine stayed to help Aaronn adjust to the new situation; she stayed to help distribute the lunch Cai sent daily to the school. Aaronn ate politely before he brought his plate to the collection area.

"I go play now?" he asked.

"The other children take naps now, Aaronn. Are ye sleepy?" the teacher asked.

Aaronn thought, then shook his head. Leaning closer to the teacher and Morgaine, he said quietly; "Only babies and sick people need naps. These boys and girls not babies, not sick. Why they need naps?" he asked.

"Not every child is as grown up as ye are, Aaronn. These children's parents are dead, or they are here at the King's request. They have had to travel far to reach us and so they need a little extra sleep every day 'till they grow up more," the teacher explained, while restraining the urge to grin.

"Is school over?" he asked.

"For today, Aaronn, will ye come back tomorrow?"

"Can I, sister Morgaine?" he asked eagerly.

"Of course, every day, if ye wish it," Morgaine agreed.

"I come tomorrow, Teacher," Aaronn stated firmly. "Thank ye for school today."

"Ye are most welcome, Aaronn," the teacher said seriously, although the twinkle in her eyes belied her voice. "Good day."

"Bye, bye," called Aaronn softly as he took Morgaine's hand and left the room where the other children napped soundly.

He and Morgaine visited the squire's quarters, and the newly sanded practice arena. As the day was fair, the older boys now gathered there were working against wooden pells, practice figures, with wooden or blunted swords. Aaronn watched with keen interest for quite some time, then he and Morgaine proceeded to his room so that he could wash and change for supper.

"Well Aaronn, how did ye like watching the squires work?" Morgaine asked as she laid out a purple shirt and sturdy black trous for the lad.

"I do that when I grow up!" Aaronn stated firmly. "Wanna learn to fight back!"

Morgaine was surprised at the vehemence in his voice. "Why?" she queried, wanting to understand him.

"Too many strong men pick on weak people. Someone have to fight back for them," the boy said slowly.

"Aye, Aaronn 'tis why God and Ceridwen have made Arthur the King," Morgaine sighed heavily. "He has come to rule Britain by the Light, instead of by Darkness."

"No more hunger, no more poor people?" Aaronn asked seriously.

"Arthur will bring new wealth to the land, Aaronn. No one will have to suffer so that the King can eat, those who have been treated badly will be protected," Morgaine told the lad, who listened intently, then nodded.

"Then I serve Arthur!" he pronounced.

"If the Goddess wills, Aaronn," Morgaine reminded. "Do ye have dreams sometimes?" she asked, handing the boy the clean trous as he came out from behind the privacy screen, freshly washed and in clean unders.

"Aye, sometimes," Aaronn answered, hesitantly.

"Do they come true?" Morgaine pressed gently, while helping him into his shirt.

"Sometimes," he admitted slowly.

"Do ye know which ones will?"

"Most the time."

"Do ye hear things that other people do not hear sometimes as well?" Morgaine asked as Aaronn pulled on his boots.

"No, only have dreams," the boy answered honestly, looking somewhat fearful.

"Have no fear, Aaronn. Ye have a gift, the Sight, we of Avalon call it. 'Tis a good thing and something ye should learn to use properly," she chuckled softly.

"Ye teach me?" queried the boy.

"'Tis a better way, Aaronn, ye could go to a place where young, talented boys can go to learn to use their gifts in the service of the Light," Morgaine proposed.

"Where?" Aaronn asked, curious.

"'Tis called Dragon Island, Aaronn, and 'tis not too far from Camelot."

"Then I go there soon, want to learn to use gifts for Arthur!" the boy stated firmly.

Morgaine's eyes opened wide at the earnest statement, and again the image of an older, broader Aaronn clad all in black flashed into the young woman's mind.

"If the Goddess wills, Aaronn," she said to him.

Aaronn nodded, finished pulling on his boots and stood. "We go eat now?" he asked and Morgaine heard the faint but insistent growling from the boy's middle.

"Of course, Aaronn," laughed Morgaine softly and took his hand. Together, they went to table, ate their fill and Aaronn retired early.

The days went on like this until just before Aaronn's sixth birthday. The boy had confided to Morgaine the date he had always celebrated as the anniversary of his appearance. It was in the first week of the eleventh month and Cai had planned an elaborate party, reckoning that the lad had never had a birthday party in his whole short life.

In the midst of the planning had come a terse message from a coastal watcher of a sail he had sighted recently in the short channel that separated Britain from Lesser Britain. The watcher reported that the sail bore an insignia that was unfamiliar to his experienced eye and that he feared it was a Saxon spy ship. Arthur put together a short patrol force consisting of himself, Sir Gawaine, Sir Tristan as well as a few others of the healthier Knights, and left the morning before Samhain. Aaronn stood stoically by, as the King made his good byes.

"I shall be back as soon as I can, Aaronn," Arthur assured him.

"Aye, Sire," Aaronn replied with a very mature attitude.

"Give me an embrace boyo," chuckled Arthur.

"I dreamed ye will be safe while ye are gone. 'Tis a true dream," Aaronn told him and slipped his arms around the King's neck, squeezed a bit then let go and stepped back. Arthur grinned, saluted Roman-style and mounted up. When he looked back, he saw that the lad had imitated the salute and Arthur's heart swelled with a brotherly fondness for Aaronn.

"Come, my Companions. The sooner we go, the sooner we are back," he said and urged his horse forward through the huge oak gates of Camelot Castle. The Knights trailed after in columns of two, the gates creaked slowly closed behind them.

When the gates were barred again, activity returned to the court. Aaronn now spent all day in school, the teacher having designed a course of independent study for him and the boy was making good progress. After only five weeks, the boy's language skills had improved to beyond most children his age. He had also taken to wandering into the kitchens of late and so Cai had started teaching him the simple tasks of washing tables, scrubbing root vegetables and cleaning the easier pots and pans. Cai watched carefully and as soon as Aaronn showed the seneschal that he could do the tasks well by himself, he was left to them. As he spent time with Cai, the details of his former life emerged. The Seneschal learned how Aaronn had "helped" his mother by picking pockets, begging on street corners and burglarizing private homes. Cai's gentle heart tore in empathy as the story emerged of the years spent wandering the length and breadth of Britain, stealing a meal here, begging one there, watching his mother dance at cheap taverns and disappear with men for a few hours while the lad tried to sleep on the hard benches of the common room.

"'Tis much better here," Aaronn finished his recitations. "I am very happy to be living here with ye."

"We are very happy ye are here with us too," Cai answered, tousling the boy's raven-black hair.

Aaronn smoothed the locks back into place, washed his hands and went back to washing the roots in the basin before him. Finishing his task quickly and thoroughly in light of his young years, the boy carried the basin carefully and set it onto the drain board. The now-clean roots were given a final rinse by Gwenna, swiftly pared into bite-sized cubes before being stirred into the simmering stew pot for the supper meal.

"Can I help more, Uncle Cai?" asked Aaronn.

"'Tis all for now boyo, I thank ye for the help, we needed it," Cai answered, slipping an enormous cookie to the boy to send him on his way. The boy went quietly to his own room, where he played with a set of twelve wooden knights and horses, carved with skill and stained with dyes derived from barks and roots. Aaronn had never had toys of his very own before, so the set was precious to him. When Morgaine came to collect him for supper, he quickly and willingly picked up his things, put them away and washed up. Supper was quiet without the King and all excused themselves immediately after the meal. The castle slept soundly that night, upon the next morning they awoke to find that a viciously cold storm had moved in from the north. Sleet, driven by the blustering winds, pounded down on the tiled roofs of Camelot, Cai prayed silently and aloud that Arthur and the Knights were not out in it.

Out in the midst of the blowing, frozen rains the King and his men huddled in a group tent, drinking hot tea and chewing on dried, jerked meat. All were wet, clammy and cold; however despite their miserable state the men left on their chain mail and kept their swords at hand. Banking their fire, all but the first watch huddled under their blankets and tried to sleep. The alarm sent had turned out to be a false alarm, after breathing a collective sigh of relief the patrol headed off towards Cornwall and Land's End. They had only just crested the top of the limestone cliffs when the first clouds had come into view and the large, cold raindrops had spattered them. Quickly, the Knights had located a small grove surrounding a small, bubbling spring; they combined their small tents to make a large, common room. Sheltering their mounts on the lee side of the tent, the horses had been liberally fed and blanketed against the wind before a loose picket line had been staked for each. The warsteeds calmly ate their grain, drank a bit of the clear spring water and then had readied themselves to stoically wait out the storm.

In spite of the blustering winds and pouring rain through the night, the men and horses slept well enough, they all awoke to clearer skies and calmer winds. Gawaine emerged from the tent, sniffed the air and grinned. He could most definitely smell bacon or ham frying, he thought, and he ducked back into the tent to wake Arthur and share the news with him. Within the quarter-hour, the tent was struck, horses saddled and the men aboard them. Following their noses, they found the Inn at Land's End a bare five miles away. Arthur and the Knights laughed aloud once they realized just how close to comfort they had all been the night before. When they rode into the Inn's forecourt, the ostlers employed by the innkeeper ran to take the weather-weary horses into the warm stables. The innkeeper ran out with a tray of warmed mugs of mulled wine for the High King and the Knights of Camelot. They were brought into the warm, cozy common room and seated on comfortable, padded seats. Heaping plates of sizzling bacon and ham, scrambled eggs with cheese, fresh cake-like scones split and dripping with butter and honey, as well as fresh griddle cakes topped with blueberry syrup were set before them and they fell to with appetites made hearty by the fierce cold. When their cups were empty, the Knights were all brought mugs of steaming tea, fresh with the taste of mint and blackberry leaves, well sweetened. The cold, clammy men ate ravenously, then sat back to enjoy a last cup of the tea. When the innkeeper's wife came to clear their table, Arthur stood and handed her twelve pure gold coins of Roman mintage. She looked at the coins, gasped, then smiled and winked at the young King.

"This pays for all and I owe ye change, Sire," she said. "An' I'll not hear a word to the contrary, 'tis an honor to serve the son of Igraine."

"Thank ye, gentle mother. My temper is greatly improved as a result of this meal. I am sure my knights agree," Arthur chuckled as he watched Gawaine tuck a few of the excellent scones into his pockets. "As far as the change ye owe me, keep it in reserve in case my Knights or I need to seek refuge here again."

"Yer horses have been rubbed dry and re-saddled with clean blankets from my stables, My Lord. Nay, do not object. Ye kin just send the loaners back by messenger and I'll return yers," the innkeeper announced, striding into the room.

"Thank ye, both of ye. Would ye consider carrying the royal sign on yer door?" asked the King, smiling.

"We would be honored, Sire," the two answered happily in unison.

"I shall send the woodworker to tend to the carving of the Royal Seal on the door then. All I ask is that ye treat yer patrons fairly and keep the quality of the fare as excellent as 'twas this morning," the King requested. Vigorous nods of assent were all the answer that Arthur needed from both husband and wife, the three of them clasped hands on the agreement.

The horses were brought and the men mounted, feeling much restored for their time in the inn. They pulled out in columns of two behind the King, as they left the courtyard, the clouds opened up again and water pelted them in great icy drops. The pace of their march fell off considerably, but Arthur was determined to reach Avalon by at least nightfall. Hours passed by in silence as the horses slogged through the ever-increasing mud.

Finally, the rain stopped and the clouds parted briefly to allow for a spectacular sunset. Arthur began to see the familiar landmarks of the road to Avalon. He made the turn and the rest of the patrol urged their weary mounts forward, anticipating a cheery night on the Isle. Just as the last orange-red glow faded behind the western treetops, the Lake appeared to their left. A stranger blocked the road; they could see he was clad all in white enameled steel, even to an unmarked shield. He calmly sat his horse, helm closed, until the Knights were close enough to comfortably exchange words.

"Give ye good evening, Sir Knight," Arthur called out, impatience tingeing his words. "Please, move aside and allow us to pass."

"Why?" asked the stranger, and his voice carried an unfamiliar accent.

"I need not explain my reasons to ye, a stranger in this land, Sir Knight. I only require that ye move aside," Arthur answered, his impatience growing.

"If ye wish to pass, then ye must give me yer reasons. No man has ever yet beaten me in battle, Sir, and I must warn ye that if ye continue to insist on being head-strong, ye will meet me in combat!" the man in snow-white told Arthur calmly.

"I tire of this banter and I order ye to clear the road!" the King barked. Gawaine moved to enforce the King's order but Arthur waved him off. "I can handle this, Sir Gawaine."

"Aye, Sire," Gawaine answered and fell back into the column.

"I shall not clear the road. I am waiting for someone," the white knight insisted.

"Whom?" asked Arthur.

"'Tis not thy concern, ye lout. Now leave off or charge me if ye dare!" the stranger shouted.

With a roar, Arthur drew Excalibur and rode towards the unknown knight. The man spurred his horse forward as well; they met with a clash of steel. Arthur's pent-up frustration had at last found a vent in this unexpected bout and he strove hard against the stranger, but found that the white knight was easily his equal. This fact seemed to spur Arthur further, in his anger he called upon the special magick of the meteor-steel blade, causing it to glow brightly for a few seconds. As if the weapon knew its special power was being wrongly used, the blade flickered and dimmed, causing Arthur to cry out as if in pain, but he could not stop the swing of the sword. It clashed against the white knight's sword and sent it flying, momentum carrying it further. The young King knew its force was diminished but still strong enough to cause his opponent a severe injury. In horror, he watched Excalibur's dull-shaded blade crash into the side of the white knight's helm and break into two pieces. The man fell like a stone from his horse's back, a huge dent in the right side of the helm. Arthur quickly bent, carefully untied the straps under the man's chin and lifted the helm off his head. Blood flowed copiously from the knight's temple, Arthur saw, and he could detect no breath from his fallen opponent. Weeping furiously in self-recrimination, Arthur picked up the pieces of Excalibur and strode quickly to the side of the Holy Lake.

"Great White Ceridwen, I have broken a law most precious. I have taken the life of an honest knight while employing Excalibur's special magick, to no good cause but my own ego. I am no longer worthy of such a blade, so I return it to ye," he called out over the water and to the dismay of the Knights, he threw the pieces into the water. They arched up over the moon-silvered waters and two distinct splashes could be heard. Arthur stood on the lake's shore, hanging his head in shame and apologizing over and over again silently. Suddenly, the Merlin was there beside him and the King jumped a bit in surprise.

"Well boyo, ye have done it now," the old man chuckled wryly, pointing out over the waters of the Holy Lake. Arthur's eyes followed the Merlin's gesture and gasped aloud. There, rising out of the water was Excalibur, whole again. A large, strong, feminine hand emerged as well, garbed in shimmering metal chain mail. With a smooth motion She sent the sword flying towards Arthur, turning end for end. Arthur could see that the blade would not reach the shore, so he waded out until the waters reached his waist, held up his hand and caught the hilt of the meteor-steel weapon. Blue lightning ran up the blade at the touch of his hand, and Arthur carefully knelt on the shore after he exited the water.

"Thank ye, Mother Ceridwen, for this second opportunity! I shall master my emotions from this day forth," he prayed aloud. The half-moon shone brightly for a few more moments on the blade before the thick clouds again blocked the orb's light. Arthur realized that this was Samhain night and he laughed aloud. Truly this man and the test he had brought were Goddess-sent, he thought and took the blade more firmly in hand. Striding to the fallen man's side, he spoke softly to the blade and set the now-glowing tip against his head for a moment. The fallen knight stirred and moaned then his eyes opened wide as Arthur knelt in front of him.

"I crave yer pardon, Sir Knight. I was impatient and arrogant. I should have explained my mission to ye and implored yer aid. I have unjustly injured ye and I owe ye for that. Please, come with me to Avalon, where the Lady of the Lake will see to yer wounds and heal ye," Arthur spoke courteously.

"I could well use my Mother Vivaine's healing skills at the moment," the white knight spoke ruefully, rubbing his aching head.

"Vivaine is yer Mother?" Arthur asked, astonished.

"Aye, she made the Great Marriage with my father, Ban of Lesser Britain," the man explained. "I am called Lancelot of the Lake because of that."

"No wonder no one knew the device on that sail in the short sea!" Arthur exclaimed. "'Twas one of yer Da's personal ships with yer own sign on the sail?" Arthur asked. Lancelot smiled faintly and nodded as the King helped him up on his horse and mounted his own royal steed. "Men, meet our royal cousin, Lancelot du Lac. His mother is the Lady of the Lake, Vivaine, and my mother was her sister," explained the young ruler to his patrol.

"Ye are Arthur Pendragon?" the newcomer suddenly realized out loud. "I have come to find ye, test ye and find out for myself what sort of man ye are," Lancelot went on.

"Not as good a one as I would like to be," Arthur commented ruefully.

"But a man who knows a mistake, then admits and corrects it. I like ye, Arthur Pendragon, and I offer my sword to thee, if ye will have it."

"If ye will vow to defend the Light, the Lady and the Land, then welcome ye are in Britain. I am in dread sore need of replacements in my army," Arthur said seriously. "We desperately need remounts as well."

"My father has both and sends ye this message," Lancelot began, but just as the words left his mouth, the clouds opened up and rain again deluged them. "Let us seek shelter Sire, where we can discuss things more comfortably," Lancelot suggested.

"Aye, cousin," Arthur laughed and they went forward to Camelot as it was late at night and there was no barge awaiting them at the docking point.

Some six hours later, close to midnight, the soggy patrol returned to Camelot. Hot baths awaited them and Cai's delicious food, all the while

Lancelot and Arthur spoke quietly of the situation in Britain. Lancelot understood most of the political hodgepodge that bound the petty kings to Arthur's will and what he did not know was quickly explained. By breakfast time the next morning, the son of King Ban was thoroughly familiar with Arthur's state of affairs. As the King sat at the morning table with Lancelot, Aaronn wandered in with Morgaine and, with a delighted whoop, the lad ran to Arthur.

"Good morning, Sire," the boy stopped before Arthur's chair and knelt there momentarily. "I am glad ye are back in time for my birthday!"

"Me too, Aaronn!" laughed Arthur. "I want ye to meet Sir Lancelot of the Lake, Aaronn. He is my newest Knight and he is also my cousin."

"Good morning, Sir Lan-ce-lot," the boy faltered over the unfamiliar name. "Ye will serve Arthur, for always?"

"For as long as he is a good King, aye," Lancelot chuckled. "Who is this delightful lad?"

"My ward, Aaronn," Arthur introduced.

"Did ye say ye were having a birthday soon?" asked Lancelot.

Aaronn nodded vigorously, his excitement clear. "I'm gonna be six years old!" he asserted.

"Not yet six years old and already at court as well as the ward of the High King, not many lads can say the same!" Lancelot chuckled again.

"Aaronn, go and sit with the others now and eat yer breakfast. Sir Lancelot, the Knights and I have a lot of plans to make, so I shall be busy all day," the King explained carefully, not wanting to hurt the boy's feelings. "Will ye come and tell us when the supper is almost on the table?" he asked.

"Aye, Sire!" the boy excitedly agreed, gave Arthur another quick hug and rejoined Morgaine at the children's table.

"He is a delightful boy, is he an orphan?" commented Lancelot.

"Nay, he was abandoned at my back door by his mother some time ago. He had a few peculiar habits in regard to other people's possessions, but he seems to have overcome those fast enough. Come Lance, we have strategies to plan, horses to bargain for and men to recruit. Winter is short enough and at first sign of spring, the Saxons will be raiding us again. This year, we stop them!" Arthur finished passionately.

"Aye, My King. It sounds as though if we start planning now, we may have all in place in time," Lancelot agreed as they left the table.

Arthur smiled grimly as they entered the war room, with its huge bas-relief map of Britain, an inheritance from Uther. Aaronn watched them go, sighed and turned back to the steaming porridge before him. Morgaine showed him again how to spoon up the honey without spilling and put the sweetened spoon into the cereal.

"May I try tomorrow?" he asked plaintively.

"Of course, Aaronn, if ye think ye can do it without spilling. The Goddess frowns upon needless waste of good food, especially when we have so little," Morgaine explained.

"I eat too much?" Aaronn asked, concerned. "Someone else here goes without?"

"Nay, Aaronn. Everyone has enough to eat, but we cannot afford to waste even the littlest bit of food." Morgaine clarified the situation for him, and the lad calmed.

"Auntie Morgaine, ye spoon up the honey for me, 'till I can do it?" he asked after a few moments of heavy thought.

"Assuredly, Aaronn, and when ye are old enough to do it without spilling, 'twill be wonderful!" she replied, smiling down in approval of his decision.

"Aye!" he answered and fell to his meal. He carefully wiped his mouth with the napkin when he was done, drank the remainder of his milk in his cup and wiped his mouth again.

"I am ready for school," he announced quietly and together the priestess and her charge deposited their empty cups, bowls and spoons into the collection area, then went to the schoolroom.

"Good morn to ye, Teacher," Aaronn greeted the middle-aged woman.

"The same to ye, Aaronn," she returned, smiling fondly at the boy. He had proven to be a quick study, and his memory abilities were incredible in one so young. He was already doing simple sums with amazing accuracy, and his sentence structure had improved to practical perfection, for someone of his tender years. She gave him his work for the day and he went directly to his table to begin. The other children entered, including a new student, an older male fosterling some nine years of age.

"Good morning to ye, boyo," the teacher greeted him courteously. "What is yer name?"

The boy's attitude was pompous and he sniffed imperiously before answering in a deliberately annoying tone; "I am Prince Bertran. My father, King Caw, sent me here to acquaint me with 'Lord' Arthur," he said with an insulting emphasis on Arthur's title.

The teacher sat back, awaiting the response of the other children to the bully's attitude. Bertran was well known for his hateful actions towards any he considered beneath him and she wanted the other children to put him in his place.

"Arthur is King of all Britain," said Aaronn's voice quietly.

"Some people say so, and how dare ye interrupt me, peasant?" the spoiled Bertran answered.

"My name is Aaronn."

"Who is yer father?" asked the bully and Aaronn spoke up defiantly.

"I am the King's own ward. Sit down and study quiet, like everyone else."

"King's ward, eh?" Bertran asked cruelly. "So, ye do not know who yer father is, eh bastard?"

The teacher made to stand and put an end to the exchange as Aaronn's face reddened. Before she could say anything, the other children took up the chant, as children will without interference from a wiser adult.

"Enough of that, all of ye!" the teacher spoke with authority. "Bertran, ye owe Aaronn and all the class an apology for yer rude manners," she looked the nine-year old straight in the eye.

"I shall not apologize to any bastard for calling him what he is!" Bertran shrilled.

Aaronn could no longer stand it. The black rage boiled up inside him and he jumped onto the bigger, older boy with fists flailing. The teacher pulled them apart, with assistance from a newly returned Morgaine. When all the dust cleared Aaronn proved to be unhurt, while the spoiled Bertran had a bruised eye. The younger boy noted, with satisfaction, that the eye was beginning to purple nicely despite the cool cloths Morgaine applied.

"He has bruised my eye, I shall be blinded!" the bully railed, weeping noisily.

"What did ye expect, calling him a name like that in front of the other children?" Morgaine admonished crisply. "How would ye like it if the situation were reversed?"

The boy stopped snuffling for a bit as the thought turned over in his bright, but ill-used mind. "I suppose I would not like it at all," he finally said.

"Of course not!" Morgaine agreed pointedly. "Some things while true, are better left unsaid, Bertran. For example, in the days of Ambrosius, yer father's life would be now forfeit to the High King for his treasonous actions, allying with Lot and Uriens."

The look on Bertran's face was pure horror, clearly he had never before considered this and he began crying for real. "I am sorry, Aaronn. I should not have said that word, and I will not say it again," the lad said and held out his hand in apology.

"I am sorry I hit yer eye, Bertran," Aaronn said and took the outstretched hand without hesitation. "Can we be friends now?"

"Ye bet!" Bertran laughed. "Anybody who fights like ye do can be my friend for always. My eye is going to be positively green in a little while!"

All the other children offered their apologies as well and the classroom settled down for the rest of the day. Bertran proved to be a good student, despite the fact that his education was obviously lacking in key areas, such as mathematics. More than once, he quietly asked for Aaronn's assistance with his sums. They all studied quietly together until the lunch was served, then they enjoyed the recess together peaceably. Near the end of the day, Bertran's trainer came to collect him for his weapon training.

"Good day, Teacher. I very much enjoyed our time together today; I hope to have the same experience upon my return on the morrow. Good-bye, all my new friends," the boy said and took his leave with the astonished retainer. Bertran's temper was very much improved all that day, and all the days to follow. He acted like the prince he was for the remainder of his life and Aaronn learned a very valuable lesson: Bullies back down when confronted with their own cowardice.

Four days later was his sixth birthday and Aaronn was made prince for a day. He received presents from everyone however it was Arthur's present he treasured above all. The King took him out to the stables after a sumptuous breakfast of griddlecakes, wild blueberry syrup, eggs, bacon and warmed milk sweetened with honey and cinnamon. Once at the stables, Arthur went up and down the rows of stalls, examining each of the first twenty-five fully trained warsteeds sent from King Ban. Lancelot had also sent for reinforcements, which would arrive in the late winter. Arthur once again thanked the White Goddess of Britain for saving Lancelot's life and for the lesson he had learned that day. Never again would he use Excalibur's special powers with anger, he reminded himself as he came to the stall where a small, dapple-gray pony waited.

"Open that stall, would ye Aaronn?" the King asked nonchalantly.

"Aye, Sire." the boy answered and reached up for the latch. By carefully balancing on his toes, Aaronn was able to push up on the latch to release the door. A gasp told Arthur the pony had been discovered.

"Happy birthday to ye, Aaronn," he said as he smiled down at the awe-struck boy.

"My Lord 'tis a beautiful pony; 'tis truly mine, my very own?" Aaronn stuttered, joy welling up in him at the King's generosity.

"Of course, how else will ye learn how to ride?" Arthur laughed. "We found this sturdy boy at a burnt out homestead last year. When the farmer and his family left, they must have been in a hurry and so this lad was forgotten. We took him in, fed him up and found that he had been trained for saddle and cart. I have had no one to care for him 'till now."

"I shall take good care of him, Sire," Aaronn said slowly as he stroked the pony from forelock to hindquarters, feeling the play of the animal's muscles under the silky-soft hide. "I thank ye so very much! I shall name him Liath, for his grey coat reminds me of the Liath Macha in the tales of CuChulain!"

"Ye have been a very good boy since coming here," the King began hesitantly. "Now, 'tis time to think of continuing yer education beyond what the teacher here can do. Morgaine has told me ye possess the gift of Sight. She should know, she has trained at Avalon and she has the same gift. She has spoken to ye about Dragon Isle, the college of the Druids?" he asked and received the boy's confirming nod. "Soon, 'twill be spring, Aaronn, and the wars will begin again. Ye will be safer with the Druids with the other children we are sending to them and the ladies of Avalon. With all the children away, I can focus on this year's campaign and the winning of it. Do ye understand my boyo?" he asked the young lad who stood before him, stroking his new pony.

"I shall go to Dragon Isle, My King, and learn all I may so I can come back and be yer Knight," the young Aaronn pledged solemnly.

"Thank ye Aaronn, for yer pledge," Arthur said seriously. "I hope I stay alive long enough to collect on it."

"The Goddess will watch over all of ye, Sire. She will make sure ye live," the boy stated firmly. "I saw 'twas so in my dreams."

"Thank ye, 'tis good news, Aaronn," the King grinned faintly. "Now, let me show ye where Liath's saddle and bridle are."

The two went to the tack room, where ostlers worked leather oil and saddle soap into the horse's dressings. The sturdy miniature saddle and light bridle hung on a peg with Aaronn's name carved on it. There was also a pair of riding boots beneath the tack, their satin finish glowing softly in the light of the oil lamps.

"Boots too?" exclaimed Aaronn, who kicked off his almost-too tight everyday boots and slipped on the bigger and better-fitting knee length boots. "They fit real g…, I mean very well, Sire!" he pronounced after walking around the straw-covered floor. "My other boots are almost pinching," he admitted quietly.

"I shall speak to the cobbler at once, Aaronn. Ye will have good footwear before ye go to Dragon Island, I can afford at least that much for my ward," he told the boy dryly as he knelt down to receive a fervent hug from his brother.

"I love ye, Arthur Pendragon. Ye gave me a home and made me part of yer family. I shall always owe ye for that," Aaronn wept happily as the King returned the embrace.

"I love ye too, Aaronn. Ye remind me of myself at yer age. I did not know my father was Uther Pendragon 'till I was fourteen," he revealed to the boy.

"Will I ever find or know my father?" Aaronn asked softly as Arthur carried him from the stables.

"I do not know, Aaronn, but if yer father could see ye now he would be proud of ye," Arthur lied about the first part, but not about the last. Aaronn clung to him for a few more moments before he asked to be put down.

"When do we go to the Druids?" he asked after wiping his eyes and blowing his nose on a proffered cloth.

"Not 'till the raids start again, so ye will be here with us 'till then. Remember, 'tis still the Winter Solstice celebration coming soon, with lots of sweets and presents for all," Arthur laughed.

"Good! I like Uncle Cai's cooking better than any I ever ate before," Aaronn laughed with him.

The King and his ward spent the rest of the day together as Arthur told Aaronn a bit of his life before being made King. When supper was served, he sat on Arthur's right for the meal; roasted wild fowl stuffed with native grains, fried mushrooms, noodles dressed with olive oil, herbs and garlic and whole new carrots and turnips. For dessert was an enormous wedge of dried blueberry and apple pie, topped with sweetened thick cream for each diner.

The time came for the Knights to present Aaronn with the rest of his gifts. The lad's collection of wooden knights with horses grew by twos and he received new clothing as well as unders, hose and even a set of wood and leather sandals from Morgaine. The boy, who put each present aside carefully before he opened the next, delightedly thanked each presenter. After that came a rendition of the birthday song, accompanied by Morgaine's harp.

"Thank ye all so much, 'tis my best birthday ever!" the boy said, yawning a huge gaping yawn. Pulling the King's ear close, he said quietly: "I am sleepy now, may I go to bed?"

"Of course, Aaronn," the King grinned.

"Will ye take me, just this once?" Aaronn requested.

"Of course boyo, come on and wish everyone a good night," the King agreed.

"Good night all ye Lords and Ladies, I thank ye all again for all the fine presents," Aaronn spoke up sleepily.

"Good night, Aaronn," each of them called as the King led him away. It took just a few minutes to get Aaronn into bed and tucked in.

"Did ye truly have a good day, Aaronn?" the King asked as he banked the fire and lit the night candle.

"O aye, Sire, the best day in my whole life!"

"Good, I am pleased. Sleep ye sound, Aaronn," Arthur told him, patting his wavy black locks.

"G'night, Sire," the boy murmured as he passed into restful slumber. Arthur slipped out and closed the door, then returned to the dining hall. The men played chess or read to relax while the women sewed and chatted among themselves.

"Good night, my brothers and sisters, 'tis been a long and pleasant day and I am ready for bed," he announced.

"Good night, Sire," they all chorused and the weary young man trudged off to bed. When he entered his room, he found the fire crackling merrily, a carafe of warmed wine beside the hearth and the smell of perfume faintly wafting around the room.

"Thank ye, Mother Ceridwen," he whispered as the woman came from the dressing room holding his robe.

"Good evening My Lord," she said evenly. "Sir Cai asked me to see to yer bath and massage this evening."

"I should be glad of a good massage, Lady...?" he asked for her name.

"My name is Gwendolyn, My Lord," she supplied and began to help him undress. He let her do so and then let her assist him into the hot bath. The Goddess was well worshipped by the pair and late in the next morning, the woman was treated to breakfast. She was shown to the door afterwards, a bag of good silver coins in her hands and a hearty thanks still throbbing in her ears.

"Ye should return again, Lady, and soon," the young King told her as she was dressing. "I very much enjoyed our time together."

"I also enjoyed it, My Lord," she replied and tried to refuse the bag of coins.

"Please, use it to buy a new gown, then return to show me what ye bought?" he entreated.

"As My Lord wishes," Gwendolyn agreed and slipped out the door. She had been gone only a few minutes when Lancelot rapped at the door.

"Artos, are ye still awake?"

"Aye, Lance," Arthur's voice came through the door, sounding well rested and calm.

"May I enter?"

"Of course Lance," Arthur answered and unbolted the door for him.

"The supply ships are here from Lesser Britain, Artos, and here is more good news. My cousins, Bors and Lionel are with the ships, along with a full detachment of King Ban's personal guards. These men have for a trainer the same former Praetorian Guard as I did, so they are very good," Lancelot crowed triumphantly. "Also, with the supply ships has come a mail packet from my contacts in Arabia. In it, my friends in Arabia talk of horses with does' eyes and silken mouths and hooves swift as the wind."

"So tell me, my cousin, how is this important?" Arthur asked, curious. He had never seen the impeccable man so excited. He was speaking a lover's poetry about horses of all things, Arthur thought amusedly.

"Do ye not see, My Lord?" Lancelot's voice pleaded for understanding. "We breed our big, slow but intelligent mares with the smaller, faster and intelligent desert stallions. The offspring will be faster, smarter and easier to train. Ye shall see, Artos. I shall underwrite the entire venture from my personal funds, so 'twill not drain the Crown treasury one tittle; the voyage there, and the acquisition of the stallions," Lancelot went on. "We will need more peaceful times for such a venture, however."

"Agreed, Lance," Arthur said blandly.

"So, we must begin this Spring to secure the realm, aye My Lord?" asked the newly made First Sword of Camelot.

This latest decision had come during the days preceding Aaronn's birthday. After hearing the news, a very angry Gawaine burst into Lancelot's quarters after the King had retired.

"Who d'ye think ye are t' replace me as First Sword, Lancelot o' th' Lake!" he had blustered.

"Gawaine ap Lot, I hold ye no malice. Calm down, man, and let's talk this out?"

"I'm nae a talkin' man, boyo," Gawaine said slowly. "Ye'll have t' show me wha' yer made o'!"

"Friend, brother Gawaine, ye were there at the Lake with us. Ye saw that Arthur and I are close to each other in ability with the sword. I know ye are at least that good," Lancelot tried to reason with the burly Orkneyman.

"Who said anythin' aboot swords, Du La'?" the wily Gawaine asked and took a defensive posture.

"Not here Gawaine, we will continue this outside," Lancelot suggested, seeing that this was inevitable. They went outside to the great room's rear entrance, and then off came shirts and boots before the two faced each other in hand-to-hand combat. Lancelot was a mighty man, but Gawaine was nine times champion of all Orkney in weaponless combat. He used every trick he had learned in his numerous bouts to best Lancelot, but to no avail. Finally, he stepped back, breathing heavily.

"I'm sorry t' ha' t' know who was truly th' better man. Now I know why th' King wants ye as First Sword, an' I kin ha' nae more objections," he pronounced. "Friends from here on?" he asked and stuck out his hand.

"Of course, brother Gawaine, and I hope my strength and skills are never so tested again. Ye are a mighty man, brother," Lancelot laughed and clasped forearms as true warrior brothers. Gawaine had gone to Arthur the next morning, early and insisted that Lancelot be installed as First Sword.

"'Tis enough fer me t' serve 'tall, an' be th' King's cousin, Artos," he had ruefully chuckled and walked away, rubbing his ribs. Arthur shook his head and made the appointment later that afternoon.

Chapter 3

The army began training under Lancelot in late winter; even Arthur took part in the formation drills and sword practices. Soon, then men began to work together as teammates and their hard work was put to the test in the early spring. Arthur had decided to clear the old Federation lands of all Saxon landholders, fearing renewed treachery from that quarter. Long ago the false king, Vortigern the Red Dragon, had signed treaties with the border clans of the Saxons; promising them farmsteads in return for service in his Red Dragon army. His rival for the throne, the War Duke of Britain Aurelius Ambrosius and his brother Uther Pendragon, broke the backs of the Federated tribes and drove them back into Vortigern's lands. The false king himself, along with his wives and children, had been trapped within the walls of his great castle atop a rocky crag in Northwestern Wales. Offered a peaceful treaty that renounced his claim on Britain's High Throne, Vortigern had laughed and sent Ambrosius' embassy back to him, in pieces tied to his own saddle.

Ambrosius' answer had been typical of his style of war. He ordered rows of archers forward and had them apply pitch to their arrowheads. Flights of flaming missiles were then launched from advantageous points around the Castle of the Red Dragon. Presently, the keep was alight and screams of terror could be heard.

"Come out, Vortigern. Yer family and ye can leave Britain in safety, this I vow!" Ambrosius had called out and all those around him heard Vortigern's roared response:

"I'll roast in hell first! Me an' mine'll never bend the knee to ye, or any Roman spawn!"

"Yer choice then," Ambrosius called back and signaled for the final wave of arrows to launch. New flames shot up and then more screams were heard, shriller this time. They stayed, Ambrosius and Uther, until the screams ceased, they left the castle to burn to rubble. The brothers then smashed the resistance among the petty kings and their noble allies, leaving Ambrosius to ascend the High Throne as War Duke.

Now Cerdic Elesing, a man five years Arthur's senior, had been chosen the new Federated "Cying". He insisted that Vortigern's treaty be honored, while Arthur maintained that since a false king had signed it, the agreements were null and void. At the center of the controversy were the vast, fertile river bottoms and grain fields that bordered the Severn River. The river had traditionally been the border between Saxon and British lands, and it was here that they sailed their longboats and began the raiding season. Also in this area were the old Royal granaries, which unbeknownst to Cerdic were now empty, the grain having been relocated to Camelot.

This was part of Arthur and Lancelot's three-part plan for the year, to await the Saxon longboats at their traditional landing point and stop them as they disembarked. The second phase of the plan would be implemented during the summer. The Crown would acquire the farmsteads occupied by Saxon families, through fair market re-imbursement. In extreme cases, the Crown would condemn the land with a cash pay-off then relocate the tenants so that there would be no place for the Saxons to hide and re-supply, as was so often the case. Phase three would be enacted after the Severn border was secured, a system of strategically located guard posts to be established to protect the British folk that would surely flock to the rich farmlands. Once friendly forces occupied the land, Britain could again be self-sufficient; growing its own food reserves. Arthur sighed as he mentally went over it all again; he wondered how long it would really take to get the job done. Lancelot's professional estimate, when the King had asked for it, was three, perhaps four years.

"But with the Goddess to assist us, Artos, perhaps the time will be shorter. I certainly hope so," the First Knight had added with a sigh.

Rousing from his reverie, Arthur looked again at the message that had come two days past from Tristan, who spoke Saxon and looked wild enough in a beard and rough skins to pass easily amongst the tribes. An early raid had been planned, he wrote, before the Equinox, and they would strike at the old granaries. The winter had been harsh in the Saxon camps, and they were hungry. "I shall meet ye at the granaries as soon as I can. Come with all who can ride, Artos, 'tis the beginning!" Tristan's hasty note finished.

Now Cai was packing dried beans, grains, flour, leavening, bacon, hams and all manner of staple provender while the Knights inspected their gear and mended rips or parted seams in their chain mail and other gear. Swords were oiled and sharpened, travel bags were packed and extra prayers said as well. The children were bundled into carts, those that did not ride, along with the pregnant ladies and their attendants. All were sent to Avalon, and once there, the boys were separated from the girls and only the lads of six years and more were allowed to go on to Dragon Island. The Merlin conducted the interviews, when he saw Aaronn he smiled fondly and nodded approval to the boy's unspoken question.

"Of course, Aaronn, we wish for ye to come to us," he said, chuckling at Aaronn's enthusiastic response.

"Will there be a school there?" he asked.

"Dragon Island is a school, Aaronn. There are many boys there and we do not care if they have a father's name or not. As long as they wish to learn, all are welcome there in peace," the Merlin assured him. "Ye will not need to blacken anyone's eye while with us."

Aaronn blushed. "Well, he asked for it," he murmured.

"True enough, boyo. Now come along, 'tis a long journey to the Druid Isle from here, but not so far as to overtire anyone's legs. I see ye brought yer pony along. Very good, I am sure ye can use the practice with yer riding skills."

"Are we going now?" the boy asked with excitement.

"Aye, Aaronn. Just as soon as the rest of the boys are ready," the Merlin of Britain, the High Druid laughed.

Fortunately, Aaronn's wait was not a long one. The small caravan departed as soon as they were assembled, with the Merlin in the lead cart and two other Druids to ride at the rear of the group. The pace of their travel was relaxed and easy, just fast enough to challenge the leg muscles of the boys who walked without tiring them overmuch. As sunset approached, the humble brick-walled, thatch-roofed buildings that housed the Druid brothers and their College of Lore came into view. Aaronn felt his skin prickle with excitement as they approached the tight circle of buildings surrounded by a huge grove of ancient, immense oak trees.

"Welcome lads, welcome among us," the Druids called out when the wagons and group of ponies had entered the courtyard and halted. All those who had their own mounts were led to the horse byre, where they scrubbed the trail dust off their hands and face, then combed their hair after tending to their animals. Aaronn followed the older man who stayed with him to his place at the table. He was seated in-between two younger men whose faces, while serious, were wrinkled deep around their mouths and eyes, as though they laughed loud and often.

"Hullo, I am called Aaronn," the boy spoke up. "I am King Arthur's ward."

"Hullo, Aaronn. I am Brother Dreer and this man beside me is Brother Michael. He does not speak."

"I am happy to meet ye. Can ye teach me fighting skills here?" the boy asked eagerly.

"Why fighting skills, Aaronn?" asked another older but wiry man sitting across from him.

"So I can become a Knight and help Arthur keep Britain safe," the six-year old stated simply.

"To learn to fight is good, Aaronn, especially if 'tis for the good of the realm," the wiry man said seriously.

"What else is there to fight for?" Aaronn asked innocently.

"There should be nothing else, my boy, for nothing else is worth the effort. Service to the Light, in whatever qualified form is still service to the Light," another Druid, a wiry man answered as he took a seat with them. "I am Brother Drusus, Aaronn. I have some knowledge of the kind ye seek. Ye still have so much else to learn first, lad, and when those lessons are firmly in yer head we will start on the other skills, if ye still want to," the older man finished.

"How long will that take?" Aaronn sighed, picking at his food in disappointment. He had supposed his trip to Dragon Isle meant that he was ready to learn swordplay and all the other warrior skills.

"Not so long as it seems, boyo," Drusus laughed. "But come and eat up so thy body will grow strong and healthy. Ye are very young, son. Be not so quick to grow up."

Aaronn sighed again, then picked up his spoon and tasted the simple foods on his plate: grilled fish, cooked lentils and new wild greens tossed with butter. Cups of milk were also served and Aaronn drank two cups of the delicious beverage.

After the meal was over, he was taken to the barracks building and given a lower bunk in a cell of six, stacked double bunks. The others who were assigned with him were of the same age and the boys quickly made friends amongst themselves. After washing hands, faces and brushing their teeth, they all crawled wearily into their bunks and said their goodnights, then fell fast asleep. When Michael and Drusus came to pass out extra blankets, they found the softly snoring boys and tenderly covered each of them with a thick, goose down comforter, banked the small hearth and left, quietly shutting the door behind them.

The next morning, the boys wakened just after dawn. Quickly, they washed and dressed in clean unders and sturdy clothing before following Brother Michael to the breakfast table. A quick blessing over the simple porridge, sweetened with honey, then the hungry boys fell to with gusto.

After consuming their fill, the boys were divided again into age groups and assigned to individual Druids. Brother Michael and Brother Dreer were the instructors in Aaronn's group and they all went walking with the men, who taught them the guidelines of the Brotherhood of Dragon Island. These men believed that all life was sacred, right down to the tiniest insect and that only to defend one's own life and limb, or that of someone else, should it be taken.

"Always remember that all life is Ceridwen's and She should be thanked if life must be spilled for sustenance, or even by accident. Blood spilled on the earth should be offered to the Goddess at once, so that the vital energy cannot be used in the cause of darkness," Brother Dreer told Aaronn's group that day.

So it was that Aaronn began soaking up information like a sponge absorbs water. Each day was a new adventure for the boy, a day-by-day discovery of a wealth of knowledge. As he matured that year, he learned to read and speak better Welsh; he also picked up a rudimentary understanding of Latin. Just before his seventh birthday, the library of the Druids opened to him and his life was doubly fulfilled. When his formal lessons and everyday chores were done, he retreated to the building and its many rooms full of books on every subject imaginable. He read and asked many questions about every book he read, expanding his knowledge exponentially.

Meanwhile, out on the Severn plains, all was progressing slowly forward. After assembling his army of Britons, Faerie folk from the hollow hills and King Ban's light cavalry, the young King had awaited the first wave of raiders. It came a full week or so after Tristan's return and it was to be the battle that set the tone for the entire campaign that year.

They came just before true dawn, twenty longboats with over-full crews just as Tristan's note had warned. They headed straight for the storehouses, seven tall stone and mortar towers and all could hear the scrape of the keels as they ground ashore. Cerdic alighted first, pointed out to Arthur by Tristan. A tall, broad man with a thick mane of blonde hair, his bulging muscles were clearly seen by all, he wore the signs of his authority, two thick gold armbands, one on each arm.

"The Armbands of Thor, Artos," whispered Tristan, as he handed the King his weapon of choice for the moment, not Excalibur, which was on his back, but a great, heavy-peened hammer of bright steel with a thick oak handle. "Go to it, boyo!" Tristan grinned, closing his own helm.

Arthur and his Knights, backed by the ranks of foot soldiers recruited from amongst the common folk, moved out into the misty morning. Some said it was only luck that served them then, but Arthur Pendragon knew and he thanked Ceridwen profusely for the bright morning sun that broke through the light spring mist. The brilliance reflecting off their chain mail at just that moment, surrounding each Knight in a halo of bright light, as the Saxons looked at them, they looked like angels in the light.

"My Saxon brothers, I give ye greetings!" Arthur called out in their tongue. Taking the time to learn the language was proving to be well worth it, Arthur thought, as the entire raiding force stopped dead in their footprints and listened. Arthur rode forward, swinging the great hammer.

"Who be ye?" Cerdic called back, his eyes squinting against the glare.

"One who would stop this before it starts, Cerdic. We are both intelligent men, why should we war instead of making peace?" Arthur called back as his line advanced to protect him. They halted in formation and the King dismounted, striding forward to the first granary tower. He hoped that the Merlin's little engineering feat would work as well as promised by the Druid and Sir Lancelot. Taking firm hold on the stout handle of the hammer, he swung it back. The Saxons looked on, confused, and the howling of the berserkers quieted a bit.

"There be no food for ye here, brothers, nor will there ever be here again for ye. No longer will there be Saxons here to hide ye, or feed ye when ye come a' raiding on our land anymore! This be Brit land, forever!" Arthur shouted out and struck the base of the first tower a ringing blow. The structure trembled, and then collapsed inward upon itself. The young King went to the next tower, then the next, repeating the gesture. By the time the seventh tower fell the Saxons, whose fierce fighting reputation was unequaled and entirely earned, stared in disbelief. Was this Thor, helping the Brits, or was this new King of theirs a god himself? As one man the horde ran back to their longboats and pushed off, rowing fast down river. Arthur heard Lancelot's deep chuckle, then Gawaine's merry guffaw then the entire army took up the laughter. Cerdic heard it for miles and in his sleep for many, many nights. As for Arthur and the Knights, they slept well that night, although they knew it was only the beginning that year.

It took the rest of that spring and into autumn before all the border farmsteads came into the holding of handpicked British farmers. These men's fathers had dreamed of one day farming the rich earth of the Severn plains and they each thanked Arthur profusely. One overwhelmed man, whose young wife was five months with their first child, grabbed Arthur's hand and pumped it furiously.

"Ye keep them Saxons away, Sire, and watch these plains bloom. We'll be feedin' Britain within a crop year, M'Lord!" he vowed.

"We will keep them out, man. Ye just grow the food," the King grinned at him and later sent a message to Vivaine at Avalon to send a few midwives to the Severn. He reckoned that there would soon be a great need for them.

True to his word, each new landholder went about the business of readying the land for the next spring planting. True to Arthur's word, the string of guard towers along the river were nearly complete and staffed before the raiding began. Arthur's army grew rapidly that season. Mighty fighting men, Knights in spirit if not always in name, found their way to Camelot from all over Britain. It became a matter of honor and pride for the noble houses to boast to their fellow nobles that their son served with Arthur Pendragon.

Gawaine officially swore fealty to Arthur that fall, so to keep the treaty between Arthur and Orkney valid, his surly brother Agravaine came to Camelot. He was as Gawaine had been upon arrival at Camelot; unkempt, unclean and decidedly unmannered. He and Gawaine fought it out in several vigorous wrestling matches and Agravaine finally came around to the idea that personal hygiene and manners only improved one's manliness, instead of reducing it. Agravaine limped a bit, a matter of a pronounced short left leg, but on horseback he was as good a swordsman as anyone. Once his attitude had been adjusted, Arthur put the black-haired man in charge of a division of light cavalry and the man proved his wiliness by capturing several Saxon divisions during the second summer of the Severn contest. These destructive men were all caught trying to burn crops or planting insect larvae amongst the now-verdant farm fields. They were ransomed back to Cerdic, whose treasury Arthur now labored very hard to drain. When his treasure was nearly spent, the Saxon leader ordered a virtual stop to the raiding very early in the season. By Samhain of that year, the crops were harvested and for the first time since Ambrosius, the granaries and storehouses groaned with plentiful food. Arthur watched the tribute from the petty kings roll by the wagonload into Camelot's gates with great satisfaction.

The children returned to Camelot for the winter, all but a few came willingly. One of those few was Aaronn, who stayed by an exercise of his own will.

"I have so much yet to learn, Sire," the boy wrote in a letter to the King. "'Tis not that I do not wish to see ye, but that I wish more to stay and finish my studies."

Arthur read the note and chuckled at the earnest tone in the boy's words. He sent Aaronn some new clothes, boots, and a cloak for the winter in the return package, along with a letter telling the boy that he understood and approved of Aaronn's decision.

"O and Aaronn, my boyo. Happy Birthday number eight," the King wrote, hardly believing that three years had already passed as he sealed the missive under the Royal Seal.

Aaronn was pleased when the package arrived, delivered by the Merlin who had been with Arthur that year in the Severn. The High Druid was pleased to see a much taller, broader Aaronn, and he smiled to see how much the lad reminded him of a young Arthur.

"Hullo Aaronn. Have ye been studying hard for examinations this year?" he asked the boy.

"Of course, Lord Merlin," Aaronn said with assurance and Taliesin grinned when he heard the confidence in his voice. "How are the King and all the other Knights?"

"The King sent ye a package," Taliesin chuckled, tossing it to him. "Go on, off with ye now. I have serious business to attend," he mock-scolded, then chuckled harder as Aaronn smilingly gave him the Roman salute and ran off, clutching the package to his chest.

Entering his room, he found only his new close friend, Olran, who had come to Dragon Island a few weeks after Aaronn had turned seven.

"What's up, Aaronn?" asked Olran, the slightly younger of the two by four months as Aaronn flopped down on the lower bunk. He was the youngest Prince of Westerland Keep, and his dialect reflected his homeland. He had worked very hard, however to conquer the defects in his enunciation.

"The King has sent me a package!" Aaronn told him excitedly, as he quickly and deftly untied the knots holding the package closed. Upon folding back the wrappings, he found several shirts, three pairs of trous, three sets of snow-white unders, hose, and a pair of shoes. Finally, he pulled out the cloak, which was pinned with a small bronze torque at the neck.

"Do ye suppose 'tis a Saxon torque?" asked a wide-eyed Olran as he fingered the design with his long, sensitive fingers.

"Of course, he has been fighting in the Severn for two years now! He must have taken many trophies!" Aaronn replied archly

Olran arched that one eyebrow of his and looked blandly at his friend for a moment and Aaronn blushed.

"Sorry Olran, I did not mean to…"

"All right, I am not offended," the thin, gray-eyed lad responded with a faint smile. "Let us go have supper now," he suggested as his stomach grumbled.

"Aye, I am very hungry," agreed Aaronn. He quickly and neatly put his things away before they went to table.

Finding their places quickly, Aaronn and Olran each accepted the plate handed them by Brother Michael and the cup of milk poured by Brother Drusus. The blessing was offered before the hungry boys dug into the simple but delicious egg custard, heavily flavored with mellow cheese, some of the first from Cai's cellars, the mound of vegetables and the slab of coarse brown bread liberally smeared with fresh, sweet butter. Seconds were asked and served up with fond grins from the two instructors. Of all the newest students, only Aaronn and Olran showed any potential for the warrior teaching both men could offer.

Brother Michael, though he never spoke in front of the students, was fully capable of speech. He preferred to allow the boys to believe him a mute, for it offered him the advantage of close observation without seeming interest. Michael was also the finest knife thrower and smith in all Britain, a man whose interest in perfection bordered on the obsessive. He saw that Aaronn, with his already blooming athletic physique, was a candidate once the boy learned to better master his darker moods. Michael watched as Aaronn used the last crust of bread to mop his plate completely clean, something most children learned later. Aaronn did this naturally because of his earlier life, and because he understood that to waste even a crumb of bread was offensive to Ceridwen.

"All finished, Aaronn?" asked Drusus.

"Aye, sir," the boy answered, wiping his lips then folding his napkin neatly before putting it aside.

"And ye, Olran?"

"O aye, sir," the lad answered, as he put aside his own napkin.

"So, what news of the King, Aaronn?" asked Brother Drusus. "Or is it private?"

"Some was," was the careful answer. "He says the Severn plain has bloomed and that the harvest is heavy. The Knights have all made it through the season without major injuries. Also, the first snow has fallen at Camelot," he went on.

"Thanks be to Ceridwen for the harvest, and that all our defenders have come through alive. Truly, the Goddess' rewards are great, eh Aaronn? Already She rewards Arthur for cleansing the Severn plains of the Saxon scourge. If only they would live in peace with us, the both of us would prosper! Stubborn, greedy fools!" Drusus finished emphatically.

"Calm yerself, Brother Drusus," came the Merlin's sonorous voice.

"Lord Merlin, I am sorry to have brought disharmony to ye. I am glad that the Severn is almost secured."

"Let us celebrate that, Drusus. How are Aaronn and Olran's lessons going?"

"Very well, actually, these two seem to accelerate each other's learning. They are quite a team already," Drusus chuckled with him. "Now that they understand that cheating is bad, their progress is much better."

The Merlin looked at Aaronn accusingly. "I thought we discussed all that at Camelot, boyo," he said sternly.

"'Twas not totally Aaronn's mistaking, Brother Merlin," Brother Drusus told him.

"O?" the Merlin shifted his withering gaze to Olran and the young princeling wilted a bit.

"It seems that our young prince here has the gift of the piercing eye, Brother Merlin. We caught him using it to win against a group of older students, he was winning big too," Drusus struggled not to laugh.

"Dice or cards?" asked Taliesin, who was similarly gifted and had been prone to use it to earn living money in his younger years.

"Dice," Brother Michael supplied.

"Can ye do it with other things as well, boyo?" asked Taliesin, who was secretly amused at Olran's chagrined face.

"Nay sir, at least I have never tried anything else," Olran answered slowly.

"I assume that yer instructors have explained to ye both why 'tis wrong to use the gift this way?" asked the Merlin sternly.

"Aye sir," the boy answered earnestly. "I shall not do it again, unless 'tis necessary."

"If ye feel it necessary while still here, boyo, then see one of thy instructors, agreed?" asked the Merlin.

"Aye, sir," Olran agreed heartily.

"And ye, Aaronn, no more arranging games for profit," the Merlin admonished the King's ward, who blushed and mumbled; "Aye, sir."

"Now off with both of ye, ye rascals!" Taliesin said, waving his hand in a dismissal. The boys sprinted out of the dining room; only when they were gone did Michael allow himself a chuckle.

"Those two are quite a pair. 'Tis a good thing they came to us so young and that they have a good direction to go in, otherwise, they could have turned out very badly," he said in his well-cultured bass voice. "That Aaronn, he is a quick lad. Cai told me he was a cut-purse at four."

"'Tis true. For days at Camelot, we used to search him at night 'till he learned the consequences of stealing," chuckled the Merlin as he remembered.

"Now he arranges games amongst the other boys and Olran. I tell ye Taliesin, the young prince from Westerland has a tracker's eye. He can already follow easy trails and his sense of direction is so good that when we were out in the woods this Summer I could not lose him, no matter how hard I tried. Every time I attempted, I had to take him many miles and over a winding path until I was nearly lost myself and still he found his way home. He can set a workable snare, one 'tis quick and painless, and he can find shelter against sudden inclement weather. The boy is good and could be better with the right atmosphere and training, neither of which he can get at Westerland Keep!"

"Do ye think he would be willing to live with us, full time?" asked the Merlin. "And what about Aaronn, do ye think he would be willing to stay?"

"They should be trained together," Michael proposed. "Which means playing the stalling game with Westerland," he added, smiling faintly.

"Aye, 'twould be best. Let it be done and let them be housed in the student's quarters rather than in the fosterlings barracks," the Merlin ordered.

"Of course, My Lord Merlin, right away," the two replied, already planning their first letter to Olran's father, the petty King Warren of Westerland Keep in the northwest of Britain. They would tell him of the Brotherhood's wish to keep the lad a bit longer for testing. The fat old man would probably begin to sweat profusely in anxiety over what his son might be telling the Druids, for it was well known that Warren secretly supported the alliance against Arthur, though it could not be proved by anyone's word or letter.

"Tell us, Brother Taliesin, what truly transpires out on the Severn?" asked Drusus after a moment or two, the warrior in him thirsting to know.

"Well, ye know Cerdic is positively fuming at losing the Severn and all his allies there. Still, the first harvest in twenty years or more is cause enough to celebrate," the Merlin began. "Ye should have seen it, Michael, that day when the granaries fell and the Saxons broke ranks and ran. Arthur toppled each of those towers with one mighty hammer blow; the howling of the berserkers just petered out after that. It was like the lemmings' run for the cliffs when they ran for their boats and all the Knights laughing at their backs. Why, they nearly left Cerdic behind in their haste! From that day on, the raiding parties were small, quick ones which were mostly annoying rather than destructive. Agravaine himself captured several whole raiding parties with his division and Arthur plans to knight him personally during the Winter Solstice celebration this year," Taliesin related.

"That means Lot will have to send another son to Camelot to secure the treaty. Gaheris is his name, as I recall," mused Drusus.

"Morgause will probably have fits about that!" the Merlin laughed coldly. "I wish there was something that could be done about her."

"Someday, she will make too great an error and Ceridwen will act. 'Till then, we can only watch and wait," Michael spoke up.

"Aaronn and Olran must go back to Avalon next year. They are old enough to start the lessons that the Ladies there can teach best. We must call together the entire Brotherhood to meet at the Spring Equinox to decide what must be done about the more questionable Lords and petty Kings in Britain. We must send watchers into these suspicious houses to gather the information we need to make educated choices as to their fates," Taliesin told them and received nods of assent. "The summons must go out now so that all can be here in time."

"The work will commence immediately, Lord Merlin," Michael said seriously. "'Twill take us that long to recall some of them."

"I shall leave the matter in yer capable hands, my Brother. 'Tis time also to prepare for the Winter Solstice. We must divine the Goddess' weather will for the coming Season, and implore Her aid to send us a properly cold winter to eradicate any pests in the earth, followed by sufficient rainfall to ready the ground for the spring sowing," Taliesin went on. "Hopefully, those kind of conditions will aid Arthur as well, but he told me that the crops must flourish this year," Taliesin grinned as he recalled Arthur's first and only imperious command for the Merlin to produce good weather for the next day. The rain shower that had followed had seen the crops gain two inches afterwards.

"Ye see Artos, my boyo," the Merlin had giggled with delight to see the King slogging it out in the mud with his Knights. "The crops flourish, 'tis good weather, aye?"

"Not for fighting, Lord Merlin," the King had grumbled in return.

"Is that what ye wanted? Ye only commanded good weather," Taliesin had nearly fallen from his pony's back, so hard had he laughed.

Arthur was only irritated for a bit before he had joined the Merlin's mirth as another cloudburst drenched them. Since this occurrence, Arthur had only asked to know what the weather would be upon the morrow and Taliesin had worked what magicks could be done to assure the proper amount of sunny days for both war and agriculture.

The next day Aaronn and the Merlin walked together in the forest. The boy walked confidently along with them, alert and observant as he gauged his surroundings.

"Tell me, Aaronn, what think ye of yer life here on Dragon Island," Taliesin asked.

"I like it here, but I miss Sir Cai and the other Knights. Of course, I would like to spend some time with the King, but I know he is too busy," Aaronn answered with a sigh. "It felt so like home at Camelot."

"I know, boyo, and as soon as this mess in the Severn is cleared up, perhaps they will come for a visit," the Merlin proposed.

"'Twould be nice," Aaronn said slowly and quietly.

"What is wrong, lad?" asked the Merlin, concerned over Aaronn's melancholy attitude.

"Some boys say 'tis a lie when they hear I am the King's ward."

"O, truly?" the Merlin queried, his eyebrow a-quirk.

"Aye, Lord Merlin. I do not want to fight them, but I will not let them call me a liar either!" Aaronn stated emphatically.

"Who says these things?" asked the Merlin.

"I am not a tattletale either!" Aaronn grumped.

"Why do I not pay a 'surprise' visit to yer classrooms? Perhaps I shall witness the truth of what ye have told me and clear up the matter for these boys," the older man assured the boy, giving him a quick embrace. Aaronn was obviously relieved.

"Thank ye, Father Merlin," the lad said quietly, his face taking on a very familiar stubborn mien. Taliesin had seen this very expression on the young Arthur's face every time his parentage had arisen during their sessions in the Perilous Forest.

"Is there more?" the Merlin encouraged gently.

"I thought I was to learn to fight here, Father Merlin," the boy stated simply. "'Tis what ye told me, and so did the Lady Morgaine. I am almost eight and I want to start learning so I can help Arthur."

"I know ye are impatient to learn, boyo," the Merlin chuckled at his earnestness. "It just so happens that ye and Olran will be moving yer things into the Student's Quarters, at least until springtime. After that, we older Druids will have much to do, so the college will close next year, or at least until things settle down a bit. Ye will have all the training ye need, Aaronn, but ye must work hard on yer studies as well. Brother Drusus tells me that yer work in mathematics and astronomy has suffered of late," the Merlin chastised mildly. "A true warrior develops his mind as well as his body while a solider concentrates only on the body. A scholar sometimes neglects his health in favor of his mind. I believe ye are suited to the warrior's way, but only time will tell the Goddess' will on that."

"I shall study harder, Father Merlin," the youth avowed, and the Merlin heard the echo of the younger Arthur in the boy's voice. It was a good thing that this boy was already so loyal, the Merlin thought again as they walked back towards the College. If he were not, there would be more trouble for Britain than a shaken wasp's nest. When he was finally told of his heritage, there would be no more loyal man in the entire realm, Taliesin thought with satisfaction, turning his attention back to the boy fidgeting in front of him.

"Go on, find Olran and help Brother Michael and Brother Drusus move all yer things into yer new room," he said and watched his nephew run off, shouting for his friend. He sighed again in satisfaction as he entered the dining hall, thinking that Ceridwen's Will was truly wondrous to watch unfold. He entered to the mass greeting of his brothers.

"Brothers, we have much to speak of. The next year will be crucial to establishing Britain's claim on the Severn. The Saxons are hardly defeated, only driven back and humiliated. We all know they will return, sooner than we want, and we must be ready. In addition, rumors have begun to circulate amongst the people of certain petty kings and nobles conspiring again. We will have to place a member of the Brotherhood in each of these suspect households to watch and report their doings, both secret and open. Any who feel the call for this service, please see me soon. Now, down to other business," he went on after a brief pause. At the close of the quick meeting, the Druids had begun the task of recalling their far-flung membership. To each went a short, terse missive;

"Return to Dragon Island for the Spring Equinox; Ceridwen and the Horned One call, Brothers. Answer their call."

Within the twelfth month of that year, the general portion of the Druids had already returned and Aaronn reveled in the abundance of new information each of them brought. The celebration of the Winter Solstice, the time of preparation for the re-birth of spring was a somewhat solemn occasion, punctuated frequently by bursts of riotous levity. Brother Michael put on an exhibition of knife throwing that dazzled the young Aaronn; the lad decided then and there that this was the way he wanted to learn to fight. Brother Drusus set up a series of archery targets and hit a bull's eye at each one, no matter how hard his assembled friends and former students tried to disturb his concentration. Olran decided that he would like to train with the bow so impressed was he by Drusus' demonstration. Finally, the Merlin put a halt to the show by wheeling in a keg-cart, on which was mounted a chilled and sweating cask of apple ale, already tapped as evidenced by the foaming tankard in the Merlin's hand.

"Come my brothers," he called out. "Join me in a cask of the Brotherhood's best!"

A rousing 'Aye!' answered his suggestion and they clustered around the cask. Aaronn watched, his attitude wary as the cask emptied, still there was no fighting, no arguing, and no bad tempers amongst them. They remained the same sweet-tempered and serene men Aaronn had always known. He wandered over to the Merlin and was invited to sit on the High Druid's lap.

"How come ye and the others do not get mad when ye drink ale?" he asked quietly. "I remember some of the alehouses where my mother worked and the men there were always either mad or sleepy."

"Ale takes away a person's thin layer of civilization. Men become what they are inside under its influence," the Merlin explained, not looking or acting like he had imbibed a drop. "'Tis getting late, my lad, ye had best take Olran with ye and head to bed," the older man finished and gave Aaronn a fatherly embrace.

"Goodnight, Father Taliesin," Aaronn murmured and slipped off his lap.

Aaronn's new quarters were spacious and comfortable with only two beds in a cell designed for four older boys. The room had running water that trickled into a basin over a drain hole, keeping the reservoir constantly full but not stagnant. It was an easy matter for Aaronn to light the small hearth and build a tidy fire. He and Olran then carried a bucket full of water over to the glowing hearth and hang it from the kettle hook to heat over the fire. By morning, the water would be nice and steaming hot for a cup of tea and a quick wash up before breaking fast. Once finished with that chore, the boys stripped down to unders and climbed into their cozy beds, pulling the covers tight under their chins.

"Did ye hear anything new about the Brotherhood's plans, Olran?" Aaronn asked eagerly.

"Nay, just that 'twill be Druids in every suspect house in Britain by spring," the thin lad answered, yawning hugely.

"Why would anyone want another High King?" Aaronn wondered aloud. "Arthur is King, both by the Goddess' Hand and by the Christian God's. Why do the others fight so hard against him? 'Twould be like fighting against the Goddess Herself."

"We'll have to be older before it makes any sense, Aaronn. Adults get so much stuff mixed up, 'tis hard to get the truth of anything from them. My father, mother and brothers all hate Arthur with a red passion, but I do not know why and they will not explain," the gray-eyed Olran answered, sighing audibly. "I hope Father doesn't call for my return, ever. I like it here with the Druids, maybe I will even become one of the Brothers when I'm old enough."

"Ye cannot do that, Olran!" Aaronn said, dismayed. "Ye have to come with me to Camelot so we can be Knights together."

"How do ye know I want to be a Knight?" asked Olran contrarily.

"Ye just have to be, otherwise, who will help me with my sums?" Aaronn asked plaintively. Olran's grasp of numbers was excellent, so much so that the others had teasingly called him "Olran the Abacus." Olran did not care for the nickname, Aaronn knew as he lay there musing over the problem. He had come to the thinner lad's rescue a few times already when the teasing had escalated into beatings. After a long time thinking, Aaronn fell asleep after finally coming to the decision to consult the Merlin.

The next morning, he did just that and the Merlin was most emphatic that he would take the matter in hand.

"Ye need not worry over it any more, boyo. 'Tis my problem now."

Later that same day, as the boys played together, the teasing of Olran began again much more violently.

"Ye stop that, or I shall get the Merlin to make ye stop!" Aaronn said to the bully quietly.

"Come on, he's not worth it!" the bully said to the others in his group and they walked away.

Aaronn assisted Olran to his feet. After helping him to wash away the spittle and mud the tormentors had thrown at him, Aaronn helped Olran get back to his room for a change of clothing.

"Are ye all right now?" Aaronn asked.

"Aye, I'm just as mad as a whole shaken hornet's nest!" Olran answered hotly, then Aaronn watched as Olran's whole demeanor calmed and he continued, cold as ice. "But I don't get mad, I get even!"

"What are ye gonna to do?" asked Aaronn curiously.

"I do not know yet. I shall watch and bide my time, just like at home. I'm sure if I watch enough, I'll get my chance," Olran chuckled and he was right.

The night before the Winter Solstice, Olran found out that the older boys were going to try and sneak into the Merlin's quarters to poke around a bit. Olran and Aaronn went to the Merlin with the news and received a hearty chuckle from the High Druid's secretary, Osric and his brother Aleric.

"Aye, we tried that too, but the Merlin is a crafty fellow and I am certain the lads will receive more than they bargained for. They have no idea what they are about to unleash upon themselves."

"What will happen to them?" asked Olran.

"That group of spoiled princelings has been the bane of us all during their tenure here, lads. All that is going to come back to haunt them now," Aleric laughed heartily. "We will come to get ye on that night, boys, and ye will get to see their fate, if the Merlin agrees," Osric invited and sent them on their way. Two days later, the Druid pair brought Aaronn and Olran into their room and ate supper with them.

"Did ye tell the Merlin about the raid?" asked Aaronn as he and Olran munched on a rectangle of sweet-spicy gingerbread.

"O aye and he is very grateful for the information, to be sure. He has been looking forward to punishing Prince Thomas for quite some time," Osric chuckled.

"Prince Thomas?" Aaronn shrilled, his voice breaking a bit.

"Aye, ye remember his brother, Bertran," Aleric said, his eyes a-twinkle. Aaronn nodded, blushing a bit at the memory of the boy's black eye and waited expectantly for the tale to continue.

"Both have their sire Caw's belligerent attitude, however Bertran has been cured. Thomas continues to be a thorn in everyone's sides, though he is the apple of his mother's eye. Spoiled rotten when he arrived, he has learned nothing during his time with us, at least 'till tonight," Aleric finished, amusement plain on his face.

"Come along, ye two, 'tis time," Osric said and opened the door. He led the way, the boys behind him and Aleric bringing up the rear as they walked towards the vantage point chosen earlier by the brothers. The High Druid lived apart from the others in a stone house built directly in front of a large cave. In fact, the house was built right into the cave entrance, so that the Merlin could access the cave without leaving his domicile. The Crystal Cave, a place of ethereal loveliness where any light was magnified by the millions of natural quartz crystals that lined its walls, was where the Merlin "saw" the happenings all over Britain. To find one's way inside was challenging enough, and usually only attempted with the Merlin's blessing. The sacrilege of entering covertly was minor enough, and the Merlin now planned to use this opportunity to teach the group of bullies the lesson of their young lives. The lads would be allowed to enter the "seeing" chamber, once they were inside Ceridwen would do Her part to ensure that they changed their attitude towards life and how to live it. The Merlin chuckled under his breath as he awaited the "raid."

The bully Thomas crept towards the High Druid's house, followed by his covey of like-aged and minded accomplices. He planned to find the Cave of Seeing and remove one of the crystals from the wall. What a trophy, he exulted in his mind, and how the others would admire him, these were the thoughts as he slithered forward on his belly until he reached the semi-concealed entrance.

"C'mon boyos, we're almost there!" he whispered. "Just wait 'till ye see the size of some of the crystals in there."

"Let's just hurry Thom," one of the others whispered nervously. "I don't want to get caught by ye know who."

"That old goat, he couldn't stop a fox in a hen-house," Thomas whispered back, contempt wreathing his hushed voice. Just the same, he moved along faster through the entrance. The others followed closely behind and carefully they all crept down the darkened hallway.

Meanwhile, from their vantage point Osric, Aleric, Aaronn and Olran saw the group enter and the two young lads sighed with disappointment.

"Now we cannot watch anymore," Aaronn complained, just a bit.

"Of course we can, Aaronn," Osric chuckled. Turning to his right, he pushed away some underbrush to reveal a small spring, one of many that bubbled out of the ground on Dragon Isle.

"Come on boyos, and watch the fun," invited, patting the ground lightly on either side of him. The two sat cross-legged before the pool and peered into its depths as Osric indicated. With a shock, the two boys saw Thomas' image in the waters, along with the rest of his gang of bullies. They were just rounding a corner and Olran and Aaronn heard Osric chuckle deeply;

"It should happen any time now; they are just entering the Crystal Cave."

Aaronn and Olran saw the others creep around the corner and peer into a small, barely man-sized opening. They could see the walkway for only a short distance before it disappeared into the gloomy depths of the cave.

"We need that candle, Rufus," Thomas whispered.

The wax stub was passed forward and Thomas produced a fire kit. Striking the stones together, he sparked the wick to life. Instantly, the cave magnified their one tiny flame to millions upon millions of flames and the High Druid's voice rang out;

"Death, death to the infidels, they have seen that which must remain unseen, the great mystery, and for that, they must die!"

"NO!" shrieked the boys. With eyes wide with terror, they all ran from the cave, falling over each other in their haste to leave. Aaronn and Olran saw, in the magicked waters, the form of a gigantic swordmaine stride forth from the glare, She swung Her sword so that the weapon sang. Dropping the stub of a candle, Thomas streaked from the cave to avoid what he thought was certain death. The watchers giggled soundlessly as the bullies bolted pell-mell from the side entrance and fled for the safety of their rooms. After a few moments, the Merlin came out the same way, followed by a gorgeously arrayed Vivaine, the Lady of Avalon. Both were on the verge of collapsing from suppressed laughter and Vivaine sank gracefully onto her knees, unable to hold it back and longer. The Merlin sat beside her, his rich tenor blending with her delightful soprano for a most pleasing combination. Osric and Aleric brought their young charges down the hill to join them. Their laughter rang out then and the six finally gasped out a final guffaw and wiped away the last trickle of tear.

"O Goddess, I have rarely laughed so hard," Vivaine was finally able to giggle out. "Did ye see their faces?"

"Aye, Lady Vivaine, we did. I must say, they were all white as new-fallen snow!" Osric answered. "Ow, my sides hurt."

"Mine too!" Aaronn chirped.

"My jaws hurt too!" chimed in Olran. "D'ye really think that Thomas is truly cured?"

"We will see, Olran. Ye two will keep an eye on him for us, aye?" the Merlin chuckled.

"Aye sir, that we will," avowed the two as one.

"All is well then, and now ye two are due for bed. Off with ye now!" the Merlin laughed. "Take them to their beds, Osric and Aleric, the day has been a long one."

Aaronn went to leave, but turned back to the Merlin. "Lord Merlin, I have a question. What we saw in the waters, 'twas truly the Goddess, or was it the Lady Vivaine all dressed up?" he asked earnestly.

"What did ye see, Aaronn?" asked Vivaine, curious.

"I saw a huge Lady, dressed up in…well…armor," the boy faltered. The Merlin and Vivaine exchanged glances, for the image they had projected was that of the Furies of Greek mythology.

"Olran, did ye see that as well?" questioned Vivaine.

"Aye, Lady," the other lad confirmed.

Again, the two exchanged a long, curious glance before Vivaine answered them.

"Aye, ye two, 'twas indeed the fourth face of the Goddess ye saw. We call Her, 'Vengeance', when She projects that face. The others only saw their own fears in form," Vivaine explained. "A very rare thing 'tis, I must think on it at length," she said this last part aside to the Merlin.

"We must both consider this long and well, Lady," he returned quietly.

"Is it all right that we saw Her?" asked Aaronn, somewhat afraid.

"Of course 'tis all right, Aaronn," laughed Vivaine reassuringly. "'Tis a rare sight to see Her so, but 'tis always for good reasons. She has blessed ye, Aaronn and Olran, be sure to thank Her."

"I will not forget, Lady," Aaronn yawned.

"Go on to bed now, my dear lads. Sleep ye both sound," Vivaine said with a smile and gave them each a peck on the cheek to send them to their nightly rest.

"G'night, Lady Vivaine," Aaronn and Olran each mumbled as Osric and Aleric led them away.

"So, 'tis true, the vision I saw. The Goddess has at last made Her choice known. Aaronn ap Uther Pendragon and Olran ap Warren of

Westerland are the Black Knight and the Black Hunter, the Champions of
Ceridwen," murmured Vivaine, almost in a trance. "They must be properly
prepared, for they will walk the secret paths in the future."

"Aye, Lady Vivaine. They both will come to Avalon this spring,
along with all the students. The situation in the Severn is critical this year
and will require all the assistance we might be able to render," the Merlin
said seriously. Since the Goddess has shown us the weather patterns for the
Spring and Summer, we have been able to divine the best way to use the
coming conditions for our advantage, both for farming and fighting."

"We at Avalon pledge our assistance as well, Lord Merlin,"
Vivaine said, giving him a smile that cheered his heart, as always. "This
year, the rites of Beltane are even more essential!"

"Aye," agreed Taliesin, rising and offering a helping hand to her.
She put her graceful hand into his and he pulled her into a furtive embrace.

"Ah, my love, 'tis hard to live the life we must. Soon, the times
will be better, after Arthur defeats his enemies and the peace can be
maintained," he murmured passionately into her ear.

"Our lives are in Ceridwen's hands, my dearest," Vivaine
whispered throatily in return. "We have known happiness at times in the
past, when the Lady's Peace was on the land, we will have joy again," she
continued and kissed him softly, just below the ear. They stood like that for
a few moments before retreating into the Merlin's house, locking the side
entrance securely behind them.

The next morning, Prince Thomas came to see the Merlin, along
with his clique. Individually and then as a group, they apologized for all
their pranks and cruel jests. From that day forth, the boys appeared to be
the models of decorum and studiousness. They read together and discussed
all their daily lessons until all six of them were approached by different
Druid brothers and asked to stay on at Dragon Island after the younger
boys went to Avalon in the spring. All agreed to stay and when Thomas
wrote home to explain to his father, the petty king Caw, the old man finally
lost his resolve to plot against Arthur any more. He signed a much sought-
after life treaty with the High King, and Arthur breathed a bit easier after
that. Things got tense for just a little while when Caw's plain-faced eldest
daughter arrived at Camelot during the winter of Arthur's seventh year on
the throne, with the obvious intent of moving into the royal suites. It had
taken Morgaine many hours to explain to the dull girl that no one expected
her to act as a slave. Finally, the girl had taken quarters with the married
women and soon she found a man who thought she was the perfect woman.
Arthur added to her paltry dowry from Caw and gave her a wedding that
was the talk of the land that year. Cai's skill in the kitchen brought him
much renown and soon all the noble houses sent their cooks to Camelot for
training in Cai's method of cooking. His way of cooking without as much

oil and making sure all was completely spotless were quickly adopted by all he taught and the rates of infectious diseases went down as a result.

Aaronn came to spend that winter at Camelot and as he and Olran were both eight years of age, they went to work as pages, a position of much work and few hands. Aaronn's organizational skills surfaced when he and Olran took tea and cakes to the women, learning to serve the light meal expertly. They found themselves fascinated by the chatter of the women, being always full of bits and pieces of information. Within two weeks of beginning this service, Aaronn and Olran knew nearly all the doings of everyone at the Castle. One day as they assisted Sir Cai in the preparation of vegetables for supper, Aaronn let a piece of gossip slip out.

"Sir Cai, why do the ladies all say that no decent woman would have ye to husband?" the curious lad asked innocently.

Sir Cai looked up, startled and Aaronn realized that the information was news to the seneschal. "Is that what they say?" he asked in return.

"'Tis what Lady Irene says," Olran confirmed.

"O, 'tis so?" Cai laughed sardonically. "What else does the eminent Lady Irene say?" he asked.

"She says that there must be something wrong with a man who went from warrior to woman's work," Aaronn quoted.

"Truly?" quipped Cai, now grinning in rapacious anticipation of confronting the busybody Irene, the betrothed of Sir Lionel, Lancelot's cousin. The boys in deep conversation spent the next hour with the seneschal. By the time supper was ready to be served, Cai knew all the gossip the boys could remember. He developed a course of attack for the following day. Preparing a tray, he sent it to the snobbish woman, along with a note.

"My dear Lady Irene, please join me in the kitchens later? I am in need of yer valuable advice. Caius Ectorius."

The woman arrived some half-hour later and the seneschal was waiting by the soup pots. He poured her a cup of tea, offered her a pastry, and then sat across from her at the table.

"So, what in yer opinion is wrong with me?" he asked sweetly, taking a bite of the crusty, current-stuffed shell.

"Pardon me?" the elitist coughed.

"The words ye used, I believe, were something to the effect, 'There must be something wrong with a man who cooks rather than fights,' " Cai calmly informed her, then took a careful sip of his current-leaf tea. "So, I ask again, Madam. What is wrong with me, the High King's foster brother?" he asked, watching her expectantly.

The snobbish woman's face turned red with shame, then white with the realization of the blunder she had committed, then red again. "I beg thy pardon, Sir Cai. I spoke out of turn and cruelly so. My mother always said my gossiping tongue would be my downfall, now I see she spoke truth. I shall try harder to govern my sharp tongue," the shame-faced woman spoke contritely, but the wise Cai saw the scorn in her eyes.

"Ah, my dear lady, ye speak fairly but yer eyes tell a different tale indeed," Cai began quietly, his rage tightly reined. "Perhaps I should inform Sir Lionel that ye question my manhood. I would be doing him a favor to let him know ye have such a cruel streak now, before ye are married to him. 'Twould be wrong of me to withhold such a fact 'till ye are wed and the ring is on yer finger," Cai went on, still quietly intense.

"Ye...ye would not tell him, would ye?" the woman asked, unbelieving. "The contracts have been signed and the betrothal gifts exchanged. If the marriage is not forthcoming, my entire family will be disgraced!"

"I know that, Madam. I just wanted ye to understand the position ye are in," Cai remarked casually. "I think 'twould be a favor to a man I call brother for me to tell him his life could be a misery because of a gossiping wife." She stared at him, horrified that he would even consider it, while Cai nonchalantly finished his pastry and tea. "Perhaps if the gossiping were to end, once and for all, Lady, I would have no reason to go to Lionel with this...distasteful piece of information," Cai proposed after letting her agonize for a bit. "Perhaps if ye acted more like a noble woman instead of a scullery maid, I could keep silent."

"Please, My Lord Cai, I shall try," Irene said and the seneschal heard the honesty in her voice at last. "Please, at least give me a chance to change?" she asked with hope in her voice.

"If ye will honestly try, Madam, ye will honestly succeed. The reason I became Arthur's seneschal is because of an injury to my leg, and because 'tis no one else to do it. Arthur's house must run smoothly and as Arthur has no Queen to manage his house, a seneschal must suffice. I was unkind to Arthur when he was first fostered in my father's house; I feel this service is making amends for my cruelty. Does that explain all?" he asked her, chucking her under the chin with a crooked finger in a playful manner.

"Ye hold me no ill-will?" she sniffled and smiled prettily.

"Nay, Madam. Just remember to treat others as ye wish to be treated and ye will always choose rightly," Cai said kindly and let her embrace him quickly.

"Thank ye, Sir Cai," she said, relief evident in her voice. "I shall not forget today's lesson."

Indeed she did remember and only participated in the talk of children and pregnancies, marriages and engagements as she sewed with the other women. When they gossiped, she remained noticeably quiet. She and Sir Lionel were married that spring, before the warring began again. Three months to the day of their honeymoon night, she sent Lionel the news of the Goddess' blessing to him. He received the message at the height of the final battle for the Severn and he threw his arms around the Druid messenger in unrestrained joy. Since this was totally out of character for the usually taciturn man, his whoops of joy brought the entire camp awake as they rested after a day of chasing groups of raiding Saxons around in the hot summer sun.

"What is amiss cousin?" asked Lancelot. Lionel, in his excitement, could only express himself in his native tongue and Lancelot had to translate the joyful babbling for the rest of the Company. "'Tis his bride, Irene," Lancelot tried to follow his cousin's stream of staccato words. "She is with child!" he finally understood and yelled out the last.

"Congratulations, Sir Lionel!" Arthur said at once, sticking out his hand to the happy man.

"Ah, ye are th' rascal, Sir Lionel," Gawaine teased. "'Tis only a bare three month since th' honeymoon."

"Father will be pleased to have youngsters in the house again, Lionel," Sir Bors thumped him on the back soundly. "Ye are a fast worker."

"'Tis joyful news indeed, brother Lionel. Lance, break out some of that 'medicinal' wine I have stashed in my quarters. This news calls for a drink!" the tired King suggested. Lancelot sprinted for the royal tent, returning swiftly with two bulging skins of rich, red wine. "To the prospective father," Arthur offered after each Knight had a cup in hand. "May thy woman carry the child easily and in full health."

"My Lord could we send to Avalon for a priestess to tend Irene? 'Tis our first child, after all," he asked, concerned for his mate.

"Of course, Lionel, I shall send a messenger right away. Congratulations again, brother," Arthur told him, drained his cup and walked back to his tent. Upon entering, he took out a small piece of parchment and carefully inked a short message to Vivaine, asking her to send a skilled midwife priestess to tend Irene. As well, he told her the news of the war so far that year.

"It goes well, Lady. Ceridwen has blessed our efforts to rid the land of the Saxon scourge. The season has brought us only a series of raids so far, now this welcome news of Irene's pregnancy. 'Tis a good year, Lady, but I fear 'twill not last beyond this season. If they do not make a major raid soon, then next year will be a bad one. Goddess bless us all, Lady. Peace be with ye, A. Pendragon Rex Britannia."

The message was sent with a Druid brother, by morning the next day it was in Vivaine's hands. She read it, sent for a young midwife and her able assistance, and sent them to Irene's aid at Camelot.

"Take care of the Lady Irene well, Bridgetta," Vivaine told her proudly. "'Tis the first child of the Round Table and the pregnancy must go uncomplicated."

"I shall do as I have been taught, My Lady," the young woman replied with a bow, then took her leave.

The war season went on, into the fall and early winter until finally at the end of the eleventh month, Cerdic sent a private message to Arthur.

"Pendragon, I must bargain with ye for food. My folk are hungry and I cannot stand the cries of the young ones any longer. We need grain and hard beans for the people, since ye deny us farmlands to raise our own. Name yer price, damn ye, and I'll pay. If ye want that treaty, I'll sign it. Anything so my people can eat! Cerdic Elesing, Cying"

Arthur invited his rival to Camelot for the Winter Solstice and told him to bring packhorses. He commanded that sacks of provisions be prepared for Cerdic and that Lancelot and a company of Knights escort him to Camelot with honor. Cerdic was surprised, for he expected to be treated as a prisoner. He rode at Lancelot's side into Camelot's gate just as a major snowstorm began to drop small, dry flakes onto the bare, frozen ground.

"We welcome ye, Cerdic Cying, to Camelot," Arthur called out and came to him holding out a steaming mug of mulled wine. Cerdic looked shocked and uncertain, but Arthur drank first to reassure him before he offered it again. Cerdic watched Arthur carefully for a few moments, then took the cup, and drank deeply.

"Ah, that puts heart into a man, by Thor's beard!" Cerdic commented. "My thanks to ye Pendragon."

"Come into my house in peace, Cerdic Elesing of the Coiled Serpent Tribe, Cying of the Federated Tribes," Arthur said formally. "Share my table and let us discuss peace," he invited and led the man into the great room. "Sir Cai, please see to the horses and men, then join us within?"

"Of course, Sire," Cai answered, bowing slightly and limping off quickly. Cerdic blanched a bit as he turned to Arthur with an apologetic look on his face.

"I never did tell ye how sorry I am about yer foster brother's leg, Pendragon. I was aiming for ye."

"I know, Cerdic. Ye have noticed I do not let ye get that close any more."

"Aye, I've noticed," the burly Saxon grinned.

Arthur poured his own cup of wine and they sat, looking at each other uncomfortably.

"Let us not waste each other's time bandying words, Pendragon," Cerdic began. "Ye want peace and I need food fer my people. What are the terms for this treaty?"

"Ye know the terms, Cerdic. Renounce Vortigern's treaty with yer people and negotiate with me fairly," Arthur listed quickly and earnestly.

"An' where then do my people farm? Where do we now hunt and fish?" Cerdic spoke harshly, impatiently, calming himself with an effort.

"Cerdic, 'tis what the negotiations will decide! Let us refrain from fighting for a year and try to live in peace?" Arthur asked reasonably.

"I'll talk for three months, Pendragon. If we cannot work it out by then, we never will," Cerdic countered.

"Cerdic, our people have been enemies for decades. Do ye truly think that all our differences can be worked out in three months?" Arthur asked, incredulous that he could ignore such an opportunity for peace.

"That's all I can promise, Pendragon. My people need land by spring. If they don't have it, the raids will start again," Cerdic said, brutally honest. "Now, let's eat! I haven't had a meal for two days," he grinned wolfishly. They sat at table then and Cerdic ate for three-quarters of an hour, then ate a final bite of dessert, burped politely into his napkin, and sat back. "Ahhh!" he sighed, accepting a steaming cup from Sir Cai. Sipping, his face assumed a surprised, pleased expression. "What is this?" he asked.

"'Tis called 'caffe,' Cerdic," Arthur informed him, and sipped his own portion of the rare and delicious beverage.

"Well Pendragon, do I sleep in a guest room or in the dungeons?" Cerdic asked abruptly.

"Ye are my guest, Cerdic," Arthur chuckled and showed him to the warm, spacious room personally.

"Would ye care to bathe before retiring?" he asked the Saxon.

Cerdic wrinkled up his brow as he asked in a perplexed tone; "Why would I want to bathe? I ran through a rainstorm just before Samhain."

Arthur chuckled all the harder at the dichotomous man, Roman-educated but so very Saxon about his personal habits. He took his leave, calling a cheery goodnight to his rival and nodding to the two Knights who now stood on each side of Cerdic's guest room door.

"Make sure he stays in there all night, Agravaine and Tristan. I am putting ye both here because I trust the two of ye to take proper precautions to insure that he stays in his room. Good night, ye two, and stay on guard, the both of ye," Arthur cautioned quickly and quietly. "And Tristan, remember. No wenches!"

"Aye, Sire," Tristan grinned back toothily. "Be sure ye tell Sir Cai to send up some food first thing though, aye?"

"Aye, Tristan, I shall tell him," Arthur laughed quietly.

"Good night then, Artos. Sleep ye sound," the two men said as he took his leave, then they both assumed an "on guard" stance and remained alert till morning.

Arthur went down to the kitchen, where Cai was assembling the emergency rations and now stood with inventory list in hand. He counted everything twice, readying the bags and bundles for their long trip to Saxon territory on the backs of the sturdy packhorses.

"Is it ready, Cai?" Arthur asked.

"Almost," the seneschal sighed. "It looks like such a lot, but will it be enough?" he asked, scratching his head.

"It only has to be enough to keep them alive through the winter. 'Tis no sense in keeping them too strong, though," Arthur sighed heavily, realizing the strategic importance of not giving the Saxons any more than they absolutely needed.

"'Tis a pity they will not ally with us, the both of us would be the stronger for it. This war is bad for all of us, Brit and Saxon," Cai agreed.

"I am for a bit of sleep, Cai. I need ye fresh in the morning, so do not stay up too late," Arthur told him.

"Have no worry, brother. I just want to make sure 'tis all here before I retire," Cai replied wearily. "Good night, Artos."

"Good night, Caius. Sleep ye sound," the young King replied, affection in his tone. "What would I do without ye, my foster-brother?" he asked as he embraced the older man.

"I dare say ye would have been happier without me, at times, especially when ye first started doing chores for Mum," Cai chuckled, a bit misty-eyed.

"Aye, ye were hard on me, Cai, but it taught me to be tough. That training has come in handy since I became King, believe me," Arthur told him honestly. "And 'tis kind of my fault about yer leg and everything."

"Nonsense, Artos!" Cai pooh-poohed it all. "If I had been more watchful where I was riding, that Saxon would have never slashed my leg with that seax."

"If ye had not ridden in-between me and Cerdic, 'twould have never happened," Arthur countered. "And while I miss yer familiar puss on the battlefield, I muchly value the service ye now perform here at Camelot. Because of yer organizational skills, the castle runs smoothly and efficiently, just like Ector's house did. Thank ye Caius, for being my seneschal. Ye bring us all honor," the King finished, gave Cai a final hug and then released him. "Good night, foster-brother."

"Good night, Artos."

The next morning dawned clear and cold, snow lay deep on the ground. Despite the difficult traveling conditions, Cerdic insisted on leaving immediately after breakfast. He spoke not a word except a terse "Good bye," to Arthur and the Company as Lancelot, Gawaine and the rest escorted the long pack train from the castle. They rode as quickly as the laden animals could move through the knee-high snow, just before full dark they came to the shores of the Severn and into a clearing.

"Ho there, it's Cerdic!" the Saxon leader called out, and fifty or so ragged people emerged from the snow-covered underbrush. They saw the line of Knights, each leading a trio of pack animals laden with sacks of grain and beans. A weak cheer of "Hail, Cerdic!" went up at the sight. Immediately, the men came to pull a sack of oats and a sack of hard beans from the first pack-frame, while Lancelot and Gawaine helped others chop through the thinly frozen waters of the Severn for water. Carrying the huge kettles to the newly built fires, the Knights assisted the starving people in preparing the quicker cooking oats and wheat for that night and soaking the hard beans for the morrow. Finally finished with their charitable work, the Knights prepared to take their leave.

"We thank ye, warriors of the Pendragon, fer yer help. Ye'd best begone though, those of the other tribes might not understand if they find ye here," Cerdic told them. "I just can't control them all, especially when they are hungry."

"Very well, Cerdic Cying, may the Goddess watch over ye all," Lancelot agreed tiredly. "Come on, boyos. Mount up, now," he called to the others. Moans of protest went quickly silent and the mailed warriors climbed aboard their mounts. At Lancelot's order, they all moved out in a single column. Once across the Severn, Lancelot heard Cerdic's hail and turned about to answer. He saw Cerdic pull a piece of parchment from his vest, wad it up and throw it into one of the cooking fires.

"There's yer treaty, boyo! I only needed it to feed my people. Ye all watch yer mailed asses next year come spring, we'll be a-raiding again!" the Saxon leader's voice roared across the thin frozen water. The assembly with him cheered their defiance as well, even as they wolfed down the cooked porridge they had made from good British grain.

"Ye'd best watch yer own asses!" roared Gawaine in answer. "If we catch ye in British territory again, ye'll be dead men!"

Laughter rang out then and the weary Knights rode off, headed for the only town for miles and the inn there. Upon arrival at the small inn, the Knight's weary horses went willingly to warm, hay-filled stalls, where they were grained and watered. Blankets soon covered the groomed horses as they ate and drank gratefully, every man's horse lay down as soon as their hunger was sated and fell at once asleep. The Knights were similarly treated, soon the entire patrol slept soundly. On the shores of the Severn, scores of hungry Saxons ate heartily of the good British grain they had tried so hard to keep from growing the summer before.

Lancelot's patrol returned with packhorses in tow the following afternoon, and it was a disheartened First Knight who related Cerdic's renunciation of the treaty. Arthur sighed, turned, and slowly trudged back to his private room, where he spent the next hour in frustrated rage. After his fit, he wiped his eyes and coolly began to plan the strategy for the next spring. Go ahead and raid, Cerdic, he thought. We'll be here, waiting for ye.

The rest of that winter the land lay in the grip of a cold spell, while Aaronn grew and matured. The boy's athletic build was beginning to show while Olran's body stayed thin and wiry. The two of them had been at Avalon now for just over a year, with time outs for visits at Camelot, and their training in the arcane arts had begun. Aaronn was just able to "see" in the pool, while Olran was a past master of the skill since age five. Much more difficult for him was to mix herbal potions for healing or sleeping, while Aaronn was fascinated by the smells of the stillroom, where Brother Michael stored his pharmacopeia of dried herbs and liquid tinctures.

Brother Michael was also beginning to teach Aaronn the exercises to build his hand-eye coordination; while Brother Drusus had started Olran's tracking lessons. The two boys discussed everything they heard. When the news of Cerdic's broken treaty came to Avalon, Aaronn was enraged. "But why did he do it, Brother Drusus? Why?" the lad asked.

"Because Aaronn, he never meant to keep his word. He only did what he had to for his hungry people. He had to tear it up and in front of them, so he could save his honor and remain their ruler. Cerdic is no fool, Aaronn. He is Roman-educated, speaks and writes Latin as well as any Druid and has read Caesar's Commentaries. Do not make the same mistakes Uther did, Aaronn. Do not ever, ever underestimate Cerdic or any of his kin," Drusus spoke heatedly. "We warned Uther, but he was stubborn and would not listen."

"I am listening!" Aaronn responded, nodding while he catalogued this bit of information. Drusus gave him a few moments to do so before he began the barrage of questions again.

Meanwhile, the political situation in Britain continued to develop. Arthur's new alliance with Caw brought tough fighting men from the North into the ranks of the Pendragon's army and Lancelot wasted no time drilling them along with the others. Caw's men fit right into the battle plan, adding lines of heavy infantry to the swelling army.

During the heavy snows of winter, the petty Kings and noble houses sent droves of eligible young maids to Camelot, pestering the High King endlessly with proposals of alliances through marriage. Poor Arthur, already pre-occupied with planning the defenses for the Severn and all the other strategic sites around Britain, felt driven to distraction by the endless and often maddeningly mindless prattle of the young women. Finally, he ordered Cai to keep them busy somehow. The seneschal found work for them all and any that would not bend to the labors went home in disgrace; those women who stayed struggled to accustom themselves to working despite never having to do a bit of real labor before. Soon, Cai had a well-trained and beautiful workforce, and the morale of the Knights improved noticeably as they enjoyed the kind and tender charms of the flowers of Britain. Many a noble house settled for a knightly marriage instead of the royal one for which they had hoped.

Arthur brought Aaronn home to Camelot and Olran came as well. The boys celebrated Aaronn's ninth birthday with the King and the Company helped make it special for the boys. Aaronn received his first practice sword, complete with scabbard as well as new boots, and a thick, black hooded cape clasped at the throat with a bright copper pin.

"Aaronn, I have news for ye," Arthur announced when he and Aaronn had a private moment.

"Aye, Sire?"

"I have arranged for some fostering for ye and Olran at Lothian Castle. My own half-sister, Morgause, is queen there. Moreover, Lot has sons so he should know how to train them. 'Twill be another lad with ye as well, his name is Dalren and he recently lost his family and home. Will ye try to be friends with him?"

"But Lothian is so far away from Camelot, Dragon Isle and Avalon," Aaronn complained a bit.

"I know, but I have no idea how bad the fighting will be this year. It might be only more raids or a return to real war, but either way I still need all the help of the Druids as well as Avalon. I had hoped ye would be more pleased at the news," Arthur explained.

"No Druid college then this year either?" Aaronn asked, sadly.

"Nay Aaronn, not this year," answered another, deeper voice behind them.

"Lord Merlin!" Aaronn exclaimed delightedly.

"Hullo Aaronn, happy birthday, boyo," the Merlin greeted them each. "Greetings, My Lord Arthur."

"Thank ye, Lord Merlin," answered Aaronn.

"Well Aaronn, 'tis time for bed," Arthur said, rising from his chair.

"Already?" Aaronn asked, reluctant to leave the still-active great room.

"Aye, boyo," Arthur chuckled. "Poor Olran is asleep already," he finished and lifted the wiry lad from his seat with his strong warrior's arms. Aaronn followed after, yawning hugely all the way until the boys were abed.

"Good night, Aaronn. May the Goddess give ye good dreams," Arthur said softly to his ward, his brother.

"Good night, My Lord Arthur," Aaronn murmured back and Arthur wondered at the ease of the formality on the nine-year olds' lips. Soft snores soon sounded from Aaronn's bed and Arthur sat beside him for a bit longer, watching him sleep. Soft whispers of lace whispered behind him, and knowing feminine hands wound round his neck from behind, gently massaging his tightly corded muscles.

"My Lord?" her voice whispered into his ear, causing the heat to rise in him.

"Where did ye come from, Dawn?" he softly asked, rising to take her in his arms.

"I followed ye from the great room, My Lord. Do ye need a bath tonight?" she asked, suggestively untying the laced front of Arthur's shirt.

"Ah Dawn, it sounds tempting," he gently restrained her long fingers from the lacing and tying them again. "But such pleasures must wait 'till later, much later. Go on to bed now, my dear, and I shall send for ye later if 'tis not too late," he reluctantly sent the pliant wench on her way with a gentle slap on her shapely bottom. She blew him a kiss and giggled out the door, the lace of her undergown whooshing down the hall. Arthur took a moment to compose his emotions by splashing a bit of cold water from Aaronn's pitcher onto a washcloth. Sponging his face and the back of his neck to remove the sheen of passion sweat, he stood by the open window until he felt calmer. He then took his leave, quietly shutting the door behind him. Walking quickly and purposefully to the war room, he entered and found the Inner Circle awaiting him.

"Thank ye for spending so much time in this room, my brothers, especially since Cai has recruited such a lovely group of servers. 'Twill all be worth it if we can keep as many men-at-arms alive through the next year as possible."

"Aye, Artos," yawned Agravaine. "So tell us agin where th' most likely attacks'll be an' how we'll array oursel's against 'em."

The others chuckled with him and even Arthur joined in. "Have I been so repetitive?" he asked, somewhat dismayed.

"With the abundance of eligible women around ye, Artos, ye could relax just a bit," Tristan drawled lazily, but all could see the sparkle of humor in his eyes. "After all, spring is still three and a half months away."

"Aye, and even though vigilance is always a watchword, Artos, relaxation would be a welcome change from all this business," came Lancelot's voice from the right side of the table. All heads swiveled to regard Lancelot, the pure and "Impeccable Knight" with astonishment. In all the years, they had known him; the man had never taken so much as a glance at a woman to their knowledge. In that light, his remark seemed very out of character.

"Why Lance, 'tis amazing from ye!" wondered Arthur aloud.

"My Lord, even a man whose duty is as solemn as mine comes to a point where relaxation is essential. I have reached that point, and I do not want to work anymore!" he stated firmly and sat down.

Silence reigned for a few moments until finally Arthur began to laugh uproariously. The Knights all joined in and the war council dismissed. Within minutes, they had dispersed to their own amusements for the night.

For Arthur's part, the King went to his chambers climbed into bed and slept for sixteen hours straight. Finally, he woke and sent to Cai for breakfast. After a bit, a soft rap sounded and a woman's voice called out huskily, "My Lord?"

Arthur quickly opened his door, pulled the courtesan inside, and closed the portal, locking it. "I would like that bath now, if yer willing, Lady," he suggested, embracing her and pushing the soft lace of her dress aside.

"Perhaps later, My Lord," she purred as he took the tray from her and set it aside. Carrying her to his bed, he carefully removed her thin wraps and again caught his breath at her generous and beautiful shape.

"Thank ye, Ceridwen, for Thy gift," he murmured as he buried his face in her wealth of sun-gold hair. No one saw the King until the next morning.

When Aaronn awoke, Olran was already up and preparing a pot of tea for them both. It had become something of a ritual for the boys since beginning their lessons with Brother Michael and Brother Drusus to have this morning libation and discuss the plans for the day. In the winter, Olran wouldn't do without a cup of something hot, and Aaronn found it a pleasant way to wake up his stomach for breakfast.

"Did ye hear what the King said?" asked Aaronn, somewhat excited by the news. "We are to be fostered at Lothian Castle this spring and summer."

"What was that ye said? We are to go to Lothian Castle?" Olran asked, almost spilling his tea as he sat down next to Aaronn on the hearthrug.

"Aye, with the King's own half-sister to mother us for a season," Aaronn told him.

"Ye mean Gawaine's and Agravaine's mother, ye know," Olran pointed out. "I have heard my Da say that she is beautiful, in a whorish sort of way," he recited for Aaronn. "I wonder what he means by that?" he mused, still innocent at nine.

"I suppose we will have to find out," the faster-maturing Aaronn answered, feeling a warm rush wash all over him when Olran said the word, "whorish."

While the boys had lived on Avalon, they were taught about the simplest of mysteries, the why behind the differences between male and female bodies. Aaronn wondered what it would be like to touch their soft skin and stroke the wealth of hair that most women sported. As he sat considering this, he felt again the warm glow wash over him. With difficulty he dismissed such thoughts from his mind. There was no sense thinking of such things, in any case, he mentally chastised himself. No woman is going to let a nine-year old find out anyway, so I shall just have to wait till I am old enough to find out.

"Hey Aaronn, what is this?" asked Olran as he wandered the room. Aaronn rose and walked to where Olran was staring at the wall.

"Ye mean this?" asked Aaronn running his fingers over a slightly indented design that was barely noticeable. He pressed on the small, carved dragon cleverly concealed in the patterns of the wood. The panel recessed, and then slid noiselessly aside. Both boys' eyes opened wide in surprise, Aaronn stepped boldly through the barely man-sized opening.

"Olran, come on," he breathed in astonishment at finding the hidden passageway. "There are three ways to go, help me choose one."

"Aaronn, tell me true. Are there any creepy-crawlies in there?" Olran asked with trepidation. Aaronn looked about carefully, knowing that his friend would not enter unless all the dangers were known.

"I see a few cobwebs, Olran, but naught else," he said after a few moments.

"All right then, I am coming in," Olran answered eagerly, lighting a candle he stepped through the opening. "Should we leave this open so we can get back out?"

"'Tis got to have an exit somewhere, Olran. Just leave a marker and let us get on with it."

Olran dropped a kerchief on the floor in front of the doorway, then searched and found the closing mechanism inside the corridor, when he pushed gently he watched as the door slid noiselessly shut.

"Let us go, Aaronn," the thin lad urged, then grinned. "Which way to the kitchens, do you think? I'm starved!" Aaronn and he set about investigating the passageways, Aaronn watching in fascination by Olran's display of ability as his friend searched then stood smelled the air. Finally after a bit, Olran pointed down the center passageway and said; "This way I think."

"Let us see if yer right," Aaronn grinned and he walked with Olran down the narrow corridor.

Aaronn followed, committing the route to memory as they walked along carefully and quietly. The corridor turned right, went down several flights of stairs and then they were in front of a door.

"Where do ye think we are?" asked Aaronn in a hushed whisper.

"I am not sure, we could be anywhere. But I think we are near the great room," Olran answered, his heart racing with excitement.

"I am for it, let us find out!" Aaronn chuckled as he found the dragon sign. Pressing it, he watched the panel slide aside and the boys peeked out. They saw the great room and realized they were but a few feet from the kitchen entrance.

"Come on, before we are seen," Olran whispered. He blew out the candle as he exited, placing it in his pocket as he pulled Aaronn behind him. They quickly closed the panel, composed themselves, and then calmly entered the kitchens.

"Good morning, Sir Cai!" they both greeted the busy seneschal.

"Good morning, boyos, 'tis a busy day today and I shall need yer help," Cai said warmly. "King Lot, King Uriens and their wives are coming to explain why they are refusing to send their treaty conscripts for training with the army. I am preparing a banquet to greet them; I wish Arthur could spare a man or two for a hunting expedition though. All I have are dried meats and we should have fresh," he worried a bit, unable to help himself.

"We could go, Sir Cai," Aaronn volunteered. "We have seen plenty of hares about and both Olran and I can set snares and…" he went on, hoping Cai would give his permission.

"Can I trust you not to get yerselves lost?" Cai asked, concerned.

"We have been out in the woods both on Dragon Island as well as on Avalon and we've never gotten lost. We will not go over the River Cam," Olran put in, anticipating some exercise outdoors.

"Very well, but eat hearty before ye go, and dress warmly," Cai fussed as he set steaming bowls of his best grain porridge before them, along with a cup of tea. Both boys wolfed the meal before they dressed in the wraps Cai brought them.

"Go quickly boyos and do not dawdle. Taliesin said there would be snow later today and I trust his weather eye. Just three fat hares would be enough for the formal meal, if ye can find them. Goddess keep ye both," he said ruffled both boy's hair a bit before settling their caps on their heads.

"Have no worry, Sir Cai," assured Aaronn in a most grow-up tone. "We will be back soon, with all the meat we can carry."

"Just do not get caught out there in the snow, boyos. I mean it!" Cai warned as they went out the scullery door, closing it carefully behind them.

The day was gloriously sunny, and the cold bit into their bare cheeks and noses. They walked purposefully down the hill to the River Cam before turning north to follow the upriver course to the edges of the deep green forest surrounding Camelot. Almost immediately upon entering the scrub and underbrush, the keen-eyed Olran found a busy rabbit trail and began following it.

"How many do ye see, Olran?" asked Aaronn after the two had followed the game trail for a while.

"I see at least twelve, mostly adults with the last of the fall bunnies. I also see four sets, possibly five of big male tracks," the hunter reported.

"We cannot use the snares then, we would not want to catch any of the bunnies," Aaronn observed.

"We will not have to use snares, look what I brought," Olran whispered and pulled a small but powerful bow and a quiver of arrows from his pack. "Brother Drusus gave this to me before he left to help the King."

"'Tis beautiful, Olran. Can ye really use it?" Aaronn asked in the same quiet voice.

"Come along and see for yerself!" Olran grinned as he turned his concentration on the trail. The boys followed the tracks until they found the first male's den. The huge hare was just outside the rabbit hole's opening, nibbling on some dried grasses. Aaronn watched as his friend knelt down, soundlessly strung the bow, nocked an arrow, sighted quickly and carefully before he released smoothly, as if all in one motion. The hare jerked only once before it lay still, dying without making a sound. Aaronn nearly broke cover to fetch it then he saw the second hare, even bigger than the first, hop out of his hole. Olran had also seen, and another arrow flew from the boy's ash bow, piercing the hare through the ears. A third rabbit appeared and Olran got that one too, impaling him from chest to fuzzy tail. The fourth hare came hopping along the trail behind Olran, when he saw it Aaronn acted without thinking, whirling and casting his single light knife, a gift from Brother Michael. He caught the hare in the throat, nearly severing its head just as Olran shot his final flint-tipped arrow and took out the largest and last of the males.

"We got them all, Aaronn!" he crowed as he stooped, slit a rabbit's throat and retrieved his arrow. This process repeated until all the weapons were cleaned and replaced in their proper places. The hares were taken away from their holes, field-dressed and tied together by the feet, three for Aaronn and two for Olran, then slung over each boy's shoulders.

"Come on Olran, that sky is clouding up something fierce. We should be on our way home," Aaronn urged.

"Aye, this way," the tracker pointed and led the way back. Within a half an hour, the boys were back at the castle and entering through the scullery door. A few minutes later big, fluffy flakes of snow began to fall in rapid quantity.

"Welcome home, boyos," Cai greeted the cold, hungry boys. "The Goddess was kind today, I see," he smiled.

"Aye, Sir Cai, we got five big ones," Aaronn told him excitedly.

"So I see. Nice neat arrow holes, Olran. Aaronn, ye must have gotten this one, 'tis been slain with a knife," he went on, looking the hares over with a battle-experienced eye. "Ye lads must be learning something with the Druids after all," he chuckled as he ladled out two bowls of delicious-smelling lentil stew, handing them to the hunters. Big cups of milk, slabs of bread and cheese came a few moments later, Cai watched in utter admiration as the hearty fare disappeared in a few minutes, followed by requests for more. Meanwhile, the hares found their way from dressing table to the cold room to await their roasting time.

"Thank ye boys. 'Twill be a fine addition to the deer Tristan just surprised me with. Now 'twill be plenty for all," Cai thanked them gratefully. "Please go and wash up now and change into yer livery. We will need all the help we can muster when Lot and Uriens arrive, and I shall need ye two to serve in the great room," he finished and sent them on their way with a huge oatmeal cookie. As they walked through the great room munching their cookies, the boys watched the activity. The Knights were assisting the staff in hanging up the first of the new tapestries, a pictorial of Arthur's crowning. The boys disappeared into the secret door they had found earlier and retraced their steps back to their rooms. They quickly washed themselves from head to toe before dressing in the colors of Camelot's service corps. Once adorned in the blue and silver surcoats, black trous, black hose and their boots, they returned to the great room the same way as earlier.

"We are going to map out all these corridors, aye?" Aaronn whispered as they approached the secret door and pressed the release.

"Of course we will, but would it not be easier to just ask the Merlin? After all, 'twas he that designed the building and the Druids built it," Olran replied.

"True, but 'twould not be nearly as much fun if we just asked," Aaronn chuckled. "We are going to have to do more hunting together. That was fun to watch, what ye did with that bow."

"That knife throw was no accident, either. Ye have been working hard," Olran turned the compliment back. "We make a good team."

"For always," Aaronn answered, holding out his hand to Olran. "Ye do not really want to be a Druid, d'ye?"

Olran took the hand offered him. "Nay, I suppose not, although I could and be happy. Our service will always be for the Lady, for Arthur, and the Land?"

"Aye, for Ceridwen and Arthur for all our lives," Aaronn agreed firmly and they clasped forearms as equals, the renegade prince and the king's bastard.

"For Ceridwen and Arthur for all our lives," Olran echoed and they both felt an inner "click" deep within their souls, as if a piece of the universal puzzle had just been fitted into place right there in that room. Each boy stared at the other in astonishment and wonder.

"Come on, Olran, let us go find out where we can help the most. Maybe we will get to serve the High Table tonight if we work hard enough. I would like to get close enough to the Lady Morgause to see if she's 'whorish,' " Aaronn laughingly proposed, winking broadly at his friend.

"Why?" asked Olran innocently as they entered the busy great room, unseen by any.

The boys reported to Cai and immediately set to work setting flatware onto the new, spotless linen tablecloths that draped each of the long tables. Each cloth was embroidered on the corner with Arthur's silver dragon crest, along with a similarly decorated napkin, folded neatly. Atop the napkin, they placed a steel spoon and fork, making sure the drinking vessel was in the correct spot at each table setting. The boys had barely finished that task when Lot and Uriens arrived, along with their wives and servers.

Arthur came to meet them immediately; he was dressed all in white, edged in blue cord. He offered each of the royal guests a cup of welcome from Sir Cai's handy tray.

"Welcome, Sister Morgause and Brother Lot, to Camelot," he greeted formally. "King Uriens and Queen Althea, we welcome ye in equal proportion. Drink, my allies, to the regaining of the Severn at last and to the success of our campaigns against the enemy. Be ye welcome in my home. Pages, would ye please take our guest's wraps and put them to dry by the fire?" Arthur said to Aaronn and Olran, who happened to be at hand. Lot nonchalantly dropped his wet, heavy bearskin into Olran's arms; the wiry lad caught and held it with no trouble. Aaronn went to Lady Morgause and held out his hand for her gorgeous ermine-trimmed velvet cloak. When the Queen of the Orkneys saw the young lad, her eyebrows rose with sudden interest, why, he looks like Uther she thought briefly, before dismissing the thought as ridiculous. With my secret powers, she thought further, I would have known of any more of Uther's bastard sons. The randy old goat had sired many daughters, all of who lived at Avalon, most of them promised to noble husbands and a royal dowry pledged for them. Still, the resemblance was remarkable and impossible to ignore for the ever-curious woman.

Uriens and Althea gave their soggy wraps to the pages before turning to the warm, blazing fire in the hearth to warm frigid fingers and toes. Talk was sparse at first, until Lot and Uriens had warmed up to another cup of cheer, while the ladies retired to rest and bathe before supper.

"Well Pendragon, thanks to ye the Severn's safe at last," Uriens commented at length. "Vortigern was a fool to sign it away!"

"We are agreed there, My Lord Uriens. Now that food will again flow from the breadbasket of Britain, we have all that much more work to do to keep them out. The army must be at full strength by spring, My Lords, so we will number enough to man all the new forts along the river borders," Arthur said carefully, leashing his anger that these two men always inspired in him. They had opposed him from the day of his king making, and reports of their treasonous alliances only made dealing with them harder.

"Aye, an' coom spring th' troops'll be there, Pendragon!" Lot growled. "I've given ye me word on it."

"I told ye to have them here by Samhain, My Lord Lot. Why are they not at Camelot for training?" Arthur said carefully.

"Look ye here, Pendragon, most o' those I send ye are farmers an' family men, as are those sent by Uriens here. We cannae joost order 'em away frum their families durin' th' winter! Who'd be providin' fer 'em while they are goon?" Lot responded, his anger growing. He was only here to stall Arthur after all. Once the spring campaigning began, he meant to withhold his troops altogether from the battles, along with his taxes. His plan was to weaken Arthur's forces enough to make him renounce the throne, if Uriens' commitment to the plan was as strong as his own, Lot thought happily. Knowing that to fight Arthur alone was a fool's game, he had long ago enlisted Urien's support for Gawaine's elevation to the High Throne. Now their alliance must hold together, even in the face of Arthur's sure anger and vengeance, he mentally grumped as he let a young pageboy fill his cup.

"Thank ye, lad," he murmured and took a full pull of the potent, warmed libation.

"Ye are welcome, My Lord Lot," Aaronn replied politely and moved to fill Urien's cup.

"As for winter sustenance, ye are the kings of yer territories and so obliged to make recompense while the conscripts are away from their families," Arthur replied coolly. "So, My Lords, when do the treaty troops arrive?" he pressed, wanting to know.

Lot spluttered into his cup. "D'ye have any idea wha' tha'll cost, boyo?" he exclaimed, choking a bit as Aaronn brought a damp cloth to wipe the beads of wine from Lot's fire-red beard.

"Aye, well do I know the cost," Arthur sighed. "Remember, the foot soldiers in my army get a full share of any booty captured during an engagement. As well, the Crown pays a certain stipend to the men. Having no need for money while with the army for all is provided they can put their stipend away in the Royal Bank. It, and any interest they earn, goes with them when they go home. That should help defray the costs, My Lords," Arthur said warningly. He knew Lot meant him ill will and he meant to head it off right now.

"Now Lot, ye told me naught of such a generous offer," Uriens finally spoke up. "My men will be here in a month," he pledged.

"Mine will be here in spring, no sooner," Lot growled and stood up, his mere bulk dwarfing Arthur slightly.

"My Lord Lot, ye will send them before spring, or the treaty between us is null and void!" Arthur spoke quiet and deadly. "I have no further patience to bandy words, Lot. Send 'em or fight me."

"I shall thin' on't, Pendragon. An' ye kin joost wait fer m' answer as well," he said, belligerently throwing his glass on the hearth. Instantly, a ring of steel surrounded him, his own son's swords at his throat as well.

"Send 'em Da," Gawaine insisted quietly.

"Aye Da," Agravaine added. "We need 'em."

Lot looked around him and found Arthur still standing and sipping his wine impassively. "Aye then, mine come when Urien's do. Will tha' suit ye?" he spoke harshly to Arthur, but looking at Gawaine and Agravaine.

"Aye, My Lord," Arthur answered. "'Twill do."

"We ha' mooch t' speak o' when next ye two coom home, boyos," Lot menaced his sons quietly.

Gawaine seemingly ignored him, as did Agravaine; everyone put their swords away. Cai appeared with the small foods just at that moment, and the ladies returned to the great room to find Arthur and the Knights chatting easily with King Uriens, while Lot glowered in the corner.

"My Lord Arthur, this new castle is marvelous!" the matronly Althea gushed. "Imagine having one's own screened privy area, complete with running water, right in the room! One would think 'twas Rome itself."

"Indeed, my royal brother. Ye must share the secrets of yer plumbing system," Morgause laughed her rich, throaty laugh.

"Ye will have to ask the Merlin and his Druid engineers, my sister Morgause," Arthur told her with a smile on his face; however the Queen of the Orkneys did not miss the hint of steely warning in his voice. "Would ye care for a plate of small foods?"

"Thank ye, brother mine," Morgause said and took his proffered arm as they went to the sideboard. Arthur over-loaded a plate with cheese, bread, pickled artichoke hearts, shredded pickled cabbage, hard-boiled eggs and olives. They spoke together for a few moments quietly, then Morgause snatched the plate from Arthur's hands and stepped away, her black eyes snapping sparks.

"How dare ye, Arthur!" she declared quietly, but furiously. "Ye cannot make us send the treaty troops in the middle of winter!"

"I suggest ye speak to yer sons, Madam, about what I can or cannot do! I am High King in Britain, ordained by Ceridwen and the Christ and I rule here! Those men will be here in a month, or tis war between Orkney and the army of the Pendragon!" Arthur answered in a voice low and harsh. "If ye have any influence over yer husband, Madam, I suggest ye use it! I must have those troops."

Morgause gave him a long and measuring look before she stalked away, headed for Gawaine's side. Arthur sighed, gulped his wine, and went to Cai for more. It was going to be a long night, he thought.

It was indeed a very long and tedious evening, culminating in a screaming tirade from Morgause directed at poor Aaronn. The lad, being temporarily distracted by the depths of Morgause's neckline, had spilled a drop or two of hot tea into the Orkney queen's lap. The lad just stood there, shock on his face as the woman began to shriek, much to Arthur's and the other Knight's hidden amusement.

"Ye clumsy fool! That tea is hot, and now I am burnt to the skin!"

"I…I…I…" Aaronn stammered as he tried to dab the wet spots dry. "I am sorry, Queen Morgause, I did not mean to spill," he finally got out.

"Aaronn, please go to the kitchen and report to Sir Cai," Arthur instructed him coolly and gave the boy a gentle push towards the door.

"He should be soundly whipped, my brother," Morgause whimpered. "My legs are burned all over."

"Sir Cai will send up a pot of healing salve, made by our sister Morgaine. My ward will be instructed so this does not occur again," Arthur consoled her.

"Very well," she pouted. "My Lord Arthur, husband, I am going to bed. I want to go home tomorrow, this whole business of war and troops is so very tedious and boring," Morgause went on, pettishly.

"Ye may go if ye please, Lady," Lot told her. "I mus' stay an' talk a bit longer wi' th' King."

"Perhaps a stop at Londinium Market on the way home would cure my mood, My Lord," Morgause suggested, her manner brightening a bit. Lot sighed and nodded in agreement as Morgause flounced off, her "painful burns" hardly even slowing her progress. Lady Althea took her man off to bed a short time later. Before she left, however, she stopped in front of Arthur. After curtsying a bit and Uriens bowed, she leaned forward and spoke quietly;

"If ye need more troops, I'll make sure ye get them," she said and winked conspiratorially. "My sons, Maegwyn and Accolon will bring them and stay to assist. I would be proud to say my sons serve with the Pendragon. Also, watch out for Westerland Keep," she spoke with warning. "They hold ye no love at all."

"Thank ye, Lady Althea, for the warning. I shall be extremely careful," he grinned.

"I see thy wretch of a father in that scoundrel's grin, Lord Arthur. May the Goddess bless ye, and thy Company of Knights. Ye may also seek extra troops from our neighbor, Lord Leodegrance. He is being carefully neutral and might need ah…persuasion to enter the conflict."

"What sort of persuasion?" asked Arthur, curious as to what the older woman's words were about.

"Althea, 'tis time for bed, my dear. Lord Arthur needs no more of yer gossip," Uriens called out sleepily.

"On the morrow, My Lord," she said to Arthur, curtsying deeply. "I am coming, my husband," she called out to Uriens and gracefully walked to him. Arthur waited until their footsteps were gone, then he dropped onto his seat.

"I need something strong to drink," he murmured loudly.

"Aye, Me Lord Arthur," Gawaine chuckled and pulled a flat flask from inside his tunic. Crossing to the King's cup, he uncorked the bottle and poured a generous portion into Arthur's cup. Agravaine reached under the table pulled out his own stash, a full stoneware jug full of the potent Orkney liquor they called whiskey, the other Knights clustered about him, holding out their cups as well. Arthur drank his portion and another before he felt any relaxation at all, then he removed the simple gold circlet that he favored over the heavy formal crown and rubbed his aching head. Aaronn came out of the kitchen, clearing tray in hand, concern clearly on his face.

"Come here, Aaronn," Arthur called and the boy came immediately.

"I am sorry, Sire. I truly did not mean to burn the Lady Morgause," Aaronn apologized earnestly.

"Of course not, boyo, however perhaps next time ye should pay more attention to the cup and less to the lady's neckline," Arthur chuckled.

"Aye, Sire," Aaronn blushed and hung his head.

"Good lad," Arthur complimented his attitude. "Now go on to bed, ye and Olran. Good night."

"Ye forgive me?" Aaronn asked.

"Of course, Aaronn," Arthur told him and hugged the lad. Aaronn embraced the King tightly for a long moment.

"Thank ye, Sire. Good night!" Aaronn told him before going back to the kitchen to fetch Olran. His friend was stretched out on a bench, asleep. The two boys went off to bed, as did the Knights and Arthur. The King wearily trudged off to his room looking forward to a few hours of sleep. Pushing open his door, he found his hearth warmly blazing, a sweet-smelling bath before it. A grin crossed his face as Dawn appeared before the fire, the diaphanous gauzy gown only highlighting her delightful, womanly figure. In her hands, she held a decanter of amber liquor and two small cups.

"I heard what happened, My Lord. I thought ye might enjoy a nice massage," her lovely voice came to him across the fire lit room.

"Ye are a most thoughtful woman, Dawn. A bath and a massage would be most welcome," Arthur said and crossed to her. "Ye are a welcome sight, my dear."

"I am glad ye are pleased, My Lord. I wove this myself," Dawn said and brought Arthur a drink. He took it and kissed her lightly on the lips.

"'Tis a thing of beauty, as are ye, Dawn."

"Thank ye, My Lord," Dawn said, looking pleased.

Arthur sat down, another cup of whiskey in hand, and allowed the skilled woman to help him remove his finery and hang it within the clothespress. He got into the tub and Dawn began to scrub him all over, starting with his back.

"Dawn, ye are getting yer new gown sodden," Arthur noted after a bit and the sight of the wet material clinging to her form gave him an idea. "Why do ye not remove thy gown and join me in the tub?" he suggestively asked, pulling at her dress a bit.

"My Lord!" she cried out in mock-dismay; however her face reflected a smile. "If it would please ye, then I shall of course" she acquiesced.

"'Twould not only please me, Dawn, but I think ye would also find pleasure," Arthur grinned seductively as the woman skillfully removed the damp gown and stepped into the hot, sweet-smelling water. Eventually, they were clean, dried and much loved, the Goddess given their worship. Arthur slept well for the few hours left in the night and woke as the early morning sun touched his east window.

"Dawn, my dear, ye must awake. Morning is upon us and I have much to do," he whispered into her ear. The woman stirred, awoke with a smile on her full, pink lips, and nodded her understanding. "Enjoy the day, My Lord. Will ye have need of me later?" she asked hopefully.

"I do not know, Dawn. If the opportunity arises, then certainly," he answered. "Thank ye, Dawn, for the assistance ye render, 'tis truly a Goddess-sent blessing to find ye here occasionally with a bath waiting."

"'Tis my duty, My Lord, no more," Dawn said with a wide smile.

"And ye perform it well, my dear," Arthur grinned and gave her a small bag of silver coins.

"My Lord?" she questioned, weighing it in her hand. "Why give me this, when the realm is so poor? Please, take it back and use it to pay for the defense of the realm."

"Ye are a good woman, Dawn," Arthur caught the bag as she threw it, halved the contents, and tossed it back. "Weave yerself another one of those gowns, girl and make it thinner. One can hardly see yer body through the one ye are wearing," he requested, winking outrageously.

"Ye are a scoundrel, my good King Arthur Pendragon," Dawn laughed as she caught the bag. "The gown should be ready soon."

"I sweat in anticipation, my dear," Arthur chuckled. "Now, go on with ye, I have serious work to do."

"So do I," she giggled back, and he heard the massive oak door click behind her. A few moments later, Cai's familiar knock, unlike anyone else's for security reasons, sounded at Arthur's door.

"Aye Cai, 'tis clear," the King chuckled in spite of himself. "Come on in!"

The seneschal entered, with Arthur's pre-breakfast tray laden with a plate of oatmeal cookies and a huge mug of blackberry tea.

"Good morning, Artos," Cai greeted and Arthur eyed him expectantly.

"What is it, Caius? Ye said Artos, not Sire," he asked, immediately anxious.

"Sire, the Lady Althea died overnight. Uriens awoke and found her on her back with a slight smile on her face," Cai reported, breaking into tears. "Uriens is pretty bad off, Artos. Morgaine appeared out of nowhere to stay with him and he is almost asleep now. Morgause acts upset, but who can tell with her for sure, and Lot is grumbling about cursed luck," he finished up, then wiped his eyes a bit. "Sorry Artos, but I really liked her. She taught me how to cook oysters the way ye like them, broiled in the shell over a slow fire," he explained bleakly.

Arthur sighed. "I wonder if she meant what she said last night."

"What did she say to ye, if ye can discuss it, I mean," asked Cai.

"She warned me about Westerland Keep, how dangerous King Warren and his brood all are, as if I did not know that already," Arthur told him. "She also said something about her sons coming here with additional reinforcements. I wonder if they are coming, or if she wanted them to come. O dear me," Arthur sighed again.

"What?" asked Cai.

"She mentioned Leodegrance and that he could be persuaded to come over to our side for a price. I know Leodegrance has a mighty fine army of his own, but he has already signed a treaty with me and he pays his taxes on time. He even sent those wagons of food during the Unification, remember?"

"Aye, all that salted fish," Cai shuddered at the memory. "Still, it kept us alive."

"Ah, Great Goddess," Arthur sighed again. "What was Althea trying to tell me?" he wondered aloud before he turned briskly to Cai. "Sir Cai, dress the castle in mourning. Make sure each of the household wears at least a black ribbon on their right arm to honor the Lady Althea. Find my black tunic and cloak, and have my best boots shined. We do honor to a great and loyal lady, all must be done correctly to comfort Uriens and ally ourselves stronger with him!" he ordered.

Cai snapped out a Roman salute and hurried to make all the arrangements for Althea's death feast. Within hours, Camelot was draped in simple black mourning. All wore their black clothes or a black ribbon, and spoke softly to honor the feisty Queen of the Western Shores, as she had been known. Later in the day, Uriens asked for a change in Cai's somber plans.

"She would have wanted a gay feast, Sir Cai," the older man sniffled bleakly. "Can it be done in this winter season?" he asked hopefully.

"I think that we at Camelot may oblige ye, King Uriens. I have prepared a feast already, all that needs to be done is to change the table dressings for more of a grand party," the seneschal told the widowed and grieving King.

"My thanks to ye, Sir Caius Ectorius, for this," he said gratefully, turning to Arthur. "Ye are kind to an old and foolish man, especially one who has fought against ye all these years, My Lord Arthur. Our sons, Maegwyn and Accolon are fair commanders; they are both hungry for war and glory in the Pendragon's army. What say ye Sire, would ye take 'em and an extra hundred men?" Uriens asked. "Please Sire, for her memory? She always spoke for ye, supporting ye against the alliance with Lot and the others. 'Twas her fondest wish for the boys to serve with ye," he urged.

Arthur was astonished for it was only two years past that Uriens had refused to even discuss the matter.

"Of course, My Lord Uriens, glad I am to have them too!" he agreed and the two clasped hands on the pact. "Send them along with the others in a month."

"Thank ye, Sire," Uriens said, kneeling humbly. "I am yer man from this day forth. Ask and I shall come or send another in my place. Anything ye ask, Arthur ap Uther Pendragon, I shall try to grant ye, from this day on until I die!" he swore fiercely.

"Thank ye, Uriens ap Lexor. The West is yer protectorate, as it always has been. We shall build forts within yer lands to insure the safety of our subject there. Ye will have the right of access to Crown granaries in time of need as well," Arthur pledged. "A Britain united is far stronger than one divided. Now, would ye please join me for a cup of wine to yer lady's memory? She was a good and noble woman. Hail Althea, Queen of the Western Shores!" he toasted and raised his cup. As one, the Knights of Camelot raised their cups as well.

"Hail, Lady Althea, Queen of the Western Shores!" they all roared out and drank deep from their cups. Thereafter, the mood of the party was changed and Uriens drank himself into oblivion. It was the young Aaronn who asked of Arthur much later in the evening; "Has anyone seen King Lot and Queen Morgause?"

No one had seen either of the Orkney rulers, a quick visit to their suite showed their possessions gone. Their horses were also absent from the stalls where they had been stabled. Arthur was very puzzled as to the why of the sudden disappearance and sought out Morgaine, finally finding her in the very room where Althea had died.

"Morgaine my sister, are ye avoiding me?" he asked gently as she turned a white face to him.

"Artos," she answered tiredly. "'Tis good to see ye at last."

"Aye sister, so, have ye?"

"Have I what?" she asked in return, her voice puzzled.

"Have ye been avoiding me?" he asked again, realizing at last that she hadn't heard him.

"Nay, Artos," she answered; again Arthur heard the weariness in her voice. "I needed to be alone for a while. Is Morgause gone?"

"Aye, and I am wondering why. I have never known Lot or Morgause to miss a free meal," Arthur confirmed.

"Althea was fine the last time ye saw her, aye?" Morgaine pressed.

"That I could see, aye, she was fine. What are ye driving at, sister?"

"I think that Morgause killed Althea by either magicks or poison, to keep her from persuading Uriens to join with ye. He did it anyway, because he loved her enough to believe what he heard as she died were her final words," Morgaine spoke harshly, as if she were weary beyond endurance.

"What are ye saying, sister?" Arthur whispered.

"I know Accolon. He is a Druid. We have spoken many times of Uriens reluctance to send troops into the army. Accolon told me how his mother felt and when I 'heard' Althea's call to Ceridwen for aid, I returned to Camelot through the Mother's secret ways. Finding Althea in her death throes beside Uriens, I listened to her whispers and learned what she told ye. Knowing that her time was short, I woke Uriens and hid myself on the floor beside the bed. I did as she asked, imitating her voice, while Althea held onto life for the last few moments before she expired in Uriens' arms, a happy woman," Morgaine explained. "I am hungry and tired, brother mine, I need a sip of something strong and warming," she said, collapsing in Arthur's arms. He took her to his room, with Dawn's help he prepared her for bed and laid her on his own mattress. Arthur poured Morgaine a tiny cup of potent Orkney whiskey, which Morgaine sipped cautiously, while Dawn went to fetch food for the ravenous woman. Cai brought a cart laden with light, simple and restorative foods; clear vegetable broth, light unleavened wafers, dried fruit and hot mint tea. Morgaine consumed nearly the entire portion offered her, then sat back and yawned.

"My thanks, Sir Cai, I feel much better now. Magick is draining work," she chuckled. "If someone will show me to a room, I would like to sleep for a few days."

"Tell me true, Morgaine. Did Morgause have a direct hand in Althea's death?" Arthur asked insistently.

"I cannot say for certain, brother, but in my opinion she is highly suspect," Morgaine yawned.

"Thank ye sister, for yer help and opinion. I shall not forget this, ever," Arthur expressed his gratitude warmly. "Come, I shall take ye to a quiet room where ye can rest."

"Right now, brother, I could sleep on a plank in the noisiest brothel in Camelot-town," Morgaine laughed sleepily as Arthur lifted her from the royal bed. It was only a short distance down the hallway, Dawn opened the door he indicated and held the door open. Entering the room, Arthur took her to the bed at the back of the room. "Artos, this room, 'tis lovely!" the priestess exclaimed as Arthur laid her on the soft, pastel pink sheets. As Morgaine looked around the room, she observed that the rest of the room was dressed with complimentary hues and that the furnishings were crafted of beautifully grained rosewood.

"Aye, Cai hopes that one day this room will house my royal lady," Arthur told her as he lit a small fire in the pink-tiled hearth.

"'Twould suit any woman well," Morgaine said softly. "Ye should marry, ye know. There are several eligible young women at Avalon who would fit the requirements of an excellent co-ruler."

"Morgaine, please," Arthur objected with a smile. "At least allow me to truly secure the realm before lining up the flowers of Britain for my wedding," he chuckled harder when he saw her smile.

"We would not want to rush yer decision, O Mighty High King of the Britons," Morgaine said, yawning wide. "Good night, my brother, may the Goddess grant ye pleasant dreams."

"Good night, Morgaine, may yer sleep be sound."

Her breathing quieted immediately, Arthur noted, as he left her to her rest. Taking Dawn with him, he returned to his room and locked the door behind him.

"Come here, wench," he said, soft and low. "Send me to my sleep relaxed."

"Of course, My Lord, 'tis why I am here, after all," Dawn laughed seductively and came into his arms.

Once again, the courtesan proved her worth to the Crown, allowing Arthur to release his suppressed emotions in a most pleasant way, and then rubbing his back until he fell asleep. Once he was softly snoring, Dawn slipped from the bed and poured herself a cup of wine, went to her robe and pulled out a small, bound set of parchment leaves, her diary, and made her entry for the day. She then secreted the diary and returned to her place beside the King. Before she slept, she thought again of destroying the document, which was a complete and detailed record of her days since accepting Sir Cai's discreet invitation to dine with the King. She smiled softly as she recalled that night, two years ago, when the seneschal of Camelot escorted her to the High King's private rooms.

The supper had been excellent; a lightly broiled pheasant stuffed with rice and herbs, lightly steamed carrots and a beautiful salad of wild greens dressed with olives, shredded carrots, as well as slices of cucumber dressed with basil and olive oil. Firelight shone from the hearth, playing on the youthful King's face, glinting from his sun-bleached hair and the light chain mail showing from under the casual black shirt and trous. The simple gold circlet around his head only enhanced the masculine lines of his face she remembered fondly, the only other ornament he wore was the royal seal and a gold torque at his throat.

"Did ye enjoy the supper, Madam?" Cai asked as he cleared the empty plates, preparing to make his exit from the room.

"Aye, Lord Seneschal, 'twas delicious," she answered quietly. She watched as Arthur walked him out, the two murmuring quietly to each other. She heard Sir Cai answer, then he left the room and she heard the sound of the locking bolt sliding home.

"The cook here is very talented," she began, trying to begin a casual conversation.

"I am sure Sir Cai would be very pleased at yer compliment, my dear," Arthur chuckled. "Would ye care for a sip of wine or whiskey, perhaps?" he asked, going to a side cabinet built into the wall.

"Wine for me, please My Lord?" she called to him.

"Whiskey helps me sleep, wine only keeps me awake," the King chuckled more.

While he was nervously pouring, Dawn took the initiative and removed her outer gown, revealing a thin cotton undergown that laced up the front. When Arthur turned back around, she was just taking down her luxuriant blonde hair, she heard a cup hit the floor and shatter.

"Are ye well, My Lord?" she asked, letting humor color her rich voice. She looked up at him and met his incredible azure eyes with her ice-blue eyes, saw his discomfort and anxiety and smiled. "Am I so hard to regard?" she laughed, going to his aid.

"Indeed not, my dear, ye are most pleasing to my eyes. 'Tis not often I see such beauty in these chambers," Arthur replied, his voice somewhat husky.

"Please, My Lord Arthur, allow me to assist ye with that," she said, disentangling his hands from the cloth he held and finishing mopping up the mess. Arthur took full advantage of the opportunity she gave him to view her generous bosom.

"By the Goddess, wench ye are beautiful to behold," he whispered as she put aside the glass-filled cloth on a tray atop the nearby table. When she had cleaned and wiped her hands on a clean cloth and put that aside as well, Arthur took her gently into his sword-hard arms and held her carefully against him for the longest time, then he tilted her head back and softly kissed her lips. Dawn, experienced courtesan that she was, could hardly believe his gentleness, responding warmly and honestly to his caresses. "Come with me, woman. I have been at war so long, I need some beauty in my life," he whispered and led her to the enormous four-poster oak bed, its thick mattress piled high with warm cozy quilts and comforters. Quickly and skillfully, Arthur unlaced her undergown, allowing it to fall aside to reveal her lush form. He took a deep breath, expelling it slowly as she removed the thin garment, hanging it over the back of a nearby chair. Returning to his side she assisted Arthur as he readied for bed, which proved delightfully stimulating for the both of them.

"Come My Lord, let me massage thy neck and shoulders," Dawn invited when Arthur brought new cups of wine for them. "We have all night, after all."

"Aye, my neck and shoulders are sore indeed," he chuckled a bit before downing a small mouthful of the potent and delicious beverage. He lay on his stomach and Dawn straddled him, skillfully kneading the knots from the King's neck muscles. She would have done his back as well, but Arthur turned over abruptly and pulled her lips down on his.

Sometime later, they lay drowsily in the comfortable bed and Arthur made her a proposition. "Tell me Dawn, would ye mind living here with me for a while? I cannot pay much, but ye would have private quarters, clothing and good food to eat. There could be much benefit to such an arrangement for ye."

"Ye wish to purchase my contract, My Lord?" she asked, astounded. She knew well what the cost would be, and what her Madam would say.

"I think that Arthur Pendragon could persuade Madam Carolyn to be generous in her dealings with the Crown," Arthur chuckled assuredly into her ear. "After the time of the war is past, and I marry, ye would be a free woman," he added.

"Ye would free me from my obligations to ye?" she asked, incredulous.

"Of course, as soon as my name is on the new contract," he assured her. "What man would prefer a slave over a free woman?"

"I would be most pleased to serve here in the Castle, My Lord. If my presence brings ye ease and pleasure well, 'tis my honor and duty to serve so," Dawn replied.

"One thing must be clear though, wench," Arthur went on, brutally honest. "I shall always be fond of ye, but 'tis all there can be. Also, there can be no child between us."

"I understand, My Lord," Dawn laughed, her tones clear and genuine. "I have a tincture that I take daily, made for me by the Ladies of Avalon. It prevents the joining of male and female essences, therefore preventing pregnancy. I have no wish of a child yet, so ye need have no worry, My Lord."

"As long as we understand each other, Dawn, I would like to be friends, at least," he smiled boyishly, yawned, stretched, kissed her lips gently, then turned over and fell asleep almost immediately. Dawn had begun her diary the next day, when Arthur burnt her old contract, fairly purchased from Madam Carolyn at the persuasive prodding of Gawaine and Tristan. Arthur drew up a new contract, which he signed and sealed with the royal ring seal on his finger. Since that day, she had made daily entries into the diary of everything Arthur had said and done in her presence. Dawn sighed and lay back, closed her eyes and prepared for sleep at last. The diary must be kept, she thought, after all kings break their word as often as other men. 'Tis a wise woman who protects herself, besides, the Lady Vivaine finds the diary so entertaining every time I go home to Avalon to replenish my supply of the contraceptive potion, 'tis worth keeping just for that. With a soft giggle, Dawn floated off into sleep.

She was gone when Arthur awoke the next morning after Althea's death, he found Cai already pouring his morning tea.

"Sleep well, Artos?" he quipped, handing the King the prepared cup of beverage with a sly smile.

"Of course, why would I not?" Arthur chuckled, sitting up in bed and accepting the steaming cup. "The Lady Morgause is suspected of causing Lady Althea's death to stop Uriens from sending his sons and troops to Camelot, then Morgaine confessing magick in persuading Uriens to do it anyway. Just the sort of situation to promote restful slumber," he went on, chuckling harder all the while until both of them were laughing to the point of tears.

"Ah, I feel so much better," Arthur finally chuckled to a halt, wiping his eyes as he did so. "A good laugh to start a difficult day is a blessing indeed."

"Aye," answered a now more composed Cai, though his eyes still twinkled with mirth. "Here are this morning's dispatches Artos, also Tristan is back this morning. He says ye will want to speak with him, right after he stops eating," Cai went on efficiently. "Judging from the way he is stuffing himself, that could take a while. Great White Goddess, ye do not think he could have picked up a tapeworm while in Saxon lands, do ye?" Cai asked, chuckling a bit.

"Is Morgaine still about?" Arthur asked as he bit into the apple doughnut, savoring the sweet/tart flavor of the fruit and cinnamon.

"As far as I know, Artos, one can hardly ever tell when she is here and when she is gone. I wish she would stay on permanently, for at least she can be trusted," Cai said, sighing.

"Thanks Cai, for this and the dispatches. Tell Tristan to eat 'till his belly is full before he comes up."

"Aye...Artos," Cai's voice answered, suddenly distant. "Look ye foster-brother...at yer eastern window," he pointed in wonder. Arthur's eyes went at once to the window Cai indicated. There, on the windowsill was a spring songbird, a wood thrush, looking in at them.

"Hullo, little one," Arthur greeted the tiny bird. "Have ye come home early to sing in the spring then?"

As if on cue, the sweet song trilled forth from the bird's beak, bringing to mind pleasant spring days filled with warm, flower-scented breezes and soft sunny days. The High King and his Seneschal stood transfixed by the glorious song for several minutes until the bird ceased his song, looked at his audience in the room curiously, and then flew off headed for the forest.

"Great Goddess, thank ye," Arthur breathed. "The invasion comes again, Caius, this time they will threaten our forests, the realm of Ceridwen Herself. Come ahead, Cerdic, if ye dare!" he whispered fiercely.

Camelot's army spent the rest of the winter in intensive training. The reinforcements from Uriens arrived a week early, Maegwyn and Accolon proved to be just the burst of energy the others needed to inspire them. A pair of pranksters, the two played their first caper on the occasion of Arthur's birthday. Stealing down to the kitchens, the pair took two large wooden spoons and two obviously older and dented stockpots. They found Lancelot's quarters and positioned themselves on either side of the First Knight's door. At a wink from Maegwyn, the two began pounding on the bottom of the steel pans, raising a huge clamor. The pair sped off towards the great room, still banging and screaming wildly as they passed each of their brother Knight's doors. Lancelot appeared with sword in hand and clad only in his unders, as were all the others with the exception of Gawaine, who usually slept in the nude. Even as he came from his room, he struggled to both hold his sword and don his long unders.

"Get them, boyos!" Lancelot called as he led the entire group after the pranksters into the great room. The others, now out of breath and laughing so hard they could barely stand, set upon the two brothers, and a vigorous wrestling melee ensued. Arthur and Cai appeared at length, astonished to find even the usually unflappable Lancelot participating in the tension-venting exercise. Suddenly, the Merlin appeared and was surprised to find the finest warriors in all of Britain laughing and grappling on the floor of Camelot's great room. He sat, poured himself a cup of tea and watched as the King and his Company of Knights laughed and wrestled for supremacy, then Aaronn appeared carrying a tray of pastries. The lad's eyes went wide as he watched the King and the Knights on the floor, acting like boys of a much younger age.

"'Tis all right, Aaronn, 'tis only a bit of spring fever," the Merlin assured the astounded boy.

"Can ye cure them?" Aaronn asked in a very concerned tone.

"Have no worry, boyo. It cures itself after a bit, just watch," the Merlin chuckled as he munched a fat pastry. Presently, Arthur happened to notice the Merlin sitting there, Aaronn on one side, Olran on the other, all three of them watching the bedlam with interest.

"Hullo, Taliesin." Arthur greeted him loudly so the others would hear. "How long have ye been there?"

"Long enough to want to wager on the winner," the Merlin laughed and helped Arthur to his feet. The others struggled to their feet, feeling somewhat abashed at being caught acting like children by the Merlin of Britain, they took seats at the tables while Cai brought out tea and honey for them all.

"Ye all must be terribly bored," the Merlin commented tartly. They all hung their heads slightly until he laughed. "Perhaps we should find something for ye all to do?" he asked, looking at them all one-by-one. Hurriedly, each man picked up his mug, grabbed a few pastries and hurried out the door headed for their rooms to change and prepare for their various duties. Arthur made to make an escape as well, but the Merlin caught him before he could rise too far from his seat.

"Wait, Artos. I must speak with ye, alone," he said urgently. "I have had the most startling dream."

"Very well, Lord Merlin, will my rooms do for a private spot?" Arthur sighed.

"Aye, well enough."

"Come along then, Lord Merlin," Arthur said and led him away. They went up the stairs to Arthur's suites, entered and locked the door behind them. Arthur quickly dressed and stirred the fire in the hearth, then sat and motioned the Merlin into the opposite chair.

"Now, tell me what dream has ye so disturbed," Arthur invited.

"As I sat, puzzling over the cause of the Lady Althea's death and the mystery behind her statement she made to ye concerning Leodegrance, I 'saw' his castle forecourt. A young girl was playing outside, a radiant blonde child. I saw Lancelot approach her, side-by-side with ye, and she put down her dolls and stood to face ye both. She ran to ye both and for a while, the three of ye stood embracing each other as friends. Lancelot suddenly broke the embrace with ye and the girl and backed away. She called out his name, as though her heart was broken, and she grabbed for his hand. Ye took ahold of her free hand and she was pulled between ye both for a moment or two, as though neither one of ye would let her go. A mist or shadow grew up around her, and I heard a voice say, 'Beware the White Shadow!' I awoke suddenly at that, drenched in a cold sweat," Taliesin told Arthur in a hushed voice.

"What does it mean?" Arthur asked wonderingly.

"Something is awaiting ye in Leodegrance's kingdom, boyo, something that will appear to be beneficial, but will come between ye and Lancelot and cause ye to grow apart," the Merlin said, shaking his head. "Just remember to examine any offers from Leodegrance very carefully."

"As long as ye are by my side, how can I make a mistake, Lord Merlin?" Arthur asked boyishly.

"I shall not always be at yer side, boyo. Ye will always have the counsel of the Merlin of Britain, but that may not always be me," Taliesin told Arthur seriously. Arthur's face lost its humor and he grabbed for the Merlin's hand.

"Ye will tell me before ye are to go, aye? I could not stand it if ye just…disappeared," he asked, anxiously.

"I shall let ye know before I go," the Merlin reassured him.

"Ye make sure ye do. I care for ye, old crow," Arthur tried to make light of the love he felt for his tutor.

"How many times have I told ye, Arthur, my name is Merlin, Merlin," Taliesin answered in a teacher's voice, as if he were addressing a much younger Arthur.

"Aye, Uncle," the younger man chuckled and threw his arms around the older man in an impulsive gesture

"Ye know, I am hungry, ye think Caius would scramble a few eggs for me?" the Merlin spoke brightly.

"I bet he would, especially if I send Dawn to ask him to make a portion for both of us. I bet he would throw in a beefsteak as well," Arthur chuckled at the delight on the older man's face. "I would like ye to sit in on the war council tonight. The raids will be starting soon, and I want to be absolutely certain we all know what to do and when. The forts are completely manned at last, and patrols will start with the Equinox. With the Mother's help, we will keep the raiding bastards away from Her sacred forests," Arthur went on, passionately striking his fist into his palm.

"Who is Dawn, Artos? Someone I have not met?" the Merlin asked, changing the subject.

"Ye will see her soon. She is currently gracing my private quarters with her lovely presence. Ye will like her, she keeps a diary although she has no idea I know she keeps one. Just be careful what ye say."

"Is she a spy?" the Merlin chuckled.

"Nay, she keeps it to insure I keep my word to her," Arthur chuckled with him and went to the door. "Page!" he called out to the passing lad, who as it happened was Aaronn.

"Aye, Sire," he answered, saluting smartly.

"Go to the Lady Dawn and ask her to bring up some breakfast for the Merlin and I, would ye Aaronn?"

"Aye, Sire, right away. Are ye in trouble with the Merlin for what happened in the great room?"

"Nay, Aaronn. Neither the Knights nor I are in trouble. The Merlin understands that even grown men need to play once and awhile. Now, go on and deliver my message to the Lady Dawn."

"I am on my way, My Lord Arthur," Aaronn replied, grinning as he sped on his way.

Arriving quickly outside the lady's door, he knocked and stood back politely. The door opened and he beheld the woman currently in Arthur's favor. She was not as tall as Arthur, and she had long, sunny-blonde tresses that fell to just below her back when they were braided, as they were now. She had sparkling clear, pale blue eyes, rosy-pink, full lips and a most pleasant laugh, Aaronn thought.

"Aye, little Aaronn?" she asked, motioning him inside. "What may I do for the King's ward?"

"The King wishes ye to go to Cai and bring a private breakfast for he and the Merlin," Aaronn reported, saluting crisply.

"I see," she replied, smiling wider. "Would ye come and assist me?"

"Of course, Lady," Aaronn agreed immediately. He took her heavy quilted robe from the peg on the wall and held it out for her.

"Why thank ye, Aaronn. What a gentleman ye are already," Dawn complimented, letting the boy try to help her with the long, flowing garment. "Women's things are such a bother, aye?" she asked, completing the job herself without making Aaronn feel small. He held the door for her and walked her all the way to the kitchens, where Cai fixed a huge plate of scrambled eggs, two rare beefsteaks, toasted bread and a pitcher of cool milk.

"Here Aaronn, would ye wait for Olran, then go with him down into the cool room? I need a wheel of that yellow cheese," the seneschal asked as he prepared to go with Dawn and serve the King's breakfast. "I shall be back in a few moments, then ye and Olran can be excused for the rest of the day."

"We can have free time?" Aaronn asked with delight.

"Aye, and earned it ye have too!" laughed Cai as he wheeled off his cart, Dawn beside him with the beverage tray.

A few moments after the adults left, Olran entered the kitchen and Aaronn helped him put away the huge armload of neatly folded napkins. As they did so, Aaronn told him of Cai's request, and their promised reward.

"Thanks, Aaronn!" Olran said when he was relieved of his burden. "We should go and get that wheel of cheese, I want to go exploring!"

"Aye!" Aaronn agreed wholeheartedly.

The two boys went down through the trap door in the kitchen floor into the cold room under Camelot. The Druid engineers, when they were excavating for the foundations, had found a frigid cold spring. Taking advantage of the natural gifts of the land, they had designed this cold room to maximize the storage capacity of the castle. No matter how hot it was during the summer months, the foods stored in the cold room came out nearly frozen. Aaronn and Olran thought it a lovely place to hide out among the casks of wine and ale aging there. They quickly found the huge wheel of yellow cheese, of Camelot's own making and carried it up the stairs into the main kitchen, where Cai was even now awaiting them.

"Good work, lads," he complimented, helping them close the heavy trap door, then lending a steadying hand to the cheese wheel as they carried it over to the slicing table. He fed them each a huge oatmeal cookie and a cup of milk, while they ate Aaronn turned to Sir Cai.

"Sir Cai, will we still go to Lothian in Orkney for fostering?" he asked.

"Aye, Aaronn, most likely," Cai sighed. "I like it not, but the Saxons are going to be raiding and Arthur thinks they will try and gain a foothold in the forests. 'Tis going to be nasty work if they do and we will need every hand around a sword this year just to hold them off," he laughed under his breath. "Ye will be safer in Lothian with the others. The Saxons don't often raid in Orkney, 'tis less in Lot's kingdom that in any other kingdom in Britain, after all." The two boys sighed and chewed their cookies, accepting another from Cai to finish their milk. "Now, ye two are excused for the rest of the day. Thank ye for doing yer share, plus a bit more. Go on and have some fun now," he urged, making a shooing motion with his hands.

"Thank ye, Sir Cai!" the boys exclaimed as one, bolting from the room. Heading for the secret door in the great room, the two boys entered the maze of corridors and soon emerged in their shared quarters. Grabbing packs, parchment, a pair of half-candles and a stick of charcoal from the hearth, the boys went back out into the secret ways and looked over their crude, but legible map.

In the last two months, the pair had explored, "The Maze," as they called it now and had found that there were secret doors in one out of every three rooms of their level of the Castle. There were also corridors that led to just outside Lancelot's door, the King's door, Gawaine's door and into

Cai's sleeping quarters. Some corridors led out of the castle and into the partially finished terraced orchard, one door even emptied out into the stable causeway, leaving just a short distance to walk to the giant barn. Still, with all that, there were still plenty of areas not yet explored. The passageway they entered today was one of those; the two curious lads had to find out all about it. Aaronn lit one candle stub, saving the other in case they wished to explore longer, then he marked his position on the map and set out toward the unexplored passageways. Olran followed behind, slowly tracing a charcoal line on the parchment as he walked along.

"Aaronn look, this passageway is different from all the others," he pointed out, and his companion nodded agreement.

"No doors, no branch corridors, just this straight causeway" Aaronn observed and walked on more slowly. The passageway bent sharply left, ending in what appeared to be a blank wall. The boys looked around carefully, finally locating the small trigger mechanism and grinned at each other, hearts racing as they pushed the small dragon in and watched the door slide open. The light from their little candle flickered at the usual rush of air that accompanied the opening of an unused room. The light steadied quickly and penetrated the dusty gloom, both boys' eyes opened wide with amazement and shock. Piles of gold coins, gold bars and assorted rings, bracelets, torques and ornate swords with scabbards glittered in front of them. There was nothing but the finest gold and silver work in the room, except for the copper and bronze inlayed with precious gems.

"Aaronn, I think 'tis the royal treasure room!" Olran breathed slowly.

"Aye," the other said shortly, eyeing the hoard.

"There must be hundreds of coins worth of just gold in this room," Olran went on quietly, not noticing the change in his friend's voice.

"Aye," replied Aaronn, who could only stare at the vast amount of Arthur's treasury. He had never before seen such riches; he could not help fingering a large gold coin of considerable weight, stamped with the likeness of Caesar. Olran, raised in a king's house, was used to such sights and had been beaten many a time for filching gold coins from his father's treasure room.

"Come on, Aaronn," he said, growing bored. "We should explore some more."

"Ye can, I have had enough for today," Aaronn said, his voice bleak as he turned abruptly. Stalking away, he left Olran in the dark and the princeling frowned. It looked as though Aaronn was suddenly in one of his black moods, Olran sighed as he started after his friend. Following the fading glow of Aaronn's candle until he finally had to light his own to avoid being swallowed up by the darkness, he called out to Aaronn;

"Come on, Aaronn, wait for me!"

Hearing only the opening of their door as it echoed down the passageway, Olran proceeded quickly, by the time he reached the portal, he was more than slightly miffed and he threw his pack into the room, ducked through and entered the room.

"What is wrong now?" he asked crossly. "It must be something really bad to make ye leave me in the dark, alone."

Aaronn said nothing, remaining curled up as he was on his bunk, face impassive.

"I shall go to the Druids, Aaronn," Olran went on, growing even more cross. "At least they will not walk off and leave me without a partner or light!"

"Shut up, Olran," Aaronn responded, his voice thick with suppressed rage. "Just…go away and leave me be."

"Leave ye be?" Olran shouted back, his slow-rising temper at last roused. "Shut up? Dammit Aaronn, I…"

He said no more, for Aaronn suddenly rose up from his bunk, took the thinner boy by the arm and twisted the limb up behind his own back.

"Aaronn, do ye really want to fight me?" Olran asked in a voice suddenly cold and intense.

"If ye do not shut up and leave me alone, ye will have to!" Aaronn answered with difficulty through the black rage boiling in his heart. "Now…go…to…yer…room!" he ordered and pushed Olran into his own separate inner chamber.

"Ye owe me, Aaronn!" Olran said, angrily struggling over Aaronn's superior strength. "Do not forget, I get even."

"Fine, tomorrow ye can beat up on me, but now, just leave me alone!" Aaronn answered as he closed Olran's door and locked it from the outside.

"Aaronn, ye open up that door, right now!" Olran raged, pounding vainly against the solid oak door. "I will not stay in here for long!"

Aaronn did not respond, so enveloped by the black passion within him, he could not hear. He just collapsed back onto his bed, tucked up his knees and rested his chin on them, thinking.

His first years of life had been rough; he had learned some very tough lessons about the nature of man early on. He had seen only hatred, lust, fear and greed in the taverns and ale-houses where his mother had danced; he had decided that absolutely under no circumstances would he ever go without riches or love a woman once he became an adult. Coming to Camelot had changed all that, for he had come to trust and love those living there. Comfortable beds and plenty of hot food had helped some of the pain of those early lessons to fade, but the sight of Arthur's treasure room had reawakened his desire for his own, independent source of income. He had remembered suddenly the cause of why he had come to

Camelot, because he had no father and his mother had abandoned him when she had no further use for him. Olran's presence had only further served to remind him of his own lowly position, for Olran was a prince no matter how much a renegade. Aaronn sat there, fuming impotently about his situation until the hot and unwanted tears began to flow and the nine year-old sobbed silently, mourning his lack of a father.

As he sat there, silently crying, the secret panel slid aside to admit a furious Olran, the princeling's anger quickly faded when he saw his friend's emotional condition.

"All right, suppose ye tell me what that was all about?" he requested, flopping down beside Aaronn and handing him a handkerchief.

"I am sorry my friend, for my temper," Aaronn began. "I just saw all that treasure and it made me remember all the time with my mother, and the fact that I do not have the slightest idea who or where my father is! I am sorry to leave ye in 'The Maze' and about yer arm. Is it all right?" he asked, concerned.

"I suppose so, though I do not know why," Olran grumped. "However, I found a doorway out of my room, so all is not in vain. Just remember brother, I am yer friend. The fact of yer parentage or lack thereof makes no difference to me!" he declared loyally. Aaronn smiled to hear him so emphatic about his declaration, and he blew his nose again, then tossed the soaked cloth into the laundry hamper.

"Thanks, brother. What would I do without ye?" Aaronn sniffled.

"Probably fail yer sums," Olran replied tartly, but his smile belied his acid remark and laughter followed. Aaronn just could not help it, Olran's laugh tickled his own sense of humor every time. He joined in, letting the humor cleanse away the remainder of his black mood and he clasped arms with Olran in apology.

"Forgive me?" he asked hopefully.

"Aye, of course," Olran laughed. "But I still owe ye one."

"I'll bet 'twill be a whopper too!" Aaronn chuckled.

Both boys' stomachs grumbled loudly just then, they grinned as the supper bell sounded faintly through the thick walls of the room. Washing up quickly, the two boys sprinted down the halls, racing for the great room. Speeding as one into the hall, they arrived just as the soup was being served.

"O boy, my favorite, beef and barley soup!" Aaronn exclaimed happily, all traces of his black mood gone now.

Olran grinned, relieved that his friend's mood had returned to normal. He joined the others in spooning the thick, tasty soup into his mouth, enjoying the taste of well-prepared food. The food at Westerland was not as good, by any stretch of the imagination. By the time Aaronn and Olran finished their meal, they were stuffed full of the soup, Cai's special crisp-roasted chicken, stewed onions, turnips and carrots, along with loaves of fresh, chewy bread smothered with sweet butter. After all had finished their meal, Cai brought out whole long oven pans filled with delicious baked fruits, topped with sweet, fluffy biscuit.

"Ahhh," Aaronn sighed after the last spoonful was thoroughly chewed and swallowed. "I feel much better now."

"I hope so," Olran replied, a mischievous grin lighting his gray eyes.

Aaronn grinned in return and swallowed hard. "Olran, I am sorry to have left ye in the Maze. I guess I just lost my head."

"I know that we have led hard lives, brother, but 'tis all changed now," Olran told him, wise for his nine years. "Ye are the ward of the High King and he loves ye as if he were yer elder brother. We are to be fostered with the King's own half-sister at Lothian Castle, not the ideal place but still an ancient and noble house. The King's own foster-brother and all the Company think well of ye, as do I. Ye have been taught at Druid Isle and Avalon by some of the best minds in Britain. What does it matter if no one but Ceridwen knows who yer father is?"

"I suppose it should not matter with so many blessings, but somehow it does way down deep inside me. Maybe I shall get to find him someday," Aaronn replied sadly. "'Tis why I have to serve Arthur, I have to win my knighthood, so it no longer matters to anyone about my parentage."

Olran smiled sadly. "Having a family and parents is not the answer, Aaronn. I know, remember?"

"'Tis why we should be a team, we are brothers, like the King and the Knights are. Such a brotherhood is rare in the world. I am proud to call ye friend," Aaronn replied and the two shared a quick forearm clasp.

"Come on, we need to help clear tables, then go study," Olran proposed. "Ye could probably use some work on yer sums."

"I have been studying on my own, brother. Ye might be surprised," Aaronn laughed.

"Such a miracle would be pleasant," Olran quipped in return and they both laughed at that.

Chapter 4

The days passed quickly, soon Beltane Eve arrived. The raids began at dawn that day, the Saxons striking Land's End by sea, destroying the royal inn as well as the entire fishing village. Arthur went at once and found the raiders camped some distance up the western coast. The Knights fell upon them, after a brief struggle the Saxons were captured and the group of young British boys and girls with them were returned unharmed to their families, saved from a life of hard slavery among the Saxon tribes. Days later, five longboats hit several villages along the Severn. A week after that, Lancelot's routine patrol stumbled onto a raiding camp, just a half-day's ride from Londinium. The Saxons were completely surprised and all thirty of them surrendered to be marched off to the holding cells of Camelot, where they remained until they were ransomed. Lancelot's patrol shuffled wearily into the Castle forecourt on the eve of the Summer Solstice, after all the reports were made, the Knights wearily bathed, ate and retired to sleep the next day away.

All the male fosterlings had been sent to Lothian Castle after New Year's Day. Aaronn, Olran and their new friend Dalren settled in quickly, however uneasily. Things were very different at Lothian, there was no doubt, but the abundance of decent food and plenty of time to run and play amongst the misty crags that bordered the sea shore compensated at least a little for their homesickness. As summer progressed, the boys took full advantage of the rocky coastline, sporting in the cold seawater until they could swim strongly.

Summer came and went, bringing the frigid north winds back to Orkney, confining Aaronn inside with the rest of those living at Lothian. He and Olran set up practice archery targets in one of the halls, firing so many flights of arrows that their arms grew sore. Finally, in the dead of the winter, the two adventurers found the secret staircase that honeycombed the Orkney castle. One could enter through the scullery and ascend all the way up to Morgause's private tower, a place feared and avoided by all. Even the ever-curious Aaronn's skin crawled whenever he saw the Orkney queen.

Morgause ab Gorlois, the Queen of Orkney, the mother of Gawaine and his brothers, was a beautiful and lush woman. From her mother, Igraine of Cornwall, she had inherited rosy-gold hair and milk-white skin, of which she was inordinately vain. Long, graceful fingers, a generous bosom, small waist, good hips and legs were her weapons, she knew well how to get the power she craved by employing them. Lot was completely bewitched by her; she carefully manipulated him through careful use of herbal potions and young, virgin bedmates. Morgause was slowly gaining the crown of Orkney as Lot relinquished his responsibilities one by one into her greedy hands. All the training she had received at Avalon was bent on keeping herself young and beautiful, so as to add to her power base instead of assisting others and adding to her wisdom so she could assist more, as did the Ladies of Avalon.

Now that she had the King's own ward here at Lothian, she studied the boy carefully at every opportunity. His face reminded her of someone, although she could not quite place who it was. She watched as the handsome lad gained in co-ordination, outstripping her own sons Gareth and Gaheris at the annual Orkney summer games that year in every event except the sheer strength tests such as wrestling and log throwing, the two events the native Orkneymen excelled in. Perhaps after he gains another year, he should be introduced to the fine art of satisfying me in bed, she thought as she assessed him.

Meanwhile, Olran and Aaronn worked to teach Dalren all they knew of hunting, the three spent long hours in the thick forests surrounding Lothian. As time passed, periodic dispatches arrived and were read aloud by Morgause. Aaronn and Olran heard them all, agreeing that the tone of the reports was dire at least. The two boys prayed constantly to the Goddess for the survival of all the Knights and most especially Arthur.

That winter, the ninth of Arthur's reign, fighting men from everywhere found their way to Britain's shore. Romans, weary of fighting in the remnants of the legions, Greeks, Iberians, Moors and even those wanderers from far Cathay appeared at the rebuilt and larger Royal Inn at Land's End, asking the way to Camelot. They were sent on their way with a smile and a polite recitation of the road, only to be found and tested along the way by one or more of the Knights. Those who survived the initiation were taken before Arthur and the Merlin and questioned at length about their reasons for seeking out the Palace of Light. The form of the answers might vary, but the content of each was consistent; to fight for the Light and attain the warrior's perfection. By the time spring came again, Arthur's army was twice what it had been in the fall, and as a result the new forts along both coasts were easily manned. Cerdic tried a few raids, but they were met and halted before any real damage was done. The superstitious Saxons began to fear "Artur and his Magick Knights," who could it seemed be anywhere at any time, so the raiding season was very short that year. The tribes, Arthur figured, needed extra time to forage for food stores to last out the winter. Cerdic and his warchiefs wanted no part of bargaining with the enemy for food again. As a result, Arthur felt safe enough to travel to Lothian for Aaronn's eleventh birthday, the boy waited anxiously for his guardian's arrival on the appointed day.

"Come on, Aaronn, relax, 'tis only the High King, after all," Dalren drawled with a grin.

Aaronn grinned in return, knowing the boy was only jesting, for Dalren had dressed as carefully as Olran and himself. Even now, Aaronn could see the fine sheen of excited and anxious sweat on the former's forehead. Olran suddenly came rushing into the room, breathless and excited.

"I saw 'em from the parapet. 'Tis the King and all the Company!" he shouted out, his speech lapsing into the Westerland dialect. "C'mon, let's go and meet 'em!"

"Aye, Olran, I shall race ye!" Aaronn proposed and the two raced away headlong down the hallways and stairs that led into the castle's forecourt, Dalren following at a more leisurely pace.

"Ave, Arthur!" Aaronn called out as the King's snow-white and mud-dappled stallion entered Lothian's gates.

"Aaronn, 'tis good to see ye too, boyo!" Arthur greeted in return, alighting from his horse and catching the boy's joyful embrace full in the chest.

"Thank the Goddess, ye are all right!" Aaronn said quietly. "I prayed day and night for the safety of ye all."

"I am certain She heard then," Arthur laughed and set the boy down. "Good Goddess, Aaronn, ye have grown heavy since I last saw ye," he complained lightly. "Ye are almost too big for me to pick up any more."

"Aye Sire," Aaronn replied, looking down at his feet. "I'll try to remember."

The King smiled fondly at his ward, then turned and gave his orders to Lancelot, quietly. "Get the horses bedded down comfortably, Lance. Threaten the stablemaster if ye must, but make sure they have plenty of food, water and fresh bedding. Once ye are sure of their comfort, adjourn within. Gawaine, Agravaine, ye are with me."

"Aye, Sire," the two saluted and flanked him as they walked to the doorway..

"Greetin's, Me Lord Arthur, will ye join me in th' coop o' welcome?" Lot's voice boomed.

"Right willingly, My Lord Lot," Arthur called back genially. With Gawaine and Agravaine beside him, he went to where the Orkney King stood with his Queen, Morgause. Taking the proffered drink, Arthur saluted Ceridwen with a few drops on the ground before he tilted the huge horn of stout Orkney ale back and drank 'till it was drained.

"Ahhh, 'twas fine, Lord Lot," he said truthfully, handing the empty vessel back.

"Ye remind me of yer Da when ye drink like tha'," Lot said, remembering watching Uther at work.

"Why thank ye, Lord Lot," Arthur said brightly. "I think 'tis the nicest thing ye've ever said to me."

Lot inwardly groaned, for that was not what he had meant by the statement, but he let the moment pass, having suddenly changed his plans from antagonizing Arthur to enjoying his time with Uther's son. After all, he reasoned anyone who could lead his men and drink like Uther Pendragon couldn't be all bad.

"Morgause, sister," Arthur turned to her and gave her an airy kiss on the cheek. "How has Aaronn been behaving?" he asked as he ruffled the boy's hair fondly.

"Very well, for someone ten years of age. He knows how to work hard, I have never caught him or his friends loafing or stealing. All three of them are studious and serious about their schooling," Morgause reported honestly. "I wish these three could teach such good habits to all boys their age," she laughed.

"Good for the three of ye!" Arthur complemented. "May we go within now, My Lord Lot? 'Tis getting colder all the time and I could use a hot bath."

"O'course, ri' away, M' Liege, Morgause ye will make th' baths ready fer our guests?" Lot asked, his tone making it sound more like a command.

Arthur watched his sister's face as Lot made his request, what he saw there made his stomach turn. Loathing and disgust wreathed her face, though she quickly quelled it. The King resolved to question the Merlin at length as to what exactly Morgause had been taught of potions and magicks on Avalon.

"Come in, My Lord Arthur Pendragon," Morgause invited formally. "All has been made ready for the King and the gallant defenders of Britain."

Aye, Arthur thought, it sounds more like the spider's welcome to the fly. Great Goddess Ceridwen, protect us all while we are under Morgause's roof, he thought to Ceridwen as he walked through the arched doorway and into Lothian's great room.

After a wash up and a few cups of Lot's excellent ale, Arthur and his Knights sat down to a pleasant meal and decent conversation. Lot, who had suffered a bout of pneumonia during the previous winter, had not been with the troops during the summer campaigns and questioned Arthur at length about the encounters with the Saxons. The questions went on until Arthur's head grew muddled with fatigue and he could no longer hide his yawns.

"My Lord Lot," he said, standing wearily. "'Twas a long ride here and I need a good rest in a comfortable bed before I discuss any more military encounters," he yawned.

"Aye," Lot agreed easily. "'Tis time fer us all t' get a good rest."

"Good night then, My Lord Lot and My Lady Morgause," Arthur said politely. "May the Goddess give ye all sweet sleep and pleasant dreams."

"To ye also, My Lord Arthur," the two wished in return.

"Come along, Aaronn," Arthur called gently to the boy, who was curled up in one of the huge chairs in front of the hearth. "Show me the way to our rooms, would ye boyo?"

"Huh, what's that, 'tis bedtime?" answered a sleepy Aaronn.

"Coom on Sire," Gawaine laughed. "I'll show ye th' way."

The Knights all bowed politely to Lot and Morgause, then Gawaine led them away to their beds and welcome rest.

Olran woke first in the morning, finding Aaronn still asleep and snoring softly. Dalren woke soon after and together the two stirred the fire and heated water for tea. When the flavorful herbs hit the hot water, their odor tickled Aaronn's nose and he stirred.

"Time to wake up, Aaronn," Olran called gently, standing over him.

"Huh?" Aaronn questioned sleepily as his friend tipped the ewer of icy-cold water slowly onto Aaronn's chest and legs. Olran had been planning this since Aaronn had left him in the maze at Camelot. Last night, he had filled the ewer and set it out on the window ledge to thoroughly ice over. Aaronn sat up abruptly, spluttering that he was cold.

"Got ye Aaronn! Happy birthday!" Olran said simply, tossing his friend a warm dry towel before dissolving into silent laughter. Dalren's laughter was a bit louder and soon one of the Knights was knocking at the door to ascertain the reason for all that raucous laughter.

"What are the three of ye up to?" asked Bedwyr, coming into the room hurriedly. He saw the boys still laughing, Aaronn sitting in a slightly soggy bed with Olran standing over him, still holding the empty ewer. "Since when do ye sleep in the bathtub, Aaronn?" he asked, chuckling despite himself.

"Sir Bedwyr!" the boys gasped and tried to compose themselves as they grabbed for robes and trous swiftly.

"Come on, Aaronn. The King wants to see ye," Bedwyr beckoned.

"Aye, Sir Bedwyr," Aaronn replied and hurried to dress. Olran and Dalren assisted; within a few moments the King's ward was beside Bedwyr and on his way to see his guardian. After a cup of hot tea with Arthur, the two went down to the stables, after first robing themselves against the bitter cold.

Entering the horsebarn, Arthur closed the doors and led Aaronn down the causeway to where the horses of Camelot were stalled. Stopping in front of the huge white stallion he rode, Arthur fished an apple from his pocket and cut it into quarters to feed the quiet warsteed. The horse took the fruit carefully from Arthur's palm, a quarter at a time while Arthur stroked and patted him fondly.

"Ye know, Aaronn, ye are now eleven and old enough to begin training as a Knight," Arthur began slowly. "Ye could even apply to be a squire."

"Can I squire for ye?" Aaronn asked hopefully, wishing that Arthur would agree. The King smiled and patted his ward on the head.

"I wish that things were peaceful enough to allow that, Aaronn. What I was going to suggest was that ye join me at Camelot in the spring. Olran's father has recalled him, and Dalren's uncle has at last defended the boy's land claim against those who challenged it. He can return home any time. I want ye home with me, boyo, so I can watch over ye better. After all, ye are Cai's favorite, he would never forgive me if I left ye here another year without due cause. What about it, boyo?" he asked, grinning wide.

"Can I really come to Camelot to stay?" Aaronn asked.

"Aye, Aaronn, when ye come home this time, 'twill be a long while before I send ye away again," Arthur chuckled and embraced him.

"O, thank ye, My Lord Arthur!" Aaronn exclaimed joyfully. "'Tis the best birthday I have ever had!"

"I hope so, boyo," Arthur answered, motioning towards the stall behind them. Gawaine and Lancelot led out a sable black pony, some fourteen hands high and well-muscled all over.

"For me, another pony?" Aaronn asked, unable to restrain the urge to stroke the pony's neck.

"I daresay ye have long outgrown yer little gray Shetland. This nimble fellow will be easy to guide around the rocky shoreline," Arthur explained.

"He is just beautiful, and black all over. Not a white spot on him anywhere!" Aaronn breathed as he inspected the horse's lines. "Olran will be just green with envy!" he chuckled. "Thank ye, so very much."

"Tha's nae all, boyo," Gawaine chuckled. "Happy Birthday, Aaronn," he went on and put a small, brightly colored cloth package into the boy's hands. Aaronn opened it, finding a piece of Saxon booty, a bright copper torque. Lancelot gave him a brooch of twined gold, silver and bronze, worked into the shape of a running horse. The other Knights suddenly materialized in the stables, emerging from their concealed places, each man handed Aaronn a piece of treasure. Cai brought some of Aaronn's very favorite pastries and the boy bit in hungrily, missing the taste of the seneschal's fine cooking.

"Thank ye all again," Aaronn sniffled a bit, unable to help himself. "Ye are so good to bring such an abundance of gifts all this way, just for my birthday."

"Come Aaronn," Arthur laughed heartily at the boy's statement. "Let us see what Morgause has planned for yer breakfast this morning."

The Knights walked the boy back up to the hall, only to find that Morgause had made no provisions for Aaronn's special day.

"Madam, ye understood very well that I would be here for my ward's birthday," Arthur began, his voice low and angered. "If not for the boy's sake, at least there should be decent foods on the boards for the Knights of Camelot! Send yer people away, Morgause, and thank Ceridwen that Sir Cai is with us,"

"But my brother...Arth..." Morgause began, but Arthur held up a hand.

"Lancelot, would ye please take Aaronn up to my room and stay with him while he opens the rest of his gifts?"

"Of course, My Lord. Aaronn, come with me."

Once Aaronn was clear of the room, Arthur turned back to the Orkney queen. "How dare ye treat the boy so, and on his birthday too!" he started, the pent anger boiling over. "First, ye make me and my Knights wait for supper last night, then the meal was plain. Now to try and spoil Aaronn's special day! For shame Morgause!" he scolded hotly. "And furthermore, if I ever hear again or have any cause to suspect that ye have used what ye learned on Avalon to further Lot's or yer own schemes again, I shall tie ye to the burning post and set the pyre alight myself! Aye, Morgause, I know a bit of what ye have been up to, and I have had ye watched," he fudged a bit on the last part, hoping to flush her out.

"Beware, Arthur Pendragon," Morgause hissed like a roused adder, dropping her façade at last. "I have a long arm."

"My arm is Ceridwen's, Madam. Her arm is longer," Arthur told her seriously. "I would have no qualms about seeking the Goddess' judgment on ye. Vivaine said to tell ye that the oaks in Traitor's Howe are waiting for ye."

Morgause blanched, knowing exactly what he meant. She abruptly whirled and disappeared into a side doorway, just as a whistling Sir Cai appeared through the kitchen door.

"Well, well now," he said brightly. "Now that the garbage has been disposed of, perhaps some decent food can be prepared."

"Quickly, Caius," Arthur whispered. "For the sake of all our stomachs, please hurry," he chuckled.

"Aye, Artos. All will be ready soon," Cai assured and went back to the kitchens, while Arthur poured himself a pot of tea and took it upstairs with him.

Opening the door to his quarters, he found Aaronn sitting amongst piles of warm and sturdy clothing; trous, shirts, unders and hose, along with two new sets of boots, one just for riding, made by Lancelot himself and modeled after the First Knight's own.

"Thank ye ever so much, Lord Arthur!" Aaronn greeted him happily. "Everything is so fine, I needed all new clothing!"

"I am glad ye are pleased, Aaronn. Does everything fit?" Arthur grinned at the boy's enthusiasm. "Why do ye not gather up all yer new things and take them to yer room? Try everything on to make sure will ye? I bet Olran and Dalren have presents for ye too!"

Aaronn quickly re-folded everything and Bedwyr helped him carry it all to his quarters. The older Knight returned quickly to the company of grown men, after assuring himself that the King's ward and his friends were secure.

When Lot finally appeared in his own great room, he was quite confused. Morgause was nowhere to be found and the kitchen wenches were scurrying about the long table, setting it as for a feast. Sir Caius Ectorius was in Lothian's kitchen, preparing griddle cakes, eggs, sausages and a great ham was being sliced and fried.

"Wha' in th' name o' all creation is happenin' in me house?" he shouted above the din.

"Ask yer lady, Da," Agravaine drawled as he slurped his tea and munched the pastries on the sideboard. "First she made us all wait fer supper las' night, then this morn' she fergot a birthday breakfast fer th' King's ward," he added, his tone caustic concerning his mother.

"Ye've grown a vile tongue a' Camelot, Agravaine me boyo," Lot growled as his second son poured a cup of tea and sweetened it for his sire. "I've nae fergot tha' ye an' yer brother held swords a' me throat, sidin' wi' th' Pendragon aboot th' treaty troops," he muttered, accepting the tea.

"We needed 'em Da," Agravaine said honestly. "Otherwise, ye'd ha' two less sons t'day."

"Aye, an' there'd be nae Pendragon too," Lot muttered under his breath as he turned away.

He thought that Agravaine had not heard, but he was mistaken. The taciturn Orkneyman now knew that his father did not feel the same family loyalty he expected from his sons, he resolved to speak to Gawaine about it as soon as possible. The rest of the time, he kept his eyes and ears on Lot while he was home.

Arthur, Aaronn, Olran and Dalren came downstairs after a time, the remainder of the Knights with them. Aaronn whooped when he saw the feast being spread out on the table.

"It all looks so delicious," he whispered to Arthur, pulling his guardian's ear down to his lips. "Can we eat now? I am really hungry!"

"Sit down and fill your stomachs, lads," Sir Cai called back, chuckling as he appeared from the depths of Lothian's kitchens. "All is prepared and 'tis plenty for everyone."

Lot glowered as he sat beside Arthur's left hand, but he bowed his head sincerely as Arthur offered a short but earnest blessing. The food began to circulate, Aaronn's plate was soon stacked with delicious griddlecakes and other foods, his cup kept filled with hot, sweet tea. After four plates of food and two cups of tea, Aaronn sat back and burped quietly, then sighed with contentment.

"Is that cavern in yer middle full at last?" Arthur laughed aloud.

"I could not eat another bite, Sire," the boy said sincerely, although the thought of perhaps just one more griddlecake was a little appealing.

"Well, Aaronn, what would ye like to do now?" Arthur asked. Aaronn thought of how much he would like to go and play with his friends, but since the King was there he wanted to spend time with Arthur as well. As he squirmed in his chair, Arthur saw the boy's discomfiture and took the pressure off him.

"Go on, play with yer friends, after all, 'tis yer birthday," Arthur laughed.

"Thank ye, Sire!" Aaronn exclaimed and the three boys ran off to their fun, after first excusing themselves from the table.

At a cursory glance at the scullery maids from Sir Cai, the table was quickly cleared. The seneschal however, followed them all into the kitchen to continue their lessons on how to keep a proper kitchen. His caustic comment to Lot was evidence of how he felt.

"If yer lady cannot keep the Castle properly, my Lord Lot, I suggest ye get yerself someone who can. Never have I seen such a filthy, disgusting place to prepare food in."

"I dinnae marry Morgause fer her housekeepin' skills, Sir Cai," Lot answered with a snicker, turning to Arthur. "Still, what yer man says is true, Pendragon. I should git a seneschal t' run m' kitchens an' Castle like yer foster brother does fer ye."

"We could send to Druid Isle for a capable young man," Arthur suggested.

"I want nae Druids here," Lot objected. "I'll find me own man."

"Suit yerself then, My Lord Lot," Arthur said strongly. "I want no more fiascoes like this morning's for my ward."

"I'll ha' one as soon as I find th' right man," Lot growled.

"Very good, now I want to see yer ledgers for the last two years," Arthur requested.

"Why?" Lot asked innocently.

"Because my ledgers show ye delinquent in taxes for the last two years, My Lord," Arthur finally and quietly exploded. "Ye know the Crown needs those funds, Lot. They could make the difference between life and death for yer sons."

"All right then, let us go t' th' tally room an' check, Pendragon. If we a' Lothian are in arrears, I'll make it right!" Lot gave in and stood. "Then perhaps ye will help me tap a keg of well-aged ale."

"I would enjoy that very much, My Lord Lot," Arthur sighed. "Perhaps ye will share some stories of my father with me?"

Lot grinned and went with Arthur to the counting room. It turned out that Lot was late only one year and the Orkney King made the amount immediately available to Arthur. The King handed the seven bags of precious gold and silver coins over to Lancelot, who put them under his bed. Lot and Arthur went down into Lothian's cold room and tapped a keg of mellow ale. Once they had consumed a few cups, they carefully carried the cask up to the great room, where the other Knights dipped out great mugfuls of the potent libation.

"My Lord Lot, 'tis without a doubt the finest ale I have ever consumed," Arthur toasted an hour later. "I thank ye for the sharing of it."

"Aw, 'tis naethin' Pendragon," Lot chuckled. "Merely hospi...hospi...hospistality," he faltered, comically inebriated. Cai appeared just then, a tray in hand, he sat the offering before Arthur, winking privately at his foster brother.

"I have made up some small foods, My Lord Lot. I hope ye do not mind," Cai spoke courteously to the grinning Orkney King, who sampled immediately.

"Nae 'tall," Lot answered through his mouthful, while Cai kept his face carefully neutral, despite being disgusted by Lot's table manners. "We miss ye in the ranks, boyo, but if ye kin cook like this, 'tis good service yer doin'. I wish I had someone like ye a' Lothian," he sighed, taking up another snack and biting into it with relish.

"I can arrange for it, My Lord," Arthur spoke up, taking a bite of his own appetizer. "The Druids..."

"I tol' ye, I want nae o' yer Druid spies here," Lot chuckled. "Good try, Pendragon." Arthur could not help but chuckle with him as the maids brought out more trays of small foods for the Knights.

Meanwhile, Aaronn, Olran and Dalren had dressed in tough, dark-toned clothing, packed day bags with candles, flints, rope, dried snacks and bandages, just in case. They entered the secret staircase for an afternoon of snooping around. The boys had been witnesses to many things, including a few of Lot's many extramarital affairs, which only served to fuel Aaronn's active adolescent imagination. Today, however, the boys found an overhanging ledge above the great room and stretched out on their stomachs watching the King, the Knights and King Lot talk and eat.

"Did ye hear, Olran?" Aaronn whispered, not thinking. "Arthur just told Lot about recalling me to Camelot this spring."

"Aye, I heard," Olran answered dully. "I was hoping that my father would just forget about me altogether."

"Do ye want me to speak to Arthur about it?" Aaronn asked.

"Nay Aaronn, he cannot interfere right now, lest my father pull his troops from the Army. Nay, I shall go home and all will be as 'twas before, except I shall make them pay if they hurt me," Olran told his friend fiercely. "I shall survive it."

"I am glad ye can go and live in yer house now, Dalren," Aaronn smiled at his newest friend.

"I bet my sisters are all just spitting mad, too!" Dalren grinned ferociously. The boys giggled quietly as Olran held up a hand for silence.

"Shhh, ye two! I hear something," he said alertly and went up the stairs a bit.

When the other two boys concentrated quietly, they could definitely hear words of some sort echoing down the tight staircase. They went off in search of the source, climbing carefully, fully aware that they were headed towards Morgause's tower room. Suddenly, they turned a corner and found themselves in front of a narrow doorway. Olran put an ear to the wooden portal and listened carefully, then his brow furrowed in puzzlement. "I do not know for sure what 'tis, Aaronn," he whispered. "'Tis very like the chanting the Ladies of Avalon practice at Midsummer's Eve."

Aaronn's face mirrored Olran's confusion, the two boys sat there, trying to figure it out, while Dalren hovered between staying and escaping. Not as adventurous as the other two, he at least would come along on their forays for companionship and the inevitable fun. They heard clearly the sound of small, cloven hooves, the bleat of a young goat, then after a moment or two more of chanting, a scuffling sound followed by a soft thump.

"What was that?" Aaronn whispered.

"I do not know, and I do not want to find out," Olran whispered in return and he turned towards the staircase. "Let us get out of here!"

"Aye," a fearful Dalren muttered, leading the retreat down the corridor. As his friend's footsteps faded, Aaronn bent to the door and listened carefully. What he heard chilled him to the bone.

"Take this blood, O Dark Master. Give me the power to kill Arthur Pendragon!" Morgause's voice called in entreaty, the malice in her voice was evident even to the young lad listening at the door. There was a pause before Morgause's voice continued through the door, purring in exultation. "Ye have come at my call, Master, at last."

An eerie, gravelly, evil masculine voice answered her. "Aye, bitch! Now, satisfy my needs with yer body and I may even grant yer desire."

"It would be my pleasure, Master! I would do anything to assure that Arthur Pendragon dies!" Morgause laughed lustily. Aaronn waited no longer, he rose and rushed down the staircase, passing Olran and Dalren.

"Aaronn, hold up!" Olran called after him, but the former did not stop. He burst into the great room, only to find Arthur and the Knights making ready to leave in an obvious rush.

"Sire, where are ye going?" the boy panted. "We have not eaten my birthday supper yet!

"I am sorry to rush off, Aaronn, but we just got word that Saxon sails were seen along the western coast, not too far from here. If we hurry, we can intercept them before they do any real damage," Arthur told him swiftly. "I guess this means no rest for the weary this year," he chuckled ruefully.

"This year, we should pursue them across the Severn, so they cannot forage for food close to British territory, aye Sire?" Lancelot asked tersely, as he handed Arthur's helm over.

"But Sire, I have to tell ye…" Aaronn began.

"Another time, boyo," Arthur cut him off sternly.

"Aye, Sire," Aaronn said, hanging his head. "But ye should have heard…"

"Send me a letter about it, Aaronn," Arthur cut him off again. "Now, boyo, be good about this, will ye?" he began, thinking that Aaronn was only wishing for him to stay. "If what I think is about to happen does, 'twill be no coming to Camelot in the spring. I shall write to Olran's father and ask him to allow the boy to stay on here. 'Till I can send for ye keep yer clever eyes on Lot for me, will ye?" the King asked.

"But 'tis not Lot…", Aaronn persisted as Arthur stood and turned to go. "Wait, Sire!"

"Aye, Aaronn?" Arthur questioned and Aaronn could see his was impatient.

"Take good care of yerself and the Knights, My Lord," the boy said, trying not to be bitter. "May the Goddess grant ye victory." Arthur half-grinned, then Roman-saluted the lad, Aaronn returned the gesture crisply and watched them all go, with Olran and Dalren waving with him until they could no longer see the Company.

"Darn those Saxons!" Aaronn grumped. "What a stupid time to attack!" he went on, kicking a lump of dirt hard with his new boots. A white flake fell onto the freshly exposed dirt, then another and another. Soon the boys were standing in a snowstorm and Morgause's syrupy-sweet voice was calling them inside.

"After all, we do not want for the King's ward to catch a chill," she said, handing him a towel. "And the King was so right; we do need a seneschal in the castle to run things. After all, we will all have more work to do come spring, eh, Aaronn?"

"Aye, Lady Morgause," answered the lad, then he went up to his room, followed by Olran and Dalren.

"Aaronn, what took ye so long to come down the stairs, and why the hurry?" Dalren asked.

"Why nothing, nothing at all, Dalren, except the desire to race for the great room," Aaronn passed it off.

That satisfied Dalren, but Olran heard more in his voice and later pressed Aaronn for some details. Aaronn told his friend all and the princeling's eyes went wide as he described what he had heard.

"We should write Vivaine a letter and tell her all of what ye just told me," Olran whispered.

"Aye, but how can we send it without Morgause knowing?" Aaronn asked.

"We will use the old ways, Aaronn," Olran told him. "Drusus told me that if I ever needed to contact the Druids I should leave a letter in the closest oak grove."

"Morgause would not let us near her oaks," Aaronn pointed out.

Olran grinned, pulled out an arrow and patted it reassuringly. "We will not have to get very close, my friend," he chuckled and Aaronn grinned.

The day before the full moon, the two boys left the castle towards evening and secreted themselves close to the ring of huge and ancient oaks planted by the Druids decades before. The altarstone in the center was several pounds of beautiful rose-pink granite; years of benign use by the holy men had polished the top to a smooth and flat surface under the light covering of moss. Olran stopped some twenty yards from the circle and knelt among the shrubbery, Aaronn by his side.

"Are ye sure ye can hit the stone from here?" Aaronn asked as his ally carefully tied the leather square around the parchment note already wound round the arrow in his hand.

"Surely, 'tis not a difficult shot," Olran assured him confidently.

Fitting the arrow into the bow, Olran drew it slowly and carefully sighted down the shaft, then released smoothly. The two boys watched the arrow soar through the air, then land upright in the light covering of fuzzy green moss atop the altarstone.

"What a shot!" Aaronn marveled as he thumped his friend between the shoulder blades.

"'Twas nothing," Olran grinned and put away the small, but deadly bow and matching quiver of arrows. "Let us see if we can spot them taking the letter."

They waited and waited until Dalren finally came looking for them. "Supper is finally ready, ye two. Come and eat," he announced quietly.

"Aye, Dalren, we are coming!" Olran responded and gathered up his gear.

"Ye two go on, I want to wait just a bit longer," Aaronn said distantly.

"All right, but do not be too long," Olran reminded. "Ye know Morgause's rule about meals."

"It will be worth missing supper for if I get a chance to talk with one of the brothers," Aaronn responded, turning his attention back to the center of the circle of oaks. He heard the other two walk away through the snow, then all was again silent. The sun dropped into the western tree-tops, then the full moon rose slowly, casting its silver-white shadow over the oak circle and illuminating Olran's small ash arrow. Nothing happened for the longest time and Aaronn's stomach began to insist upon being fed. He made to leave before he caught the slight motion of a shadow in the grove. He ran swiftly and silently down the hill, halting just outside the ring.

"Brother!" he called out urgently in the Old Language. "Wait, 'tis more to know than is said in the letter."

The Druid master materialized out of the shadows, Aaronn saw with a start that it was Brother Michael, his trainer. "So, tell me little Aaronn. What is so secret that ye did not write it in this missive?" he asked, startling the boy with his rich, bass voice.

"I thought ye could not speak!" he accused, admiring the Druid's stealth in fooling him all these years.

"Ye were told that I did not speak, not that I could not," the older man chuckled. "Now quickly boyo, before she discovers my presence, tell me what ye must about Morgause."

"It concerns what happened after I heard something go 'thump', as I said in the letter," Aaronn began, Michael nodding encouragement as the lad spoke. "She said to the voice that she would do anything to gain the power to kill Arthur. The voice then commanded that she satisfy him, and then it might assist her."

"I see," Brother Michael mused, stroking his tightly groomed beard. "Is there ought else?" he asked, his voice betraying none of the disgust he felt for the daughter of Igraine.

"She said that she would do anything, as long as Arthur dies!" Aaronn finished his report.

"Ye have a good memory to keep that all in mind, Aaronn," Michael complimented him. "Do not worry; Vivaine will hear all of what ye have told me."

"Thank ye, brother," Aaronn said gratefully, then he impulsively threw his arms around his trainer.

"Happy Birthday, Aaronn," the man laughed as he handed the boy a small, but heavy package. "Do not open it 'till ye are sure ye are alone. Remember what I have always told ye, practice makes perfect."

"I shall remember, Master," Aaronn replied earnestly as he watched the man melt back into the shadows, then he turned and ran like a deer for the Orkney castle.

Michael watched him go from his hiding place; only when Aaronn entered the Keep did he break the seal on the scroll and read. Combined with what the boy had just told him, the letter was a condemnation of Morgause, pure and simple. Vivaine was not going to like hearing what her niece was up to, the tall Druid thought as he re-rolled the parchment and stowed it in his large leather pouch. Opening the "door" into the Mother's secret ways he entered, leaving only the faintest of footsteps to indicate his presence. Moments later, he arrived in Avalon and knocked discreetly on Vivaine's door.

"Lady, 'tis Druid Michael. I have returned from Orkney with fearful news," he called quietly.

The door opened and Vivaine appeared in a long, flowing amethyst colored gown, her hair down. "Come in, Michael," she invited, her rich, full voice filling his ears. "I wish to have the truth of what my niece is doing in Orkney."

In the morning, Vivaine rose from her meditations and made her private devotions to the Divine Feminine and Her Daughter, Ceridwen. "O Great Goddess," she began, her need to speak to the Goddess very great indeed. "Thy daughter Morgause has turned traitor to Thee and to all we taught her here on Avalon. Please Mother; send us someone to combat the very great evil she plans to do, for Thy Black Knight and Black Hunter have not gained a majority of years or ability. They will need a great Teacher to assist their maturation. Help me to thwart Morgause's plans until then, please Mother?" she pled and bowed her head. "So mote it be, Mother."

"Do not worry, daughter Vivaine," came Ceridwen's comforting voice into her mind, and Vivaine felt Her warm, loving presence. "Morgause cannot hurt Me or Arthur, just yet. By the time she is ready, My Champions will be able to defend the realm and Avalon against her. The oak grove in Orkney must be locked against her now. The Merlin can easily accomplish that. All is as well as it can be, for now, my daughter."

"Thank ye, Mother. I shall continue to trust in Yer Divine wisdom," Vivaine answered mentally. There was no more from the Goddess, so Vivaine put on hot water for her morning cup of tea.

"Got enough there for two, My Lady?" the Merlin's deep resonant tenor called through the door.

"Always, if the other is ye," Vivaine's silvery tinkle of a laugh echoed pleasantly in his ears. "How goes the winter campaign?"

"'Tis bad, Lady. We have lost many horses, there are many more that might be lost if ye do not come with me to Camelot's stables," the Merlin told her seriously.

"Of course, I shall come at once, right after breaking fast?" Vivaine assured him.

"I was hoping ye would ask," the Merlin winked outrageously and sat expectantly at her table. She laughed and called to her attendant priestess to bring a meal for them both quickly.

After they had eaten their fill, the Merlin assisted Vivaine with a hurried job of packing and they departed Avalon. Vivaine called the Elder Sister to her, explaining that she must watch over the others well while she was away at Camelot. The younger woman nodded gravely, wishing them every success in the veterinary work. Arriving at Camelot through the Mother's secret ways, Vivaine was welcomed gratefully by all.

"My Lady Vivaine, 'tis good to see ye at last," Arthur greeted her wearily. "Can ye save our gallant horses?"

"We will see the poor beasts first, My Lord Pendragon. Those we can save we will tend first, the others Epona will take to her Sacred Pastures in reward for their valiant service," Vivaine smiled gently. "Prince Olran's family just brought a whole herd of fine war-horses in from the Scotti's pastures. I am certain ye can depend on them for remounts."

"I had no idea that Westerland Keep had allies among the Scotti," Arthur wondered aloud. "I need someone to spy on that group, I suppose," he sighed.

"'Tis why ye have we of Avalon and the Druids, My Lord Arthur," Vivaine told him, still smiling gently. "Now take me to the stables, I have work to do."

Only a few of the valuable animals were hurt too grievously for Vivaine's skillful hands to mend, to those she gave a mercy drink to speed them painlessly on their way to their reward in Epona's pastures. The rest were stitched, bandaged and dosed into healing sleep. Tired and hungry, Vivaine and the Merlin walked slowly up the causeway to Camelot, where Cai handed them welcome cups of warmed, spiced wine.

"I shall ever be grateful for this, Caius Ectorius," Vivaine said after wearily taking a few sips of the restorative drink. "Now, if ye would take me to some quiet table, I should like very much to partake of the fine food for which ye have gained such a reputation."

"Would ye care to bathe first, Holy Mother?" the seneschal asked, concerned for this very special guest.

"Perhaps later, my boyo, just bring the food," she laughed tiredly.

"At once, Madam," Cai saluted and took his leave, returning with a plate of small foods for each of them. "Supper will be served in a bit, Holy Mother."

"I thank ye, Sir Cai."

"So, how many of our valiant steeds will be rideable soon, Holy Mother?" asked Lancelot.

"All but twenty, my son," she responded warmly to the son she had borne for Ceridwen in the Great Marriage with King Ban of Lesser Britain. "Of course, fifteen should be ready to ride in a few weeks. I told the King that Westerland Keep kept a large herd of fine warsteeds in Scotti territory. I also know that the herd was recalled two weeks ago, they should be arriving any day. Certainly, if someone were to appeal to that house in the proper way, they would agree to remount all those whose mounts are either still healing or dead."

"Aye, an appeal wi' th' flat o' me blade woul' do nae harm at all," Gawaine laughed and Vivaine could see why her priestesses reported to her that no maiden was safe within an arm's length of the handsome and witty Orkneyman.

"Perhaps we should make a 'routine' patrol of Westerland's realm, eh Gawaine?" asked Arthur's voice, sounding much more rested. The Knights immediately made room for him at the table, and he knelt before the Lady of the Lake. "Thank ye, Holy Mother, for coming to my aid, again," he said respectfully as he kissed her open palm in ritual greeting.

"'Twas and will always be my pleasure to aid ye, Arthur Pendragon," she answered softly, feeling true affection for her nephew.

"And I think 'twould be in yer best interests to send that patrol immediately," the Merlin put in. "Would ye like me to go along?" he asked grinning.

"I would welcome the assistance of the High Druid, Lord Taliesin," Arthur laughed. "The King of Westerland Keep can be an intractable man at times."

"Aye," Gawaine muttered quietly, putting his sword meaningfully on the table. The other Knights nodded and muttered amongst themselves. Prince Olran's father, Warren, had refused to house the Army twice during the winter raids, only the fact that Lancelot had forced the issue at sword's point, backed by Agravaine and Gawaine, convinced the surly petty king to change his mind the second time. All the Knights were now anticipating the "bargaining" for remounts from Westerland.

"Perhaps I shall 'request' my treaty troops include half as many farmers and twice the horses," Arthur mused with a smile as he imagined the reaction such a request would elicit from Warren. The petty king would be positively apoplectic.

"Supper is served, Lords and Ladies. Please, come ye and sit at table," Sir Cai called out and the diners quickly found their places.

"Holy Mother, would ye bless our meal?" Arthur asked.

"Of course," Vivaine readily agreed. She stood then and her small figure seemed to tower over them, so powerful was her presence. "Great

Mother, please bless the defenders of Thy Realm with health, strength and wisdom, so that their struggle against the Saxons and Darkness may be won soon here in Britain. Thank ye, beloved Mother. So mote it be," she intoned and they all echoed the last sentence.

The soup was served then, a light cabbage-based broth, flavored with diced basil, oregano and dried peppers. Small loaves of fresh, lightly crusted bread came around also; Vivaine found that it complimented the soup perfectly. After the soup a fluffy egg custard was served, some flavored with smoked fish and some with a combination of cheeses, all were spiced with garlic and dill. On the side was a cooked lentil salad, tossed with carrot slivers and dressed with olive oil and wine vinegar. More of the bread came out and all Vivaine could hear were contented eating noises. The Lady of the Lake ate her fill along with the Knights, then sat back and drank the last of her one cup of wine. The plates were cleared and tea came out, hot and well flavored with strawberry leaves and currents. Arthur courteously honeyed Vivaine's tea for her, while Cai slipped a small wedge of dried apple pie, sweetened with raisins, cinnamon and honey onto her plate. Vivaine finished the rare treat slowly, savoring the indulgence, waving off a second cup of tea.

"Please, Caius my son, no more. 'Tis time for bed, if I have any more to drink, I shall do no sleeping," she yawned. "Good night, Lord Arthur, Knights of Camelot and yer ladies. Sleep ye sound and may the Goddess bless ye with sweet dreams. Sir Cai, if 'tis not too much trouble, could I impose upon ye for that bath now?" she asked, turning to him.

"Of course, Lady, I have the water heating already, the boys will bring up the tub, aye brothers?" he appealed to the Knights of Camelot.

"For the Lady of Avalon, nothing could be too much trouble," Lancelot spoke for them all. "Come on, Gawaine and Tristan, help me would ye?" he asked, receiving nods of assent. "Bors and Lionel, would ye take the first stable watch tonight?"

"Certainly, cousin," they both answered.

"Gareth, Bedwyr, relieve them in three hours?"

"Aye, Sir Lancelot," Gareth spoke quietly, still adjusting to life at Camelot.

"Of course, First Sword," Bedwyr grinned and went off to catch a few hours of sleep.

Once the tub and hot water were delivered to Vivaine's room, Lancelot went to Arthur's quarters to check on him. The King had been prone to nightmares of late, waking up calling for Dawn occasionally. The First Sword had appealed to Sir Cai to contact the courtesan, who had returned home to deal with a family problem, and ask her to return at once to Camelot. So far, she had not returned, so Lancelot had taken to checking Arthur's door every night. As he turned the corner, he heard the soft whisper of silk in a side corridor. He turned sharply putting his hand on his sword before he saw Dawn's beautiful face. The woman started at his approach, quickly regaining her composure.

"O My Lady Dawn, I am very happy to see ye returned," he greeted her gladly. The woman was intelligent and pleasant company, when she was with Arthur, the King thought and acted with a clearer intent.

"My Lord Lancelot, ye startled me. I have only recently returned to Camelot. Is the King within?" she asked with a smile.

"I shall check, Lady, if he is within he will wish to see ye, right away," Lancelot smiled as he turned to knock on Arthur's door.

Arthur answered after a moment or two, his face looking haggard and drawn with stress. "O, hullo Lance, I was just..." he began, his eyes finally lighting upon Dawn. "Good evening, Lady," he finished, his whole attitude changing. Lancelot smiled privately, he well recognized the look on Arthur's face, and he stepped aside to allow Dawn to pass within.

"Goddess give ye good night, Artos," the First Knight bid the King, his friend.

"The same to ye, Lance. Wake me at the fourth hour and bring the morning's dispatches. Would ye also ask Cai to make up Dawn's room?" Arthur asked.

"Of course, Artos, good night Lady and again, welcome back to Camelot."

"Good night, Lord Lancelot. Thank ye for yer welcome," the woman answered softly.

Arthur closed and locked the door, leaving Lancelot to perform his tasks before retiring to his own bed. Dawn removed her cloak and Arthur took it from her, draping it carefully over the back of a nearby chair. Under the heavy wrap, she was wearing only a frock of even thinner gauze than any she had ever worn before. Arthur said not a word, but took her gently into his arms and carried her to his bed, covering her mouth with his own in a gentle, but passionate kiss.

Vivaine awoke early the next morning, turning to face her beloved Taliesin, the Merlin of Britain. Their times together were sparse, but it only made the time they had sweeter when the Goddess contrived for them to be alone.

"Taliesin, we must wake," she murmured. "'Tis time for devotions."

"Is the sun risen yet?" he asked sleepily.

"Nay, but soon," she answered, rising from her place and reaching for her robe. Taliesin turned on his side to watch her, running his assessing eye over her mature, ripe figure. He sighed inwardly, for to him she was shaped in a more appealing way now than when she was younger. He smiled and rose as well, pulling a robe over his own body quickly, but not so fast that Vivaine missed her opportunity to sneak a peek at his still lean and muscular form. Together, they faced east and spoke the ancient words of greeting to the sun. Afterwards Vivaine yawned and stretched back out onto the bed.

"I am not ready to go downstairs, just yet," she smiled as she snuggled back down into the mattress. "Perhaps 'twould be a good morning to sleep in, My Lord?"

"Perhaps ye may be right, My Lady," Taliesin chuckled, then yawned wide himself. "A person should indulge such a whim, occasionally."

He lay back down beside her and they spoke of Morgause. Together, they decided that the defiant woman definitely needed a good scare to warn her away from the dark path she was walking.

"I shall take brother Osric with me. His eye for detection of subtle presence has no equal in the Brotherhood; certainly his help will make doing the deed much easier."

"Very well," Vivaine sighed. "I had hoped this would not be necessary, but the girl has forced the issue. Teach her a hard lesson, Taliesin, for her own good as well as for the good of Arthur," she added, hoping that this experience would forever quell Morgause's lust for power at any expense.

A discreet knock sounded rapidly on the door, Taliesin answered to find Sir Cai standing there, putting together a collection of pastries and other goodies from his rolling cart.

"Good morning, ye two," he smiled, handing Taliesin the plate of pastries and taking in the pot of tea himself. "Breakfast will be ready in about an hour and the King wants to see ye both. I have sent the clothing ye wore while working on the horses to the laundry, but I have brought clothing from our stores to borrow 'till yer own are dry. I hope they both fit all right and that the color suits ye," he bustled around, laying out the clothing on the bed, chatting pleasantly as he did so. Vivaine held up the robe he laid out for her, admiring the deep rose hue and smiled warmly at the seneschal.

"I only hope that 'tis big enough to cover all my less attractive areas," she chuckled.

Cai's ears turned a sudden red and he hurriedly left the room, realizing that he had probably interrupted a rare, private moment between the Lady of Avalon and the High Druid. "Please excuse me, Lady Vivaine and Lord Merlin. I did not mean to intrude. As soon as ye are ready, please join us in the great room for breaking fast."

Vivaine laughed outright and stood up on her tiptoes to kiss the flustered man on the forehead. "Thank ye, Sir Caius Ectorius, for thy service. Ye are truly a rare gem among men," she said. "Goddess bless ye, always."

"Thank ye, Holy Mother," Cai answered quietly.

"How is the leg, Caius?" she asked, noticing the still visible limp in his gait.

"It still pains me, from time to time," he answered honestly. "Perhaps ye might have an ointment or salve I can rub on it when it aches?"

Vivaine herself had sewn up the nasty seax slash, stitching the length of his leg from outer left knee to just below the groin area. Despite the fact that the Lady of Avalon had used the last of her silk thread and applied many healing and softening herbal oils on the wound, she considered Cai's healing one of her few failures. "Aye, Caius, I brought something in my bag just for that. I shall leave it for ye, remember to rub it on at the first twinge of pain, right along the stitch line," she instructed, handing him the jar of sweet, pungent herbal salve.

"Thank ye, Lady," he said gratefully, tucking the jar away in his apron's pockets. "I must be off now. Good morning to the both of ye," he said, still a bit flustered. He practically ran from the room, pushing his cart of morning sweets and tea quickly down the corridor towards Arthur's suite.

"He is such a dear man," Vivaine observed after Taliesin had shut the door. "I wish that I had been able to fully heal that leg!" she sighed regretfully.

"It took ye four hours to sew up the wound, Lady, and after he had ridden the whole day to reach Avalon. If ye had been on the battlefield that day, perhaps things would be different, but ye were on Avalon, where ye were needed more. Ye must know 'tis the Goddess' judgment on him for the mean treatment of those lesser than himself in his earlier days. Ye could do no more for him than repair most of the damage, the Goddess did the rest."

"I know, but still his leg pains me almost as much as it does him," she sighed again. "However, since his natural organizational skills have been accelerated, I suppose 'tis not all bad," she consoled herself by biting into the flaky pastry stuffed with a sweetened curd cheese and apples tossed with honey and cinnamon.

"Anyone who can cook like this needs feel no shame or dishonor," Taliesin grinned and took another treat in hand.

After consuming their morning wake-up snack, the two dressed in the finery Cai had brought. Vivaine's gown, the man noted, was scooped low in the front and gathered into soft folds at the waist, causing it to drape attractively over her hips and thighs. It was floor-length and made of thick felted velvet, Vivaine felt as though its warm folds were embracing her. Taliesin made a mental note to contact Arthur's tailor and contract a few more gowns of similar pattern as a gift for his lady.

Meanwhile, Cai was knocking on Arthur's door, to be admitted by Lancelot. Dawn was nowhere to be seen, but Arthur was working intently with his scribe, Sir Bedwyr, on the day's dispatches. At the first whiff of food, he rose and walked to Cai's cart, still dictating while he filled his plate with pastries and accepted his mug of tea from Cai.

"Thanks Cai," Arthur said gratefully. He looked much better Cai noted and sent a whisper of prayer to the Goddess for Dawn's return. "Are the Merlin and the Lady of Avalon awake?" Arthur asked after finishing one dispatch and asking Bedwyr to begin another.

"Aye, Artos," Cai answered, his cheeks blushing red again.

"Do not be too concerned, Cai," the King chuckled, recognizing the look on his foster-brother's face. "I am certain they are used to interruptions by now."

Cai only blushed harder, he poured himself a cup of tea and took the smallest pastry on the plate. He sat with Lancelot and Arthur, discussing things in Britain candidly with the King and the First Knight.

"Shall we send the King of Westerland Keep a 'request' for remounts, or shall we just appear on his doorstep?" asked Arthur, grinning widely as he anticipated the response.

Lancelot's handsome face twisted into a look of loathing, with difficulty he straightened his features and answered impassively. "I vote we just appear, in full armor. King Warren is Caw's second cousin; 'tis no reason not to believe that he keeps a larger fighting force on hand than he lets on. I think also, now that he has recalled Prince Olran, we should assure ourselves of the boy's well-being at home. Remember when he first arrived, he was quite withdrawn and how we found all those welt scars all over him? I think because he speaks in support of ye, Artos, that the boy is subjected to the kind of abuse designed to change his mind," Lancelot expressed his opinions quickly and succinctly.

"I agree, Artos," Cai spoke up when Arthur looked at him for his opinion.

"Bedwyr?" asked Arthur.

"Aye, I agree Artos. I think this should be a formal visit, however. Strict protocols, bodyguards for the King, make 'em treat ye as the High King. Put heat to the iron, I say!" the blacksmith's son gave his opinion rapid-fire.

Arthur had been King for bare weeks before the quiet, dark and handsome man had appeared at Caerlon, Uther's stronghold. Bedwyr had pledged eternal loyalty, the nineteen year-old rode at Arthur's boot against the Irish. Young Arthur had acquitted himself well, neatly removing the head of the Irish King with a single blow of Excalibur. His men, screaming in superstitious panic, scrambled back to their boats, not to return again as a raiding force. Bedwyr had remained beside Arthur like that until Lancelot's arrival. Seeing Lancelot's prowess, Bedwyr had quietly stepped aside. Indeed, he had encouraged Arthur and Lancelot's friendship, staying in the background by choice. Still, he was one of Arthur's closest companions; the King would trust only Bedwyr with the responsibility of being royal scribe. He was expected to attend every war council, all the other Knights respected him for his no nonsense attitude towards war and the enemy. Once, just after Lancelot's arrival, the two had headed a patrol along Britain's main highway, finding a day camp established by raiding Saxons. The few Knights hid their horses, secreted themselves around the camp, and then ambushed the twenty-five Saxons, slaying them all. When Lancelot had wanted to gather wood for a pyre, Bedwyr took him aside and refused, saying only;

"Would ye deprive good British scavengers the right to salvage perfectly acceptable food? The worms must eat, as do the wolf and bear. Leave 'em lie."

He would hear no objections, only giving the order to mount and continue the patrol. Cerdic, coming upon the site two weeks later, dissolved into a cursing tirade when he found the remains, for among them proved to be his first cousin, a well-loved warchief. How was he to explain that the man was denied a proper burial because he went a-raiding, and who would care that he had no permission from Cerdic to do so? Bedwyr earned Lancelot's respect that day, when the latter man was elevated to the status of First Knight; he went to Bedwyr to talk it over with him.

"So, Artos has finally made his choice eh?" Bedwyr said, offering Lancelot his hand in congratulations.

"Ye are not angry with me?" Lancelot questioned, amazed.

"Why should I be?" Bedwyr drawled in response. "I could care less. I am a Knight of Camelot because I love the Goddess and Artos, not because I covet some position among the Knights."

"Are we friends then?" Lancelot asked, taking Bedwyr's hand.

"Aye, we are friends as long as ye are loyal to yer oath, Lancelot du Lac. Let anything violate that, and I'll be after ye, sword drawn," Bedwyr answered, blunt as always. Since then Bedwyr and Lancelot often shared confidences, having grown very close, no summer campaign was complete without a rendering of Bedwyr's comic and bawdy rendition of "Arthur's Ballad."

Now the King listened intently, to their conversation and nodding agreement. A knock sounded and Cai opened the door to admit the Merlin and the Lady Vivaine.

"Greetings, wise counselors," Arthur said at once, rising to greet them. "We were just discussing the destination for our next royal visit."

"Ye mean to Westerland Keep to see King Warren?" asked Vivaine as she chuckled softly. Arthur shook his head, grinning widely.

"I should have remembered, Lady, that no conversation is secret from ye," he said ruefully.

"Ah, but I hardly need the Sight to figure out this one, Arthur Pendragon," Vivaine laughed as Arthur led her to her chair, pulling up a low stool for himself. "I think 'twould be a good thing to allow King Warren to 'host' the High King and the Knights of Camelot. Be sure to take thy ladies as well, to add weight to the group. We want to test the stores of Westerland, to see if they are bountiful," she giggled a bit as she pictured Justine's reaction. The screaming tirade would be truly magnificent, surely a wonder to behold, she smiled inwardly. "I would send Sir Lancelot ahead as herald, along with Sir Cai, Sir Bedwyr and Sir Gawaine, just to be sure that the King of Westerland, along with his lady Justine, prepare properly for a royal visit. And for Goddess' sake Artos ap Uther, take Dawn with ye, discreetly wrapped up of course. Let there be an aura of mystery about her, encourage it even! That ought to screw Warren's head on right again. Once the expenses start adding up and ye let it drop that such visits will be a regular practice unless Camelot is properly supplied according to signed and sworn treaties, they will see that 'tis cheaper to tithe properly than to host the royal court once a month," she finished in triumph.

Arthur could only nod his head in agreement. King Warren and his brood were an annoying thorn in his side, as they always had been to Uther. With Westerland as their base, he and a group of major and minor nobles along the borders above Londinium generated enough gossip about treason to occupy five Kings, Arthur sighed to himself. One day, I am going to have to find a reason to break that group up, he thought to himself, then turned his attention back to the discussion at hand.

"I agree entirely with the Lady Vivaine. Caius, start the wheels in motion for a royal procession to Westerland Keep. I want total secrecy for the time being, so say nothing to anyone not holding yer absolute trust. Lance, draw up the escort assignments, I want twelve Knights in full armor at my side. Be sure ye all take yer formals; we will be wearing only the best while at Westerland. Lance and ye also, Bedwyr will attend me in all public and private meetings, I want Gawaine and Agravaine standing guard at my door. And Lance...," Arthur stopped for a moment.

"Aye, Artos?" Lancelot smiled.

"Be sure that Tristan stays at Camelot this time. Ye know how it is with him, no maiden within smelling distance will be safe at Westerland," Arthur instructed, grinning. "I want both he and Gareth to follow us the day after we all leave, just in case things get dicey with Warren and his sons."

"Aye, Artos," Lancelot smiled slowly, agreeing with Arthur's plans.

"We leave in a week, gentlemen. Lady, with the Goddess' blessing, this year, the Saxons will face a more united Britain than they have ever faced before!" he declared firmly.

The preparations were made and, three days before the King's departure, Lancelot, Bedwyr, Cai, Agravaine and Gawaine left as all the warning Arthur wished to give. The four Knights rode hard for a day and a night, arriving at Westerland Keep just after dawn the second day.

"King Warren of the Westerland Keep, I abjure ye in the name of the High King to open thy gates for us. We are Knights of Camelot, with word from Arthur Pendragon, High King of the Britons," Lancelot called up to the watchtower courteously and crisply, despite only sleeping a few hours in a borrowed bed at one of the garrisoned towers Arthur had built since gaining the High Throne.

"What business do ye have here?" a surly voice called back. Lancelot recognized the voice of Warren's eldest son, Kevin.

"We have come to bring ye glad tidings. Ye will have the honor of hosting the High King and the Knights of Camelot for a few days. Please, allow us to enter and make thy castle secure for His Highness?" Lancelot called back, still allowing the flowery phrases to fall from his lips, while in his heart he chuckled with glee at what he imagined the young man's reaction might be, as did the others.

"Is this all the advanced notice we are to receive?" Kevin called back rudely.

"We are the heralds, Prince Kevin. The High King left with the vanguard three days after us, so he should be here soon. Ye see we have even brought the Seneschal of Camelot with us." he finished, indicating the stone-faced Cai. The seneschal's leg throbbed fiercely, after two days a-horseback, but he ignored it by promising himself a thorough leg massage with Vivaine's miraculous salve.

"Very well, Sir Lancelot du Lac," Kevin's voice sneered as he said the title. "We will open the gates."

Lancelot turned swiftly to his companions. "We are Knights of Camelot, boyos. Act the part, completely, right Gawaine? No drunken sprees?" he warned.

Gawaine appeared shocked at Lancelot's warning before he grinned brightly. "Aye, Sir Lancelot, but we'll all wan' t' relax after hours, won' we?" he slyly suggested, patting his saddlebags before schooling his features back into sobriety, waiting with the others outside the gates of Westerland Keep.

Finally, the great oak doors creaked open, revealing a tight-faced King Warren and his queen, Justine. Kevin, red-faced with drunkenness and barely-controlled rage, stood alongside with the second son, Sean and the third son, Marcus. Olran stood in back, Lancelot noted that the youngest prince was very happy to see the Knights, though he said nothing.

"Greetings to all at Westerland Keep in the name of the High King, Arthur Pendragon of Camelot," Lancelot began the ritual.

"Bah, skip that courtly bullshit," Warren said loudly and rudely. "Why's the Pendragon coming here?"

"I am not here to discuss that with ye, My Lord Warren," Lancelot responded vaguely. "I am here to assure a proper welcome for the High King," he went on coolly and professionally. He dismounted and gave the others the order to emulate him.

"Damned inconvenient and rude too, we are only now preparing for the Winter Solstice feasting," Queen Justine grumbled.

"Of course, Madam," Lancelot replied, handing his reins to Gawaine, who took them without hesitation. The silent message to the nobles was that Lancelot was unquestionably in charge. "'Twas due to the festive spirit of the holiday season that the King chose to spend time with ye, to feast and share in the warmth of his ally's home."

"WHAT?" Warren, Justine and their sons all shouted at once. "But we've made other plans, invited special guests and family…!" the petty woman went on, stopping herself too late to avoid Lancelot's next sally, he pounced on the opportunity to wield his words as well as he wielded his sword.

"Wonderful, 'tis exactly the chance the High King wished for, to meet with yer family and guests. 'Tis his greatest pleasure to converse with his subjects and discuss many lively topics. We have brought, as I said before, Sir Caius Ectorius, the Seneschal of Camelot, to assist in yer kitchens, My Lady Justine. Surely, that combined with our own efforts, will suffice for yer house to welcome the King, the Knights and their Ladies? We Knights are accustomed to hard work, we will not fail to accomplish our mission," he finished meaningfully, all the while smiling politely.

Warren and Justine exchanged a look of resignation and defeat. "Very well, Sir Lancelot, if the Pendragon wants to play dress up, we will oblige him. How many can we expect?" Justine asked.

"The King, along with twelve Knights and their ladies, children and squires, of course; 'twould make the number thirty-five, plus we four," Lancelot answered, making a quick tally in his head.

"Very well, My Lord Lancelot. Quarters for thirty-nine 'tis, I suppose they must be together on the same floor?" Justine sighed, thinking of all the extra help she would have to hire from the town. The rooms were far from ready; indeed they hadn't been opened for quite some time. She knew that they would need more than a cursory cleaning. She prayed for Warren to bargain for all he could get for those horses, this holiday season would be more expensive than she planned, she thought meanly.

The preparations began at once, Cai supervising a thorough cleaning of the Keep's kitchens and pantries. That meant only cold meats, bread and cheeses all day and no hot meal at night. Finally, after midnight, most of the cleaning was accomplished; the castle was nearly ready for Arthur's visit. The four Knights took short soaks in the natural hot springs for which Westerland Keep was famed before they washed up in the accompanying blue-tiled Roman-style bath. The room was decorated with a mural of a naked and sensuous Venus rising out of the sea with Neptune in his chariot, the Goddess attended by mermaids and sea-nymphs. The four shared a room, when they were all within Gawaine revealed the secret of his saddlebags, a crockery jug full of potent mead, called meglithin and a jug full of Orkney whiskey.

"Where'd ye get this?" asked Bedwyr as he held out his cup for more.

"From 'ome," the Orkneyman chuckled. "An' if ye thin' me Da was fierce wi' me o'er th' troops, wait 'till he takes stock o' his liquor locker," he laughed harder, almost spilling a bit of the potent liquor. "I an' Agravaine pinched twelve jars o' whiskey, twelve skins o' ale and ten skins o' meglithin. Drink ye hearty, laddies."

Warren's earlier invited guests made loud and merry that night, the Knights drank a good cup or two, just to get to sleep. Agravaine stood first watch, followed by Gawaine three hours later. Bedwyr took the third watch and Lancelot woke early to allow the man to get additional rest. Bedwyr could work until all was done, then fall asleep immediately wherever he was. It was a skill not yet fully acquired by the others, being how they had not been with the Army as long as Bedwyr. Cai, having worked the longest and hardest, was allowed to sleep the full night so as to ready himself for the next day's labor.

It was Olran who brought up the breakfast tray of hot tea, cereal with honey and toasted bread with butter. The boy was so happy to be alone with the Knights that he burst into a rare display of tears as soon as Lancelot let him into their room.

"Easy now, boyo, yer with friends now," Lancelot comforted him, handing Olran a nose cloth.

"Aye, Sir Lancelot," Olran agreed, blowing his nose loudly. "Is the King coming for the horses?" he asked with curiosity.

"Aye, Olran, and more, say nothing to anyone?" Lancelot chuckled.

"Of course not, especially not the King's secrets!" the ten and a half year old asserted.

"What kin ye tell us o' th' horses, laddie?" Gawaine asked.

"They are here, arrived yesterday early in the morning. Warren paid the Scotti off in gold, they left riding hard for the border. All the steeds seem sound, nearly all the mares are in foal. The family plans to sell them to Lord Merin and Lord Corwin," Olran reported quietly.

The news brought a malicious gleam to Bedwyr's eyes. "Someone is going to have to slit that bastard Merin's throat for him one of these days. He's a snake, and a damned sneaky one at that. Only someone more skilled at trickery is going to catch that eel, I say," he muttered darkly, fingering his belt knife.

"How many in the herd, boyo?" asked Cai.

"More than a hundred, all together, Warren sorted out forty big yearling stallions and stashed them in the stud barn. The foaling mares are in the birthing barn now, and the lead stallion is a big, coal-black brute in chains in the cow-byre. He is a wild one for certain and he won't let anyone near him!"

"What's Warren planning to do with him?" asked Bedwyr suddenly.

"He says if cannot break him, he will eat him," Olran reported, choking up again. "Sir Lancelot, ye will not let him do that, will ye? That horse is Epona's own, for certain!"

"Nay lad, I will not let him hurt the black one. What say we let him loose?" he suggested conspiratorially.

"I want to, but if I get caught, Warren would beat me to ribbons," Olran replied matter-of-factly. The Knights all noted how the boy would not use the honorific "Father" or "Da" for Warren. "I have been able to avoid that happening since I got home, I should like to keep on avoiding it."

"Very well, Olran. We will figure something out," Lancelot sighed and let the boy gather the dishes onto his tray.

Unfortunately, he did not get out the door before Prince Kevin knocked and called out crossly; "Olran, ye puke! Is my laundry done?"

"Of course, 'tis in yer room, Kevin," the boy answered quickly.

"Sniveling around with the Pendragon's men again?" Kevin sneered, catching hold of the younger boy's hair and pulling him out the door with it. "Wait'll Da hears, ye'll be whipped again," he laughed and yanked the boy off his feet. Dishes and scraps went flying and landed on the floor, making one big mess of oatmeal and plate shards. "What's the matter, lose yer balance?" Kevin chortled, laughing so hard his eyes puddled with tears. The Knights had all seen enough at that, and an angry Gawaine took matters into his own hands. Striding over to the fat, hulking man, the even larger Orkney Knight picked him up by the front of the shirt throwing him backwards into the wall to his right, pinning him against it with easy effort.

"Now, listen 'ere laddie. All th' boy did was bring us a tiny bite o' breakfast, then stay an' visit awhile wi' his friends. King Warren needn't hear o' this, an if he does, ye'll settle wi' me, Kevin," he growled at the now-fearful and dazed bully. "An' tha' means after we leave too!" he added, dropping the man forcibly down on his feet. Kevin looked at the Knights who were now all glowering fiercely over him and he broke, running quickly back up the hallway.

"They will just wait 'till Spring, or whenever the raiding or wars start up again," Olran sighed. "I really want to go back to Lothian with Aaronn. At least they did not beat me up there."

"Arthur will hear all of this, have no worry, Olran," Bedwyr assured the boy as they helped him clean up the broken plates and cups. "He'll help."

"The best way to help me is to get me out of here, permanently," Olran said sadly as he embraced each man hard. "Thanks anyway, for stopping Kevin this time. He's been in a foul mood ever since ye showed up," he said, taking up the tray. Accompanied by Cai and the Knights, Olran went back down to the kitchens to resume his chores for the day. Cai let the lad help in the kitchens all day, where he could keep a watchful eye the family's actions. The princeling proved to be his usual helpful self, mixing eggs, grating cheese, sifting dried ingredients into bowls, fetching needed materials from the pantries and keeping Cai's teapot full all day. When the royal party finally arrived in later afternoon; wet, cold and uncomfortable, the young Prince was chosen to bring the cup of welcome to King Arthur.

"We welcome ye, Arthur ap Uther Pendragon, King of the Britons and all thy train, to Westerland Keep. Take and drink, Sire; enter my house in peace," King Warren spoke in ritual greeting. He noted a bundled form being whisked from a white palfrey by Sir Bors and Sir Lionel into the kitchen entrance, he wondered what piece of pretty the son of Uther had managed to smuggle into his home.

"In peace we come, Warren ap Daffyd, King of Westerland Keep. I thank ye for this most welcome cup," returned Arthur as he quaffed the warm, sweetened spiced wine. Sir Lancelot fell in behind the High King on his right, Sir Bedwyr on the left. Into Westerland Keep they followed Warren and Justine, where the rest of Warren's household and guests waited to greet the High King.

"My Lord Arthur, ye know my sons Kevin, Sean, Marcus and of course the youngest, Olran. It seems he cannot stop comparing our humble home to the shining grandeur of Castle Camelot," Warren began, a slight sarcasm in his voice.

"Prince Olran is young and easily impressed, King Warren. All new things are likely to cause wonder in such a one," Arthur carefully passed off the baited statement. "However, he and my ward have become fast friends since being fostered together. Perhaps ye will return yer youngest to Druid Isle or, ye might consider returning him to Lothian 'till I recall Aaronn," he went on as he handed his soggy wraps to a servitor and accepted another cup of the warmed wine from a comely maid.

"Not damn likely, Pendragon, I may be a bit rough on the boy, but I'll not send him back to Lothian, whether Morgause is yer half-sister or not!" Warren said emphatically. "And far as the Druids are concerned, I'm sure we have plenty of tutors here at the Keep to teach him what he needs to know to survive this world." Arthur listened, but he also watched Olran's face unobserved by Warren. When the suggestion of fostering had arisen, the boy's face remained unchanged, except for a slight smile at the corner. When Warren had refused to allow it, Arthur noted the boy's face was absolute granite, even the usual sparkle of mischief disappeared. Ah, but what is the nature of yer teachings, Warren, Arthur thought, resolving to speak to Lancelot on the subject. "Come My Lord Arthur, I want ye to meet some of yer fellow revelers. Ye know Lord Merin of Darkensdale?"

"Aye, I appointed Lord Merin to his land grant," Arthur responded stiffly and Warren's face reddened.

"Of course," the petty King harrumphed. "Come, Sire let us begin the celebration?" he questioned.

And so began the "party," Cai's small foods saved the night for Arthur, he and those of Camelot ate heartily but drank sparsely. The High King waited to bring up the subject of remounts until four hours later, during the main course, when Warren and the others were well into their cups.

"Aye, the raiding in the forests is deadly business. The Saxons are now aiming for the horses rather than at the Knights. We've lost too many horses to lose more, we need remounts if we are to effectively patrol the realm," he began, still speaking conversationally.

"That's too bad, Pendragon," Warren guffawed, along with many others. "Where are ye goin' to get 'em?"

"I thought the vast plains of yer lands, long fabled for excellent horseflesh, might supply a few King Warren. 'Tis mentioned in the treaty we both signed that Westerland will support the Army," Arthur answered, pressing carefully.

"I pledged men, Pendragon, I said naught about horses," Warren reminded. "And besides, I've none to send anyway."

"But Da, what about that herd ye brought in yesterday?" Olran spoke up loudly as he poured more wine for the High Table. "There must be over a hundred in the compound now."

"Ye have over a hundred, how much for the lot?" Arthur asked innocently.

"Ye want them all?" Warren asked, incredulous. He had no idea the Pendragon's pockets were so deep.

"I need 'em all, Warren ap Daffyd, how much?" Arthur repeated strongly.

Lords Merin and Lord Corwin, the cousins to Warren, shot daggers at the young Olran, then at Warren for even considering changing the oral deal they had already struck. The arrangements were secret, the two treacherous Lords knew well that anything they might say to object would implicate them in the treachery and Arthur would be immediately suspicious.

"Well, Pendragon, I won't sell them all. Most are breeding mares, ready to drop foals in late winter. I have a few yearling stallions I could let go, but no more than forty. They are good stock too, so they won't come cheap," he warned, rubbing his hands together mentally in greedy glee. After all, he had already accepted full payment in gold from Merin and Corwin for the yearlings, now to get paid twice for the same goods. Perhaps the royal visit would be profitable after all, he thought.

"How much?" asked Arthur, slowly and deadly serious.

"The price is fifty gold sovereigns for each yearling," Warren announced, having finished his mental reckonings.

"But Da, ye were going to charge Lord Merin only ten for each yearling, and twelve for the brood mares," Olran's voice rang out in the suddenly quiet feast hall.

"Olran, ye git to yer room, I'll speak to ye later!" Warren ordered loudly.

"Hold, King Warren," Sir Lancelot's voice countermanded the order. "Why send the boy away now? I think the High King needs to hear more, aye My Lord?" he finished, stressing the title meaningfully.

"Well Warren, what is this all about?" Arthur asked mildly, although he was furious with the petty king.

"I had already struck an oral deal last fall for these, Pendragon. The extra cost is a reflection of needing to break those agreements," Warren explained hastily. "These are the only horses I have to sell, so of course I began the bargaining on the high side."

"Da, yer forgetting the herd ye sent to Lyonnesse when the wars started?" Olran called out once more, impatiently. "We sent fifty, there must be triple that number by now."

Warren cursed violently under his breath, for those horses and his agreement concerning them was how he had kept Leodegrance out of the war so far. The Westerland King had sent ten of his biggest and best stallions, along with forty hefty-framed mares to the man in hopes of breeding up to even larger progeny. Leodegrance, a fussy perfectionist had desired nothing more than to breed fine horses and find a good catch as a husband for his radiantly beautiful daughter Gwenhyfar. He wanted to stay out of fighting the war personally. There was talk of an alliance between the two houses through marriage of the young girl and Olran, but nothing had come of it, though both houses favored the match. In any case, the ownership of the herd had become a somewhat muddled matter between the houses, so it had become accepted that the entire herd would be a wedding present to the couple upon completion of the nuptials. Now, Warren thought in frustration, he would have to compensate Leodegrance for Westerland's share in boarding costs for each animal. The amount was seemingly astronomical, Warren's temper exploded, all pretense of courtesy gone.

"Olran, ye get to yer room boyo, now! Ye've cost the family plenty with yer wagging tongue and ye'll pay for it," he shouted. "Kevin, Sean, git to yer horses and ride for Lyonnesse. Tell Leodegrance what has happened and that he'll be compensated fully for his time and feed stocks then bring back every one of those horses! Pendragon, ye can have all the remounts, the treaty troops as well, but if ye ever come back to my Keep, bring yer sword. Now get out, ye and yer whole party! This royal visit is at an end!" he finished his tirade and sat, then drank his cup to the dregs.

"Wait, Lord Warren, 'tis one more thing. Have Prince Olran's things packed and ready to go. We will also take Prince Marcus. Once the horses are delivered, ye will be returned that which is yers," Arthur's voice grated tightly.

"Very well, Pendragon," Warren acknowledged. "But this tears it, no more treaty, no more retainers from my realm, no more food tithes. I say that yer reign is a false one, that ye are no true King to use one of yer subjects as ye have used me. I deny ye are the son of Uther, therefore any treaties ye have signed with me are invalid!" Warren shouted.

"Ye'd best think that through, me wee little man," Gawaine's voice drawled out behind him.

"Aye, Warren ap Daffyd, Westerland Keep and it's lands can always be stripped from ye, and then where will ye go?" Arthur asked in a purring tone rife with cunning.

"Ye...ye wouldn't dare Arthur ap Uther! Ye cannot!" Justine whispered, appalled.

"Wouldn't I? Couldn't I?" Arthur asked softly and threateningly. "Remember, my Crown came to me from both the Mother's hand and the Christ's. Who is the Land, Warren ap Daffyd? Ye or the Goddess?" he pressed, bending over the now-seated and pale man. Warren and his brood were visibly shaken by Arthur's words, they sat wan and quiet in their chairs. "Ye have tried my patience for the last time, Warren of Westerland," Arthur began. "Ye have what stallions and fillies not suitable for breeding in my stables two weeks from today. If they are not there on that day without good cause, 'twill be a formal revoking of thy family's land grant, which the Lady of the Lake will attend. Ye can explain to Ceridwen why ye have been treasonous to her chosen King. I am for bed now, I expect to sleep undisturbed in my suites 'till a proper time in the morning. Upon arising, the baths are to be made available to my entire entourage and then breakfast will be served. Only after that will I depart, taking my entourage with me. Good night, My Lord Warren, My Lady Justine and honored guests. Goddess grant ye all good dreams," he flung his words at them, impatient to be away from the nest of vipers.

The Knights and their ladies made formal good nights, took their children with them and left the great room, following Arthur, Gawaine and Lancelot up the stairs to their assigned quarters. Once they were all gone, Warren poured himself a full cup of whiskey and drank it straight down. All he could think was that he was ruined in both fortune and reputation, ruined because of his blabbermouth son.

Arthur bedded Olran down in Bedwyr's room, for the boy's own safety. After all, who could have guessed that the lad was privy to such secrets considering he was so tight-mouthed concerning the situation at his home. Only when Warren had tried to cheat Arthur had he spoken up and at considerable risk to himself. The High King returned from tucking the princeling into a rough bed made from donated quilts from all the other Knights and found the Inner Circle awaiting him. He looked from face to faithful face, glad to see them assembled around him.

"Well, we have stirred up a hornet's nest, aye boyos?" he grinned and let the laughter cleanse the darkness from his soul.

"Aye, Artos, tha' we ha'," Gawaine agreed. "It just so happens tha' I ha' th' perfect remedy fer it!" he laughed and poured some liquid into a cup. Arthur tasted and smiled slowly.

"Gawaine, I am proud of ye, from Lot's own store to my cup here in Westerland," he chuckled.

"Well, Artos, I am yer man now, nae me Da's," Gawaine chuckled with him.

"Aye, Gawaine, 'tis glad I am of it too," Arthur responded seriously as he accepted more whiskey from Gawaine. "Ye and yer brothers are irreplaceable men."

"Ye have torn it with Warren now," Lancelot suddenly changed the subject. "And what of Leodegrance, could this be what Lady Althea meant?"

"That crafty old lion, I should have realized he was playing both sides for maximum profit," the King chuckled wryly. "Lance, I need ye to be my embassy to him. Let him know I shall pay plenty if he would sell me that herd direct."

"I shall leave tonight. Warren's sons left some hour ago, I shall have to ride like Epona Herself to catch them!" the First Knight said and drained his cup. Just as he was picking up his gear, the door burst open to reveal Sir Tristan and Gareth, each holding a squirming Westerland Prince by the nape of the neck.

"We found these rascals riding like demons towards the south," Tristan announced loudly as he strode into the High King's room, thrusting Kevin before him.

"Ye stop that!" Sean shouted as Gareth neatly tossed him after his brother. "Our Da will make ye pay!"

"Truly, 'im an' wha' army?" Gareth answered with contempt.

"O, we won't have to confront any Knights, brother mine," Kevin said coolly. "We always have our dear brother, the King's man, to 'talk' to about Camelot."

"Ye woul' nae, a great hulkin' oaf as yerself, an' him barely o'er ten," Gareth said, unbelieving. "I'll kill ye meself if I hear ye've hurt him."

"If ye hear of it," Kevin snickered.

"Well, boyo," Gawaine spoke up, rising from his chair. "Maybe 'tis time ye foun' out wha' 'tis like t' be beat oop by someone bigger."

"Aye!" answered both Bors and Lionel, also rising from their places and rolling up their sleeves. Fear finally dawned upon the two bullies as the sword-hardened Knights took off surcoats and shirts, revealing bodies honed by years of campaigning. Only Arthur eschewed any action, other than retiring to his inner chambers and shutting the door firmly behind him. The last sight Arthur had of the brothers was Lancelot tying gags firmly over the two cruel men's mouths to muffle any cries of pain. Only the sounds of severe pummeling were heard for the longest time, then Tristan and Bedwyr slung the unconscious, bruised and battered bullies over their shoulders, down through the kitchens and out into the stables. Leaving them in the stalls of patient old geldings, the Knights removed the gags and exited the horsebarn. Upon returning to their rooms, the two men drank a final cup of whiskey to each other and their brother Knights, then lay down and enjoyed a wholly restful sleep.

During the night, a form materialized just outside the stables, then entered and lit a candle lantern. The light revealed Lady Morgaine's beautiful features, which were schooled into passiveness. She had seen the events of the day in her meditations, and came to help protect the reputation of the King and his Knights. The two men were just regaining wakefulness, so she quickly opened the herbal vial in her pocket and poured a few drops into each man's mouth. Waiting until she was certain the mildly hypnotic potion had taken full effect, she leaned over the two and spoke quietly and swiftly into their ears.

"Hear me, Kevin ap Warren and Sean ap Warren. By the Power of the Goddess, ye will remember only that ye were set upon by brigands on yer way to the Lion's Den. They wanted yer horses, and beat ye soundly to get them. Ye managed to escape and wandered back home. Ye must have become confused and lost consciousness, due to exhaustion and lack of blood, and collapsed here in the stalls. Ye will remember only my words," she instructed.

"We were beat up by horse thieves, aye," mumbled Kevin.

"The beat us up, took our horses," Sean whispered through swollen lips.

"Very good, now sleep, wake very late in the day tomorrow, long after the King's party is gone from Westerland," she further instructed.

"Wait 'till long away," they echoed and began snoring softly.

Morgaine grinned with delight and blew out the lamp, perfectly able to see in the pitch dark. Releasing Kevin and Sean's horses from the stalls she exited, locked the stables from within with the door bar and melted into the shadows, leaving no evidence of her presence.

All went smoothly in the morning and Prince Olran left home mounted up behind Bedwyr, while the spoiled and whining Marcus preferred to ride in the wagon with the luggage. Olran, overjoyed to be headed for even a short stay at Camelot endured the long ride without fussing, while Marcus complained and nit-picked about each little bump. Once they were well away from Westerland Keep, Sir Lancelot, Sir Bors and Sir Lionel left the main party, headed at their best pace to the kingdom of Lyonnesse. The First Knight carried with him a letter from Arthur explaining his dilemma and offering a goodly price per head for any extra yearlings and non-breeding fillies. He also carried a hefty gold advance in Roman coinage to tempt the man into agreeing to the deal.

Kevin and Sean appeared from the stables after Arthur was long gone, groggy and bruised green, black and purple from head to toe. All they could remember was that there had been trouble on the road to Lyonnesse, no matter how Warren questioned them they could only repeat the story suggested by Morgaine.

Meanwhile the rest of the King's party went on to Londinium and the new Royal Inn there. The beds were firm and comfortable, there was a large bath available and the food was quite acceptable as well.

By the next morning, Lancelot, Bors and Lionel arrived at Lyonnesse. Leodegrance was pleased to hear the King was in need of steeds, he showed off his horses proudly to the First Knight. They sat down and began the dickering right away. When Kevin and Sean arrived to inform Leodegrance of Warren's instructions, they found Lancelot and the others fully engaged in counting out the advance and sealing the bargain with a glass of wine. There was much arguing and threats thrown about by Warren's sons, before they were "escorted" out by the First Knight of Lyonnesse. The bargain had been struck and the Old Lion would not change his mind. He saw now a better match for his Gwenhyfar, possibly even the High Throne itself, he was determined that she should have the opportunity at least, to seek her fortune. Westerland could just go to Hades, Leodegrance thought as he watched Lancelot walking with his daughter.

Lancelot spent much time with Gwenhyfar; she even charmed him into playing ball with her several times. The thirteen-year old girl had wormed her way into the First Knight's heart, now when he regarded her budding figure, sapphire eyes, and the wealth of silver-blonde hair that tumbled to her waist when it was unbound, his heart pounded. He knew this girl would be something very special once she matured a bit more. Gwenhyfar was naïve and innocent, but she was also well read and intelligent, witty and extremely graceful, just the qualities the "Impeccable Knight" desired in a woman. He took his leave of her reluctantly, but necessity forced his hand and leave he did, driving fifty young stallions and thirty fillies. All were of good lines and breeding, Lancelot could see, each horse stood at least fifteen hands high at the withers, giving a large height advantage to its rider. None of the horses were even gentled to the halter, for as Leodegrance told Lancelot; "The deal we made with Warren said to breed 'em and feed 'em, not to train 'em. That would've been extra."

Lyonnesse's herd arrived in Camelot ten days later, and the Knights all cheered when the saw the fine horses filling the pens. Arthur welcomed the three Knights home personally, handing each of them cups of warmed wine to drink after their cold journey. Lancelot handed Arthur the letter sent by Leodegrance, offering more troops and trained horses to swell the Army, for a price. Arthur choked when he read Leodegrance's proposal and Lancelot could hardly believe his ears.

"To the High King at Camelot, Arthur ap Uther Pendragon;

Greetings, My Lord, I hope these few poor animals will assist My Lord in these current troubled times. I have often said that if the High King were my son, there would be no end to the assistance I could offer him. Think well on it, My Lord Pendragon, and send thy answer soon. Leodegrance of Lyonnesse."

"A betrothal, is he joking?" Arthur blurted.

"'Twas my impression that Leodegrance is a serious man, Artos," Lancelot said, swallowing his own feelings and thinking only of Britain. "The girl is lovely, but barely thirteen and very naïve. On the positive side, though, she is quite beautiful already and shows good training as well as intelligence. She is witty as well, charming and graceful with silver-blonde hair and sapphire-blue eyes," he sighed, remembering.

Arthur looked as his First Knight and saw much emotion on his face. He saw the man's secret, that he cared for Gwenhyfar dearly. Truly, this would be a difficult decision, for he did not wish to hurt Lancelot. Well, enough time to consider this later with the Merlin's guidance.

"Tell me Lance, how many trained troops does Leodegrance have at the Lion's Den?" he asked.

"Enough, his private army is nearly as big as yer own. Well-equipped too, Leodegrance has a huge smithy in the Keep and employs five smiths year round, or so he claimed."

"And the horses?" Arthur pressed.

"Ye saw them, tall with nice broad backs to sit on, strong legs and teeth. I can hardly wait to incorporate their lines into my breeding project," Lancelot reported efficiently, glad to be off the subject of Gwenhyfar.

"I see, Lance, that I am going to have to visit Leodegrance to see the marvels of his Keep. Who knows, by the end of the year, I may be a married man!"

Lancelot said nothing, only nodding and trying to smile at the suggestion. He was hardly amused, however, the feelings he had for Gwenhyfar were very new to him, but strong. While he understood that Leodegrance lusted for a royal marriage for his daughter, he wondered if he would accept something less grandiose for her. He swallowed again and answered as impeccably as possible. "Only Ceridwen can tell, Artos."

Warren sent his tribute within the required time and Prince Marcus and Prince Olran were recalled, immediately. Arthur had no choice but to fulfill the terms he had set down and the stone-faced Olran climbed without a word into Westerland's carriage. In saying his good-byes the night before, he had begged Arthur to send Aaronn the letter he pressed urgently into the King's hand.

"Of course," Arthur had readily agreed. "I am sorry at having to send ye home, ye know that boyo. I know 'twill be bad for ye there, as soon as I can, I shall find a way to get ye back to Camelot."

"I know, Sire," Olran replied simply, his voice breaking a bit with unshed tears. "Please, I beg ye to hurry."

Arthur sent the letter to Aaronn the same day, without reading it. A week or so later, Aaronn broke the seal on the envelope and read the long missive carefully. It detailed to Aaronn how his situation at Westerland had steadily worsened and how Olran feared for his life.

"I shall not be able to send another letter this way, brother. Warren or one of the others are reading everyone's mail now, so I shall try to leave letters in the oaks. Pray for my salvation from this hell I live in, brother, pray for Arthur's victory. Olran."

Aaronn cursed impotently after reading the end of the letter; due to observing Lot's own rages some of his invectives were quite colorful. He sat heavily on the bed that used to sleep his friend. "How could he? How could Arthur let them take him back?" he fumed to himself. "The King knows well how they treat him there. I shall run away, get him out of there and we will go back to Avalon!" he vowed to himself, stashing the letter in the ditty bag he always kept packed now.

After composing himself for the day's doings at Lothian, he left his room and went up to the high parapets that rose up beside Morgause's tower. He leapt up onto the narrow catwalk that edged the tower and began practicing the routine of exercises he had learned from Brother Michael as he balanced on the tiny ledge. When the routine was complete, he executed neat flips and cartwheels along the perilous route. He heard Gaheris call, ignored him and went on with his work, knowing well that his foster-brother would come looking for him in a few minutes.

"Aaronn, damn it, I know yer up there, now coom down!" Gaheris' voice floated up the stairs. "Da wants t' go a huntin' an' yer t' coom wi' us."

Aaronn said nothing in return for he was busy concentrating on his newest stunt, a full back flip from the ledge to the parapet floor, three feet down. When Gaheris poked his head through the doorway, he saw Aaronn flip backwards, landing cat-like on the balls of his feet.

"Quit yer screwin' aroun', Aaronn. Da wan's t' see ye," Gaheris said gruffly, secretly admiring Aaronn's graceful, athletic abilities. "Time t' go get fresh meat!"

"Why not just use horse meat?" Aaronn answered caustically. His black pony had taken a misstep and damaged his right front tendon. It was not a major injury, but time-consuming to treat, so Lot and Morgause had ordered the horse destroyed. They claimed he would consume too much time and effort, and that there was no use in doctoring since he would never recover fully. Aaronn was heartbroken, but he had taken the responsibility himself for felling the animal with a quick and merciful slice across the jugular vein with his birthday knife.

Later, at supper that night, Aaronn found a piece of meat in his stew, which still retained a tuft of black hide. "Ye cooked my pony?" he accused, spitting the meat out of his mouth. "Is that why ye would not doctor him?" he went on, outraged.

"O'course nae, boyo," Lot answered, chewing unconcerned. "When a pawny's leg be damaged tha' way, th' animal is ne'er right agin."

"And 'twould have been a waste to just burn all that fresh meat as well, Aaronn," Morgause purred as she filled her bowl again to the brim.

"Ye all make me *sick*!" Aaronn shouted to them, his voice breaking into a deeper, mannish tenor and he had left the table, furious.

Now, Gaheris sighed. "Aw c'mon, Aaronn, I dinnae know, an' I ate nae more o' the stew after I knew," he consoled.

"I know, but Morgause and Lot stuffed their stomachs full with it. I shall never forget or forgive for that!" the adolescent vowed fiercely. "We better go and get some venison so that no more horses end up in the stewpot," he added as he went to the stair head.

The hunting trip proved successful, as it usually did with Aaronn along. The King's ward himself managed to bag a full-grown stag of enormous proportions. For his assistance, Aaronn was given the honor of carving the freshly roasted venison at the table. He always watched carefully when meat was carved at the table, he knew he could easily manage the task, and so confidently sliced off perfect portions of the well-roasted flesh. Lot noticed and complimented him.

"Good work there, laddie, I coul' nae done it better meself."

"Thank ye, My Lord Lot," Aaronn answered politely. Supper finally finished, after evening chores were done, Aaronn went to his room, locked the door and sat down to answer his friend's cry for help.

"Brother, I got yer letter today. I know what ye are enduring. Just try to keep out of the way 'till summer. I am going to run away to Avalon as soon as the snows clear. I shall come and get ye on the way. I miss yer company brother; I cannot wait to start training together again. Aaronn."

Early the next morning, Aaronn crept out of the castle, hurrying to the oak grove. Secreting himself just outside the circle of ancient oaks, Aaronn assured himself of privacy before he crept to the altarstone. He was just about to leave the leather-wrapped missive on it a hand dropped onto his left shoulder. He whirled, drew his knife and crouched into the ready position before he saw Druid brothers surrounded him.

"So, Aaronn, what note is so secret that ye should resort to sending it this way?" asked the Merlin of Britain.

"I cannot be sure that my letters get to where they are supposed to go without being read first, Lord Merlin. 'Tis Olran, he is in trouble with his family again for holding to his loyalty to Arthur. Will one of ye take it for me?" Aaronn explained, his voice breaking several times, even though he tried to control it.

"Of course, Aaronn," answered the Druid Drusus. "What started it this time?"

"Ask the King, he can tell ye!" Aaronn answered sarcastically. "All I know is that Arthur sent him back there, even though he knows well Olran's family situation."

"I shall ask the King, Aaronn. Something will be done to help if we can," the Merlin assured Aaronn while Drusus took the missive and stowed it away. "Now, go on with ye. This oak grove is no longer safe to leave with Morgause; we are here to close it against her evil. Ye will not be able to leave another letter here, do ye understand?"

"I understand, Lord Merlin, and I agree," Aaronn nodded. "Can I stay and watch?"

"Nay, Aaronn, I am expecting interference from Morgause, and we cannot risk it falling upon ye. Go off somewhere by yerself for the day, and do not come back 'till just before dark," the Merlin advised, then bent a bit and embraced the rapidly growing boy. Taliesin could see that Aaronn had inherited Uther's stature, but that the boy's mother had contributed a classic athletic physique. The pair's bloodline had combined well, giving Aaronn the best of both genetic lines, just as the Goddess had planned.

"Will there be classes at Dragon Isle this year?" Aaronn asked hopefully.

"Nay, Aaronn not with the Saxons raiding so close to Avalon. We Druids must gather in force to protect the Mother's Holy Isle, Lake and Forest," the Merlin told him gently. "Perhaps next year will be peaceful enough for classes to resume."

"I hope so, Lord Merlin," Aaronn replied firmly and went his way with a final wave. Once he was out of sight, the Merlin turned back to the twelve Druid brothers with him.

"Well brothers, we haven't all day. 'Tis much to do, our labors must be quick if we are to finish by noon."

"Aye, Lord Merlin," they all answered, taking their places around the pink altarstone. By an hour after noon, they were finished, when Morgause went out to perform her planned rite to the Dark Ones on the beautiful stone she found it gone and the oaks grown up around where it had been. She could not get through the tangle of branches to the center of the circle and ranted in frustration as she realized what had been done. The Merlin and those other interfering Druids had "closed" the grove against her, spiriting away her altarstone as well!

"They shall pay dearly, every one of them!" she vowed darkly, not seeing the small, boy-sized figure that observed her from the far side of the grove. Aaronn stepped from the shadows only when he assured himself she was truly gone. He began to chuckle, then he laughed outright. The Witch Queen lost a valuable tool forever, he thought happily, then went down to the seashore to collect oysters, whistling all the while.

The Saxons began raiding heavily again in the second month of the year, all other problems became secondary to halting their incursions so that the farmers could plant the vital food crops without worry for their lives and stock. Arthur rotated the Knights from garrison to garrison, each time anticipating Cerdic's every move. The plan was mostly successful until spring came and the raids became small wars. Only the valuable information supplied by the Druids and the assistance rendered by the Faerie folk kept Arthur's forces one step ahead of the wily Saxon ruler. Arthur made sure that those who brought him useful information were rewarded generously with food and gold after each victory.

The Summer Solstice came, bringing Leodegrance fully into the war without costing Arthur any promises. Ulf, Cerdic's next eldest brother, led a raid into Lyonnesse, which was intercepted by Lancelot. The First Knight, acting on a tip from a Faerie hunter, was awaiting them with Leodegrance's army and a squad of Knights. Ulf's forces were crushed, and the Saxon warchief was captured by the heroics of Bedwyr. While in full galloping pursuit the blacksmith's son leapt from the back of his horse, still arrayed in heavy battle dress, landing atop the running man and squashing him flat to the ground. The Knights of Camelot and Lyonnesse did not kindly treat Ulf, although no permanent damage was done. He was clapped into irons and paraded into Camelot's gates, a great prize of war. His ransom was set, very high; nonetheless the full amount was paid by his family, leaving Cerdic to explain how his plans went awry.

The rest of the summer was divided into quelling the smaller raids that followed while assisting the farmers of Britain in harvesting the rich bounty bestowed by the Goddess that year. The Knights often exchanged their swords for scythes; they all worked tirelessly until all was stored away in granaries and cold rooms all over the countryside. The people breathed a large sigh of relief as they began to plan their Samhain celebrations in the shadow of plenty instead of hungry.

Bumper crops blessed Orkney as well; Aaronn's body grew more muscular as he assisted in caring for and the harvesting of the enormous amount of peas, beans, grains and other crops. The fruit trees too bore heavily and Aaronn climbed up the orchard trees, agilely picking the ripened apples and pears. He picked pecks of berries and grapes as well, and went with Lot and Caeside, the new seneschal of Lothian, to fish for fat salmon making their way from the oceans to their spawning grounds upriver. By mid-autumn, the harvest was in and the people began preparing for the Samhain feasts, which offered thanks to the Goddess and to their own ancestors, for the bountiful harvests and Arthur's victories over the invading Saxons.

Morgause too, was planning Samhain rites, and it was a dark thing she planned to do this season. Earlier that year, she had obtained a few wisps of hair from Aaronn's hairbrush and performed a ceremony that had revealed much about his sire. Morgause gasped as the image of a dragon appeared in the flames as the answer to the question, she realized that fate had brought her the solution to her dilemma. The dark angel she had attracted to her was no longer satisfied with small doses of animal blood; as a result she had been obliged to offer it human blood instead. Servants began to have mysterious accidents as Samhain approached and still the evil being's thirst was not sated. Finally, her master revealed its true desire.

"I must have noble blood to work the magick ye have in mind. Bring me a fatherless child of noble blood, bitch and ye shall have what ye desire."

She now planned to use Aaronn for this, seeing the image of the dragon had convinced her that somehow Aaronn was related to Arthur, through some chain of nobility. She had planned to seduce him and keep him as her lover for a time first, so that she could use her influence to keep him quiet during the rite, but Aaronn had so far resisted her charms. Now that Samhain was near, she grew desperate and began to pursue the budding young lad harder. Aaronn however, wanted nothing to do with her, to resist her he began taking his meals alone in his room. Morgause waited as long as she could, and formulated a plan to make sure he was in her tower room on Samhain night.

When darkness fell that night, Aaronn locked his door as usual and went to bed. Later, he awoke to find three men standing over him, before he could roll from the mattress, they fell on him. Aaronn resisted as well as he could, but he was vastly out-muscled and some vile liquid was forced down his throat. He struggled not to succumb to the effects, but soon he was groggy and one of the bullyboys threw him over his shoulder and took him from the room. As they passed Aaronn's night table, he reached for and grabbed his knife, tucking it into his sleeve. The table teetered and crashed noisily to the floor; the leader of the three punched his fellow and told him to be more careful.

"Ye keep him quiet," he whispered and stomped on the candle to extinguish the small flame it caused on the rug. Entering the secret staircase, they climbed up the spiral way to Morgause's tower room. The leader knocked in a distinct patter, Aaronn heard the evil woman's voice answer;

"Bring him in."

The door opened and he was carried into the candle-lit room, where Morgause awaited, dressed only in a sheer-to-the-skin black silk robe. "Well, little Aaronn, since ye find me so unattractive, I am sure we can find some use for ye after all," she gloated over him. "Put him in the pentagram and make sure he is tied securely," she ordered, smiling when the men leapt to do her will. Perhaps one of them was careless, or perhaps the Goddess distracted them, for none of them searched thoroughly enough to find the small knife Aaronn had snatched from the table. Morgause ordered them all out and locked the portal behind them.

Aaronn continued to play groggy, but he was feeling ever more alert and the cool reassurance of the knife steel against his wrist kept him calm. Moving slowly, cautiously, he used his clever and nimble fingers to withdraw the blade and slide it between the ropes and his skin. The razor edge of the blade cut the bindings without much effort and Aaronn lay still, waiting for his chance. Morgause stood in front of her black-draped alter, taking no notice of him while she chanted in ever-increasing volume. Aaronn saw his opportunity and took it, using his free hand to cut the rest of his bonds. He stood, shook himself carefully, and then crept for the door. He found the latch and opened it soundlessly, entering the passageway and closing the door behind him. He ran for his room at that point, reaching his door just as he heard the shrill screaming of Morgause as she found him gone. The alarm would be heard throughout the entire castle, Aaronn knew he only had a few moments to grab his things and depart before the way was sealed against flight. Grabbing his ready clothes pack and ditty bag, he used his mattress to set a fire and exited, closing the door behind him. He ran down the stairs, through the scullery, out of the castle and into the hen house. Only then did he pause to dress in his warmest black clothes and put on his boots, strapping on his belt knife. He fled for the ferry landing, making good time despite using the less traveled paths. Once aboard the ferry and out into the narrow channel, Aaronn began to breathe more normally and he used the opportunity to relax a bit. The ferryman said nothing, but he recognized the King's ward and supposed there would be reward from Lothian if this boy were returned unharmed. When the ferry docked, however, a knife pressed into the ferryman's back quickly dispelled any plans for ransom.

"Tell no one ye have seen me, lest the Goddess punish ye," he spoke harshly and as deeply as his breaking voice would allow, pressing harder with the blade. "If ye say nothing, ye can expect reward from the King, who is my guardian."

"So ye say, youngling," the ferryman said roughly and made to turn on the boy.

Aaronn leapt nimbly aside, kicking the man behind the knee with his booted toe so that the older man fell heavily on his back. Aaronn straddled him, held the knife firmly against the ferryman's throat, momentarily angered by this attempt at betrayal.

"I said ye would be punished, ye bastard!" he said, quiet and deadly. "Now ye shall reap what ye have sown," he went on, then slit the man's cheek, just enough to leave a permanent scar on the left side.

"Ye little piece of dung, ye've cut me!" the ferryman screamed in pain, but he could not rise for Aaronn's knee was firmly planted in the middle of his chest.

"Would ye like one to match it on the other side?" Aaronn menaced, feeling more powerful than ever before.

"Nay."

"Then get this tub out of sight, quick as ye can," Aaronn ordered and let him up. There was no more trouble after that, and Aaronn made sure Morgause could not physically pursue him. He tossed the ferryman's wife a piece of his booty, a good bronze torque, before slitting the man's sails into shreds. "Ye might speak to yer mate about the folly of betraying the King's ward," Aaronn spat out as he ran off into the night. "If he tries it again, it might be the end of him."

The man had to listen to her persuasive arguments before she would agree to stitch up the wound in his cheek. By the time the task was done, shouts of rage could be heard from the Orkney side of the channel. The voice was feminine and enraged; Morgause cursed foully when she learned of the condition of the boat's sails. She was wild with rage for days, then one day she appeared from her room, composed and calm.

Aaronn's name was never again mentioned in her presence, until many years later.

Aaronn went directly overland to Westerland Keep, using the many skills he and Olran had developed on their forays into the wild forests to orient himself as he went. He hunted when he was hungry, and kept moving to keep ahead of the full onslaught of winter. He found an oak grove along the way and left a note for the Druids, telling them that he and Olran were on their way to Avalon. The thought of coming to the aid of his friend, the renegade prince, drove him on until finally he came to the village of Daffydsdown. Three weeks had passed since his thirteenth birthday; he had matured greatly in those days, his skills with bow and arrow improving daily due to use.

Hearing a great commotion in the middle of the village, Aaronn approached the square from a side path, keeping himself concealed in the shadows. He caught a glimpse of the attraction and was horrified at the sight. There, tied on his stomach, naked and spread-eagled to a whipping frame, was Olran. He had blood running all over him, his face and body showed signs of efficient pummeling and still he did not cry out in pain. He held a defiant silence, even when he was lashed again by one of his tormentors.

"Still won't change yer tune, eh Olran?" the drunken Kevin guffawed and sent the heavy whip singing towards the princeling's already muchly-striped back. Aaronn took off his pack and withdrew Olran's old practice bow and arrow; these tools had brought him relief from hunger pangs many times in the last three weeks. Pulling a worn shirt from his pack, Aaronn quickly made a rough mask from the cloth, cutting eyeholes in it and tying it around his face to protect his identity, hoping they would take him more seriously that way.

The whip was passed to Warren; the petty king was dangerously drunk, and administered three quick, sharp blows to his son's back, opening new cuts that bled furiously. He prepared for another series, but the whip was knocked from his hand by a well-shot arrow. The Westerland family turned in the arrow's direction, seeing a tall, nimble looking fellow, holding a small hunting bow.

"Hold there, Warren of Westerland! Put down that whip," the lad called out in a voice more powerful than usual. Olran recognized his friend's voice and turned his head painfully to see if he were imagining it. Tears formed as he saw that Aaronn truly stood there, masked and unrecognized by his family.

"Ye can't shoot us all, fellow," Kevin laughed and rushed him. Aaronn pulled and released, striking the fat man full in the left thigh and dropping him howling in pain. Olran had put barbs on the steel heads of the arrows so that they would stick into their prey's flesh and quicken the kill. Now the pain-wracked Olran found the strength to chuckle slightly as

Kevin rolled on the ground in pain, struggling furiously but still unable to remove the arrow.

"Perhaps not, but I can kill the next one to hurt Prince Olran. Now ye, Warren, cut him loose carefully," Aaronn ordered from under his makeshift hood, loading another arrow pointedly. Warren cast another look at Kevin and took out his belt knife. Walking slowly to the whipping board, he cut Olran's bonds and stepped away, allowing Olran to try and stand on his own. The princeling sagged slightly, trembling from pain and cold and Aaronn quickly walked to where he stood.

"Bring out some warm, sturdy clothing, do not forget hose and boots," Aaronn ordered, training the loaded bow on Warren's flabby face. The outfit was brought and Aaronn held them all at bay while his friend slowly dressed himself and pulled on his boots. "Can ye ride, brother?" Aaronn whispered.

"I shall damn well ride out of here, even if it kills me!" Olran whispered in return as he struggled to control the violent spasms of shivering the beset him. A woman servant from the Keep brought him a thick gray woolen cloak and he swung it round him, pulling up the cowl over his head.

"Horses, Warren, and a purse for the boy, right now!" Aaronn ordered, pulling the bowstring taut.

"All right, just don't fire that thing at me!" Warren answered, true fear in his voice.

The steeds were brought, saddled and packed with provisions. Olran swung up, stoutly ignoring the immense pain of his body then Aaronn swung up as well and the boys put spur to flank, galloping swiftly from Westerland Keep. They put plenty of miles between Daffydsdown and themselves before they found an abandoned hut and cow-byre. They housed the horses, grained them from the stores in the saddlebags, then Aaronn filled water buckets and put them into the stalls. Olran managed to make it inside the hut before he collapsed from weariness into a handy pile of hay that once had served someone as a mattress.

"Are ye all right?" Aaronn asked as he helped his friend peel off the bloodstained shirt he wore.

"Look at me, do I look all right?" Olran moaned, adding contritely, "Thank ye, my brother. I do not know how much longer I could have lasted without screaming for mercy."

Aaronn lit a small fire and heated water in a copper bowl they found, then he carefully bathed Olran's mangled back until all the crusts of dried blood were removed. He searched the packs and found two rolls of bandages and a pot of salve, put there by servants friendly to the rebel prince. Carefully, he spread the pleasant ointment all over Olran's stripes and wound the bandaging around him, pinning it securely with a brooch from his own treasure hoard. Olran recovered enough strength by the time Aaronn finished bandaging him to prepare a simple soup of water and dried smoked meats. Aaronn gobbled it hungrily, while Olran simply poured off the broth and drank it slowly; claiming solid food would make him sick.

"I need to get some sleep, what about ye Aaronn?" Olran yawned, just keeling over in the thick straw. Aaronn took a horse blanket and covered him, then banked the fire and pulled the other blanket around his body, sleeping with one ear open. They awoke early, finished up the small pot of soup and took their leave of their camp just as dawn broke over the trees. Aaronn had to saddle both horses, as his companion had trouble just moving, he had to boost Olran into his saddle before mounting up himself. The two boys said very little, Aaronn due to mentally composing a letter to Arthur, Olran due to the intense pain and discomfort he was feeling. They stopped late that afternoon, finding a warm cow barn to sleep in. Olran fell off his horse onto Aaronn, who was assisting him down. Once on the ground, the exhausted boy could not be wakened until dawn the next day. The farmer came to milk his cows and found the two still sleeping in the warm straw. He grinned and gently woke the nearer of the two, Aaronn.

"Heya, boyo, ye two aren't stealing from me, are ye?" he asked softly.

"Nay, sir," Aaronn answered. "My friend here was beaten and disowned for supporting the King against his family. Ye can see his face is still bruised and ye should see his poor back! We need hot food and bandages, as well as feed for our horses. We can pay for it, will ye help us?" he asked.

"Of course, any friend of the Pendragon is a friend of mine. Bring yer friend up to the house and my woman will see to ye both," he smiled kindly and helped Aaronn bring the slightly feverish Olran to the farmhouse. The woman was good with wounds; Aaronn saw the crescent moon between her gray brows.

"Elder Sister, thank ye for yer aid," he said in the tongue of Avalon. "We are the Pendragon's men."

"Aid ye shall have, little brother," she smiled crookedly at him, then bent to her task.

Carefully unwinding the bandages Aaronn had applied, her face darkened at the damage she saw. Rising from his side, she quickly brought warm water, scented with herbs, and soft cloths to the bedside. Aaronn watched in admiration as she skillfully treated each stripe, applying salve and spider silk to each cut to hold it closed until it healed. She sat the unconscious boy up and wound clean bandaging around his torso, fastening them with Aaronn's pin. She fed Aaronn and brewed a restorative tea. "For the pain when he wakes," she explained.

Olran awoke sometime later and sat bolt upright in his fever fear, not recognizing his surroundings.

"Easy, brother," Aaronn reassured him. "We are with family."

"Are ye sure?" Olran asked, and Aaronn waved towards their hosts for explanation. Olran could see the crescent moon between the woman's brows and smiled. His apprehension now comforted, he found the strength to smile wanly as he lay down again on the soft sheets.

"Aye, the woman who treated yer wounds wears the crescent moon between her brows," Aaronn confirmed, squeezing his friend's hand. "She says Avalon is no more than a bare day's ride from here."

"I am glad, Aaronn," Olran said gratefully as he reddened with embarrassment when his stomach grumbled.

"Here, drink this, little brother," the woman said as she came to their side with a steaming cup. "'Twill feed thy body and also help to deaden the pain. The strength ye need to ride to Avalon is in this, and 'twill aid in yer recovery."

"Aye, and I have a letter for Arthur, detailing our experiences. He will punish Warren and the others," Aaronn told him.

"Aaronn, do *not* send that letter," Olran said coldly. "I told ye before, they are mine! Warren and his sons are traitors and somehow, I am going to get the proof I need to present to Arthur. Then they die, one by one!" he vowed, his voice low and deadly. "As for Morgause, ye can tell the King what happened, but she is a traitor too and deserves to die. What better way than by yer hand?"

Aaronn had considered this while writing the missive to the King; now what Olran was saying was making good sense to him. He smiled slowly as he considered that evil was often done in secret, shadowed places, knowing well that was where it must be combated. He suddenly crumpled the letter and threw it into the fires, watching it blacken and whither.

"We have to get back to Avalon, my brother. We have lots to learn before we can work on preventing all the treason in Britain. I wager that Brother Michael and Brother Drusus can help us."

"If they will not, we will just have to teach ourselves," Olran vowed, wincing as he moved his arm to smack his right fist into his left palm.

"Now, don't ye go and get those stripes all bleeding again, Prince Olran," the goodwife laughed as she came into the room. "Or I'll beat ye myself."

The boys both chuckled at her imperious tone, but Olran kept calm and quiet the rest of the day to give the healing she had done a chance to work. They slept the night in the cozy house and awoke to a hearty breakfast, which Olran wolfed ravenously since his fever had abated during the night, then they were on the road before the day had barely began. Keeping the pace easy out of consideration for Olran's back, they found the small, deep lake surrounding Avalon just as sunset faded from the sky. The barge awaited them and they led their horses aboard, where a priestess stood in the prow of the boat, robed and silent. The boat broke through the clinging fog to find Avalon bathed in glorious silver light from the intense full moon overhead. Vivaine met them, the Merlin by her side; she gently embraced first Olran, then Aaronn as he led the horses on shore. Druids came to assist the boys to the House of Healing, Olran's wounds were seen to first and Aaronn was relieved to find out that his friend would suffer no permanent ill effects. He was asked to leave Olran to a long rest before he was taken to bathe and change into a loose, soft robe. Served an enormous plate of food, he was allowed to eat until replete before any questions were asked.

"Now Aaronn, suppose ye tell us exactly what has happened?" the Merlin asked.

"I decided that Lothian was too cold in the winter. I tried lighting a fire, but that did not help so I left," Aaronn explained casually. The Merlin looked at him, eyebrows raised, but the boy would not elaborate.

"And Olran?" he questioned.

"Ye saw his back and ye can see they beat the stuffing out of him! I went to Daffydsdown and found them in the village square, whipping him to make him stop supporting the King. The last letter he sent me said he was afraid for his life. It appears he was not exaggerating," Aaronn replied calmly, then yawned and stretched. "Can I go to bed now? I think I could sleep for a week!" he asked.

"Of course, Aaronn ye should sleep right away. Brother Michael?" the Merlin called softly to the Druid brother standing close by.

"Come on, boyo. We have a room all ready for ye."

"Good!" Aaronn said happily and went with his mentor, after first wishing Vivaine and the Merlin good night. Taliesin watched his secret nephew go before he went to the Healing Hall to speak to Olran.

"Do ye want to talk about it?" he asked as the healer-priestess washed his wounds with an antiseptic tincture, causing him to squirm a bit as it stung his stripes.

"'Tis nothing new to tell, Lord Merlin, other than they got drunk after tax time, started cursing Arthur, then the beating started. This time, they went too far, I am through with them, I shall not go back ever!" he vowed coldly. "At least 'till 'tis time for them to die!" he added almost beneath the Merlin's hearing. The boy's voice sounded like a taut bowstring releasing in the Merlin's ears and he shuddered involuntarily.

"Olran ye know well that vengeance is the name of the Fourth Face of the Mother, 'tis Her realm not man's," he warned.

Olran turned painfully to level a long, measuring look at the Merlin. "Then I shall just have to become the Mother's Hand, aye?"

The Merlin had a sudden flash of the Sight, "seeing" Olran older, standing atop a moving pile of bodies, aiming an arrow at the head of a Saxon berserker with a beautiful ash bow. The arrow neatly skewered the man just behind the ear and blood flew everywhere when the arrowhead pierced the artery there. The man's mouth worked silently and he dropped. The vision dissipated, leaving only a young and muchly troubled youth now snoring softly as the attending priestess continued her work. Some of the wounds were deep, however due to the care they had received while Olran traveled all but a few were beginning to close. Those few were quickly and painlessly stitched closed with silken thread, covered with a light sheet of gauze bandaging. Finally, she covered him with a thick blanket and left him alone with the Merlin, who sat with the sleeping boy for a long time. Vivaine joined him and they quietly left Olran to his dreams.

"Did ye get anything out of Aaronn?" he asked, concerned.

"Nothing, but 'tis obvious something disturbing has happened to him. He hates Morgause with a passion for certain," Vivaine answered. "If he does not talk about it..."

"'Tis plenty of time for that, Lady, right now they both need time to rest and heal. Let them have the time they need for themselves. In the meantime, they should resume their lessons and training with Michael and Drusus," the Merlin returned.

"I agree," Vivaine nodded, laughing a bit. "Aaronn said that he would revenge Olran's treatment as soon as he was able. When I reminded him that revenge belongs to the Goddess, he responded thus; 'Then I shall just have to become Ceridwen's avenger, won't I?' then he fell asleep."

"Olran said something very similar concerning his situation," the Merlin said, then recounted his conversation with the renegade prince and the vision he had experienced. The Lady of the Lake smiled slowly as she heard his words.

"I saw something as well, but 'twas Aaronn wading into a melee of Saxons. He was throwing knives like a whirlwind, then he drew his sword and began to cut a swath towards Knights of Camelot who wore Lesser Britain's standard as well as the Pendragon's," Vivaine related.

"So, 'tis a true answer to the prophecy then," the Merlin grinned. "Ceridwen told us She would choose Her own Champions and She has, or so it appears."

"There can be no doubt of it, Lord Merlin. The prophecy clearly states that a spur of the royal line will become the ears and eyes for Ceridwen, and that his companion will always be at his side. If that does not describe Aaronn and Olran, I cannot imagine who 'twould be."

"Well, let them go on with their training, for certain, until Ceridwen calls," the Merlin sighed and put his arms around his ladylove comfortingly.

Olran and Aaronn lazed about until they were fully recuperated and rested from their ordeal. They had a chance at last to fill each other in on the events leading up to Samhain. Aaronn's face tightened noticeably as his friend described his experiences and Olran smacked his fist against his palm as Aaronn detailed Morgause's attempts at first seduction, then sacrifice to gain a measure of dark powers.

"But I cannot understand why she wanted me specifically," Aaronn asked, still puzzling over it.

"Why ask me?" Olran answered, returning to soak again in the hot mineral springs that bubbled up from the hot depths of the Earth. Aaronn saw that most of the stripes on Olran's back were fading, again he thanked the Goddess for Her assistance on the day he had boldly stepped forth to defend him in Daffydsdown. "Maybe it was because ye are still a virgin," Olran added after easing his thin and wiry body into the hot, healing waters.

"Probably," Aaronn sighed. "Vivaine said that virginity is a powerful thing for both girls and boys. Maybe Morgause needs that extra something to accomplish her foul plans."

Joining Olran in the steaming water, Aaronn relaxed again and allowed his quick mind to puzzle over the problem; due to lack of experience he was unable to put any sense to it. At length, he put it aside to enjoy the feeling of peace and contentment, a thing quite rare in his life so far.

The Saxons hit hard along the British coastline in mid-winter that year. Cerdic gambled in an all-out attack, once again Arthur was ready for him. The coastal garrisons were alerted by carrier pigeons trained by patient Druids just for this purpose. Arthur himself, leading the Inner Circle and supported by Leodegrance's troops, met Cerdic's hordes as they waded ashore off the Cornish coastline. The Brits fell on the Saxons; slaughtering tens of Saxons and recapturing Ulf along with two other warchiefs named Gunnar and Ivarr, both kin to the Saxon "cying." The raids never stopped, not even when the icy snows buried Britain, so the Knights were obliged to fight in all conditions. Once again, Leodegrance stepped in, providing access to his armory for any of Camelot's Knights to make repairs in their well-worn chain mail suits. The head smith was quite good and made his repairs such that they could barely be seen. Arthur's own suit suffered much abuse from flying seaxs, so Leodegrance made him a gift of a new one in the spring. Arthur looked over the heavy, chained suit with a practiced eye, but he could find no error except where the smith had made his signature flaw.

"Why mar such a beautiful work, Master Smith?" he inquired of the taciturn, black-haired and brawny man, who was one of Leodegrance's sons.

"Only God works true perfection, Sire. I am naught but a mere man, my work is naturally flawed. I only make sure they happen in non-essential places," he finished his explanation.

"Well, nonetheless, 'tis noble work and I thank ye for it," the King said graciously and donned the shiny, flexible suit. He saw the way the rings of metal had been sewn, one by one, onto thin pliable leather before all was lined with soft, comfortable cattail fluff and cotton covering. There would be less chafing and binding in this suit, Arthur thought gratefully as he finished dressing and pulled the full hood over his face.

"Make a note to find out what it would take to lure that man into the service of the Crown, would ye Lance?" Arthur said with a grin that night to his First Sword.

The spring and summer months were busy times for all that year and Arthur meant to go to Lothian and Westerland to investigate the Merlin's charges of abuse and dark magick. The occasion never arose due to constant fighting all that year. Arthur and the Knights fought into winter again. The raids suddenly stopped just after the Winter Solstice and gratefully, the Knights retired to Camelot to rest and ready themselves for the next onslaught.

Aaronn and Olran spent all the days with good weather out in the woods of Avalon, in the foul weather they were in the classrooms with their tutors. The boys ate, slept and breathed training, by the time they took their winter break, the fourteen year-olds were two inches taller and several inches broader of chest. When letters from Arthur came, there was usually a special package for Aaronn. Once, it was a gold Saxon torque, another time a double string of freshwater pearls. Slowly Aaronn was amassing a store of treasure, which he planned to use for purchasing more weapons for his small, but growing arsenal. Already, Brother Michael had given him his first set of twelve throwing knives and had shown his pupil the steps and exercises to accelerate his speed and accuracy in delivering them to their targets.

On Beltane that year, Aaronn took Brother Michael to his private target area and showed him the result of their work. Each knife found a place in the inner target area; however bull's eyes were still rare. In all, Michael thought happily, the lad shows definite innate ability. If only my own skills showed this kind of potential, he smiled inwardly.

"Ye have made an excellent start, boyo," he congratulated. "With such dedication, ye cannot help but gain speed."

"I have only to apply all ye have taught me, brother," the boy said modestly, but he could have burst with excitement and proper pride.

As Aaronn learned, so did Olran. Drusus made the boy track him through the marshes, forests, meadows and hills on Avalon, sometimes even taking the boy hunting in the thick tangle of Celidon Wood that bordered the Holy Lake. On one such occasion, the boy drew a bead on prey that Drusus couldn't even see with his sharp, Druid-trained eyes. When the missile found its mark, the buck dropping without even a jump and Olran sprang to its side to neatly slit the throat.

"For the healing of the Earth, Mother Ceridwen," the boy murmured as the crimson flood spread at his feet. "Please, forgive the taking of thy life, brother stag, but we must eat. We honor ye, and the sacrifice ye have made."

Then he took up his hunting blade and began to field dress the kill. Drusus hung back until he saw the lad had the task in hand before going to cut poles for a carrying sling to cart the heavy carcass home. Olran heard him go, and then returned to his labor. As he worked, he heard the bushes rattle and looked around casually, expecting to see Drusus. What he saw instead was a full-grown black bear, standing on all fours and sniffing the air.

"Hullo, my great brother Ursus. I shall share with ye, but this kill is mine!" Olran spoke quietly and firmly. The bear looked the young man over, and then rose on his two hind legs, growling horribly. Olran did not hesitate; he loaded his bow, aimed and fired, striking the bear square in the chest. It dropped to all fours, but kept coming for him, now angered from the pain. Olran loaded and fired twice more, scoring additional hits on the upper chest and neck area. These new wounds only seemed to further anger the bear, it roared fiercely and charged. Olran stood his ground, reloaded and fired coolly, finally able to get a clear shot at the bear's head. The arrow penetrated the enraged animal's skull through the right eye, the steel point of it emerged from the base of his skull and the bear staggered another step before it fell to all fours, then to its front knees. Olran leapt onto its back, leaned over and pulled up the bear's head, then drew his sharp hunting blade across the jugular. Blood spattered everywhere and the bear relaxed suddenly, causing the young hunter to roll from the bear's back as the inert body fell. The boy landed in the growing puddle of blood just as Drusus appeared, red-faced and panting with the effort of running to assist his student.

"Olran, my boyo, are ye all right?" he shouted and sprang to Olran's side.

"I think so," the boy answered slowly, trying to breathe and slow his pounding heart. "I believe 'tis all the bear's blood," he grinned.

"Olran, 'tis a full-grown boar bear!" Drusus exclaimed. "What happened?"

"It wanted the deer, and I told it I would share, like you taught me. It must have been hungry, or sick, or looking for a fight to attack me like that," Olran explained, struggling to his feet and beginning to field dress the huge bear's carcass.

"Look at the teeth Olran, 'tis no young bear," Drusus pointed out the wear on the molars.

"'Twas looking for easy prey then, Master," Olran agreed, then he paled and put down his knife. "It was not after the deer at all, was it? 'Twas after me," he realized.

"I have no doubt of it, boyo. But this time, it chased after the wrong man," Drusus observed, taking out his own knife and bending to assist the boy. Several Druids came along just as they finished their task of dressing both carcasses; the meat was divided and carried home in equal shares. The skins were taken to the tannery as soon as they returned to Avalon's compound, where they were stretched, scraped and salted, beginning the process of preservation. Venison steaks were cooked and served to those who partook of flesh foods, while the bear meat went into a thick stew. Even Vivaine pared off a tiny portion of the liver of the stag. The story of the hunt was shared after the meal had ended, questions were asked of the boy. Olran answered until his throat was tight and dry before he asked to be excused. He walked quickly away, anxious to seek the privacy of his room, Aaronn following closely behind.

"Ye are not going to ask me a bunch more questions, are ye?" Olran asked after they reached their quarters and locked the door behind them.

"Nay, brother, I think ye have answered quite enough questions for now," Aaronn chuckled. "Look what I found," he continued, holding up a half-full skin.

"What is in that?" Olran asked suspiciously.

"I think 'tis wine, but I do not know for sure. I just grabbed the first one I could pick up," Aaronn answered and poured himself the first cup. The contents of the skin poured out dark, deep red, and the sweet bouquet of the wine tantalizing their nostrils. Each boy poured only a half-cup of the purloined booty before Aaronn stashed it under his bed.

"'Tis good wine, Aaronn," Olran grinned as he carefully sipped the potent spirit. "Thanks for sharing it with me."

"I thought ye would enjoy a nice relaxing cup before bed," Aaronn chuckled harder. "What did it feel like, standing down that bear?" he asked, unable to stop himself.

"Truly, Aaronn, I do not remember feeling anything other than the need to make that bear leave me and my kill alone," Olran told him. "After he was dead, I almost peed in my britches, though, for 'twas when I realized that I was his intended prey," he confided with an abashed chuckle. The boys finished their drink, rinsed out the cups and went to bed, sleeping soundly until morning.

Arthur and the Knights arrived unscheduled the next day, hungry, tired and cold. The large bowls of thick, hot bear stew helped them feel warmed from the inside out after skirmishing in the frozen woods, the foaming tankards of good Druid ale did their mood no harm either. Aaronn and Olran were astonished, exchanging a look of wonder at the workings of Ceridwen between them. Were it not for the "chance" meeting of hunter and bear, the Knights would have had to wait for hot food, they each thought, feeling an eerie sensation pass over each of them.

"Aaronn! Olran!" the King shouted and beckoned the boys to his side. "Come here lads, let me look at ye! Goddess, ye are nearly grown men!" he exclaimed, measuring their growth in his mind's eye.

"My Lord Arthur, 'tis good to see ye too. Yer beard is growing in nicely, Sire," Aaronn grinned and embraced his guardian.

"Ye see, Lance. I told ye he would notice," Arthur called laughingly to his First Knight, who grinned and tossed his king a heavy silver coin. Arthur caught it easily, winked at Lancelot and bit the coin as if to check its purity, then stashed it in his purse.

"So, Olran, tell me about yer bear hunt," the King turned to the young archer, who blushed a bit.

"'Tis really very little to tell, My Lord, I had just shot a buck and was field dressing it while Brother Drusus prepared the carry sling. I heard the bushes rattle behind me and turned expecting to see Brother Drusus. I was surprised to see the bear and started just loading and firing until I scored the hit through the eye. Then, after he was down, I jumped on his back and slit his throat, 'tis all the tale to tell," he concluded modestly.

"Laddie, tha's th' best bear stew I've eaten fer sometime," Gawaine complimented and accepted a third bowlful.

"Aye, and he must have been a fat old bear too," Bedwyr commented, as he mopped up the gravy from his bowl with the last crust of bread. "Thanks for the stew, 'twas good!" he said after slowly chewing and swallowing the last mouthful.

"Are the Saxons close about?" Aaronn asked, pining for news of the war.

"Nay, not very, thank the Goddess. The Faerie folk keep them out of this part of the forest, at least for now. They want this part of Celidon Wood because of the abundance of game and fruitfulness of the forest. 'Tis the Goddess' Wood, it must be protected from the Saxon's incursion," Arthur explained. "We ride patrols through here all the time now."

"Ye could house troops on Dragon Isle, Lord Arthur," the Lady of the Lake put in, entering the room.

"Holy Mother! I greet thee in the name of the Goddess," he rose and bowed slightly, then resumed his seat. Vivaine sat beside him, everyone else in the room moving down to accommodate her slight bulk.

"'Twas that very subject I meant to speak to ye about, Mother," Arthur began. "I want to build a garrison tower to protect the Lake."

"Nay, My Lord. Ye cannot build a garrison here. The Goddess' Law forbids it," Vivaine protested.

"Not on Avalon proper, then," Arthur added. "On the shoreline to protect the access to the Lake," he explained.

"I see. Can ye show me where, exactly, ye wish to build this garrison tower?" Vivaine asked.

"Ye choose the site, Mother. Wherever Ceridwen would allow it."

"We will divine where the proper site will be, My Lord Pendragon," Vivaine agreed. "But only the Druids may build it."

"If 'tis what is necessary, fine, but that garrison should be in place before too long," Arthur nodded, satisfied. "Now Mother, may we rest here for a while?"

"Of course, My Lord Pendragon ye know ye are always welcome. See to their rooming, Maevin?" Vivaine called to one of her attendant priestesses.

"Right away, Mother."

"Thank ye, Holy Mother," Arthur said gratefully and kissed her open palms in respect and filial love. "Come my Knights, we will rest awhile in Avalon before we rejoin the fray," Arthur rose and spoke to his men. A weary "Aye" answered him and they filed out, guided by priestesses skilled in massage. Each man took his turn in the hot springs, was massaged thoroughly, and then tucked into bed. For those unmarried men, all they need do was ask and they shared the Mother's blessing before they slept, eased by the release of stored passions. The men slept late into the next day, finding their armor and weapons awaiting them, freshly cleaned and polished. In some cases, unders and hose had been replaced with new sets; boots had been re-blacked and polished to a satin sheen. The Knights thanked the Lady of Avalon, for the new clothing and stocked saddlebags.

"Pish-posh, gentlemen," Vivaine played down the gifts. "Ye needed those things, we make them here. As for the armor, it stunk worse than its owners, so we cleaned it out of consideration for our noses," she laughed, her infectious humor causing the men to break into spontaneous riotry.

"Thank ye, Ladies of Avalon. Holy Mother, would ye offer a blessing on the Knights and their steeds before we go?" Arthur implored.

"Of course," Vivaine readily agreed. The Knights of Camelot knelt, sending their heartfelt thanks along with the Lady's prayer. "Great White Goddess, grant yer blessings to these men, thy defenders. Guard them and keep them safe with Thy watchful eyes. Grant them holy victory against those who would destroy the Mother's Holy Isle and Her worship,"

Vivaine called out, raising her hands in benediction over them. A corona of blue light surrounded her, and bolts of lightning arched skyward from her slender fingertips. An answering roll of thunder sounded from the skies, and tremors shook the earth. A great, titanic form shimmered before them, dressed in scale mail that glittered as though set with diamonds, the sword in Her hands glittered and flashed with its own inner light as she wielded it in a series of quick exercises, then held it over Her head.

"My blessing has been asked, and I grant it unto Arthur Pendragon and all the Knights of Camelot!" Ceridwen's voice sounded in their ears like thunder as She laughed a great laugh and disappeared. Vivaine sagged, but Arthur caught her before she ever touched earth and held her until she could stand. The Knights all looked at each other in awe and wonder, but none so much as the two teenage boys who stood among them. Aaronn was transfixed by the vision, and could say nothing. The sight of the swordmaine had affected him deeply, for he had heard something far different from what the King and the Knights had heard.

When She appeared, Aaronn was startled into staring, he had clearly heard the Goddess say; "Greetings, My Black Knight. I see ye have finally found the path I laid out for ye so long ago. Continue down it, ye shall have the knowledge ye thirst for. Deny it and all ye have been gifted shall be for naught. Keep thy Companion, My Black Hunter by thy side always and ye need never fear betrayal by any. Honor My Laws and protect the Pendragon from all that seek to destroy him. Hear and obey!"

In that instant, Aaronn's entire life changed. He had a purpose now, a divine mission to protect the realm from those who would end Arthur's reign through treason and subterfuge. Olran's life also changed, for though he had only heard what the others heard, he had felt the Goddess' presence shoot through him like an arrow, he found he could forget the pain his family had caused him. All he could think of now was to practice always, so that he would never, ever miss.

"Well, Olran my friend," Aaronn began, turning to him. "We have lots more work to do from this day forth."

"What makes ye say that?" Olran asked, startled at the sound of Aaronn's voice. For the first time in months, his friend's voice had not cracked, and it never did again after that day.

"Come on, we have to talk, Olran," Aaronn urged and walked off quickly as the Knights mounted up and took their leave of Avalon.

"Farewell, Aaronn!" Arthur called after Aaronn.

"Farewell, Sire may the Goddess grant victory to the Brother of the Dragon!" Aaronn turned and called back, waving vigorously.

Arthur grinned, flashed a victory sign with his right hand, spurring his stallion onto the barge. Aaronn waved until the Company disappeared into the fog, then he and Olran ran off to their quarters. Once there, Aaronn related to his friend what he had seen and Olran's eyes grew wide when his friend related what the Goddess had named them.

"The Black Knight and the Black Hunter, eh?" he mused as Aaronn pulled the wineskin from under the bed.

"'Tis what She said," Aaronn confirmed and locked their door before he uncorked the wineskin and poured two half cups of the potent drink.

"As long as it means we get to go after the bad people, 'tis fine with me," Olran grinned darkly at his friend, who raised his wooden cup in a toast.

"To the Black Knight and the Black Hunter, may they be allowed to scour Arthur's realm clean and white," he said, clinking his cup against Olran's. The two drank deeply, thus cementing their relationship. Aaronn's life, as well as Olran's had taken a decidedly important turn. Neither lad, however, could begin to imagine where this turn would take them.

The wars stopped suddenly, again just before the Winter Solstice that year, the Knights breathed a collective sigh of relief, counted their losses and began to plan for the next year. On the day of the Solstice, Arthur lounged lazily in his room with Dawn, enjoying the rare holiday. At twenty-eight he was fully-grown and beginning to show more signs of resembling Uther. His chest broadened, his shoulders filled out and the rest of his form trimmed and tightened into something very athletic. The poor tailor, having made Arthur's winter wardrobe from the previous year's patterns had rent his hair in frustration when the King tried on a shirt, but could not move due to the tightness in the shoulders. The tailor carefully cut seams to allow Arthur to escape the too small shirt and the King struggled not to laugh as the nervous and fussy man re-measured him all over to prepare for the alterations necessary.

"Again, Sire, I apologize," the tailor fretted anxiously. The whims of kings had left many a tailor without his employment or even his head, the man knew and so he was understandably nervous.

"Please, Master Tailor. If I hear that again, I shall dismiss ye!" Arthur chuckled, relieving the tailor's fears. "I think the entire incident rather amusing, I can hardly wait to tell this story," he laughed outright.

Arthur's Solstice finery were among the items needing re-fitting and now he awaited its delivery with Dawn, who poured his tea for him while they played chess. Dawn was a good player, but her beauty made her a dangerous opponent. Arthur became accustomed to her power plays of distraction and could steel himself against most of them. Only when she removed her outer robe to expose her filmy undergown, claiming the room was too hot, did Arthur's eyes wander from the board. Once he did, she usually outmaneuvered him within a move or two, having the advantage of superior weaponry.

"Ye are cheating, Dawn," he chuckled when she checkmated him with her bishop and rook.

"I only use the tools given me by the Goddess, My Lord Arthur," she smiled wanly but accepting his embraces willingly. Kissing her deeply, he began untying the laced front of her thin gown when Cai's knock sounded, then the seneschal's voice called though.

"Artos, 'tis urgent, ye must come at once!"

Dawn pouted a bit, and the King sighed as he watched her whirl her robe around her and sash it shut. She went out the side exit and back to her own room.

"All right Caius, what's up?" he called and admitted the seneschal into the room. Bedwyr and Tristan were with him, and Arthur's heart began to pound. Between the two Knights, securely tied with stout ropes, was Cerdic's vicious younger brother, Celdrin. He was muchly battered and abused and he noted that the two Knights looked quite pleased with themselves.

"Well, well," Arthur said, deadly and quiet. "To what do we owe the pleasure of a visit from Celdrin Elesing?" he asked, coming up close to the younger man. Celdrin said nothing, struggling in the ropes seemed to take up his entire attention span.

"Heya boyo, the High King of Britain is talking to ye," Tristan reminded Celdrin by twisting his ear a bit. "Show some respect."

"Eat my shit, Briton!" Celdrin growled before spitting a huge glob of phlegm at the minstrel Knight. Bedwyr simply pulled on the binding ropes bending Celdrin's arms in a most uncomfortable way, forcing him to his knees. Wrapping his gloved fingers in the Saxon's unruly black hair, Bedwyr pushed hard and suddenly on the back of the captive's head, causing it to bend forward until he was just over the puddle of spittle that had missed the King and fallen on the floor.

"Now, what did ye say to the High King of Britain?" he asked quietly, almost gently.

"I said he could eat my sh…" Celdrin said, but he could not finish, for Bedwyr pushed his face into the floor, thoroughly smearing the gooey mass all over the Saxon's furious face. When Gawaine and Lancelot appeared Celdrin was remanded into their custody after they had congratulated their brother Knights on their catch.

"Coom on, boyo," Gawaine said to the speechlessly enraged Saxon. "Ye smell like a shithouse and ye've somethin' foul all o'er yer face. I thin' he needs a bath, eh Lancelot?" he asked, baring his teeth in a wolfish grin.

"I do not know, Gawaine," Lancelot replied as they took Celdrin away between them "I think the shithouse might smell better than he does. We'd best use the brushes and lye soap in the laundry room."

"Ha' I e'er tol' ye tha' yer a darlin' man, Lancelot du Lac?'" Gawaine's voice floated back to the King's ears before Cai closed the door. Arthur grinned at their enthusiasm, turning back to the other two.

"Where did ye find him?" he asked, waving the two over to the liquor cabinet. Tristan grinned, grabbed a stoneware crock from the depths of the shelves and poured three cups of the potent Orkney whiskey. The two Knights then sat with the King on the hearthrug.

"Trying to set fire to the stables, Artos," Bedwyr reported, tossing back the small draught of the whiskey and pouring himself another. "'Tis damn cold out there, ye know," he wiggled his eyebrows comically.

"Tell me," Arthur ordered, grinning at Bedwyr's antics.

"We were tending to my horse, Artos," Tristan began. "Bedwyr was helping me salve the stitches and put on a clean bandage when we heard rustling outside. When we investigated, we saw that little savage Celdrin, just tossing a lit candle into a manure pile. Of course, the fire did not light right away and we jumped him. Unfortunately, we also ended up pushing him on top of the tiny flame and finally got his arms pinned back while he was distracted by the burning. Ye Goddess, he is a scrapper; he almost bit off my ear! A timely cuff from brother Bedwyr here saved me from a new nickname, One Ear Tristan," he finished his report. "Now, I think our brother Knights might need a bit of help with our captive. Come along Bedwyr," he grinned fiercely and went out, shoulder to shoulder with Bedwyr.

Arthur grinned and sat his writing desk to pen the ransom letter to Cerdic. A hefty sum could be demanded for the Saxon leader's brother; Arthur tried very hard to name a sum he knew they could only raise by beggaring the Federation. Calling to him an older boy of some eighteen summers, Arthur charged the boy with delivering it to the Druids on Avalon. Gaheris had finally joined his brothers at Camelot, serving now as Arthur's personal messenger until he proved himself worthy of Knighting. The young Orkneyman took the letter, saluted smartly, turned crisply and strode from the room with purpose. Leaving immediately, the young man pushed his horse hard and gained Avalon's shore by dusk the next day.

"Why, 'tis my nephew Gaheris!" exclaimed the Lady, looking into the seeing pool. "Make ready the barge! Maevin, ye take it over to meet him," she instructed, rising carefully from her chair. Vivaine's joints began to ache during the winter cold that year; only periodic trips to the healing mineral springs brought her any relief. How I wish I had access to the Mother's holy Herb, she thought wistfully, recalling past pleasant experiences with the heady and potent substance. When Gaheris was ushered into her presence, Vivaine was better prepared and more mobile. She chatted amiably over supper with the now better-mannered

Orkneyman, all the time thinking what a good-looking fellow he was, as well as being a really nice man.

"So tell me, Squire Gaheris ap Lot, what message brings ye to Avalon?" she asked as he dabbed the napkin on his lips trying hard to observe all the new rules for mealtime.

"I ha' coom a' th' request o' th' High King, M'Lady Vivaine," he began courteously. "He asks if this letter kin be taken t' Cerdic Elesing."

"We can see to that, Squire," Vivaine assured him as she took the proffered missive. "What is it?"

"I dinnae know, M'Lady," Gaheris answered. "But I thin' it has somethin' t' do wi' th' fact tha' 'is younger brother is a guest a' Camelo'," he speculated, winking in a conspiratorial fashion.

"Are ye tired, Squire?" she asked when he pushed away his plate burping quietly into his napkin before he folded it and put it aside.

"Aye, Lady, but first I must see t' me horse," he said, and made ready to leave the table.

"Squire, yer horse is tucked into our own stables and is probably asleep by now," Vivaine chuckled. "Ye get yer tired butt off to a bed, boyo," she grinned and shook her finger in his face, very mother-like.

"Aye, Mum," the impudent eighteen year old answered as he swiftly followed Maevin out the door.

"Goddess give ye sweet dreams, ye rascal!" she called after him and heard his laughter in return. Dismissing her group of younger attendant priestesses, Vivaine wove a quick but powerful spell of protection to her room and carefully eased open the letter. She smiled slowly as she saw the terms for the ransom set the amount high. With great satisfaction, she re-sealed the missive carefully so that none would ever know it had been tampered with. When she finished the task, she called for Brother Michael, as soon as he appeared she explained what needed to be done and handed the letter over.

"I shall go on the unseen ways, Lady, and return as swiftly as I may. Cerdic shall have his ransom note in short order, that I promise," he told her, tucking the letter into his pouch.

"Be cautious, Michael. The Saxons hate the Druids as much as they despise Arthur," Vivaine warned him. Michael smiled faintly, remembering the year before Arthur took the throne. He, Drusus and the Druid Master Blayse had come upon an oak grove, desecrated by the Saxons in a most horrible way. The trees had been set afire by dousing their bases in liquid sheep's fat, on the altarstone was stretched a Druid Elder, pinned through the heart with a stake of holly. He had been set alight as well, his body still smoldered in the cold morning air. Blayse had carefully removed the Elder's body, freeing his soul from the binding that had been inflicted cruelly upon it, finishing with a clean cremation. Turning their attention to the pain-wracked trees, Blayse had prepared himself for the ordeal to come. He went to stand before the seed tree of the grove, the Mother Tree and laid his hands carefully on the charred trunk. A look of despair crossed his features and he took his hands away quickly.

"The Mother Tree is dying, we must first strengthen her before the others may be attended," he wept silently and held out his right hand. Michael grasped it with his left and the Druids joined right hand to left as they encircled to suffering tree.

"Peace, sister oak. We greet thee in the name of the Mother. We feel thy pain, and we offer thee repair or release," he intoned softly in the secret language of the Druids. The three felt the tree's answering tremble, then the answer tickled inside their heads.

"I must stay, for the children," they all heard in the depths of their minds.

"In Ceridwen's name then, Mother Oak of this grove, I say; LIVE AND GROW!" Blayse commanded and Michael felt the energy rise up his spine warmly. Brilliant emerald light burst forth from the ground at the base of the tortured tree, enveloping the trunk and spreading slowly upwards. Green buds appeared from blackened branches and the charred bark fell away as healthy bark pushed its way through. When they were sure the tree was capable of sustaining itself, the Druids performed the same ritual with each of the other surviving oaks in the grove until it again quietly hummed with life.

"Now, she and the children she has sown are well again," Blayse muttered and swayed a bit. His brothers steadied him, and Drusus gave him a drink of a restorative tonic. The three rested a bit before they prepared to cleanse the altarstone. More Druid brothers appeared from out of the surrounding forest, as if summoned, and all encircled the stone. Blayse and his companions stood in the center of the ring and laid their hands on the stone. "Almighty Light of the Universe, Feminine and Masculine, we ask that ye come forth and cleanse this stone of the great evil done upon it. Great Ceridwen make what was pure, clean and whole again by fire, by water, by air and by earth. This circle is closed, not to be used again 'till its full healing is accomplished. Guard it well, little brothers and sisters of the elements," he pronounced and withdrew his hands sharply. A soft, purple glow surrounded the stone and the Druids chanted softly together until the glow faded and seemed to be withdrawn into the stone. Blayse collapsed, exhausted by the energy outlay required by such high magick, the others took him away through the secret ways to Avalon. The portal closed behind them, leaving only the barest imprint of their feet in the soft grass.

Now Michael prepared to enter Saxon territories, but he was only mildly concerned. The Mother's pathways existed everywhere, even in Saxon lands; Michael had long ago mastered the art of opening the doorways to that place where time ran so very differently than on the physical plane. He traveled quickly, found Cerdic's camp and located the "cying's" tent, then stooped and entered, finding Cerdic beside the fire, eating a bowl of some sort of stew.

"Cerdic Cying?" the Druid spoke quietly and put his hand on a knife blade, prepared for any reception. The Saxon man only glanced up tiredly, started a bit at the sight of the Druid before him before turning back to his meal.

"Aye, and what business have ye with me, sorcerer?" Cerdic asked wearily, his Brit clean and barely accented.

"I am no sorcerer and well ye know it! Yer foolish younger brother has made a serious mistake, Cerdic, now 'twill cost yer people. Arthur Pendragon sent ye this," Michael explained and handed over the missive. Cerdic paled and took it, broke the seal and read. Inside was Arthur's ransom demand, four times Celdrin's weight in gold, silver, copper and gemstones, along with a record of Celdrin's naked weight.

"Damn it, Cerdic!" Arthur's letter finished. "Let us end this destructive war and unite our people! Ye can keep yer gods; all we ask is that ye respect ours. If ye would work with me truly this time, I would forgive the ransom and only retain Celdrin here as a guarantee of treaty maintenance. Ye know and I know how 'tis going to end and I hear the Saxon children crying for their fathers and brothers. I hear Saxon women wailing over dead fathers, husbands and sons. I see fire and hunger rampant all through the Federation lands. I hear and see this all as clearly as I now hear British women and children. Let it be over, Cerdic. For the sake of us all, let it be over. Arthur Pendragon, Dux Bellorum."

Cerdic cursed silently and struggled for control as he gave his oral answer. "I answer the only way I can, listen carefully and take my words to the Pendragon, sorcerer. The ransom will be collected for my stupid brother for there can be no permanent peace without a land grant, well do ye know it, Artur. Without that assurance, I cannot stop the raiding. We would rather plant grain than Brits, so give us fertile lands and the fight is over. Until then, we fight until we can farm. I'll send word as soon as the payment is collected. Harm my brother with a scar and fifty of yer Knights will die very unpleasant deaths. Ye got that, sorcerer?" Cerdic finished tiredly, repeating the insult to Michael, even though he did know better.

"Aye, Cerdic Cying. I have it all, but think on it a bit further, I implore ye. Is it worth all the deaths, Saxon and Brit?" Michael asked, ignoring the insult and sighing within.

"Ask a man who grows his own food, Druid," Cerdic answered softly. Michael sighed and turned to go, Cerdic took him by the arm and the Druid turned back, ready to draw his blade. He stopped himself when Cerdic held out a small silver ingot.

"Give this to yer High Druid, will ye?" he asked. "I heard about an oak grove that was burnt a long time ago, and that a Druid master was burnt with it on the altarstone. I never ordered that, and I don't need yer Goddess wroth with me personally. As soon as I finish finding everyone responsible, ye can have them to punish as ye please. Will that satisfy Her?"

"I am gratified to hear 'twas not yer order that caused the harm, Cerdic. I was wondering if all that fine Roman education was going to waste," Michael replied caustically.

Cerdic snorted for answer, "Get ye gone, sorcerer. If the others catch ye, I cannot save ye," he warned.

"Very well, Elesing. Have it yer way," Michael sighed and melted into the shadows. Cerdic did not know for sure whether the Druid was truly gone but he laid down his head and slept for a few hours, just a few blessed hours, he thought wearily.

The ransom was gathered from the tribes, Cerdic's family putting in the largest share as was proper, for the boy had acted on his own without orders. Hungry for glory and recognition, the vile Celdrin had several times forayed into the Summerlands of the Severn Valley to kill and rape with his hand of bullyboys. Several times Cerdic had belted the boy soundly and confined him to camp, but there were those tribesmen who believed the boy's actions were laudable. They had constantly led Celdrin away from Cerdic's calmer influence and into the fanatic worship of Thor the Thunderer. Now Celdrin hated everything and anything Roman, continually mocking the unusual education Cerdic had acquired and wished to share with his brothers.

The exchange for Celdrin's ransom between Arthur and Cerdic took place at a crossing the Severn. While the mood was intense, everything proceeded peaceably. Cerdic refused to even speak to Arthur however. Once they were back at camp, he tried to reason with his hotheaded younger brother. It was time to tell him, Cerdic thought, just what it cost me to ascend to my position.

"Take yer faggot education and shove it, Cerdic. Thor is my father and 'tis from Him my strength flows," the young man cursed hotly.

"If ye say so, Celdrin," Cerdic sighed. "But ye are confined permanently to the family compound. My guards will escort you to meals and Thor's meetings; they will be under orders to bring ye directly back here. If I catch ye anywhere else, I'll kill ye myself. Understand brother, I got the 'Armbands of Thor,' because I was ruthless enough to get rid of those who would have challenged me for it," Cerdic pressed on and his brother's face paled. "Aye, Celdrin, ye begin to understand at last. Our uncles had to die so I could be Cying. If ye threaten my authority again, boyo, ye die by my hand. Think on it while ye sit here in the tent for a few hours 'till mealtime."

"But they were found spread-eagled and staked out over anthills! Ye said the Britons had done it," Celdrin whispered, shocked.

"What else could I say, brother? We needed tribal unity and we got it with their deaths. The tribes follow only me now and that is the way it must be! If we raid by ones or twos, we all die. Only when we are together do we stand any chance of winning the Severn Valley as our own. Do ye hear me, brother?" Cerdic asked sharply. Celdrin nodded, white-faced and went directly to his place in the family tent. When his bullyboys came around to rescue him, he sent them away with a word of warning.

"Don't do anything to defy Cerdic's orders, lest ye suffer a horrid fate. Let us wait to raid until the Cying orders us to."

There was no further raiding from the Saxons until the snows stopped, as soon as the thaw began they infiltrated the forest again, trying to build small hidden bivouacs amongst the thickets. Meat was slaughtered, skins stretched and tanned, then all was sent back over the river to feed meat-hungry mouths that waited. Arthur was brought news of the incursions by the Faerie folk and he sighed heavily. This was Cerdic's final answer to Arthur's proposition of peace, the King thought as he sent a royal page for Lancelot, then turned back to the Faerie hunter that stood uncomfortably before him.

"Tell me, Gwydorn, my old friend. Are they taking the does from the herds?"

"They take anything old enough to mate, Great Pendragon. All is sent over the Severn and the raiders stay to harvest more," the man answered flatly. A knock sounded and Arthur called out to enter.

"Ye sent for me, My Lord?" Lancelot asked after entering and saluting smartly.

"Aye, Sir Lancelot. The Saxons have come a-raiding in Celidon Forest again and their hunger for deer meat is without end, it seems," Arthur told him. "Ready the entire Company and assemble them in an hour, armed for full battle. We will fall on them and the whole group will be kept for hostages. Meat and skins will come back to Camelot, we need the fresh meat as much as they do," he chuckled a bit at the irony of the situation. "If they resist over much, slay 'em and skin 'em. We will send that much back to their families," he ordered ruthlessly. This example must be made, he thought privately.

Lancelot's face hardened and he nodded. "Aye Sire, shall we leave the heads attached to the skins?"

Arthur grimaced, knowing how difficult it would be for the gentle-hearted Lancelot to order and accomplish such a grim task. "I am going along, Lance, ye will not have to order the deed done," he added softly, laying his hand on his close friend's shoulder. Lancelot smiled a little at that, then saluted crisply and left the room to assemble the Company of Knights.

Three-quarters of an hour later, the twelve Knights of the Inner Circle, supported by the quickly growing cadre of the Outer Circle of Camelot, those landless and foreign knights who had pledged loyalty to Britain and Arthur. Also among that swelling number served sons of the noble houses, rejected by their clans due to their commitment to a united Britain under the Pendragon's benevolent and lawful hands. The force assembled was considerable, far out-numbering the Saxon raiders, and Arthur was content that it should be so. Too many victories had been lost due to being out-manned by the invaders, he though as he strapped Excalibur's scabbard onto his back, then slipped the huge broadsword into it.

"Come with me my brothers, one and all. The Saxons are stealing Ceridwen's bounty from Celidon again. They must be stopped, for they also steal the future fawns when they slaughter the mothers." A disapproving murmur went round and the Knights settled into their saddles, knowing what was coming next.

"Forward, for the Light and Ceridwen!" Arthur ordered and withdrew Excalibur, shining with its own peculiar power from the scabbard. Made from white buckskin and lined with ruby red silk, the scabbard had been a gift from the Ladies of Avalon. The Lady Vivaine had told him that certain protective spells to prevent excessive blood loss had been incorporated into the making of it. He had been glad of it over the years, for even the deepest sword cut had only bled enough to completely cleanse the wound.

Now he led the Knights of Camelot forth from the castle gates and down the hill into the vast green meadow that now surrounded Camelot. A thick cloud of fog lingered there, a cloud tinged with a pale, pearly luminescence and the entire group rode into it. The hoofbeats of their horses, a veritable earthbound thunder, were suddenly silenced on the meadow, as if swaddled by the fog. Inside the glowing cloud the Knights thundered on over Ceridwen's secret ways. They appeared a few moments later outside the main hunting camp where the first kills of the day still steamed in the cold morning air of early spring.

Arthur's eyes narrowed and stung, for he saw the pile of unborn fawn carcasses tossed casually aside. Outrage at the senseless carnage sounded from every man's throat and they needed no further orders from Arthur as they streamed down the small hill and into the surprised Saxons. Full battle was joined, seaxs and arrows flew thickly and shouts of orders added to the tumult as the Knights and their enemies strove against each other. Suddenly it was all over and Arthur's men cheered lustily as they regarded the result of their labors; all but two of the marauders lay dead.

"Well boyos, we've some cleaning up to do. The King's orders are…" Lancelot began. Arthur laid his mailed hand on his First Knight's arm and stepped out in front of him.

"Flay the dead ones, boyos, with the heads on. Prepare them for full display," he ordered grimly. "Make them watch!" he pointed at the survivors, two young lads just barely fourteen who had served as message runners between Saxon camps. Without a word, Bedwyr whipped out his skinning knife, pulled the furs off the closest dead man and began the task. The others bent to the labor, however unwillingly; even Arthur participated while clenching his teeth against the bile that rose in his throat. When the grisly task was done, the carcasses were thrown without any ceremony into a fire along with the offal pile and the remnants of the hunter's tents. Booty was sorted into gold, silver or bronze, the salted meat was loaded into the Knight's saddle packs. When all was clean in the area again, the two Saxon lads were brought before Arthur. They trembled with fear, but stood straight and proud before the British King as he told them in their own tongue his message to Cerdic.

"Tell him I have offered peace for the last time. He has burnt too many treaties, farms and bridges behind him. If he would have made peace, we could have made room for everyone within the fertile portions of our lands. But, since the raids, rapes and murders have continued, Ceridwen has pronounced only the first of Her judgments against yer people. What has been done here today is only the first installment on what the tribes owe in blood to the Goddess in payment for the slaughter of Her children, especially the unborn! As long as the raiding continues, so will the repayments!" he said crisply and watched the lads' faces pale as they heard his words and understood his meaning. "Go on now, both of ye. Yer lives are spared to carry this message straight to Cerdic. If we find ye still within our borders at the end of the day, ye will suffer the same fate as did these men," he told them, signaling to Lancelot and Gawaine to release them. The two boys sprinted off towards the Severn, disappearing quickly over the hills. Arthur turned to Lionel and Agravaine and gave his orders rapid-fire. "Follow them, boyos. Make sure they go all the way home!"

"Aye, Sire," the two responded and leapt to their saddles. The rest of the patrol rolled up the flayed skins, stuffed them into oiled leather bags and slung them over the cantles of their saddles. Mounting up, they heard Arthur's orders.

"On to the next camp, my brothers!" he called out and urged his horse forward.

They spent a month rooting out the seemingly innumerable hunting camps and either capturing or slaying the occupants, depending on the size of the camp. When they at last located the main bivouac, just out of sight of the British side of the Severn, Cerdic barely escaped with his life during the pitched battle along with his warchiefs. Arthur watched them splash across the river, sighed then ordered the survivors taken to Camelot to await their ransom. The catches of salted deer meat were hauled back to Camelot's cold room, where Cai continued the drying process, then jerked the venison for dry stores and travel rations.

The Saxons were sent messages of warning in a very convincing way, or so Arthur thought. At the Summer Solstice, the flayed, tanned skins of the all the Saxons slain so far were taken to the edge of the Severn, mounted on special display trees, the dried and shriveled heads stuck precisely on pike poles. At the feet of the boards were small clay representations of does and fawns, some looking remarkably convincing in poses of nursing, sleeping or even being born. Arthur waited until dawn, then drew Excalibur and walked in front of the effigies.

"Cerdic Elesing, Cying of the Federated Tribes! I return thy men to ye, as well as proof of why they were dealt with as they were. If this poaching had continued, the whole spring fawning season would have been lost, leaving few deer for both our people. If such is the normal practice of yer people, 'tis no wonder yer people starve! Stay out of the Goddess' forests, unless ye come to speak for peace!" he called out and raised Excalibur. The sword's bright blue aura sparked a light and lit the effigies and skins, making them clearly visible to those assembled. Howls of rage and despair erupted and Arthur smiled grimly, sheathed Excalibur and stalked back to his horse. They all saw a seax flying from the Saxon side of the river, but Lancelot spurred his horse forward in easy time to catch it. The Company rode away silently and angrily, as a score of women came weeping forward to claim the remains of their husbands, brothers and fathers. Afterwards, they all gathered outside Cerdic's tent, a mob angry and demanding an explanation from the man most unable to give it to them.

The raiding stopped, replaced by war fully-blossomed; the summer was hot and desperate. Leodegrance sent his best-trained troops into the fray, men trained by the Lion King's own team of stray Roman trainers. But his munificence was not without its price. He sent Arthur the troops, but demanded in courtly phrases, that the King think long and hard about the betrothal question. Arthur reluctantly agreed to allow the girl to visit Camelot during the coming winter, "sometime," as he vaguely put it in his reply letter. He had no idea what he had unleashed upon himself and the staff of Camelot with that answer. Lady Jolynda, Leodegrance's wife and Gwenhyfar's mother, arrived just before Samhain, with her gaggle of noisy attendant ladies. Cai's tight schedule went to pieces within two days as Jolynda ran the seneschal ragged with her attempts to make "this bachelor's lair" livable for her precious daughter. Cai appealed to Arthur in desperation, and the King went to Lancelot.

"Please, Lance, we must find something for this overbearing, puffed up old gossipy hen to do so she's out of Cai's hair!" he asked plaintively. "I have not had a decent cup of tea since she and her ladies arrived."

"Of course, Artos," Lancelot chuckled, remembering his last visit to Lyonnesse and Jolynda's pompous and arrogant manner. "I shall keep them so busy they will not have time to bother our poor brother Cai."

The First Knight was true to his word, as usual, organizing a few of the Knights into a contrived work party. They made a great show of "cleaning" an unused housing section of the Castle. In due time, Cai and the Lady Jolynda passed by, accompanied by her ladies; the women were aghast at the mess the Knights were making of the cleaning job.

"I know, My Lady Jolynda, but someone must do these jobs. As understaffed as I am, I just do not have the staff to spare for these extra jobs," the seneschal sighed, exaggerating his tone while he crossed his fingers behind him to compensate for the small fib.

"Well, My Lord Cai, why did ye not just say so before?" Jolynda asked compassionately. "My ladies and I can contribute to this part of readying the castle. Men who protect all Britain from the raiding, raping Saxons should not have to spend their rare free time scrubbing walls and floors. Come, my ladies, we have much work to do," she announced to her entourage. The women returned to their suites, changed into working clothes, commandeered cleaning supplies from the kitchen and went to work in the dusty, stuffy rooms. Cai breathed a sigh of relief and put his staff back on schedule. By the time Gwenhyfar arrived with a full division of Lyonnesse's knights as escort for her heavily-curtained litter, the castle truly sparkled from parapet to scullery.

No less than full honors for her visit were proper, and Lancelot ordered the Company out in full formal armor. They stood at attention as her litter passed and they all saw her peek cautiously from behind the heavy, warm velvet draperies that cocooned her inside the litter, which was more like a fancy wagon that trundled behind the four matched white horses that pulled it. Arthur stepped forward to meet her, the Lady Jolynda beside him. The beautiful, petite fifteen-year-old stepped out from the litter, placing her fingers delicately into his sword-callused hand to allow him to assist her down the steps.

"Greetings to ye, Arthur ap Uther Pendragon, High King of the Britons. I am honored to be invited to Castle Camelot for the Solstice celebration this year," she said after the formal introductions had been made, then she curtsied deeply in her radiant pink gown.

"Greetings to My Lady Guinevere, in the name of the Mother, I welcome ye to Camelot. Will ye come with me into the great room? Sir Cai has prepared a hot drink to warm ye after yer long, cold trip," he nodded acknowledgment and led her inside. Sir Lancelot awaited them, holding the small cup of mulled wine to welcome her officially.

"Thank ye, Sir Lancelot," Arthur said, taking the cup from his hand and offering it to the young lady. By partaking, she made herself a protected guest of the King and no harm could come to her. Any of the Knights would now defend her honor or body with their strength of arms, lest their King be dishonored.

"I thank ye, Sir Lancelot du Lac," she said, smilingly handing the empty cup to him.

"Ye are welcome, My Lady Guinevere," Lancelot answered, smiling warmly in return.

"My Lord Arthur, Castle Camelot is all that Sir Lancelot said 'twould be. I never expected fighting men could be so gentle and courteous," the young princess went on, handing her heavy wrap to a page who, as it happened, was Aaronn.

Arthur had finally recalled him to Camelot for the winter and the newly sixteen-year old gloried in spending "manly" time with the Knights, hearing them exchange tales of deeds done and maidens won. The Company accepted him as one of them now, they gladly answered he and Olran's many questions about styles of fighting and sparring techniques. Lancelot and Gawaine had taken them under their wings, so to speak, beginning their training in the sword. The two experienced Knights were very surprised at their skill and unusual style of wielding the heavy broadsword that was the common weapon of the Company. The boys had developed a style that, while effective, could be considered less than knightly. When Lancelot reprimanded them for what he considered to be errors in form and technique, Aaronn had answered very seriously and simply.

"But Sir Lancelot, 'tis not the idea to win one of these encounters? I have trained myself to win."

"Aye, Sir Lancelot. We fight the Saxons, they cheat constantly. One must be flexible after all," Olran added, grinning nastily.

Lancelot shuddered at the lack of emotion in either boy's voice, while Gawaine rolled his eyes skyward in resignation. No one else ever questioned the boy's sword tactics again, although there were many in the Company that held the opinion their style would never win them any Tournaments. Two of those were Bors and Lionel, older by far than any of the others; they were stalwart men whose strict adherence to established rules and techniques was complete. Only Arthur, Bedwyr and the Merlin stood by and made no comments as they watched the two at practice.

Now Aaronn put Gwenhyfar's heavy wrap away in her room and returned quickly to his post in the great room, where Lady Jolynda stood embracing her daughter.

For supper, Aaronn and Olran were assigned to serve the High Table, the King finally found a moment to introduce Gwenhyfar to the two unusual boys.

"My Lady, I would like ye to meet my ward, Aaronn," he said, motioning him to his side.

"Welcome to Camelot, Lady Guinevere," Aaronn said smoothly, being sure to pronounce her name as he had been told she preferred.

"Thank ye, Aaronn," the girl returned smoothly. "And who is yer quiet companion? 'Tis Prince Olran ap Warren, aye?" she asked with a faint smile.

"'Tis indeed I, Lady Guinevere," Olran answered.

"What are ye doing here at Camelot?" the petite girl asked, not knowing the lad's situation.

"Prince Olran has broken with his family to support me as High King," Arthur explained quietly.

"Good for him! I have thought for a long time 'twas something nasty about Westerland Keep," Guinevere answered.

Olran inclined his head in thanks for her support, then he added fiercely; "Do not worry My Lady, Warren's day will come."

Guinevere stared at Olran, hearing the hate in his voice she wondered what could cause him to dislike his family so. He levelly returned her sapphire gaze with his own gray eyes as she sat there, between Lancelot and Arthur. With his developing gift of Sight, he saw her as a white shadow hovering between the King and his First Knight. Inwardly he gasped, and he nudged Aaronn to urge him to take his leave. Respectfully, the two bowed and returned to the kitchens for more bread.

"Aaronn, how does one say her name in the Old Tongue?" Olran asked, whispering.

"Gwenhyfar, it means 'the white shadow', why?" Aaronn asked in return.

"I just had a vision of her, hovering as a white shadow between Arthur and Lancelot. She suddenly moved from between them to clinging to Lancelot. What does it mean?" Olran said, still whispering.

"I do not know, we will have to talk to brother Drusus about it," Aaronn answered, concerned at the pallor of Olran's face. "Are ye all right?"

"I have never before experienced a touch of the Sight this strong," Olran answered, taking a seat. "I am feeling a bit strange."

"We will speak to someone about it very soon then," Aaronn decided. "We have to know what this forebodes."

The two boys had their chance to ask the Merlin, for the High Druid arrived the next morning. He paled when he heard that Leodegrance's fair daughter was housed in the rosy pink room that was beside Arthur's private quarters.

"What is *she* doing here?" he exploded all over Arthur when the King finally arranged his schedule to meet with him. "I thought we agreed to discuss and consider very carefully all offers from the Lion's Lair together."

"Excuse me, My Lord Merlin. I suppose the High King should wait upon the conveniences of Dragon Isle to make snap decisions vital to the winning of this war!" Arthur snapped in return. "Ye were nowhere to be found when Leodegrance demanded that I at least see his daughter before I rejected the betrothal. I have promised only to talk with the wench, not take her to my bed!" Uncle and nephew, King and Counselor stared hotly at each other for long moments before Arthur looked away and sighed heavily. "I am sorry, Taliesin. But I had to do this to satisfy one of my staunchest supporters. He has given so much to the realm, surely the King can at least entertain the girl and ascertain her fitness to rule beside me," Arthur reasoned.

"I suppose so but do be careful. The Old Lion is a crafty man, as Uther found out almost too late. He actually managed to talk yer father into extending Lyonnesse's borders into Uriens' lands when he was drunk and feasting. When I found the document, I burnt it in front of Leodegrance and Jolynda, warning them not to try it again. They are both charming, ruthless and undoubtedly thirsting for the High Throne through their lovely and fragile Gwenhyfar..." he trailed off.

"Guinevere, Lord Merlin," Arthur corrected. "She dislikes the pronunciation in the Old Tongue."

"I do not doubt it, Artos. Gwenhyfar means 'the white shadow,' when the glyph appears in the runes it always portends strife between close companions," the Merlin warned. "Please Artos, my boy, be very careful. She may be queenly material, but she may not be best for the High Throne. If Leodegrance could be persuaded towards one of the noble Knights as a suitor for her, possibly Lancelot or Gawaine, perhaps 'twould satisfy both honors."

"We are in agreement, Lord Merlin. But to hold the allegiances of the Christian lords in Britain, I may have no choice. We need them to support the garrisons and the hostel system throughout the realm. We need them to repair and maintain the road system so that the Knights can ride on roadbeds instead of muck and mud. The Army has shaven response times to alarms since the roads were repaired, I would like to keep it that way," Arthur finished, sighing. "Are ye very cross with me this time?" he asked after a moment.

"Nay my boyo, how could I be?" Taliesin answered sadly. "I have been absent of late, I know. Perhaps 'tis time I retire to Dragon Isle and pass on the mantle of the Merlin to someone younger."

"I need ye, Taliesin, Britain needs ye. Do not leave us just yet, please?" Arthur implored as he poured a cup of wine for the Merlin, then one for himself.

"How can I leave?" the Merlin chuckled dryly, accepting the wine. "Look at the trouble ye can get yerself into when I leave for only a few weeks!"

"Still 'the Wart', eh?" Arthur chuckled with him, remembering the days when the Merlin had come to tutor him at Sir Ector's keep in the Perilous Forest of South Wales.

"Nay my boyo, ye are the High King Arthur Pendragon now. No more time to be 'the Wart'," the Merlin sighed and embraced his nephew warmly.

"'Twould be fun, just for a few hours though," Arthur chuckled, recalling the many misadventures while Sir Ector fostered him in secret.

"So tell me, what think ye of the girl?" the Merlin asked.

"I've only just met her, Uncle," Arthur laughed outright. "So far, she seems intelligent enough and is well informed on the political situation. She even commented favorably on Olran's defection from Westerland Keep. She also happens to be very pretty, well-shaped from what I can see with her clothes on and smells of apple blossom all the time," Arthur told him. The Merlin frowned briefly, but Arthur did not see. "I could be content with her to wife," he added, mischief lighting his voice. He could not keep a straight face when he saw the Merlin's face blanch white, he added reassuringly; "I told ye, Uncle. I shall consider all the advantages and disadvantages of the match. If she is in any wise wrong for the Throne, I shall refuse the offer on such grounds. I'll propose to the Old Lion that he accept a matching between her and one of the princelings we have riding about in armor all over Britain. With all the noble blood around Camelot, she ought to find one Knight who is a match for her," Arthur returned to the original subject.

"Ye are the High King, boyo. Listen to the council of yer true heart, for 'tis the voice of yer Divine self. If ye always listen to that voice, ye cannot go wrong," the Merlin told him, evasively.

"And what is the opinion of the Lord High Druid?" Arthur asked.

"Do ye really want me to say it?" the Merlin asked in return.

"I would not ask if I did not want to hear it," Arthur retorted. "Please, give it to me straight from the heart."

"Then talk to her, be with her and if she wishes, share the Mother's Rite with her, Artos. If she truly is Ceridwen's choice for the throne, all will be as She wills," the Merlin advised, even though he heard his inner self scream for Arthur to send the Lion's whelp back to her father's den.

Gwenhyfar stayed at Camelot until the snows abated, her ready hands and willing spirit of service made her welcome indeed. Her clever mother and ladies worked unceasingly at the looms in Camelot's workshop and their crafty needles worked tirelessly, embroidering beautiful designs onto stacks of tablecloths, napkins, runners and towels for the private necessity areas in each Castle suite.

Gwenhyfar also dined with Arthur privately and often. They spoke of Arthur's fostering, of the wars and of the treaty situations. Arthur was very impressed by Gwenhyfar's ready grasp of political nuances; her quick mind was a match for his own. She played chess with the enthusiasm of a man, rather than using her young, innocent beauty as a weapon, and Arthur began to grow fond of her. When the time for the spring rains approached, Gwenhyfar prepared to return home and Arthur presented her privately with a farewell gift the night before she left.

"Please, Lady Guinevere would ye accept this small token of my esteem? It may not be the betrothal that yer father wants, but 'tis a gift from a grateful High King to a very lovely subject. Thank ye for lighting Camelot with thy fair and graceful presence," Arthur said and handed her a small, linen-wrapped package.

She opened it carefully, finding within a delicate, silver-white dragon pin with a small but practically flawless diamond mounted for an eye.

"Ooooo!" the girl breathed in wonder and appreciation. "Sire, surely 'tis is too fine a gift for only friendship," she reproached him gently. "What will folk think when they see me wear it?"

"Only that a very dear friend has given it to ye," Arthur smiled gently, leaned over and carefully covered her sweet, full, virgin lips with his own. Her response was much more than he had expected, for she threw her arms around his neck and returned the kiss ardently. Both of them were breathing heavily when Lancelot's voice warned them of his approach, they quickly composed themselves to meet him.

"Come, My Lady. Thy litter awaits," Lancelot said, his eyes only on her, though she saw not.

"I thank the High King for his gift," she turned gracefully and curtsied. "Truly, I shall wear it with pleasure; 'twill remind me of the lovely days I spent with the King at Camelot."

"Fare thee well, My Lady Guinevere. May the Goddess watch over thee as ye journey home," he gave the ritual closing, immediately wishing he had not.

"I need no heathen goddess to insure my safety, My Lord Arthur Pendragon! God, the Christ and the Angels guarded my journey here, they will see to it as I return home!" she responded, highly offended, turning to follow Lancelot.

"My Lady, do not cross the Goddess," Arthur warned. "She and the Christ put me on the High Throne of Britain through similar and just as sacred rites. I rule this country accordingly. If ye know nothing of Her, I suggest ye seek knowledge and quickly."

"Never will I seek knowledge of such filth!" Guinevere retorted harshly, quickly following Lancelot to where her wheeled litter awaited. Arthur followed a moment or two later, smiling and wishing all a good journey home in the Goddess' name, when the girl was gone he retreated to his suite, already missing her quick and witty company.

A week after Gwenhyfar's visit, the Saxons sailed fifty longboats up the Severn, falling on the farms there. Arthur arrived with the Knights early the next day, finding the common storehouses empty, even to the sowing seed for the next year's planting. The raiders had killed no one, however, and the farmer's daughters escaped the unwanted attentions of the marauders.

"Hit us, cleaned out the storehouses, locked us within and went off towards the next farm," was the tale the Knights heard over and over again. Arthur was very concerned and sent Bedwyr and Tristan off in pursuit. The two Knights returned just after dusk, thirsty and tired.

"They are headed for central Celidon, Artos. They get in there solid an' we'll be all spring and summer roustin' 'em out!" Bedwyr reported.

"Damn!" Arthur swore, smacking his fist into his palm. "Well, boyos, 'tis it, we have to beat them this time. This year, we do not stop 'till we have Cerdic by the balls, tightly! The Saxon's retreat across the Severn will be halted and they do not go home 'till they are defeated or dead, to the last man! I am tired of war, so 'tis time to end it, here and now! What say ye, Knights of Camelot?" he called out to them in his best battlefield voice.

His answer came back, loud and strong from each man's throat; "Victory for the Pendragon is Victory for the Light!"

"Then go after them, boyos, and chase them 'till they beg to go home!" Arthur laughed lustily, the War Duke of Britain once again.

Chapter 5

It was long before they laughed again, for the Saxons fought harder than usual, using the forest as their best weapon. Patrols were ambushed, horses slain, Knights killed or captured and the hot summer dragged on endlessly. Arthur's letters to Aaronn were dark and depressing; the maturing young man threw himself into his training with renewed and frustrated energy, hoping that this would be the year Arthur called him to serve with the others. When the letters stopped coming just before the Summer Solstice, Aaronn began to plan his departure from Avalon, where he had returned after Gwenhyfar's visit. Try as the young man might, he could not stop himself from referring to her by her name in the Old Language, so he refrained from speaking about her altogether except to Olran.

As he continued his training under Brother Michael's tutelage, Aaronn broadened and matured much; the Druid noted with quiet pride the skill he exhibited while practicing his knife-throwing regimen. The centers of the targets now showed much sign of being hit repeatedly by Aaronn's razor sharp blades; Michael noting that Aaronn hardly ever missed. The lad's sword work was unequaled by any of his other students, except for Olran's. The best either lad could manage against one another was a draw in every mock bout they engaged in. Aaronn wielded a definitely heavier blade, but Olran's speed and finesse closed any advantage gap offered by the heavier blade. The pair's tempers never flared while they sparred; instead each encouraged the other towards perfection and always discussed each bout at length, pointing out flaws in their defenses and offenses. Finally, Drusus and Michael took them aside and offered each of them the chance to wear the blue woad Serpent tattoos of the Druids.

"Nay, Brothers, I cherish the offer greatly as well as all ye have taught me. The Serpents mark a man, I would not mark my body with such a notable identification sign," Aaronn refused politely after thinking a moment.

"And ye, Olran?" Drusus asked, turning to the princeling.

"Would ye teach me how to paint them on?" Olran hedged. He too, was proud of all Drusus had taught him and wanted to honor them by wearing the marks. Frankly, he thought to himself, the pain of the tattooing process was all the discouragement he needed.

"Of course, little brother," Drusus laughed, nodding his head. "I understand yer reasons for answering this way; I daresay yer skin has been marked well enough." Olran's face tightened just a bit, only those who were close with him could have seen it. He relaxed in a moment, joining his teachers and sword brother Aaronn in a toast.

"To Ceridwen, and Her Justice," Michael proposed.

"Aye," they echoed and drank.

"Does this mean I am ready to assume the mantle of the Black Knight, Brothers?" Aaronn asked.

"Aye, Aaronn. Ye and Olran know everything ye need to assume yer roles," the Druid Masters assured them. "Come with us, boyos. We have something to give ye."

"But Brothers, ye have given us so much already," Olran protested.

"One last set of gifts, boyos and then we will have nothing left to give," Drusus chuckled, propelling him forward. Going to Michael's room, the four entered and locked the door.

"Here Aaronn, 'tis for ye," Michael indicated a large, lumpy package on the floor. "And this one is for ye, Olran."

"What could it be?" the gray-eyed lad asked.

"Open them and find out for yerself," Drusus laughed.

The boys complied, carefully flipping back the voluminous amount of black cloth that swaddled the contents within.

"Teacher…Brother!" Aaronn breathed in wonder as he revealed the set of chain mail, light and strong links sewn onto flexible hide, lined with goose down and covered with absorbent cotton batting. With it was a new broadsword, custom balanced for his hand alone and a matching sheathe that was a perfect fit for his back. The crowning touch of the weaponry was a crossed black leather knife harness, complete with a new set of thirty-six knives. Each of the blades had just the barest hint of a hilt that looked like a button, each was wickedly sharp and only the trained eye could discern the weapons behind the decorative disguise. Aaronn realized that he could wear them anywhere, even within the great room at Camelot, where weapons were forbidden. Also included was a pair of flexible black leather boots, fitted with a dagger in each, two pair of sturdy black trous, two shirts and two full sets of sable black unders and hose. The cloth the whole package was wrapped in turned out to be a full-length hooded black cloak and an acid blackened silver brooch to pin it.

Olran's package was nearly identical, but in place of the throwing knives, Drusus had made a beautiful black-dyed ash bow and black leather quiver full of ebony colored mistletoe arrows, fletched with raven feathers. He was struck speechless and could only run his hands over the smooth, strong wood of the weapons. His sword was slightly lighter and thinner than Aaronn's, but it was balanced and weighted so that the thinner lad could wield it effectively.

"Thank ye, Masters, for these weapons. We will always try to wield them with honor, in the service of Ceridwen and Britain," Aaronn said as he ran his hands over the weapons, caressing them as lovingly as he ever touched a woman. Aaronn had found favor in Ceridwen's eyes last Beltane and a skilled, mature priestess had patiently guided the boy through his First Rites. As far as Michael knew, his student was still receiving occasional instruction by the same priestess. The Black Knight would need such skills as much as any others, Michael grinned privately, for information could be gathered through them as well as through more painful means.

"Go on, boyos, try them," the Masters urged and the two raced to see who could dress first. The clothing was form-fitting, soft and warm, the weapon rigs fit snugly without binding.

"The harness looks well on ye, Olran my boyo," Drusus commented as he circled Olran, adjusting a fastening here and there. Michael did the same for Aaronn before both teachers stood back and nodded approvingly.

"Tomorrow, ye must work with yer new weapons. Ye must get the feel of 'em before ye go into battle," Michael said finally. "Thy roles as Ceridwen's men must be secret, even from the King, the Company of Camelot and from any lovers or wives ye choose to take over the years. To all, other than the Lady of the Lake, the Merlin, we yer teachers and those ye choose to entrust as yer operatives, ye must remain only Aaronn and Olran. Ye must learn to think of the Black Knight and the Black Hunter as completely separate identities."

"Aye, Brother Michael, ye have taught us well the importance of such secrecy," Aaronn acknowledged, Olran nodding his understanding as well.

"Now, off to bed with the both of ye. Ye still have much work to do before ye and yer weapons are as one," Drusus laughed and pointed towards the door. "Sleep ye sound, boyos."

"Sleep ye sound as well, beloved Masters. Thank ye again for the weapons and the skills to use them," Olran called back as they exited the room, laden with their presents.

The two young men retired to their room, packed away the extra clothing in their always ready bags, hung the cloaks on pegs in the clothespress and stowed the armor and weapons on the armor-tree. Olran pulled out the wineskin they now kept openly in their room, for it was impossible to hide anything from their Druid Teachers. Their Masters had found the lad's first purloined half-skin within three days of the theft.

"Be careful how ye use it, boyos," Drusus had warned. "More than one warrior has lost himself within a wineskin."

The boys usually limited themselves to one full cup upon occasion, tonight was a special occasion and Olran poured their cups full again after the first and raised his own cup in a toast.

"To Ceridwen's men, the Black Knight and the Black Hunter, the scourge of all evildoers!" he pronounced, grinning wide.

"Aye!" Aaronn returned and they tapped their cups together before draining them to the last drop.

"So, now that we are ready to do this marvelous work, how do we get started, and when?" Olran quipped, pouring his glass full a third time.

"We wait, we watch and when the opportunity presents itself, we act," Aaronn answered, watching Olran pour a third cup of wine for him. He was very surprised at the authority in his voice.

"Do we get to choose our targets, or does Ceridwen choose 'em?" Olran wondered aloud.

Aaronn chuckled softly as he answered. "All will be made clear to us when the time comes, my friend,"

"Good! I would not want to make a mistake and kill the wrong man," Olran returned emphatically.

The next day, Aaronn and Olran awakened at dawn, after a light breakfast the Druid Masters took them on an extended run around the whole island of Avalon. Their teachers had spent many hours setting up traps and blinds, each lad avoided all but one or two minor hits along the way. Targets sprang out at them; each one was hit by either arrow or knife, sometimes both in a vital area. When they at last returned to the housing compound, they were thoroughly exhausted.

"So, ye are not in as good shape as ye thought after all, eh boyos?" Drusus and Michael laughed uproariously. All their students could do was grin wryly and start stretching their tired muscles to avoid cramping. Every day, this ritual was repeated and the trials grew more difficult. As the weeks wore on through the long, dry summer, Aaronn and Olran labored zealously to acquaint themselves with the heft and feel of their weapons.

Other skills were also honed and Olran finally lost his virginity to a willowy blonde priestess who had quietly pursued him for a year. Aaronn thrived on manhood and tried to wait patiently for Ceridwen's call. Finally, in the late summer of that year, She did.

One hot morning Olran awoke, his head aching and spinning. Aaronn brought him a cup of hot blackberry tea, laced with willow bark powder, but it did not relieve the pounding that disabled the young princeling. Aaronn was ready to run for Drusus but when Olran tried to stand and stop him, the renegade prince fell to his knees, clutching his throbbing temples.

"Aaronn, 'tis a 'seeing'," he gasped out finally through the aching and tried to calm himself as he had been taught. Slowly, the pain lessened and he could hear the terrified neighing of horses, along with the clashing of steel on steel. He saw a battlefield, recognizing a portion of Celidon Wood that stood just beside the Severn. Arthur's battle standard fluttered wildly above the men as the battle raged on. Olran heard clearly, as the pain cleared and faded he heard a familiar voice reverberate in his head;

"Go, my Champions! Join the battle for the Light! Win thy Knighthood at Camelot, I command it!"

As Aaronn watched his friend struggle with the powerful vision he finally heard the same in his own head. Instantly, he was shown the same vision Olran had seen, and heard the words of Ceridwen.

"Olran, are ye well?" he asked, helping the thin young man to his feet.

"Aye, Aaronn. The pain has gone," he answered, still somewhat shaky. "I hope Ceridwen's warning does not affect me this way every time, I felt like throwing up there for a moment," he managed to chuckle as he struggled to his feet.

"Come on then, let us dress and go. I know the area and we can be there by late afternoon. At last, the time has come for me to repay Arthur for all he has done for me," Aaronn urged excitedly, starting to put together his things. Olran sat on the bed, composing himself as the last shreds of the vision faded into memory. Aaronn saw him still sitting and was concerned. "Ye are coming, aye?" he asked.

Olran grinned wanly and pushed himself off the mattress. "Of course I am. A man who is landless and clanless must earn his keep in the world, after all," he replied as he pulled his always-packed bags from under his bed. "Being in the victorious army at least buys me a room at Camelot. After that, who knows?" he grinned and mocked a bow-string thrum as he released an imaginary arrow.

When they were almost ready to depart, they heard the sounds of shod hooves outside their window. Grabbing bags and cloaks, the young men sprinted outside to find two horses standing there, fully dressed for travel. Their trainers, Michael and Drusus each held a set of reins and smilingly extended them.

"Here, take these steeds for the journey. When Arthur grants ye new ones, just send them home. They know the way," Michael smiled.

"Make sure ye take good care of them while they are in yer care," Drusus added, mock-serious, for he knew the animals were in good hands.

"Thank ye again, beloved Masters. Thank ye for everything, the training, the weapons and now the loan of horses too," Aaronn began, moved close to tears, but unwilling to shed them. "I shall always strive to be worthy of what ye have taught me."

"As long as ye serve the Light, Ceridwen and Arthur, in that order, ye will do fine. Just come and visit us once and awhile, will ye?" Michael sniffled and dabbed his eyes a bit. "We count it as our honor to teach such willing students as ye have been, Aaronn and Olran. Go on now, do yer duty!"

"Right willingly, Masters," the two saluted smartly and sprang into their saddles, touched spur to flank and sped off to where the barge waited.

The journey over was quick and as they crossed Aaronn and Olran offered devout and silent thanks to the Light for this opportunity to prove their worth to those who had sponsored and taught them through the years. Aaronn fretted a bit, impatient to be about his work at last. All the negatives in his life forgotten, Aaronn only wished to go forward and build a new life, finally free of the stigma of being without a father. Surely once I am knighted it will not make any difference to anyone that I am a King's ward, he thought happily.

The barge scraped ashore, the two led the horses from it, and then Aaronn solemnly thanked the men who poled it before mounting up. Olran thanked them as well and was silently handed a vial of thick black liquid. His eyebrows questioningly rose at the gift and the leader spoke for them all.

"For thy arrows, Black Hunter, certain death for Ceridwen's foes lies in the fluid. All ye need do is to cause a small scratch on their skin for them to die."

"I see. May I return to learn this secret?" Olran asked, tucking the vial away in his belt pouch carefully.

"We would be honored, Black Hunter. May good fortune follow ye both," the Faerie man answered before they took the barge away.

After Olran mounted up, he and Aaronn galloped off towards the southwest. Traveling overland to avoid the roads saved much time and miles, by the time the sun dipped below the tree line, the two spied the campfires of the Pendragon's camp. They could see the sentries already in place and knew that the Knights had retired to their beds for the night.

"Let us not go in just yet, Olran. What if we go and find Cerdic's camp and cause a little trouble for him?" Aaronn proposed, grinning widely in the gathering dusk.

"What kind of trouble?" Olran asked as they led their horses away and stripped off their weapons and bags.

"I am sure we can think of something to cause them difficulties, brother. "Go home, blessed of Epona. Thank ye for bearing us here quickly and comfortably," Aaronn told the animals. Pricking up their ears, the horses tossed their heads and trotted away through the forest, back towards Avalon. "Come on brother and help me tickle a few Saxons," Aaronn chuckled and led the way.

The two crossed the border after stowing their supplies and found the noisy, boisterous Saxon camp without trouble. There was much dancing and singing, ale flowed from cask to horn in an unending stream. Clearly, they were elated about the day's events.

"Perhaps we can dampen their good humor?" Aaronn whispered, making ready to enter their camp in secret.

"Wait, we can cause them sufficient trouble right from here," Olran returned and strung his hunting bow. Taking from his quiver of arrows, he loaded a missile and drew, carefully sighting down the shaft. He released it smoothly and both of them grinned in satisfaction as a reveling Saxon clutched at his throat and dropped twitching to the ground. Another shaft flew into the crowd and another man fell, mouth working soundlessly as he died. A third man managed a short shriek before he dropped and a great commotion broke out in the crowd as they found the three dead men among them. A man called out in panic for Cerdic and the Saxon leader appeared. He strode to a position in front of the main fire and stood questioning those closest to the dead men, presenting a clear and perfect shot that Olran could not resist taking. His hands trembled a bit from excitement and the arrow missed the vital spot that he had targeted. It did, however, bury itself in the meat of Cerdic's upper right arm and the hooked barbs on the steel head burrowed into the flesh. Cerdic howled with pain and the two young men ran laughing into the shadows of the forest. Aaronn and Olran rested in Celidon Wood, sleeping easily and comfortably in the warm summer night under the stars. They awoke early, breakfasted on spitted game hens and chose a vantage point from which to watch the events of the day.

Arthur also awoke early; Cai brought his breakfast and Lancelot with the daily dispatches. "Are they still out there, Lance?" he asked, still tired though he had slept decently.

"Of course Artos, ye know they are," Lancelot responded, equally weary. "Bedwyr says that during the first watch last night there was some kind of trouble in Cerdic's camp," he added.

"Indeed?" Arthur perked up a bit. "Cerdic is not dead, is he?"

"Nay, but Bedwyr reports that this morning he is sporting a very bloody bandage on his sword arm," Lancelot grinned wolfishly.

Arthur laughed outright and ate ravenously, then donned his battle dress. Gawaine peeked in, flashed Arthur an obscene gesture and moved on, laughing. Arthur grinned and exited his tent, his long cape fluttering behind him. His horse was brought and Arthur stepped onto the saddle, trotting over to where the army was now gathered to attack the Saxons once again in an attempt to break them and scatter the tribes. That, at least, would halt this battle and possible end the entire raiding season as well, Arthur sighed mentally. As he was ready to give the order to move out, he heard the screams of the berserkers. The horde spilled over the lip of the small rise that sheltered Arthur's camp and battle was joined. It was messy, bloody and totally brutal; Arthur grew concerned for his victory as the hot day wore on.

Aaronn and Olran watched with interest as the Knights and infantry worked together, trying to surround the Saxons, while the Saxons constantly worked against them. It was Aaronn who noticed that off to the left, Sir Bors and Sir Lionel had somehow gotten cut off from the main force and now struggled to rejoin their brother Knights. Cerdic's berserkers now surrounded them and Aaronn saw a pikeman work his way close to Sir Bors, trying to hook the Knight's chainmail. In a flash, Aaronn was up and running madly down the hill, Olran behind him. When the two hit the berserkers from behind, a path instantly opened under a flurry of arrows from Olran's bow. Arthur saw, but could hardly believe his eyes as knives flew from Aaronn's hands, mowing down the huge men like so much wheat. Olran's bow thrummed until his missiles were nearly exhausted, with the last one he leapt up onto a pile of still moving bodies and coolly fired the arrow at the pikeman who was trying to unhorse Sir Bors. The arrow neatly skewered the Saxon through the jugular, when the steel head appeared Bors' horse was spattered liberally with Saxon blood.

Once Aaronn's knives were spent, he pulled his broadsword, as did Olran. Cutting and hacking their way quickly and efficiently through the horde, the two opened an escape route for the beleaguered Knights. Sir Bors reached Olran, while Sir Lionel hauled Aaronn up behind him and they were able to escape to the British lines. A great cheer arose when the four reached the army and Lancelot himself led a renewed counter-charge. The Saxons, stunned by the result of Aaronn's and Olran's relentless form of battle, retreated across the Severn with the entire Company in pursuit and the chase was on. It continued for a whole day to insure the marauders were thoroughly scattered, then the Knights returned to British territory to celebrate their victory. Aaronn and Olran were taken to Arthur's tent immediately and ushered inside the darkened space.

"Aaronn! Olran! Where in the name of Ceridwen did ye come from?" Arthur asked, still shocked at their sudden arrival. "And may I add, thank ye for saving Sir Lionel and Sir Bors. If ye had not stepped in just then, we might have lost two very valuable men, let alone the day."

"We have been watching from the lip of the rise all day, Sire. There did not seem to be anything for us to do 'till Sir Bors and Sir Lionel got cut off from the main force," Aaronn explained. "It seemed then was the right time to act."

"Indeed so, and now I have to act. Come with me, ye two," he ordered, solemn-faced. The two followed him out to where the entire Company awaited. "Today we have ended an entire summer's campaign with a rousing Saxon defeat. 'Twould have been impossible without the brash and heroic deeds of our two young friends, Aaronn and Olran. Kneel before us, ye two," he commanded, pulling Excalibur from his back. Hearts pounding wildly, the two complied with eyes closed. "Aaronn and Olran, I, Arthur Pendragon, War Duke and High King of Britain, name ye Knights of the Company of Camelot. I pledge ye a home, arms and horse for the defense of the Light, Ceridwen and Britain. Rise, Sir Aaronn and Sir Olran and welcome, both of ye," he pronounced, nearly bursting with pride for his secret brother Aaronn.

"Sire, we are truly graced by thy generosity. 'Twill be our honor to serve the Light, Ceridwen and of course Britain, who is Arthur Pendragon," the two responded in one voice as they felt the cold steel of a glowing Excalibur touch on their shoulder. The sword's touch tingled warmly on their skins, and afterward Arthur raised each young man and embraced him, warrior to warrior. A cheer arose from the throats of every Knight and infantryman and Aaronn and Olran were congratulated over and over again.

When all had said their heart's feeling, the work of cleaning up began. While the dead were gathered, piled into separate pyres and set alight, Arthur called the army together and tapped a cask of ale.

"Now my friends, we have much celebrating to do. The wars are over for the year and we have two new Knights to welcome properly into the Company," he called to the assembly, who cheered loudly and dipped their mugs in turn into the recaptured British ale. Food was available in plenty and every man wanted to toast Aaronn and Olran. Tristan finished his first plate of food, filled his cup again and brought out his lap harp. He strummed a few notes, tuned the strings then launched into his rendition of, "The Ballad of Arthur;" "Once there was a King named Uther, who loved another's wife..." he sang the bawdy tune as loudly as he could. The others could not help joining in and soon they were all singing their favorite campaign songs, performing appropriate suggestive pantomime to accent the off-color lyrics. They ate, drank and sang until their throats were sore and before it was over, Aaronn and Olran fell fast asleep, snoring where they sat. Lancelot and Gawaine picked them up and carried them off to sleep in one of the Company's tents where they slumbered peacefully for the rest of the night. The others sat around the campfire with Arthur, discussing the event and each thanking Ceridwen continually for sending the two in such a timely fashion.

Bors and Lionel were still shaken and offered even more fervent thanks to the Goddess and to the Christ. Both men had continually criticized the pair's unusual fighting style and choice of specialty weapons as dishonorable. In the morning, the two rose early, dressed simply and brought Aaronn and Olran breakfast. The two older men served the meal in silence and with great skill, then cleared the empty dishes and put them back on the tray. Over Aaronn and Olran's protests, they knelt before the two and thanked them for saving their lives.

"We are very grateful, Sir Aaronn and Sir Olran, that ye did not let our prejudice towards yer fighting styles dissuade ye from perfecting it. We have spoken against yer choice of weapons for years due to our lack of understanding of yer motives. Now we see the value of them and we apologize to ye, our new brothers in arms," the two spoke as one.

"Please Sir Bors, Sir Lionel; ye should thank the Goddess for yer lives, not us. We only did Her will," Aaronn told them and Olran nodded his agreement. The two older men got up from their knees and offered the warrior's forearm to each young man, each took it and clasped firmly.

"Any slights are forgiven and forgotten, brothers," Aaronn grinned. "Ye need never worry over it again."

The two older men looked relieved and they left the tent with a much lighter step. Aaronn and Olran dressed quickly before running up the hill to fetch their packs, cached in the forest. By the time they returned, the tents were nearly packed and Cai was hooking up the supply wagon. When the seneschal saw them, he flashed a broad smile and a victory sign.

"The King wants to see ye, boyos," he called out and clambered out of the wagon bed. The two walked quickly to Arthur's tent, as they got there the structure collapsed as it was struck before packing.

"Sire, ye wanted to see us?" Aaronn called when they saw Arthur.

"Aye," he grinned. "What can ye two tell me about Cerdic's bandaged right arm?"

Olran blushed and cleared his throat nervously, but Aaronn spoke quietly and boldly. "He got caught in a storm, Sire, a storm of arrows from brother Olran's bow. He lost three men in that storm," he chuckled as he recalled the incident.

Arthur's eyebrows arched, but he only nodded and changed the subject, knowing well there was more to the incident that he would investigate later.

"How did ye two get here from Avalon?" he asked as he turned and walked towards the picket lines.

"The Druids loaned us some steeds, but we sent them home, Sire," Olran explained, having recovered his composure.

"I see. Well, one of the Knights will let ye ride behind back to Camelot. When we get home, ye will both come with me to the stables to choose mounts," Arthur ordered. "Aaronn, ye can ride with me, Olran, ye ride with Bedwyr."

"Aye, Sire," the two responded and ran to toss their belongings into the wagon. The Knights sang all the way back to the Castle, when they arrived they were welcomed with cool cups of ale and hot baths. Cai went immediately to the kitchens, where a full banquet was in the midst of preparation. Cai embraced his assistants heartily, congratulating them on the excellent job they had done so far. He then went to his room off the kitchen, closed the door and removed his trous. Quickly he opened the jar of healing salve Vivaine had given him, dipped a double fingerful of the unguent and started rubbing it liberally on his aching and scarred leg. A knock sounded on the door and he pulled a robe over his knees.

"Aye?" he asked.

"'Tis me, may I enter?" his assistance Claudia's voice came through the door. "I know yer leg is aching, and I want to assist."

"I do not require assistance to tend my aches, woman," Cai answered tartly.

Claudia entered despite his acidic response for she was, in spirit, the sister he had never had. She was the daughter of Ector's cook, a woman of prodigious skills in the culinary arts and Cai's earliest teacher thereof. Now Claudia served as head breadmaker and while Cai enjoyed her company, he did not see her as a romantic interest, which suited them both.

"I am not pursuing time in yer bed, Caius Ectorius," Claudia answered indignantly. "We will need ye to co-ordinate the serving of the meal and when yer leg aches ye have too sharp a tongue. Now, let me help ye, if not for yer sake, for everyone else's."

Cai grinned and handed her the jar without another protest. She pushed him back onto the bed, flipped the covering aside and without embarrassment applied her strong fingers to the task. Before too long, Cai noted the scar line had stopped twitching and that his whole leg felt relaxed and painless.

"Thank ye, Claudia. My leg feels much better now. Let me clean up and change, then I shall come and see to the serving. Be sure 'tis plenty of ale on ice, for we have two new Knights among the Company, Sir Aaronn and Sir Olran."

"Ye mean little Aaronn, the King's ward and Prince Olran, of Westerland Keep?" Claudia asked, amazed.

"Aye, they saved Sir Bors and Sir Lionel from certain death at the hands of the berserkers. I have never seen anything like the way they fight. Aaronn's knives flew like pollen grains on the spring winds and Olran's arrows took a quick and deadly toll among them. Ye should have seen it, Claudia old girl," Cai sighed and pointed to the door, indicating she should leave.

"Old girl?" she asked, eyebrows arching. "Ye have seen more summers than I, Caius Ectorius!"

He laughed and shooed her from the room, reminding her to check the breads and chill the ale. When he was alone, he quickly washed and dressed in clean white clothes, laced on his boots and went out to the busy and humming kitchen to put the finishing touches on the feast foods his staff had skillfully prepared.

Meanwhile, Aaronn and Olran were in the stables with the King, choosing mounts. Aaronn checked over several horses carefully, running his sensitive hands over rumps, back and front legs and along their backs. Finally, Arthur grew impatient and tapped Aaronn on the shoulder.

"Is there nothing here to yer liking, Aaronn?" he asked.

"They are all fine animals, My Lord," Aaronn began diplomatically. "But I feel no emotional connection with any one of them, so far."

"Well then, follow me boyo. Perhaps we might have a suitable animal in our stables after all," Arthur grinned suddenly, impressed with Aaronn's discriminating tastes in horseflesh.

They went outside where Lancelot held five horses by their halter ropes. Aaronn's eyes lit, for the young, barely gentled stallions were almost all completely coal black. All five were subjected to the same complete inspection while the King and the First Knight leaned against the corral fence, watching him. Finally, Aaronn took hold of a halter rope and led a stallion forward, smiling broadly at Arthur.

"May I have this one?" he asked.

"He is thine, Sir Aaronn," Arthur answered, bowing a bit at the waist.

"Sir Olran, have ye made a choice yet?" asked a grinning Lancelot, turning to the princeling.

"Aye, First Sword. That one over there suits me," Olran replied, turning and pointing at a separate pen. Within its circle stood an ill-tempered, ugly and jug-headed horse, its hide a non-descript dark blue roan color. No one had yet ridden this horse and Lancelot had thought more than once about drawing his skinning knife across its jugular vein, but could not get close enough to try,

"Sir Olran, are ye sure?" Lancelot asked. "He is a stubborn, mean, nasty, ass-biter of a horse. Not even I can get into the pen with him!"

"He's an ass-biter eh?" Olran asked, grinning with relish at the challenge. "Let me have his halter, and then we will see."

"This should be a good show," Lancelot said aside to Arthur as he motioned for a sturdy, leather halter and a length of good stout hemp rope. Handing Olran the apparatus, Lancelot and a fast growing crowd of Knights, including Aaronn and Arthur, followed Olran to the pen.

"He will never get the rope on him," Lancelot said to the King in a quiet voice.

"Do not be so sure, First Sword. Olran has been around horses all his life, even as ye have. I would bet on him rather than any horse," Aaronn broke in.

"How much would ye wager that the roan dumps him, brother Aaronn?" Bedwyr asked, eager for entertainment after the long summer's campaign.

"I would not steal yer money, brother Bedwyr. Olran is a sure bet on this one," Aaronn chuckled, then settled back to watch.

Olran eased through the bars of the pen and walked slowly around its inner perimeter. The roan watched him, curious and cautious, as the young man walked towards him, showing him the halter and rope openly.

The Jughead eyed this person suspiciously, but stood quietly as Olran fed him an apple and rubbed the halter all over his back and rump. Only when the horse was completely at ease with the feel of the leather and the rope did the princeling slip the leather restraint over the horse's nose and ears then buckle the throat strap. Holding the halter rope loosely in his hands so that it could be dropped quickly, Olran fed the horse the last quarter of apple, then fished another out of his pocket and tugged on the halter rope, just a bit. The stallion followed, lipping for the fruit, which Olran fed him a bit at a time as he motioned for the gate to be opened. It swung wide and they went through, with the placidly chewing stallion following right at Olran's shoulder, anticipating more apple pieces. Down to the River Cam they went, the crowd following behind at a safe distance so as not to spook the horse and spoil Olran's chances, though the muttering among them increased in volume.

Olran led the horse into the slow moving river up to above the roan's knees and stood with him, patting and speaking in gentle tones for a long time. The horse drank deeply, enjoying all the attention he was getting until Olran vaulted up on his back without warning. The stallion tried to buck, then tried to rear up onto his back legs, but the muddy bottom and the water itself slowed his movements enough to allow the horse-wise Olran to stay aboard with little difficulty. Only when the animal was completely exhausted did Olran urge him up and out of the river onto the bank. He slipped from the horse's back and patted him all over.

"See, ye have nothing to fear from me, do ye?" he spoke gently and the horse gave the newly knighted man a look of sheer surprise. "Now, we can either be friends or ye can be meat!" Olran added, drawing his belt knife and laying it gently across the stallion's jugular vein meaningfully. The horse rolled its eyes and stared at the slight lad before him for a moment before laying his head wearily on Olran's shoulder. "Ye have made a good choice, my friend. We will find a name for ye tomorrow," Olran chuckled and led the stallion away slowly. Lancelot turned to Aaronn and grinned, but the latter saw that the First Knight was astonished.

"I have never seen the like! Where did he learn that technique?" he asked.

"At Westerland, I imagine," Aaronn chuckled. "Sir Olran's education is exceptionally varied."

"This calls for a drink, Sir Lancelot," Arthur laughed outright. "And I need a long, hot bath."

"Aye, Sire, if ye smell anything like I do, then definitely so," Lancelot replied, wrinkling his nose.

"Well, Sir Lancelot," Bedwyr chuckled. "Ye can go last. After all, how bad can the Impeccable Knight smell?"

They all laughed at that, when Sir Olran returned from the stables the group went to the bathing room and slipped into one of the many wooden tubs there. As fine as most Roman-type baths were, Arthur saw them as a waste of fuel and water. The Merlin, therefore, had designed the heating vat as the central piece in the room, with pipes leading from it into several large, four-person tubs. Each tub had a control valve that allowed a small flow of fresh, hot water to constantly trickle into the tub, as well as its own drain way. The soapsuds and dead skin floated away down the drainpipe before it emptied into a settling reservoir. The solids were separated from the water, the latter being used to water the ornamental shrubs and flowers in the formal gardens Cai was trying very hard to persuade to live and grow. The solids were emptied every day from the settling tank and incorporated into Cai's growing compost area, where time and nature added to the formal gardens as well.

Aaronn eased his body into the hot water, soaped himself thoroughly twice, and then ducked under the water to rinse his head. Once clean, he settled back and let the hot water soak his weary muscles. A trio of serving maids wheeled in a cask of chilled ale and a tray of mugs. Aaronn accepted the cooling drink and let his eyes feast on their obvious charms. Women were beautiful and deadly creatures, he thought with a sigh, and was glad of their presence. Soft, strong hands applied a semi-stiff boar bristle brush and soap to his back, he groaned with pleasure at their welcome attentions.

"Thank ye, my dear. That felt marvelous," he told her as she poured another mugful for him.

"I am certain yer muscles must be all sore and stiff from yer labors on behalf of Britain, Sir Aaronn," she answered, playfully stroking his strong muscles with her fingertips. Aaronn felt her caress, then grabbed her hand and kissed the palm, gently and lingeringly.

"What are ye called, and what is yer fee for massage?" he asked.

"My name is Isolde, Sir Aaronn," she supplied, giggling slightly. "And for ye, 'twould be no fee asked."

"Well, we must discuss this later, Isolde," Aaronn smiled warmly at her. "Can ye visit me after supper?"

"Aye, Sir Aaronn, that I shall," she promised and winked as she left the room. Aaronn could hardly wait.

After their baths, Aaronn and Olran wrapped up in the plain white cotton robes hanging on the pegs in the wall before they went to find where their quarters would be. Sir Cai himself took them up to the Knight's quarters, opened up a familiar-looking door and bid them enter.

"Aye, 'tis yer old room, boyos," he chuckled. "We knocked out the wall to the corner room beside it to give ye more room after ye went back to Avalon. Now, supper is on the way, so ye should get dressed quickly if ye want any small foods. Ye know the routine, eh boyos?" he winked and chuckled.

"Thank ye, Sir Cai. 'Tis good to be home at last," Aaronn told him, truly glad to be back at Camelot.

"'Tis good to have ye both back. I always knew ye would win yer knighthood, and ye know how proud Artos is of ye, aye?" Cai said seriously. "Now, hurry it up the both of ye, or the party will start without ye," he grinned and strode away, whistling a tune of his own making as he returned to the kitchen.

The two made short work of dressing in their best new clothing and boots. Camelot's corps of pages was still in top form according to the shine on the leather, Aaronn noted as he laced on the satin-finished knee-high boots.

"Are ye ready, Olran?" he called into the separate chamber occupied by his friend.

"Aye, just let me get this one…boot…on!" Olran answered, stamping vigorously. "There, now I am ready!" he announced. After taking turns inspecting each other's appearance, they left the room, headed for the feast. Arriving in the great room, they were announced and a great cheer went up when their names were heard over the noise of the crowd already there. Mugs of good, stout ale were handed to them, after a few sips they saw Sir Bors' wife come to speak with them.

"I have heard the good deed ye have done for my husband, Sir Aaronn and Sir Olran. I add my thanks for saving my man and the father of our children," she said warmly, stood on her tiptoes and planted a soft kiss on each man's cheek.

"'Twas my honor and pleasure to serve my King and the Company in such a way, My Lady," Aaronn replied.

Olran said nothing, but he bowed and walked to the sideboard where the small foods were laid out. The thin young man had not eaten since early that morning, now it felt like his stomach was rubbing against his backbone. He loaded a plate with halved boiled eggs, varied pickled vegetables from small pearl onions to tiny, sweet cabbages and cucumbers, unleavened crackers and sliced cheeses. Filling his mug once again, he ate enough from the heaped plate to stop the grumbling in his stomach as he circulated among the Knights and ladies present. He was asked at length about the final arrow shot at Celidon, he could only reply thusly;

"Certainly, 'twas Ceridwen's doing."

He could not recall even thinking about it and could barely remember even doing it. He could see the shot in his mind's eye, knew it had come from the bow in his hands, but it was as though someone else's hands had loaded, nocked, and released that last missile.

After some time had passed, supper was announced and everyone took his or her place at the tables.

"Great Father and Mother God, this day we thank ye for these gifts; Thy blessings of food, shelter and brotherhood. May the bonds that bind us together in the defense of Britain only grow stronger through the years. Great Ceridwen, White Goddess, Thy Forest is safe, Thy Land is whole again, and Thy enemies have fled before us in defeat. May Thy Victory bring peace, prosperity and freedom to every corner of Britain! To Holy Victory!" he said with much passion and raised his glass.

"To Holy Victory!" replied the Company as they drank with the King. At that signal, Cai began to serve the much-anticipated meal. Aaronn and Olran were seated at the High Table, along with Lancelot, Bedwyr, Gawaine and of course Arthur. The soup was light and flavorful made from the broth of cooking beans with slivers of onion, carrot and parsnip floating in it. Crusty hard rolls came around too, and Aaronn used them to soak up the delicious soup to the very last bite. The second course was fried trout; the fish was deliciously crisp and the flesh sweet and tender. Blanched green beans accompanied and Aaronn munched contentedly, savoring every bite of the tasty fish. The main course was an impressive rib roast, slowly baked overnight in a special rock salt and herb coating. It was crackling brown on the outside, rare and tender on the inside and Aaronn couldn't help taking a third serving of the roasted beef. A green salad came with it, dressed lightly with olive oil, minced garlic and red wine vinegar. Dessert came out only after all had finished their meal and the adults had a hot cup of strong tea in front of them. Cai wheeled out huge apple and dried blueberry pastries, well-seasoned with cinnamon and cloves. Aaronn sat back after downing a large one of the sweet treats, sipping his tea and relaxing contentedly.

Sprightly music sounded from a far corner of the great room, the ladies swarmed together and went to hear it. Dawn came to stand before Arthur, smiling questioningly.

"Would ye care to dance, My Lord?" she asked.

"Aye, Lady," Arthur smiled gently down on her before turning to Aaronn. "Well, boyo, we should join the ladies for a bit of pleasantry. Ye will have no problem finding partners for there are at least two ladies for every man here at Camelot."

"Sire, 'tis good news," Aaronn chuckled with him. "I confess to being a bit rusty at dancing, I hope the ladies are patient."

"For someone as well-built and handsome as ye are, Sir Aaronn, I am sure any lady will be at her maximum patience," Dawn answered with a giggle as Arthur led her away towards the music. Aaronn and Olran following behind and starry-eyed young women anxious to find a husband among Camelot's knights mobbed the two. The rest of that evening and into the night the revelry continued until the musicians needed a break to rest their fingers. The Merlin appeared from nowhere, or so it seemed, a stool was brought for him to sit.

"Good evening, King Arthur, Knights and Ladies of Camelot. May I offer most hearty congratulations to Sir Aaronn and Sir Olran? We Druids saw the victory at Celidon, we saw the Saxons flee in a total rout. Mother Ceridwen is well pleased with what ye have done and if all goes well then the peace shall stand through all the years of Arthur's rule and Camelot's existence. If they return, they must find only steel awaiting them. Blessed be ye all," he said in a prayer and benediction combined. He ran his skillful fingers across the strings of his great harp and the finely tuned instrument sang at his touch as the assembly found seats and prepared to listen to the Merlin of Britain.

He sang old love songs with a depth of feeling that moved even the sternest Knight to wipe stray tears from his eyes. When he was done with the first round, he went onto something more amusing, a comic recitation of the Knightly Company's names and deeds. When he finished that, someone called out for the tale of Maximus. When that was finished, he sang of CuChulain and his epic fights. On and on the songs went until the musicians were well rested and retuning their instruments. Sir Cai finally appeared, rolling an ale-cart loaded with cups before him.

"Ah now, tha's wha' I been waitin' fer!" Gawaine's thick brogue rolled out. "Coom on, laddies, let us see how fast we kin drain it!" With much laughter and jesting the Knights served themselves and raised their cups in a quick offering to Ceridwen, then drained them dry. Dancing music began again and the mood of the party accelerated into riotry. The Knights danced with gusto and Aaronn watched, happy to be among them. A light touch on his arm caught his attention; he turned to find Isolde, arrayed in her finest pale yellow gown. "Greetings, Sir Aaronn. Would it be too forward of me to ask ye for a dance?" she inquired in her light, pleasant voice.

"I would be delighted to take a turn on the floor with ye, Isolde. As to being forward, how could ye know unless ye ask?" he replied charmingly and led her onto the floor. From that moment on, Aaronn had to keep a list of women's names in his pocket, so many wished to partner him. Olran watched him work, sitting in utter fascination as Aaronn narrowed his choice for serious pursuit. By the time the younger man retired to his room, weary beyond reckoning, Aaronn was fully engaged in the hunt. Olran made sure his own chamber door was carefully closed and locked before he fell, face first and fully dressed into the warm, firm bed. Much, much later, Aaronn followed. He quickly checked Olran, put his inert and snoring body between the covers and then crept from the room.

"Come in Isolde and be quiet. Olran has his own chamber, but he normally sleeps very lightly," he cautioned the girl when she entered the room. They went to Aaronn's bed and lay down, both weary. Isolde's roommate had locked her out, so Aaronn had offered to share his bed. He was far too tired for anything beyond sleeping even though he was tempted greatly and closed his eyes, falling asleep almost immediately. Isolde snuggled closely, and they both enjoyed several hours of undisturbed slumber.

The entire company slept late and Cai prepared a simple, light breakfast of two-grain porridge and various leftovers from last night's banquet. Singly and in groups the Knights appeared, sat at a table and accepted cups of hot tea. Lancelot came to table and sat with Bors, Lionel, Gawaine and Bedwyr and they spoke of horses, his passion.

"Those horses Leodegrance sent are big and strong, but so few of them have any spark of fire to them. If there was a way to introduce the blood of the Arabian horses, we could get that extra quality of heart into Camelot's steeds," he was saying, the others with him smiling as they heard the now-familiar refrain.

"Aye Lance, boot how are ye gonna do it?" Gawaine answered. "Those mares frum Leodegrance are o'er sixteen 'ands 'igh. Ye said th' tallest Arab stallions barely grow t' twelve 'ands. Are they gonna jump oop to mount th' mares?" he chuckled at the image in his head.

Lancelot sighed. "'Tis a problem," he said in mock-dejection.

The others laughed quietly at his expression of despair. Olran and Aaronn appeared, somewhat bleary-eyed, saw the group and joined them.

"Good morning, ye two. Heads all right?" Bedwyr asked, pouring them each a cup of tea and pushing the honey pot towards them.

"I shall be fine, right after breakfast," Olran replied, yawning.

"I feel fine," Aaronn replied brightly, grinning from ear to ear.

"Ye are in a bright mood, Aaronn," Lancelot commented, trying to hide a grin. "It would not be due to the almost irresistible charms of the lovely Isolde, would it?"

Aaronn looked at them all, very calmly as he sipped his tea. Finally, having appeared to give the matter thought very carefully, he cleared his throat and answered. "Truly 'tis none of yer business, First Sword," he replied simply and dug into the plate of food Cai set before him. The senior Knights assumed surprised expressions and silence reigned at the table. When Aaronn was finished, he and Olran politely took their leave and went out to the stables. The senior Knights watched them go, grinning at each other in appreciation of Aaronn's comment.

"He is a good man, not to kiss and tell," Lancelot pronounced, wondering what kind of man "little" Aaronn had become.

Aaronn and Olran waited until they were well outside the earshot of the older men, then the both of them broke out in peals of delighted laughter.

"Aaronn, 'twas prime what ye told them, ye sure stopped them in their tracks with that retort," Olran finally gasped out, wiping his eyes.

"Well, 'twas not any of their business. I have heard the Ladies of Avalon complain that men share too many intimate details among themselves. I resolved long ago that I would have no part in idle gossip. Besides, they should all know better," he added frostily.

Olran grinned as they proceeded down to the stables. As they walked Aaronn patted himself down, his routine assurance that all his weaponry was in place. He stopped short just inside the stable door, face wreathed in dismay.

"By the Goddess, brother, I have lost a knife!" he said, somewhat shaken.

"'Tis probably in Saxon lands by now, Aaronn, 'tis no sense in looking for it," Olran said, knowing his friend's way well.

"I am going anyway, are ye coming with me?" Aaronn asked, determined to find his lost weapon without which he felt somewhat naked.

"Aye…if only to say I told ye so," Olran grinned. "Our steeds are not yet ready to ride, so I shall see if we can borrow some."

"Thanks brother," Aaronn smiled in return, grateful for his assistance.

Just then, a short, hard-looking man strode by, leading Arthur's white stallion to his stall. He stopped, looked first at Olran, then at Aaronn very carefully.

"I've not seen ye two before, I reckon," he began. "I am Sir Ulster, the stablemaster. What kin I do fer ye?" he asked respectfully.

"Good morning, Sir Ulster. I am Sir Aaronn and he is Sir Olran. We need to borrow two steeds to take a little ride back to Celidon."

"Of course, ye'll need 'em 'till yers are trained. Ye are the ones who took over training those two wild ones," Ulster agreed readily. He called into the tack room, summoning a tow-headed gangling lad. "Heya Pwyll, saddle up a couple of the spares fer these two, will ye?" he ordered, then turned back to Olran as the lad sprinted down the corridor. "So, what do ye think yer real chances are with that jug-headed roan?" he asked, a trace of youthful wagering spirit in his voice.

"Why, looking to make odds, Sir Ulster?" Olran grinned, seeing the older man's start of surprise. Clearly, Olran had guessed the man's motive correctly, quite to the shock of Ulster.

"Aye, ye've caught me. So, what think ye?" he smiled a small smile of admission.

"Ye can bet on me safely. Lead them a bit, but settle on four to one," Olran told him, a serious look on his face, though his eyes twinkled with reckless humor. The young ostler returned quickly, leading a red-white paint and a liver-colored horse, fully dressed and ready to ride.

"Thank ye, Pwyll, 'twas efficiently done. Ye have a lad with some smarts there, Ulster," Olran complimented, but checked out the girth strap and other rigging before he mounted. Both stableman's eyes rose in questions, and Olran quickly explained his caution. "I had a family full of practical jokers. They thought 'twas funny not to pull the straps tight. I learned to ride bareback that way," The two men nodded, but made no comment.

"Thank ye for the loan, Sir Ulster," Aaronn said, leading the horse outside. "We will have them back by nightfall."

Olran followed and they mounted up, urging the horses into a steady canter. The animals were well trained, their gait comfortable and conducive to discussion.

"So, here we are, Aaronn, junior Knights of Camelot and Ceridwen's men," Olran began as the miles slipped away. "Ye have already told off the First Knight and his subcommanders, what is next?" he grinned.

"We need to set up practice areas that are private and quiet to keep our skills honed," Aaronn proposed. "And we need to know the 'Maze' inside Camelot's walls much better than we do now."

"Aye and our clothespresses need false bottoms for our working weapons and clothing," Olran added.

"As far as our secret work goes, we should begin doing some snooping around here and there," Aaronn went on.

"I know just where to start," Olran muttered quietly. "Westerland Keep."

"Yer father is hardly the realm's worst enemy, Olran," Aaronn chuckled.

"True, but if only half of what I suspect of him is so, 'tis good as any place to start," Olran said seriously.

"Ye should tell me all about it Olran," Aaronn stated, his curiosity piqued. "Ye have made a lot of inferences over the years, but told me naught of the truth of it all."

So Olran told him, finally cleansing his soul of all the secrets he had suppressed during his years at Westerland Keep. Aaronn listened, incredulous as his friend rattled off names of major and minor nobles who had frequented his family's hold during Arthur's reign. Olran's memory was amazing, Aaronn thought, as he listed the many times King Lot and Lady Morgause had played "trade yer wife" with King Warren and Lady Justine.

"It sounds like Westerland and its allies are our first case after all," Aaronn grinned when Olran finished his recitation.

"I told ye so," the latter chuckled, without humor.

They topped the small rise that bordered the battlefield, pausing for a moment to recall it all. Aaronn tried to remember where he had been during the times he had used his blades as he rode down the short, steep hillside. Dismounting when he reached the bottom he began his search, while Olran remained aboard, on guard with bow and arrows in hand.

"Come down here and help me look, Olran," Aaronn said exasperated after a bit.

"The Severn is only two miles away, Aaronn. Someone should remain on guard," he returned, stubbornly.

Aaronn sighed, knowing it was useless to argue the point further, especially after Olran strung his bow and loaded an arrow casually. He searched carefully, finding a small bag of booty in the process, but failed to locate the missing weapon. Finally, he gave up and remounted, whispering a prayer to Ceridwen to somehow return the blade.

"Come on, brother. Let's go home," he sighed sadly.

"Aye, Cai was cooking up some nice fat pheasants, stuffed with wild rice," Olran replied wistfully. "Aaronn, do ye think I'll ever gain any weight?"

Aaronn's mouth quirked into a half-smile as he replied; "I do not know, brother, but if anyone's cooking could help, 'twould be Cai's."

"I can taste those birds already, Aaronn. Come on, I shall race ye!" Olran laughed and urged the horse into a fast gallop. Aaronn could only follow in his wake, for the princeling had ever been able to get more out of a horse. It was just past sundown when they returned to Camelot, and they only just had time to wash up, change into clean clothing and dash downstairs for the common supper always served in the great room. They sat at the places marked for them, knowing that the assignments were permanent, laying the napkins across their laps.

"Would ye care for wine, Sir Aaronn?" Isolde's smoky voice asked invitingly.

"Thank ye, Isolde." Aaronn answered, refraining from letting his eyes feast on her form under the gown. "Some wine would be welcome indeed." She poured for him, all the while trying to make eye contact with him, which he strenuously avoided. He hoped to maintain the aura of secrecy he had established that morning. To the others and the girl, it seemed his was resisting Isolde's considerable charms with little difficulty. Isolde moved on, but her eyes were confused and Aaronn resolved to speak to her later about public displays of affection between them.

The salad that night was boiled lentils, seasoned with garlic and bay leaves, dressed with fresh minced basil, red wine vinegar and olive oil. Whole roasted pheasants, stuffed with wild grains, fried mushrooms and field greens followed, eagerly Olran bit into the crackling brown skins. Delight wreathed his face as he chewed in silent contentment. Aaronn also enjoyed the meal all the more, watching his friend ravenously consume half a pheasant plus extra servings of the accompanying vegetables and cheeses. Dessert was an enormous cake, heavily flavored with cinnamon and orange water. Pots of hot tea came around with it, talk around the table included Lancelot's pet project, importing Arabian stallions to improve the bloodlines of British war-horses. Those at the table with the First Knight sighed collectively, Aaronn and Olran picked up their cups, wandered over to the table and sat across from the First Knight, listening.

"I tell ye, Artos, if we could obtain excellent bloodlines from Arabia, we could alter horseflesh forever in Britain!" he went on excitedly.

"Aye, Lancelot, I agree," Arthur chuckled, smiling broadly. "Ye should write yer friends in the desert and tell them yer coming for a business visit."

"Wha…what?" asked Lancelot, surprised.

"Ye heard me. If ye go now, ye will easily be back in time for the spring raiding season. Go, bring us back some of Arabia's finest and take yer squire. Sir Olran seems to have an eye for horseflesh, so he should go as well. Leave as soon as possible and hurry back?" he ordered and was enveloped in an embrace from Lancelot.

"Thank ye, Sire. I shall return and with a shipload full of Arabia's best as quickly as the Goddess will grant. Ronald, come with me boyo. Ye have a letter to take to Land's End for me," he ordered as he left the table.

"Aye, My Lord Lancelot," the boy answered and all could hear the excitement underneath his calm voice.

"Sir Olran, get a bag packed and keep it so. We may have to ride hard to catch the tide," Lancelot ordered crisply.

"Aye, First Sword," Olran replied, already daydreaming about horses running swiftly over the desert sands. Lancelot went to his room, with Ronald running to keep up with him.

"I am for bed too, Aaronn," Olran yawned sleepily and turned to the King. "Good night, Sire. May the Goddess grant ye deep rest," he said formally, saluted and strode off slowly.

"And ye, Sir Aaronn?" Arthur grinned.

"I have some errands to run before I sleep, Sire. I wish ye good night and pleasant dreams," Aaronn responded dryly, saluted and strode off after Olran. He caught up with his friend and together they found the small, inset dragon key in a side corridor off the great room. It slid aside noiselessly and they slipped inside, closing it behind them. Up to their shared room they went, and when they reached their doorway, they entered through the sliding panel, locking it behind them.

"'Tis nice to know it still works, eh Olran?" Aaronn chuckled.

"Aye," Olran agreed, yawning again. "Ye want me to lock my door tonight?" he asked, grinning from ear to ear.

Aaronn smiled with him. "I suppose 'twould be a good idea. Isolde likes to be assured of privacy."

"Tell her to be quieter this time, would ye Aaronn?" Olran said, straight-faced, but his eyes twinkled with mischief. "'Tis what woke me this morning, ye know. I am sorry if my grouchiness was overwhelming."

"I shall tell her that," Aaronn acknowledge, a smile creasing his face.

"Good night, Aaronn. Success in the hunt," Olran said over his shoulder as he entered his inner chamber, closed the door and turned the lock shut. Aaronn inspected his dress completely before he went looking for Isolde. He found her quickly and led her away from the group of gossiping women in the sewing room to a more private doorway.

"'Twas very kind of ye to seek me out, Sir Aaronn," she began, her voice clearly angered and affronted. "But I believe ye explained yerself very well at supper."

For answer, Aaronn took her in his arms and pressed a gentle, passionate and lingering kiss onto her full red lips. She was all but breathless when he released her mouth from that embrace, so Aaronn continued to hold her while he explained.

"I was asked by others if we had shared the Mother's Rite, Isolde. I told them 'twas none of their business. I had to seem only passingly interested in yer very effective display. 'Twas most difficult to seem distant, I assure ye," he chuckled softly into her ear before he pressed his lips against her neck. "Also, I should have explained that I do not hold with overt, public displays of affection between lovers."

"O, ...I see," the aroused woman panted into his ear as his well-trained hands ran over her body, everywhere at once or so it seemed.

"Am I forgiven then?" Aaronn asked, smiling, for he knew her answer before it was given. "Come, Isolde, let me make amends?" he asked softly.

"Aye, Aaronn," she managed to reply. He took her by the hand and led her back to his room, wanting to avoid questions for both their sakes. Entering, Isolde began untying the laced front of her gown and Aaronn stopped her after first locking the door.

"Please, allow me?" he spoke tenderly and took over the task. The Mother's blessing was shared between them and afterwards they slept comfortably until Aaronn was awakened by a soft thump. He looked over the edge of the bed and found Isolde on the floor, looking very sleepy and confused.

"Shhh," Aaronn whispered. "Ye fell out of bed, my dear. 'Tis a bit narrow for two, aye?"

"Aye," she yawned. "I had best be dressed and gone before Sir Olran awakens. He was so grouchy last time he found me here with ye."

"I meant to speak to ye about that. It seems ye are a bit noisy when engaging in the Mother's rite, 'tis why he awoke prematurely and was grouchy."

Isolde's face reddened, but she said nothing and quietly got dressed. Aaronn wrapped up in a warm robe and saw her back to her room.

"Do ye think I make too much noise?" she asked in a whisper when they were outside her door. He smiled and answered carefully.

"Perhaps, but at least I know for certain that ye are enjoying yerself as much as I am during our time together."

"I shall try to be less vocal, My Lord, truly. Ye are like no one I have ever met, Lord Aaronn. I am not yet ready to marry, as I am sure ye are not. Our time together will at least teach me to please the man that chooses me to wife," Isolde spoke her heart.

Aaronn embraced her for her honesty. "I am sure we have much to learn, Isolde, good night."

"Good night, Sir Aaronn," she answered warmly and with a last furtive embrace she fled within her room.

Aaronn walked back up the hallway, looked around carefully, and then ducked into a side corridor. At the end, he found a blank wall and felt all over it with his palms. Sure enough, he found the dragon key and pressed. The whole wall slipped back into the secret passageway and closed up tightly when Aaronn found the inner mechanism. He went carefully, trying to remember where he was, finally locating the passageway back to the Knight's wing and his own room. Entering, he found his bed remade and a kettle steaming beside the hearth. Olran appeared, freshly washed and dressed from behind the privacy screen. He took up two mugs, handed one to Aaronn without a word and poured for the both of them.

"How long have ye been awake?" Aaronn asked as he sipped the brew after adding a generous amount of honey.

"Since Isolde fell out of bed," Olran chuckled. "I am going to have a word with my horse, the Jughead. He is going to have to wait 'till I return from Arabia for the real fun, but I shall ask Ulster to continue his lunge line work," he laughed a bit as he honeyed his tea and sipped carefully.

"Good idea," Aaronn commented, realizing that Olran was leaving with Lancelot. "Do ye want me to take care of yer horse?"

"Nay, ye will be busy with Ceridwen's business, Aaronn. Evil will not wait," Olran returned. "Just try not to do it all before I return?"

All Aaronn could do was chuckle and sip his tea. When he was finished he dressed and followed Olran down to the stables. His friend took up a long length of line and a halter before he went to the stall where his mount stood placidly in his stall. The second Olran was in with him, the ugly jugheaded stallion tried to pin him against the side of the stall and Aaronn cried out in alarm.

"Olran! Are ye all right?"

"Of course, 'tis not a horse in all of Britain that I cannot train and ride," his friend's tight voice answered as he pushed the Jughead's body away from him. "I used to sneak out into the horse barns and ride the greenest horses when I was younger. Every horse that came to Westerland eventually accepted me on its back! This one may be mean and nasty, but he has a brain and courage too. 'Twill be a glorious fight, but I shall win or he will be dead. Just ye watch!" Olran answered as he brought his knee under the horse's belly, hard and sudden. The wiry young man was stronger than he appeared, Aaronn knew, but even he was surprised when the horse grunted in pain at the impact and stepped aside, eyes rolling as he thought about what had just happened.

"Well, do ye want more or shall we go and train for a while?" Olran asked irritably.

The horse made no attempts to hurt his rider until Olran slipped the halter on and fastened the line securely to the ring under the horse's jaw. He led the Jughead out of the stall, then into the training arena where he began to work the horse, teaching him to stand and follow. Aaronn watched, fascinated as his friend's expertise with equines was revealed. He observed carefully, trying to fix in his head the procedure Olran was demonstrating for him. After an hour had passed, the stallion was panting and wet with lather, so Olran walked him until the sweat dried before taking him to bathe in the Cam. The horse sported and splashed in the slow moving waters, even getting to his knees and rolling in the shallows before he was finished. Olran and Aaronn could only laugh until tears rolled down their cheeks at his antics, then they pulled him from the water and turned him loose in his isolated paddock.

"There now, ye have worked hard and had yer fun, eh?" Olran crooned affectionately to the stallion. "As soon as ye can behave yerself like a gentleman, ye can be with the others."

The horse cocked his jughead around to eye the other war-horses, the proceeded to turn his flanks in their direction and lift his tail to emit a loud expulsion of internal gases. That set Olran off laughing hard again, at length the fit subsided and he gasped to Aaronn. "He thinks himself superior to all the other Knight's horses, 'tis why he is so hard to get along with."

"'Twould take some doing, to be better than all of them," Aaronn laughed along with his breathless friend.

"He had best prove it now, Aaronn," Olran returned, wiping his eyes with a large kerchief. "I am going to work him 'till he is," he vowed.

"Can ye help me with my horse?" Aaronn asked. "All I need is for ye to show me what to do."

"Surely, Aaronn," Olran agreed readily.

They went to fetch the warsteed, the animal turned out to be malleable enough and at the end of his hour the stallion had learned to walk, trot and stand on command. Aaronn repeated the river treatment with his horse; while the stallion seemed to appreciate the bath, he was very dignified about it and barely muddied the waters. Shaking each hoof carefully as he emerged from the river, he then shook the rest of the water from his hide. The huge black stallion walked to Aaronn and nudged him a bit, then looked at him a bit askance.

"I'll remember an apple next time, big fellow," Aaronn apologized, smiling. "How about Eclipse for a name, in recognition of the spot on yer heel?" The horse nodded his head vigorously, then trotted away, feet high and tail flared, towards the adjoining corral of fillies.

"He is like his rider, eh Aaronn?" Olran commented dryly as he watched the stallion strut and snort for the fillies' inspection. Aaronn only grinned wider as he rubbed his growling stomach.

"Come on Olran, I need something to eat," he urged. Olran sprinted away, laughing, but Aaronn caught up quickly and the two arrived at the Castle shoulder to shoulder. They ran up the secret stairs to their room, washed, changed and returned via the regular route.

"Good morning, ye two. Breakfast is nearly over and lunch is still two hours away. Try to be a bit earlier tomorrow?" Cai reproved gently with a smile. "And when ye need apples for training rewards, take them from the front baskets, not the back ones please?" Cai's voice had taken on an instructive, pleading tone that Aaronn remembered well. He just could not help replying quietly;

"Aye, Uncle Sir Cai."

Cai's face blanched, then the grin returned even broader. "Good boy, little Aaronn," he answered just as quietly and moved off, after serving two bowls of oat porridge, a pot of honey and two mugs of tea. The two wolfed the food, drained the mugs and returned to the out of doors. Aaronn determined to locate a site for his practice targets, a place protected from the winter snows and summer heat. The two spent the rest of the day in the woods surrounding Camelot, scouting and evaluating sites until they found one that Aaronn found suitable.

Quickly, the two cleared a rough circle amongst the tall maples and oaks. When they finished, Aaronn marked a rune sign carefully on an oak tree, after first offering a quick prayer.

"Brother Oak, please allow me to mark this area with a protective rune sign, only into thy outer bark. I shall not pierce into the inner lining or the wood, but I must be able to guard this place and find it. Sister Dryad of this tree, I wish thee no harm," he spoke gently to the tree, then laid his hands on the place he wished to mark, just as Brother Michael had taught him. He felt the tree's lifebeat faintly, and no objection surfaced in his mind.

"Thank ye, I shall work quickly and painlessly as possible," he told the tree then pulled out his boot knife. Working as quickly as he could, Aaronn marked his sign unobtrusively in the oak's outer bark. When he was done, he stood back and inspected his work. Olran's stomach rumbled loudly as he waited for his fastidiously careful friend to assure himself that the mark was adequately hidden. Aaronn heard, adjusted a bush branch one last time and stood, finally satisfied with the screening effect.

"There, that should do it, eh brother?" he commented, trying not to laugh.

"O, I don't know, Aaronn," Olran replied in a lazy tone. "I think we should dig up and replant the whole grove, just to be safe."

Aaronn broke out in a rare series of loud guffaws and put his arm around his friend's shoulder. "I think the Mother's hand has done a fine job here already. I know ye must be famished, so let us be off," he chuckled and led his friend away.

The baths were hot and steamy when they returned to the Castle, gratefully the pair sank to their necks in one of the deep wooden tubs. Slowly, their weary muscles relaxed and unknotted, they enjoyed the tall, cool mugs of Orkney ale that Isolde brought them. Nodding their thanks, the two sipped carefully of the cool drinks while in the hot tub, not wanting to distress their already tasked bodies.

The Orkney brothers occupied the tub directly beside them; Gawaine leaned over and addressed them.

"Aaronn, Olran, good day t' ye both," he greeted. "So tell me Olran, will ye be able t' train tha' Jughead ye've chosen as yer mount?"

"Only the Goddess' own steeds are beyond mortal man, brother Gawaine," Olran replied seriously. "All others are both biddable and trainable when handled by the right man."

"I'll lay ye ten gold pieces ye won't ha' him ready t' take inta battle by Spring," Agravaine proposed, not being able to help himself. He had been one of those bitten by the nondescript horse when he had tried to claim the beast himself.

"I'll take soom o' tha'," Gawaine chimed in. "Tha' Jughead bit me on me arse when he firs' arrived."

The others in the baths chuckled heartily, a few more made noises about wanting in on the wager.

"I only ask one consideration, fellows," Olran added after everyone had spoken. "Sir Ulster is going to be training his gaits for me while I am with Lancelot in the desert. Does anyone object to that?"

A general nay sounded around the room and Olran grinned smugly, turned to Aaronn and whispered triumphantly; "Now I have them. They do not know me very well, do they?"

Aaronn could only grin in answer as the two finished their soak, rinsed off with clean water and toweled their bodies dry. Wrapping up in the soft cotton robes, they scurried for the secret door. No one was in the hallway, and they swiftly entered the hidden corridor and went in silence to their room. Once there, they dressed in clean, plain clothes, tied back their growing locks into neat queues. Olran's stomach grumbled loudly as did Aaronn's as they left their room. Once in the great room, the two went directly to the sideboard and piled plates full with thinly sliced roasted venison, fowl, bread and cheese and whole boiled eggs. The two ate as they made the rounds of the great room. Some of the noble houses had sent more of their daughters to invade the bachelor King's home, the beauties now decorated Camelot's great room nicely, Aaronn thought to himself. At least I shall not have a problem diverting myself from more serious work, he grinned inwardly.

"Aaronn, look there, bless me if 'tis not King Caw's youngest daughter, Julia. My, she has grown to be a chesty one, aye?" he chuckled. "I remember when she braided her hair into two long braids and had a chest flatter than mine."

"Then she has grown!" Aaronn whispered back, his eyes feasting on the raven-haired beauty. "Introduce me Olran, duty calls," he urged his friend.

Olran walked to her and engaged her in conversation, then escorted her back to the table to acquaint Aaronn with Caw's virginal third daughter. She thrived on their attention; Aaronn played the perfect gentleman while keeping the chit's wineglass full.

"Why, Prince Olran!" she gushed when Aaronn sat her between them. "'Tis so good to see ye again, Westerland during the holidays was so dreary without ye."

"I am Prince of Westerland no longer, Julia, only Sir Olran of Camelot," Olran informed her, smiling carefully.

"O!" Julia answered, wonderingly. "Why have ye abandoned yer family?"

"I have three brothers, Julia. Westerland Keep will never fall to me, so I bid it farewell. I can earn a land grant for myself here at Camelot. All I can ever earn at Westerland is abuse," Olran informed her frostily.

That ended the girl's curiosity, the rest of the evening she spent in the glow of Aaronn's attentions. He worked hard to charm the girl and get her to talk about Caw's business activities. Julia knew more than she would openly admit, by the time Aaronn escorted her to her chambers he had a good idea whom the petty King did most of his business with. Time and time again, the name of Lord Evin Merin came into the conversation causing Aaronn to wonder just how deep into the shitpile of dirty dealings Merin really was. He resolved to investigate the man further.

"Good night to ye, Lady Julia. I have enjoyed yer company tonight, very much, I hope to enjoy it again soon," he spoke quietly with intensity.

"I hope so as well, Sir Aaronn. My father and mother will be joining me here at Camelot sometime after Samhain. I hope to be able to talk with yer parents soon as well," Julia responded, shivering with the excitement of being alone with this very handsome man

"I am the King's ward, Julia. My parents are…gone," Aaronn improvised quickly.

"O, I am sorry, Sir Aaronn. It must be awful to lose one's parents so soon in life," she said sympathetically and moved closer to him. Aaronn put his arms around her and let her snuggle against him for a bit. She suddenly stood on her tiptoes and softly brushed her lips against his neck. Aaronn bent and answered her timid advance, boldly pressing his much more experienced lips against hers. Obviously, the young girl had never been kissed by a man before, so Aaronn took his time and made sure she was good and aroused before he released her, enjoying the experience.

"Sir Aaronn, I know I am supposed to slap ye now, but I know I asked for that. Growing up in the Northlands under Christian priests was very hard, they tried their best to teach me proper and ladylike behavior…" she tried to explain, halting when she saw Aaronn smile and hold a finger up to her lips.

"I know what the black robes say is the proper and seemly way for a woman to act, but I was raised on Avalon and Dragon Isle. I have therefore, a somewhat different attitude. I would never take anything from ye that ye were not willing to give," Aaronn responded warmly, keeping his voice soft. "But there are those men, not of Camelot, who would have taken more than a mere kiss from ye after that shy, sweet little advance. Please, Lady Julia, be more careful in the future?" he warned and kissed her hands, one at a time.

"I thank ye for the warning, Sir Aaronn. I shall take it to heart, I assure ye," Julia answered, liking him very much.

"Good, I cannot abide a stupid woman!" Aaronn answered with a small smile.

She blushed and went to her door, opened it a bit before turning back to him and kissing him on the mouth again. When they parted, she went inside her room and shut the door before her resolve to remain a virgin until marriage fled her. Aaronn grinned widely, took out a kerchief and made sure to remove any trace of cosmetics from his face before launching a search for Isolde. Julia's virginal kiss had affected him much more than the chit knew, he thought, Isolde's company and comfort was now necessary to heal his disquiet of spirit. He went down to the great room, found her clearing the last of the supper dishes from the table and spoke with her.

"Isolde, can ye come with me? I have something to show ye, 'tis a surprise," he said invitingly.

"Can ye not show me here?" she asked wearily.

"Isolde 'tis a big surprise, I should like to give it to ye in private," Aaronn insistently pulled on her arm.

"Sir Aaronn, I have been working all day. I am hot, sweaty and tired, and I need a nice, long soak," Isolde said stubbornly.

"I can arrange for that, Isolde. Get yer chores finished then come up to my room for yer surprise. I am certain ye will like it," Aaronn persuaded, using a more gentle tone. Isolde looked at him, questions in her eyes, then she nodded assent.

"I hope so, Sir Aaronn, and ye best not be jesting with me," Isolde said warningly, while wagging a finger at him. "I am too tired to abide one of yer famous jokes."

For answer, Aaronn kissed her palms lingeringly before he strode away, his mind working fast. Entering the kitchen, he found Sir Cai consulting his huge recipe book, the seneschal looked up when he heard the footfalls approaching.

"What can I do for ye, Aaronn?" he asked, pleasantly.

"Is there a tub I can take up to my room for a private bath?" he asked.

"Of course, I shall have Flynn and Gwynn bring up some nice hot water and an herbal packet. Do ye need food also?" he asked, guessing Aaronn's motives.

"Maybe just cold meats and bread, perhaps some wine too?" Aaronn answered, hopefully.

"Of course, and ye will be needing two glasses?" Cai queried, knowingly. Aaronn grinned widely and nodded. "Then go on and make yerself all pretty for Isolde," Cai chuckled quietly. Aaronn looked at him, a bit surprised, receiving a wink from the seneschal. "Well, boyo, ye know nothing much happens around here without my hearing of it. Besides, Isolde's temper has been improved of late, and she has been asking a lot of questions about ye. Ye need have no worry though, I am a discreet man and I shall not break yer confidence to any but Arthur, but only if he asks. Pax?" he declared and stuck out his arm.

Aaronn clasped forearms with him, and then embraced the older man hard and with affection. "Thank ye, Sir Cai, 'tis nice to have someone to trust. Who better than the seneschal of Camelot castle?" he grinned fiercely.

"Who better indeed?" Cai chuckled with him and made a shooing motion with his hands. Aaronn dashed out the swinging doors, ducked into a secret door and ran up the hidden way to his room. He found Olran packing some final things in his bag.

"Where are ye going?" asked Aaronn as he shut the panel behind him.

"Lancelot has found passage to Arabia and wants to leave on the next tide. We are to sleep at Land's End Inn tonight and leave in the morning," Olran explained, no trace of weariness in his excited eyes. He tied his bag closed, added his quiver and bow by way of lashings sewn on either side of the soft-sided leather bag, then slid his sword and scabbard onto his back.

"Well, Sir Olran," Aaronn said, proud for his friend to be included on such an important mission. "Be careful, aye? I do not want to lose ye before we even get started."

"Of course I shall be careful," Olran chuckled. "What do ye think I am anyway, an unseasoned boy?" he added, mock-indignantly.

The two embraced hard and wished each other good fortune as well as the Mother's blessing. "Aaronn, do ye want me to bring something back from the desert for ye?" Olran asked as he went out the door.

"Ye could bring home one of those exotic dancing girls to entertain me privately," Aaronn laughed.

"I shall look into it. Tell Isolde hullo for me, eh?" Olran called back over his shoulder.

"Surely," Aaronn called back and waved one last time as Olran turned the corner and disappeared.

Aaronn sighed, already missing his best friend's company. He stepped back into the room and straightened up a bit. A knock sounded some ten minutes later, and Aaronn opened to admit Gwynn and Flynn, the huge twins from Ireland who did most of Cai's heavy work in the kitchens.

"Evenin', Sir Aaronn. Sir Cai said ye'd be needin' a private bath t'night?" one of the huge, bulky men asked.

"Aye, are ye Flynn?" Aaronn questioned.

"Nae, I'm Gwynn," the speaker laughed heartily as he rolled the tub through the door. A line of older pageboys followed, each carrying a large, steaming bucket of water. Flynn brought up the rear, adding a final large kettle of water and throwing in a packet of dried rose petals, lavender sprigs and honeysuckle blossoms to steep in the water. The fragrance was delightful, Aaronn observed as he thanked them while they filed from the room. A few moments passed before a light tapping came on the door and Isolde's voice asked to be admitted. Aaronn, now freshly robed and wearing comfortable slippers answered, holding a cup of wine for her and offering it as soon as the door was secured.

"Thank ye, Sir Aaronn," Isolde accepted the glass gratefully as she saw the steaming tub in front of the hearth. "A private tub, just for me?" she asked, surprised.

"Aye, Isolde. Ye said ye needed one, I thought it might be just the thing before I give ye yer surprise," Aaronn answered softly.

"The bath is surprise enough, Aaronn, and very thoughtful of ye too," Isolde responded and sat tiredly to remove her shoes. Aaronn assisted in her undressing, then helped her into the tub and took up brush and soap for her back. Both people found this most pleasant, soon they were both in the tub scrubbing each other. The Mother was well worshipped and granted them Her blessing of calmer spirits and relaxed bodies, the two slept well with only pleasant dreams. Waking easily before dawn, Aaronn woke Isolde with a gentle kiss then helped her dress.

"That surprise ye arranged was very nice, My Lord Aaronn. No one has ever done anything so thoughtful as providing a private bath for me, and I thank ye for it," Isolde spoke slowly, trying to find the right words. "Ye know I have some small skill at massage, if ye should ever need those services, ye have only to ask."

"Can ye visit me tonight?" Aaronn answered and warmly embraced her.

"What are ye going to do about Lady Julia?" asked Isolde impishly.

"She is but a virginal girl; ye are a warm-blooded, experienced woman. I much prefer the latter of the two," Aaronn stated emphatically. "Lady Julia can only be a diversionary tactic. If they all think I am wooing her, they will not be looking at us," he explained to her at least part of the truth. The rest that he withheld from her was that Julia was a vital source of innocent information within Ravensdale, Caw's castle. She knew who was there and when; with such information the Black Knight could act with informed decisiveness.

"Can I see ye tonight, if Sir Olran does not mind?" Isolde asked.

"Sir Olran is sailing for the desert with Sir Lancelot at this very moment, Isolde. Come as soon as ye get my note, I shall be sure to leave it somewhere where ye will be sure to find it," he assured her and kissed her quickly, then quickly propelled her out the door.

Dressing in working black, he made himself a cup of tea, already missing Olran's presence as he drank it. He went downstairs, breakfasted quickly on ham and griddlecakes with more tea before he sped away to his secret practice area. He was quite surprised to find the Druid brother Michael there waiting for him.

"Ye have made a good choice, boyo. This place hums with the Mother's energies. It should aid us in our work," he said after embracing his student.

"Work, my Master?" Aaronn questioned.

"Of course, son, did ye truly think I taught ye everything I know?" Michael laughed heartily. "Now, lend a hand here and let us set up some targets for ye."

The two spent all that day clearing the circle more completely, replanting several stands of brush. In his mind, Aaronn could hear Olran's laughter as clearly as if his friend were standing right beside him, 'I told ye so, brother,' while he dug and replanted to increase the screening effect. Finally, as the sun dropped into late midday, he was able to plant the target's bases firmly into the ground. The two stood in the center of the throwing area they had created, at last satisfied as to its total security.

"Ye should have no problem keeping this place secret, Aaronn. Congratulations earning yer knighthood so very quickly."

"Thank ye Master, for all yer help. I was wondering how I was going to do this without Olran's assistance," Aaronn expressed his gratitude. "Is his journey going to be a safe one?" he asked of his teacher.

"He is with Lancelot du Lac, Aaronn. He could be no safer except in Ceridwen's arms," Michael chuckled comfortingly. Aaronn grinned, assured that his friend would be returning from the desert safely.

"Will ye help me train my horse, Eclipse? Arthur gave him to me greenbroken, and Olran taught him a little before he left, but he needs so much more training. The Black Knight needs his steed trained and ready to ride as soon as possible, eh?" Aaronn asked, hoping that Michael would agree. The Druid Master laughed a bit and nodded his assent.

"Of course, but bring him here. No one is to know that I am even around, understand?" Michael instructed firmly.

"Aye, Master," Aaronn agreed, embracing the older man again, glad to have his teacher with him. It would make the long months without his best friend much easier to bear.

"Now go on and wash yerself. 'Tis time to be Sir Aaronn again. Ye watch yerself among the daughters of the Christian lords, boyo. They have a totally different agenda where men are concerned, most of them just want to find a husband and raise fat babies. If ye violate their chastity, even with a simple kiss, it could be the basis for a forced marriage," Michael warned him. "A girl's first time should be blessed by the Mother and her parents, after her instruction in the Mysteries."

"Aye, Master. Aaronn shall not be known as a rude despoiler of virgins, I assure ye," he laughed.

"Ye show great wisdom for someone so young, boyo," Michael replied. "I must go now. See ye here in the morning, boyo, and bring yer steed with ye."

"I shall be here early," Aaronn replied brightly, waving as his Master walked slowly away. Aaronn only blinked once and the Master disappeared from sight, as was his habit.

Out on the ocean, Olran gloried in the brisk salt air, once his body had accustomed itself to the constant rolling motion of the ship. As he watched the seagulls play on the trade winds, he "saw" Aaronn clearing the new target area and thought to himself, 'I told ye so!' He hoped that Aaronn would not do all the work before he returned to Britain, then smiled as he realized just how much work there would be for the both of them for years to come. Lancelot's voice called him below for supper, after the meal he played a game of chess with the First Knight. Predictably, the senior Knight beat him soundly, but it took quite some time for him to do it. Congratulating Olran on the game, Lancelot called his squire to him and the two retired to their beds. Olran was too excited to be sleepy; he went above and heard the sound of sailors gambling with dice, the clinking of gold coins. Nothing sounds like the music of gold, Olran grinned to himself as he walked over to the huddled circle.

"Hullo boyos, wha'cha doin'?" he asked innocently in a Westerland drawl.

The sailors moved aside for him, winking at each other conspiratorially. He hunkered down among them, out of the cool breeze.

"We're just playin' a game of dice, youngling. Wanna bet a few coins on a pass or two?" the one-eyed First Mate asked.

"I do not have any coins, but perhaps this would do?" Olran replied, pulling a solid silver torque from his belt pouch.

"Is tha' solid silver, laddie?" the mate asked, looking at it with longing in his eyes. Olran laughed to himself, seeing the greed in the man's eyes and knowing him for what he was.

"Aye, took it off a slain Saxon myself!" Olran boasted to complete the image of a spoiled boy he had built in their eyes.

"I'd put a value o' fifty gold denarii?" the Mate proposed. Olran nodded and the small weight coins were piled in front of him. The dice were also passed and Olran carefully took their measure in his palm. They seemed a bit off, so he bet carefully on the first pass. They rolled to a three and Olran nodded to himself. He glanced at them again, taking a quick and closer "look" at them, "seeing" the extra weights hammered into the number dots and concealed by carefully applied paint. He compensated for the extra weights with techniques learned in his young years, scoring seven straight times. Not only did he win back his torque; he managed to impoverish the sailors as well. He then purposefully lost all the coins except for the original fifty and the torque, throwing seven straight losses so as to avoid a reputation for winning too often among the sailors.

"Well fellas, I am off to bed now. Thanks for the games, though. Sleep ye sound and may the Goddess watch over ye," he said, yawning in truth. He went below; those sailors not on watch went to their bunks as well.

Once in his quarters, Olran gleefully stashed the gold coins away in his quiver and blessed the Goddess for his good fortune. He extracted from his luggage a set of his own personal dice and put them in his pouch, then went to bed. In the morning, he dressed and took a quick meal with Lancelot and Ronald before walking up on deck. The Second Mate waved to him, as did several of the crew and Olran waved in return. He walked over to where the Second was working and pulled him aside.

"I played some interesting dice last night with the First Mate," he commented.

"Ye played dice with the First Mate?"

"Aye and I think his dice are fixed. I cannot abide a cheat, so I am going fix him for good. Would ye like to help?" Olran proposed, figuring these men preyed on each other like sharks. All he would have to do is bloody the water to start a feeding frenzy.

"Sooooo! That's how th' bastard's done it. He's stolen good gold coins from everyone on this ship, we wondered a' his luck, but could never prove a thing!" the Second Mate whispered, hate in his voice.

Olran grinned inwardly before making the wound deeper; assuring that it was bleeding freely. "Personally, I think his honesty should be tested. I have an honest set 'tis an extra that I always carry, take 'em and test him, with my blessings," he offered blithely.

"Ye leave it to me, laddie. He's cheated his last," the Second Mate laughed nastily and took the proffered dice. Shoving them into his pocket, he limped away from the princeling on his wooden left leg, back to his duties. Later after Olran had gone below, he heard a commotion on deck, a loud shriek of terror, followed a splash. The young, gray-eyed man chuckled softly and turned over in the bunk, slipping easily back into sound sleep.

In the morning, the Captain made a great scene of losing the First Mate overboard, then promoted the Second and dismissed the whole incident as the justice of the sea. Olran continued to play dice all through the long voyage, slowly acquiring a sizable stash of gold and silver coins.

Finally, they reached the port of Constantinople, named for Rome's last great emperor and the man most responsible for creating the now very powerful Catholic Church of Christianity. This church sent scores of black-robed priests and prudish nuns to Britain to convert the "heathen" practitioners of the Goddess's religion. Olran generally despised the flea-bitten, unclean men and women, never missing an opportunity to bait them with their own Bible, which he and Aaronn had studied while under the tutelage of Michael and Drusus. The Druids taught that all Gods were derived from one Source, that all Goddesses were also derived from the same Source. Therefore, if They had made mankind in Their image, then the Source must be both male and female. Men and women were therefore equal in God's eyes and were accorded the same respect. The Druids gave respect to every religion of the Light they encountered due to this philosophy and could not understand why the Christians were so bent upon forcing everyone they encountered to accept their version of the Christ as supreme.

Olran's eyes fastened on the wealth of colors, peoples and unfamiliar styles of architecture as the ship docked and the varied smells of the open-air market filled his nostrils. Lancelot took them on a long tour of the huge agora, letting them investigate the many stalls offering everything from exotic spices to unusual live fish. While they purchased suitable desert robes and boots, they heard music. Almond-eyed, veiled, silk-garbed dancing girls swirled in the plaza, their master sitting back in the shadows listening to the clink of coins into his collection jars as passing men expressed their pleasure for their considerable skills at performing the ancient, sensual dances. While the three Britons watched for a bit, Lancelot was approached by the slavemaster about purchasing one of the lovelies. Lancelot had been in Constantinople before, so he politely refused and walked on. Ronald could not help glancing back one last, longing time before he sighed and followed his knightly sponsor.

At last they found an inn whose reputation was known as favorable by Lancelot, they took a large room with three beds at the clean, airy inn. Ronald and Olran hauled all their gear up the narrow stairway while the innkeeper led the way. When the man was gone, Lancelot locked the door and put a chair under the latch to prevent it from being opened from the outside.

"There, that should discourage anyone from bothering us," he said, eyeing the arrangement with obvious satisfaction. "There are many in the city that would cheerfully kill us for our weapons alone, if not for that chest of gold under the bed there," Lancelot warned.

"What happens next, Sir Lancelot?" Olran asked brightly.

"We wait," Lancelot yawned and sat on the bed closest to the door. "My contact will meet us here either tonight or tomorrow. After that, we will be on our way. We should change into our desert garb though, it takes a bit of getting used to wearing," he suggested and began the process.

Lancelot was very patient and showed the two younger men how to wear the voluminous robes in comfort. Olran, however, could not be convinced to part with his chainmail, even though it was hot and a bit uncomfortable. He did not feel safe without it. Lancelot considered and donned his own mail suit under the robes, making sure that Ronald did the same.

"Could we please get something to eat now, Sir Lancelot?" Ronald asked, his stomach growling loudly. The squire had not adapted well to shipboard life, losing several pounds due to persistent nausea. Since hitting dry land, however, the lad had eaten constantly since smelling the marketplace.

"Of course, boyo, brother Olran, are ye hungry as well?" Lancelot chuckled.

"I can always eat, First Sword," he answered eagerly.

"Very well, then let us sample some of the best this city can provide," the First Knight said grandly and unlocked the door, after first remaking his bed so that the covers draped over the side to hide the small chest. "Please, guard this room and its contents, little elementals," Lancelot invoked the unseen personalities of air, fire, water, and earth. Olran felt a sudden tension in the air, like just before a severe thunderstorm, and he was surprised to see the First Knight use magick, until he remembered just who Lancelot's mother was. They left then, Lancelot making doubly sure the door was secure before he would depart the room. The inn's common room smelled uncommonly good, they ordered couscous, flame-roasted lamb, a salad of cici beans and cucumbers in a sweet vinegar marinade and a sort of flat, soft unleavened bread. Lancelot laughed when the two young men looked for utensils before he showed them how to use the bread with the proper hand, tearing the bread into large pieces to use for scooping the food into their mouths. Within minutes, the large platter of delicious food was devoured to the last crumb.

Their plates were barely taken away when the doors of the tavern swung open and a group of swarthy, dusty, desert-robed men entered. At the head of the group stood a tall, noble-looking Bedouin man, whose robes were of the finest quality. He saw Lancelot and strode over to him, embracing him with definite familiarity.

"My good friend Lancelot, I thought ye would never arrive! Thy journey, it was good?" the Arab asked, concerned. "This dog of an innkeeper, he has not charged ye too much?" he went on, glaring at the innkeeper.

"M...My Lord...Lord Sejuni, I had no idea these were thy friends," the innkeeper quavered.

"Everything has been most cordially done, Sejuni my friend," Lancelot assured the Arab prince. "I am sorry to be late, but only Allah controls the winds, eh my brother?" Lancelot laughed, letting his normally formal speech lapse into something a bit more casual.

"Aye, my northern brother," Sejuni agreed, chuckling with him. "I recognize Ronald, thy squire, but who is this other young man ye have brought with ye?"

"This is Sir Olran, recently elevated to knighthood by Arthur's own hand," Lancelot introduced.

"Welcome to Constantinople, young one," the Bedouin laughed, bowing a bit at the waist. He turned back to Lancelot, eyes bright with suppressed excitement. "Ye have come for the horses?" he asked.

"Aye at last, my brother," Lancelot chuckled with him as they escorted the group out into the dazzling sunlight of late afternoon. "I hope ye have the will to part with a few."

"I think we might spare ye a few of the stallions, my brother," Sejuni laughed. "Ye are garbed properly this time; I see ye have taken my advice to heart at last. Then let my men load yer belongings and we will be off! My father will be stopping at an oasis not too far from here, but we should be on our way before nightfall."

His men brought out all of the Knight's belongings, Lancelot and Sejuni carrying the trunk of treasure personally. Olran followed them out, slinging his bow and quiver of arrows over his shoulder and across his back as well as his broadsword. Passing into the bright sunlight, he stopped and stood still, struck silent with amazement. Twelve odd-looking animals knelt in front of the inn, their appearance like some strange cross between a horse and a cow. Olran's mouth dropped open wide in amazement.

"They are called camels, Sir Olran. Truly, these strange animals are ships of the desert, for they carry cargo from our seaports to the very interior of the deserts. Silks, spices, oil, and all sorts of other commodities travel on their backs, as well as men," Sejuni laughed softly. "Now watch as I mount, and do as I do,"

The Bedouin carefully approached the head camel and warily put his foot in the stirrup, swung aboard and urged the animal to stand with a light smack of his camel crop. The beast rose reluctantly, and then tried to bite the man holding its halter rope. Instantly, Sejuni pulled its clumsy head around and lashed it twice savagely across the muzzle. The camel merely blinked and resumed chewing its cud. "Well, brother Lancelot, shall we be off?" he called, a slight challenge in his voice.

"Aye!" the First among Camelot's Knights answered and expertly climbed aboard one of the ill-tempered beasts. Ronald followed, and then Olran clambered aboard. With Lancelot leading the treasure and gear-laden camel, the group pulled out of the city. Olran suddenly realized that this was the day of Aaronn's birthday; he silently wished his sword-brother a happy day and hoped he was having a good time.

Aaronn's birthday was fun enough; he found that the only thing to mar it was Olran's absence. Still, Cai's planning was excellent and Aaronn's eighteenth birthday was non-stop gaiety. He received many gifts from the Knights of the Round Table, the best being a new set of jet-black formals. The shirt, trous and boots fit like none ever had before, thanks to all the measurements that were made by Isolde while he slept. Cai had rewarded her greatly for the favor, knowing the gift would not have been possible without her assistance. The elegant black cloak's silver trimmings barely touched the floor as he walked; Arthur's contribution was a sturdy hammered silver pin in the form of a flying dragon. The final present was a small, unmarked box.

"Whose gift is this?" he asked, holding it up.

"Open it and find out, Sir Aaronn!" a much-loved contralto voice called back. Complying, he found inside a small silver dagger with his rune sign worked into the hilt.

"Morgaine!" he cried out with excitement. The priestess, garbed in a courtly dress of rich fabric appeared suddenly by Arthur's side, laughing heartily at his expression of surprise.

"Would I miss the eighteenth anniversary of yer appearance?" she laughed softly and embraced him. Aaronn felt her petite, firm body against him and the feel of it sponsored other than mere friendship.

"The gift is beautiful, Lady Morgaine, as are ye. I shall treasure it always," Aaronn thanked her courteously.

She took it from him and, whirling swiftly even though encumbered by the gown she wore, Aaronn heard the "thunk" before he even saw the quivering blade stuck firmly in the wooden beam directly opposite them. "'Tis functional as well!" she laughed gaily as she went to retrieve it. "Let me offer my congratulations on gaining yer Knighthood! No one worked harder for it than ye, ye should be proud of yerself; 'tis yer right to be here at Camelot with the King and the others. Now, where is that rascal Sir Olran? I have a gift and congratulations for him as well," she finished and turned to search with her keen eyes for the renegade prince.

"Ye do not know?" Aaronn queried wonderingly. "He has gone with Sir Lancelot to fetch home to Britain some of Arabia's finest horseflesh," he informed her, snagging two new wine glasses off a passing tray.

"Well now, 'tis fine for him!" Morgaine smiled fondly. "Such a trip will help settle him, I think. Have ye heard yer brother's thoughts in yer mind while he has been gone?" she asked her voice so quiet only he could hear.

"I think sometimes I do, but I am not sure, My Lady," Aaronn whispered to her.

"Well then, I shall have to work a bit harder to smooth the day for ye, I have to do Olran's share too," she laughed. "Here's to the birthday boy. Nay, a boy no longer, I beg yer pardon. A man stands before me today, look at ye, Aaronn, all grown up and a Knight at eighteen! 'Tis a mighty big accomplishment for a fatherless orphan," she quipped and raised her cup again in a silent salute. They drank and Aaronn's eyes only saw Morgaine as he wondered what it would be like to share the Mother's Rite with her. She was so much more experienced and Aaronn found himself intrigued as never before.

"Morgaine, 'tis true I am no longer "little" Aaronn," he responded, adjusting the tenor of his voice to a more seductive tone. "Perhaps we could go somewhere private and discuss *all* the ways I have matured?"

Morgaine's mouth curled into a little smile, she laughed gently. "Well, one thing is certain, ye have changed the topics of conversation ye care to discuss. I bet 'tis many ways ye have matured," she added, stepping back and casting a mock-speculative eye over him.

Aaronn's temperature raised quite a few notches; he leaned over to whisper in her ear. "We should continue this discussion in private."

"I should slap yer face for making such a suggestion, Aaronn of Camelot!" she responded lightly, turning back to the party. "I feel very close to ye as a sister, Aaronn. Let us not spoil the rare friendship that we share?" she added seriously.

"Can we not be friends and lovers?" Aaronn insistently pursued.

"I am not for ye, Aaronn. Besides, I am old enough to be thy mother!" she objected, slipping the knife into his hand. Aaronn stowed it in the empty sheathe in the harness, with a prayer of thanks to Ceridwen for its replacement.

"The Lady who taught me of the Mother's blessing was of yer age, Morgaine. I do not mind a little experience," Aaronn pursued.

"She must have taught ye that when a lady says no, it means no?" Morgaine said frostily. Aaronn was a mighty handsome fellow, she thought to herself, but he is Arthur's half-brother and his mother is my aunt, which makes him kin.

"I hope ye will not be angry with me, Morgaine, but unless a man asks, how can he know?" Aaronn concluded his statement on the subject. "I value yer friendship highly, I shall try not to bring it up again. 'Tis going to be difficult, though," he sighed heavily, escorting her back to the others. "Now, come and sit by me? Ye have to keep me company tonight, especially since Olran is not here!" he tried to laugh.

"That I shall do, and gladly," she declared, glad he was dropping the whole subject. "Ye almost had me persuaded, though," she added playfully.

"I could try harder next time?" Aaronn teased carefully in return, hoping to restore her smile and good humor.

She grinned and responded with obvious humor, "Ye are a smooth rogue for one so young, aren't ye?"

"Aaronn the Rogue, eh, I like that!"

"As long as ye serve Ceridwen and Britain, ye can be roguish all ye like," Morgaine laughed and the two clinked glasses to reseal their friendship, then sat talking until supper came around.

The thin soup of the first course calmed Aaronn's stomach, settling his mind and spirit, which had been excited by the bantering word play and Morgaine's unconscious sensuality. A light salad followed, a mix of winter greens steamed and dressed with olive oil and sweet vinegar, with garlic and cracked black pepper, and Aaronn enjoyed the texture and flavor very much as he munched it with half a loaf of fresh, crusty bread.

The next course was oysters on the half shell, with a serving of poached sole in a garlic and butter sauce, along with steamed tender broccoli. The fish resulted from a day of frivolous angling, when Gawaine insisted that Arthur accompany him fishing. Of course, the Orkneyman was into his third cup of ale when he woke the King and bade him dress for a day of fishing, but Arthur had been very easy to persuade. So the two had returned to Camelot, filthy and smelling of fish, but the fish had been cleaned and packed properly to assure their freshness. Cai had stowed them immediately in the cold room, then ordered the two into the baths for a long soak, sending them cups of ale to sip while they cleaned their bodies of sweat and the scent of dead fish.

After that, Cai wheeled out a pair of yearling boars, whole-roasted to a crackling brown, Aaronn was given the hunter's portion. The young Knight had brought them back to Camelot the day before, having packed them onto a now better-trained Eclipse. Wearily hauling their field dressed carcasses into Cai's spotless kitchen, Aaronn had deposited them one at a time on the butcher's table.

"By the Goddess, Aaronn, what have ye been up to out there in the forest?" Cai exclaimed, pouring him a full tankard of cold ale and setting it in front of the tousled young man. Aaronn drank the entire contents of the cup before setting it gently down on the tabletop.

"I was in the forest, training Eclipse to track and follow me. He suddenly stopped, pricked up his ears and went "on guard," as I have been teaching him. I trust his eyes and nose almost more than my own, so I listened for what was amiss. I heard a tremendous bass squeal, followed by another, and then all Hades broke loose! These two boars were so intent on killing each other over a huge sow, they never even heard me. Most certainly, they never saw what hit them!" he explained, pointing to the tankard meaningfully. The seneschal grinned, refilled it, handed it back and watched as Aaronn consumed half its contents.

"One knife took a boar in the throat, but it took me a couple more to bring down the other one. The sow got away unscathed, I was glad she did for Eclipse would not have carried another carcass, 'twas bad enough just trying to get those two on him. Are horses just afraid of pigs, or do ye think 'twas just the blood?" Aaronn finished his recitation and held forth his cup in a silent request for more of the ale. Cai filled it again, Aaronn finally feeling a bit of relaxation wash over him before excusing himself. "I need a bath and just look at my working clothes! Rent and ripped when I tried to make Eclipse stand so I could load those porkers aboard him. I finally had to tie him to a tree after he first made me carry one carcass and run after him. I guess 'tis time to see the tailor," he chuckled, too tired to be upset. "I am off to the baths now, Sir Cai. Would ye send someone every ten minutes or so with a fresh tankard? I shall let ye know when to stop."

Cai chuckled with him and nodded agreement, then shooed the dirty, filthy man out of his formerly spotless kitchen.

Now the porkers graced Aaronn's birthday supper. It was a rare treat, for Camelot's Knights usually had more important things to do than to hunt dangerous feral pigs. All enjoyed the flesh, except Morgaine who ate no such foods. With the pork came whole turnips, carrots and small onions, baked in butter as well as fried cabbage. Steamed grains, barely moistened with crushed herbs and olive oil were also served, along with pitchers of thin cream sauce. When all had feasted on the delicious meat, the plates were cleared away and a hush fell over the crowded tables. Cai wheeled out, after the proper theatrical wait an enormous cake, deeply moist and sweet, drizzled with a topping made from a syrup of dried berries. Aaronn pronounced it delicious, as did all the Company.

Dancing music sounded and every lady married or not, demanded a turn on the floor with the dark, handsome man. Even Claudia, Cai's assistant, asked for a dance and Aaronn found the muscled woman very graceful for her size. Claudia was definitely not fat, Aaronn found as he held her against him, just big. His interest was sparked and he decided to test the waters.

"I have never known ye to attend a dance before, Lady Claudia. 'Tis a shame, for ye are very graceful indeed," he complimented easily.

"Am I?" she responded. "Would ye be tryin' yer charmin' wiles on me?" she laughed. "I am almost as old as Sir Cai!"

"Perhaps, but older women are my preference. They always have such good timing and responses, one always knows when they are truly enjoying themselves," Aaronn responded, guiding Claudia through the complicated pattern of the slow-paced tune.

"Ye *are* tryin' to seduce me, ye young rascal!" Claudia replied in a mock-scolding but delighted tone. "Are ye serious?" she asked, smiling softly at him.

"Most assuredly, Lady," Aaronn responded. "I do not ask for what I do not want."

"Be careful, Sir Aaronn. Ye may get more than ye bargained for in me," Claudia laughed, but she felt the attraction between them. "It can only be this one night, though."

"Ah, but one night could equal many, Lady," Aaronn responded.

They did meet later and the lovemaking was warm and passionate. Ceridwen gave Her blessing to them as well, and they slept comfortably together in Aaronn's bed. In the morning, Claudia was out of bed first and fixed tea for them both.

"That bed is much too narrow for a man yer size, Aaronn. I shall get Flynn and Gwynn to bring ye up something more suitable," she promised and kissed him gently on the cheek. "I want to thank ye, Aaronn. A long time has passed since I spent the night with a man, for not many count age or physical strength as womanly qualities to be desired."

"I think such an attitude is too bad," Aaronn responded, embracing her warmly. "I think both add depth and fire to a woman. Flighty virgins are too much trouble," he laughed and kissed Claudia a final time. She finished dressing, pinned up her hair and scooted out the door, humming happily as she went. Aaronn waited a bit before he exited the room through the secret panel. Arriving in the great room before Claudia, he sat beside Morgaine, Arthur and Gawaine.

"So, Sir Aaronn, what occupies yer days here at Camelot?" asked Morgaine as she cut her stack of griddlecakes and put the generous bite into her mouth. The blueberry syrup dripped a bit, Aaronn picked up her napkin from the table to dab her mouth. She grinned as he did so and took the napkin from his hands, taking over the job herself.

"I practice, I train my horse and enjoy being here with those who serve the Light, Lady Morgaine," he answered, accepting a heaped plate of griddlecakes, slices of reheated pork and fried eggs. Aaronn was famished, so took a second, then a third helping of everything. Morgaine and the others at the table with her watched in sheer astonishment as the young man consumed his meal hungrily, but neatly. When he was done, Aaronn wiped his mouth a last time, burped very quietly into his napkin and pushed away the clean plate.

"Ahhh!" he commented. "I wish my griddlecakes tasted that good."

"I can show ye how to make them, Sir Aaronn," Claudia's voice came from behind him. She was washed, dressed and aproned as usual; Aaronn inwardly applauded her for her aplomb. She met his eyes easily, winking at him so that no one else saw as she picked up an armload of plates.

"I would forever be in yer debt, Lady Claudia if ye would teach me such knowledge. 'Tis good to have someone about whom cooks well when one is out on patrol," Aaronn answered, remembering his recent first patrol assignment with a chuckle.

Eclipse had hardly been trained at all, so Aaronn made do with a trained remount from the stables. The patrol had been an easy enough assignment, at least until the men had to fend for themselves.

When Aaronn tasted the tasteless gruel that Bedwyr made for supper, he quickly put it aside.

"How can ye *eat* this?" he spat, taking a drink from his water skin to clear his mouth of the taste.

"'Tis all we have, Sir Aaronn, unless ye can do better," Bedwyr replied, placidly chewing his mouthful.

"Stoke up that fire and set up a spit for fowl. I shall cook all the meals from now on, if no one has any objections?" Aaronn volunteered and everyone agreed.

Aaronn left the camp, returning some hour later with a big, fat goose, as well as a pair of ducks. He also had a fat bag of cattail roots, acorns and all manner of wild herbs and greens. The two Orkney brothers, Gawaine and Agravaine, took up the task of cleaning and picking the feathers from the birds. They were careful not to stain the feathers with any blood or body fluids and packed them loosely in a burlap bag for return to Camelot. The others washed and scraped the roots, putting them to boil in a small pot Agravaine produced from his saddlebags. Tristan searched around a bit and found several handfuls of mushrooms he knew were edible and tasty. Aaronn assembled everything and produced a large, deep iron pan from his dittybag, along with a jar of bacon fat, a bag of mixed crushed pepper and salt mixed with dried garlic. The game birds were seasoned with the mix, then spitted and hung over the fire to cook. Agravaine watched over them, basting them periodically with the olive oil and seasoning mix, producing a crackling brown skin.

The mushrooms were tossed in along with the acorns, Aaronn fried them slowly and carefully so as not to scorch them. After the wild greens were seasoned liberally, olive oil was quickly drizzled over then as a dressing, which Aaronn and his famished companions quickly consumed. As soon as the greens were gone, the other Knights sat and salivated as the odor of the roasting birds, combined with the mushrooms and acorns tantalized their nostrils. Disdaining plates in their hunger, the Knights squatted around the frying pan and spit, carving pieces of the perfectly cooked birds and stabbing chunks of mushroom and acorn out of the pan. The cattail roots had been boiled, Aaronn sprinkled his seasoning mix over them, offering them as a side dish. After all their hungers were sated, there were even leftovers for morning and Aaronn packed them away after assuring himself they had thoroughly cooled. The cooking dishes were cleaned and put away as Aaronn stretched out in his tent, thinking that his days of tending horses or standing watch were done. In the morning, Gawaine made it official, while Aaronn made a strong tea from blackberry leaves, currents and honeysuckle blossoms.

"I vote tha' Aaronn be our camp cook on any patrol he's on frum now on. As a consequence, I'll do 'is share of th' other chores."

"Me too!" Bedwyr offered at once. "What ye prepared last night was a very tasty meal, laddie," he grinned as he tasted the tea that Aaronn brought him.

They drank their tea, finished up the leftovers that Aaronn heated into a hashed breakfast; they were on their way after making sure their camp was well policed. Any food leftovers were neatly piled in the center of the camp and left as an offering. "Take this offering in thanks for the use of the clearing and for the abundance last night," Aaronn said quietly before mounting and riding away. Their patrol came to an end just as the first snowfall had drifted down upon the land.

Back in Arabia, Olran wished for a cold river to swim in or possibly some snow to roll in. It was so hot here in the desert and in the sheik's oasis camp there was little relief. He mopped his brow, replaced the head cloth and band, and then went off following Lancelot.

"Come, Lord Lancelot, Sir Olran and ye also, young squire," Sejuni's father gestured to them, indicating that they should take caffe with him. Olran didn't truly care for the taste of the strong drink at first, but time drinking it had accustomed his palate so as to make the drink tasty to him. Besides, one just did not offend the man who was about to grant Lancelot's fondest desire. "So now, my eccentric son tells me ye are in need of horses. He also says ye want only the stallions. Why?" the Sheik asked.

"Our stallions are much too big to mate with yer delicate mares. Also, yer son informs me that ye desert men are loathe to part with thy mares," Lancelot explained, knowing that the wily Bedouin was testing him yet again.

"Come then, o men of Britain, and ye will see what wonders we breed here in the desert," the Sheik said and clapped his hands. The walls of the sheik's tent rolled up, and the three British men could only stare in amazement. The tent was surrounded by hundreds of Arabian horses; bays, blacks, red roans and satin whites. Soft whickers and occasional ringing neighs punctuated the quiet as Olran rose and approached the nearest animal, overcome with the desire to touch the wondrous creatures. Lancelot made a move to warn the young man of their wildness, but the Sheik held him back, motioning for his own herdsmen to stay close just in case. The renegade prince came closer, but remained cautious as the young golden-bay stallion watched him, wary of concealed ropes. Olran had only a piece of sweet bread, but he offered it on a carefully flat palm. The horse started a bit, pricked up his ears at the sound of Olran's crooning entreaty to eat, allowing the young man to approached and slide his hand under the stallion's muzzle. As the horse nibbled the rare treat, Olran reached out slowly with his right hand to stroke soft and silky hide with utter delight. He grew bolder after the offering had been consumed, caressing the horse's legs and back, crooning softly all the while. The horse stood, flicking his ears back and forth, listening and studying the unusual human before him. Olran glanced at the Sheik, longing on his face, silently begging permission to try and mount the stallion, the Sheik nodded once in consent. Grinning wide, the thin princeling wrapped his hands in the mane and vaulted aboard the bay. Instantly the animal's untrained nature became apparent, with a shout or two, Olran was carried off into the desert at a full gallop. Lancelot saw his face as he flashed by and the First Knight saw no fear, only intense excitement. A short time later, he reappeared, controlling the bay by knee-pressure around its barrel and hands on its neck. A great cry arose from the throats of the desert men.

"By Allah's beard, Sir Olran, somewhere in thy blood lies that of a King, for certain!" the Sheik exclaimed, gesturing to a slave girl. "Only a prince can ride like that!"

He took from the girl a mug, filled with fruit juices iced with the snows brought down daily by runners from the mountains. Olran took a spoon and ate carefully of the ice-cold treat, which soothed his parched throat and cooled his sweating body. "I say to all, that since Sir Olran rode him, that the bay is his!"

Olran was overcome by the man's generosity. "But Afendi, he belongs here!" Olran protested. "He is the noblest horse I have ever ridden!"

"Still, he is thine," the Sheik chuckled. "Here he is only one of many."

"I thank ye, Afendi," Olran gave in, knowing he had protested enough for courtesy's sake. "Truly, he is among the blessed of Allah and Epona."

"The British Goddess of horses?" the Sheik asked curiously. "What care would She have for horses of the desert?"

"All Gods are One, Afendi, and all Goddesses One," Olran replied conversationally. "Why would She not lay Her hand on the horses of the desert?"

"Ye are a philosopher then, Sir Olran?" the Sheik asked as Olran washed his hands and face in warm, jasmine-scented water, then patted dry on the scented towel brought by the attendant slave girl. "Come now, Sir Olran. Tell me truly; ye are some sort of prince, aye?" the Sheik pressed, curiosity evident.

"Aye, 'tis true. I am the fourth son of a minor king's family. As such, I had no chance of winning the lands of my father, so I pledged my sword to Arthur's cause. Now I serve as a junior member of the Company of Camelot. If I distinguish myself, there may even be a land grant for me. 'Till then, I am still young and eager to slay the enemies of my Goddess and King," Olran explained all he cared to and the subject did not again present itself.

Supper was served, chunks of lamb, onion, red pepper and baby squashes skewered on long, thin steel spikes and quick flame broiled to delicious tenderness. A large dish of falafel balls accompanied, with a sectioned platter of cucumber slices, tomato wedges, white creamy goat cheese, greens and flat bread. Cool ripe grapes and dates, oranges and assorted melons were also brought, along with flasks of cooled wines. Olran ate until replete, burped twice loudly to thank the host for the food and washed his hands again. When all the dishes were removed, a large water pipe was brought out and the Britons were offered a smoke of powerful hashish. The Sheik took the barest puff as his goblet was refilled, then the pipe was offered freely to whomever wished to participate. Only after the pipe had gone around the circle twice did the wily Sheik bring up the subject of horses, how many and how much.

"How many of my children would ye take from me off to Britain?" he asked, beginning the bargaining.

"How many would the Afendi part with?" asked Lancelot, motioning unseen to the others to be silent and listen. Olran paid close attention as the two men bargained back and forth.

"I could manage to part with several dozen, for the right price," the Sheik hedged.

"I only need a few, Afendi. If ye have a few extra, I might take them as well, if I get the right price and my pick of them," Lancelot answered, getting right to the point.

The Sheik smiled slowly, knowing that he had met his match in the bargaining. They struck an arrangement, after both parties had compromised enough to seat the bargain. Lancelot made partial payment for twelve, handpicked stallions.

"The rest of the money is in the city with a friend, Afendi. With such a long trip over the open sands, I was concerned about carrying a large, obvious chest of gold. When we reach the city, I shall send the rest back with Sejuni. Agreed?" Lancelot explained, playing his trump card at last. This way, he guaranteed eager guards for the long trip over the desert.

"Agreed, and sensible too, Sir Lancelot," the Sheik nodded his assent. They spit on their palms and shook hands to bind the deal before Lancelot made his mark in the wax tablet the Sheik used to record his business dealings.

"Now, to bed for me, may I offer thee one of my wives for thy night's comfort?" he asked courteously, each man politely refused. "Very well then, may Allah bless thy sleep then, my friends."

"Sleep ye sound, Afendi," the three responded and bowed at the waist. Wearily, they retired to soft cushions and warm coverlets where they slept comfortably through the night.

Waking in the morning, Olran found new robes and boots, along with a note from the Sheik.

"A prince should dress as a prince, especially if he rides a noble horse." Olran grinned, packed away his stained travel robes and slipped into the snow-white robes, pulled on the calf-high camel leather boots and set the full scarf and the matching headpiece in place before he strode out from the shade of the tent. There stood the bay, fully dressed in the desert style and standing without a handler. Olran's eyes filled with emotional tears, for the first time in a very long while. He stepped into the saddle, feeling its comfort and knowing that this saddle was designed for long days of travel. He could not help making a few circles of the oasis, when he returned there stood Sejuni and his father in front of the main tent, smiling widely.

"Afendi, all this for me, again, I must thank ye for yer generosity. May Allah reward ye."

"Anyone who rides the way ye do should have the proper equipment. Ye have many miles ahead of ye, so the saddle and other gear will make the journey easier for ye," the Sheik laughed. "Come now, and break thy fast with me."

"Gladly, after I tend the stallion."

He did that, then and there, undressing the horse and sponging the sweat from his silky hide, then picketing him in the shade of the palm trees. Sitting with the sheik and consuming his share of melons and grapes, Olran satisfied his hunger. Accompanying Lancelot and the Sheik as they picked the dozen horses that would accompany them to Britain, Olran said nothing while the two older men engaged in their bargaining. Lancelot eyed them all expertly, choosing quickly as he was impatient to return home in time. He chose a pair each of blacks, roans, golden bays, paints, blood bays and whites. Halters were placed on them, and then Olran led them out to where the squire held them until the full group was chosen.

"Now, Lord Lancelot, one final thing as a gift for thy King, the Pendragon. He must be a remarkable man to be King over such as I see before me," he laughed and clapped his hands. A dazzling white mare was led forth, prancing and strutting nervously.

"Afendi 'tis one of thy precious war-mares!" Lancelot breathed in amazement. "Surely, 'tis too great a gift, too great a sacrifice, even for one as generous as yerself!" he tried to protest as the Sheik waved him off.

"I must insist that ye take her! Otherwise, I shall have to part with her in donation to the dowry of one of my nieces. The family she has decided to marry into has ever lusted for my mares; I know they will insist on one like her for the dowry. 'Tis purely political, this marriage, I am loathe to ally myself so closely with such a greedy tribe. Please, for a favor to an old man, take her and make her part of the dowry for yer King's marriage, whenever he might be betrothed," the Sheik entreated.

"Afendi, thou art truly generosity incarnate. We will take her and Arthur shall hear naught but praise for ye from us. She is magnificent!"

"Aye, by Allah's beard, she is that!" the Sheik agreed laughingly, glad that Lancelot was taking the purebred mare. "And now, let us see to yer caravan's camel packs," he said as he guided them to where five of the beasts were being loaded heavily, Olran noted.

"Afendi, what is all this?" Lancelot asked, his voice wreathed in amazement. "Surely, all this gift giving will beggar even such a wealthy man as ye!"

"Nonsense, I am merely sending gifts from one King to another. In the packs are bolts of silks, to be made into dancing costumes for the King's entertainers, as well as hashish to smoke to clear the mind of worries, date wine and a few bricks of fresh dates. Please, take these extra provisions, with my blessing."

"Many, many thanks, Afendi. Thy name will live in honor in our hearts forever for thy kingly gifts and royal hospitality," Lancelot embraced the older man heartily.

"'Tis good that warriors such as the Knights of Camelot live, aye, even to the lowliest squire like yer man Ronald. May the blessings of Allah follow ye all the rest of yer lives," he wept openly and then embraced the stallions, one by one. Lingering at the mare's side, he crooned a few words in her ear before he turned back to Lancelot.

"Remember, her name means 'Wind over the Sands.' The stallions are thine to name," he added, wiping a stray tear from the corner of his eye.

"I shall remember, Afendi," Lancelot replied, misty-eyed over the affection the dark Arab chieftain showed for the horses. "We will likely never again meet in this life, Afendi, but if ever ye should have sons or other worthy men to send to Camelot, send them along. We will be glad to have them among us."

"Thank ye, Lord Lancelot. This will surely be a tale to be passed from campfire to campfire, the story of how I sold horses once to the Knights of Camelot," the Sheik smiled. "Ye will spend a final night with us?" he asked, truly hopeful that they would.

"Of course, Afendi, one more night among yer tents will be welcome indeed," Lancelot accepted the offer gladly. Much gaiety was shared around the Sheik's fire that night, only the comeliest of his wives danced in diaphanous silks the wild and sultry desert dances long into the night. The three Britons drank and smoked until they were too sleepy to keep their eyes open. When Olran stumbled into his quarters, there was an almond-eyed, dusky-skinned woman awaiting him, a jar of sweet-smelling unguent in her hand. She helped him undress, then dabbed him all over with a sea sponge and gentle oil soap. After washing the residues from his body, the woman undressed down to skimpier clothing while Olran turned face down so she could massage his back.

"Ye have strong shoulders, My Lord. Are ye an archer?" she asked after a bit of working the scented oil into his muscles.

"Aye, how did ye know?" Olran murmured, the pleasure of relaxation coming upon him.

"My brother was fond of the bow, My Lord. Yer muscles are similar to the touch," she explained and her voice chimed nicely in his ears. "I should like to see ye shoot a flight or two before ye go on yer way," she went on.

"I would be happy to give such a demonstration, my dear," Olran responded, letting go of his muscular control, but not his mental readiness while her skillful hands took all the pain from his body. She massaged him to sleep, afterward she lay down beside him as she had been instructed and fell asleep snuggling against him comfortably. When he awoke, he found the mostly naked girl beside him and rare desire flared in him. They shared the Mother's Rite, a quietly pleasing experience for them both, and then the girl dressed hurriedly and departed, leaving him with a lingering kiss to remember her by. Aaronn should have been here for this, Olran grinned wryly after she was gone, then he sponged off and dressed again in his new robes for the day's travel. Breakfast with the Sheik was quickly consumed; afterward Olran brought out his quiver and bow.

"Afendi, I have seen thy desert archers shoot the light horse bow and have been mightily impressed with their skill and accuracy. In return, allow me to introduce ye to the British bow?" he said amongst murmurs of interest around the table.

"We would like to see this weapon in use, Prince Olran," Sejuni spoke out, with his father's tacit permission.

Olran nodded, strung his ash bow and tested the gut-string for tautness. The dryness of the string concerned him, but he reckoned that it had been conditioned enough to resist the desert's effects. He loaded his first arrow, pulled and aimed down the shaft at the first target the Sheik's servants set up some fifty paces away. After easily scoring a bull's eye, he moved on to the next of the ten targets. Scoring ten perfect hits, he retrieved his arrows to a light patter of applause from the assembled men in the Sheik's tent.

"Any man could hit a standing target with such accuracy. What about testing him with moving targets?" a voice asked. A general agreement was heard and Olran nodded his agreement.

"Test me then, but remember I shall not kill on a sheer whim," he declared.

"Sejuni, ready the test," the Sheik ordered, beginning the wagering himself. Olran heard Lancelot's voice agreeing to odds and he gave the First Sword a knowing wink. Lancelot smiled faintly, nodded in return with total privacy and bet an additional amount of gold coins.

Sejuni and several of his warriors mounted their personal war-mares, loading their arms with over-ripe melons. Spurring their horses into a hard gallop, they held the fruit over their heads and rode directly at Olran. The archer coolly loaded and fired one arrow at a time, hitting a melon square with each missile, causing its seeds and juices to spill out over the bearer's head.

"By Allah's beard, Prince Olran, that was fair shooting indeed! Never have I seen such accuracy and speed, and ye are but a stripling!" the Sheik called out with delight. "Come here young man!" he motioned, laughing, and Olran drew nigh. "This is what I lost wagering against ye!" he chuckled, handing a very heavy bag of gold to Lancelot. The First Knight grinned and quickly tucked away the bag within his robes. "Such hard work and dedication as ye have shown should be rewarded!" he grinned slyly after pulling an empty larger bag from his robes. He went to each of his lieutenants and collected his winnings, sending half of the coins to be loaded onto the pack camels for Olran.

All said formal farewells to the Sheik and his tribe, remembering to thank all for their hospitality, they mounted up and took their leave of the oasis while the sun was still cool. Soon, it would be too hot even for the camels and they would have to take a rest through the middle of the day.

Five days later found them on the outside of the limits of Constantinople. Lancelot gave Olran a quick reminder about the nature of business workings in the city before turning him loose in the agora. Olran spent two full days walking up and down the street of smiths, selecting a brawny Guild steelworker from Damascus at length. He used part of his stash of gold coins to invest in dozens of detachable steel arrowheads. The renegade prince used every bargaining trick he had ever learned to reduce the final cost of the beautiful arrowheads. When he went to collect them, he found them well laced with the filigreed pattern so characteristic of master-forged steel. So pleased was he with the work that he ordered two matched pairs of similarly worked boot knives, insisting that the hilts be wrapped in plain, black leather. When they were finished and paid for, Olran's eyes gleamed with the anticipation of presenting a set to his knife-loving ally. He stashed the weapons in his quiver, making sure not even Sir Lancelot knew of their existence.

Olran also spread a few tales of Camelot around, being sure to include a hint or two of the Black Knight. He crossed his fingers as he embellished the truth a bit, reckoning it acceptable to do so in order to scare off those of evil intent. The boat finally arrived at the end of their fourth week in the city, Olran took the opportunity offered by the loading process to bargain for and purchase twenty bags of roasted caffe beans. He could hardly wait to see Aaronn's face light at his first taste of the strong, delicious brew. Once their gear was stashed aboard, the Knights and Ronald undertook the task of loading the spirited Arabian horses into the special stalls below decks. The mare and Olran's bay stallion entered rightly enough, but the rest needed blindfolds before they would set a hoof onto the boat's ramp. The Sheik had sent along a mild, calming potion and

Sir Lancelot sprinkled a few drops into each animal's water bucket. Within a short time, they were pliable enough to be led aboard and secured within the confines of the padded stalls. The horses just lay down to sleep while the ship pulled out of Constantinople on the tide, into the Mediterranean Sea. Olran was glad to be at sea again, on his way home he returned to his habitual black shirt, trous, boots and chain mail under all, just for protection.

"We are on our way home, brother! May the Goddess send us fair weather and winds enough to speed us home to Britain!" he thought wishfully to Aaronn as he stood in the prow of the ship, the breeze blowing his long, brown hair away from his face. Olran took out a leather thong, combed his fingers through his straying locks and tied them back with the thong into a neat queue.

"Heya, boyo, wanna play some dice with us?" one of the crew asked and Olran turned to examine the man's face. It was not familiar, he thought, and nodded his agreement.

"Some dice would be fun. I am always more relaxed at sea after rolling a few passes with friends," he responded in a friendly voice. The trip home was definitely looking less boring already, he thought as he followed the man to the stern and squatted down out of the breeze to take his turn at the dice.

In Britain, Winter Solstice had come and gone, but Aaronn had not enjoyed the holiday as he usually did. Gwenhyfar had come, Leodegrance and Jolynda with her to discuss a formal betrothal for the girl and the King. Things had not gone well for the chit had changed somehow, Aaronn thought to himself as he reflected on the last month's happenings. She seemed much more ambitious and crafty than before. Aaronn stalked her a bit, just to annoy her and make her drop her guard. Predictably, she had done exactly that by dissolving into a screaming tirade over "having that fatherless bastard of Avalon following her everywhere," as she put it. Of course, most of it had been innocent enough, easily explained away by Arthur and Gawaine as coincidence, the chit let herself be soothed by a simple apology volunteered by Aaronn.

"I am sorry, Lady Gwenhyfar, I did not mean to bother ye. I shall try to avoid annoying ye in the future," he said coolly, bowed at the waist and took his leave of the castle gladly. Out on patrol, he could forget the girl's pettiness among the company of other men as he unwound and settled into the routine of riding the west coast rode from Land's End to the Orkney ferry. Bedwyr said there had been possible sightings of Saxon sails, so they all watched the seashore very carefully. By the time he returned to Camelot, Gwenhyfar and her parents had departed, everyone was noticeably more relaxed.

The weeks passed and Aaronn's dossier on Lord Evin Merin grew fatter. From peasant farmers at Darkensdale, Merin's family keep, the

Black Knight heard tales of the cruelty Merin practiced to keep "order" as he called it. Undue taxation, confiscation of valuable meat animals no one ever paid for, wives forced to serve at the Castle, sons and daughters sold into slavery to pay their parent's debts. The Black Knight's blood boiled, but he listened calmly, writing down everything for his records. Acquiring confirming evidence proved difficult until Arthur conveniently installed Sir Llew Stonecutter, an aged campaigner from Uther's days, as Merin's seneschal. The Black Knight waited a few weeks before going to see the aged Knight. Choosing a moonless night in the second month of winter, the Black Knight stashed a nervous mount in a thick copse of birch trees and blanketed him against the cold before he crept away on foot. He traveled the short distance to Darkensdale quickly, hiding in the shadows until the lights all dimmed in the kitchens. Creeping carefully in through the scullery door, the Black Knight found the older man in front of the main hearth, banking it skillfully for the night.

"Sir Llew Stonecutter?" he asked in a whisper.

"Who's there?" the older man asked, startled only a bit. The Black Knight noticed with a grin that the old campaigner's hand was on his belt knife.

"I am the Black Knight of Avalon, Sir Llew. I have reason to believe that Lord Merin is a traitor. I would appreciate any information ye can provide. I shall see to yer protection, as well as any family ye have with ye here at Darkensdale," Ceridwen's champion told him. Sir Llew peered into the shadows, but could only discern the outline of a tall, wide-shouldered fellow, with a narrow waist. Something about the voice made Llew think of Uther, but he dismissed it as coincidence and old ears.

"I am alone here, and I have seen some things that are quite out of the ordinary since coming to Darkensdale. 'Twas no way for me to get word to the King, so I am glad that ye are here," Llew answered, relaxing a bit. "Sir, ye have no idea how often I have prayed for Ceridwen to send someone like ye among the people."

"Ceridwen has indeed sent me, Sir Llew. The King does not yet know of me, I would prefer to keep it that way for now. Our conversation, therefore, must be strictly private. I must have yer sworn word as a Knight on this," the Black Knight told him and the oldster could hear how very serious he was. Rightly so, the very senior Knight thought with approval. Whoever this was, he knew his business right enough, he nodded to himself.

"Ye have my word, Sir Black Knight," Llew swore. "None shall know of our conversations from me."

"So then, tell me what ye have seen," the Black Knight urged, pulling a stool carefully over to him and sitting comfortably. From the old man's lips came a listing of who had been at Darkensdale within the last few weeks and what they had done while in Merin's company.

"I asked him once for extra help in the house and he sent his bullyboys out into the countryside. They brought back a group of comely, but very frightened women and girls, all stolen from their husbands and fathers in the night. Never was I more disgusted when I saw how they were clothed or unclothed, more rightly, to serve at the banquet that night. Barely clad, all of 'em bare-chested, they were groped and fondled, some even raped on the table while that auburn-haired bitch from Orkney sat in Merin's lap and drank wine from his cup," Llew related, his face curling into a grimace of revulsion. "I tried to send the virgins away before the meal and I managed to get most of them at least into the forest before Merin's men caught me. I received a severe pounding from his First Knight for my trouble, but he didn't get a peep o' pain out of me!" Llew finished proudly.

"What happened to the others?" the Black Knight asked.

"The women who served that night were released in the morning; I've heard that the priestesses of Avalon sent a pair of healers to the villages. I know if I had a wife or sister return from here, I'd want the priestesses to look her over, very carefully."

"Thank ye, Sir Llew," the Black Knight said respectfully. "What ye have told me only confirms what others have already said," the sable-clad man went on as he put the stool aside and made ready to go.

"D'ye need for me to keep a diary?" Llew asked quietly. "My memory isn't what it used to be."

The Black Knight grinned though the older man did not see and answered. "If it puts ye in no danger from Merin, I would be most grateful."

"How often should I expect ye?" the aged seneschal asked a final question.

"Expect me at the dark of the moon each month," the Black Knight answered and melted into the shadows. Llew sighed and thought that the man had appeared at just the right moment, thank the Goddess!

Ceridwen's man rode back to Camelot heart-heavy but glad for the old man's honesty. Once back in his room, Aaronn pulled out the tidy pile of parchment leaves and made a new entry. He read over the entire compilation and decided the time had come for the King to hear all about Lord Evin Merin. Taking the notes with him, the Black Knight entered the maze and took the passageway that led to an exit just beside Arthur's door. It took but a few minutes before he knocked quietly on Arthur's suite door. A few moments passed, then he heard the King growl sleepily;

"Aye, who goes there?"

"My Lord, please allow me to enter and quickly. I am the Black Knight of Avalon, Ceridwen's man," he responded. Long moments of silence passed, Ceridwen's man began to think of finding another entry into Arthur's quarters. Finally, the locks clicked and a bar slid aside, then Arthur's rumpled appearance in the doorway, holding Excalibur at the ready.

"I have heard a bit about ye," the King answered, peering at the shadowed figure. "Certain nobles have begun complaining rather noisily about yer recent activities. Please come in," he invited, holding the door open wider. The Black Knight entered and Arthur closed the door, locking it securely. "Please sit Sir Knight, would ye like a drink?" the King asked courteously.

"A glass of wine would be nice, My Lord Pendragon, if ye would allow me to pour," the Black Knight responded, taking the proffered carafe of deep red wine. Pouring two cups, he gave one to the King and sipped off his own after the two silently saluted the Goddess.

"So, what is so vital about yer questionable activities that ye would finally consult me?" Arthur asked tartly.

"Let us first understand each other clearly, My Lord Pendragon. I am first and foremost Ceridwen's man, after that my allegiance lies with ye. The Goddess has assigned me the honor of eliminating all traitors and all treason from Britain. That puts me in your service as well. Ye are the War Duke of Britain, the ruler of the Land, therefore when ye are betrayed, so is the Land and Ceridwen," the Black Knight told him succinctly.

"I see," Arthur mused. "Are ye at my command then, if the Goddess has no objections?"

"Exactly!" the Black Knight confirmed.

"Very well then, we understand each other. Have ye something for me then?" Arthur nodded, accepting any assistance offered to keep the rebellious nobles in line as well as true to their treaty vows.

"Aye, it concerns Lord Evin Merin, a cousin of Caw. He over-taxes his own people grievously, yet he files petitions to be excused from tithing to the Crown. Daughters disappear from their father's house in the night, never to be seen again. Wives are coerced into serving at obscene orgies, when their husbands object, they die," the Black Knight reported efficiently. "Also, it seems that the Queen of the Orkneys is a frequent overnight visitor at Darkensdale, without the company of her husband," he added, causing Arthur to choke a bit on his wine.

"Do ye have anything else?" Arthur gasped out after the fit of coughing had subsided somewhat.

"Not at the present, Lord Pendragon. Do ye have anything ye wish for me to check on for ye?"

"The only thing I would like to know is who ye are. Ye have my word, I shall swear on Excalibur if ye like, that I shall never tell any of yer identity," Arthur grinned.

"I would like yer word, on Excalibur if ye please," the unknown knight responded matter-of-factly. Arthur grinned widely at his boldness, but complied.

"I, Arthur Pendragon, High King and War Duke of all Britain, in Ceridwen's name and in the name of the Christ, vow never to reveal the identity of the man known as the Black Knight." he vowed solemnly.

"Then know me, Artos," Aaronn replied and pulled the leather hood from his head, and gratefully for the thing was hot and a bit uncomfortable.

"Aaronn, how, and when did this mantle fall on ye?" Arthur exclaimed, surprised.

"When I saved myself and Olran from the abuse of our caretakers, My Lord," he answered with a trace of rage in his voice. "Such persons as Morgause and Warren should not be suffered; they should be eliminated after ascertaining their guilt, of course. Instant justice, enacted by Ceridwen's man for the good of all," he stated simply.

"Nasty business, but a valuable service nonetheless," Arthur sighed. "Is being a Knight of Camelot going to interfere with what ye do?" he asked, concerned.

"Not at all, Sire. In fact, being Sir Aaronn is to the Black Knight's advantage," Aaronn chuckled and finished his wine. "I love Britain and the High King is the Land. Ye took me in and made sure I was trained and loved like a son or even a brother when ye knew naught of me. Let me repay some of that debt I owe ye by being of service in this wise?"

"As long as ye do naught to harm the Throne," Arthur laughed a bit. "Of course, Ceridwen would not allow that."

"Of course She would not, My Lord," Aaronn stated with assured confidence.

"We see things the same then; I can see no conflicts between us. Please, feel free to consult me anytime," Arthur yawned. The Black Knight pulled his hood back on and made ready to leave, taking the hint Arthur's yawning suggested.

"Good night then, My Lord. Tell Lady Dawn that if I find any reference to our conversations in her diary, I shall rip them out," he said this last part rather loudly. Hearing the sound of ripping parchment with satisfaction, he called out; "Good night, Lady Dawn. Remember, the Pendragon's oath also binds ye."

He slipped out the door then, making sure he heard Arthur turn the locks and slide the bar into place before he crept down the hall and entered the Maze through the secret door. Quickly, he returned to his room and put away the file, then lay down on the enormous oak four-posted bed. He sighed as he stretched out fully on the comfortable mattress, blessing Lady Claudia for her thoughtfulness. He knew for a fact she had raided one of the royal guest suites for the bed; he had protested when she, Flynn and Gwynn brought the bedstead into the room, one piece at a time.

"Nonsense, ye are the King's man now and first among the Outer Circle of Knights! As such ye are entitled to such a bed!" Claudia had harrumphed.

The bed was quickly set up and a thick solid straw ticking set into place above the planks. Atop that went a down and feather mattress, then a number of fluffy new quilts. Claudia did a quick accounting of comfort pieces in the room and decided to remedy their lack. The next day, a thick bearskin rug was in place in front of the hearth, new wall hangings hung on his walls. Candle-lamps, a new tea set appeared as well as a set of fine silver goblets, worked with a small dragon insignia on the outer surface. Aaronn, at the end of that week was feeling much more at home in the room due to her ministrations. He easily fell asleep, drifting blissfully into Ceridwen's cradling arms with a last prayer that Olran was on his way home, soon.

Lancelot's letter finally arrived at the beginning of the third month of winter. All eagerly clustered around Arthur as he read the missive, then whooped wildly;

"They have the horses, and are on their way home! Sir Lancelot wrote these words eight weeks ago, in Constantinople, he says to expect him in twelve to sixteen weeks. They should be here in a month!" he called out. A cheer went up and excited chatter broke out among the residents of the Castle. "We must make ready for their return. Sir Cai, can ye plan a merry welcome for our weary travelers?" Arthur called out over the babble of voices. "Someone fetch Sir Ulster up here, the stables must be ready and waiting for the Arabian stallions Lancelot is bringing home!"

The time flew by, what with all the busy hands working furiously to finish the breeding wing of Camelot's stables. New steel buckets were crafted and hung in the corners of the stalls, fresh hay stored in the new lofts above the stalls. Tiles were laid on the floors of the corridors for ease of cleaning, and golden-bronze tether rails were installed. The stables looked palatial when they were done, Arthur was satisfied as he inspected them a week after they were finished.

Aaronn joined the hunting parties, and between his efforts and those of the Orkney brothers and Bedwyr, ample game was harvested from the forest. Arrangements were made for delivery of fresh oysters, live crab, lobsters, and fish from the coastal towns, Sir Cai saw to it that preparations included a last minute run to procure them.

Amidst all the preparations, Aaronn received a pigeon message from the Land's End innkeeper, telling the Black Knight of a ruffian band that was terrorizing a local village repeatedly. When Ceridwen's justice was carried out upon them the Black Knight coldly left the cutthroats bodies' where they fell, tossing a token onto the chest of one of them. He returned all that which had been stolen to the village elders, receiving their thanks in return. It was quite late by then, and the Black Knight slept the night in the offered shelter of a horsebarn, sleeping comfortably on clear, salt marsh straw. The goodwife fed him generously enough, but when he made to leave a coin behind on her kitchen table, she pressed it back into his hand with a silent wink, then shooed him out her door like one of her sons. Since he was close, he went to Land's End for the latest gossip and saw a mass of excited men gathered on the dock. A white sail could be seen far out in the channel and his heart began to pound. Taking off his mask and stowing it in his saddlebag, he rode down hoping and praying that the sail meant that Olran was back. Taking a table in the inn, he waited for two hours, until finally the ship was close enough to hail. The word was that Sir Lancelot and his party was aboard. Aaronn ran joyfully out of the inn and down to the dock, where he found the last lines being tied to the pier posts.

"Aaronn!" he heard a very familiar voice call out. He looked up to see the well-tanned and familiar features of his best friend. Olran was just disembarking, laden with baggage; he dropped all in his rush to embrace his much-missed ally.

"Welcome home Olran my brother!" Aaronn answered, clasping him heartily and thumping him hard on the back.

"I need a nice, long, hot bath, and then I have so much to tell ye!" Olran said excitedly. "We brought home some real beauties as well as gifts for Arthur from the Sheik, kingly gifts! Wait 'till ye try this new brewed beverage I brought home, brother. I have missed being home, but I am so very glad to have gone! 'Tis so hot in the desert, ye cannot even believe it!" he went on as they stood there on the dock. The horses were unloaded as they watched; they stood a bit unsteadily on their normally nimble legs after such a long time at sea.

"Sir Olran, would ye go up to the Inn and bespeak stables for our steeds?" Sir Lancelot called out from the deck.

"Of course, First Sword, what about quarters for us?" he called back.

"Aye, those too for I am too tired to ride to Camelot tonight. O, hullo Sir Aaronn!" he called back in a belated greeting.

"Welcome home, Sir Lancelot and squire Ronald. 'Tis good to see ye home at last," Aaronn called back as he took some of Olran's baggage in hand. With Olran talking the entire way, they walked up the short hill to the inn.

Rooms were made available to the Knights, as well as the bath bespoken before Olran and Aaronn climbed the short flight of stairs to their room. Aaronn opened the door, Olran staggered in behind him, putting his loaded ditty bag down on the floor. It made a definite thump when it hit the wooden boards. Aaronn's eyebrows rose a bit at the sound, but he started a bit more when Olran dropped his quiver and bow on the bed and a chinking rattle could be heard when it bounced slightly.

"Here Aaronn, 'tis for ye," Olran grinned and handed him a hefty, silk-wrapped package. "Happy Birthday!" he added.

Aaronn opened the wrappings and his mouth dropped open in surprised awe. The two boot knives gleamed darkly against the black silk they were wrapped in, Aaronn held first one, then the other, then both. Each were weighted exactly the same and their balance was perfect, Aaronn could tell just by holding them. The patterns of the worked steel fascinated him and he breathed softly; "These are the most beautiful knives I have ever seen. Thank ye, my brother."

"I knew ye would like them!" Olran grinned happily. "Now, I want ye to look at these!" he grinned even wider and upended his quiver. Dozens of Damascene steel arrowheads spilled out, making a kind of deadly music as they hit the soft blanket. He held one up, his face alight with sheer, calculating delight before handing it to Aaronn for inspection.

"Be careful brother. They are absolutely razor-sharp. I had them barbed too, just like my old ones," he warned. As Aaronn continued his study, Olran unpacked the pair of small brass pipes Sejuni had given him at their parting in Damascus. The Arab had pointed to tight little packages strapped to his personal bag, saying only that he would soon find use for the gifts he was now giving him. As soon as Olran had found a moment alone with his luggage, he found that Sejuni had provided him with gifts of the heady Mother's herb. Olran's own purchases of the herb had been considerable as well, the amount in his possession would last the two for at least a year, with conservative use. Olran pulled a pinch or two of the herb from the bag and stuffed both pipes full, then took a brand from the hearth and lit Aaronn's.

"Be careful, brother, with the first few puffs. Yer lungs will feel very hot at first, but ye will appreciate the effect," the archer warned his ally.

"So, what is the Arabian name for this?" Aaronn asked as he sat back, enjoying the relaxing effects of the dosage.

"I cannot pronounce it, so I have taken to calling it the Mother's Herb," Olran chuckled. The two shared a few more bowls, Aaronn began to feel more relaxed, but still able to function unlike when he imbibed too much liquor.

"So, Olran, take off yer coat and tell me all about yer trip," Aaronn prompted.

"My coat, I almost forgot!" Olran grinned ruefully. "I have had it on so often, I am used to the weight."

"How much can a coat weigh?" asked Aaronn and Olran's deeply tanned face creased into a wide rapacious grin.

"Watch and see," he replied and began pulling small bags of gold from inner pockets, setting them on the floor. Aaronn counted fifteen bags before casting a questioning look at his ally.

"I am a rich man now, brother!" he declared with a laugh, with that he launched into his tale of the journey to Arabia. Aaronn listened intently as Olran spun his yarn through the bath they both needed, then through supper as well. The tale took some time to tell, they stayed up until late into the night before Olran finished telling the story. They finally fell asleep somewhere between midnight and dawn, Aaronn having vivid dreams of being at sea and in the desert, almost as though he now shared Olran's memories.

In the late morning, Olran rose and started hot water, then ground some of the roasted caffe beans with his mortar and pestle. He waited until the water boiled, then preheated the teapot before brewing the potent black beverage in the glazed clay vessel. He measured the fine powder carefully, poured the hot water over it, then covered the teapot and allowed the mixture to brew. Aaronn's nose twitched a little at the aroma as it gently wafted across the room, fanned gently by Olran, and he opened his eyes. Inhaling deeply of the rich odor, he asked sleepily;

"What is that?"

"'Tis called caffe, Aaronn. 'Tis ready, do ye want a cup?" Olran replied, chuckling.

"Of course!" he heard Aaronn's ready reply.

Olran poured them each a cup, spooned honey into it and handed Aaronn a cup. Aaronn took a cautious sip, rolled the hot beverage around over his tongue, swallowed and took a bigger sip.

"Delicious!" he pronounced and Olran laughed outright. "'Tis good to see ye laugh again, brother. I despaired of ever seeing joy on yer face again," he added gently.

"Aye," Olran agreed. "I lost all my excess rage out in the desert, I think. The heat just burnt it all away," he said softly.

"I'm glad 'tis gone. 'Twill make ye that much more effective in our work," Aaronn told him, laying a hand on his knee. "Now pour me another cup of that caffe, 'tis a very good drink!"

The two finished their drinks before they went down to the common room. Olran's mouth watered at the smell of sausages, griddlecakes and fried eggs, he and Aaronn ate prodigious amounts. When they were at last stuffed full, Olran took his friend to show him the beautiful Arabians.

"Just look at them, Aaronn! They are everything Sir Lancelot said that they were, swift, strong and smart!" Olran said proudly as he led the bronze bay out into the weak winter sunlight. The horse strode out of the building and looked at his new surroundings alertly, flicking his sensitive ears back and forth as he listened to and watched his surroundings intelligently. Olran noted that his coat had already begun to thicken with extra hair against the cold of Britain's winter.

"By the Goddess, Olran, he is a beauty! What are ye going to do with him?" Aaronn asked as he looked the Arab over, only slightly envious.

"I am going stable him next to the Jughead. Maybe Habib here can inspire him to behave like a real gentleman, eh boyo?" he crooned to the stallion. The stallion whickered softly and lipped Olran's pocket, looking for the treat that usually was there.

"Sorry, boyo, I have naught for ye right now," he chuckled wryly. The horse butted him back a step with his regal head, then sighed and shook himself all over. The innkeeper's wife passed by at just that moment, she held a bushel of wrinkled, winter-soft apples in her arms. The Arab's nostrils flared a bit and he stepped after her, straining pointedly at the halter rope, whickering softly in anticipation. The goodwife could not resist his obvious entreaty, after silently gaining Olran's permission with a glance; she offered one of the small, shriveled apples. Habib took her offering from her hand with his soft lips and crunched down on it, chewing with abandon.

"Is he always this gentle?" Aaronn asked. "I thought Sir Lancelot said these horses have fire and spirit!"

For answer, Olran leapt up on Habib's bare back, gathered up the halter rope and galloped away at full speed. He turned back smartly and thundered straight at Aaronn. Olran reined in gently but shortly, setting the Arabian back on his heels and causing him to rear up to full height. Olran hopped off, once the stallion had set down on all fours again, grinning sarcastically. "All right, brother, I get the message. He has fire and spirit in plenty!" Aaronn laughed. Together, they walked him back to where the other horses were being roped together in a long herd line.

"Good morning Sir Olran," greeted Sir Lancelot. "Good morning to ye as well, Sir Aaronn. Are ye two going on ahead?" he asked.

"If 'tis what ye wish, First Sword," Olran told him. "We can send some ostlers back to help with the horses."

"Very good, we will wait two hours before we come on ahead. Ride hard, ye two, I am anxious to sleep in my own bed again," he grinned, but exhaustion clearly showed on his face.

"Of course, First Sword, come on, Aaronn. Let us be on our way!" Olran grinned and signaled the ostler to ready their mounts. A short time later the two laden men returned, divided their luggage between Eclipse and Habib, who shouldered their burdens without objection. When all was ready, they told Lancelot they were on their way and urged their steeds onto the main road back to Camelot. Once down the road a mile or two, Olran let out an exultant whoop.

"Great Ceridwen, 'tis good to be home again!" he laughed.

"'Tis good to see ye home, my son Olran," a great thunderous voice echoed back and they both heard.

"It seems She is glad to welcome Her Black Hunter home. Listen brother, I have much to fill ye in on before we return to the Castle," Aaronn began the briefing, telling his ally all that had transpired in Britain in his absence.

"Ye already have a contact in Merin's household then?" Olran asked alertly.

"Aye, old Sir Llew Stonecutter. Ye remember him, from our early days at Camelot," Aaronn responded.

"Is he safe there?" Olran asked, concerned. Sir Llew was over sixty, after all.

"Safe enough, no one knows he is working with the Black Knight, I have made a habit of dropping around there once a month, just to be sure," Aaronn assured his ally.

"I shall start making additional visits," Olran told him reassuringly. "The Black Knight must protect those who work with him," Olran replied strongly.

"Agreed, thank ye for yer assistance in this, brother."

Six hours later they were in the forecourt of Camelot and Arthur was embracing them in welcome, handing each a goblet of good wine from Ban's vineyards.

"Thank ye, Sire. 'Tis been fun to travel, but my eyes ached for the green fields of Britain. Sir Lancelot and his squire follow, with twelve spirited horses. Could ye send some ostlers to assist them?" Olran requested.

"Sir Gawaine, Sir Bedwyr and Sir Gaheris, take some ostlers, go and meet yer brother Lancelot and his squire for us, and take a skin of good wine to ward off the chill of the weather?" the King requested. The three sprinted for the stables, horse hooves clattered on the cobblestones of the forecourt, then pounded away down the road.

"Blessed Epona! Sir Olran, 'tis one of the Arabs ye are riding?" Arthur asked in wonder as he ran his hands over the patient Habib's hide.

"Aye, My Lord. He is special, aye?" Olran smiled, pleased that Arthur had an eye for fine horseflesh. "Wait 'till Sir Lancelot arrives with the others. He has something very rare and special in his bags for ye, gifts from Sheik Harimun," Olran promised, laughing.

"I can hardly wait!" Arthur grinned. "Now, come in and let us welcome ye properly."

"I need a bath first, My Lord, and a chance to change into some really clean clothes," Olran hesitated. "Such a long time on the road requires a thorough cleaning afterward."

Arthur laughed all the harder. "Of course, Olran, of course. I suppose all of Camelot can wait until ye have had a proper bath and a clean set of clothing."

"I am certain that all of Camelot's noses will be eternally grateful, My Lord," Olran responded dryly and bowed, then took himself off to the bathing room. While he cleansed himself, preparations began on the welcoming feast. Once he felt clean enough for his fastidious nature, he went up to his quarters with Aaronn through the Maze.

"Ye have done some remodeling, brother," he commented humorously upon seeing the renovations. "I see a female's touch in here."

"The room is much cozier, aye?" Aaronn answered, grinning.

"Ye did not let her touch my room, aye?" Olran asked with concern, for his privacy always imperative to him.

"Of course not," Aaronn answered, indignant.

"Thank the Goddess. I have been dreaming about sleeping in my own room since we left Constantinople!" Olran sighed, relieved. He found his gear stowed neatly outside the main locked door and brought it all inside. Carefully, he unpacked it all and found places for everything. He kept out the pipes and herb, dressed in his ever-present chainmail, best black trous, and a dark purple silk shirt from the marketplace in Constantinople before he rejoined his ally in their sitting room.

"One more gift, Aaronn," he said and handed his friend a large package of resin-coated herb.

"Why thank ye, my friend. How much of this did ye bring back?" Aaronn asked as he opened the bag, smelled deeply and broke off some to stuff in his new brass pipe.

"All I could buy or contract for in Constantinople. I also arranged for periodic shipments of rare spices, silks and good olive oil for Sir Cai," he chuckled in triumph, taking a long pull from his pipe.

"I'm sure he will be grateful," Aaronn remarked and they both grinned widely. "I judge by yer expression that ye also spread some tales of the Round Table and the Black Knight?"

"Of course, would I miss an opportunity to keep malcontents out of the realm? I hope Cai will join our secret service. We are going to need his aid, after all," Olran said slyly.

The light dawned on Aaronn's face as he took a thoughtful puff. "I had not thought of that, brother. 'Twould be handy to have Sir Cai working with us," he agreed. "Arthur knows about me now."

"I reckon that as a good occurrence," Olran nodded. "'Twould be bad if the Crown took an unfriendly stand towards the Black Knight's activities."

"Aye!"

"Well, are we ready to feast?" Olran asked, putting away the smoke and pipe. "I am hungry for Sir Cai's marvelous foods!"

"Let us join the Company then. Cai's been preparing for weeks in anticipation of yer return. I hope yer appetite is enormous!" Aaronn laughed and re-combed his hair into a neat queue.

"Are ye joking, Aaronn?" Olran asked, laughing outright as he opened the door. As if on cue, his stomach rumbled loudly, sending both men off into peals of laughter.

Appearing in the great room, the two were offered goblets of wine. They began working their way through the crowd to the sideboard. Lancelot was already there; head still damp from a hurried bath, loading a plate with all manner of small foods; cold roasted meats, breads made from different grain flours, an array of cheeses, pickled broccoli spears, cucumbers, mushrooms and marinated artichoke hearts. Olran filled a plate to heaping, grabbed a fork and began to consume the small foods ravenously.

"Mmmm!" he murmured contentedly and put the plate into a collection bin, hunger sated for the moment. Aaronn grinned and nibbled as he did so, just glad to have his best friend home at last.

"Aaronn, look there, isn't that the fair Julia, Caw's third daughter?" he asked, knowing that Aaronn's interest had been high when he left.

"Aye and ye can see that her parents are with her," Aaronn growled.

"Tell me about it later, would ye?" Olran asked. His concern now was roused due to the expression on his friend's face.

"Not much to tell, except that King Caw believes that he can do better for his little girl than the King's ward and a junior member of the Round Table," Aaronn sighed, remembering how Caw had come to him just after Olran's departure and told him bluntly that Julia was not for him.

"I've no doubt that yer a fine enough man, Sir Aaronn, but ye've no name, no properties. Can ye truly be serious about my daughter's hand when ye be landless, fatherless? How would ye live, boyo? How would she live, a pampered Princess who's been groomed to marry well?" Caw asked, trying hard to remain calm. "Stay away, Sir Aaronn, far away from me daughters!" he warned and without giving Aaronn a chance to respond, he stalked away. It was not the fact that Caw had refused, it was why he had refused that angered Aaronn and sent him on a four day drinking binge. He had finally wandered back to the Castle, where Cai had helped him wash up and then into bed before scolding him soundly.

"Imagine, ye being out of control?" he ended his harangue acidly. "I would have never guessed ye would be so sensitive still of yer parentage! For Goddess' sake, Aaronn, ye are a Knight of Camelot now, high in Arthur's esteem! Is that not enough?"

"Ye are right, of course, Sir Cai," Aaronn responded, head aching with the volume Cai put behind his battle-trained voice. "I did a stupid thing!"

"Aye, ye are right about that!" Cai answered hotly. "See to it that this never happens again, at least for a long time!" he said and stalked from the room, slamming the door behind him.

"That sounds like Cai, all right," Olran chuckled. "Try not to let the petty kings bother ye with all their snobby behavior. They all see their lovely and generally empty-headed daughters beside Arthur on the High Throne. Not even Lancelot is good enough for them. Yer in good company, Aaronn," he finished and sipped the last of the wine in his cup, set the used goblet down on a gathering tray and picked up two more from a passing server's tray. He handed one to Aaronn, winking and raising his cup in a silent toast to a gay celebration.

The feast that Cai prepared was equal to the events of the day. First out of the kitchen was a light stock, rich with the flavors of roasted garlic, onion, and ocean fish. Fresh warm bread came with it and Olran tried to eat slowly but could not stop himself wolfing the delicious appetizer. Next came all manner of baked, broiled and poached shellfish. The oysters were particularly tasty and all savored the lobster claws and tails along with quick boiled crab. Bowls for the shells were provided, along with extra napkins, Arthur set the example by picking up an oyster in the shell and, after loosening it a bit with his knife, slurped it down after chewing to enjoy the salty taste. When the bowls were filled and the plates cleared away, finger bowls came out offering the diners a chance to clean the residues of butter and fish stock on their hands.

Next came the fowl course, eagerly Olran dug into his portions of stuffed pheasant and quail, served with fried onions, mushrooms and a salad of greens that Cai had nursed along in the kitchen's window sills.

The main course was roasted venison, tender and done to perfection. Olran happily tucked away a slab or two, along with a large portion of wild rice, sighing in contentment after cleaning his plate thoroughly with a last crust of bread.

A rich, unfamiliar odor preceded the teapots of brewed caffe that Cai and his staff brought out next, accompanied by pitchers of honey and thick cream. When each adult's cup was filled, Lancelot was pressed for the tale of the journey, he launched into the telling with the ease of one trained in the bard's art. When he related Olran's archery demonstration, he was interrupted by applause after telling of how well the young man had performed. The High King called for a general toast of caffe in appreciation for a deed well done, while Olran blushed a bit and mumbled shy thanks. Only Aaronn saw how much the quiet young man was moved by the recognition of his ability, silently he thought that it was about time.

After the toast had been given and celebrated, Lancelot stood and motioned to his squire, who opened a side door. In trotted the fully dressed war mare, every mouth dropped open in awe of her beauty. The mare halted in front of the High Table, nodded to Arthur, then dipped her delicate muzzle into the King's water goblet and sipped a few mouthfuls of the liquid.

"By Epona, what is this, Sir Lancelot du Lac?" Arthur breathed, wonder-struck. "Surely, 'tis a horse from the Blessed Isles?" he went on, rising from the high-backed chair. The mare watched him, curiosity evident in her tensed muscles and flickering ears. "Whoa, my beauty, stand easy and let me look at ye," the King crooned to the war mare. She ceased all movement, except for an occasional prance and the flickering of her ears.

"A gift for ye, My Lord, from our host in the desert, Sheik Harimun," Lancelot explained, joining him beside the mare. "Her name means; 'Wind over the Sands.' "

"I bet she is that, Lancelot," Arthur chuckled lightly as the mare lipped his straw-blonde hair as if investigating the unusual color.

"Aye, My Lord," Lancelot grinned, motioning for the horse to be returned to the stables. "Now, if ye please, one and all, excuse me. I have been on the road for a long while; I hear my warm and comfortable bed calling me, entreating me to sleep. Good night, My King, brother Knights and assembled ladies. Sleep ye all sound," he bid them and went wearily up the stairs to his quarters. Never had he been so grateful to open that familiar doorway and let his eyes feast on that little bit of home, with its eclectic furnishings. Rome and Britain blended together in the impeccable knight's quarters, maintaining his sense of balance. Only here and on the battlefield was he free from the thought of Gwenhyfar, the memory of her fair voice and lithe, petite body. He sighed with relief and closed out the world. But he was not to be spared this night, vivid dreams of the wisp of a girl floated through his mind, causing him to twist and turn in anguish in his bed. Finally, Ronald could take it no more and woke his master, carefully.

"My Lord, Sir Lancelot?" he spoke quietly in the great Knight's ear. "Please Sir, wake from yer nightmare," he implored, shaking him a bit. Lancelot came suddenly awake, shouting; "Take yer hands from her, ye will not have her!" Sweat poured from his face in a steady stream of beads, he woke completely and sagged against his squire for just a moment.

"What is amiss, Ronald my boy?" he asked gently, still breathing heavily.

"Ye were shouting in yer sleep, Sire, and tossing and turning frightfully. I couldn't stand to see ye suffer so, and I woke ye. Have I angered ye?" he asked, hoping he had done right.

"I am sorry, Ronald. I was riding some nightmare, eh?" he tried to laugh. "Go on now, back to yer bed. I am all right now," he told the boy quietly.

"Good night, My Lord. Goddess grant ye peaceful dreams and sound sleep," Ronald grinned lopsidedly before wandering back to his own cot.

Lancelot rose, sponged off the sweat residue and donned fresh unders. His were soaked through with sweat salt, he grinned ruefully as he tossed them with a soggy thump into the laundry basket. Once he was back in bed, he went right off into a dreamless and healing sleep, waking blessing Ceridwen's mercy.

Chapter 6

The days passed and winter's chill was at last broken by Spring's arrival on the Equinox. All Britain celebrated the coming of the warm weather and took advantage as soon as the snow melted to plow their fields, small and great, readying them to receive the Goddess' Beltane blessings. The Britons were hardly the only ones to make ready for spring, however. Cerdic had spent all winter trying to convince all twelve Tribes to join the Coiled Serpent band in raiding fruitful Britain. They planned to make their base atop a tall, cone-shaped hill called, laughingly, Mount Badon. Surely, Cerdic thought triumphantly, the Pendragon would never lay siege to such a natural fortress, for it would mean weeks of battling uphill against fortified positions. Badon was where Vortigern had been turned back, and Cerdic used this historical fact to cap his arguments to the other war leaders. The idea had been discussed all winter at the council fires and had won so much support from the leadership that the people believed heartily that this summer would see the end to all wars. The berserkers, fanatical worshippers of Thor, had been working themselves into frenzy, now on the day the Britons celebrated Beltane, they reached a fever pitch.

The first stage of the attack was carried out at dawn, a massive ship landing all along the southern and western shorelines, the bulk of the junior Knights, under Tristan and Gawaine, were dispatched to handle what seemed to be another series of raids. It was Aaronn and Bedwyr who rode full gallop into Camelot's forecourt, threw themselves out of their saddles before even coming to a full halt, shouting that the landing was but a diversionary tactic. Arthur cursed violently, and then sent for the Merlin.

"Where are they?" he shouted when the older man appeared eight hours later. "Why was there no warning?"

"They have dug in on Mount Badon, Artos, where else?" the Merlin answered calmly. "Badon is where they made the treaty with Vortigern, after all."

Arthur turned back to the giant bas-relief map in the war-room and looked at the situation with a war-duke's eye. Cerdic had chosen to make his stand on a most tricky battlefield. Being classically educated, Cerdic would most certainly employ the deadliest of fortifications; pitfalls, deathtraps and spiked fences with trenches behind them. Arthur sighed heavily and called the senior Knights together. Sir Aaronn and Sir Olran were included, due to their rather special choice of fighting style. The two listened intently as Arthur set up the offensive measures to contain the Saxons at Badon.

"Sir Tristan, Sir Gareth and Sir Agravaine, I want ye to surround that hill for twenty miles. No one but our forces goes in there or comes out alive without a royal pass, understand? No one!" he ordered. "Sir Lancelot will co-ordinate with Sir Cai for secret supply lines for us."

"Aye, My Lord," they all answered. "Sir Bors, Sir Lionel and Sir Gaheris will stay here at Camelot and assist Sir Cai. We will need good, dependable messengers to send back and forth, boyos and ye are my choices for such a task," he grinned, having deliberately chose the two eldest and one youngest at the Table because of their lack of stamina or experience in Gaheris' case.

"Sir Bedwyr, Sir Aaronn and Sir Olran, I am assigning you three the job of harassing the enemy and making their very existence a misery. Make sure they fear going into the forest for game or water by whatever means Ceridwen provides. I want all three of ye back to celebrate our victory with us, understand?" he chuckled coldly.

"Be assured, Sire," Aaronn returned in a voice just as icy. "Ye will have us back to annoy ye in no time."

Arthur shuddered inwardly, secretly hoping they would find and eliminate Cerdic, for good.

Aaronn and Olran packed carefully, taking only enough clothing to provide a change when that which they wore became too soiled for comfort. They spent the night honing weapons and attaching the beautiful, deadly Damascus arrowheads to the stack of black-dyed mistletoe shafts so thoughtfully provided by the Faerie folk. Olran made sure to include the vial of fatal toad poison, just in case he had to make less than a sure killing shot. When Bedwyr knocked on their door, his bags in hand, the two were packed, dressed and eager to go.

"Come on, ye two. I've been waiting for this a long time," Bedwyr grinned. When they sat down to breakfast, Cai set a stuffed food sack beside each of them.

"Now, 'tis dried meats in there, along with that spicing mix we use on patrol," he began efficiently. "As well I have packed flour and oil, leavening for biscuits, hard beans, dried onions and carrots as well as a good wedge of hard cheese."

"Thank ye, Sir Cai for the supplies, doing the dirty work will be a bit easier knowing we will eat well. Ceridwen keep ye," Bedwyr told him, anticipating the long weeks ahead eating Aaronn's and Olran's delicious meals. The three rode out, hours before the rest of the Company, arriving at Badon just after dark. Easily escaping the attentions of the Saxon guards, they found a huge, hollowed maple tree just a quarter mile away and set up their camp on the site. A small, fresh spring stood at the base of the small rise, Aaronn grinned as he realized that the camp was right in-between Badon and the water source.

"Go on now ye two, snoop around that Saxon fortress. Find out what they are up to. I'll finish up here," Bedwyr ordered.

"What should we use as our pass-sign?" Olran asked, mounting up on the Jughead, whose nickname had stuck due to his mean sense of humor, despite his recent dependability.

"Can ye make the owl hoot?" Bedwyr asked.

Olran demonstrated and convincingly so, they agreed on it. Aaronn mounted up on Eclipse and the two rode back to Badon Hill, quiet and swift on the paddled forest floor, until they could see the campfires of the Saxons. Slipping on their new black linen hoods over their heads, the two smeared charcoal around their eyes to conceal any white skin and donned half-finger gloves to cover their hands. Eclipse's white ring was also blackened with charcoal, thus disguised they crept into the outer rings of Saxon defenses. One sentry died without a sound, the other dropped twitching as the Black Knight's accuracy in the dark was again proven. The pair continued on their deadly way, after first springing the two pitfalls the two Saxons had defended. Up and up they climbed, only seen as a flickering shadow here, or a stray breeze there, until they had nearly reached Cerdic's tent, boldly atop Badon's gentle peak. A single sentry stood negligently leaning on his pike pole outside, the Black Knight motioned for his ally's bow and pointed out the target. The Black Hunter saw the man was practically asleep as he leaned there; a cold smile crossed his face as, without a sound, he pulled out a single shaft, sighted carefully and released. The missile flew silently and struck the sentry, who suddenly turned to a convenient angle, full in the chest. He only managed a quiet gurgle of alarm before he died.

As he fell, the two were already flying down the hillside towards their mounts, screaming in Saxon as they ran, "Brothers, the Cying is under attack!"

Reaching their picketed mounts unmolested in the panic they had created, the two covert specialists leapt aboard their horses, spurring them away. The shouts of, "Invaders!" echoed behind them and the pair broke out into peals of laughter, almost able to mentally see Cerdic's frustrated and enraged face.

Every night for two weeks in the almost constant rain, the pair went to cause havoc amongst the Saxons fires. Once, they poured half of Olran's vial of toad poison into a kettle of food for the Saxon war-chiefs and were satisfied to see them all fall deathly ill. All but one died, the incident caused Cerdic to hold new elections for replacements. Another time, they ran off the Saxon cattle herd, used more for fresh meat than for milk, making sure the frightened animals ended up in the care of Camelot's forces. Another time, the Black Knight got close enough to neatly slit the throat of a newly elected Saxon war-chief.

Bedwyr, meanwhile, concentrated on studying the Saxon fortifications, using Olran and Aaronn's keen eyes to confirm what he suspected. By the time the Pendragon's army appeared, the three presented a full report to Arthur, as well as the herd of captured beef.

Supply lines across the Severn had obviously been affected by whatever Tristan, Gareth and Agravaine were doing; Bedwyr told the King when he made his report. A few days later, the trio dropped unexpectantly into the camp. They all looked exhausted and thinner than usual, but they led a twelve-mule pack train behind them. Bags of hard beans, flour and oats were unloaded from the frightened and tired beasts, along with rashers of bear bacon, huge pork hams and leather sacks full of cured sausages.

"Woul' ye feed us, brothers? 'Tis been naught but cold rations for a week, an' we came upon this yesterday. Thin' we brought ye enough t' do th' job?" Agravaine chuckled tiredly. Aaronn tossed each man a towel and bar of soap.

"Why not take the opportunity for a wash before supper, boyos?" he suggested dryly, while Olran made suggestive sniffing noises as he stood a good distance away.

"Come on boyos. Let 'em work while ye take off a layer or two of grime. It'll be worth it, I promise," Bedwyr backed him up, leading them off to the small pond at the bottom of the gently sloping hill. When they returned, sometime later, they found a meal like they had dreamt of many times in the last two weeks; crisply fried bacon, thick sliced, a whole roasted ham, liberally basted with butter and ale from the captured supplies, along with a pan of oat porridge and light, fluffy biscuits baked in a cast-iron oven in the coals of the fire awaited them and they sat to eat, talking amongst themselves of the situation in Britain. When they were replete, Bedwyr took them to see the King, along with most of the supplies from the mule train, while Aaronn and Olran cleaned up and went out to harass the Saxons. The two had finally located Cerdic's hidden water cistern, the two now determined to attack and at least drain it.

Donning their face hoods and concealing clothes, the two rode around Badon's base until the located the huge wooden cistern. Ordering their steeds on guard, the Black Knight and Black Hunter crept on their bellies towards the structure, but were halted by the sound of sentries talking among themselves.

"How many do ye think, eh my friend?" Ceridwen's archer whispered.

"Six, perhaps eight," the Black Knight calculated after a few moments. "Think ye can take them all?"

He felt rather than saw the withering glance his ally threw at him under his hood, he smiled in anticipation of watching his ally's work. Coolly, the Black Hunter fitted a black shaft to the string, sighted his first target and fired. A moment later his victim fell, but the Black Hunter was already loaded and firing again, knowing that the man was even now dying. When the second man fell, the archer rose up from his hiding place, firing again at his third target. As that man fell dead, the Black Hunter began walking towards the confused, superstitious and frightened men who were now running about wildly, shouting that "the demon of the wood" was back. The Black Hunter targeted and felled men almost faster than his movements could be seen. Arthur's troops took advantage of the distraction at Cerdic's rear to send in a full-force night attack, led by Bedwyr and Lancelot against the first line of Cerdic's fortifications. Cerdic swore impotently, for he could not deploy his own archers in the dark as the Knights moved into the first two rings of fortifications and captured over sixty men. One of his men brought him a retrieved arrow from one of the cistern's guard's body and Cerdic swore even fouler oaths as he registered the trademark black shaft, the head broken off.

"Who are ye!" he screamed out in anger, his rage almost to the point of apoplexy. "Is this place truly haunted?" he sighed to himself and ordered the pull back to the third level of rings.

Arthur's Knights spent the rest of the dark hours before dawn finding and filling in the pitfalls, trenches and springing the death traps, then moved their own encampment into the rings. A major victory was won that night, when Arthur heard of the distraction provided by the Black Knight, he blessed Ceridwen's name before laying down to a restful sleep that night.

The next month was spent by the Pendragon's army in mass rushes up the hillsides at all hours of the day and night. Slowly, even the hardy Saxons tired and the lack of abundant food hardly helped their cause. None of the Saxon hunters sent out for game returned alive, but their dead and neatly scalped bodies appeared regularly either back in their own tents or in front of Cerdic's. The hunters among the raiding force lost their desire to ever venture into another British wood. The talk of evil spirits and demons in the surrounding forest got to the point where Cerdic wearied of it and ordered the High Skald to perform an exorcism. At the height of the ceremony, the aged man stepped in front of the fire at just the right angle, the patiently waiting Black Hunter took him in the throat. Gurgling horribly, the old man fell squarely in the bonfire.

"Find that dammed archer!" Cerdic roared out the order, but not one man moved. Their eyes were filled with terror and many fingers made the sign against enchantment.

"Go home, Cerdic of the Coiled Serpent!" a voice mocked him from the woods. "Go home and take yer men with ye, lest Ceridwen come in the night for *ye*!"

That was enough for the men, the usually hardy Saxons scurrying for the shelter of their tents, where they all huddled fearfully and recited chants to ward away evil spirits.

The next morning was the Summer Solstice and the Pendragon's army at last won two more levels of fortifications. All the traps were again disarmed and the Knights settled in again amidst the thick mud. Bedwyr was recalled to Arthur's side, leaving Aaronn and Olran to continue their deadly and demoralizing attacks.

That Summer was the rainiest anyone could remember, the squires were constantly busy removing rust from chain mail suits of all the Knights. Cai sent new sets of unders as fast as the ladies could make them, but all of the men chafed endlessly anyway. All the moisture in the air and the muddy ground made it impossible to do anything but feel and try to ignore the scratching, burning sensations. Even Lancelot grew cranky under the constant tension and Arthur grew concerned. Ceridwen saw to their entertainment, however, it arrived just in the nick of time.

The next day's fighting was as usual and it rained all day, as usual. Due to the constant downpour, cooking fires were too cold to cook over, the Knights prepared for another night of cold rations. This was the fifth time in as many days they had chewed on dried meats, tonight they ate the last wedges of cheese with yesterday's breads. Just as most of them handed their chain mail suits over to the squires and donned clean but tattered unders in their tents, two great wagons hallooed the camp and were passed gladly by the sentries. Arthur heard and emerged from his own tent, a weary and wan smile spreading over his face. In the front wagon sat Sir Cai, Lady Morgaine beside him.

"Morgaine my sister, 'tis good to see ye!" Arthur exclaimed as he assisted her from the wagon seat. "Cai, 'tis good to see ye as well. What have ye in those wagons?"

"A feast, Artos, and some lovely company provided by Sir Dalren there in the second wagon. I thought the Saxons might enjoy watching us having a good time," Cai chuckled.

Indeed, the young women who now piled out of the back of the second wagon were beautiful and the music of their laughter proved a tonic for the weary Knights of Camelot. Morgaine went from fire to fire, chanting and tossing fragrant herbs upon each one, causing them to burn hotter and brighter with her magick. Within a short time, the smoky layer that hung thickly over them was lifted from the British camp.

Around the main fire Cai set a pair of huge spit irons, loading onto them a whole steer, the flesh well-marbled and tender. Over some of the smaller ones, Cai boiled a combination of cracked wheat and oats, seasoning the porridge with fresh thyme, garlic and dill weed. Pans and pans of pre-made biscuits appeared and were put under clean dishcloths to wait until the main course foods were done. When the beef was nearly done, Cai made a mixture of flour, eggs, mushrooms braised in wine and olive oil, cheeses and chopped greens, then gently fried small spoonfuls of the loose batter in hot olive oil until they were patties. Piling them onto huge platters, they were served as soon as all were ready. Cai lined up steel plates, forks and spoons, the Knights and ladies lined up as he carved the perfectly rare cooked beef right from the spit, serving themselves of every other food offered. The women served the skins of wine, red and hearty, as the Knights ate the feast foods ravenously, thanking Ceridwen for Cai's generous and thoughtful use of his marvelous culinary skills.

"So, Caius, who is running the castle while ye are here?" asked Arthur as he took a long pull from his wine cup.

Cai blushed and answered quietly; "The Lady Gwenhyfar and her mother, Lady Jolynda."

"WHAT?" Arthur exclaimed, nearly choking on his mouthful of food.

"They came last week, alone but for an escort of three Knights so old they must have been dug up from their graves," Cai began, smiling in spite of himself. "The young miss found out what the situation here was and insisted that we bring ye whatever comfort was possible. Of course, Sir Dalren's idea of entertainment was hardly what she meant, but what she does not know will not hurt her virgin moral sensitivities. I know what a fighting man needs when he has been campaigning for months, in the rain. I know 'tis not a group of flighty, inexperienced girls," he chuckled as he watched the women improve the morale of the Pendragon's camp. Even the foot soldiers were now in a mood to relax a bit, their stomachs full of good food and wine, soon the Inner Circle joined in the sing-alongs, most of them understandingly bawdy, laughing and joking with the farmers and other from the common ranks. Up above the camp, Arthur and Cai knew, the Saxons were watching and salivating over all the festive offerings.

Cai stayed with the Army, knowing his place was with them now that the siege was truly joined. The King sent his personal thanks to Gwenhyfar. He also sent along a private message to Sir Ulster, the aged stablemaster, instructing him to provide a suitable steed for the Lady to ride. When the stablemaster received and read Arthur's message, he interpreted the command of the King to mean the war-mare, "Wind Over The Sands". When he showed the spirited animal to Gwenhyfar, telling her that the King himself had ordered this steed to be made available for her use while at Camelot, she protested coyly.

"Surely 'tis too much, Sir Ulster, I am certain the King meant that some horse other than his gift from the desert."

Gwenhyfar saw it as more than just a friendly gesture, being Leodegrance's horse-wise she also saw the animal's worth, and Jolynda saw it as the answer to the betrothal question.

"The King said to provide a suitable mount, Lady Gwenhyfar, she is the best animal we have in the stables. She is also the best trained, otherwise ye'd have to break yer own mount, like the Knights do," he explained simply, disgusted by the avarice apparent on both women's faces.

The first time Gwenhyfar attempted to mount and ride the war mare however, the horse would have none of the spoiled princess on her back. She was thrown none too gently, to the sands of the training arena; afterward, she refused to have anything to do with the Arabian. Gwenhyfar and her mother stayed at Camelot all that summer and everyone at the castle prayed at one time or another than Sir Cai would soon return home.

The summer dragged on, humid and hot, and during the waning months of the season and early autumn, the rains finally stopped. The insects, however, swarmed over Saxon and Brit alike. Due to the Knight's cleaner personal habits, the blood-sucking gnats and mosquitoes that bedeviled the Saxons did not bother them. So many of the pests laid their eggs in the Saxon's newly cleaned cistern that finally it had to be drained and cleaned once more in a desperate attempt to clear the camp of the annoying bites. Many of the berserkers began to suffer from some sort of fever, in the end those afflicted died terribly, ranting and raving in a high fever. In a panic, Cerdic ordered all the stored water in the camp replaced with fresh from the spring. They drained and re-filled the huge cistern laboriously before retiring for the night.

When they awoke in the morning however, they found the cistern's waters fouled by blood seeping from the bodies of three scalped sentries, courtesy of the Black Knight and Black Hunter. New cries of "demons in the dark" went up, just as Arthur's army attacked without warning. It was an all-out assault that went on for a solid seven days. The Knights wearied of charging uphill, fighting hand to hand all the way, only to hear Cerdic rally his men with shouts of, "Thor!" and "Odin!" and finding themselves pushed back. Every day, however, the Pendragon's forces won another few feet of ground until the day came for the last great push.

The onslaught began at the crack of dawn on the Autumn Equinox; they all struggled hard to end the wearying conflict. Aaronn and Olran, from their base camp, watched for their opportunity. It came just as the sun sank below the treetops. The glow cast an eerie, reddish light over the battlefield; Arthur stood and wondered if he should pull back for the night.

Suddenly, great cries of, "the demons, the demons!" rang out from the Saxon ranks, Arthur's forces rallied as Aaronn emerged suddenly from the growing shadows and engaged Cerdic's personal guard, point-blank. Arrows flew from an unseen vantage point, scoring killing hits among the blood-guard of the Coiled Serpent. Arthur saw what the two were doing and pushed his horse through the melee, trying to reach the top. Suddenly, the arrows stopped flying and Arthur saw the sable-clad and filthy junior Knight engage Cerdic himself, sword in hand. Cerdic was not unskilled with the broadsword, Arthur knew, and could be devilishly tricky with the seax that always hung on his belt. In that moment, Aaronn's blade flashed and cut a nice, deep slice in Cerdic's sword arm, causing him to drop the heavy sword and whip out the small and deadly sharp seax. Aaronn caught the small, wicked ax deftly on the crossguard of his sword, then pulled Cerdic in close, both of them striving against each other in a deadly match of, "king of the hill." Cerdic heard his closest lieutenant shout; "Kill 'im an' leave 'im, Cerdic! The Pendragon is on us!"

The Saxon leader chanced a quick peek, indeed, Arthur's army was swarming over the stake fences and earth works. He redoubled his efforts to break Aaronn's grip on him, finding that the junior Knight had a death grip on his right hand. Only Arthur was able to ride up and take the Saxon leader into custody for Aaronn was experiencing a bit of battle-madness. At first he would not release his hold on the Saxon leader even when Arthur came cautiously to his side.

"Easy on there, Aaronn boyo," Arthur said softly as he attempted to loosen Aaronn's grip, but the younger man clearly could not hear. The King saw the slightly crazed look in Aaronn's eyes, as did Gawaine, who had seen the look often enough on other Knight's faces. Temporary battle-madness possessed the best of warriors occasionally, so Gawaine took the best possible action. He swung his great right fist hard, connecting with Aaronn's jaw, felling the junior Knight where he stood. Only then could Cerdic be taken into charge by the Pendragon's forces.

"C'mon, Cerdic 'Cying,' we've a loovely cell awaitin' ye a' Camelot," the giant Orkneyman said in a conversational and friendly tone as he pulled Cerdic away to the medical tent to have his wounds tended. Morgaine herself stitched the slice in his right arm, noting with satisfaction that it took thirty stitches to close up the slice to her satisfaction.

Aaronn was taken up by six of his brother knights and transferred to the medical tent as well. He woke some hours later, finding himself restrained in case his madness remained. Morgaine heard him groan and brought him a cup of watered wine.

"Sir Aaronn?" she questioned before handing him the cup, well-laced with pain reducing herbs.

"Aye, Morgaine. What happened, why have my arms and legs been tied to the cot?" he asked, trying to sit up and finding himself restrained.

"Ye were a bit overzealous and looked a bit too crazed for our brother Gawaine. He had to bless ye with his good right fist before ye would release Cerdic into his custody. Are ye all right now?" Morgaine explained, looking at him skeptically.

"I feel fine, except the right side of my jaw aches," Aaronn answered, rubbing it gently when Morgaine freed his hands from the restraints.

"How does yer mind feel?" asked the priestess. For answer, Aaronn pulled her into his lap playfully and tried to kiss her full lips. "I would say ye have recovered yerself well enough, Sir Aaronn," she laughed gaily and untied his feet as well. "Now go on with ye and get bathed. Sir Cai is using the Saxon's cistern for a bath, ye are among the last to use it. I would say ye were a bit overdue," she sniffed and wrinkled her nose fastidiously. Aaronn took the hint and went quickly to the makeshift baths, where the last of the Knights lounged in the hot water.

After the battle ended, the army of the Pendragon began the long work of cleaning up and restoring the battlefield. Pyres were set up, well away from the healing tent, the bodies of the slain Saxons were laid upon it with the respect they were due. Lightning bolts from the Merlin's hands set them alight; the men of the Pendragon's camp then turned their attentions to those who had fallen in defense of Britain. Foot soldiers and knights were laid upon pyres by the loving hands of their fellows, a tear or two shed for their passing and the ritual parting words of, "Goddess receive ye, brother, into the Blessed Realm," whispered over them each.

Blue bolts again arched from the Merlin's fingertips, igniting the wet wood available. Instantly, the entire pyre was alight, sending off a fierce heat and very little smoke. Prayers were offered to the Goddess, then the work of filling in the remaining pitfalls and traps began. When Badon's hillsides were returned to a close semblance of their former state, Arthur caused a great granite stone marker to be planted on the site where Cerdic had been captured. It was marked with a warning that read, in both Saxon and Briton,

"Beware, all ye invaders of Ceridwen's Holy Land. She Watches, She Hears, She Avenges!"

With Cerdic tied to a spare horse and led by Arthur, the Knights of Camelot followed the King back to the Palace of Light, the rest of their captives in tow. All the local nobles and petty Kings had heard the joyous news, even now they were on route to Camelot to greet and honor their heroes. King Ban of Lesser Britain had arrived with his regular shipment of trade goods, along with his tithe of wines and foods for Camelot. Now he waited, dressed in his finest, beside a gorgeously arrayed Gwenhyfar at the main entrance to the Castle.

"My Lord Arthur Pendragon, 'tis true what we have heard?" King Ban asked when Arthur wearily dismounted and pulled off his helm. "Are the Saxons defeated at last?"

"Well, My Lord Ban, we have captured their leader along with their war Thanes and a goodly amount of their menfolk. I suppose ye could say that the war is over, for now," Arthur grinned tiredly. "I know ye would all like to feast us and celebrate, but we are all bone weary. Can it wait 'till tomorrow?" he asked, as many of the Knights nodded their weary agreement.

"Of course, My Lord," Gwenhyfar answered, stepping forward to take the King's arm solicitously. The weary man accepted any help offered, Ban took the other arm and the three walked slowly into the Castle, where warm cups of mulled wine awaited every man. The ostlers came and took the steeds off for a much-needed bath, rub down and good feed, then a long sleep on clean, soft straw. Even Olran's Jughead went willingly with the horseboys, head lowered in weariness.

Finding that there was only a thin lentil soup boiling over the cooking fires, Cai went immediately to the kitchens to find out why. Claudia related to him, in the privacy of his office, how Gwenhyfar had refused to believe the early messengers until Sir Lionel had arrived with the official message. By then, it was too late to prepare any kind of feast foods and only lentils would cook fast enough to provide any kind of hot food for the Knights of Camelot. Even the mulled wine had nearly been late due to Gwenhyfar's desertion of her adopted kitchen post in order to bathe and dress herself to greet the victorious King and Army. Sir Cai went directly to Gwenhyfar's private chambers, quietly exploding in her face.

"How dare ye interfere with my orders to the staff, girl!" he began, his anger evident as he paced back and forth in front of her, showing no sign of his limp. "I specifically left Claudia, my best and most trusted assistant, in charge of the running of Camelot in my absence. The entire victory feast was planned down to the last detail before I left to serve with the Army, now all is ruined! As a result of yer interference, 'tis no proper supper laid on the boards for the victorious King Arthur and the Knights of Camelot, men wearied by nearly a year of grueling campaigning to keep yer pretty ass from falling into Saxon hands!" shouted Sir Cai, unable to restrain himself so greatly was his ire aroused.

"I could not waste resources of the Castle on some unofficial messenger exited, but possibly overestimated report of victory…" she tried to defend herself, but Cai was relentless.

"*I* sent that 'excited boy', Lady! If Claudia had been allowed to speak with him, as I instructed, she and the staff would have easily been able to provide an excellent meal for homesick Knights and King! As 'tis, Camelot is disgraced, and in front of our best ally, Ban of Lesser Britain! Imagine if King Lot and Queen Morgause or any of the other rebellious nobles had arrived instead? Poor Arthur's reputation and image would have been tarnished for years to come!" he went on, after snorting derisively. "And ye wish to be High Queen? Ridiculous! Never will ye again set foot in Camelot's kitchens, I shall see to it!" he finished, turned smartly and Roman-marched, still without a visible limp, back to the kitchens. Claudia, knowing his mood, already had begun the cleaning, the lentil soup had disappeared somewhere to cool. He smiled at her intuition, poured himself a cup of wine and sat for a few moments to calm his temper before beginning on the pastries. The entire noble class of Britain would soon be within Camelot's walls, all must be perfect for their arrival; Cai thought and set the maids to cleaning all the guest rooms in the Castle. He ordered fresh linens for all the rooms, opened the windows in each and burnt incense to improve their atmospheres. Setting the Castle staff humming about their tasks, everyone noted that within hours the tight schedule that the Lord Seneschal of Camelot maintained was again in place, much to the staff's utter relief.

Meanwhile, the entire Inner Circle, with Aaronn and Olran, "escorted" the Saxon prisoners down to the holding area beneath Camelot. The bulk of the fighting men they had released at Badon, only those of some rank were still prisoners; twenty-four sub-chiefs, twelve war-chiefs and Cerdic himself. Arthur quickly drafted the surrender treaty and sent it off with the sub-chiefs as an act of good faith, with a warning that the rest of the prisoners would die if no answer were received within a month. After seeing Camelot's fortified strengths, the sub-chiefs were glad to be spared further British "hospitality," when they were released they literally ran across the green sward, their Knightly escorts from the Outer Circle giving chase to insure they crossed the Severn River, post haste.

For Cerdic, the Inner Circle had planned a very special welcome indeed. He had been constantly pummeled and punched while under the "care" of the Orkney brothers, now the entire set of senior Knights followed, eagerly awaiting their chance to repay the Saxon most responsible for the suffering of the British people all these years. The man was not bound with restraints and he tried hard to defend himself against the flurries of punches directed to various places all over his well-conditioned body. In the end, Cerdic ached all over; hardly a place on his body was free of bruises.

"All right, boyos, ye have all had yer turn at Cerdic now," Lancelot ordered. "He is going to be here for a long time yet, the King gave the tribes a whole month to respond to the Treaty, after all," he added for Cerdic's benefit. The Saxons leader moaned and rolled onto the cot in the cell, hoping they would go away now and forget all about him.

"We will assure that he is all tucked in, Sir Lancelot, then how about meeting at the Royal Inn down in town? The first round is on me," Aaronn proposed.

"Aye!" the others accepted and left the holding area to change into clean clothes and prepare for a boisterous night. The two young Knights went to Cerdic's bedside and bent over him, knowing full well he could still hear them despite appearing to be asleep.

"Good night, Cerdic 'Cying,' " Aaronn said quietly. "Be assured if one day beyond the month passes, ye will be fed to the demons in the wood."

Cerdic opened one puffed eye, regarded the two with blurred vision and moaned again. "Leave me be, haven't ye all had yer fill of hurting me yet?"

"We could keep ye here for the rest of yer days, Cerdic, and hurt ye every day like this. It could never, ever be enough!" Olran hissed. Cerdic paled visibly under his cuts and bruises and then shuddered.

"Come on, my friend. He has the message, for now anyway. Surely he will not make any trouble, aye Cerdic Elesing?" Aaronn urged. Olran got up to leave; he turned back and spat a huge blob of spittle onto Cerdic's face.

"Now, I am ready to leave," Olran announced and sauntered out the cell door. Aaronn followed, shut the door, locked it securely and hung the key outside the main door, after sliding the locking bolt home across the heavy, iron bound oak door.

"Sleep well, Saxon brothers. I hope yer not scared in the night. Do not have any trouble with demons in the dark!" he taunted as he went out, laughing heartily with Olran as they went. The candles all burnt out at the same time, leaving the captured men no option but to try and sleep.

The Knights and their King met at the Royal Inn and spent the next few hours drinking and celebrating. The innkeeper wisely closed the common room to the public before rolling out a cooled keg of good ale as well as a smaller cask of well-aged wine. Platters and platters of sizzling rare steaks came from his open charcoal grill, accompanied by a boiled cracked wheat salad and loaves of crusty bread, and still the ale flowed. Only when they could drink no more did they return to the Castle to fall gratefully into the arms of their patiently waiting wives or into comfortable if empty beds. All slept easily until almost noon, except for Sir Cai. He had been up all the night, cooking and making the castle ready for the onslaught of visitors sure to invade Camelot on the heels of the victory at Badon. As each person came down to the breakfast table, they were greeted with their choice of hot tea or caffe, griddlecakes, fried eggs and sausages.

"Now, go on all of ye Knights and Ladies, and make yerselves ready for tonight's victory feast!" Cai told them, then went off to his own bed for a few hours of blessed sleep. Before retiring, he made sure all understood that only Claudia's orders were to be followed except Arthur's, of course. The Knights suspended all other activity except that of hosts for the day and donned their formal wear in acceptance of their role.

Guests flocked to Camelot, soon every available bed in the Castle and town was filled. The petty Kings met with Arthur late in the afternoon to hear the recounting of the battle as well as the terms of the Saxon surrender. All agreed on the simple terms:

I) All lands on the east bank of the Severn were designated Saxon land.

II) The Saxons would no longer raid into British lands for any reason, on pain of death.

With that business done, the celebrating went on and the games began. Some of the junior Knights, working with Aaronn and Olran, had organized a few games of skill and strength. Now they competed in a friendly manner while the Court and guests watched and cheered. The senior Knights as well watched and could not resist answering the tacit challenge offered. Stripping off formal tunics, they joined in and that made the games much more interesting. Mock-bouts of swordplay, archery, horse racing and even lively partner dancing were among the events held that day. Ceridwen's electric-blue sky and warm autumn sun added to the guest's thirst, Cai's assistants rolled out many iced ale and white wine casks, the cool beverages slaked their dry throats and added to the pleasure of the day.

Gwenhyfar finally made her appearance, on Sir Lancelot's arm. She was radiant as the Spring Maid herself, or so many thought, in her gown of rosy pink gauze lined with matching silk under the filmy fabric. All the ladies envied the girl, both for the gown and for her quite handsome companion. It was obvious to all that the First Knight of Camelot doted on Leodegrance's daughter and gossiping tongues began to wag. All wondered where, or more rightly, from whom the rare and expensive silk had come. Olran saw her parading around the green meadow, caught Aaronn's eye and motioned him over.

"Ye see that?" he asked, gesturing obliquely.

"Aye, Gwenhyfar of Lyonnesse has a new gown, what of it?" Aaronn asked, once he returned his gaze to his friend.

"Lancelot bought a whole bolt of that same color silk in Damascus. He spent a pretty hefty sum, as I recall," Olran informed him. "I wondered what pretty had finally caught his eye."

"Aye, Lancelot loves her, but she only has eyes for the throne," Aaronn observed alertly. "She is a cunning little lion cub, a true daughter of Leodegrance, aye?"

"Poor Lancelot, he is headed for heartache with that chit," Olran sighed, turning as his name was called to join the archery contest. Try as the others might to out shoot him, he won by easily splitting his own bull's eye with his last missile. He and Aaronn then wandered over to the wrestling competition. It had come down to Tristan and Gawaine, the Orkneyman stood on the downwind side of the circle. He stood quite alone, his body hair plastered to his body by some shiny substance. The breeze changed, Aaronn's nose twitched in response to a suddenly foul odor and he glanced at Gawaine. The Orkneyman was grinning wide; he winked and nodded at Aaronn, who realized that Gawaine had smeared his upper torso with rancid grease of some sort. Gareth appeared, holding a foamy tankard and laughing softly.

"What is our brother Gawaine up to now, and what is that smell?" Aaronn asked.

"Bear grease gone rancid, 'e's been savin' it since las' fall, when he brought 'ome tha' big, mean killer bear," Gareth chuckled so hard he could hardly speak. After composing himself, he wandered off to place a few more bets. Aaronn and Olran found an ale-cask, filled two mugs and sat on the sidelines, after first determining the most prevailing wind direction. Tristan stepped into the ring, starting violently as the incredibly noxious odor emanating from his opponent.

"Ye'll not win that way against me, brother Gawaine. I've lived among the Saxons and they smell even worse than ye do at times," he commented and crouched into the ready position.

The marshal's hand dropped and the two closed with each other, Tristan striving to get a grip on the greased Orkneyman, while Gawaine maneuvered to get inside Tristan's longer reach. Meanwhile, the sun gained strength, as did the smell wafting off Gawaine's sweating body. Finally, Tristan caught hold of Gawaine's belt, throwing him face first into the dust, jumping atop of him. Gawaine grunted a bit at the weight of his opponent, then struggled and squirmed, effectively keeping Tristan from turning him over to pin his shoulders to the ground. The match went on and on until finally the marshal stepped in and stopped the match.

"I have smelled that foul odor long enough, Sirs," he exclaimed. "I declare the match a tie!"

"I say 'tis good enough fer me, how 'bout ye, Tristan?" Gawaine grunted.

"Aye, I think 'tis good enough indeed!" Tristan agreed and assisted Gawaine up, after rising himself. "We should go and wash up, change clothes and rejoin the ladies at the dancing square, aye my brother?"

"Aye, tha's worth cleanin' up fer!" Gawaine agreed. The crowd cheered as the pair of grease covered and smelly men linked arms and walked off towards the baths, both whistling a sprightly tune in harmony.

"Sir Aaronn?" he heard Morgaine's beloved voice at his back.

He turned to see her, dressed in deep royal blue, trimmed with thin silver ribbons, which also tied the neckline of the gown. "Are ye coming to the dancing square?" she asked with a smile.

"Only if ye will partner me, Lady, ye have the lightest feet at Camelot," he grinned after delivering the compliment, which all knew for a fact.

"Flatterer," Morgaine laughed. "But then, no one else has asked me. Of course, I shall be yer partner."

"Then come with us, sister. We have something to share," Aaronn returned and led her away, Olran with them. The three found a private, tree-screened area and Aaronn produced his pipe, while Olran fished out the bag of herb. He stuffed the barest pinch of the heady herb into the bowl of the pipe, lit it with a brand from a brazier nearby, and let Morgaine take a small, experimental puff. While she held it in for a bit, they were surrounded by the smell emanating from the brazier, which Cai lit to keep away insects, burning a special mixture of strong, aromatic herbs. Morgaine finally exhaled and smiled.

"O my 'tis some of the finest herb I have ever had the pleasure of sharing. Sweet, delicious and moist, where did ye get it?" she asked eagerly.

"Ask our brother Olran," Aaronn chuckled as Olran took his share of the herb. Morgaine turned to him, questions ready, but Olran merely held up a finger and took his turn. Only after he was finished did he pull out another, smaller black leather bag.

"For ye, Sister, may it bring ye peace," he said quietly and handed it to her.

The bag, she found upon opening the strings, was completely full of the sweet, pungent herb and she hugged Olran hard, adding a kiss full on his mouth.

"Thank ye, brother. May the Goddess reward ye handsomely for this act of generosity. But I have no pipe," she sighed.

"O, I forgot," Olran added, handing her a pipe similar to the ones he and Aaronn had. "I thought ye would need one, so I had this made for ye."

"Ye are perfect, Olran. Thank ye for yer kindness."

"Thank ye for yer teachings," he returned, smiled and blew her a kiss.

They all shared another round of the herb, then put it away and rejoined the others. When the music began, Aaronn led Morgaine out onto the floor for the first medium paced dance, accustoming themselves to each other's movements. The next piece and many others after that were sprightly and quickstepping tunes, after the first few the elder Knights, Bors and Lionel, retired to the sidelines with their ladies. Their wives brought them cups of wine and plates of small foods Cai's liveried staff were now laying out on spotless, white linen covered tables. Small, folded pastry shells, stuffed with a mixture of roasted, chopped venison, diced onions and other vegetables graced the tables on huge platters. Bite-sized and delicious, they were the centerpieces for Cai's array of appetite teasers; marinated vegetables, boiled and halved eggs, plates of sliced and cubed cheeses, roasted duck, served cold, whole poached salmon and bushels of clean, raw oysters on the half-shell. The sumptuous table was visited by all, the platters replenished as soon as they emptied until all was gone.

As the sun dipped below the treetops, the last set of dancing music began. Only seven couples remained now; the King and Gwenhyfar, Gawaine and some young spitfire of a noble girl Aaronn had not yet met, Bedwyr and his new, red-haired beauty that he thought he heard the men call Vondra, Tristan and Lady Christina of Caw's line, Sir Gaheris with Lancelot's younger sister Branwyn, Aaronn and Morgaine, and Lancelot with young Julia. Aaronn noted that the girl was pressing up against Lancelot eagerly, but Lancelot's eyes were distant and he was a bit stiff, even for his usual impeccable self. The last tune of the set was a slowly accelerating toss dance. This was a most challenging dance, for after executing several intricate movements, the men were obliged to lift and toss the women up, spinning the same amount of rotations every time. If even one step was missed, the dancers would crash atop each other and be disqualified. Pair after pair eventually made a misstep and either the toss or the catch would go awry. The judges would make sure no one was injured seriously before assisting the couple from the floor while the crowd cheered their effort. Finally, there was only the King and Gwenhyfar, Aaronn and Morgaine and Lancelot with Julia. The judges halted the dancing and all three couples stopped gratefully, standing still until their breathing steadied.

"'Tis a three-way tie!" the judges announced and presented each couple a pair of silver goblets as a prize.

The call came for supper, all filed in through the great room to where feast tables awaited. Once seated, the King motioned for quiet and when all noise subsided, he offered a formal blessing on the meal.

"Great Father-Mother God, the Alpha and Omega, we thank ye humbly for all ye have provided Britain. May Thy great Love, Wisdom and Power guide us always through our lives, this opportunity ye have given to us so we may prove our worthiness to serve Thee. Great Mother Ceridwen, Goddess of the World, we thank Thee for the victory ye have granted. We pledge again to Thee that evil will be kept from Thy Holy shores and that all will have the right to worship Thee according to Thy ancient ways. Grant us peace and fertile fields; watch us make Britain's hearts, minds and souls bloom with knowledge of Thy eternal Mysteries. Bless this food, Divine Ones and let it strengthen us and heal us after the long years of war," he spoke with obvious emotion.

"So mote it be," those of the Mother's way responded, while those of the Christ's way responded with, "Amen."

The soup was then served, a clear broth in which floated slivers of onion and cabbage. It was light, and tasty, the unleavened wafers served with it gave the taste, but not the bulk of bread. White wine from Ban's new vineyard filled their glasses, Aaronn found that the taste of the white pleased him as much as most reds he had tasted so far. After the soup was cleared, Cai sent out golden brown fried river trout, served with green vegetables of all sorts, quick steamed and still crisp-tender. Following that was marinated whole pheasant, roasted to crackling crispness, accompanied by steamed grains dressed with basil and olive oil. The white wine accompanied every course nicely, Aaronn thought as he let the servitor fill his cup again. The main course was platters and platters of rib roasts, slow-roasted for hours in dry rock salt and herb marinade, the juices collected and thickened carefully into a thin sauce for tiny, fluffy biscuits. Fried mushrooms, more greens, lightly steamed and tossed with sweet butter and diced onions, as well raw carrot sticks served on the side. All ate their fill, saving just the barest corner of their stomachs for was sure to be a spectacular dessert. While the plates and glasses were cleared, conversation picked up around the series of long tables, King Lot brought up the subject of what was next for Britain. Morgause sat beside him, wearing a deep ruby red gown that showed off her generous bosom, egging on the conversation by throwing out subtle jibes.

"So Sire, when have ye scheduled Cerdic Elesing's execution?" she purred, as if anticipating blood.

"We wait the whole thirty days, Lady Morgause. If I hear nothing from the Saxons, we will give him and easy death as is proper for a worthy enemy," Arthur replied tightly, trying to discourage this line of conversation.

"If 'twere me, I'd skin him alive, piece by slow piece," the Orkney queen remarked savagely.

"Quiet, ye acid-tongued tart, don't ye start on it now, here a' th' table o' victory!" Lot murmured quietly

"I shall say what I please, when I please," she responded louder than he had spoken. "No man orders me silent."

"I shall, Lady Morgause," Aaronn's voice came ringing across the hall. "Be silent, ye harpy, or leave our happy feast."

"Aye, Lot, keep yer woman quiet, especially when she only speaks such hate!" Uriens growled testily. "Let th' King be, he knows what he's doin'. Surely if Cerdic's life is spared, th' Saxons will be easier to keep east of the Severn. If he dies, he becomes a martyr."

"Thank ye, My Lord Uriens," Arthur said graciously. "Ye explained that almost better than I could," he laughed softly, the irony of the situation touching him. "Please, Sister, let us forget Cerdic for tonight?" he asked, his voice kind but his eyes hard and flinty.

Lot nudged her noticeably; she reluctantly took the hint and turned the conversation to Gwenhyfar's gown.

"Lady Gwenhyfar, that gown is stunning! Where in Britain did ye ever find so much silk?" she asked cattily.

"Sir Lancelot was kind enough to purchase a bolt for me in Damascus, along with many rare and exotic spices for Sir Cai. 'Tis not the only bolt of silk he brought home, however. There are bolts and bolts of various colors, including some scarlet that would certainly be just right for a woman of yer complexion," Gwenhyfar answered in kind. Even Aaronn had to grin at the subtle insult hidden in the innocent remark. Gwenhyfar might have some redeeming qualities after all he thought and resolved to compliment her later.

"Truly, Lord Lancelot, how much would it take for ye to part with that bolt of red?" she asked coyly, turning to the First Knight.

Aaronn thought for sure he would retch and he clasped Morgaine's slender hand so hard she tapped him on the leg to make him release the appendage.

"Easy Aaronn, 'tis not the time, not here at the table of victory," Morgaine whispered, shaking her hand under the table to alleviate the pins and needles sensation.

"Is yer hand all right?" Aaronn asked, concerned that he might have harmed her.

"Aye, no thanks to Morgause," she grumped, but accepted the last sip of wine from Aaronn's cup with a wry smile.

Caffe was served and all that partook enjoyed the rare treat gladly, sipping the hot black beverage with obvious delight. With the drink, Cai brought out great pans of apple, pear and current cobbler, as well as little pitchers of sweetened cream spiced with cinnamon.

"Sir Cai, 'tis one of th' best meals I've e'er eaten, an' when ye get t' be my age, tha's a big bill t' fill," King Lot complimented, meaning every word. A salute of caffe was offered to Sir Cai's skills by one and all to thank the Seneschal of Camelot.

"I thank ye, friends and noblemen. 'Twas an honor to prepare a real victory feast at last!" he responded, grinning widely. "And now, I believe our musicians' supper has settled sufficiently to allow a gentle tune or two," he added, hinting that the guests should leave the tables.

"Surely, the musicians' stomachs should settle a bit longer after such a grand meal!" laughed the Merlin, who had been silent and pensive up until now. "Allow me, My Lord Arthur, to entertain the Company with a few songs?" he asked formally.

"Of course, Lord Merlin, if ye would," Arthur agreed easily. Taliesin plucked his harp to insure its proper tuning before strumming the strings, a new song rising under his skillful fingers.

"On Badon's flanks they met,
The Armies of Light and Dark,
No amount of pain or wet,

Could make them miss their mark..." he began and sang the whole moving tale. Included in the verses were those alluding to the Saxon's belief in "the demons in the dark forest," and the whole senior Company was moved to express their gratitude to Aaronn and Olran for the pair's success in their assigned mission by way of a toast.

The Merlin chose a happier tune next; the one following was full of veiled warnings against rebellion of any kind. A happy love song followed and on and on. After an hour, the Merlin put away his harp, bowed and excused himself for the night. Dancing music sounded again from a corner of the great room, the court went in to finish the celebration. Aaronn and Olran grew weary of playing courtly games, so they excused themselves to retire to their room. Morgaine and the Merlin followed behind within minutes of each other, the four smoked a pipe or two of herb, exchanging news of Avalon and Dragon Isle.

"I have sad tidings for ye, Aaronn, brother Michael is quite ill. He was out in all the rain this year with the Druids getting wet and soggy constantly, trying to assist Arthur as much as possible. He has caught a cold in the lungs that has proven persistent. It does not look good, boyo, he has been asking for ye. Go to him, Aaronn, and let him see the Black Knight," the Merlin advised after Morgaine had gone.

"I did not know, Lord Merlin. Of course, I shall go to him, immediately," Aaronn vowed staunchly. The Merlin stayed a bit longer, before he left the two as they prepared for bed and sleep. They fell wearily into their beds, falling asleep quickly and spending all that night in restful slumber.

Upon rising, Olran boiled water and made caffe for the two of them. The odor roused Aaronn, who also rose and dressed for his trip to see Brother Michael. Olran also made ready to go, for Brother Michael's teachings on history and military strategies had been two of Olran's favorite classes. Besides, one did not just let one's best friend attend his mentor's deathwatch alone, he thought as he packed a pair of compressed bricks of the potent herb.

"Where do ye think yer going?" Aaronn asked, surprised to see Olran packed and ready to ride.

"Brother Michael is special to me too, ye know," he answered, seriously.

"Of course he is. I just did not think ye would want to come with me," Aaronn replied contritely, glad to have him along. They went down for a quick breakfast of last evening's leftovers before walking quickly down to the stables. Aaronn saddled up Eclipse, who stood quietly as usual and gave him no trouble. Olran quickly dressed Habib, who had only worked on the lunge line since the Badon siege commenced. The golden-bronze Arab stallion pranced a bit, then stood still while Olran placed the pad of sheepskin, then the camel-hide saddle on his back, tightened the girth strap, the slipped on the horse's gentle bridle.

"Where are ye off to, Sir Aaronn and Sir Olran?" asked Sir Ulster.

"To Avalon, Sir Ulster, to see my Druid teacher and discuss points of improving my skills," Aaronn replied.

"Go with the Goddess, then," Ulster said approvingly. "Sir Olran?"

"Aye, what might I do for ye, Stablemaster?"

"What would ye ask for yer stallion's stud fee?" the stablemaster asked slyly.

"Ye mean 'The Jughead'?" Olran asked, astounded.

"Nay not at all, I mean that beautiful golden-bronze Arab yer aboard," Ulster replied, laughing. "Think on it for a while, then when ye come home, we'll discuss it over a pint or two."

"I shall think on it, Sir Ulster. But I warn ye, 'twill not come cheap," Olran replied.

"That I can believe," Ulster laughed harder and waved them off as he walked away to his next task. The other two led their steeds out into the warm autumn sun, mounted up and pointed their horse's noses towards Avalon. They passed the Celidon battlefield on their way, Aaronn couldn't help stopping and searching for his lost blade. It was futile, he knew, but even with Morgaine's replacement the harness he wore still felt slightly off-weight. Sighing in resignation, he mounted up again and headed towards Avalon.

They arrived at mid-afternoon the next day, finding the barge awaiting them. Vivaine's attendant priestess, Raven, was in the front of the barge as the two led their steeds aboard and took their places. The bargemen poled off and headed towards the ever-present bank of fog that hung like a curtain between Britain's shore and Avalon's. Once the veil was parted at a word from Raven, the two regarded shining Avalon. The smell of warm, ripe apples from the huge groves wafted out over the Lake into their noses, as intoxicating as the good apple ale the Druids made from these very same apples. Vivaine greeted them before she walked over to Habib, a perfect piece of fruit in hand.

"Hullo and greetings, swift one. Welcome to Avalon, the Isle of Apples," she spoke quietly to him. The stallion's head and ears perked up as he regarded the surrounding groves. He let out a ringing neigh and delicately took the apple from Vivaine's hand a piece at a time, crunching happily. The younger priestesses came and took the horses into Avalon's stables.

"How is our brother Michael?" Aaronn asked.

"He is in the sun today, Aaronn. Only then and when he is in the hot springs does he feel no pain. Come, he will be happy to see the pair of ye," Vivaine said as she led them to where the aged and ill Druid lay on the padded cot in the warm sun.

"Aaronn, my boyo!" he said in a glad whisper, and Aaronn nearly wept at the echo of his master's strong and resonant voice.

"Master, I did not know…, I…" Aaronn tried to explain as he knelt beside the man.

"I asked that they not tell ye, for ye were more needed at Mount Badon than here to watch me waste away. Ceridwen calls, boyo, even I cannot ignore that summons. I only wanted to see and speak with ye one last time," Michael said, a very fatherly tone in his voice. "Ye are the son I never had and ye are the very best student I ever taught. Pass on what ye have learned and do not ever turn down a chance to learn more, no matter who the teacher might be, as long as they are of the Light. I wish I had been more knowledgeable, but I taught well what I do know," he finished proudly and laid his hands atop Aaronn's head.

"I shall miss ye, Master. Ye have been and shall always be a friend and my mentor," Aaronn replied, choking on tears he fought to withhold. "Is there anything I can do for ye?" he asked, regaining a little control.

"Ye can tell me about the demons of the dark forest," the Druid replied, laughing carefully to avoid a coughing fit.

"Of course, dear Master," Aaronn replied. Wine and food were brought as the two young men related their campaign of terror against the hardy Saxons. Even Brother Michael flinched a bit when Aaronn told him of capturing the Saxon hunters one by one and slaying them by either sword or arrow, then neatly removing their scalps from their skulls.

"Did ye keep the scalps?" the Druid asked.

"Of course, I thought I would make Cerdic a present of 'em, or more rightly, the Black Knight will," Aaronn chuckled.

"Tell me true, boyo. Was the scalping planned or spontaneous?" asked Michael.

"It seemed the right thing to do to keep them out of the forest and away from the deer. It just happened, I did not plan it," Aaronn admitted.

"And when ye battled Cerdic?" Michael pressed.

"It looked like Arthur's forces would be stopped before they crested the final fences and ditches. All I meant to do was divert the Saxons attention long enough for the Knights to break through. I had no thought to engage Cerdic personally," Aaronn said, grinning wide before he went on a bit more hesitantly. "When his steel met mine, I went a bit mad, however. I remember thinking, "Ceridwen please aid me now!", and then I looked up in the sky and thought of how much it reminded me of bloody water. Then I do not remember anything until a big, meaty fist hit me on the jaw."

"Ye have experienced the rapture of Vengeance, my boyo. Remember how I told ye the Fourth face of the Mother is the most terrifying?" he asked and Aaronn nodded and Michael went on. "When ye ask for Her aid, She sends Vengeance. Sometimes, unless a warrior is very strong in his mind, he can be lost entirely in that rush of direct Goddess energy. I have trained ye well, for ye are intact and whole despite the experience. I am content," he sighed. "Could I have a sip of wine, please, my boyo?" he asked after a moment.

"Of course Master," Aaronn agreed and held out his own cup to Michael's lips. The Druid sipped carefully twice, then swallowed and lay back.

"Thank ye, boyo," Michael said and closed his eyes.

It was a full hour before Aaronn realized that Michael was gone to his reward in the Blessed Isles.

"Fare thee well, Master. Remember me when I follow after ye," he wept a few rare tears.

Olran heard, looked, saw the tears running down his friends' face, then ran for Vivaine. The High Priestess of Avalon came with the Merlin and the seven Elders of the Druids to take the body gently away. Olran led Aaronn to the hot springs, where a combination of the soothing waters and herb melted away most of Aaronn's immediate grief. When the pair of them emerged sometime later, they were ready to celebrate Michael's passing as only the Druids could. All of the past Master's favorite foods were prepared and a cool cask of apple ale stood at hand to toast Michael's memory. An empty place was set at the head of the table where Michael's formal ritual robe draped over the back of the chair. A full ale mug stood at the place and periodically it was passed around as those who held it offered small tales of remembrance of their brother and co-worker. When the pyre was ready, Aaronn was granted the honor of lighting it to send Michael on his journey to Ceridwen's realm. The wood crackled merrily and burnt hot, with a great puff of sparks and smoke, the body of the Druid ignited and burnt entirely. Aaronn distinctly heard Michael's great infectious laugh as the hot flames consumed the Druid's mortal remains.

They celebrated long into the night, retiring only after the entire meal was consumed and the ale cask empty. Aaronn and Olran slept the whole day through, rising in the late afternoon and eating a huge meal. When the Merlin and Brother Drusus joined them, Olran produced his pipe and a brick of herb.

"Where did ye get this?" asked Drusus as he smelled the rich fragrance.

"In the Arab lands, brother, would ye care for a pinch?" Olran asked coyly.

"What are ye waiting for, boyo?" Drusus asked, grinning wide and producing his own pipe. The brick was looking a bit chewed on by the time Vivaine joined them, her eyes lit on the rare treat and a pipe was handed to her. The talk drifted onto the subject of the Black Knight.

"So, now that the Saxons are rendered meek and mild, and they fear Britain's forests, what is next for the Black Knight and the Black Hunter?" Vivaine asked.

Aaronn grinned, then answered mock-seriously: "Why, kill all the traitors in the realm, of course!" he laughed. The others laughed with him, none but Olran knowing just how serious Aaronn really was. After several hours of conversation passed, the two said their good-byes, met their horses by the barge landing and led the steeds aboard. All their friends waved farewell as they disappeared into the veil of fog, reappearing in Britain just as the sun sank. They slept in the wood that night, in the morning they mounted up, returned to Camelot by the longest route and took a private supper in their room. Over the meal of fish, boiled lentil salad and eggs, Ceridwen's men discussed what would be their next move.

"The name and reputation of the Black Knight must be feared throughout all Britain. 'Twas easy enough for us to frighten the Saxons at Badon during the siege, they are mostly an unlearned people. The nobles of the Pendragon's realm, however, are not so easily frightened," Olran observed.

"Aye, 'tis sure," Aaronn agreed, knowing Olran's insight with the ruling class would be invaluable in their cause. "We must also invite the co-operation of the common folk. 'Tis they who are made to suffer for the nobleman's treachery," Aaronn said.

"We should start then, with the common folk's problems," Olran suggested. "When the noble's bullyboys start disappearing, the stories are sure to be spread far and wide. Have ye thought of leaving behind a short, concise parchment scroll or a token?"

"Aye, my brother, indeed I have. Here is the design of the token," Aaronn chuckled and handed Olran a piece of parchment. Olran grinned when he saw it.

"'Tis perfect, brother. Who are ye going to have make 'em?" he asked.

"I have a young Guildsman in mind to sponsor, through Sir Dalren, of course," Aaronn laughed.

"Ye always seem one step ahead of me, brother. Congratulations," Olran laughed with him. "Of course, a few carefully spread stories would not hurt," he suggested, rubbing his hands together in anticipation of undertaking that enterprise.

It all began a few nights later; Lord Evin Merin's bodyguards at Darkensdale were the targets. Creeping into the castle, the Black Knight killed each man where they lay, leaving a rolled scroll warning the treacherous Lord that his habits should change. Going to the slave pens, the Black Knight released cell after cell full of emaciated, weary men whose only crime was they could no longer pay the outrageous head taxes levied by Merin. Warning them all to silence with gestures, the Black Knight escorted the wretched men out of Merin's incarceration and into freedom.

"Who are ye that ye would do this for us?" they all asked after leaving Darkensdale a safe distance behind. "How can we ever repay yer deed?"

"No payment is asked, except that ye offer prayers to the Goddess for all treason to be discovered and ended in the realm," the Black Knight told them. "Know ye that I am the Black Knight of Avalon, sent by Ceridwen the White to patrol the land in search of treachery. Go home to yer families now, take this bag of gold I have for ye and use it to yer best advantage. Feed yer families and make sure the King hears of Merin's treatment of ye," he went on, handing each man a sizable bag of gold coins, appropriated from Merin's own treasury.

"Goddess bless ye, Sir Knight!" they all said quietly together, bowing to him collectively as he strode away into the night. He returned to where Ebony waited, blanketed against the chill of the night, in a copse of trees and mounted up. Riding slowly away, heading back to Camelot, several times he was sure he heard muffled hoofbeats behind him and he pulled off the road to listen carefully. Each time he heard nothing, but quickened his pace, returning to Camelot long before he had planned. Slipping into his room through the secret door, Aaronn checked at Olran's door and heard breathing, snoring noises. He opened the door and checked visually just to make sure and saw an Olran-sized lump in the bed. He watched for a few moments before closing the door quietly, sure now that the hoofbeats on the road were figments of his over-active imagination. He put off his working clothes, lay down and was immediately asleep. He could not have been more mistaken, however, about his concern at being followed.

As the Black Hunter had trailed the Black Knight from Darkensdale, where he had watched over his ally's back, he had turned off the road towards his own family keep. He had an appointment to keep there after all these years and he did not wish to be late. He tethered the Jughead, ordered him "on guard" to stay him from wandering, then made his way onto the catwalk that topped the castle walls of Westerland Keep. Right on schedule at the first pink of dawn, Justine came out of the Keep's scullery door, headed for the stables and her early morning ride. The Black Hunter assured himself that the rolled message on the arrow was tied tightly, loaded it into the ash bow, drew, sighted and fired, striking the Lady of the Keep cleanly in the upper right arm with the missile. The woman screamed with fright and pain, dropped to her knees and struggled to remove the arrow, but the barbed points of Damascene steel held fast, causing the flow of blood to increase as she struggled with it.

"Warren, Kevin, help me!" she screamed and the two came running. The Black Hunter grinned coldly, his plan coming to fruition; he drew another arrow from his quiver and sighted the most obvious target.

"Ahhhhrgh!" Kevin screamed and twisted to remove the barbed arrow from his fat buttocks. Another arrow whistled by, skewering Warren's left foot to the courtyard's dirt floor.

"Curse ye, whoever ye are!" Warren screeched like a fishwife, trying to wrench free. "Find that damned assassin!" he called to his men at arms. Nine of them died before the tenth man turned and ran back into the guardhouse.

"Beware Ceridwen's Black Knight, Warren of Westerland Keep!" the Black Hunter shouted down, his voice echoing around the inner Keep. "He finds and punishes the wicked in the name of the Goddess! No traitor is safe from the Goddess' wrath!"

Quickly, the fleet figure worked his way down from the heights, returned to his horse and hid in the wood. He laughed until his sides ached as they searched ineptly for him, then after all was quiet, he returned to the castle. He located the nine biers on which lay the bodies of the slain men at arms, surgically removed the arrowheads from them, putting them in a pouch until they could be properly cleaned of the toad poison they had been coated with. Next, he invaded the kitchens and found the three arrowheads removed from Justine, Warren and Kevin, putting them in the pouch as well. Grinning to himself in anticipation of the repercussions, he left a "gift" in the flour barrels before taking his leave.

When the cook came in to set the sponge for the next day's rising, she made such a fuss that when Warren limped downstairs to find out what was amiss she leapt on him with her full fury.

"Roaches, 'tis what is wrong, My Lord!" the cook shuddered violently. "The whole batch must be tainted!"

"Aye and we traded with Merin for this shipment. No wonder 'twas so cheap," Warren grumbled, as the Black Hunter had intended. "Well, what are ye waiting for? Set a crew to open the rest of those barrels and sift for roaches. Empty those barrels that are tainted and burn 'em, collect the bugs and use 'em for fish bait. Tell 'em in the stables I'll need my good dapple-gray team and wagon. Merin has a bit of explaining to do," Warren huffed, shouldered one of the infested barrels and limped after the servant, already planning what he was going to say to his questionable ally about the cost of the tainted flour.

By then, however, the Black Hunter was miles away and side-sore from continual laughter. He stabled the Jughead, wiped him down, watered and grained him well, covering him with a clean stable blanket before entering into Camelot through the Maze. Returning to his room, he found

Aaronn sleeping soundly, or appearing to, he quietly entered his sleeping chamber and woke the woman who slept in the bed.

"Marian, my dear, awake, 'tis past dawn," he whispered, now clad in dressing gown and slippers.

"O, I have slept late," she exclaimed quietly. "I thank ye for letting me do so, yer bed is very comfortable," she added, pulling her dress on.

"You looked so beautiful and relaxed, Marian. I was loath to wake you until 'twas absolutely necessary. Now, go on back to yer duties, lest Sir Cai come looking for ye," Olran chuckled and held open the door for her. She gave him a quick, shy kiss, then exited out the portal, and headed for her duties in the kitchen. Olran locked the door, entered his inner chamber and locked the door. He sat and methodically cleaned the dried blood from the arrowheads, then refitted them onto black shafts and replaced them in his working quiver. Pouring himself a cup of wine, he sat and saluted the Goddess, drinking deeply. "Thank ye, Mother," he thought. "For at least making a beginning in their fear," Only after the wine was finished did he lay down, falling immediately asleep.

A messenger arrived from Darkensdale four days later with a very distressed letter from Merin.

"My Lord High King, Arthur Pendragon, things are not bad enough here in this realm, now we must also bear the indignity of being subjected to a bold fellow attacking our own castle and people? This Black Knight is a vicious criminal whose end must be sought by the High Throne, lest there be no respect for law in the realm. He has casually slit the throats of twenty of my tax collectors, right here in my own castle! Also, he has freed dozens of tax evaders from my holding cells. He must be stopped, or I shall not be able to meet my obligations to the Crown's Treasury. Lord Evin Merin,"
Arthur laughed heartily when he read the missive, penning his reply while still chuckling.

"My Lord Merin, Perhaps if ye would lighten the load of yer people and be kinder to them, they would not write the Crown letters complaining of yer cruelty. We have had many testimonies sent to us here at Camelot; they are all filled with the most interesting facts. I have sent Sir Lancelot and a full detachment of Camelot's Knights to Darkensdale. They will arrive within the week to carry out a full investigation. Be sure yer books are in order and that ye are ready to pay, in full, yer taxes for the year in gold, unless ye are prepared to question yer liability. We are sure a full audit can be arranged, if ye desire, to ascertain whether or not yer present assessment is fair. Arthur Pendragon, High King of Britain."

As soon as the letter was sealed with the royal seal, Arthur summoned Aaronn to him. "So, tell me about Lord Merin?" he said directly as soon as the man was seated.

"Where should I begin, My Lord 'tis so much to discuss," Aaronn grinned, the aura of the Black Knight falling on him.

"Why not begin with his dead tax collectors?"

"The Black Knight found them all involved in the persecution of helpless peasants. This may, or may not in all fairness, be at Merin's orders, but Ceridwen could no longer tolerate their bullying those poor folk. She called for their judgment. I assume that those who came to see My Lord offered enough evidence to substantiate my words?" the Black Knight reported dryly.

"I cannot help but wonder, Sir Black Knight, if other methods would suffice?" Arthur said tightly.

"Men like Merin are afraid of little else but death, My Lord Pendragon," the Black Knight responded. "On another matter, I have a present for ye, Sire," he added slyly. "It may come in handy when ye begin negotiating for Cerdic's ransom."

"Anything helpful would be handy," Arthur laughed, glad to be off the subject of the traitorous Merin. "They have responded and the Saxon negotiators are on the way even as we speak."

The Black Knight produced a string of well-cured, scalped locks, braided together by their long tresses, handing them to Arthur. The King took them each in hand, studying each one carefully.

"I do not recognize any of them. Who are they?" he asked as he regarded the neatly presented trophies.

"These once graced the heads of Cerdic's best hunters. The Saxons are now so frightened of the Goddess' forests they will never again enter them willingly," the Black Knight laughed.

"Nice work, good trophies, Sir Black Knight. Did ye recover all yer blades this time?" Arthur questioned.

"Of course, My Lord, never again will I leave a battlefield before locating all my blades!" Ceridwen's man replied ruefully, his normal demeanor returning. "I have found 'tis far too difficult and expensive for me to find exact replacements."

"I believe that," Arthur nodded, then handed over his reply to Lord Merin's demands. Ceridwen's man scanned it, grinned wide when he read the implied threat and suggestion that the Black Knight had acted improperly, then returned the missive to the King's hand.

"He has balls the size of chapel bells," the Black Knight commented. "He is actually calling for *my* prosecution?" he added unbelievingly.

"See that ye tread lightly, Sir. I must have incontestable proof in hand to be able to shield ye from Merin's wrath," Arthur reminded. "Yer greatest protection is the Law of Britain."

"Ceridwen's Law supersedes yers, My Lord. What needs doing will get done and ye shall have whatever proof ye need," the Black Knight answered testily. "Do ye have anything ye need done for the Crown?"

"Aye, I want ye to attend the treaty signing." Arthur answered.

"Truly?" Ceridwen's man asked, surprised.

"Of course, the Black Knight should be there in case of trouble," Arthur said craftily. "I cannot think of anyone more qualified."

"I see. Do ye want me in the room or roaming about, looking for trouble?" he asked, pouring himself a cup of wine.

"Cerdic will be in the room with me, so 'tis where I want ye. Sir Lancelot will be handling normal security and I shall let it be known that Sir Aaronn is to help him," Arthur chuckled.

"So, Sir Aaronn will be conveniently occupied. None will be looking for him," the Black Knight laughed.

"Very good," Arthur laughed with him. "Now, go on. I have to dress to impress our Saxon neighbors," the King dismissed him casually.

"Be sure to wear the formal crown, Sire. I know 'tis a heavy burden, but 'tis embellished with Ceridwen's sign as well as the Christ's. Cerdic will certainly recognize both and fear because of it. He saw the Goddess' judgment at Badon."

"Aye and I have these as well," Arthur agreed, indicating the scalps on the back of his chair.

"Aye, they should help somewhat," the Black Knight rose, bowed at the waist and took his leave. After stopping at his room to stow his working clothes, he went directly to the baths and washed quickly, then robed up and returned to his room. Just as he laid his clothes on his bed, a knock sounded at the door and Aaronn opened to find a panting young page awaiting him.

"Sir Aaronn, Sir Lancelot requires yer presence in his quarters at once," he reported, stressing the last two words.

"Very well, tell the First Knight I shall dress quickly and report."

"He said for me to return with ye or be dismissed from the page corps," the young boy struggled to regain normal breathing. "Please, Sir Aaronn. I have made one mistake today of all days, I cannot be sent home in disgrace."

"Very well, yer name is Regulus, aye?" Aaronn replied and wrapped the towel tighter around him. "Lead on."

Regulus gulped hard and complied, preceding Aaronn down the hallway, through the crowded great room, then up the stairs to Sir Lancelot's quarters. Many people were treated to a full viewing of Aaronn's well-muscled physique as he strode through wearing naught but the towel.

"Go on now, Page. I shall handle this from here on. Sir Lancelot and I have something very important to discuss. What we have to say to each other is not for a page's ears," Aaronn told the boy and sent him on his way. He waited until the boy was long gone, then knocked.

"Sir Aaronn, 'tis about time," Lancelot's voice answered impatiently. "I should have that mistake of a page Regulus whipped and sent home!" he added, through the slightly ajar door.

"Aye, Sir Lancelot. Sir Aaronn, reporting at once, as ordered!" he heard the reply. Lancelot opened the door to find the mostly naked Aaronn, standing at attention outside.

"Ye could have taken a moment to dress, Sir Aaronn," the First Knight said after recovering from momentary surprise.

"Ye told Regulus to bring me at once, My Lord. He was most insistent that your will was to be followed to the letter," Aaronn replied stiffly. "I am here, as ordered. What is it ye wish of me?"

"Sir Aaronn, would ye please go and attire yerself properly before ye return for yer assignment?" Lancelot ordered, breaking into a wide grin in recognition of his own impatience.

"I only came in the haste of yer summoning, First Sword. I am always at yer service. Besides, I should not wish to be the cause of another's dismissal from Camelot, My Lord," Aaronn answered, saluted again and hastened back to his room to quickly dress. Returning at once to Lancelot's quarters, he was welcomed inside, apologized to again and then apprised of the security measures already in place.

At noon, a full division of Camelot's Knights escorted the Saxon bargaining team into Camelot. They brought wagonloads of booty to ransom their warchiefs; there was a moment or two of tension as they discussed leaving Cerdic behind to punish him for leading them into defeat. Once all was calm, the group of British and Saxons sat uncomfortably at the table, trying to relax. With Arthur sat Lancelot, Gawaine, Tristan and Bedwyr. At hand for Cerdic was his Skald Cronin, as well as his own lieutenants Gunter, Leifr and Hallr. The Black Knight slipped in from the Maze's secret entrance, remaining in the shadowed vantage point unseen by any whom sat at the treaty table. They all sat squirming a bit as Arthur cleared his throat and began:

"Please, our Saxon brothers, let us put aside all old hurts and hates. We are willing to grant ye a portion of the east Summerlands, some of the richest farmland on the island. We will provide ye seeds and assistance in re-stocking yer forest on that side of the Severn with wild game animals, so ye may practice yer hunting rites. No raiding in Britain will be tolerated, however," he told them. Surprised looks appeared on the faces of the Saxons, none of them had expected such generosity from their former enemies.

"That's mighty generous, Pendragon. But what about the hot bloods who will not be controlled?" Cerdic shot back, glancing at Hallr.

"I leave that sort of thing to Ceridwen of the Forests, as yer hunters from Badon can attest," Arthur answered coolly and tossed the braided string of scalps onto the table in front of the Saxon "Cying."

"By Thor the Thunderer, where did ye get these?" Hallr asked, horrified as he recognized each of the grisly trophies as formerly gracing the heads of his best hunters. Arthur made a summoning gesture and the Black Knight appeared from the shadows.

"I was made a gift of them by Ceridwen's man here. He said he got them from the demons in the wood of Badon," Arthur responded. "The Black Knight is the guardian of our Forests, appointed by Ceridwen Herself. I do not command him. If ye are found raiding, expect to be subjected to the Goddess's Vengeance."

"All right, enough. We understand what ye mean, Pendragon. Where's yer treaty?" Cerdic growled, white under his normal ruddy complexion. "We'll agree to yer terms, as long as ye are High King. What other choice have ye left us?" he turned to his companions and asked, shrugging.

Sir Bedwyr brought the treaty and Cerdic sighed his rune sign, countersigning his Roman name and title, "Cerdic Elesing, Chief of the Federated Tribes, Cying".

"Will ye join us in a cup of peace, our Saxon brothers? 'Tis a good stout, made by our brother Sir Cai," Arthur asked.

"I shall join ye, as will my warchiefs. Good stout is rare east of the Severn," Cerdic grinned wanly. His body had healed well in the month in Camelot's jail, due to the abundance of fresh fruit, vegetables and decent meals. No visible signs of bruises remained, although sometimes when he exercised hard, he still had a hitch in his side. Even that was nearly gone, Cerdic realized as he toasted the peace loudly with the others. He held no animosity for the beating for he would have done the same and worse to the Pendragon if the situation had been reversed. They ate and drank together in a pleasant way before the Saxons took their leave of Camelot. They were escorted by the same division that had brought them to the castle, the Black Knight and the Black Hunter watched from the forest making sure that all the Saxons stayed with the group of supply-laden wagons across the Severn and miles into the new treaty properties. The pair of Ceridwen's men watched them go, then returned to Britain's soil; once home, off came their hoods and the two clasped forearms in triumph.

"They are still our enemies, ye know. They will be back when their numbers have increased sufficiently," Aaronn observed.

"Aye, but by then we will have eliminated all their allies in Britain. We will be ready for them, barring anything that fate throws our way," Olran replied, excited. "Cai was preparing the traditional victory feast when we left; whole roasted quail, salmon and Dalren's farm provided a whole steer that Cai was just mounting on the spit when we left," he rubbed his stomach and smacked his lips.

"How long have ye been following me on missions, brother?" Aaronn asked suddenly, hoping to startle the truth from Olran. "O, and I found out about yer little 'visit' to Westerland as well," he added.

Olran blushed a bit and shuffled his feet. "I wanted to cover yer back at Darkensdale. 'Tis a dangerous place, even in the best of times," he answered. "Ye are my only friend; I wanted to be sure ye stay alive. Doing what ye did there alone would have been suicide, if any of them had awakened."

"And yer actions at yer family's castle?"

"I only wished to create a riot, so I could taint the flour shipment Warren bought cheap from Merin. Ye should have seen Merin's face when Warren dumped that roach-infested barrel of flour all over Darkensdale's great room floor. I have never been so well entertained," Olran related, chuckling at the memory. Aaronn grinned, knowing well what Merin's snobby and aristocratic face would look like in such a calamity.

"So, now 'tis animosity between Darkensdale and Westerland Keep, where before they trusted and traded openly with each other," he observed. "I could not have done better myself. From now on, however, we discuss every mission, if possible, whether or not ye are working with me or independently to spread the fame of the Black Knight. He will seem able to be in many places at once that way and be able to use more than one weapon to accomplish his missions as well," Aaronn laughed.

"We are Ceridwen's men, after all," Olran grinned and chuckled with real humor.

"Aye, that we are, brother," Aaronn responded and mounted up. "Come on, my stomach is ready for that feast!"

Olran's stomach rumbled loudly in response. "Aye!" he laughed and made to vault into the Jughead's saddle. The ill-tempered beast stepped a large step forward, despite being trained and commanded to stand. Olran landed face first in a large pile of fresh horse manure, provided by the Jughead as well.

"Why ye...ye...Jughead!" he spit through the foul-tasting mouthful. "I should use ye for bear bait!"

The horse turned his head, rolled his eyes and obediently turned to offer his ride the stirrup on the proper side. Olran took out a cloth, wiped his face thoroughly before mounting up, without a word he spurred the great blue roan into a full gallop. He forced the animal to maintain the pace all the way back to Camelot, then stabled him, wiped him down, blanketed and watered him, leaving him to wait until the horseboys regularly fed the entire stable. It was close to the scheduled time, he knew, the wait would serve the foul-tempered beast right for moving despite being ordered to stand.

Aaronn followed suit with Eclipse, being sure to wipe his white ring clean of concealing soot. The two made their way to the secret entrance that was so conveniently located to the stables and stepped through. Up to their room they went to slip off their working leathers, donning yesterday's clothes. The two went out their door and down the hall to the baths, which were crowded by laughing, joking Knights. When their turn came, Aaronn and Olran gladly took their places in a tub, moving over for Bedwyr when he appeared through the clouds of steam.

"Greetings to ye, brothers. Well, how does it feel to be at peace, at last?" he grinned, accepting a tankard of cool ale from a server.

Aaronn took his portion, sipped and answered truthfully. "I do not know, brother Bedwyr, I am not so sure we are, despite the treaty."

"Aw, coom on Aaronn," Gawaine joined in from the next tub. "Cerdic's ne'er given his 'sworn by Thor's word,' before. This be th' end o' it!"

"For now, brother Gawaine," Aaronn added. "We must remain ever alert to their thieving ways."

"Aye, tha' we will, laddie," Gawaine returned, still smiling. "But a' least we've got 'till they breed oop a bit. Did ye ever hear the final Saxon body count from Badon?"

"Did we count?" asked Aaronn, amazed.

"O' course, we always do! Th' final count was one thousand Saxon dead, if I recall right," Gawaine answered, chuckling harder.

"And that doesn't count all they lost to the 'demons in the forest'," Bedwyr laughed until tears ran from his eyes. All the others joined in and the assembled Knights toasted Ceridwen's unknown man, the Black Knight.

Aaronn and Olran finished bathing, returning freshly robed to their quarters. Dressing in their finest, the two went downstairs where the sideboard waited. They partook of the appetizers and drank mug after mug of good apple ale brewed by the Druids, provided by Dragon Isle as their contribution to Camelot's larder. All toasted the God, the Earth Mother Ceridwen, as well as the King, the Knights of Camelot, the Druids and the Ladies of Avalon and Sir Cai all through the night.

Supper was excellent as usual, but Aaronn was restless and after he was comfortably full he returned to his room. Ceridwen's favor sent the mantle of the Black Knight upon him; he left the castle and went down into the town, prowling the row of taverns and inns. He found one he had been told harbored its share of rough types, entered and took a seat in the back of the room. He sat, watched and listened, again amazed at how much men will talk when properly plied with liquor. Sorting the valuable information from the useless, he mentally discarded the latter.

"More ale, Sir?" he heard a luscious female voice at his ear. Looking up from his shadowed seat, the Black Knight was surprised to see the voluptuous redhead named Vondra standing there, tray in hand.

"Aye, my dear, and thank ye," he replied, meaning it.

The woman bent over him, exposing her most noticeable features for his inspection as she picked up his used mug and swayed away from him. He watched, pleased by the motion of her shapely bottom under her shift before returning to his work. It was difficult to concentrate however for he found his eyes watching Vondra with growing interest. When the hour grew quite late, the Black Knight decided that he would hear no more useable information and prepared to take his leave. Vondra began the work of closing the tavern's common room; clearing the tables of used mugs and scrubbing them clean of spilled ale, as was her duty. A group of hard-eyed men entered and encircled her, obviously up to no good, teasing and taunting her as she tried to do her work.

"Please men the tavern is closed. Go home and pick on yer wives, eh boyos?" Vondra tried to be pleasant, but they were in no mood to be placated. Before she could blink, one man pushed her into the arms of another. He began kissing her neck and chest with his mouthful of broken and rotting teeth. She tried to free herself, raking his face futilely with sharp fingernails, but found herself bent back over the oak tabletop, his filthy hands pawing at the laced front of her dress.

"Help me, someone please help me!" she screamed as the laces of her gown snapped and her lush breasts spilled from the bodice. Her attacker buried his dirty face between them ecstatically as she squirmed and fought vainly. The man felt a sudden, sharp pain in his neck, then the rush of warm blood before he dropped to the floor, dead. His companions fell similarly in the rain of thrown knives, each man suffering the sure knowledge of his passing before losing consciousness.

"Are ye well, Lady?" a resonant voice asked of the girl, who now cowered fearfully under a table.

"I…I think so," she answered slowly, coming back into the open. She tried to re-tie her bodice, finally giving up with a sigh. "Damn him! I just bought that gown!" she managed to say, then hawked and spit with disdain on the leader's dead face.

"Certainly it can be replaced with something finer?" the Black Knight chuckled, handing her his cloak for cover.

"Not for a while. It took me one whole night's services to pay for this one," she sighed heavily again. "I cannot always depend on that kind of client."

"Sir Tristan is known for his generosity to ladies of great beauty," the Black Knight chuckled a bit harder, unable to help himself. "I have a proposition for ye, wench. Are ye bound here?" he asked.

"Nay, not after this!" she answered emphatically.

"Good then, come with me. I have a friend who will help," he told her and escorted her from the tavern through the dark streets of Camelot-town. Arriving at a tavern he knew well, owned secretly by Sir Dalren, he took her upstairs to the room he maintained there. Wine and cups were set up on a table inside the room and the Black Knight waved her over to them. Pouring herself a brimming cupful as well as one for the hooded man, Vondra sat before the hearth, watching him light the ready pile of dry wood laid there. "Tell me, Vondra. Why are ye here, when ye should be home with surely aged parents?" he asked directly, after taking a sip of the hearty wine.

"My parents, due to a long illness, are in debt up to their wrinkled old necks. The new King's tax assessors are no fairer than the old King's, it seems. My parents have no idea of what I do here in town, they are merely grateful for the money I send home," Vondra answered, trying hard not to sound bitter. "My brothers, all five of them, died in the Pendragon's army, but not one cent of their pay came to my parents. Their commanders claimed any moneys they earned were used to defray the costs of burying them," she added.

"How much is the debt?" asked Ceridwen's man, interested. He had heard tales of such things, but never had anyone made formal charges. "Has the amount been paid to any extent?"

"Not one cent." Vondra sighed, tears forming. "I have to keep replacing my clothing. The whole amount is a hundred gold sovereigns."

"I shall pay it." the Black Knight told her, without hesitation. He bent and unlocked a safe under his chair, although Vondra could not see how he did it, then counted out the proper amount, bagged it and set it in her hands.

"Thank ye, My Lord Black Knight," Vondra managed to sputter, astonished. "What can I ever do to repay yer generosity?"

"I want to employ ye, wench, as my ally. A woman of yer abilities and beauty could entertain any man, even the King himself, and probably get him to tell ye anything. Put that inborn skill to work, woman! Put it to use in my service. In return, ye will have whatever ye need, gowns, a room here at this inn and a monthly stipend of say, twenty gold sovereigns?" he proposed, watching her face dissolve into astounded wonder.

"Why?" she asked, suspicious. "Certainly ye do not need my help after what I witnessed tonight."

"I do need yer help, Vondra. Ye would be a valuable ally and the Black Knight could certainly use a woman on his side," he told her, meaning every word.

"I see. So there are things I could find out easier than ye could for yerself?" she asked alertly.

"Aye, like who is sleeping with whom at Camelot. I know how women talk of such things only between themselves," he answered. "I know ye talk more freely amongst yerselves about the men in their life, about how they make love and any 'unusual' tastes they might enjoy."

"I see," she pursed her full, red lips. "Can I order a bath?"

"Why?" he asked, surprised.

"Surely ye wish to know exactly what 'tis ye are purchasing?" she purred and removed the cloak as well as the rags of the gown and any undergarments she wore. As she turned in the firelight for his inspection, the Black Knight's eyes were treated to a full and complete measure of her astonishing figure. She had large, full, firm breasts, a small neat waist and legs so shapely he could no longer resist. He took her gently into his arms and pressed his lips against hers in a long, slow sensuous kiss that left them both breathless.

"I think that bath might be a good idea for both of us," he suggested, breathing heavily, then called downstairs to ask after it.

The innkeeper heated a pair of large kettles of water, when they were ready he called to his servants to assist in taking the large wooden tub as well as the hot water up to the room, along with small foods and more wine. Two men stood outside the room to insure the privacy the Black Knight always insisted on. Afterwards, their lovemaking was slow and passionate, leaving them both spent and sleepy. Before they slept, however, Vondra agreed to enter the service of the Black Knight.

When she awoke in the morning, he was gone, but one fresh cut, dark red rose remained on his pillow as a token of thanks. Vondra smelled its rich odor, put it in water and called for the innkeeper to send for a good seamstress. The next few hours were spent ordering appropriate styles and colors of gowns. The woman had thoughtfully brought with her several ready-made gowns, Vondra found two that fit and suited her. She purchased them both, using some of the twenty gold sovereigns left behind by her patron. She paid half down on the order with the seamstress, telling her to hurry with the gowns.

Donning a demure green gown, the neckline barely scooped over her chest, Vondra dressed her hair simply and donned the cape that completed the outfit. She left the room with the bag containing the money to pay her parent's debt, went directly to Camelot and the office of tax collections. Gleefully, she paid off her parent's tax debts, making sure to obtain a receipt, and left the office singing. Aaronn watched her go, grinning as he saw her be approached and complimented by many a lonely single Knight. She played her role to the hilt as he watched unseen from a parapet and was satisfied entirely with his choice of an ally as she walked enticingly away down the road to the tavern.

Almost from the very first night, the Black Knight began to get complete reports from Vondra concerning the habits of certain men currently under consideration for knighthood. Many a man's nocturnal activities were duly reported to the King, who then either found convenient reasons to dismiss them or invited them to stay depending on the contents of the Black Knight's reports. For those expressing regret with any aberrations in those activities during the interviews, help from Avalon was always suggested. For those who expressed only rage at being discovered came only an escort to Land's End to insure that he left Britain, not to return upon pain of death.

Vondra also proved useful in other ways as the weeks passed, the Black Knight found to his delight. The woman had a real gift for learning the unknowable from those men she personally entertained. From Merin's nephew Corwin she heard the news of growing distrust amongst the traitorous and scheming Merin. He was now conspiring with Warren, Lot and several others of the old guard; still working for Arthur's unseating. The Black Knight left fueling that valuable feud to the Black Hunter, who knew the territory well. For himself, the Orkneys were much more interesting.

As the months progressed, reports from old Llew told of Merin's negotiations to purchase from Uriens a large villa next to Londinium. Immediately, the Black Knight was suspicious and sent Ceridwen's Hunter to investigate, while he attended to tasks closer to home. The nobles were now gathering for the Winter Solstice celebration at Camelot, the topics under discussion amongst them interested the Black Knight considerably. As he circulated among the cream of Britain's nobility as Sir Aaronn, he watched and listened, storing away volumes of little tidbits of information. King Lot and Queen Morgause were also in attendance; however the Orkney queen stayed as far away from Aaronn as possible. This, of course, delighted him and offered the opportunity to watch her work the room with her charming wiles. No wonder Lot kept her as his lady, Aaronn thought as he studied her methods. She could charm Lucifer himself with her ways, he thought with reluctant respect.

Gwenhyfar was in attendance as well and stayed close to both Lancelot and the King. Tongues began to wag again that she was now in pursuit of both men, a fact that Aaronn had tried to bring to Arthur's attention one recent early morning as the Black Knight made his latest report in the King's private suites.

"The chit is good, 'tis certain, Sire. She plies both ye and yer First Knight for some sort of betrothal, without making emotional attachments to either of ye. The Christian Lords highly favor the match for ye and her, those of the Old Religion leave it in the hands of the Goddess," he observed dryly. "What is the Old Lion up to, trying to insert this girl between the King and the First Knight of Camelot?" he wondered aloud.

"Not ye too," Arthur moaned a bit. "I have heard of naught else but talk of marriage and betrothal since Badon's victory," he half-chuckled. "'Look what happened with yer father, Yer Majesty,' and 'The realm needs an heir, Yer Majesty,' and so on. I am so weary of the talk of it and 'tis no place in all of Britain I can go to be away from it, not even Avalon, Dragon Isle or my private suite!" he went on, venting his frustration.

"Every King needs a private retreat, Sire," Ceridwen's man suggested slyly. Perhaps the Pendragon needs a hunting lodge, a quiet little place to find occasional peace and quiet?"

"Ye have suggested a very good idea, Black Knight. Why do ye not scout about the realm, no more than a couple of hours away, and find me a nice, quiet place for such a thing?" Arthur laughed aloud.

"Are ye serious, My Lord?" the Black Knight asked eagerly.

"Surely, and begin as soon as possible," Arthur smiled faintly, beginning to anticipate the peace and quiet such a lodge would afford.

"I shall begin today, My Lord," the Black Knight assured him.

"Good! Now, tell me all about what Lot and Morgause are up to," Arthur sighed and sipped his caffe as the Black Knight related the latest frolic of the King's half-sister.

No one was happier to see the nobles leave Camelot than Arthur. For three weeks, he saw no one but an occasional beautiful lady. He made it a point to do nothing but enjoy generous meals, soak and exercise his sword arm with the other Knights. Even Aaronn was asked to take his turn in the arena with Arthur, a thing he eagerly anticipated. Some hour later, the two ceased the informal training session, Aaronn's style being much improved and Arthur's respect for his quickness and intelligence much increased.

A few weeks after the Solstice, Aaronn and Olran were hunting in the surrounding woods with Gawaine and Bedwyr. A bear had awakened from his winter's sleep with a very bad temper and had gone about killing good cattle for the pleasure of it. Such a rogue animal was dangerous and had to be taken before his tastes degenerated into eating people. As they tracked the huge boar bear, the four came upon a site Aaronn felt was perfect for the hunting lodge. It had a nice flat hilltop, through which ran a swift stream that drained down the gentle slope into a large, deep lake.

"Brother Gawaine, in yer opinion, what is the King's biggest problem right now?" he asked.

"Tha's an easy question," Gawaine answered at once. "Th' poor man's got neither nae privacy nor peace at all."

"Aye, what man doesn't need privacy once and awhile?" agreed Bedwyr.

"I was just thinking the same thing, my brothers. What if we, the Knights of Camelot, built the Pendragon a hunting lodge?" Aaronn proposed carefully. "Somewhere he could go in times of stress, to be alone with other men for sheer companionship?"

"Such a thing would be a great gift indeed, brother Aaronn," Bedwyr nodded approvingly. "Let us keep this a secret among us, at least 'till Lancelot has seen this site."

"And the Merlin," added Olran.

Just then, a deep growl sounded behind them and the four turned with their weapons at the ready. The great black bear stood on its hind legs, roaring frightfully. Its two small, blood red eyes glittered in the cold winter sun as the Knights separated and encircled the raging beast.

"Stan' back laddies! This be my fight!" Gawaine shouted, stripped off his coat and shirt, pulled his belt knife and jumped towards the snarling bear. Hitting it full in the chest, Gawaine's weight caused the animal to stagger back and fall to the ground. The Orkneyman growled and snarled as loud as the bear as the two struggled and thrashed in the deep snow.

"Aaronn, I'll lay ye twenty gold coins that he slits that bear's throat before the animal lays a paw on him!" Bedwyr shouted above the din and Aaronn smiled, nodding to accept the wager.

The fight went on until finally Olran pulled his bow and nocked an arrow, hoping to score a weakening wound in the bear. Gawaine saw and waved him off.

"Don't ye dare, boyo, ye'll ruin th' hide!" Gawaine shouted, laughing aloud. He struggled a bit more, then found himself in a position to get up onto the bear's back and pull the head towards his burly chest. Encircling the throat with one burly arm, Gawaine drew his blade quickly and deeply across the bear's jugular vein. Even though he leapt quickly aside, he was unable to entirely avoid the fountain of blood that spurted forth to bathe him from waist to foot on the whole of his right side. "Than' ye, Mother Ceridwen," the Orkneyman whispered reverently. "May th' blood spilled here bring health an' abundance t' all o' Britain!"

"So mote it be," intoned the others before they bent to the task, pulling their skinning knives to divest the bear of its thick, warm hide. Afterwards, Gawaine bent over the stream to wash the crimson from his sweaty body before quickly pulling on his shirt and coat.

"Wait 'till ye taste the bacon I make from this great beast!" the Orkneyman exulted. "Ye've nae tasted anythin' better."

"Make sure all the grease gets used before it goes bad this time, eh Gawaine?" Bedwyr commented dryly. "That last batch was horrible."

"Aye 'twas a' tha'," he grinned and began quartering the well-marbled carcass. When the laden hunters returned to Camelot, the fresh meat was hustled into Cai's kitchen, laid on the butchering table to be sliced into thick, tender steaks. A giant kettle was filled with the scraps and water added just to cover, along with leaves of bay myrtle, garlic, onions, chopped cabbage and dried carrots for a delicious and hearty stew.

That evening around the Knight's table was one for open discussions. Aaronn reveled in listening to the King and the Knights discuss the Mysteries of God. Among the Company that night were representatives of many religions and cultures, visiting through the winter season. Their new ideas and informal teachings intrigued Aaronn, he found that indeed, many doors and roads lead to God and that God indeed might have nine hundred and ninety-nine names, each equally valid. This is what Aaronn loved most about Arthur as King, his tolerance for other beliefs and creeds, as long as they sought the Light of God. If only everyone in the Kingdom was so patient and thirsty for knowledge, he sighed.

"Good night, My Lords and Ladies, Brothers of the Round Table, Sire," he said, standing after a very long time and bowing respectfully at the waist. "May the God and Goddess grant ye all a good sleep."

"Good sleep to ye as well, Sir Aaronn," Arthur returned. Aaronn went up to his room, where Olran sat nursing a cup of whiskey.

"Are ye all right?" Aaronn asked, concerned.

"Aye, my brother," he answered. "Want a snort before bed?" he asked with a smile.

"The whiskey is from Orkney, aye?" Aaronn asked.

"Aye, and a good ten years old too," Olran grinned wider and poured a good measure of the mellow liquor into a silver wine cup, then handing it to Aaronn before freshening his own cup. Aaronn tasted, grinned and asked the obvious question.

"'Tis good, where did ye manage to acquire it?"

"Where else would one get ten year old Orkney whiskey except from Lot's own storeroom?" Olran asked, grinning intensely. Rising from his seat, he strode over to his chamber door and opened it, bringing out two large stoneware jars, clearly marked with its bottling date and Lot's own rune sign. "I took these from Westerland's store house, of course. 'Tis only part of the shipment that arrived at Westerland Keep five days ago. I estimate a couple of hundred of these in the storeroom, along with barrels and barrels of salted fish. Salt marsh hay now covers the Keep's garden beds for the winter," Olran reported. "Lot has just received new saddles for both he and Morgause."

"He has bought a matching pair of blacks for their personal steeds, I thought I recognized the pair from Westerland's training pens," Aaronn added to the ever growing activities of the Orkney royals.

"How long do ye think those poor beasts will last in Morgause's tender care, Aaronn?" asked Olran, shuddering.

"Not too long, if I know the Witch Queen. She seems to favor horseflesh on the table during winter," Aaronn responded tightly. Olran shuddered again, violently, and took a steadying gulp of his drink.

"Don't worry, brother. Those two noble horses won't grace Orkney's table if I have anything to do with it." Aaronn assured his horse-loving ally as he sipped his whiskey thoughtfully. Perhaps it was time for Morgause to meet the Black Knight, he mused, and learn at last that she was not invulnerable. He planned carefully, wanting to go alone on this mission. This was between the Goddess and Morgause, he knew, and he prayed for an emotionless performance of his duty.

On the chosen night he arrived in Orkney, ground-tethering his horse and ordering him "on guard" before leaving him in the shadows of the dead oak grove not far from the Lot's castle. Gaining the scullery door easily, the shadowed figure entered and found the familiar secret stairs to Morgause's private tower room. He stole up the stairs, found the correct door and opened it, after first picking the lock with a belt knife. The woman lay asleep on the bed and Ceridwen's man left his token, a decorative pin made of acid-blackened silver, the end stained with blood-red copper, pinning it to the inside of her bed curtains, right at eye level. Morgause stirred at the whisper of the curtains and the Black Knight swiftly clapped his gloved hand over her mouth. Stopped from screaming for her guards, Morgause ceased her struggles nearly at once and regarded the hooded man with a speculative eye.

"Nay bitch, I am not here for yer over-ripe body. I would rather cut yer black heart out and feed it to ye," he snarled, before asserting calm over himself. "Ceridwen is watching ye and She knows what yer up to. If ye do not keep yer meddling hand out of British politics, I shall have no choice but to return and slit yer throat," he whispered in a rasping voice. "I would enjoy that, very much," he added and pressed a knife blade against her soft, white throat. "O, and since ye have a taste for horseflesh on yer table, I shall be taking those two perfect blacks as tithe to the Mother. I am certain She will not abuse them, nor drink their blood in some perverted rite."

"Ye cannot take them!" Morgause whispered as her fear showed clearly on her face and in her voice. "They are Lot's pride and he'll blame me for their disappearance."

"Too bad!" the Black Knight said with a nasty tone. "I'm sure ye will be able to lie yer way out of this too, as usual."

"Lot will go to Camelot for yer punishment! Arthur will have no choice but to act against ye!" she whispered cunningly.

"I think not, bitch!" the Black Knight answered coldly. "Perhaps 'twill be ye who are called before the High Throne to answer many, many questions concerning the rumors of yer black sorcery."

"Who and what are ye?" she asked, terrified now.

"I am the Black Knight of Avalon, Ceridwen's hand of Vengeance, Morgause ab Gorlois. I have watched for many years and have seen yer mis-use of the gentle teachings of Avalon. I answer first to Ceridwen, and then the Pendragon. Ye know his laws are subject to Her Will. Remember, if ye refuse to turn from yer dark path, 'twill be no escape for ye," he answered and slipped away from her bedside, then down the stairs before she could recover enough to scream for her guards. He was halfway to Britain, laughing all the way, before they could even leave Lothian Castle in pursuit. By morning, he was riding into Dalren's farm; the golden-haired and jovial man welcomed his friend and partner, Sir Aaronn. Being a rare and welcome guest, he was treated to a huge meal of well-aged beefsteak, fresh eggs, warm biscuits and gravy. Aaronn even downed two cups of cold milk with the meal before retiring for a welcome nap in one of Dalren's guest beds.

When he awoke, just before sunset, Dalren asked about the Black Knight's latest mission. The half-Saxon man was well acquainted with Ceridwen's champions for he had been recruited into their service just after the victory at Badon. With Dalren's easy nature and talent for investments, both Aaronn and Olran had seen their fortunes increase by immense proportions. With all the gold, silver and other treasures confiscated from those caught breaking the law the two always had spare coins to invest in profitable enterprises. The three owned the tavern where Vondra was now based, although the deed was in Dalren's name, as well as two wagon freight companies and the building housing the Guild forge in Camelot-town.

The three also sponsored an orphan child adoption house, allowing the Ladies of Avalon a place to distribute children needing adoption to loving and kindly folk. Much wealth that would have fueled attacks or physical harm to the Crown in any way was channeled through the Black Knight into more positive uses. The common folk therefore loved the mysterious figure and none of them would turn him away from house or hearth when he came to them. He was always quiet and courteous, those houses he visited always prospered. One family needed a new barn that year; they found a sum of gold left on their kitchen table to pay all the costs. Another family's oxen were confiscated by their Lord; the Black Knight delivered a new pair on the day of their wedding anniversary. There was even a mysterious bag of gold coins on a Londinium family's doorstep, with a note suggesting that it be used for their daughter's upcoming dowry and wedding. All these acts of charitable kindness endeared the Black Knight to the common folk. While the nobles squirmed under his scrutiny and demanded the mysterious man's death in every letter they wrote to Arthur, the common folk who lived in their territories extolled his virtues whenever news of a Crown investigation spread throughout the Land.

During the second month of winter, Aaronn took the Merlin and the King out to the site for the lodge. As Arthur walked the perimeter with a glowing Excalibur in hand, the Merlin by his side, he related the tale of Gawaine and the bear. The two then walked down to the lake and back up the slope, while Aaronn stood on guard.

"I like it, Lord Merlin. 'Tis peaceful, a veritable fortress could be built here without causing uproar. What say ye?" the King asked of his trusted advisor.

"'Tis a blessed site for certain, Artos, with the stream running beside and the lake below. The forest feels friendly; I saw spoor and sign of many food animals as we walked. Now that I have been told the tale of the bear's blood being spilt, I believe the Goddess has inspired Sir Aaronn's choice. She would favor any building done here. Would ye allow me to draw up plans for ye?" the Merlin replied, chuckling.

"I was going to insist," the King laughed with him.

"Good! Ye have an excellent eye for strategic sites, Aaronn my boyo," the Merlin complimented, turning to him. "Perhaps the King would consider assigning ye to the panel now planning the system of royal hostels across Britain?"

"I think that Sir Aaronn would be a proper addition for such a group, Lord Merlin. Are ye agreeable, Aaronn?" asked Arthur.

"If ye need any of my services, Sire, ye are welcome to them," Aaronn accepted. "I am at the Lord Merlin's disposal, always."

"Let us return to Camelot's warmth, my toes are freezing out here!" the King suggested and whistled for his war-mare. She loved the feel of the snow crunching beneath her feet; Arthur was certain she regarded it as some sort of cold sand. The mare was swift like the wind and sure-footed beyond any British horse he had ever ridden. He had ridden her rarely, but had resolved to remedy that situation now that the peace looked secure.

The three returned to Camelot, sat in the kitchen drinking Cai's mulled wine, discussing the needs of the new lodge. Arthur put Cai on the project, knowing his foster-brother would pester him endlessly anyway until he was included. The four of them took supper together with Sir Olran, talking like brothers until very late. Bedtime called at last and they all retired to rest and dream in comfort through the remaining hours of the night.

Chapter 7

About a week later, an excited runner came from Land's End to report that an unusual ship had grounded on the reefs off the coast. Assistance was needed to salvage its crew and cargo before a predicted great storm tore it all apart and killed those aboard. The King dispatched Sir Bedwyr with a group of unruly and bored pages to assist. Just before sundown, they all returned wet, hungry and cold, but successful in rescuing all the bales and bundles from the ship's hold. They also brought an aged Oriental man, wrapped in sturdy woolen blankets, but still shivering and miserable. Arthur handed him the customary cup of warmed, mulled wine, which the unusual visitor accepted and drank gratefully.

"I thank ye, Arthur Pendragon. I am called Huan, and I am from Szechuan province in far Cathay," he introduced himself after consuming the entire cupful. "I have come to trade silks and rare spices, as well as to learn of thy culture."

"Welcome to Britain, brother Huan. Stay at Camelot in peace and learn of us, while ye teach us of ye," Arthur invited with a smile, instinctively liking the man. "Ye are the first of Cathay to visit Britain's chilly shores."

"I thought as much. Not since Damascus have I been stared at with more curiosity. And far Cathay is a country of many climes. In Szechuan Province, we grow hot and spicy peppers to eat. We need their fierce heat in our food to ward off the cold rain and frigid winters," the wiry Oriental laughed with delight.

"Come lads, bring in all those bales and bundles thee all worked so hard to save from the sea," the King ordered.

The procession began and in a short time later, an impressive pile of packages wrapped in oilcloth lay neatly stacked around his chair. The old man began opening them, one by one, looking oddly like Father Winter distributing gifts to children during the Winter Solstice celebration. The ladies' mouths all dropped open, for in crate after crate were bolts of brightly colored silks, thick damasks from Damascus, filmy cloth from Gaza and hand-woven rugs from the Berber Arab tribes in the stony desert hills. From other crates came fine porcelain jars and vases, and hand-blown glass herb pots, labeled in Arabic and filled with rare and fragrant spices and herbs. Aaronn was most interested in the small, black lacquered cask within one of the crates. It looked mysterious and the way the old trader tried to divert everyone's attention from it made it that much more intriguing to the ever-curious Aaronn.

Supper was served presently, a homey meal of pea soup, fresh biscuits and warmed, buttered milk. Huan ate and drank copiously, amazing everyone by surpassing even Gawaine in the quantity consumed of Cai's excellent provender. All through the meal, Aaronn felt eyes on him and whenever he glanced up, the Oriental's black eyes met his.

"Aaronn, he is staring at ye again," Olran observed about halfway through his second bowl.

"I know, but why?" Aaronn answered. "Have I got food on my face or a blemish between my eyes?" he asked uncomfortably.

"I have been watching him too, and I tell ye I am not the only one who is. Olran smiled faintly before continuing. "Bedwyr's eyes have not left him since he opened those bales of silk and Arthur's eyes have watched him as well. I would say this "old trader" is something or someone more than he appears to be."

"Is that not true of everyone?" Aaronn chuckled dryly.

After supper, they talked of Huan's homeland. He spun tales as he circulated among the Knights and their ladies of beautiful temples of pure gold set against nature's beauty, where talented and sincere men and occasionally exceptional women trained to perfect body, mind and soul according to the ancient ways of the Taoist philosophy. Encountering Aaronn at last in a quiet corner, the aged man looked him up and down, finally speaking quietly in a knowing voice.

"So, 'tis ye at last, I have heard many tales of thy deeds in the agora of Damascus, Sir Black Knight."

"Ye flatter me, father. The Black Knight is a bold and restless fellow. I am only a simple, landless and fatherless junior Knight of Camelot, a former ward of King Arthur, just trying to serve King and country out of extreme loyalty," Aaronn protested.

"Ye need not play yer game with me, O Black Knight!" Huan laughed merrily, keeping his voice low. "I have come a long way to find thee. I have certain knowledge thee might find useful."

Aaronn couldn't help it as he grinned wide and took the old man outside, leaving Olran unofficially on guard to deflect any others away from his private conversation with the wizened-looking old man. Huan had appeared half dead when first brought to Camelot, but a hot bath, clean clothes and plenty of warmed wine and hot food seemed to cause an incredible transformation in him. He now carried himself as if never having been drenched and frozen in the waters of Cornwall at all.

"So, tell me what would bring ye all the way to Britain to find a myth ye heard in a Damascus market?" he asked.

"My curiosity mostly for the tale reminded me of others I heard of in Cathay and on the Silk Road. There are tales of evil men dying in their sleep, throats neatly slit or by poison everywhere along the ancient highway's length. I know ye are he and I can help in thy cause, the protection of thy Goddess's people and thy King," Huan related.

"I can see ye have much to teach me, Huan of Cathay," Aaronn chuckled. "How do we begin?"

"Let me settle in for a week before we start our discussions. I can see now that Britain's reputation is far below what it should be in the area of recreation. I am glad to be here among right-thinking people," Huan laughed outright as he bowed grandly and excused himself to continue circulating among the Knights and ladies. Aaronn was left standing there, silently awed by the workings of Ceridwen's Will.

"So, what did he want?" Olran's voice whispered into his ear.

"He knows, my friend. Somehow, he knows about the Black Knight. But...how?" he wondered softly. When Olran's eyes got wide, Aaronn indicated they should say their goodnights and retire for the night. Returning to their rooms, they changed into loose, comfortable clothing and slippers, then poured two small cups of mellow Orkney whiskey.

"So, he is much more than he seems," Olran chuckled wryly. "Did he just come out with it?"

"Aye and he told me he heard a few tales of the Black Knight in Damascus. It seems that the stories ye told are spreading," Aaronn told him.

"How else to make potential visitors think twice if they have negative intentions at heart?" Olran told him.

"I agree with ye, my friend and how better to spread those warning tales than to tell them in the marketplace of Constantinople? Truly, ye are the best companion the Black Knight could have!" Aaronn laughed, enjoying the humor of the situation.

"So, what does he want here, to be ally or foe?" Olran asked.

"Ally," Aaronn responded firmly. "He is offering knowledge and learning to aid Ceridwen's cause. He also mentioned an obscure Temple somewhere in Cathay that trains warriors with similar skills to ours."

"Did he mention the name or identifying marks?" Olran asked pointedly. "He must be one of them!"

"We will see, my brother," Aaronn yawned and finished his drink. "I am too tired to worry over it now."

"Be sure to double lock that door and I shall put the latch on the Maze. That old man is not to be taken lightly," Olran stated emphatically and went immediately to accomplish that task. Going to his inner chamber, he closed the door and Aaronn heard the bar slide shut, and the scraping of a chair as his friend added a further obstruction to bar the entrance. Taking similar precautions with the main door before stretching out on his bed, Aaronn closed his eyes and relaxed into sleep.

"Sir Aaronn, wake up and let me in. We must begin thy education as soon as possible," an unfamiliar, commanding voice called through the door just at first light. Aaronn roused at the light tapping on the thick oak door, wrapped up in his robe and opened.

"Master Huan, have ye any idea of how early 'tis?" he asked sleepily.

"Of course I do," the Oriental man laughed. "Now, let me in there before someone sees me."

Aaronn grinned widely and opened the portal wide enough to allow Huan to slip through, then locked up again.

"Would ye like some tea, Sir Aaronn?"

"'Tis my custom to drink something hot upon rising, Huan," Aaronn chuckled. "See, I have hot water ready."

"Good, ye can pour me a cup as well as one for thyself, and sprinkle this powder in," Huan instructed. "This herb is 'yang,' or male orientated. 'Tis called ginseng and it strengthens a man's blood," he went on, showing Aaronn how much to add to his tea. It was clear to Aaronn that this man was a Master; the knowledge he displayed as he spoke and moved evidenced a great mass of learning. Once the tea was steeped enough, the old man sipped his portion slowly, without adding honey to it. Olran emerged from his inner chamber and headed straight for the necessity, upon emerging he poured his own portion and sweetened it liberally, as Aaronn had.

"Honey weakens the herb's potency, but then thy education is just beginning. Sir Aaronn, would it be possible to speak with the person responsible for yer training?" Huan asked. "He or she must have been someone extraordinary to have produced someone like thee!"

"Aye."

"I am a Master of a secret and fabled Order of warriors. We are constantly searching the world far and wide for prospective students such as the two of thee. Do not make such a face, my boy," he said, turning to Olran. "Sheik Harimun had naught but mighty praise for that bow arm of thine!" the old man cackled in pure delight.

Olran stared at him hard, as did Aaronn, then all three men burst out in gales of laughter. "How is the Afendi?" Olran was finally able to ask.

"Very well, now he is Caliph Harimun. Sejuni is hereditary sheik now and both send their regards," Huan answered. "It seems I just missed thee among his tents. The very first night I was with him, Sejuni returned and the tale was told."

"I should send him a letter. I meant to keep in contact, but I have been very busy of late," Olran chuckled and went to the door. Today was the Christian Sabbath and Olran wanted no part of the stiff, formal sermon that all mouthed, but not a one of them seemed to understand. It had become the pair's habit to order breakfast delivered to their room, Olran knew that the pages would soon be too busy running errands for the sermon-goers. Right on schedule, an older boy dressed in page livery passed the door and Olran waved him down.

"Aye, Sir Olran?"

"Page…I am sorry, I do not know yer name" he said after returning his smart salute.

"I am Daniel, Sir Olran."

"Ye are new to Camelot, page Daniel?"

"Aye Sir, my parents were killed in the wars, 'till a month ago, I lived in Avalon's orphanage. Sir Gawaine saw me there and recommended me for fostering and page duty," he related to avoid questions. "I am hoping to become squire someday."

"Well, if such a thing could happen, 'twill at Camelot, Daniel," Olran smiled encouragingly before he continued. "Sir Aaronn and I would like breakfast for three as soon as possible, please?" Olran asked.

"Of course, Sir I shall fetch it right away!

"Off with ye boyo, we are hungry!"

The lad was on his way at once, going quickly to the kitchens he passed on Olran's request to Cai. The seneschal was used to this routine and so had his cart already prepared, the plates and bowls were loaded swiftly and covered with a clean linen cloth. The seneschal let Daniel take the wheeled cart out of the kitchen without escort, a measure of trust for Cai, the page was quickly back in front of Aaronn and Olran's door. He knocked and identified himself, and was immediately admitted.

"Good morning, Sir Aaronn, Master Huan. The Goddess blessed us with a sunny morning!" he reported. "Sir Cai asked if ye Knights would please come and see him as soon as ye are up for the day," the page chatted easily as he poured caffe for all three.

"Thank ye, Page. We can handle the food now, I am sure Sir Cai has many things for ye to do other than waiting on us," Aaronn dismissed the boy.

"Aye, 'tis sure, Sir Aaronn, good day to ye and I hope ye all enjoy yer meal," Daniel said in response and wheeled the cart from the room, closing the door behind him. The three chatted on, discussing everything from herbal potions to poisons as they ate the fine meal. Once Huan had finished his food and washed up, he produced the black lacquer box and opened it to reveal packets, jars and bottles of oddly colored powders and whole roots that smelled strongly potent.

"Ah, but 'tis what I came to teach ye. Poisoncraft is a specialty of mine and with the ingredients ye see in front of ye, I can extract and prepare all sorts of substances to produce many virulent poisons," Huan finally revealed. "I have one recipe I favor most, I have employed it on a few occasions to eliminate otherwise unreachable men. One simply sprinkles the tincture into a man's love sheathe, leave it on a handy table and stand aside. It usually works within incredible speed, by the time he is found, the poisoner has the time to slip away to be with company to provide the perfect alibi."

"What of the woman?" Aaronn asked, amazed.

"Such is the true beauty of this potion, my boy," Huan laughed triumphantly. "It only kills on tactile contact, not through liquid interaction. The potion does not affect the woman, although it might be a bit unsettling to witness the results on the man."

"Marvelous!" Aaronn exclaimed excitedly, his mind already fixed on a target for the potion. "How is it made?"

"O ho, Black Knight and Black Hunter, what would ye pay for such knowledge?" Huan asked craftily.

"What is yer price, old man?" Aaronn responded, wary now.

"Only knowledge of yer Goddess and the Brotherhood of Druids," Huan told him with a smile.

"I can easily arrange for that, after ye meet the High Druid. Of course, he has final say over who knows what of the Brotherhood."

"Then make the arrangements right away. I must leave here on the first day of summer. Ye are not the only one I was sent out to find," Huan laughed and bent to finish his breakfast.

When they were finished eating, Huan went to Cai to see about his need for spices in Camelot's kitchens, while Aaronn and Olran went out for their daily exercises. Going through the dual workout in silence, both their minds worked on the proposal Huan had made to them. Knowledge such as he offered had never been easy to obtain, both men wanted it for their secret work. A poisoned arrow was, indeed already had been a valuable too, but the lethal toad poison was difficult and messy to collect. With roots and leaves, the process was sure to be easier. Again they wondered about exactly who had sent him all the way from Cathay, a very long journey under the best of conditions. The question occupied their thoughts all day, making both pensive and silent until supper. The Merlin returned to Camelot that night, Arthur entreated him to speak to the strange, crafty old man. Taliesin sighed, asked for a cup of ale and complied, finding to his delight an equal in the old trader after an hour or so of intense conversation.

"Ye need not worry, Sire," he reported later after all had sought their beds. "Britain has nothing to fear from him. I have rarely met his equal in the Mysteries of the Light, yet he says he has come to meet the Goddess and Her servants. I want the Lady Vivaine to meet him, so I am taking him to Avalon. She sends her regards to ye, Arthur Pendragon, and says to please forgive her long absence during the holidays. Old bones ache during the winter cold," he sighed heavily.

"Is the Lady well?" Arthur asked, concerned at once.

"Well enough for a woman who has borne so many children for the Goddess. The hot springs are comfort enough for now," the Merlin answered as Vivaine had bid him. "A hot bath would suit me well this night. Good night, My Lord."

"Good night to ye, Lord Merlin. Thank ye for yer assistance," Arthur said warmly and embraced the older man fondly.

"'Tis my everlasting pleasure and honor to do so, Artos," he responded, just as warmly.

"Whew, ye do need that bath, Uncle!" Arthur grimaced, laughing despite the offensive odor.

"Why nephew, would ye wrinkle yer nose at the body odor acquired while laying out the foundations for yer new hunting lodge?" the Merlin laughed.

"The ground is hardly ready for such work surely," Arthur remarked.

"Aye, 'tis true. But we can and did lay out the markers, now the logs must be harvested. We will need many big, strong, bored Knights on the axes and teams of strong obedient horses to haul them to the staging site. Stones must be quarried for the foundations, hearths and chimneys as well. Certainly there are those among the Table who would volunteer to assist?" the Merlin suggested.

"I would imagine so, Lord Merlin," Arthur chuckled harder. "Feel free to ask among them."

"I was hoping ye'd say that."

In the morning, the Merlin asked for volunteers to cut logs for the lodge walls. The entire Inner Circle eagerly complied, of course, and sat with Aaronn and Olran to put together a lumbering crew. It was decided that Lancelot would head up the hauling, while Gawaine would direct the cutting operation guided by the Merlin. Aaronn and Olran would assist where needed and perform the cooking and hunting duties. By the time they had arranged everything a week later, the Knights were eager to begin this latest project. Arthur visited them as often as possible, assisting when he had the time and walking among them as he had during the wars. Mostly, he was involved in the business of running the Kingdom. The load was enormous, growing every day and Arthur began to long for someone to share it with. The Christian Kings applied more and more pressure for Arthur to marry a suitable girl and the more he considered the available noble women the more Gwenhyfar's name came into his mind. She was pretty, intelligent and of good family. Since it was an official marriage, one girl was as good as any other, he thought. Love would come later; the Goddess would see to it, he sighed as he came to a final decision.

Writing the letter personally, he made his offer of betrothal to Gwenhyfar, carefully folding it and sealing it with the royal seal. He sent it off to Leodegrance, in the care of Lionel and Bors, three days later, the answer came back the same way. Predictably, permission was granted to commence the wooing of Gwenhyfar. Leodegrance listed the immense dowry of his only daughter; it included the use of his troops and forges, gifts of horses, gold and silver coins and sacks of precious gems, as well as one large round oak table.

"This table is large enough to seat the entire Inner Circle, Sire, and it comes with matching chairs. 'Tis an heirloom, which I have no son to pass to and none of the rest of my family's children is worthy to inherit. Please, accept it as the son ye will become when ye are joined with my precious daughter," the letter explained. Arthur sighed, it seemed as though the match was the right one, after all.

The news was kept secret until Beltane that year. When the King made the announcement, Lancelot went into his tent at the lumbering camp, pulled out a wineskin and drank, very deeply. He brought it out and offered it to Gawaine with the following words;

"To the health of the Pendragon, may he be blessed with much happiness. Our brother and King, Arthur, is to be wed to the fair daughter of Leodegrance of Lyonnesse, Gwenhyfar!"

"We offer this cup to the health of King Arthur and his betrothed, the Lady Gwenhyfar! Long life t' ye both an' may there be many heirs!" Gawaine answered gravely and drank, passing the skin on. All the Knights drank to the King's health, then two wagons trundled into their midst. Arthur was driving the first set; he leapt down somewhat clumsily from the wagonseat due to the amount of drink he had already imbibed.

"My brothers, I have come to feast my betrothal with ye, my only friends! I hope 'tis plenty to eat, I am starved!" he said gaily. Lancelot swallowed his emotions down and embraced Arthur with warm affection.

"Congratulations, Artos! She will make the realm a wonderful Queen!" he said, trying to smile for his friend's benefit. Inside, his heart felt torn to shreds and he felt his spirit torn as well. But "The Impeccable Knight" would not allow himself to falter in front of the one man he respected most. He kept thinking over and over to himself throughout the night; "I shall not stand in the way of Artos' happiness."

Aaronn and Olran prepared supper that night in a state of shock. Both had seen the blank look on Lancelot's face at the announcement and they both empathized with him. The other Knights never noticed, not even Bors and Lionel as they celebrated the impending marriage. Still, they could hardly believe what they had heard; surely Arthur could have chosen someone of more neutral alliances for his queen. A lady of Avalon would certainly have been more appropriate was the thought that ran through both men's minds as the game roasted and biscuits baked. Still, they congratulated the ever more relaxed Arthur in their turn, wishing him the Goddess' blessing.

"He will need all the blessings he can get with that shrew in his bed," Olran muttered as he ladled the basting sauce over the whole stag, beside which several fat geese roasted. Wild grains boiled with herbs and butter in a kettle, while a fresh berry cobbler baked in an oven in the ashes to round out the meal. When all was done, they all ate and drank too much, Arthur most especially. Lancelot put him to bed in the large tent and took the first watch. He caught a few hours of sleep after Aaronn relieved him before personally escorting the still-weary King back to Camelot after the morning meal. The others went back to work, raising the walls of the lodge. The first floor was up already and raising the walls of the second story was the job at hand. Teams of oxen hauled away on the ropes and slowly the heavy logs lifted up and were settled into place, after the notches were fine-finished. The Merlin watched in satisfaction for over an hour before he wandered into view as the final trusses were hauled into place and pegged fast. Aaronn handed him a cold mug of ale, chilled in the stream's glacial waters as he stood and admired the view.

"It ought to be ready by the King's wedding, eh Lord Merlin?" Aaronn commented.

"Wedding, what wedding?" the Merlin asked in alarm.

"The King's marriage at Summer Solstice, to the Lady Gwenhyfar," Aaronn informed him casually, waiting for the explosion. It was thunderous, as expected.

"What? When did this happen?"

"Just two days past, My Lord. We were up late last night, celebrating. Lancelot left not too long ago to escort the King back to Camelot," Aaronn told him.

"I need a horse, Aaronn, a very fast horse," the Merlin said tightly.

"Come with me, Lord Merlin," Aaronn responded and headed off to where he knew Olran was digging a garden bed for roses on the south side of the lodge. "Brother, the Merlin needs to borrow yer horse. He needs to get to Camelot at once and talk to the King."

"Aye, I'll call him," Olran agreed immediately, knowing only the Merlin had a chance of changing Arthur's mind about marrying Leodegrance's daughter. Whistling to the golden-bay Arab, Olran only waited a short time before he appeared, trotting quickly towards them. Olran dressed him and trustingly handed the reins to the Merlin of Britain, then spoke to Habib.

"Take the Merlin quickly and comfortably, Habib. Watch where ye step, boyo," he murmured affectionately to the Arab stallion, patting him lovingly. The Merlin expertly urged him away, the galloping hoofbeats quickly fled into the growing dusk. Olran turned to Aaronn and grinned, knowing just how furious the Merlin was at the news.

When Taliesin appeared at Camelot, he went directly to Arthur's suite and knocked very loudly. The door jerked open, revealing a very sleepy Arthur, sword poised for trouble.

"My Lord Merlin!" he exclaimed, lowering the weapon.

"I am glad ye still remember who I am, Arthur Pendragon, or should I go back to calling ye, 'the Wart'?" he spat sarcastically. "And why, when there are so many more acceptable girls in all of Britain, are ye marrying Leodegrance's cub?"

"Because Taliesin, my very dear uncle," Arthur began, waving him inside. "I weary of the long days of Kingship, alone. Because the petty kings and major nobles add more and more pressure each day I tarry over my decision of when to wed a girl of good family and produce an undeniably legitimate heir. Surely Gwenhyfar is no worse a choice than any of the other daughters of noble house, she is without a doubt the loveliest and most intelligent of them all. Even Lancelot favors the match."

"Have the banns been read, the dowry recited?" the Merlin asked quietly.

"Aye, the wedding will be on the Summer Solstice, here at Camelot," Arthur told him.

The Merlin sighed heavily. "Well, 'tis no breaking the contract now, without disgracing ye and the Crown. I am sorry, nephew, for barging in where I am no longer needed. Ye are a grown man now, only in the matters of the realm do ye need this old wizard's council," Taliesin sighed heavily again.

"Ye will do the wedding ceremony, aye?" Arthur asked, feeling that their relationship had somehow altered, just the slightest bit.

"Will Gwenhyfar accept me at her wedding?" the Merlin answered with a question.

"I care not if she accepts ye, I am still High King and I am asking if ye will do this for me. Will ye perform the wedding ceremony, side by side with Bishop Patricius?" Arthur asked insistently.

"Of course Sire. If ye wish for me to, I shall," the Merlin agreed.

"Thank ye, Uncle," Arthur said, gratefully. "I shall need ye there, just to keep me calm. I always thought to marry for love, but it seems a King must do most things for love of his country more than for his own pleasure," Arthur sighed. "Still, as I said, she is witty and intelligent. Perhaps 'twill not be so bad."

"Ye watch her, Artos. As I warned ye before, she is Leodegrance's cub. The Lioness is always more dangerous than the Lion," the Merlin warned, feeling helpless and impotent for the first time in a very long while. Maybe it was time he retired to Dragon Isle after all, he thought as he accepted the glass of wine Arthur offered.

"I shall be careful, Lord Merlin. I do not love her, after all," the King said seriously.

"Goddess bless ye, Artos Pendragon. May She smile on this match," the Merlin toasted, but he could not rid himself of the dark foreboding that chilled him inside. He went back to the lodge site in the morning to facilitate the building's completion by the Summer Solstice. The Knights labored on and in the final week before the wedding, the last touches were put on the lodge and the hearths finished in each of the rooms. Most of the furnishings would have to wait upon the royal carpenters and the Knights made sure that plenty of logs waited on the site for their uses. Inside the one fully finished suite however, they made a four-posted canopied and curtained bed, matching clothespresses, several comfortable chairs and handy tables. The ladies came from Camelot and finished decorating the large, airy room for the royal couple's honeymoon, including making up the bed with new ticking and comfortable mattresses, soft sheets, warm blankets and quilts. Over all went a huge, thick coverlet with Arthur and Gwenhyfar's personal rune signs embroidered into it.

"'Tis a lovely room, 'tis so quiet and so very private; ye have done a miracle, Lord Merlin," the Lady Enid exclaimed when they had finished. "The King and his Lady should enjoy their time here. I know that I would." she sighed happily.

"I hope the new Queen will enjoy this as much as I know the King will," was the Merlin's tactful reply.

Back at Camelot, the pages flew down the halls, cleaning women bustled and the kitchens steamed constantly, while the preparations for the wedding went into double-step march. Gwenhyfar and her attendants arrived from Lyonnesse, escorted by Lancelot, Gawaine, Bors and Lionel. She was immediately ensconced in her own private suites, well away from the King's room. Her dress was brought to her the next day, the seamstress took the final fittings in a long and tiring session, whisking away the yards of creamy, pearly-white silk and lace back to her workshop to finish sewing the final seams.

Gwenhyfar was visited all that day by a steady stream of noble women from all over the realm, she began to long for the peace and quiet of her own small room back at Leodegrance's castle. Gwenhyfar also received a visit from the Lady Vivaine of Avalon. The petite and snobbish princess hardly contained her disdain for the High Priestess of Ceridwen, a representative of a religion that Gwenhyfar had been taught was comprised of naught but obscene orgies and strange sacrifices. Vivaine knew she was being tolerated, but tried to treat Gwenhyfar as she would any candidate for the position of High Queen. She tried hard to show Gwenhyfar this was so by presenting her the traditional gifts for a royal marriage, a hand-woven, lacy nightgown for her wedding night, perfume custom designed by Vivaine herself, made of the concentrated essences of lilac, rose and honeysuckle, as well as soft-bristled brushes, the work of many hands on Avalon to make Gwenhyfar's honeymoon night memorable.

"Thank ye, Lady Vivaine, I am sure I can find a place for this, along with everything else," Gwenhyfar said in a haughty voice, pushing it all to one side negligently. Vivaine's temper was roused by the rude treatment of Avalon's gifts and blessing, she gathered up all the gifts carefully as she pounced on the snobby princess.

"Leodegrance and Justine should have taught ye better manners, young Princess of Lyonnesse! If the gifts of Avalon are unwelcome, then ye need not trouble yerself to accept them, or Ceridwen's blessing on yer marriage either," Vivaine raged quietly and, gifts in hand, she swept from the suite. She went directly to Arthur, strode up to him regally and told him of his betrothed's rudeness. "I shall not stay another moment while Ceridwen's blessings are thrown aside like so much trash. May the Goddess watch over ye, Arthur Pendragon, and may ye have much happiness from yer white shadow."

"Lady Vivaine, wait!" Arthur called after her slight figure. "I have no intention of allowing any slight to Ceridwen's High Priestess."

"Gwenhyfar thinks these handmade gifts are…inappropriate for her wedding night," Vivaine retorted, angry and offended.

"'Tis so? Please come with me, Holy Mother," Arthur said as his eyes narrowed with displeasure.

They went back to Gwenhyfar's quarters, Arthur carrying Avalon's gifts reverently. The King pushed aside the clucking old hens bestowing gifts on the bride-to-be.

"My Lady Gwenhyfar?" he called out harshly, using the Old Language's pronunciation of her name. "I require yer attendance, at once!"

"Aye, My Lord Arthur?" she answered prettily, until she saw his tightly-controlled rage.

"Am I to understand that ye revile Avalon's gifts for our wedding night?" he asked, unconcerned by the shocked gasps of the so-called Christian women around him.

"I do not need things crafted by heathens for my wedding night, Sire," she replied in a pettish tone. "And I do not want her or her kind at my wedding celebration."

"Indeed?" Arthur challenged. "The Lady Vivaine is the High Priestess of the Earth Goddess Herself. I daresay she is more highly educated than ye are yerself. Her life is an inspiration to all proper women; ye would do well to imitate her. How many orphans have yer Roman Church found homes for in Britain? How many of the women raped and battered by the Saxons have been made welcome in yer Christian sanctuaries? How many mentally injured folk, especially children, have the slave nuns in Christian churches cared for and nursed back to health? How many babies has Bishop Patricius delivered alive, despite the mother's difficulties? How many, My Lady Gwenhyfar, how many?" he fired his cascade of pointed questions in ever-increasing volume, until Gwenhyfar could not help herself. She broke out in tears, fell to her knees and covered her face to hide her shame.

"I am sorry, My Lord. I did not know," she wept, and he saw that her tears were genuine.

"Save yer apologies for the Lady Vivaine, girl," he growled. "Never again do I wish to hear that nonsense from yer lovely mouth. I would now be within my rights to beat ye, here and now, for giving offense to Ceridwen, and send ye back to Lyonnesse still unmarried!"

Gwenhyfar stared at him, truly afraid he would disgrace her in front of all the noble women. Gulping her tears down, she bowed her head and offered a humble apology to Vivaine. "Please forgive me, My Lady Vivaine. I can see there is much for me to learn. May I please smell the perfume ye brought?" she asked contritely.

"'Tis a better attitude ye are showing now, My Lady, much better. Need I remind ye 'tis traditional to model the nightgown as well? See that ye honor Avalon by doing so. I want to see ye in that, or nothing on our wedding night!" he admonished her. "Ladies, please excuse me. I must attend to other business," he said, just barely polite, and pushed his way out of the room. They all curtsied, very low, and the gifts of Avalon were presented anew. Gwenhyfar did put on the thin, gauzy shift of the finest cotton lace, all the women saw how it covered but revealed all.

"Anyone can see 'tis beautiful work, Lady Vivaine," Gwenhyfar complemented timidly. "Could I impose upon Avalon's ladies for two more?"

"Open that last bundle, my dear," Vivaine smiled genuinely. Gwenhyfar complied, finding three more gowns in pink, blue and yellow pastels. "The colors stand for love, strength and wisdom, my dear. I am glad ye like them."

"I truly do like them, very much", Gwenhyfar told her, meaning it. "Please, Lady Vivaine, would ye bless me?" she asked suddenly.

"Of course I shall my child. The Mother would not withhold Her blessing for the betrothed of Her chosen High King. May Ceridwen smile on ye, Gwenhyfar ab Leodegrance. May thy children be many and strong and may peace and freedom follow ye all yer days," Vivaine pronounced and laid her hands atop Gwenhyfar's head.

"Would ye stay for tea, Lady Vivaine? I want ye to tell me all about this perfume and the bath powders, how they were made, I mean if 'tis not a secret," Gwenhyfar invited, meaning it.

"I would like a cup of tea very much, daughter," Vivaine smiled gently. The rest of the afternoon passed quietly, there were no more outbursts of that sort to mar the festivities. That night, however, the prospective bride received a very unusual visitor, the Black Knight.

He slipped into her room via a hidden entrance from the Maze. After assuring himself she was indeed alone and that the door was securely locked, he strode to her bedside. He grinned as he regarded her, laying on the narrow bed clothed from head to toe in a long, sleeved nightgown. It was obviously too hot for comfort, she was covered in a light sheen of sweat despite the chill of the early summer night. He briefly considered improving her comfort by removing the nightgown, but refrained from indulging himself. Instead, he drew up a chair, lit her bedside candle and laid a gloved hand over her mouth. Instantly, she was awake and struggling until she saw his masked face. Fear showed clearly in her eyes then.

"Be quiet, wench. I have not come to do anything but deliver a warning this time, although I am tempted. I can see now what 'tis the King sees in ye, although I have seen better," he chuckled boldly. "Now, listen carefully, Gwenhyfar of Lyonnesse, the White Shadow of Britain, I am the Black Knight of Avalon. I have heard of the insult ye gave to Lady Vivaine, no more such things will be heard lest I return and take the Mother's vengeance from yer lovely hide. I can find ye anywhere, anytime and get to ye just as easy as I got to ye tonight, remember that, wench. Be a good and gracious ruler for all yer subjects, as Arthur has done, whether they follow Ceridwen's creed or the Christ's. I shall have no argument with ye if ye follow that simple rule. May yer marriage be long and fruitful, Gwenhyfar," he told her in a pleasant tone, pinning his token to her pillow. "My gift to ye, Lady," he laughed lightly and disappeared into the shadows.

Waiting 'till she was sure that he must be gone, she unpinned the token and put it among her jewelry, then returned to her bed. "Sleep well, My Lady Gwenhyfar," she heard then. Terrified, she dove back under the layers of blankets and hid until morning. She said naught of the Black Knight's visit, but was thereafter very careful what she said to whom about the Goddess, for a time.

The day of the Solstice dawned bright, warm and clear, a good omen for the wedding ceremony. Cai had the bride's breakfast ready and loaded onto a tray, along with three-dozen perfect pink roses in a vase. As well, he set his wedding gift to her, a lovely light silver tiara with a flawless pink-toned ruby of half-carat weight set in the center, putting the box on the tray with her breakfast and taking it up to her room himself.

"Good morning, My Lady. All is perfect outside for the ceremony," he informed her when she opened the door and invited him inside.

"Good morning, Sir Cai," she exclaimed, delighted to finally see him in person again. "Is that tray for me? I am absolutely starving!"

Cai was inwardly surprised at her warmth and entered, setting the tray down on her small table. "Aye, My Lady, I have brought ye a little breakfast," he answered.

"Sir Cai, these roses are beautiful. May I carry them for my bouquet today?" she asked, honoring him.

"They are thine, Lady. Carry them if ye wish, with my blessing," he agreed, touched by the gesture. "I wish ye and my foster brother good fortune in thy wedding, My Lady Guinevere," he added, indicating the box on the tray.

She opened it, her mouth making a perfect 'O' when she saw the delicate silver circlet. "Sir Caius Ectorius, 'tis beautiful!" she breathed as she picked it up. "How thoughtful of ye to provide a lighter circlet for after the crowning. I am sure the formal crown is quite heavy," she said, grateful for his good will. "We have gotten off to a rocky start, let us begin anew. Let us be partners in the running of the castle, as well as the realm?" she asked, hopefully. "Can ye begin, after I return from the honeymoon, to acquaint me with the proper scheduling procedures as well as yer way of running things?"

He smiled warmly. "Of course, Lady, I am here to serve, after all."

"Thank ye, Sir Cai. Ye are a most generous and gentle man," she said gratefully and tried on the circlet. It fit perfectly and looked well on her, he noticed with satisfaction.

"Enjoy thy breakfast, My Lady," he said pleasantly and took his leave, giving her a small but respectful bow as he went.

She acknowledged his gesture as he closed her door, and then enjoyed her light meal of poached eggs, toasted bread, butter and jam with her tea before the attendants came and there was no more quiet time.

Things were the same for Arthur and when the time came for the wedding however, they both managed to appear calm and composed before the hundreds of guests assembled for the wedding. The vows of the Christian ceremony mingled with those of the Old Religion, Bishop Patricius was surprised the words were nearly the same. The wedding feast was served when the ceremony was over. Cai served a meal with so many courses most of the guests lost count. First was a simple soup, then fish, fowl and roast venison, beef and so on. The untouched platters were gathered up and taken to the poor tables to be distributed among the folk gathered there. After two hours of eating, drinking and many toasts, the wedding cake and caffe were served. The confection was many layered and in-between the pristine white layers were slices of fresh strawberries, glazed with caramelized honey. The same dressing decorated the top and the juices slowly drizzled down the sides, making everyone's mouth water despite the amount of feast foods they had already consumed.

After the meal, the Merlin sang many songs, accompanied on some by Lady Morgaine's lovely contralto voice. She had arrived after ceremony and offered the royal couple her good wishes, then changed into courtly garb and joined the festivities. Being Arthur's half-sister meant sitting at the High Table with the royal couple, along with the Merlin, Lot and Morgause. The Orkney Queen had done nothing but eat her and drink her fill while speculatively eye each young handsome Knight at the feast.

Now that the dancing was about to commence, Morgaine saw Aaronn's beckoning and came to share the dance floor with him. They and all the guests danced and toasted the King's marriage until almost dark, then Arthur and Gwenhyfar boarded the royal carriage and rode away to the lodge, escorted by a full division of Knights. For the next week, the two newlyweds were scheduled for nothing but rest, relaxation and time to acquaint themselves with each other. Lancelot left for his estate in Lesser Britain, Joyous Garde, that very same night. The First Knight had informed Aaronn that he would be gone for a month, recuperating from the stress and work of the wars and after, but the Black Knight knew better. Lancelot was still madly in love with Gwenhyfar, since it was a first love; it would be a long time healing, Ceridwen's man surmised sadly and was sorry for him.

The party went on without the royals, far into the night. Aaronn had partnered Morgaine exclusively, slipping outside occasionally for some fresh air and a puff of the Herb. On one of those occasions, he took the opportunity to try and persuade her to accompany him to his room.

"Aaronn, thank ye so much for being my partner this night, 'tis nice to be stared at in envy rather than with revulsion. After all, I am dancing with one of the most handsome men at Camelot," she laughed lightly and took another quaff of wine.

"Let us leave all this noise behind, Morgaine," Aaronn suggested bluntly. "'Tis much quieter in my room and no one will stare, except for me, of course."

"Aaronn, are ye still chasing me?" Morgaine asked, just as blunt. "I am so much older than ye and in no wise as beautiful as some of the other ladies here tonight. I can give ye nothing…" she went on until Aaronn interrupted her by encircling her in his strong arms.

"Ye can give me the strength of yer comfort, Morgaine of Avalon. Ye can give me the wisdom of yer mind and the love of a friend. I ask no more than that," he said in a voice hushed by passion.

"I am not for thee, Aaronn. Even so, I am flattered by yer pursuit," Morgaine laughed softly, then stood on her toes and pressed her warm lips against his cheek. "Are we still friends?" she asked.

For answer, he embraced her hard against him, fighting back tears of longing. "For always, dear sister Morgaine," he said with difficulty.

"But I am hardly going to give up the chase so easily," he added, trying to use the joke to compose himself.

"Ye are an incorrigible wretch, Aaronn!" she laughed and pushed him away. He let her go easily and returned with her to the party. Olran had already departed with feminine company, Cai reported somewhat unsteadily, Aaronn noticed. Morgaine also took her leave, with Aaronn as escort, but found the door to her assigned room locked fast.

"Come sister. Ye shall sleep in my own bed and I shall sleep on the floor," he told her with authority.

"Right now, Aaronn, I would sleep in the stables. Ye are kind to offer," she said and took his arm.

"I only wish I could share it with ye," he thought to himself, but said nothing.

Opening the door to his shared room, he found Olran's inner door locked tight. He did the same with the main door as Morgaine carefully shed her court finery. Aaronn obligingly unlaced the back of her gown before excusing himself to the necessity while Morgaine hung the gown over the chair back. When he returned, she was comfortably cuddled under the thick blankets.

"Are ye sure ye want to be alone in that great big bed?" he asked suggestively.

"Quite sure, Aaronn, and I thank ye again for the use of it." Morgaine answered firmly. "Good night, brother."

"Good night, sister," he answered.

With extra comforters and pillows from his storage closet, he made himself comfortable on the thick bearskin in front of his hearth. It took a while for him to fall asleep, what with Morgaine within reach in his own bed. The wedding also swirled around in his head; finally he was able to slip into restful sleep. When he awoke in the morning, quite late, Olran and Morgaine were chatting easily over fresh, steaming caffe and still-warm pastries from the kitchen.

"Good morning, brother," the priestess greeted him with a friendly kiss, handing him a mug of the black beverage.

"'Tis good to see thy lovely face in my quarters first thing in the morning, I only wish I had been beside ye to wake ye," he said, sitting up to take the mug from her.

"I bet ye do," she laughed, bantering with him in kind. "Eat this instead."

He made a great show of slowly devouring the crumbly, layered sweet, smacking his lips and licking his fingers, one by one, free of the sticky residue. Morgaine watched without being seen, and since no one was paying any seeming attention, Aaronn ceased his display. If only he had been able to hear her thoughts, he would have never stopped.

Morgaine had been mightily tempted to take Aaronn up on his offer to share his bed. He was tall, darkly handsome with intense eyes, well-muscled and proportioned, as well as being possessed with a reputation for high accomplishment at lovemaking. Morgaine was priestess-trained, estranged though she might be from Avalon right now. The Blessing of Ceridwen brought mental healing and quiet to the body, enabling those who shared it to perform their daily duties free from stress. It had taken a high resolve to push the magnetic man away the night before. Now, seeing him bare-chested in front of her, she was tempted to send Olran on a short mission for her and push Aaronn back onto the soft bearskin. All this went swiftly through her mind as the three of them shared their breakfast caffe and pastries.

"Well, ye two 'tis been a pleasant experience spending overnight in the room of such a pair of men," she grinned impishly. "I shall be the talk of Camelot for at least a week!"

Aaronn and Olran smiled with her, knowing it was true and anticipating listening to the old hens' gossip through the walls of the Maze. Aaronn quickly dressed and escorted Morgaine back to her assigned room, unseen by any. The door was now unlocked and Morgaine hesitated before going in.

"Thank ye, brother," she said quietly before opening the door and slipping into the room. "Ye are a good friend."

"If 'tis all I can be to ye, then 'tis good enough," Aaronn teased a bit. "Enjoy the morning."

"May ye also, my dear brother Aaronn."

After the door clicked shut, Aaronn returned to his room and proposed to Olran that now might be a good time to visit Dalren. They packed bags, told Cai of their plans and went down to the stables. Huan was awaiting them, stroking Habib's soft nose and talking to him softly. The two saw the old man was garbed in traveling clothes and realized that this would be good-bye.

"Well, ye two rogues. I have tarried here long enough, I must be off. I have more work to do before I return to my home. I need a horse, however, do ye know of where I might find a decent horse to buy?" he asked, looking directly at Olran. The young man met his eyes evenly before both men glanced at the gold-bronze Arab stallion.

"Please Master, do me the honor of taking Habib," he offered the old man. "He is a desert horse and I know he will be happier in warmer climes. He is my gift to thee, for all that ye have taught to us," Olran spoke up for both men, with Aaronn's blessing. "I know ye will take good care of each other," he added, swallowing his fondness for the Arabian stallion.

"I shall take good care of him, Sir Olran, when I return to my Order he will receive only the best of food and care," Huan vowed.

Swiftly, before he changed his mind, Olran dressed the Arabian and handed Huan the reins. "May he carry ye as well as he ever did me."

"He is a gift worthy of a prince, Sir Olran. I accept, gratefully. Now, listen ye two, I shall not return to these shores, but one comes after me who can further yer education far beyond what I can," he told them in a hushed voice. "Ye will know them when you see them."

He chuckled then, hugged them separately to him like sons, and then took up the Arab's reins.

"Fare thee well, Master Huan," Aaronn said in parting, then was startled when the man thrust the black lacquer box into his hands.

"For the Black Knight, should ye see him," the Master chuckled harder.

Olran was embraced next and received a packet of fletching feathers unlike any he had seen before.

"These will make thy arrows scream in flight. 'Tis a very frightening sound, I assure ye. I thought the Black Hunter would find these of great use on some appropriate occasion. Watch for the one who follows behind me, ye two, if ye want yer skills to be perfected."

"We will watch, Master," Aaronn responded. "Good journey to ye, may the Goddess bring ye safely home," Aaronn gave the ritual parting phrase in true hopes he would be safe in his travels.

"Good journey, Master," Olran echoed, then embraced Habib one last time. "Carry the Master well, golden one. He will be thy caretaker now. Farewell," he whispered and nearly wept as Huan mounted up and rode away, unnoticed by any but Ceridwen's men. It would take the Master many months to return to his Order, but he had done what he had been sent to do. The potential of the Black Knight had been tested and found worthy of expansion, as the Elder of the Temple had foreseen. Huan chuckled to himself as he boarded the ship at Land's End, after first stabling Habib carefully in the hold. He rubbed his hands in sheer delight every time he thought of the Elder's joy when he learned that the tales of Britain were true.

Chapter 8

Olran worked harder with the Jughead every day after losing his beloved Arab, it seemed all the extra training finally tamed the ugly horse's twisted sense of humor. However, the first mission the Black Hunter took the blue roan out on was a disaster. He was tailing the Black Knight to Aquae Sulis, trying to cover his ally's back uninvited when the Jughead suddenly took the bit between his teeth and began galloping wildly after Eclipse. Passing his ally, the Black Hunter was only able to shout out a quick plea for help as he thundered past, then was unceremoniously dumped off the horse's back to land butt first into the thick, slimy muck of an irrigation ditch.

"I have had enough of yer ways!" Ceridwen's Hunter growled out to his horse for the animal was now staring at his rider's predicament with obvious enjoyment. The Jughead's teeth were opened as though he was yawning, the Black Knight saw as he rode up, and a parody of a laugh came out of the orifice. The Black Hunter simply took out his skinning blade and suddenly drew it across the horse's throat, dropping him where he stood.

"Beloved Ceridwen, take this blood and bless it. Use it healing of the earth and thy People," he said simply, then laughed harshly. "Who is laughing now, stupid?" he addressed the still-twitching body as he bent to strip off all the gear.

"Ye want a ride to Londinium?" the Black Knight asked.

"Aye, I should be able to 'borrow' a ride back to Camelot," his ally answered, stiff and sore all over. "Ye've yer wish on this mission. Be careful, will ye?"

"We could ride double to my appointment. I could use yer help, thinking it over," the Black Knight offered. His ally stepped up behind him, gear and all; they rode to Londinium without exchanging many words. Once in the walled city, they took a room at the inn of a confederate before they went to meet with those who had sent messages of entreaty to the Black Knight. The Black Hunter secreted himself amongst boxes and crates along the line of warehouses in the shipping district of Londinium. The Black Knight felt comforted by his ally's keen-eyed presence as he met with those who told him a tale of goods stolen from the warehouses of legitimate shippers and re-appearing on the black market.

"Ye say even Sir Dalren's shipping company has suffered losses?" the Black Knight asked.

"Aye, all the cartage companies have been stolen from, Sir Knight, but most especially the royal shippers," the tallest of the three merchants said nervously. "There are rumors that the horses used to pull the dishonest wagons bear the mark of Westerland Keep."

The Black Hunter's ears perked up at the mention of that name and he listened closer. Suddenly he noticed a flitting shadow skirting the edge of the lamp-lit circle as he watched. He began working his way silently toward it very carefully keeping his black arrow at the ready in case it was needed.

"Thank ye, gentlemen, for sharing this information," the Black Knight was saying in parting. "Stay close to home for the next few nights so that I may more easily protect ye from retaliations."

"Aye, Sir Knight," they all answered and the spokesman answered quietly. "With my door locked tight and my daggers sharp."

The Black Knight walked to the lamp and as he bent to blow it out he heard the whispered 'whiz' of an arrow past his ear followed by a 'thunk' as it lodged solidly into something behind him. He turned swiftly and swung the oil lamp to ward away the attacker, noting the black arrow protruding from the man's chest. The light source struck the thug's right arm, breaking and spilling the flammable oil all over the man. One spark was all it took and the dying man was set alight. He was dead before any real flesh burning began, however, and the Black Knight left his token close to the charred remains, where it was sure to be found. Mounting up double on Eclipse, they made their way back home. "Ye made a great shot back there, my friend," the Black Knight complimented. "Did ye know the deceased?"

"He was one of Warren's men, Cynus ap Maed'wen," Olran confirmed. "I missed him before when I delivered the Black Knight's warning to Westerland. When the news of his death gets around Londinium, Warren's gold will not buy horse manure!" he laughed.

The Black Knight's eyes narrowed a bit in scrutiny as he headed Eclipse back towards Camelot. "Ye are enjoying this all a bit too much," he stated carefully.

"Ye did not feel the beatings, my brother," the Black Hunter returned, suddenly sober. "But I shall re-examine my motives if ye think my ego is out of control."

"Just give it a quick thought every once and awhile, brother," the Black Knight returned. "I do that myself."

They went on in silence, returning to Camelot at daybreak. Stowing their masks in their belt pouches, they tended to Eclipse's care. After all was done to comfort the horse, he was turned out into the warm, sunny and grassy pasture to sleep away the morning.

The two men walked quietly to the bathing room, stripped and soaked themselves clean. Returning to their room, they dressed in clean, casual clothes then went to the breakfast table, where Cai was just serving poached eggs on fresh biscuits topped with a slice of ham and cheese. Fresh cups of strong tea also were available and the two sat with the seneschal of Camelot. The King and Queen were expected back at the Castle the next day, he told them, and Gawaine was going out for summer trout to round out the welcome home meal.

"So Aaronn and Olran, would ye be interested in spending the day with our Orkney brother at his favorite fishing hole?" Cai asked cagily.

"When is he going?" Aaronn asked, seeing an opportunity to spend the warm, lazy day beside a stream with an occasional mug of cool ale to quench his throat. Besides, Gawaine was a friend from long ago and Aaronn missed his company.

"Ri' now, brother Aaronn," Gawaine's voice boomed from the scullery door. "Are ye coomin'?"

""Do ye have gear?" asked Aaronn, grinning, knowing the answer already.

"I've always enough fer four men, ye know tha'. Ye got tha' wee cask o' ale fer me, Cai?" Gawaine laughed.

"Aye and the basket of food ye will surely need to get through the day and still bring me back a fish or two," Cai laughed in return. "Be sure to share!" he used the old joke, taking the huge basket out to the fishing wagon Gawaine had custom-outfitted with a tarred and watertight tank to hold the fish alive until he returned to Camelot.

"Don' worry, Cai. If ye've packed enough, no man'll go hoongry," Gawaine teased. "Ye are coomin' too, aye Olran?"

"If I am invited, I am coming," the renegade prince called back.

Outings with other males always were rare occurrences while he had been a boy at Westerland Keep so as a result Olran treasured the time alone with his peers. Settling into the cushioned seats, Aaronn and Olran waited in the four-man cart for Gawaine to haul himself into the driver's seat. The Orkneyman picked up the reins to the two sturdy Welsh ponies and slapped them gently against their rumps. The two strawberry roans trotted smartly away, pulling the load easily along the newly cobbled road that ran beside the River Cam. After about an hour, Gawaine pulled off the road and put a finger to his lips.

"Shhh!" he warned, whispering. "If ye talk too loud, ye'll scare 'em." he went on, pointing to the river. Aaronn and Olran watched where he indicated and soon saw huge brown trout leaping out of the water for the gnats and mayflies that swarmed over the slow-running water. Stringing their rods with live bugs from Gawaine's collection jar, the anglers took their positions along the river and began flicking their lines over the water, trying to hook the fat fish. Olran flicked his line into a deep eddy just downstream and hooked into a fierce fighter. It took a long while for the thin man to land his prize; proudly he slipped it into the water-filled box at the back of the cart. He carefully led the horses closer, tethering them in the shade of the trees and loosening their gear for their comfort.

"Anyone for caffe?" he called out quietly and both his companions nodded vigorously. He quickly built a tidy fire and set water to boil, while he carefully measured and ground the beans with his mortar and pestle. When the water boiled, he pulled it away from the fire, spooned the roughly ground powder inside the kettle and stirred carefully. He let it sit for a few minutes, poured and strained out the spent grounds, then sweetened each mug the way he knew each of his companions preferred. Taking a cup to Sir Gawaine he found the Orkneyman held a fish for him to take to the box. After Olran deposited the squirming trout he took a steaming mug to Aaronn. The morning was spent in like manner, indulging in a cup of cool ale and catching enough fish to feed all of Camelot that night. Lunch was sliced meats, cheeses, boiled eggs and squares of last night's fruit cobbler.

"Ah Aaronn an' Olran, who'd e'er believed 'twould be this way fer us? Here we are, fishin' in th' mornin' like other men, while peace lies on th' land. 'Tis grand, joost grand, I tell ye!" Gawaine sighed.

"Peace is a wonderful gift, Gawaine," Aaronn commented. "But vigilance is the only safeguard for peace."

"Aye, 'tis sure," Gawaine answered. He said nothing for a few moments before continuing: "D'ye thin' Lancelot will return?" he asked without warning.

"Aye, he will be back." Aaronn assured him.

"I dunno, Aaronn," Gawaine expressed his doubts. "Ye dinnae see 'im before th' weddin' as soom o' us did. He worked 'imsel' every day in th' arena 'till he'd almost pass oot, then oop all nigh' drinkin'. All th' time before Arthur sent 'im off t' fetch the chit back t' Camelot, 'twas goin' on. Then th' day before he goes t' Lyonnesse, he cleans 'imsel oop proper wi' th' rest of oos, goes off t' bed early an' leaves wi'oot s' much as a g'bye," Gawaine related slowly. "I've ne'er seen 'im like tha', except fer when th' King started seein' her."

"He loves Gwenhyfar there can be no doubt of that. But he will not say a word about it, fearing that Arthur and Gwenhyfar's happiness will be marred," Olran stated bluntly. "Perhaps his knightly brothers should find some nice lovely lass to take his mind off his problems?"

"I might know someone to fit that description," Aaronn mused quietly.

"He'll nae sleep wi' her. Says 'twould take away 'is strength. I dinnae understand tha'," Gawaine puzzled over it.

"He will not have to share the Rite with this lady. All will be well, Gawaine. Ye know me well enough to know that the arrangements will be discreet as the Light itself." Aaronn assured him. "Do ye think that Cai might enjoy some fresh fowl with tonight's supper?" he asked, motioning over to his right as they all heard the honking of geese from a nearby pond.

Since the nesting season was over and the goslings were easily distinguishing from the adults, Olran took his bow and quiver to the water's edge. Secreting himself among the rushes there, he watched and waited for the obviously single geese, unmated adults. He took seven fat birds from the flock without causing the rest to panic and leave their goslings unprotected on the nests. Gawaine played retriever for him, swimming strongly and quietly to fetch the birds from the water before they sank and were lost. They field-dressed the birds, leaving the entrails for the scavengers well away from the nesting sites, then drank a few cups each of ale to quench the thirst hunting in the heat always brought on. Loading everything back into the cart, they returned to Camelot and presented Cai with the geese, as well as the tank full of trout.

"Thank ye, brothers," Cai said gratefully. "As the King and Queen have just returned, I was hoping ye would be home soon. I was headed for the chicken coop for supper," he chuckled as he fanned himself. Camelot's kitchens were a hot place to work in the late summer.

"We're off t' th' baths, Sir Cai," Gawaine announced grandly, and the three went on their way. Immersing themselves in the last available tub, Gawaine told the others fish stories until he was wrinkled as a current. Aaronn and Olran had long since departed before that, they told Cai not to expect them for supper. The two fell asleep immediately upon closing their eyes, pulling covers up to their chins.

Gwenhyfar and Arthur's return home was bright enough, the very next morning the new Queen had tea and pastries with Sir Cai. She was amazed at how strictly he scheduled the work crews in the castle, and asked how she could be of the best assistance.

"Well, if ye would please take over the castle's laundry, My Lady, I would be very appreciative. Also, I need for someone to see to the care and clothing of the many children here at the Castle, 'twould leave me a bit of welcome free time," Cai told her honestly.

"I would be happy to take all the correspondence concerning the care of the aged as well, Sir Cai," she ventured, smiling softly at him.

"If the King agrees, I shall deliver them with yer breakfast every morning, My Lady," he smiled back, relieved. "Will there be anything else I might do for ye?"

"Are there those young women here at Camelot I might have to assist me in my chambers?" she asked.

"I can think of two who would be suitable, I shall send them to ye," Cai told her, bowed and took his leave. Gwenhyfar finished her snack, dressed in her oldest frock and went directly to the laundry. She spent the entire morning there with the washerwomen, learning how they performed their tasks and taking their suggestions on what would make the operation more efficient. When Cai and Arthur passed by the washing room, they were treated to the sight of Gwenhyfar, bodice loose and dress soggy to the skin, hair trailing and cheeks pink with hard labor. The two grinned at each other, very brother-like, Arthur ruefully passed Cai five gold coins, and then they walked on, unseen by any of the laughing women.

"How do ye suppose Sir Gawaine's underwear got to looking like this?" the Queen's voice giggled behind them.

"My Lady, those are his best set!" one of the others answered, laughing outright. "Look at the holes in these!"

A peal of laughter echoed after the King and the Seneschal and a quiet suggestion was passed to Gawaine to replace his unders from stores more regularly. They need not have bothered, however.

Gwenhyfar proceeded to organize all the royal women at the Castle into mass-producing stock sizes of made-up sets. Soon they had stock-piled ten sets in each Knight's size, as soon as one set showed even the slightest sign of wear it was replaced through the laundry. The worn cloth was made into baby diapers, polishing cloths or even bandages after a thorough cleaning.

Knocking out walls in the Queen's private chambers during that Summer enlarged the sewing room and the ladies quickly requisitioned larger quilting frames, embroidery hoops and comfortable chairs from the busy royal carpenters. The sewing room became the hot bed of royal favor, if a woman wanted to be a part of court life she had to first spend more than a few hours in the sewing room. Much to the delight of the Black Knight, Vondra was eventually able to work her way into the circle of women. Many times, the clever woman was able to subtly direct the conversation into areas Ceridwen's man was interested in picking up a few clues to assist in his investigations. As a result, he was privy to all sorts of information.

Soon Vondra became his lover as well, a relationship that proved very satisfactory to each. When he increased her stipend, she immediately redecorated her quarters, bringing in fine furnishings and comfortable seating to make her rooms more comfortable and cozy. Vondra was also becoming somewhat well known for her charitable works, funded openly by the Queen and secretly by the Black Knight. The woman and her rapidly growing circle of trusted associates made sure that there were new houses for the impoverished aged, new clothing for poor children and their families, new schools for the young so that all could learn to read, write and do their sums. As well, she arranged for proper dowries for orphaned girls, allowing them to marry better than they would otherwise, all this was administered and cheerfully done by Vondra and her troop of well-educated women. This circle of beautiful and talented ladies became the most renowned of hostesses in all of Britain, funded by the Black Knight, of course. All the nobles in the Kingdom stood in line to hire them for the most important feasts and dinners. Vondra and the other women fed all the information they gathered from the usually exclusively male gatherings to the Black Knight, who added it to ever-growing files, neatly recorded in his meticulous hand. When Vondra informed him that Lord Evin Merin had paid her five hundred gold sovereigns for hosting a very exclusive buying fair, at which goods grown in each petty king's territory could be sold in field lots, he immediately asked for a guest list. It read like an inventory of his files.

"He mentioned that Caw, Lot, Uriens, Leodegrance's nephew…O, what's his name?" Vondra hesitated. "O, aye, Conrad and the rest of the Christian Kings. Also, Lord Thomas Corwin and his allies, 'twere several others as well, but I cannot recall their names," she apologized as she kneaded his shoulders expertly. Her soft, strong and skilled hands spread the scented oil all over his back and legs, rubbing gently but firmly to ease the knots she felt in his muscles.

"Ye have done well, Lady," he sighed as he relaxed as much as he allowed himself to under his hood. "I suppose I should take ye further into my confidence, Vondra," he teased a bit.

"I should hope so, Sir Aaronn of Camelot!" she laughed softly. Grinning ruefully under the mask, he turned over to face her.

"How long have ye known?" he asked.

"I suspected for a long time, but 'twas not 'till I peeked under yer mask a year ago while ye slept that I knew for certain." she confessed.

"I trust ye more than any other woman at Camelot, Vondra!" he said seriously. "Be sure ye understand well what that means."

"I understand, very well, My Lord," she answered, rising from her kneeling position. He watched, enjoying seeing her lovely body in motion, as she washed her hands free of the massage oil, then pulled a diminutive dagger from a sheathe on her bedside table. "If I ever betray ye, O Black Knight, my life is forfeit. 'Tis my understanding of our relationship and the cost of our alliance," she spoke calmly, and then made a tiny cut in her wrist before he could stop her. A drop of blood gathered and dripped into the Black Knight's right palm, and he nodded in satisfaction.

"Ye are an extraordinary woman, Vondra. Yer word is sufficient from now on," he told her, respect in his voice. She handed him a cloth to wipe the drop of blood from his hand, then wiped the dagger on the same cloth and tossed the cloth into the hearth's flames. They both watched it quickly catch and burn with a fierce flame, then Vondra returned the dagger to its sheathe.

"I shall let it remain here for now, My Lord," she stated coolly. "If I ever displease ye or break our bond, slay me with it. 'Twill look like a suicide and ye will not be blamed."

He kissed her softly on the lips and helped her cleanse and bandage the small cut.

"My back feels much better, Lady. Let yer hand heal before ye massage me again," he said softly, then removed his hood and took her into his arms. "Besides, there are better ways ye and I can find ease for our troubles."

He let her wipe the oil from his back before blowing out the candles except for one. They retired to her bed, and he was most attentive during the Mother's Rite, finding the release sufficient to bring sleep readily.

The Black Knight attended the 'buying fair' at Darkensdale, to listen and make sure Vondra's ladies were not accosted against their wills. It took all his restraint not to kill the arrogant and oily Merin right there and then, but he had no concrete evidence of treason against him. He watched, and waited patiently for his opportunity, reckoning the batch of newly-brewed lethal potion that was aging right now in his quarters needed the full two years before reaching its full and deadly potency. He grinned to himself, anticipating watching the evil man die, horribly.

"They found my man Cynus, burned to death in front of the royal carters, that damned Black Knight's token on the street beside him. What can be done to stop him?" Warren growled, his beady eyes following Vondra's ripe figure with longing.

"Find out who he is!" Merin answered succinctly. "Maybe he is that rebel son of yers?" he proposed.

"That whining wimp? He's much too squeamish to even gut a chicken." Warren answered with disdain.

"I have seen Olran at the Camelot games, Warren. He is damn good with that bow of his, his swordwork is not too bad either," Merin went on. "But 'tis the knife throwing that disqualifies him."

"Well, what about the King's pet, Aaronn?" Warren asked.

"He has acquired a nickname, 'the Knightly Knife' they call him now, but he cannot shoot at all as well as Olran. He swordwork is excellent, however," Merin passed him off. "Besides, I've seen this Black Knight closer than any of ye have, he is built bigger and broader than either Olran or Aaronn. Nay, 'tis neither one of them, it must be Bedwyr or Tristan, or perhaps one of the other junior Knights."

"We must find a way to stop him, otherwise all our plans will go awry," Warren stated firmly. "In the meantime we only do the strictest of legal business."

"Aye Warren, that much is obvious," Merin answered in a very condescending tone. "I see King Ban over there. We should go and talk to him about his grape harvest this year. If he has any at all to spare, I do not mind buying a few casks. He produces the finest wine in all the realm."

"I'll go in with ye on a bulk lot, Merin. Ban's wines are the best, after all," Warren agreed eagerly as they went to speak to the King of Lesser Britain.

The Black Knight made a mental note to speak to King Ban about the perils of doing business with the group of treacherous nobles. He continued to listen from his vantage point as the conversations continued. As a result of what he learned that night, more than a few black marketers and other underlings associated with Merin and his group turned up dead, throats neatly slit and the Black Knight's token always on hand. No protests were made, for each time the token pinned a scroll to the body, outlining his crimes and providing detailed proofs. For each man, the words on the scroll always began, "Executed for crimes against the Goddess and the Realm", followed by the list of crimes and evidences. Arthur's own investigations always proved the accusation and the gains he had made by doing business with the treacherous nobles were always confiscated by the Crown, enriching Arthur's coffers steadily. There was always a need for extra funds in the realm; the moneys were used for needful things like new armor for the Knights, weapons, bulk steel and the ever-growing network of royal hostels along the main roads. Between Cai's and Aaronn's clever planning, the network of hostels were placed at convenient places, spaced at regular intervals. Each one was simply built and furnished with a main hearth, a common privy, small kitchen and cold room as well as six to eight double bedrooms on the second story. The Black Knight found them very useful as convenient stopovers when he was out doing his work. It was fine to prepare a good hot meal before retiring to sleep on clean sheets when one was weary from a night out in the weather. His horse also appreciated the comfort of a stall, oats and hay to eat and clean straw to sleep on after long, weary missions all over the realm.

During the Samhain celebration, Lancelot returned at last to Camelot, returned to his usual impeccable self and proposing a Summer Tournament of Knightly games. He went to work at once, scrupulously avoiding any informal contact with the Queen. Arthur appointed him as Gwenhyfar's protector, a proper assignment for someone of his talents. He saw to it that she was surrounded at all times by a ring of the most formidable junior Knights on each occasion she left the protection of the Castle. When she complained about the lack of personal privacy, he explained stiffly:

"My Lady, ye are the woman chosen to bear Britain's heirs. Ye must be kept safe at all times, so those children can be born and grow up strong. 'Tis yer duty to remain safe and in good health, ye will accept no one into yer service, unless I have interviewed them first," he instructed. "'Tis on the King's orders and for yer own good, My Lady."

"I trust the judgment of the First Knight of Camelot, Lord Lancelot. Thank ye for taking such pains on my behalf," she answered quietly, accepting the situation.

"'Tis only my proper duty, Madam," he answered blandly and excused himself. She watched him go and drew a heavy sigh of consolation. He did not truly love her after all; she thought and put it away in a far corner of her mind.

Lancelot threw his energies into his duties; drawing up patrol schedules, coordinating the Knight's and squire's training times and being ever-watchful of Gwenhyfar. Somehow in his frantic schedule, Lancelot also found the time to undertake the gentling and schooling of the first yearling offspring of the British and Arab crossings. The first generation was slightly smaller than the British mares, but their speed and intelligence more than made up for it. They learned quicker and protected their riders more aggressively than their predecessors ever had. Each of the Inner Circle had their pick of the group of newly-trained young stallions and mares. Those lucky enough to win a mount in the lottery held for them confirmed within weeks all of Lancelot's claims of excellence. Arthur willingly funded the program in perpetuity, putting Lancelot and his heirs forever in charge of guiding it.

Winter was deep and cold that year, all breathed a sigh of relief that the harvest in the fall had been so huge. New granaries all over Britain bulged slightly when they were filled, the harvest was that heavy. Root cellars in many a house, both noble and common, had to be enlarged to accommodate the bushels and bushels of nourishing vegetables. Racks and racks of fruit had dried in the hot autumn sun and been stored away, along with salmon and other firm-fleshed fish. On the herding farms, beef had been dried and jerked, then put into dry, cool storage places to feed hungry workers and nobles alike all through the winter. That year's heavy harvest was famed as the Pendragon's harvest and at the Samhain festivals all throughout Britain, the people danced and offered thanks to Ceridwen and the Christ for the bounty.

When the winter holiday season began, two weeks before the Solstice, Camelot entertained the newly arrived warriors from far and wide. Arthur interviewed each of them as candidates for the Companions of Camelot, now commonly referred to as; "The Knights of the Round Table", in honor of Leodegrance's wedding gift. The immense table had to be sawed into thirds just to get it into the war-room; after it had been positioned in exactly the center of the room the royal carpenters pegged it securely back together. Stripping away the old layers of dirt and wax, the original honey color of the oak was revealed and admired, to preserve its beauty only a light coat of oil and wax was applied. Each of the Inner Circle's family crests was carved into their place and chair back. The

Ladies constructed banners for each Knight, which consisted of their personal sign under the Pendragon's dragon crest. The room was now quite satisfactory, the impression it made on visitors was obvious. Aaronn often slipped into the room unobserved, to imagine his own coat of arms hanging among those of the Senior Knights. He knew it was impossible, but he couldn't be blamed for thinking about how fine it would be. The Queen approached Olran the day before the Solstice with the idea that his family's banner should go up on the Wall of Honor, but the thin man declined coldly.

"Excuse me, My Lady, but I would not hang Westerland's banner in a pigsty! I shall earn my own coat of arms."

Gwenhyfar, of course, had heard the stories but she could hardly believe the savage cruelty portrayed by them. "Surely, 'twould honor yer ancestors to have Westerland's colors among all the others?" she persuaded innocently and was shocked to see Olran's handsome face harden even further.

"Madam, ye have asked for my permission, I have declined! Even the Pendragon's lady cannot force me to honor those who caused me much pain and grief. Family honor includes loyalty, kindness and love amongst the members; nothing could have been further from the real situation at Westerland! The people who live there have no love for Arthur Pendragon, or for ye Madam! I do, and 'tis all the discussion I shall participate in on the subject!" he stated firmly, then added. "I suggest, Lady Pendragon that ye learn to accept no as an answer!

Stalking away, he returned to his room, grabbed his bow and quiver despite the fact that he had already shot his usual quota of seven flights earlier that day. Bedwyr was working alone in the arena, trying to smooth some fancied footwork error. He saw Olran enter, set up a ring of targets at various distances, then string his bow and begin shooting furiously. Bedwyr was shocked to see the pain and fury on the usually composed Olran's face; he wandered over to him, being careful to stay well away from the line of fire. When the first flight was shot, Bedwyr picked up the next quiver of practice arrows and held it out for Olran to pick from. The archer nodded silently and resumed shooting, coldly and calculatingly aiming and firing at bull's eye after bull's eye. Tears finally began to drip down his face, though his eyes were filled with salty water, the thin man continued to score perfect shot after perfect shot. Bedwyr continued to supply arrows until, after ten quivers of arrows had been emptied, Olran finally appeared to have had enough. The young man's arm ached and his eyes burned, but he could still feel the shame of Westerland's treason hanging over him.

"What is amiss, boyo? Can ye speak of it with me?" Bedwyr asked quietly, persuasively.

"'Tis the Queen," Olran could barely choke out the words. "She wants to hang Westerland's banner on the Wall of Honor, and put my name on it."

"She doesn't know anything, boyo. She was not here when ye first came to Camelot with yer back in stripes. She didn't sit up with ye as we did, nursing ye through the fever afterward. Remember, she's been spoiled rotten since birth, raised to be a noble woman. She's a princess of a petty King, boyo. Ye know what 'tis like for a girl from such a family. Be patient with her, Olran, no one ever beat her for declaring loyalty for the Pendragon against the entire family's wishes," Bedwyr told him with kindness, handing him a handkerchief.

"Thank ye, brother Bedwyr. I know she meant no offense," Olran said after clearing his nose with a few quick and forceful blows. "I shall have this washed," he said apologetically and tucked the offensive cloth away in a remote pocket.

"Don't worry about it, Olran. Yer a good man in a fight, I can't think of anyone I'd rather have at my back on patrol," Bedwyr told him in a friendly tone. "Besides, I'll bet Gwenhyfar doesn't cook anywhere near as well as ye do," he chuckled. "Which reminds me, did ye see yer goin' out on western coast patrol?"

"I saw Lancelot post the list for the month," Olran confirmed regaining his usual composure.

"Good, that means I get to eat well!" Bedwyr chuckled harder. "Come on, boyo, a few of us are meeting Gawaine down at the Royal Inn for a few pints. He's been seeing a very spirited girl of late and we're all expecting a marriage announcement any time."

"Gawaine, the man who can smell a virgin at half a mile, is getting married?" Olran exclaimed, chuckling a bit.

"I know, 'tis unbelievable. I wager that the wench will show up at the inn to drag our brother out of there by the ear," Bedwyr laughed aloud.

"How much would ye bet?" Olran asked eagerly.

"I'd wager five in silver she shows up after an hour!" Bedwyr proposed.

The two men shook on their wager, and then Olran went quickly to wash up and change. When he was satisfied that he was presentable, and after a pipe or two of the herb with Bedwyr, the two went down to the royal inn. Aaronn was already there, with Gawaine, Tristan, Lancelot, Maegwyn, Accolon and the other Orkney brothers. All had wagered some amount with Bedwyr about the appearance of Gawaine's intended, after they had been there just over an hour a young, fiery red-head with flashing emerald eyes came stalking into the common room.

"Sir Gawaine ap Lot, I was sure I'd find ye here! Ye git yer mailed arse out of this alehouse an' up to yer room at Camelot!" she shouted and strode over to the smiling Gawaine.

"Ah lass, 'tis good t' see ye." he laughed and pinned her arms to her sides with a careful bear hug. "Ha' ye coom wi' yer answer then?" he asked pleasantly and tried to peek down her modestly cut bodice. The neckline only enhanced the girl's generous chest; Gawaine was in his cups enough to try for a harmless glance at what was under all that cloth.

"I have not, ye drunken swine of an Orkneyman!" she replied tartly and tried to squirm out of his grasp. "And stop peeking down my dress front!" she ordered. He would not release her, so she reached down as if to caress his manhood, then delivered a savage pinch to the sensitive member.

"Ow! Tha' hurt Rhian!" he protested, rubbing it comically. "I should go to yer Da right now, an' withdraw me petition fer yer han'!"

"I would not marry the lecher from Orkney if ye were the richest man alive, Gawaine ap Lot!" she replied shrewishly. "Ye are a womanizer, a drunkard and those are two of yer best qualities. Now, let me go and get yer arse home to bed!"

"Ye've a good idea there, Rhian. Let's go home," he chuckled, picked her up by the waist and proceeded to carry the kicking, biting girl from the inn's common room. Just at the door, he turned back to the Knights, who were all now laughing unstoppably, and gave them a beatific smile. "I'm gittin' married, me brothers, t' this very charmin' an' demure young lady. We'll let ye know when th' happy day is, there are problems wi' th' dowry, like always. Isn't she th' mos' beautiful thing ye've ever seen?" he asked, pulling the wench's head up by the hair to reveal her absolutely enraged and embarrassed face. "Coom along dearie, yer Da'll be expectin' ye. 'Tis after sun down, ye know, an' pas th' time fer decent, betrothed women t' be oot alone!" he said pleasantly and exited out the door, accompanied by the furious screams of Rhian.

"Let me go, ye Orkney bastard! Let...me...go!"

Bedwyr paid all his debts, for it had been after all, after an hour before Rhian had made her appearance. Olran and Aaronn each bought a round for the highly amused and side-sore Knights.

"By the Goddess, what a beauty, wherever did he find that hell-cat?" Aaronn asked, still somewhat stunned.

"The story he tells is that he was chasing this Knight in green-enameled armor, trying to catch up with him and ask him a few questions about his relationship with Morgause. He came upon the cretin in the midst of slicing away at that beauty's clothing, clearly preparing to rape her. They fought hand to hand and our brother Gawaine was victorious, he had to kill the man however. Rhiannon came back to Camelot behind him on his horse, we soon found her very worried father. Gawaine loves her dearly however she might not return his affections. The father thinks the two are a good match, or perhaps he is anxious to rid himself of a shrewish daughter," Tristan related, laughing all the way through the story. "I cannot wait 'till the wedding!" he finished, almost falling from his chair with mirth. Finally, all the men wiped their eyes, and toasted their brother Gawaine's long and hopefully happy marriage.

The two were united at the following Beltane, in a ceremony officiated by both the Merlin and Patricius, as had become the custom among the Knights since the royal marriage. The feast that followed was full of riotous fun and games, even Gwenhyfar drank more than usual on the hot spring day. Soon, she and the King disappeared, not to be found by anyone until the next day.

Gawaine took his blushing and demure bride off to the hunting lodge for the honeymoon, then back to Orkney for a long visit home. Nine and a half months to the day of the wedding, Lady Rhiannon was delivered of a ruddy-cheeked, squalling boy-child. He was named Arthur and Gawaine asked Aaronn to godfather the boy.

"Would ye help me watch o'er me boy, Aaronn? I've seen ye fight, an' I know ye kin teach soom o' tha' skill t' m' son once he's old enough. Would ye be me Arthur's godfather?" he asked simply and earnestly.

"I would be honored, brother Gawaine. I shall watch over him like the angels themselves." Aaronn vowed, grinning broadly.

"I'll sleep better knowin' yer sharp eyes are on 'im," Gawaine grinned back and turned to accept yet another hearty congratulations. The boy grew like the proverbial weed, eighteen months later Rhiannon delivered another boy, just as healthy and loud as the first.

Bedwyr found favor in the eyes of Lancelot's sister Branwyn and took her to wife that same year, during the Autumn Solstice celebration. During this time, Gwenhyfar again found herself with child. First the entire Kingdom celebrated, their joy soon turned to mourning when the young Queen miscarried after only three months. To console her and help her forget the pain and loss, Arthur took her on a winter tour of the noble's villas during the holiday season of the Winter Solstice and the feast of Saturn. The young Queen seemed to pull out of the depression that had beset her after losing the child. Soon, she found herself with child again; she carried it only two months before waking to find blood all over the sheets of the royal bed. The cruel rumors began to spread, fueled by Arthur's enemies, that she was unfit as Queen due to her inability to bear a healthy son.

The royal couple was invited to Lesser Britain for the Beltane celebration, when they returned Gwenhyfar's cheeks were again rosy and healthy. In that year, the first Summer Tournament games were held on Camelot's vast lawns. It had taken the organizing committee an entire year to put the thing together. Those who participated and watched appreciated all they had done to make the event enjoyable, each mock bout between squires, each pairing of Knight against Knight brought wild cheers and applause for both victor and fallen. Small silver cups, engraved with Arthur's sign and the year were presented to the winners of each event, participant and guest alike consumed much ale and delicious food. Dancing music sounded in the great room until late every night for a week, everyone but those participating in the next day's events enjoyed the pleasant diversion. The second morning of the Tourney, Olran awakened Aaronn.

"Brother ye must wake, 'tis someone we need to see," his ally whispered urgently into his ear. Aaronn opened his eyes to see the Black Hunter before him, dressed for work.

"Wha…who do we need to see?" Aaronn asked, forcing himself awake. "What is afoot?" the Black Knight came suddenly, fully awake.

"I saw someone who looked a lot like Morgause slipping in through the outer Maze door, the one in the orchard," the Black Hunter answered, handing him his outfit. The Black Knight donned his trappings quickly then motioned for his ally to follow. They entered the Maze through their own access; Ceridwen's men went down separate corridors, seeking the intruding Morgause. The Black Knight met no one on his way to the royal suite, nor did he see any lights from any room except the Lady Dorilynda's room. The young woman was Gwenhyfar's chambermaid, the daughter of some minor noble of Londinium. The Black Knight frowned, wondering what she was doing awake so early in the morning. He bent and peeked into a small hole in the wall, saw a flash of auburn hair and the murmur of words in a familiar sounding, over-ripe female voice.

"Have ye done as I ordered?" the voice said, impatiently.

"Aye, My Lady. I am now trusted to be alone with Her Majesty," Dorilynda's timid voice answered.

"Very good, ye have done well. Stay in her service and learn all ye can of her monthly cycles. Be sure to have the information for me when I return," Morgause's voice told her, threateningly.

"I shall, My Lady. Will our bargain then be fulfilled; will ye free my parents of their debt to ye?" Dorilynda asked, hope in her voice.

"If ye have information of some value to me, then we will talk about it. Plotting against the Queen of the Orkneys is no small crime; yer service will decide their fate. Sleep well, my dear," Morgause laughed cruelly, moving off to the door.

"What of the Black Knight, My Lady?" Dorilynda asked. Ceridwen's man grinned, noting that the girl obviously feared him at least as much as Morgause.

"If ye are not stupid, ye will not be caught, Dorilynda. Ye could pay yer debt another way, ye know," Morgause's voice dropped to an almost seductive tone. "Ye are a beautiful girl, just the type My Lord Lot might enjoy initiating into the pleasures of adulthood."

Dorilynda's voice was full of disgust as she answered. "Nay, My Lady. This way is much more satisfactory to me."

"And ye could not be persuaded to pay for yer parent's debt in my tower room?" Morgause asked.

"Nay, My Lady," Dorilynda was obviously repulsed by the very suggestion.

"Very well then," Morgause laughed, moving off to the door. She peeked out carefully, slipping out of the room and down the hallway with barely a whisper of her petticoats. The Black Hunter arrived beside his ally in the Maze at last, and was sent off in pursuit of Morgause at once.

"Find out where she is staying, brother," the Black Knight whispered. "I have to find out what she is up to here."

The Black Hunter nodded, adjusted his face hood and set out after her. The Black Knight assured himself of the presence of all his weapons before entering the room through the secret panel.

"Lady Dorilynda?" he spoke quietly.

The diminutive brunette whirled and in doing so, the front of her gown gaped open a bit, revealing her lithe, petite body.

"Wh...who is there?" she called out, fear in his voice.

"I am the Black Knight of Avalon, Lady."

"O...Goddess...no," she whispered, her pretty face wreathed in fear.

"Tell me girl, why are ye consorting with the Witch Queen of Orkney?" he asked, enjoying the view she was unknowingly affording him.

"She holds my parents in Lothian Castle's vile dungeons. Her henchmen caught my father talking witch burning in the town tavern. They took my Ma too and she whipped her right in front of both my Da and me. I told her I would pay the debt, she laughed, said I had better lest the two of them die as sacrifice to appease the vile demon she serves. She coached me for a month, gave me a wardrobe and made sure I was accepted here at the Castle. Now, she has ordered that I..." the girl related, the truth of her words ringing in the Black Knight's trained ears as he cut her off.

"I heard what she ordered ye to do, and the proposal she made as alternative. Come, ye must tell me all, girl, and for my sake, tie up that robe or we will never get any work done at all," he chuckled.

"Ye are not going to kill me?" she asked, terror in her fawn-brown eyes as she tightened the sash of her robe.

"I do not make war on little girls, Dorilynda. But as I said, ye must tell me all ye know, be sure to hold nothing back," he told her warningly. "Do ye have any wine in yer room?"

"Aye, Sir Knight, would ye like it warmed first?"

"Nay, but thank ye for the offer. Just pour me a cup, then sit here beside me and make yer report," he requested. She poured and served him nicely, then poured for herself and took a seat next to the ebon-clad man. It took a while to make a full confession of all she had done in Morgause's forced service. Mostly, it appeared that she had only passed information about the Queen's wardrobe and her personal life with Arthur.

"She has often asked for their sheets, but I have not given them to her for fear of what she might do with them with her evil magick. When she visits, she often collects hairs from the Queen's hairbrush, or a sample of the water she has passed," Dorilynda finished her report and wine.

"Thank ye girl. Ye have cleared up many mysteries that have long troubled me. Pack yer things now, ye are leaving the Castle tonight," he ordered, pulling her bags from the closet.

"But where can I go to be far enough from the Lady Morgause?" she asked in wonder. "I have no one but my parents."

"I maintain a safe house nearby. Come girl, waste no time, lest I lose my resolve and bed ye, right here and now!" he stated, smiling under his hood. She threw her clothes into the bag, filled a smaller one with brushes, combs and hairdressings, then ran behind her dressing screen and pulled clothing on faster than ever she had before.

"Are ye ready, at last?" he asked.

"Aye, Sir Knight. The rest of the gowns are Morgause's, I do not want anything to do with them," she stated emphatically.

"Then stay close behind me, girl, and be quiet!" he instructed and poked his head out the door. No one could be seen or heard in the hallway, he pulled her out the door and to the stairs. Creeping through the great room and out the garden entrance, he went with her down the road to Camelot-town and Vondra's room. The woman opened at the first knock and motioned them inside.

"Shhh," she cautioned. "King Lot is with Kristine down the hall, trying to sleep off a terrible headache. He has been drinking heavily with a strange man I have not seen before. Who is this?" she asked, after reciting her news.

"Vondra, meet Dorilynda, formerly the Queen's chambermaid. No one is to know she is here, understand?" he asked, hurriedly.

"Aye My Lord, I understand perfectly. She will stay here 'till ye return for her, or send me other instructions," Vondra nodded.

"Very good Vondra, I am glad ye have a good grasp of the situation. Sleep well and safely, Dorilynda. I may need ye to go to the King with me, so be sure to stick to this room like ye were imprisoned here," he instructed. "Those who inform on Morgause often turn up dead."

The girl paled and nodded. "Aye, Sir Knight. I have no desire to leave without yer permission."

"Very well then, ye need fear no reprisal. Good night, Ladies," he said warmly, winking at Vondra before striding away.

After closing the door, Vondra turned to Dorilynda. "Well, I have an extra bed in here, the necessity is behind this screen," Vondra showed her. "I suggest ye lay down and at least try to rest. He is very punctual as a habit," she added kindly and closed the curtains to the alcove.

"Are ye the famous Lady Vondra of Camelot?" Dorilynda asked after she was in bed.

"Am I famous?" Vondra giggled as she made sure the door was securely locked. "I did not know."

"Everyone loves ye for all the good things ye do," the girl told her admiringly. "I have wanted to meet ye for such a long time."

"Why thank ye, my dear. Now, go to sleep," Vondra answered, yawning.

"I shall try, Lady Vondra."

They slept until nearly noon, then shared a late breakfast and played dice games, sewed and talked all day. Dorilynda stayed with her a week, the Black Knight making periodic visits until finally she was taken before Arthur.

"Sire, I have someone with me who ye need to meet," Ceridwen's man said, pulling Dorilynda into the King's suites.

"Why, Lady Dorilynda! Where have ye been girl?" Arthur exclaimed, glad to see she was unharmed.

"She has been in hiding with me, Sire, and for very good reasons. Tell him what ye told me, Dorilynda, leave nothing out," the Black Knight urged. The girl told all, when she was done, Arthur sighed heavily and nodded.

"I thank ye, Dorilynda. Yer parents will be freed soon," he told her. "I shall send ye and yer parents to stay with King Ban in Lesser Britain, he is blessed by Ceridwen and will provide ye with suitable protection from any reprisals mounted by Lot or Morgause. The Black Knight will continue to see to yer safety until ye are reunited."

"Thank ye, Sire. I know I should have come to ye, but I was afraid for my parents, and Morgause said..."

"I know, child. Now, go on with the Black Knight," Arthur told her gently. "I want to speak to ye as soon as ye return from hiding her," he added to the Black Knight.

"Of course, Sire," the Black Knight agreed. When he had returned Dorilynda to her hiding place, he returned to Arthur's suites, together they spoke of how best to handle the situation.

"I cannot antagonize Lot, not now. Morgause is the only means I have of controlling him. Use what means ye might to contain her, save killing her, unless ye find her in the actual practice of black magick. In that case, she is under Ceridwen's judgment," Arthur instructed the Black Knight.

"Any means, save killing her?" he asked, just to clarify Arthur's orders.

"Ye heard me right, Sir Knight."

"Thank ye, My Lord Pendragon. Shall I speak to Sir Lancelot about his screening of chambermaids?" the Black Knight asked.

"Aye, we must be more cautions. The Queen is again with child, if she loses this one the rumors will be even more vicious than the last time," Arthur told him.

"Agreed, but she should have the Lady Vivaine at her side at all times," the Black Knight suggested.

"She will not hear of such a thing, preferring her black-robed and ignorant priest to mutter prayers all day, while fondling her rosary beads," Arthur said, wearily. "'Twas all I could do to persuade the filthy man to bathe before attending the Queen, he has been ordered to bathe daily while in residence. I cannot believe I would have to order such a thing!"

"Ye are the King, Lord Pendragon! Insist as ye did with Avalon's wedding gifts!" the Black Knight responded. "'Tis thy child as well, a gift from Ceridwen, only the ladies of Avalon have the proper knowledge to assist her in keeping the child in her womb long enough to deliver a healthy heir."

"Well I know it, Black Knight, but even if Vivaine were here, Gwenhyfar would not follow a word of her advice," Arthur sighed in resignation.

"She is acting too foolishly to be Queen, Sire," the Black Knight responded coolly. "If she loses this one, ye should divorce her and take a smarter woman to wife."

"Ye have expressed yer opinion and 'twill be quite enough, Sir Knight! My choice for Queen is my own!" Arthur said, his temper rising.

"Not when she cannot produce a healthy heir, due to incompetence and superstition," the Black Knight said calmly in response.

"Tend to yer own duties, Sir Knight, my marriage bed is none of yer concern," Arthur told him sternly.

"Thy marriage bed is Ceridwen's realm, Lord Pendragon, therefore 'tis my province to protect. 'Tis the extent of my interest, I bid ye good day, Sire," the Black Knight informed him firmly before making his exit.

He and his ally spent the rest of that day making sure that Morgause never again intruded into the Maze. They installed hidden trip wires that released darts or arrows, as well, hidden loose boards delivered a healthy blow to an invader's backside and even a pail of water balanced precariously above a ceiling beam, triggered by yet another of Olran's clever trip wires. Feeling more secure, the two planned the Black Knight's next trip to visit Morgause.

The bold woman stayed throughout the entire week of the Tournament, Aaronn was pleased to note her confusion at Dorilynda's absence. He adopted black and silver as his dress at the final feast and felt Morgause's eyes on him all night. He knew, and played it for all it was worth, with his ally's assistance.

"Tell me again, Sir Olran," he began at supper, between courses that night. "The laws of the desert Arabs concerning women, I mean. I have heard that they use enslavement as a way to teach women lessons about an over-active ego?"

"Aye, Sir Aaronn, 'tis true. When I was in the Damascus agora, the slavers came and presented a woman with a legal writ of enslavement. They locked a collar on her, right there, then stripped her naked for the assessment of her body measurements, and so the men could appreciate her beauty. Cuffing her hands and feet together with a light steel body chain, the slavers led her off to be branded. No woman ever escapes slavery, but I heard that many have earned their freedom by learning to shed their proud ways," Olran replied, trying successfully to keep the grin off his face. Morgause's shocked mien showed that she had heard every word and now at least feared such a situation, just as he had intended that she should.

One evening after the Summer Solstice, Aaronn supped lightly and retired early to his room. Donning his working clothes, he stole out through the Maze exit, down to the stables and dressed Eclipse, being sure to black out the white spot. Assuring himself that his little gift for Morgause was in his saddlebags, he headed for Londinium and the royal inn. He knew that Morgause and Lot were still staying there, due to the roof at Lothian being repaired after heavy rains had damaged it during the spring. He reached the walled city in the early morning hours, tied Eclipse nearby and climbed up the outside of the inn, using parapets and balconies to swing and leap his way to Lot's room. The Orkney King was absent, but Morgause slept inside the curtained bed. The Black Knight entered the room quietly, watching for a while to make sure she was truly asleep. Seeing no signs of her rousing, he locked the window tightly, crossing on silent feet to the door, he assured it was locked as well before approaching her bedside. Sitting beside her carefully, he invoked Ceridwen's aid in keeping the Witch Queen asleep before he withdrew the simple, strong ring of steel locked in back with a key lock and opened it. He carefully and cautiously encased Morgause's neck with it, after locking it tightly he left the scroll sealed with his sign on the pillow beside her. He carefully cut away the nightgown she barely wore with a convenient blade from his harness, using the pieces to bind her hands and feet to the head and foot boards of at the corner posts. Adding a secure gag, he looked at her spread-eagled on the bed.

"Now, ye are displayed as the slave ye are, bitch!" he murmured and left the room, leaving the door and window as had found them. When the cool night air finally awoke Morgause, she spent the remainder of the night in a futile attempt to free herself. The chambermaid was the first to find her, the frightened woman sped off to Lot in the common room, bringing him immediately to Morgause's aid, or so she thought. When he saw Morgause, Lot laughed loud and long as he bent to read aloud the delicate engraving beautifully etched around the simple steel collar.

"I am the property of the Black Knight, use me as ye will," then he unrolled the writ of enslavement left on the pillow beside her. "In light of her treasonous meddling, this female is declared slave. All her possessions are mine; she is free for the use of all men." Morgause struggled harder and Lot's eyes lit with arousal. When he began removing his shirt and trous, Morgause's eyes opened wide as she guessed his intent, and struggled all the harder.

"Fer th' use o' all men, eh?" he chuckled, climbing onto the wide mattress. "Well, we'll ha' t' see aboot soom day takin' off tha' new necklace ye've been given, although, it doos seem t' suit ye," he laughed softly and bent to kiss her body. Much satisfaction he had from Morgause that morning and her hate for the mysterious figure known she knew only as the Black Knight grew by leaps and bounds. Ceridwen's man laughed all the way back to Camelot after witnessing all, when he told his ally they forever shared the secret joke about the Black Knight's 'hot, luscious and overripe slave girl'. Arthur received a letter from Morgause a week later, describing the event in detail and demanding that he, "Do *something* about this outrage!"

He had not met with the Black Knight for quite a while, due to the Queen's latest miscarriage. It seemed to take much more out of her this time and nothing Arthur could do or say would cheer her. Her depression continued for many weeks, finally her temper turned foul. Many folk, both noble and common, felt the lash of her bereaved and vicious tongue. Trying to be of some help, Sir Cai started flower seeds in the kitchen and when they began to show signs of growing, he took them up to the Queen's chambers and filled each and every windowsill with the potted plants. Gwenhyfar was delighted, much to his relief, and took over their care enthusiastically. Soon, her room was ablaze with color and the Queen began planning a flower garden. Cai assisted gladly, setting the pages to preparing the plot as soon as the ground thawed enough to rough plow it. Afterwards, the young men and boys used hoes and shovels to break up the clods left behind, adding well-aged horse manure to enrich the somewhat rocky dirt of the only spot near the gardens that Cai could not use for vegetable production. When the weather warmed enough, Gwenhyfar planted patches of bulbs; flags, bluebells, lavender and other fragrant flowers for cutting, their fragrance perfumed the entire Castle. In thanks,

Arthur commissioned and presented Cai a new set of steel pans for his kitchen. Gwenhyfar also made one other decision, when she told Arthur of it he was heartily disgruntled despite his understanding of how she arrived at it.

"I have decided My Lord that I shall sleep in my quarters for the time being. I have lost three children in two years, 'tis almost beyond bearing emotionally. We both need the time to recover, Arthur, please understand," she said, struggling not to cry in front of him.

"There are many ways we might comfort each other in the night, Gwen. Please, do not push me away at the very time we need each other most!" he protested, gently.

"'Tis only one proper way for a man and woman to join," she replied stiffly, frowning at him. "The priests say that any other practice is obscene and perverse in the eyes of God."

Arthur sighed in resignation, knowing it was useless to argue with her. "Very well, My Lady, I shall grant yer wish and give ye the distance ye require, for a time. I want ye to consider making the separation as short as possible, however. I am a man, not a eunuch. The sheer pressure of ruling alone will force me to seek release in some woman's bed; I wish it to be yers. If ye will not, I am sure I can find comfort elsewhere," he told her seriously, calling for his personal page to assist her in moving what she wished from the royal suite into her own rooms. Arthur was a patient man and he cared for Gwenhyfar enough to grant her a time to heal. It went well enough for about four months; Arthur began to get very cranky at slighter and slighter provocations. Everyone overlooked it, of course, except the Black Knight. Ceridwen's man finally went to the King on the matter.

"My Lord Pendragon, I have come into the knowledge that ye and the Queen are sleeping in separate chambers. Personally, I would not tolerate it, but apparently ye do. Allow me to provide ye an alternative to this enforced celibacy," he came out with it bluntly, just as the Spring Equinox approached. It had been six months now since Gwenhyfar had fled the royal bedroom, Arthur felt as though surely he would explode if something didn't change soon. He face was truly agonized as he turned around to at last face Ceridwen's man.

"I would not break my sworn, sacred word, Sir Knight. 'Twould be better if the Queen could be persuaded to return to me. If that cannot be accomplished, then we can further discuss yer suggestion."

"Would ye like me to persuade her, Lord Pendragon?" the Black Knight asked. "Or are ye going to snap at everyone all summer long?"

Arthur stood silent for a long moment before chuckling a bit as he answered. "If the Goddess can spare ye from Her service, then I would count it a favor if ye would speak to the Pendragon's lady."

"Very well, Artos," the ebon-clad man answered. "Also ye should know that I spied foreign sail off of Land's End yesterday. The flood of new applicants begins early this year," he observed dryly. "All the more reason ye should have access to the Mother's Rite."

He discussed a few more pressing matters with the King, then took his leave and returned to his room. Olran was out on eastern coast patrol, so he was alone to plan. He waited until he knew Gwenhyfar was completely alone before he went carefully through the Maze to her room. He entered, staying in the shadows until he saw her sit at her tiring table to unpin her wealth of golden hair, then take up her brush and drew it through, counting every stroke.

"My Lady Pendragon?" he spoke softly and she turned, dropping the hairbrush in shock.

"What are ye doing in here?" she demanded, fright tingeing her voice.

"Lady, let us not play that game here, while we are alone. Ye know well I serve Ceridwen, the White Goddess of Britain, and that I am Her arm of justice," he stated and she nodded her understanding. "Why have ye allowed yer mate to suffer for half a year under the burden of Kingship, alone? When ye took yer marriage vows, ye promised to be Queen to the entire land. Ye have ceased in yer duty to yer Lord, My Lady, and the realm suffers for it," he told her seriously, keeping his voice gentle and calm.

"Ye know nothing of what a woman suffers, Sir Knight!" she answered, tears trickling down her face. "Three children lost, in two years! I cannot, I will not face it again."

"The Lady of Avalon can certainly assist ye in forestalling getting with child. She is a very learned woman who is falsely reviled by yer ignorant and filthy priests in their jealousy of her wisdom and power. 'Tis the Christians who teach that women are naught but pretty decorations and walking wombs!" the Black Knight derided. "They do not teach self-worth or a proper sense of pride in yer womanhood. Ye make the King's mind at ease when the Mother's Rite is shared between ye. I can imagine that yer own disposition would improve as well."

"How dare ye!" Gwenhyfar's rage finally flared. "I am High Queen of all Britain! No one speaks to me that way!"

"I do," the Black Knight insisted, quietly but firmly. "For all yer airs, Gwenhyfar, ye are still only a girl. Ye have the wants and needs of a woman, but lack the maturity to express them. Ye have heard that Morgause now wears my collar; she earned it with her arrogance. I could very easily do the same to ye. What would ye be then, Gwenhyfar? I tell ye true, ye would only be one more ego-blinded girl in a coffle. Does that frighten ye, wench, or do ye long to have yer true self revealed for all to see?" he asked, pulling the simple silver chain from out of his belt pouch. From it dangled an intricate steel key.

"What is that?" Gwenhyfar asked.

"The key for yer bracelets if ye earn them by the continued neglect of yer duty, delivering the comfort only ye can provide," he told her plainly. "Return to the royal bedchamber, lest ye find yerself replaced there and remanded to my care. I could enjoy yer presence in my quarters, very much, and you would not be able to put on such airs as ye do now, I assure ye," he went on and melted away into the shadows.

"I...hate...ye!" she screamed and threw the brush after him. She heard it strike the wall dully before she threw herself onto her bed, weeping in sheer fright and frustration. Still, it was only two more days before she moved her things back into the royal suites and sent for Lady Vivaine to come and have tea with her, "to discuss many issues of women."

Arthur was overjoyed, they spent a week together at the hunting lodge to celebrate their reunion, re-lighting the fire of their marriage. When the royal pair returned, the work of the Kingdom went on much smoother than before. The Black Knight continued to watch, waiting for Gwenhyfar's manipulative nature to surface yet again.

Lancelot came to Aaronn later in the season, asking for his assistance in training pigeons to carry messages all over Britain. It was a lengthy business, but they reckoned by winter to have a fast and regular communications system to make the Kingdom run more efficiently.

Olran finally won a permanent remount he could train, so every day he attended to the task until the two year old stallion, another mottled blue and black roan, was as fine a warsteed as any ridden by the Inner Circle. Named, "the Jughead", affectionately due to his resemblance to the first of Olran's steeds, the horse worked willingly and hard for his rider. His gaits were so smooth the archer could easily shoot from his broad back while at a full gallop and still hit his targets well enough for a kill.

The Black Hunter continued to bedevil Westerland Keep, keeping them frightened and distrustful of their allies. His latest stunt had been sneaking into Westerland's cellars and pouring vinegar into all of Warren's ale casks, rendering them undrinkable. Warren, when he unwittingly drawn off two mugs to share with Lot, quickly spat out the foul drink and grabbed for Lot's mug before he could partake.

"'Tis sour, but how?" he wondered, explaining his actions to Lot. "I followed the same recipe as always. Well, come with me into the cellars and help me tap another cask," he suggested in a jovial tone to Lot, while the Black Hunter snickered silently in his hidden spot. The two opened every single cask, fifty of them, finding each of them fouled and unfit for even swine food. Warren's rage erupted loudly upon opening the last one.

"Damn it all, what's afoot in this Keep?" he shouted. "Are we under some black enchantment? Call for that black-robed Christian priest and tell him we need an exorcism!"

The Black Hunter slipped from the building and away to the closest hostel. Once there, he uncorked the first wineskin to come to hand in the cold room and drank to Ceridwen, then enjoyed a long and long laugh as he recalled the fury on Warren's fat face. When Olran heard, through his sources, how much Westerland's 'spiritual cleansing' had cost, he chortled with glee and told Dalren to load a wagon full of his best ale and take it to Westerland. Warren bought the whole load without question, paying twice what Dalren usually charged, thus further enriching the Black Knight's coffers, assisting in funding further works. It was a rich joke that kept Ceridwen's men amused while Olran worked on another scheme to further frighten and agitate his former family. That year, after Olran had figured up the pair's profits and losses, the paperwork showed a substantial gain. The Black Knight brought his tithe to Arthur, for the first time it was more than a token amount. Arthur's eyes widened as the sacks piled up at his feet. The accounting the Black Knight presented the King with an accurate inventory of every coin and gem, down to the tiniest stone.

"Sir Knight, 'tis very welcome indeed, especially with all the noble houses in arrears. I thank ye," Arthur said gratefully.

"'Tis my honor and duty to make sure the funds go where they are most needed, My Lord. I trust all is well between ye and the Queen?" he inquired tactfully.

"All is well indeed, Sir Knight," Arthur assured, grinning despite himself.

"Good!" Ceridwen's man chuckled along with the King. "Do ye wish for me to 'assist' in tax collections from the errant houses?" he asked.

"Not just yet," Arthur answered, returning to seriousness. "I have sent them all reminders of their obligations, as well as hints of the penalty for non-payment. I hope ye do not mind, but I also dropped a hint or two about fearing Ceridwen's vengeance." After a moment of silence, Arthur said. "I thank ye, Aaronn. What would I do without yer assistance?"

"I do not know, Sire," Aaronn answered, removing the hood from his head. "I do know I am finally glad to be of real service to ye and the Goddess, and that all is well between ye and yer Lady."

"I know, Aaronn," Arthur acknowledged, pouring them each a cup of wine. "I also remember that ye and Gwen have never been friends. Still, ye support her for my sake and I am grateful."

"Ye are the High King and War Duke of Britain, Artos. I pledged my loyalty to yer Crown, she is yer chosen Queen. My personal feelings in the matter are nothing!"

"I wish there were more in the realm like ye. I wouldn't have to watch over the tax rolls like a scribe if there were," he laughed, but the idea intrigued him. What if a small estate opened up without heirs, he thought. Wouldn't such a thing make a nice reward for the Black Knight, as well as give him an independent base of operations? It would be advantageous for all, he mused as he sipped the well-aged and mellow wine. But how could he grant Aaronn, a fatherless King's ward, a sizable enough piece of land without enraging the entire noble class? 'Tis a problem, he sighed inwardly, turning his attention back to the Black Knight.

Black Knight returned the mask to his face. "How is the prosecution of those black marketers going?"

"We finished it up today, nine executions were found to be necessary. The thing will be done tomorrow in the town square," Arthur finished, sighing heavily.

"Swift justice is best," the Black Knight responded. "Who is doing it?"

"I am, of course. King's Law, King's Justice," Arthur told him.

The Black Knight nodded in approval. "Is there anything else ye want for me to do?" he asked.

"I have heard more rumors of young girls being sold into slavery to pay their parent's taxes. Find out who and where, if ye can, and put a stop to it, permanently," Arthur requested.

"I have heard that as well. I shall get on it, right away."

"Thank ye, Sir Knight," Arthur said. "Now, I have others to meet with. Would ye please excuse me?"

"Of course, My Lord Pendragon, may the Goddess watch over ye," the Black Knight said courteously and withdrew.

He was well away before Bedwyr brought in the latest traders with offers of regular shipping overseas. This was where Britain was least advantaged, Arthur wanted regular access to things from the Byzantine markets. Pressed dates, exotic cooking herbs and spices, sturdy hemp sail cloth and ropes were rare here so far north, now that the tin mines in Wales were back up to full capacity, he had hard trade goods again. Sir Ectorius, Cai's father and Arthur's foster father, had taken over the task of overseeing the mining operations, he had put his excellent organizing skills into bringing order out of the chaos of the Mining Guild. British tin was world-renowned and the finished goods made from it were highly sought after. The bargaining began spiritedly, Arthur enjoyed coming to the agreed terms.

"Now, My Lord Arthur, a small down payment will be necessary to secure our deal. Perhaps, one hundred coins of gold?" the merchant suggested.

"Quite right, Arthfael. Sir Bedwyr, will ye make out the receipt for their payment?"

"Excuse me, Lord Pendragon, but…our payment?" the merchant squeaked out.

"When the perishable goods arrive, of course I shall make my part of the bargain good. Ye wish to take the tinwork with ye, which is of course acceptable with the suggested deposit. Certainly, the amount that ye have purchased will sell for much more than what ye paid for it. I must have some security, after all," Arthur explained, reasonably, while the merchants squirmed. Finally, the headman sighed.

"Very well, My Lord Pendragon. We agree to the one hundred gold on deposit against delivery of the trade goods from overseas. Where is the contract I must sign to make the agreement legal?" he sighed again heavily, knowing he was outmatched this time. The coins were brought, counted, and then the ship was loaded with a full cargo of cookware, utensils, artwork and other items. The ship from the Byzantine traders appeared on time in Land's End, bringing passengers as well as goods.

Caliph Harimun had sent two of Sejuni's younger brothers for a visit and the strong capable men brought many a gift for Lancelot and Olran, among them a small, bound and obviously water-resistant chest for each. Opening it later in their quarters, the heady odor wafted into Aaronn's and his nostrils, bringing smiles to their faces. It had been a long while since their store of the rare and potent herb had run dry. After imbibing, the two dressed to escort Abd-Al-Karim and Abd-Al-Malik to their favorite tavern for a few rounds. The Arabs were enthusiastic drinkers, but soon were spent and returned to the Castle, leaving Aaronn and Olran to spend more time together. The focus of this night was at Dalren's tavern. Seeing them enter, Vondra seated them at the back table they liked and served them supper, her lovely presence only serving to enhance the décor as well as their enjoyment of the excellent food. After they had eaten their fill of sizzling rare beefsteaks, sautéed vegetables, hard rolls and butter, washed down with many a glass of good, hearty wine, they sat back and relaxed while discussing many things, including the harvest already underway in Britain.

It was proving to be a heavy one, already the pear trees had borne so much fruit everyone could barely stand the sight, let alone the taste of them. Cai finally ran the rest of the fruit through the apple press, now the juice stood aging in the cold room under the kitchen, four full hogsheads, and Cai pressed more every day. Aaronn sighed inwardly as he imagined the many wonderful meals the light wine would accompany. Olran related his latest exploits at Westerland and Aaronn's amused chuckles were all the congratulations the archer needed to hear.

"Next, I am going to cause the whole summer's cheese to rot!" he said quietly to Aaronn. "All I have to do is find a way to flood the aging room with water. The kitchen water is piped right in through the room's wall, so I should be able to accomplish my goals by breaking the pipe.

Once I have done that, the entire room will be filled with water!" he chuckled. "I have been planning this for a very long time, ye know," he added.

"So, the residents think Westerland is haunted and cursed now?" Aaronn questioned in a musing tone. "No wonder their allies have been jumpy lately, especially Merin. Llew told me recently that he was ordered to make a complete search of Darkensdale, being very careful to look for unusual things," he told Olran, laughing quietly as he did so. "I wonder what might be done to add to those fears."

"I am sure we can think of something," Olran chuckled with him as he finished his wine. He ordered another cup, and a pretty, willowy blonde delivered the drink with a gentle smile. The girl sat beside the thinner man for a while, Aaronn could see she was speaking quietly and persuasively to his friend. Presently, Olran rose, pulling the girl up beside him.

"See ye later, brother. I think I need a breath of fresh air."

"I bet ye do," Aaronn answered with a smile. "See ye later?"

"Aye, much later," Olran responded, walking slowly with his sinewy arm around her waist. Aaronn was very glad his friend was seeing someone at last. He was beginning to hear a lot of very nasty gossip about how much time he and the archer spent together alone. He thought about suggesting to Olran that he begin seeing more women, possibly even marrying to alleviate the gossip. He thought he knew well what Olran's reaction would be if he ever heard the sniping words to his face. Aaronn was proven quite right in his suppositions.

The harvest had barely been gathered when the first frosts blew in from the North that year. When everyone went to look out their windows the day after Samhain, they found a fresh, thick blanket of dry powdery snow had fallen. That winter was exceptionally frigid, the cold preventing anyone without urgent business from traveling. Idle hands and tongues gave rise to more and more gossip among the women of the sewing circle; finally even the Queen participated in the nasty and cutting conversations.

"So tell me about that handsome Sir Olran," one woman, an unmarried minor noble woman from Cornwall was saying as they sewed. "I would think a man of his age, from a well-landed family would be married happily by now, with a son or two around his feet."

"Sir Olran is hardly the marrying type, Lady Cornelia," Morgause answered in an insinuating tone. The Orkney queen was spending the winter at Camelot that year, claiming the roof of Lothian was hardly mended enough to house chickens, let alone royal folk. "Ye know about him, aye?" she went on, dropping her voice to a whisper.

"Lady Morgause, ye speak of a Knight of Camelot," Gwenhyfar objected, in a slightly quavering voice.

"He and Sir Aaronn, why do ye think they share the same quarters?" Morgause went on viciously. "They are lovers."

"Sir Aaronn and Sir Olran?" they all gasped in shock.

"How do ye know?" Cornelia asked.

"Sir Aaronn was fostered at Lothian for years, Lady Cornelia. He and Olran were inseparable all that time. Why do ye think King Warren whipped Olran out of Westerland Keep?" Morgause fit her lies to match the facts. "He discovered their unnatural relationship and was bound by Christian morals to scourge him. Obviously, Olran would not repent, so Warren was obliged to drive him away. Unfortunately, it seems the damage was already done and poor Olran remains Aaronn's catamite to this day. Ye never see them apart, just like real lovers," she wove her tale, sighing theatrically, adding just a bit of black magick to help set the tale into their weak minds.

"Surely, they would not be junior members of the Round Table if this were so, Lady Morgause," Gwenhyfar spoke up again quietly, hesitant to challenge the formidable Orkney queen. "The King is quite gifted at seeing the truth of a man; he regards that kind of relationship as unnatural as well as unlawful."

"Sir Aaronn is and always has been his pet. One tends to overlook negative things in one's favorite," Morgause answered. It all sounded so reasonable and believable when she put it like that, before long the nasty rumor was all over Camelot. The only persons that had not heard it were most of the Knights of the Inner Circle and Arthur himself.

Aaronn and Olran had been out on patrol all the month of Samhain, a week after the first snowfall their party returned to Camelot and its welcome hot baths. The hostels and guardtowers had helped some, so had friendly farmers and innkeepers. Still, the whole patrol party felt iced to the bone and ready to relax in the hot waters of Camelot's bathhouse. The two, as well as the rest of the patrol, were subjected to many an open stare and wondering glance until finally Olran could stand it no longer. During the appetizers before supper that night, he walked over to the Lady Cornelia and asked why she was staring at him. She blushed and hurriedly excused herself without answering, Aaronn noted as he saw Morgause smile in triumph. He knew very well, from experience, that the Orkney queen was up to something rotten.

"Easy brother," he tried to comfort his ally, who was now fuming with suppressed rage. "I shall get to the bottom of this."

"If 'tis what I think it might be, then 'tis the last time 'twill be brought up, or I leave Camelot and Britain forever!" Olran growled. Aaronn patted him reassuringly as they strolled over to Lady Morgause and King Lot.

"King Lot, good evening, have ye tried this eggplant dish Sir Cai just put out on the sideboard? 'Tis delicious, especially with the bread," he tempted Lot, grinning as the Orkney King quickly headed off towards the sideboard.

"Good evening, Lady Morgause. Suppose ye share yer secret joke with me?" he chatted in a pleasant tone.

"What joke?" Morgause tried to play innocent.

"I saw the smile on yer face when Sir Olran asked the Lady Cornelia why she was staring, I know ye have the answer to the puzzle I find myself in," he went on, still pleasant.

"She has learned the truth about ye and yer archer friend," Morgause snapped and made to leave. Aaronn caught her by the arm and pulled her off to a quiet corner nearby.

"What truth are ye talking about, woman?" he asked, his voice hushed and dangerous, although Morgause did not detect it.

"That Sir Olran of Westerland is yer catamite!" she shouted so that the entire hall could hear. Lancelot turned and ran for the King at once, as gasps went around the room. Olran's face tightened with pain and bitterness as he turned to find Lot's face among the crowd.

"King Lot of Orkney!" he called out, his voice cold and dry. "Yer wife has a vicious and lying tongue! If she were a man, I would kill her on the spot for what she just said. My name and reputation is all I have, they have now both been sullied and I claim the right to clear them of both this outrageous stain!" he went on, striding over to Lot and pulling a single gauntlet from his belt. "She is yer woman, ye will have to answer for it!" he said, once he was in front of the man. The gage hit Lot's face hard, nearly knocking the big man to his knees. "Right now, in the practice arena! I shall not rest 'till I have quelled this rumor once and for all!" he finished and strode away, headed for the arena. Aaronn went after him, with the intent of calming him, but when he saw his ally's face, he saw it was cold and dispassionate.

"Do not kill him, brother, Arthur needs him alive!"

"I have no intent of killing him, but he will be on his knees begging my mercy in the end," Olran answered through tight lips.

Meanwhile, Lot glared at Morgause, who now watched fearfully as he prepared for the honor bout. If Olran killed him now, all her plans would be for naught, she realized and went after the renegade prince.

"Sir Olran, ye cannot call King Lot to task for my harsh and foolish words. I only spoke to anger Sir Aaronn, whom everyone knows hates me. Ye are a young man, fit and strong, my Lord Lot is a man in his fifties," she persuaded in a syrupy-sweet voice before Agravaine interrupted.

"Aye, me Da is old, but I am nae, if ye wan' a fight, ye coom t' me!"

"Someone from Orkney is going to answer for this insult! If ye wish it to be ye, Agravaine, then come on! Ye, lying bitch, do not speak to me ever again unless ye have an apology on yer hateful tongue!" he finished tightly while facing Morgause, then resumed his march to the practice arena.

The great room buzzed with renewed conversation as Arthur and Gwenhyfar came downstairs, Lancelot beside them. Arthur walked quickly after the renegade prince, intending to put a stop to the bout. He did not catch up to them, however, until the bout had already started. Once begun, the thing could not be stopped until resolution was won. When he arrived breathless at the arena, the sounds of clashing steel could be plainly heard. Aaronn halted him at the entrance of the covered arena, shaking his head to indicate that this was something that he should allow to come to an end on its own. Arthur watched as Olran put a quick and honorable end to the matter, not even giving Agravaine so much as a cut in the process, but making him kneel awkwardly in the dust and admit defeat to the assembly.

"I admit me Mother, th' Lady Morgause has lied! Sir Olran be nae catamite, I will avow t' it fer I've been oot on patrol wi' him an' now he's defeated me in honorable combat. Any who say so will answer t' my blade before his, frum this day on!" Agravaine called out, then Olran held out a helping hand and pulled him to his feet. King Lot pushed Morgause into the circle and Olran put his sword to her milk-white throat, sorely tempted to push hard and put an end to her, once and for all.

"I would be well within my rights according to the ancient laws to slay ye, Morgause of Orkney, here and now. I have never spread lies and rumors about ye nor have I ever offered ye any other offense. Ye have forever slurred my reputation Madam and that demands a further, personal apology from ye, right here on the honor sands!" he demanded, leaning against the sword a bit. She gulped at the pressure and hastily complied.

"I say, here and now, in front of all ye witnesses. I was wrong to spread this vicious and vile rumor concerning Sir Olran and Sir Aaronn. I did it for my own amusement, I admit, and I apologize humbly," she said, kneeling before him, still at sword's point.

Olran trembled a bit, wanting to thrust the blade home through her black heart, but wisdom prevailed and he swallowed his anger down hard, withdrawing the weapon and replacing it in his back scabbard.

"Thank ye, Queen Morgause," he said, sneering over the title. "And I wish the rest of ye noble ladies and lords a pleasant good night!" he finished sarcastically and stalked from the arena. Aaronn went after him, but could not catch him till they were back at their room, where Olran was packing.

"Where do ye think ye are going?" he asked.

"Back to Druid Isle Aaronn, at least there, no one questions my masculinity!" Olran answered in a voice full of pain and anger.

"What of Arthur and of yer service with me to Ceridwen?"

"Arthur does not need me. I can serve Ceridwen from Dragon Isle. I am weary of hearing that old saw just because I am picky about whom I take to my bed."

"I daresay ye have made that clear enough, my brother," Aaronn said dryly. "No one will ever bring it up again."

"Perhaps not to my face, but 'twill forever be behind my back now."

"What about that pretty blonde at Dalren's tavern? Isn't she one of Vondra's handpicked ladies?" Aaronn pointed out. "She pursues ye and she does not have to sleep with anyone she does not want to. Certainly, that should mean something; after all, not everyone believes Morgause's trash." Olran stopped packing and sat down heavily, and Aaronn pressed on. "I need ye to stay, brother. The work ye do assists Arthur to stay on the throne. Who else could bedevil Westerland the way ye have? Who else do ye know that can drop a traitor at a hundred paces? Stay, my friend, lest they all say the rumor is true," he pleaded. "Ye are my only friend."

The gray-eyed man sat silent for a few moments, then sighed. "Then help me unpack. I am not staying because of Arthur or the Kingdom or any of them. I am only staying because the Black Knight, my friend and ally is asking me to," Olran said firmly and began taking his folded clothing from the bag. As they finished the task, a knock came on the door. Aaronn opened to find Arthur standing there, grief on his face.

"By the Goddess, Olran, I am sorry for that!" he said as soon as Aaronn let him in the room. "My Queen has told me she had heard the vile rumor, but she did nothing to stop it. I have pointed out to her the mistake she made by allowing Morgause to spread such a vicious story, Gwen wishes to make amends and apologize, personally. Would ye come to our suite in the morning for caffe and pastries?"

"Of course, Sire," Olran responded stiffly.

"About the eighth hour will be fine," Arthur told him. "Are ye all right?" he asked gently.

"Aye, Sire," Olran replied.

"I cannot tell ye, boyo, how I grieved I am at this incident. No one knows better than we of the Inner Circle how ye have suffered under yer family. We have no doubts of any kind about ye, ye have nothing to prove to us!" he stated, genuinely sorrowed at Olran's evident pain.

"I thank ye for that, Sire, but actions speak louder than words," Olran grinned wanly and took the King's proffered hand.

"See ye tomorrow, Sir Olran," Arthur answered warmly and took his leave, glad that Olran was not leaving because of the incident. He needed every man he had to hold Britain, especially one with Olran's special skills. He had also recently put two and two together and now suspected that Olran was the Black Knight's ally. No wonder then, he laughed to himself, that the mysterious man could be in several places at once. I'll have to invite him into my confidence, he resolved as he returned to his quarters to finish his talk with Gwenhyfar. In the morning, at the appointed hour Olran appeared at the King's door to accept Gwenhyfar's apology. By the time he had departed, the Queen was convinced beyond a shadow of a doubt that Olran was no catamite; she began at once to spread that conclusion among her ladies. The other Knights severely reprimanded their ladies as well, each man telling his wife that from now on, there were to be no half-truths or lies spread among them. Still, many of them harbored the opinion of Morgause, but they kept it amongst themselves in private, maintaining the rumor.

During that winter, Aaronn and Olran were obliged by the heavy snows to limit their nighttime excursions to the easily traveled ways. To go beyond those roads was to cause one's steed to have to plow through chest-high drifts of snow, leaving a clear trail behind. Still, the activities of the Black Knight brought him occasionally to Darkensdale and Llew's kitchen. The reports that came from the seneschal were invaluable, and the staunch and quiet support that the aged campaigner showed for Arthur was evident. Llew wrote down everything he saw and heard and his observations proved so thorough that he now held the almost complete trust of Ceridwen's men.

Sir Cai was recruited into the pigeon training program, the Black Knight began receiving reports regularly with the breakfast tray Camelot's seneschal began sending regularly to his room. It amused Aaronn greatly that nothing was ever said between them about it, that Cai accepted the matter as a fact of life. Many a late night or early morning mission ended with an exhausted Black Knight or Black Hunter entering the castle through the scullery door to find Sir Cai awaiting them with hot food and a relaxing drink. Private bathing became somewhat of a regular thing as well, especially when Aaronn plied the Queen's ladies for information. Aaronn found that many among the group of young women were accomplished masseurs; the relaxation he found under their ministrations was a comfort indeed. Besides, massage was hard labor, often obliging the lady to remove her heavy gown and petticoats down to the thin, laced-front shift. The sight of so much revealed beauty was a comfort to the Black Knight's eyes, balancing the harsh evil he saw everywhere around him.

King Warren came to Camelot at the height of the winter, blowing in with a blizzard storm to complain about the last year's many strange happenings around Westerland. The last disaster to hit the Keep before winter had struck during the Autumn Equinox feast. A pipe in the cellar walls under the Keep had burst without warning, flooding the entire cold room with water halfway up the walls. All of the Keep's aging cheese, the product of the entire summer's labor, had gone moldy and was unfit for eating as a result, as well, most of the smoked meats and barrels of salted fish had been spoilt, he moaned to Arthur.

"I paid that black-robed priest plenty of good silver to rid me of whatever evil spirit is causing all this bad luck, too!" he went on.

Arthur nodded sympathetically, keeping his reply non-committal. "I am sorry to hear that, Warren, and what a shame yer taxes are in arrears two seasons. The Crown has no extra funds to assist yer house in their hour of need. Perhaps the other Lords will extend ye credit 'till spring."

Warren glared at him, hating the Pendragon because he was right. He sighed after he had fully stuffed himself of Cai's excellent foods, after all the stored foods had gone rotten, the cuisine around his home had been rather bland of late. After Warren had gone home empty-handed, Arthur sent Olran a note, asking that he report to the royal suites before supper. Olran was surprised, but dressed carefully and appeared promptly as ordered.

"Yer King thanks ye for coming, Sir," Arthur greeted, handing him a cup of good red wine from Ban's vineyards. "Or should I be greeting ye as the Black Knight?" he smiled. Olran managed to keep his composure in place as he accepted the cup silently, but his mind worked furiously to come up with a proper response.

"I think ye have the wrong man, Sire. My poor skills can hardly compare to the Black Knight's," he replied vaguely.

"Ah, but I think they do, Olran boyo," Arthur chuckled, waving him into a chair. "I have been receiving a number of complaints about the Black Knight's accuracy in archery, especially from Westerland. It took each of them three months to heal from that first little encounter, ye know," he said and sat in the chair opposite Olran.

Olran blushed and was caught; he knew it and saluted the King's astute cleverness. "My foot is the one in the snare now, I suppose, My Lord," Olran chuckled, then sobered. "Ye should refer to me as the Black Hunter, however. No one can know I even exist, lest the Black Knight's mission be compromised. Am I under arrest?"

"Of course not, I only want ye to report to me what yer up to occasionally," Arthur harrumphed. "Please, do not let on to the Black Knight that I know 'till he asks. I want to see how long it takes before he figures out that I know about ye," the King laughed merrily.

"I will not lie to him, Sire. The resulting distrust is not worth yer amusement," Olran replied seriously.

"I do not want ye to lie, just to wait 'till he asks," Arthur explained. "Now, tell me everything ye are planning next to disrupt the alliance between Westerland and Darkensdale. I can hardly wait to hear about it!" Arthur grinned and sat back expectantly.

Olran gave him a quick briefing about his next plan, having already discussed it thoroughly with the Black Knight, of course. The amusement that Arthur garnered from the telling was surely worth the time it took.

"I am looking forward to the letter this stunt will surely generate," he chuckled as he escorted Olran to the door. The amused expectancy got him through the next few weeks until the weather warmed enough to allow the spring rains to begin thawing the ground.

The Black Hunter and the Black Knight left the castle by different roads a few weeks after the Spring Equinox, one headed for Darkensdale, one for Westerland Keep. Through Sir Llew, they had learned that Merin was shipping dry goods to Westerland secretly in exchange for young, comely girls to be servers at his monthly feasts, which were more orgies than feasts. When the Black Knight reached his destination, he found the preparations for just such a feast already in progress. When Llew left the scullery door open, he crept into the dungeons below the main floor. He found two dozen frightened young women there; they were all dressed scantily and had their faces plastered with cheap cosmetics.

"Shhh," he warned. "Where are ye all from?" he whispered.

"Our families are bound to Westerland Keep, Sir Knight. Will they be all right?" the shortest girl asked fearfully.

"They will be!" the Black Knight answered shortly. "No one but the Goddess knows I am here. Come now, out of that cell and follow close behind. Do not stop for anything, no matter what. Understand?" he cautioned and deftly picked the lock with a knife blade.

The girls filed out, then lined up in twos, clasping hands as they did so. The Black Knight led them up the stairs and through the busy kitchen without seeming to attract any attention. Everyone saw, but ignored them, knowing full well what reprisals such actions would bring from Lord Merin when he found out. Willingly the staff shouldered that burden to save these girls a lifetime of shame and humiliation. The Black Knight led them out the scullery door, loading them into a wagon just pulling into the delivery area. The driver's outline looked remarkably like Dalren; soon the wagon was loaded and away. The Black Knight watched until he could no longer see them, then re-entered Darkensdale and found his way up to the evil Lord's bedchambers. He heard moans and grunts coming from the slightly ajar door, carefully he peeked around knowing full well what he would find. There was Morgause and Merin atop her, thrusting for all he was worth. The Black Knight's sense of humor was roused; it was just too perfect a set of circumstances. Drawing one of his tokens, perfectly deadly weapons in their own right despite their diminutive size, he took aim and threw it at the most vulnerable spot. Merin cried out in pain and rolled off Morgause to pull the wickedly sharp blade out of his posterior.

"Come back to me, Evin," Morgause moaned. "Ye have not finished."

"I have for now, Morgause," Merin answered, and dabbing a cloth at the small wound that bled profusely, while looking sadly down at his now flaccid member.

"I can fix that," the Orkney queen purred seductively, rising on her knees in front of him. Merin halted her, looking down at the diminutive dagger in his hand. He gasped when he recognized the token; he hurled it away from him in fear and loathing.

"Where are ye!" he shouted in panic. "Guards, guards where are ye?"

The Black Knight ran to the stairway, ducking quickly into the doorway to the dungeons. Merin's half-drunken men rushed right past him, unnoticing in their frenzy to rescue their Lord. With an unseen wave to Llew, the Black Knight disappeared out the scullery door and ran the entire distance to Eclipse's hiding place. Jumping aboard, he spurred the steed into a full gallop to catch up with Dalren's wagonload. The man had stopped at a hostel with a bath and the Black Knight could hear the giggles and splashes of the girls as they scrubbed the cosmetics and perfumes off each other. Dalren had also come supplied by Avalon with many frocks of different sizes, as well as the rest of the clothing necessary to clothe the girls properly. He had gone first into the bathing room and deposited the clothing neatly on the surrounding benches, when the girls saw the new frocks they literally squealed with delight. Passing the garments from hand to hand, they assisted each other in donning the clothing, exclaiming all the while over how pretty and nice the new dresses were.

"We thank ye, Sir Black Knight and yer assistant," the shortest girl, who seemed to have been chosen as the group's spokesperson. "Could we go home now?"

"Ye should sleep first, girls," Ceridwen's man advised. "In the morning, after a proper sleep and breakfast, I will send ye home."

Meanwhile, the Black Hunter had arrived at Westerland Keep, where Warren and his family were now taking stock of their latest shipment of staple goods, bought from Darkensdale. Merin's mark was on every package, barrel and sack, the Black Hunter cursed as he counted and made a quick written inventory in his own peculiar coded script. After assuring that all was counted, he slit open every sack and pried off the lids of every barrel. The rats that infested Westerland Keep would do the rest, he thought grimly, as he hammered a hole through the heavy rodent-proof wall to insure that they would.

"Who's down there?" he heard a familiar, slurred voice he recognized all too well. It was Kevin, Warren's eldest and cruelest son, prowling around the cellar in search of drink no doubt, the ebon-clad archer concluded from personal experience. He drew an arrow, checked the fletching to ensure it was secure and loaded his bow.

"Da, are ye down here, or 'tis Marcus?" Kevin called out hesitantly.

"Nay Kev, 'tis me," Ceridwen's Hunter called back

"Olran, ye little bugger, what are ye doin' back here?" Kevin laughed derisively, recognizing the voice. "I thought we'd finally gotten rid of ye years ago. Ye don't learn very well, do ye, no matter how hard yer beaten? Very well, if ye've come back for more, come out of hidin'!" he answered threateningly and stepped forward, holding the lamp in front of him.

"I learn, very fast, Kev. Would ye like to see some of what I know now?" the Black Hunter whispered loudly and unstrung his bow, putting the arrow carefully back into the quiver. He removed his mask and stepped from the shadows to face Kevin. The bully started in surprise as Olran materialized in front of him. Olran took two quick swings at his brother's face, connecting both times and opening a cut over Kevin's right eye.

"Ow!" Kevin said, wiping the dripping blood away from his eye. "Ye've put on some muscle finally, haven't ye faggot?" he observed and kicked out savagely. Olran caught his leg by the knee and ankle, twisting the opposite way, hard. He heard some very satisfactory crunching, tearing noises, then Kevin screamed in real pain and dropped to the floor, writhing.

"That must feel good, eh Kev?" Olran asked pleasantly. "I bet this will feel even better. What was that?" he went on and punched him hard in the face, breaking his nose.

"Don't hurt me anymore!" Kevin screamed and lashed out blindly, knocking over the lamp and setting a nearby open sack of flour ablaze. Olran stepped back, put his mask back on and reached for his bow and arrow, knowing well there was no possibility of carrying the obese man from the flames. As Kevin screamed and begged for mercy, the Black Hunter drew his bow and sighted carefully.

"May the Goddess grant ye the mercy ye never showed anyone else," he whispered and released the arrow. The missile took Kevin through his open and screaming mouth, silencing him suddenly, then the flames leapt up and the Black Hunter fled the smoke-filled cellar. Once out of Westerland territory, he turned the Jughead towards Avalon's shore. The chance meeting with his cruel older brother had released a tide of confusing emotions; he needed to discuss the incident with the Lady of Avalon. She awaited him in the cold misty morning and held him as he sobbed like a child in her lap.

"I think I have taken personal revenge on Kevin of Westerland, My Lady!" he was finally able to say. "I wish I could say for certain what happened was the Goddess' Hand, but I cannot."

"Tell me all, Olran," she urged as she fixed him a cup of soothing tea. Olran drank slowly, relating everything as Vivaine listened intently.

"I only wanted him to be silent 'till I could escape. Then we were fighting, and I broke his knee and ankle as well as his nose. He struck back, striking the lamp and setting an open flour sack ablaze. He was so fat, I knew I could not carry him out," he went on, finally calming.

"Ye did not leave him to burn to death?" Vivaine asked.

"Of course not, Mother. I gave him a mercy arrow."

"Then 'twas not just revenge that motivated ye, ye remained the Black Hunter 'till the end, despite the fact that Kevin knew ye. I must tell ye, Olran, that Westerland's eldest son was diseased, beyond yer knowledge of the situation. Two years past, Justine came here with him, begging to know what ailed him. We found a lump in his innards, told him he only had a short time left on the earth and they left. He would have died a long and wasting death, the mercy arrow was too good a fate for someone as cruel as he, in my way of thinking, but the Goddess apparently thought otherwise. Now, he stands before Her to account for his evil. Ye may not have intended it, but ye were the Goddess' Hand in this matter. Feel no guilt Black Hunter lest ye fall prey to the disease guilt will spawn in yer heart. If ye succumb to this, ye will no longer be of any help to the Black Knight," Vivaine counseled. "'Twas Her Judgment after all, let it stand."

"I shall, but I do repent me of enjoying any of it," Olran confided sadly. "May Ceridwen assist me, and let Her help me to be stronger against such temptations in the future."

"Brother Drusus wants to see ye, my boy. He knew ye would come today and insisted we prop him up in bed. He looks very old these days, I think the Hunter will call for him soon. Go to him, Olran, before his strength leaves him as it always does," Vivaine told him gently. "Today, he seems to remember everything, very clearly. Many days have passed since he was so lucid."

Olran's eyes misted over again and he wiped his eyes free of the tears that remained. He splashed his face clean of the salt stains with the cool water in Vivaine's pitcher, when he was finished he looked like the cool and collected man he always appeared to be. One would never have guessed, Vivaine noted as she took him to Drusus' room that he was crying like a babe a scarce hour before.

She opened the dying Druid's door quietly, but Drusus was sitting up in the sun and heard. "Is he here, Lady?" he asked.

"Just as ye said he would be, Drusus," Vivaine answered gently.

"Aye Master, 'tis I," Olran told him as he sat by the man's bed.

Vivaine left the two alone; she did not see Olran again until the evening of the next day. He came to her quarters, was admitted and told her his tidings.

"He has gone to his rest in the Blessed Isles, Lady. He asked if ye Ladies would do the rites for him after he went, instructing me to light the pyre personally," Olran told her coolly. His grieving was already done, Vivaine could see, his youthful and hot blood cleansed of the great darkness that had always hung over him.

"So, he told ye, did he?" Vivaine asked, knowing what Olran's answer would be.

"Aye," Olran answered. "Imagine my relief at finally knowing that Justine was not my mother. But why wait 'till now to tell me?" he asked, pouring himself a cup of wine after looking to Vivaine for permission. "Drusus was gone before I thought to ask."

"Justine delivered a child, a stillborn. She knew Warren would blame her, and drive her out of Westerland for it, he being a Christian. One of the midwife's assistants went into labor just as her babe died and Justine arranged to substitute that child for the stillborn. I have always suspected that the assistant was pregnant by Warren, but the Goddess would never confirm my suspicions. So ye see, Olran, 'twas the Goddess who put ye into that household. I think 'twas to learn the difference between being truly noble and playing the game of it, as so many of them do," she explained. "What is Warren?" she asked suddenly.

"A traitor to Arthur and the Goddess, pure and simple," Olran pronounced and grinned wanly.

"And what are ye?"

"The companion of the Black Knight, Ceridwen's avenger," he answered quickly and confidently.

"Let it never trouble ye again, yer relationship with Westerland," Vivaine told him with a slight smile. "Now, let us send our beloved friend properly on his way," she said, taking his hand and leading him outside. Drusus' body had been washed and clothed in his best robe, his own quiver of arrows and bow beside him. Vivaine took a torch and made a gesture, the pitched end of the torch kindled suddenly, casting a warm light over the scene. She held out the torch to Olran, who took a special pitch-tipped arrow and set it into his bow, then set the end alight in the torch. Taking careful aim, he launched the fiery missile into the extremely dry wood. It burst into flame and roared up quickly, consuming Drusus' body with no smoke or odor. Olran slept awhile after eating his fill at the death feast, then rose and took his leave just as morning paled the sky. He arrived at the meeting place he and his ally had arranged, easily finding the convenient hostel between Darkensdale and Westerland.

"What happened, are ye all right?" asked Ceridwen's man.

"Aye, I am fine. I have news 'twill shock ye, though," the Black Hunter grinned under his hood. "Not here, not now, we should get these girls home where they belong."

The two did just that, with Dalren driving the wagon and the Black Hunter watching from afar to ensure their safety, delivering the girls home to ecstatic parents. To each home was also given a bag of gold to help with expenses, from each man of the house came a promise to write the King and tell him what had happened. Ceridwen's men parted with Dalren just a mile from the latter's farm, then they returned to Camelot under cover of darkness. The two bathed, took supper in their private quarters and Olran gave Aaronn the latest news.

"So, yer a bastard too," Aaronn laughed merrily. "No wonder we are good friends."

"We are two very lucky bastards, aye?"

"Very lucky, brother," Aaronn replied warmly.

The two chuckled all through the rest of the meal, sharing food and wine like the equals they had always thought themselves to be. Sir Olran was a much happier fellow after that and no one could rile him about Westerland anymore.

Chapter 9

Beltane was celebrated among masses of meadow flowers that year and soon the crops planted by the farmers showed the same abundant fertility. Those who planted green peas were rewarded for their efforts by many pickings of pods, each stuffed full of the bright green orbs. Cai's staff was out in the garden every day, picking huge bowls and buckets of the early vegetables. All enjoyed the abundance of Ceridwen and in one way or another, blessed Her name.

Gawaine's third son was born that year, squalling and crying heartily, Rhian recovered as quickly as usual from the easy labor. Most of the other Knights of the Inner Circle had at least one child at their feet by now. Camelot came to resemble somewhat of a nursery until Cai had no choice but to open the last unused wing in the Castle to accommodate the many Knights needing family quarters.

With the Spring also came the annual migration of aspirants to Camelot's Round Table. The number of contestants at the Summer Tourney caused the usually three-day event to be expanded to five. Tents and open canvas pavilions decorated the wide meadow below the Castle, looking for all the world like a collection of oddly colored mushrooms, or so Gwenhyfar thought as she looked out her window. It all went so smoothly that the suspicious Aaronn suspected something would go wrong, but no incidents marred the general enjoyment of the Tourney, as well as the accompanying Barter Faire. The Guilds of Britain planned the huge outdoor craft and art show well, so that all the Guilds found the chance for equal representation. Those who watched the mock bouts and other games also took the time to walk through the Faire; many a Guildsman was invited by a noble family to set up their shop at their personal holdings, making sure vital services were available to all.

When the whole affair was complete, Arthur and the Inner Circle, along with the Queen and the other married ladies, partook of the peace and quiet offered by the hunting lodge. Sir Aaronn and Sir Olran were also invited, with all the single serving maids about neither one of them suffered for lack of female companionship. Aaronn's intimate relationship with Vondra had ended by mutual consent, so he was again the hunter. It was not easy to find a woman who pleased him as well as Vondra, but the young woman named Isolde shared his bed almost exclusively. She began to exhibit typically jealous behavior, flying into huge rages if he so much looked at another female; he ended that relationship as soon as the vacation ended. She was quite upset and unbelieving at being rejected and tried every trick and wile she knew to regain her place in his bed, but Aaronn remained adamant.

"Isolde, please try and understand," Aaronn said gently two weeks after returning to Camelot. "We both needed someone, what we have between us has been a very pleasant sharing of balance. Now, 'tis over, ye know I never loved ye, Isolde, nor ye me," he reasoned.

She sniffled prettily, then dried her eyes and smiled wanly. "Well, if ye ever need again, Sir Aaronn, ye know where to find me," the lovely Irish lass told him honestly, kissed him lingeringly on the mouth and ran off laughing.

"I am glad she took that well," Olran quipped from behind him. "Ye must have really made an impression on her, my brother."

"Come on, we need some practice," Aaronn replied, grinning. They went to the arena at Camelot, working together with the sword for a long while. Afterwards, Aaronn ran off to his secret practice area and Olran to his, as was their custom.

Aaronn enjoyed his workout very much, breathing deeply as he stood among the targets when he was finished for the day. He ran all the way back to Camelot, meeting up with Olran in the baths, which were still empty. When the other Knights came in, the two greeted them and talked among themselves as men will. The married Knights began trading stories of their broods of growing children, and the old longing in Aaronn suddenly awoke. The scenes described by his brothers sounded idyllic, the loving way all their wives treated them in public made Aaronn wish to abandon the bachelor life to settle down with a beautiful woman who could make him happy. Olran saw his friend's face, recognized the old hunger in Aaronn's eyes and inwardly sighed, wondering what tavern he would have to fish Aaronn from this time.

At supper that night, Aaronn's eyes lit on an unfamiliar strawberry blonde sitting next to Sir Tristan.

"Who is that?" he asked immediately.

"Never seen her before," Olran replied vaguely.

"Do not wait up for me," Aaronn told his friend as he continued to watch the very shapely girl. When supper was over, Aaronn waited 'till after the first set of music to wander casually over and introduce himself to her.

"Sir Tristan, who is yer charming companion," he asked.

"Sir Aaronn, meet my only cousin, Gabriella. She has come to join the Queen's ladies," Tristan introduced warily. "Gabriella, meet Sir Aaronn, who is known among us as, 'the Knightly Knife'."

"Good evening, Sir Aaronn. I am very pleased to meet ye, at last. Cousin Tristan has always praised yer work highly, I should like to see ye throw the knives, sometime," the young lady's cultured voice sang in Aaronn's lonely ears.

"When ye have the time, Lady Gabriella, I am at yer disposal," he answered smoothly.

"If 'tis so, then partner me for the first tune of the next set?" Gabriella boldly suggested. Tristan frowned and the girl laughed and pushed him aside. "Now, ye need not make that face at me, Tristan! Are I not already eighteen and an old maid in my father's villa?"

"That I can hardly believe, Lady Gabriella," Aaronn chuckled and smoothly removed her hand from Tristan's arm, replacing it on his own. Together, the two walked out onto the floor just as the music began again, leaving Tristan in their wake. He watched them all night long, but Aaronn was his usual gentlemanly self. After the last set, he delivered the lady back to her cousin.

"I thank ye, Lady, for a lovely evening. Would ye care to go riding tomorrow?" he asked.

Gabriella did not even spare Tristan a glance before she answered with enthusiasm. "Thank ye, Sir Aaronn, 'twould be very nice. Is Mount Badon too far away for a visit? I should like to see it."

"'Twould be my honor, Lady, if brother Tristan would give permission," Aaronn replied tactfully. Tristan relaxed, having wanted to interfere to protect his cousin's reputation from the gossipmongers.

"Please, Tristan?" Gabriella pled. "'Twould be pleasant to ride through the summer flowers in the meadows. Certainly, Sir Aaronn's presence would be enough for safety's sake?" she added persuasively.

Tristan sighed heavily as he threw up his hands in defeat. "Very well, have yer ride. But stay close to Sir Aaronn," he warned. "Badon is still a dangerous place, being so close to the border."

"I shall protect her with my very life, Sir Tristan. When may I call for the Lady?" he asked, first bowing a bit to his brother Knight and taking Gabriella's hand in his, he pressed his lips warmly against the back of her hand.

"After breakfast?" she proposed, looking to Tristan. He nodded and smiled gently. "Perhaps we should take a lunch with us?" she proposed shyly.

"I shall speak to Sir Cai, Lady," Aaronn told her. "Good night and sleep well, Lady Gabriella. Goddess give ye good dreams, Sir Tristan."

"Good night, Sir Aaronn," Gabriella answered, going with Tristan back to her chambers.

Aaronn returned to his rooms, after first asking Cai about the lunch basket. He stripped and fell into bed, already anticipating spending the entire day in the fair company of Tristan's delightful cousin.

The next day dawned bright and clear, after breakfast and a light workout, Aaronn changed his clothes and called for Lady Gabriella. She appeared at the door costumed in a riding habit with an unusual split skirt. Aaronn was pleased that she was trained to ride properly instead of the ridiculous and impractical side mounted position favored by the Queen and the rest of her ladies.

"Are ye ready to ride?" he asked, smiling warmly at her. "All we need do is collect our lunch basket from the kitchen and dress our horses."

"Let us go then! I have not been riding for a long time and I am itching to get astride one of Camelot's famous wonder horses!" Gabriella replied impatiently.

"Well, just do not stand there then," Aaronn answered and extended his hand. She took it, clasping it firmly as they walked down the hall to Camelot's kitchen. Thanking Sir Cai for preparing the huge basket, they went on to the stables. Aaronn had Eclipse brought out and dressed, while Sir Ulster brought out a prancing red roan filly for Gabriella.

"She's well-trained, I assure ye Lady," he told Gabriella. "But like most young girls, she can get a bit flighty at times. Just be firm with her, she'll give ye no trouble."

"Thank ye, Sir Ulster," Gabriella smiled, taking the reins.

Aaronn tied the basket on Eclipse before they took the horses outside and mounted up. Gabriella was a seasoned rider, Aaronn noted satisfactorily, so they set out overland, not noticing the black-clad rider trailing them long distance aboard a blue-black horse. The ride to Badon was taken at a leisurely pace; they arrived at the overgrown battlefield sometime in the early afternoon. Aaronn described the final day for her as they climbed the small hill and tethered their steeds amongst the tall grasses. Gabriella saw the marker stone and read the words inscribed on its already weathered face.

"Is the King truly a Druid?" she asked as Aaronn shook out the blanket and spread it on the grass.

"Nay, Lady, though he was trained by them to be a proper King," Aaronn answered, uncorking the wineskin and pouring two cups. Gabriella took hers and together they saluted all the brave dead, Brit and Saxon.

"Ye can see the border guardhouse from here," she observed. "'Tis a bit frightening, to be so close to Saxon lands," she shuddered noticeably and Aaronn obligingly put his arm around her. He was quite surprised when she pulled his lips down on hers and kissed him, deeply and boldly. He could not help but answer the kiss as it was given, finally Gabriella pushed away, panting more than a bit.

"Be very careful, Gabriella. I am not one of those men who drool over a virgin. In my opinion, a female is not a woman 'till her virginity is gone and she gains some experience," he warned her. "I revere the Christ deeply and believe that He is the Son of God, but I am pledged to Ceridwen."

"Are ye a Druid then?" she asked wonderingly, wanting very much to kiss him again.

"Nay, but I was educated on Avalon as well as on Dragon Isle. What I consider perfectly acceptable behavior would be quite scandalous to the Christians," he told her honestly. "Come, let us eat the fine meal Sir Cai has packed for us and discuss this," he invited, opening the basket. He wanted her, very much now, but Aaronn was too much a gentleman to take something Gabriella might be offering on an impulse. He wanted such things only if they were freely and informatively given. As the two ate the simple meal of wine, bread, pickled vegetables, sliced meat and cheese, they spoke of what had happened and the loneliness that had inspired it.

"They keep me confined to my father's villa like a prize heifer locked in the breeding pen 'till just the right bull is found," Gabriella sighed. "Tristan is under strict orders to not allow me out of his sight, I know. I wouldn't be surprised at all if he is out there somewhere close right now, spying on me."

"I think Sir Tristan knows me well enough by now to trust me, Lady," Aaronn replied reassuringly, but could not help glancing around a bit, just to be sure.

"I am trapped," she went on, sighing heavily. "Soon, my father will marry me off to some rich old man who could not father a pea. I wish things were different for women," she cried just a bit, then wiped her eyes. "I do apologize for kissing ye that way. I suppose I was trying to make ye want me enough to take my virginity, so I may marry who I want, for love," she confessed, reddening a bit with embarrassment.

"Ye need not lose yer virginity for that!" Aaronn chuckled. "Enlist the Queen's aid, or the Knight's ladies, the more the better. I am certain they would all help."

"They would, truly?"

"Of course, they are all women, ye know," Aaronn replied, refilling their cups again. "To marrying for love," he toasted and they tapped their glasses before drinking deeply. "Of course, if ye are truly weary of being a virgin, we could remedy that," he suggested slyly and winking at her.

Gabriella laughed with delight. "Ye are a very nice man, Sir Aaronn of Camelot," she told him and kissed him on the cheek.

His face took on the hurt puppy dog look and he sighed comically: "Aye, 'tis the way of it, always the nice man, never the 'seducer of Camelot' role for me."

She enjoyed his sense of humor and they stayed there at Badon for a while longer, then they packed their lunch scraps away and folded up the blanket. Riding back to Camelot took a long, lazy time, which was a relief for the shadowy rider who still trailed them at a discreet distance. Sir Tristan awaited their arrival at the stables, a worried and anguished look on his face.

"Ye have been gone all day," he stated, sounding more than a bit annoyed. "I hope nothing is amiss?" he asked with double meaning.

"Cousin, ye should be ashamed to suggest such a thing!" Gabriella replied, shocked at his implication. "Sir Aaronn was the perfect gentleman all day. He treated me with the utmost respect, like a real Lady, which was a refreshing change, I might add."

"Sorry, Gaby and to ye as well, brother Aaronn," Tristan replied, apologetically. "My uncle instructed me to watch over her like she was my own sister on pain of a horsewhipping. I suppose I was being a bit too nosy."

"If I had a cousin as beautiful and witty as the Lady Gabriella, I would watch over her too!" Aaronn replied graciously. "Thank ye, Gabriella, for a lovely day," he said to the girl and kissed her hand warmly. Bowing to Tristan, he took his leave of them and took Eclipse to his stall. Courting this Lady was going to be a tricky business, he observed silently and wondered if it was worth the trouble. He went up to the room he shared with Olran then, opening the door, he caught his ally in the process of hurriedly changing his clothing.

"Ye followed me!" he accused, closing the door with a bang.

"Of course and I was not the only one, ye know. I saw Tristan leave right after ye, I wanted to make sure ye both would be all right. As ye know, our brother Tristan has a nasty temper and a big mouth," Olran reminded, grinning in the face of Aaronn's wrath. "I thought for certain he was going to run up and tear ye to bits when she kissed ye like that, but he watched and relaxed once ye pushed her away. He was breathing very hard, however," Olran chuckled outright.

"So, if I decide to court her, I can expect to find ye behind me again?" Aaronn asked stiffly.

"If I have to, aye," Olran replied cheerfully. "I have to know which tavern to get ye out of when her father says nay."

"How do ye know that will be the answer?" Aaronn asked, beginning to relax.

"I was raised a noble, remember? I know how snobby they are about marrying off their daughters," his ally answered. Aaronn turned and coolly assessed Olran, wondering if the thinner man were truly his match or not. "Do not even consider it, brother, unless ye want a full scale wrestling match on yer hands!" his ally laughed, with a warning in his tone. He knew well that Aaronn would eventually overpower him, but Aaronn recalled well how much that victory would cost in pain. "Why not change the subject? Ye should ask me about a recent and interesting conversation I had with the King, please?" Olran suggested.

"All right, I shall bite," Aaronn chuckled, unable to ever stay angered with Olran. "What did ye talk about with Arthur?"

"He has ordered the Black Hunter to report his activities directly to him before telling ye about it. He said to wait 'till ye asked about it, but I did not want to wait too long. Trust is everything between allies, eh?" Olran told him quickly.

"He is a clever man, the Pendragon," Aaronn chuckled, his respect for Arthur growing again at this display of logical deduction. "The Black Knight is going to have to find a way to repay his little joke, gently of course."

"Of course, are ye going to see Gabriella again?" Olran rejoined.

"Maybe, she is a very nice girl who needs a husband to love and have children with. I am not so sure I want that kind of relationship from a woman," Aaronn replied honestly. "She would be hurt and confused when I was gone for days on end and could not explain where I had been."

"All the noble girls are like that, Aaronn, 'tis what they have been taught from very early on to expect. If ye must marry, then do yer courting on Avalon, where they have been taught well," Olran advised.

Aaronn actually blushed and poured himself a shot of good whiskey, then one for Olran. They spoke no more of it, turning instead to their next mission to the Saxon lands. It seemed there were British nobles trading poached venison and stolen beef for the use of secret troops of Saxon warriors in the cause of overthrowing Arthur. The two planned a four-day trip into Saxon lands, using the excuse of hunting as a cover. Cerdic obviously needed reminding about the consequences of trifling with Britain's King and Goddess.

They packed carefully, storing packets of dried foods, their cooking utensils, extra whetstones and arrow fletching in the soft, flat saddlebags that tied on behind the high cantles. The next dark of the moon, the two crept from Camelot into the stables, then out into the night with their horses. Riding towards Badon, they made a quick stop to offer earnest prayers to Ceridwen for Her assistance in their cause before continuing on their way. Just as false dawn tinged the sky over the trees, they entered Cerdic's territory. Finding a secluded spot, the two pitched their tent between two large trees then Olran went hunting for breakfast. He came back quickly, carrying two fat hares, making short work of skinning them. He stretched the skins of a curing frame, being quite fond of warm rabbit skins to line his slippers. Cutting the carcasses in half to shorten their cooking time, Olran laid them on the open grill that cleverly folded flat for ease of storage. The meat cooked quickly to a moist tenderness due to the constant attention from Aaronn, the rich and tasty flesh was enjoyed down to the last crumb. The gnawed bones were disposed of by burying them deeply well away from the campsite. The two spread their thick bedrolls inside the tent, sleeping long and restfully all that day in preparation for their night's work.

Aaronn woke first, boiled water for caffe and had it ready when Olran emerged from his bedroll. He handed the sleepy man a steaming mugful with a wink that said, 'I beat ye this time, brother,' and Olran saluted him before taking a careful sip, knowing Aaronn's penchant for jokes. The beverage was sweetened just to his liking, he found as he sat down to inspect his weapons once more. Packing up the camp took just a moment or two, obscuring all signs of it took a bit longer, but when the two were satisfied with the area's restored condition, they went on their way.

The winter camp of the Coiled Serpent band was where their information said it would be. The two tethered their steeds in a copse of scrub oak and donned their face hoods. The Black Hunter took up a vantage point on a hillside closest to the small depression's center to cover the Black Knight's back, while Ceridwen's avenger stole into the raucous Saxon camp. He saw a group of wretched Brit girls, clad in tattered rags, tending the spits or serving mugs of ale and being thrown to the furs under burly Saxon men. His blood boiled as he reckoned the eldest girl's age to be no more than sixteen. He turned to where he knew the Black Hunter's bow awaited and made a signal only his ally's sharp and watching eyes would see before returning to his hiding place to watch the fun.

"Ffffft!" an arrow whizzed by close and a Saxon man screamed and dropped writhing into the dust, the toad poison on the arrowhead already killing him. Another arrow whistled by and caught a Saxon warchief in the chest, spinning him around with great force, knocking him and the man next to him into the cooking fire. Their screams of pain and terror added to the building panic, in the midst of it all the Black Knight saw a matronly and tough-looking woman herd the British girls into a tent. She then pulled her sword and set herself in front of it as a guard. The Black Hunter's arrows continued to scream into Saxon flesh, providing just the distraction the Black Knight needed, he walked quietly to where the armed woman stood, feet solidly planted like tree-trunks, her sword drawn.

"Move aside, woman!" the Black Knight ordered in perfect Saxon.

"Go back to hell where ye belong, demon!" she replied and swung the sword. The Black Knight wasted no time with her, he countered her sword and swung a fist, connecting square with her jaw. With a moan, she crumpled to the ground; the Black Knight stepped cautiously over her inert body. Poking his head through the tent flap, he called out in Brit: "Come girls, time to go home to yer families. The Goddess commands it! We must leave, now!"

He had to restrain them for a moment, so much in haste were they to depart from bondage among the Saxons. As the riot raged outside the girls, led by Ceridwen's man, quietly filed out of the camp. He led them out of the small valley, leaving the Black Hunter to cover their escape according to their plan. Putting the three youngest girls aboard his horse, the Black Knight walked with them the short time to the border and got them across unseen. Quickly finding their old camp in the hollow tree at Badon's base, the Black Knight pitched the tent, rolled out the bedrolls and bade the girls lay down for a nap.

The Black Hunter arrived hours behind them, bloody from neck to knees. His ally's eyebrows quirked up at the sight and the archer explained, quietly.

"They have packed up and left the camp. They also left their dead behind, unusual eh? I had to collect my property, but some of them were not quite ready to give it back. I had to 'persuade' some of them pretty hard," he laughed coldly as he went down to the pond to wash himself and the arrowheads clean of blood. When he was finished and re-attired, the two prepared a big meal for the thin and undernourished girls. The meal prepared, the Black Hunter took his leave before they awoke, leaving the Black Knight alone with them.

"Eat hearty, girls, we have a long way to go to Avalon. Ceridwen's people will help ye recover from yer ordeal and re-unite ye with yer families if ye should wish it."

"Aye, that we will, O Black Knight," came a sonorous voice at their backs.

The Black Knight whirled out of habit and cast a blade without thinking before he saw it was the Merlin with two Druid brothers beside him. In amazement, he saw the High Druid pluck the blade out of the air with a very quick motion.

"Lord Merlin!" Ceridwen's man laughed. "Congratulations on yer stealth, ye surprised me."

"Ye were trained to be on guard against those of evil intent, Sir Knight. Those of the Light can still surprise ye from time to time," he returned, laughing with great abandon as he returned the blade to its wielder. "Come, daughters of Britain, away to Avalon. Aye, I am truly the Merlin of Britain, these two Druid brothers have come with me to help protect ye on yer journey through the forest roads," he told the girls as they stared, wide-eyed at his harmless appearance. Most were from Christian households, raised to believe that the Druids ate children and that Avalon was a place of rampant sin. They followed nonetheless, instinctively trusting him despite what their parents had told them. The Black Knight trailed them for a few miles, assuring that the Saxons had not followed after and set up some ambush in the forest, then turned back.

"Well, two whole days to relax," Aaronn observed when he reached the camp and found Olran there awaiting him. "What will we do?" he asked as they began striking the camp and concealing the traces of the cooking fire.

"I do not know about ye, but I need a real bath and some good wine. The hunting lodge is not too far away, we should go there," Olran suggested, warily removing his hood.

"Ye have a good idea, my friend!" Aaronn agreed with enthusiasm.

They rode their horses gently over the meadows of soft green grasses, stopping once to reset saddles and bridles. When they arrived at the hunting lodge, they tended both horses completely, brushing their hides clean of dirt and sweat salt, cleaning their hooves of lodged dirt and stones, then taking them down to the lake's edge and turning them loose to swim. Eclipse and the Jughead eagerly waded in to their chests, swimming around snorting in pure enjoyment. Their riders dove in as well, swimming around until thoroughly refreshed and cooled. Horses and men waded out, the steeds shook violently, sending the excess water flying before both lay down and rolled in the tall grasses, nickering as they scratched themselves all over. Finally, they flopped over on their sides and napped in the generous afternoon heat.

Aaronn and Olran went up to the lodge, where they always kept spare clothing just in case they needed it and dressed in light trous and shirts, Aaronn retaining his knife harness and Olran swinging his skinning knife in its special sheathe onto his back. They went down to the kitchen and more importantly to the cold room under it. True to form, Sir Cai had stocked the storage area with ripening cheeses, wines and good stout Druid ale. They tapped a small cask of latter and drank a toast to Ceridwen, thanking her for the successful conclusion of their business in Saxon lands. They hauled it upstairs and outside to the stream, immersing it in the perpetually cold water to cool it more. Returning to the storage room, they filled baskets with dried beef, onions and other dried vegetables, fruits, and cheeses, taking it all up the stairs along with three skins of wine.

Aaronn immediately started the thick beef stew he prepared so well, adding the meat to water and adding garlic, salt and fresh herbs from the corner garden of the lodge. Covering the kettle, he then set it to simmer a while, before adding the dried vegetables. Olran picked fresh wild greens and washed them carefully, drained them and took them down to the cold room to crisp while everything else cooked. Deciding that fresh bread was in order, Olran put together a batch of biscuit dough from the flour, lard and leavening he found stored in airtight containers in the cabinets. After cutting a panful of biscuits to bake, he added sweetening to the remainder, using the extra dough to top a dried berry and apple cobbler.

"By the Goddess, it smells fine in here!" called a voice from the great room and Arthur suddenly appeared around the corner.

"Sire!" the both of them exclaimed. "What are ye doing out here, alone?" Aaronn added with immediate concern.

"I am not alone, Sir Aaronn," Arthur laughed merrily. "Lancelot, Bedwyr and Gawaine are with me, the rest of our brothers are on the way," he explained, enjoying the surprise on both men's faces. "But, what are ye two doing here?" he asked, accepting a cup of ale.

"We we've been hunting, My Lord," Aaronn explained.

"Aye, but what is in the pot?" Arthur asked with a smile, suspecting the two's quarry had been human.

"Dried beef stew, My Lord. It seems we could not catch anything else, other than the enemy," Aaronn replied ruefully. The three of them broke out laughing at the joke. The other senior knights entered to find their King in tears, with Aaronn and Olran breathless as well. After composing themselves, the King explained to his puzzled companions the joke about the two's hunting expedition. Sir Gawaine pulled out the bag containing his fishing gear after hearing their explanation.

"I kin git beef stew anytime," he chuckled. "But on th' way here, I got me mouth all set fer fried trout, an' I'm gonna ha' it wi' th' Lady's blessin'. Seeing as how brother Olran's here now, an' tha' he has a gift fer cookin' trout, now tha' hunger fer fresh fish ha' increased. I kin hardly wait t' catch me some o' those fat brown fellas in th' lake. Bring tha' cask along, boyos, an' put another in th' stream t' properly chill while we fish," he chuckled and went down the hill, pulling Arthur with him.

The sun was just setting and the trout could be seen jumping in the water, feeding on the insects settling on the surface of the lake. Gawaine's line tightened almost immediately and he pulled in a big, fighting trout after just a few minutes. Arthur pulled in one just as big and Gawaine landed a second fish very quickly. Aaronn stood with Lancelot on the shore, content to watch the others pull fish out of the water, lending a hand cleaning and scaling the fish. Olran provided drink support, keeping everyone's mug full and adding his assistance with the cleaning duties when Gawaine's angling skills began to overload the other Knights. When they had two huge pans full of cleaned fish, they went back up to the lodge kitchen. Olran rolled them in flour, egg and dried breadcrumbs, frying them to a deep, golden brown in hot melted butter. Lancelot tore the wild greens into bite-sized pieces as Arthur prepared a salad dressing of olive oil, a bit of ground mustard seed, wine vinegar and herbs. He then diced boiled eggs from their snack basket into the greens and tossing it all together, proclaiming it his one and only culinary skill. When the other Knights arrived, they found a meal all ready for them and gladly sat down to the platters of fried trout, bowls of stew, biscuits and salad, all served with skins of good wine. When Olran brought out the huge cobbler, it was passed around the table like the rest of the meal. The pan returned to Olran empty, he was glad he had saved a portion for himself in the kitchen.

After the supper dishes were cleaned and leftovers put away, Aaronn made caffe for all. Stories were passed around and invariably the subject of the Black Knight came up, the Knights discussed his deeds in detail.

"Ye know some news of the Black Knight came to Camelot recently," Bedwyr began, sipping his caffe. "We heard that yer brother Kevin died in a storeroom fire not too long ago."

"I do not get any news from Westerland Keep any more. Well, Goddess rest him, I say." Olran replied distantly.

"They said that an unusual steel arrowhead was found buried in his skull, when the fire was put out. I asked around in the Guilds, I was told that the thing was made in the Damascus style," Bedwyr pressed, wanting to test his theory.

"The Black Knight has good taste in weaponry then. Damascus steel is the best steel, or so say they who know," Olran answered blandly.

That stymied Bedwyr and he let the matter drop as another Knight related a tale he had heard of the mysterious man. Finally, none of them could keep awake and they retired upstairs to waiting beds and dreams, except Lancelot who stood first watch. Cai arrived very late indeed, he put the bread on to rise, then retired for a few hours' sleep before waking early to put the finishing touches on the King's meal.

At dawn, the smells of griddlecakes, sausages, bacon, eggs and new bread woke them. Thanking the Goddess for Cai's skills, they ate and discussed things of importance as they always had. The main subject of conversation was what to do about Lord Evin Merin's stubborn refusal to allow neither hostel nor guardtowers to be built on his lands.

"Perhaps we should turn the matter of Lord Merin and his allies over to the Black Knight," Sir Bors put in wearily after they had discussed it at length without resolution. "He seems to be able to convince the reluctant nobles of the realm to toe the mark."

"Aye, if anyone could summon the wretched man," Lancelot complained, just as tired. "Only the common folk seem to see him on any regular basis."

At that moment, the Merlin entered and bowed to Arthur. He had with him a very wretched looking fellow, bound in chains and bleeding all over. He pushed the man down on his knees in front of the King.

"This man is a foul slaver, Lord Pendragon. Only through the actions of the Black Knight were we able to find him. Just yesterday, Ceridwen's man rescued nine girls from bondage at Cerdic's own fires. Through the information provided by the Black Knight, we Druids found this wretch, preparing yet another wagonload of poor children for delivery across the Severn. He deserves the death of a thousand cuts for such a heinous crime!"

"I quite agree, Lord Merlin," Arthur glowered, rising and drawing his own belt knife.

"Please, Sire, do not trouble yerself with this trash," Aaronn spoke up and rose, throwing back his cloak to expose the harness on his chest. "Allow me to unlock his tongue." he continued, eagerly.

"Very well, Sir Aaronn, but take him far away so we do not have to hear his screaming," Arthur appeared to be dismissing the matter.

"Nooooo, please, yer Gracious Majesty!" the wretch screamed. "Mercy, please I beg ye, mercy!"

"What of the mercy ye did not show to those poor children ye sold to the Saxons?" Arthur turned back to him and asked savagely. "Take him from my sight!"

"I only transported the goods, My Lord Pendragon, and brought back payment!" he wept openly now.

"Who did ye deliver the gold to?" Arthur questioned.

"To an account in the Royal Bank, Sire, I know no names, no faces, truly!" he squealed like a frightened pig.

"The penalty for slaving is usually banishment with full restitution. Ye will confess to our questioner every sale, where they went and the price paid. I am sure the tin mines will provide ye an excellent opportunity to work it all off with honest labor, any wages ye earn will be distributed among yer victims and their families," Arthur pronounced. "Sir Gawaine, Sir Agravaine, take this wretch to Camelot's holding cells so we may continue this enlightening conversation," he pointed distastefully as though the man were manure. "Sir Bedwyr, Sir Olran, ye are off to Londinium to confiscate that account. I shall write ye the warrant before ye leave. Let us clean up, boyos," he ordered crisply and began clearing the table himself. The Merlin sat down and helped, cleaning platters of cooled griddlecakes, meats and eggs with a fork and a hearty appetite. When all was clean and neat, they took their leave, King Arthur and his party for Camelot under Aaronn's watchful eyes, Bedwyr and Olran for Londinium. When the latter two passed over the writ, the account was immediately reconciled and handed over. They had to commandeer a wagon to haul the bags and bags of gold back to Camelot. When the amount was stored away in the Royal Treasury, the room looked considerably fuller than before.

It occurred to Olran later that day as he took a long, hot bath, that Lord Merin had recently acquired Urien's villa outside of Londinium, which he now referred to as "Merin's Keep." Perhaps, he mused, it was time to really snoop around to see what was going on there. He had, from time to time, met with a certain woman of that villa's kitchens who had lost a daughter to the slave trade. He had kept her informed of the progress of his search to relocate the missing girl, and the woman had been a comfort to him in many ways, in and out of her bed. Her cooking skills were on a par with Sir Cai's, and her pastries were incredible. Olran decided, as he pulled himself out of the hot water, that it was time to meet again with her and do a bit of thorough searching in and around the villa.

His decision was made more urgent when he secretly learned, by way of a letter on Arthur's desk, of Lord Merin's request for more funds to begin breeding a new strain of guard dogs. The Black Hunter periodically intercepted letters to the King, reading them or handing them over to the Black Knight as the situation demanded. The letter from Merin listed a huge amount of expenses, Ceridwen's archer thought as he read over it. He re-sealed the letter so it appeared to have never been opened and informed his ally that it was time for another mission to Westerland, by way of Londinium.

"What is amiss in the walled city?" asked the Black Knight.

"I want to find out why Lord Merin needs so much money for breeding guard dogs," the Black Hunter told him. "Maybe he really will need them after my visit there," he chuckled coldly.

"Ye watch yerself. As ye have often warned me, anywhere Merin is, 'tis danger," the Black Knight warned.

"Aye, ye need not worry. What are yer plans?"

"A visit to Druid Isle, I need to speak in private with the Merlin. I am sure he must know how to properly administer the death of a thousand cuts. I would have had to improvise," the Black Knight told him seriously. Waiting until full dark, they took their leave of Camelot, each headed to do his own business.

The Black Hunter arrived at Londinium, taking a room at a rather seedy inn he and the Black Knight used when on clandestine missions in the area. As it was nearly morning, he ate breakfast, then retired to his room to sleep away the day. When dark again, he left the inn to ride the short distance to Merin's Keep. Entering through the scullery door to find his contact setting bread sponge for the next day's rising.

"Greetings, Madam Glenda, 'tis I," Ceridwen's man called out softly.

"O!" she jumped a bit, startled at the sound of his voice. "Have ye found my angel yet?" she asked, recovering her composure.

"Not as yet, though I did find others, all from Westerland," he told her. "What is Merin up to that he needs more money from the Crown?" he asked, accepting a day old pastry and a cup of tea.

"Those damned mutts!" she exploded, quietly. "He says they are purebreds, but all they do is eat and crap all over my floors. Those men he pays may be trainers all right, but not for dogs, I assure ye," she went on, clearly aggravated.

"So, if the program is not working out, why is he asking for more funds?" the Black Hunter wondered aloud.

"Lord Merin never has enough money," the cook chuckled, though clearly the name of her Lord brought her to the point of disgust. "I suspect ye'll find yer answers somewhere on the grounds here, and at Darkensdale.

There are plans to expand this villa's stables to make them twice as big. He just finished renovating the old baths here, and found a beautiful tiled mural under all the plaster. He found a smith to make him a new, bigger heater for the bath water, but he won't let any of the staff use his fancy new bath," she huffed, still reporting efficiently. "He told me this morning that he's planning a huge Samhain night celebration, the guest list includes Lot the lecher and Morgause the whore!" she finished up.

"Now, that certainly will be a bit of good fortune for me. I shall have them just where I want them, at last," her visitor chuckled. "Thank ye, lady. Ye have been most helpful, as usual. Ceridwen thanks ye."

"Thank ye, O Black Knight," she answered, warmly. "Are ye leaving so soon?" she asked wistfully.

"I have much to do, lady, I have no time to spare," he answered softly, wishing he could stay.

"Perhaps next time then, 'tis very lonely here, with my daughter gone," she sighed.

"I shall find her, Glenda," the Black Hunter vowed again. "I will not rest 'till I do!"

"I know, and when ye do, Merin's doomed! He was the one who sold her, I saw him!" Glenda's voice shook passionately.

The Black Hunter embraced her fondly before taking his leave, another pastry in hand. He passed by the kennel on the way out and the fierce guard dogs set up a loud barking. The Black Hunter smiled grimly, leapt into the kennel and began slitting throats. In the end, twelve big canine carcasses lay in pools of their own blood and the kennel burned fiercely. The token of Ceridwen's man was left conspicuously behind as he quickly checked over the huge new stables, cow byres and other barns and pens. The scale at which Merin was fortifying the villa was impressive; the Black Hunter could see why the suspected traitor was three years tardy in his Crown tithes. When he was finished with his scouting activities, he took his leave and rode on to Westerland Keep.

Arriving at Daffydsdale, the small town at the base of Westerland, the Black Hunter sat at the back of a run-down tavern where he knew Warren liked to drink. He ordered a cup of tea and nursed the hot drink along as he rested and waited. Suddenly, Sean burst in, hauling a much-abused and screaming girl along with him by the wrist.

"So, I'm not good enough fer yer family, eh bitch?" the bully laughed cruelly. "Well, after ye've served among the Saxons fer awhile, ye'll learn how to be more grateful for a British man's interest in ye!"

"Ye cannot do that!" she objected, real fear in her voice. "I am the niece of a King, he will have ye killed when he finds out what ye have tried to do this day!"

"Caw is old, fat, and sotted with drink and age! An' that peace he agreed to with the Pendragon has softened his brains! He won't even know ye've gone!" Sean laughed maniacally and swigged of a jug that the Black Hunter guessed was some kind of liquor. "Now, I'll give ye one last chance. Bed me, wed me an' be a good little wife so I can inherit the Keep, or be a slave in Saxon lands!"

"Hold yer answer, girl!" the Black Hunter growled at last, and stood to reveal himself. All that Sean saw was the outfit he was wearing and he threw the weeping, struggling girl to the aside. She landed hard on the filthy wooden floor.

"So, ye've come back have ye!" he snarled. "Ye'll pay now, for our wounds and fer Kevin!" he half whispered, the hate in his voice evident.

"Nay, Sean ap Warren, 'tis ye who will pay for all yer insults to Ceridwen, and for the heinous crimes ye have committed without repercussions all yer miserable life! Yer slaving days are over!"

With a roar, the enraged Sean leapt at him, broadsword in hand, meeting only steel. The fight was short and sweet in the Goddess' eyes, for the Black Hunter handled himself coolly and professionally through the entire incident. Sean was quickly disarmed and thrown to his stomach on the floor, where the Black Hunter tied him like a deer for the spit. He then went to where the girl lay, weeping and cursing softly.

"Are ye well, Lady?" he asked, holding out his hand to assist her from the floor.

"Well enough. Ye are the Black Knight?" she asked.

"I am Ceridwen's man, aye." he answered carefully, trying to avoid a lie. "Get ye to Avalon, girl. 'Tis closer than Camelot, the ladies there will help ye when ye show them this," he explained, handing her a cloak and the dagger token. "When next ye see yer uncle Caw, tell him what has been done to ye, what might have been done, and by whom," he went on.

"I thank ye Sir. Ye are a true knight, after all. My kinsman will hear of all ye have done to assist me. If ever ye need anything, I am the Lady Heather, and I shall assist all I may," she told him, then kissed him warmly on the lips through his hood. She then went to where Sean lay trussed on the floor and spat a huge glob of mucus and spittle into his face.

"I hope he kills ye, Sean ap Warren, very, *very* slowly," she whispered savagely into his ear, then she stepped carefully away as if to avoid a pile of manure and laughed heartily as she went out the door.

"So, it seems I have someone worth practicing on after all," the Black Hunter chuckled coldly. "I need to sharpen my skills in the art of flaying. I know ye have heard of the death of a thousand cuts."

"Nooooo! Ye can't, I am a King's son!" Sean screamed, knowing from all the whispers that the ebon-clad man meant what he said.

"So? Look what ye were going to do to that young Lady Heather, and she is a King's niece. Ye certainly do not act like a King's son. I have heard that the blood of Westerland's royal folk is the bluest of blue. I shall test that and see if 'tis true." the Black Hunter added. When Sean opened his mouth to object further, Ceridwen's archer simply stuffed a wadded kerchief into his gaping mouth. Leaving his token, he picked up the man carefully, for he was quite heavy. Slinging him over his shoulders, he strode unimpeded from the tavern, then loaded Sean onto the Jughead. Pointing his steed towards Druid Isle, he rode out of the town at the fastest pace the horse could manage, being double-loaded, arriving at mid-morning at the Merlin's cave. Making sure Sean was still unconscious the archer took him to the Black Knight.

"Brother, a body for ye to practice the ritual death of a thousand cuts upon!" he announced gleefully, binding Sean's eyes with a proffered cloth after dumping him onto the floor.

"Why, 'tis Sean ap Warren!" Taliesin observed, watching the Black Hunter carefully.

"Aye, the Slaver of Westerland," the Black Hunter agreed, removing his mask once Sean's eyes were bound. "I caught him in the act of bullying and abusing the Lady Heather, Caw's niece, trying to force her into a marriage by threatening to sell her to the Saxons. He only offered her a choice between two evils, in my opinion."

The Black Knight grinned and prepared to use the knowledge the Merlin had only recently imparted to him.

"Wake him up then. I wager I will not have to lay a knife on him before he sings like a songbird," he chuckled.

The Black Hunter bent to wake the man, but Sean was inexplicably dead. "Damn him for dying!" the Black Hunter swore heatedly. "He was the key to the whole thing! I am sorry brother for this; I must have treated him too roughly."

"Nay, he was fat and wasted. His heart just gave out, probably from fear," the Merlin said philosophically. "Ye did him no real harm, I can see that from the condition of the body," he added in a comforting tone.

"Well, 'tis always Marcus," the archer sighed. "He will be easy to scare into line at least," he went on, chuckling in spite of his regret of allowing Sean to die.

"This deed is going to cause a firestorm for us, brother," the Black Knight observed.

"Not when Lady Heather gets ahold of Arthur's ear. She will scream blood vengeance on all of Westerland, for certain!" the Black Hunter laughed, remembering her furious words to Sean.

Blood vengeance was indeed on the Lady's mind when she rode into Camelot two days later, still dressed as she had been when the Black

Hunter had seen her last. As soon as her feet touched the cobbled stones of the castle's courtyard, she began her enraged accusations against Westerland Keep, showing the now familiar token to the King. Arthur escorted her inside personally, then to his private suite, after first gaining a bit of control over her vocal volume.

"Now, Lady Heather calm down and tell me again, slowly and exactly, what happened?" Arthur asked as he poured her a cup of pear wine.

"Very well, Sire," she agreed, now somewhat calmer. "Sean ap Warren invited my father and mother to Westerland to discuss terms of marriage. Once we arrived, 'twas obvious that his family was definitely one we did not wish to ally with. I turned him down flat and we left for home at once. Sean made vague threats about how we'd soon be put in our place, but we paid them no mind, not believing he truly meant all he said. We stopped at a royal hostel, which was a bit lacking in staples I might add. Sean must have followed us, for as soon as night fell, he crept into the room where I was sleeping and kidnapped me back to Westerland's dungeons. I was there all night, tied up and forced to listen to him rant and rave about how I was too haughty and should be put in my place. He untied me after a while and tried to rape me, but I kneed him between the legs as hard as I could and ran away. I would've escaped too, but for these skirts!" Heather went on heatedly, taking a few sips of the cool, sweet wine to compose her emotions. "He then dragged me into a pit of a tavern and gave me a choice between marriage to him or slavery among the Saxons. I was about to choose the Saxons, when the Black Knight stepped in, Sire," she stopped her recitation to allow a small smile to cross her face. Arthur grinned inwardly, for the look was unmistakably one of longing. "After a brief and spectacular sword fight, Sean was knocked unconscious and trussed up like a capon on the floor. The Black Knight gave me this token and a cloak, bade me to go to Avalon for healing, then come to ye with this tale. He then rode off with Sean draped over his saddle," she finished and Arthur poured her a bit more wine. "I want that family punished, My Lord Pendragon! My uncle Caw will be as outraged as my father will be. Our treaty with the Crown guarantees equal justice under the King's Law. I demand blood vengeance on Westerland Keep!"

"Vengeance is hardy justice, Lady Heather," Arthur observed dryly. "Yer story rings of the truth, but I wish to talk to Sean ap Warren first before I render a decision. Pax?" he asked, rising and bowing slightly at the waist.

"If we do not see justice done, My Lord Pendragon, my family will be back to see ye," she told him flatly. "May I impose upon ye for a room to sleep in and some clean clothes?" she asked after her sapphire-blue eyes met his own royal gaze levelly.

"Of course, My Lady Gwenhyfar shall see to yer needs, personally. My Lady?" he called out and the antechamber door opened at once to admit her.

"Aye, My Lord?"

"Would ye please take Lady Heather in hand? She has been through a terrible ordeal. She needs a room and clean clothing. Give her anything she needs to make her stay with us more pleasant."

"Come with me, my dear," the Queen crooned comfortingly, having heard the entire story through the door. "A nice hot bath and clean new clothes will help set ye right. Some of Sir Cai's delicious vegetable soup will settle yer nerves so ye may sleep soundly. Ye look so tired...." her voice trailed off down the hall.

Sometime later, the Black Knight came into Arthur's presence, hauling Sean's dead body with him.

"Ye know, ye could bring in one of them alive to me, once and awhile," he complained after calling to have the body removed.

"He was dead on arrival at Druid Isle, My Lord," the Black Knight explained, taking the cup of pear wine Arthur handed him. "Are we alone?" he asked and received Arthur's nod of confirmation. Removing his hood, he drained the cup, smacked his lips and indicated he would like more.

"So, tell me about Westerland's involvement in the illegal trade of slaving," he asked, sitting down expectantly.

"I know we were close to identifying Sean ap Warren as the headman of the entire operation. The account at the Royal Bank of Londinium was his, although 'tis no proof of it now. He covered his deeds well, no one at Westerland would admit to anything. Sean's death will cause many repercussions I think, My Lord, but the Merlin himself will testify that he was not tortured in any way. He just died of fright," the Black Knight explained, chuckling over the last statement.

"How fortunate that Lady Heather was basically unharmed," Arthur observed. "She has called for blood, ye know."

"She made that quite obvious," the Black Knight told him, relating what his ally had said. "She is going to make some petty king's life very interesting someday, I think," he went on perceptively.

"That wisp of a girl actually threatened the Crown with a blood feud!" Arthur told him seriously. "If she hears the news of Sean's death, perhaps 'twill be enough to calm her."

"I shall speak to her tonight, My Lord, if ye wish," the Black Knight offered.

"I would appreciate it, Sir Knight. Britain hardly needs a civil war now! We also need to prevent any re-occurrence of this sort of thing. I want this slaving matter put to rest!" Arthur ordered.

"Very well, My Lord Pendragon. May I use any means at my disposal to accomplish this task for ye?"

"Ye know what means are acceptable under the King's Law," Arthur reminded.

"Is there ought else?"

"Not at the moment. I am meeting, coincidentally, with Lord Delmont Corwin, Heather's eldest brother on the morrow. It seems that he too, is now suddenly unwilling to allow guard towers and hostels on his lands. I may have more work for ye when our talks are completed," Arthur sighed and poured himself another cup of wine. "I almost wish the Saxons were still marauding. At least then the nobles were all with me instead of dividing against me."

"I could take care of that, Artos," the Black Knight suggested quietly. "I could arrange for them all to be taken care of, quickly and permanently."

"Nay, ye know it must be done through careful negotiations to win true loyalty. Ruling through fear produces a despot," Arthur told him although the idea was quite appealing. To have all his enemies removed at once would tempt any King.

"Very well, Lord Pendragon." the Black Knight sighed and drained his cup.

"I must be off. I cannot wait to hear Lord Corwin's excuses concerning the placing of royal hostels within his borders," Arthur tried to laugh. "Maybe I should set Lady Heather loose on him."

"Let me know if his answers are not satisfactory, Lord Pendragon," the Black Knight answered, then slipped on his hood and left the room.

He went to his chambers, where he found his ally still stowing away gear in their secret closet. "Need any help?" Aaronn asked.

"Nay, I am nearly done now. After this and a hot bath, I am going to put a new edge on my blade. Sean never could parry a blow without a blunder," Olran related without a trace of emotion over the death of his brother.

"Are ye all right?" Aaronn asked carefully.

"Aye, of course," Olran replied. "He was a despicable human being, a person who traded in human flesh for profit! He died much too easily, in my way of thinking, but Ceridwen's Will was done on the matter. He stands before the Her now, trembling with the coward's fear that killed him," he said in a tone that said the matter was closed. "Just think on this, Warren knows all about Sean's activities. I wonder how long it would take to get the information out of him at his age," Olran added, thinking out loud.

"Leave it for now, brother. We have some peacemaking to do. Lady Heather still wants to drink Westerland blood from a cup," Aaronn told him and poured them both wine.

"Too bad Sean is dead," Olran chuckled. "Do ye want me to handle this?"

"I do not know, is she pretty?" Aaronn laughed.

"Sean may have been stupid, but he knew a beauty when he saw one. Heather's cold, but gorgeous," Olran informed him, coolly. "Ye could have a lot of fun thawing her out."

"Such will be the right job for the Black Knight my ally," Aaronn laughed harder.

"Nay, Sir Aaronn of Camelot will have to handle this one, the handsome bugger," Olran laughed with him. "I want naught to do with that hellcat."

"I shall be sure to trim her nails first," Aaronn replied, grabbing a robe. "I am going for a soak, coming?"

"Aye, I still have not recovered from that trip to the Saxon lands," Olran replied.

"Ye never did say how many more ye had to take out to cover our escape," Aaronn hinted.

"Only two were stupid enough to give chase," Olran picked up his own robe and followed after his friend. "I guess Cerdic's going to have to elect new family members for lieutenants, though. I suppose 'tis a good thing that his family's a big one."

When news arrived at Westerland of Sean's death and the charges against him, Warren and Justine came at once to Camelot. They fussed and bothered over it, until the coolly eloquent Lady Heather made her case before the Royal Court of Justice. When the young woman was finished, pandemonium broke out and new accusations of promises made and broken rang out in the courtroom.

"Please, please," Sir Lancelot called out. "Gentle people, quiet please?"

"Aye, I want no civil wars or blood feuds in Britain under my rule," Arthur agreed. "I shall remove Westerland from yer hands, Warren, if 'tis not resolved. And ye, Lady Heather, can be sent into exile to prevent such a horrific sundering of Ceridwen's peace. I have fought too hard, lost too many fine men of Britain to enemy swords and seaxes. I shall not cheapen those brave men's sacrifices of life and limb by allowing a personal disagreement to continue!" Arthur went on. "Sean ap Warren was the head of a slavers ring that stole young girls and boys then sold them into slavery among the Saxons. Warren, ye owe the Lady Heather recompense for her kidnap and attempted rape at Sean's hands. Pay up now, and while yer at it, pay yer taxes in full. Ye have a month to remit yer taxes to the Crown, but the Lady is to be paid now!"

"But, I haven't any gold of any amount with me!" Warren protested.

"Very well then," Arthur said tersely, rising from his chair, drawing Excalibur.

"Wait, Sire…I…" Warren said haltingly, fear showing in his voice as the King approached, sword in hand. Arthur leveled the sword at Justine, who blanched as the King neatly cut the beautiful gold necklace from the proud woman's neck. The double strand of freshwater pearls came off next, right over Justine's head without so much as one lost gem. He gestured for her bracelets next, as well as her ruby rings and hairpins adorned with tiny emeralds. He only left her the thick gold wedding ring on her left hand as he collected the mass of jewelry and put everything into Heather's hands, except the heavy gold necklace.

"This sum, Lady Heather, settles the matter in the Crown's eyes," he pronounced, handing it to her. "The rest will constitute a partial payment of Westerland's taxes, now in remiss four years. One month, Warren, and make sure the entire amount is paid in that time!" he finished and returned to the throne, sheathing Excalibur onto his back.

"I thank ye, Sire," Lady Heather rose and curtsied gracefully. "The matter is settled in my eyes as well, My Lord."

"Excellent! Warren and Justine go home and take that whiner Marcus with ye. Do not come back 'till ye pay yer taxes in full," the King ordered, making a dismissive gesture. Sir Lancelot and Sir Gawaine escorted them out to their carriage and made sure they were well on the way home. All they heard while following the Westerland carriage was Justine's moans over her lost jewelry and Warren's constant admonition for her silence. They had also taken Sean's body back with them; they laid it out in the chapel of Westerland with the assistance of the corrupt and perverted Christian priest. His fee for leading Warren's family in the rote prayers and mouthed songs was an occasional night with a very frightened and newly-arrived young servant lad.

The priest said the final rites over Sean's bloated and smelly corpse, then it was placed in a coffin and nailed shut, to be buried in the morning. The despicable priest, Joaquin, was sure to lock the door securely when he left, draping the keychain around his fat, sweaty neck so he would not misplace it. Entering his room, he found a hooded man, dressed all in black, calmly going through his treasure hoard.

"What is the meaning of this?" he asked angrily. "I am a priest of Christ and that box is for the poor."

"The poor friar Joaquin, more like," the figure chuckled. "What is here could pay Westerland's taxes for a year. I thought ye men of Christ were sworn to poverty."

"I told ye, 'tis for the poor," the terrified priest mumbled without much conviction.

"I thought ye were sworn to chastity as well," the figure went on, producing a black leather bag and turning to the chest, loading handfuls of the treasure into it. "I have been to the Saxon lands recently and rescued a young lad who knows ye, very well. His name is James," he replied pleasantly.

"I know many lads by that name, what of it?" Joaquin began to sweat furiously.

"He described ye very well, Joaquin. Does Warren pay ye in any way than with a young boy's company?" the Black Knight asked, his voice clearly disgusted.

"I have no idea what yer talking about!" Joaquin protested hotly. "I occasionally council young, confused boys on the sins of the flesh," he added, trying to assume a saintly demeanor.

"A subject ye know very well, eh Friar? I have spoken to several families here about. They all tell me the same story of their young sons disappearing in the night, only to return a few days later, bruised and bleeding from ah, shall we say, unusual places and unable to function normally for a long time," the Black Knight stated, dropping the last piece of gold into the bag and pulling the drawstring tight to close it. "I have come for ye, Friar. Ye are an abomination unto the Christ ye claim to serve, ye are corrupt and perverted. Jesus would condemn ye Himself if He were here and blast ye where ye stand for yer blasphemy. He taught that perversion was wrong, that children were precious. Ye have two choices, get ye to Dragon Isle and be cured of yer sickness, or be slain where ye stand!"

"I am going nowhere, except to call the guards!" Joaquin shouted petulantly and turned for the door. A knife suddenly pinned his filthy black robe to the oak boards, his face turned white under the mass of beard that covered his face.

"Perhaps ye should reconsider that decision, brother," the Black Knight remarked conversationally and strode towards him. Joaquin began to tremble violently and he could hardly speak.

"Where can I find these Druids?" he finally managed to say.

"Come, I can take ye to them," the Black Knight told him as he swung the heavy bag over his shoulder. He went to the door, exposing his back. Joaquin thought he saw an opening to escape, he worked furiously at the dagger pinning his robe to the floor. Once armed, he rushed the mysterious man's back with every intention of killing him to keep him from telling anyone what he knew. Ceridwen's man heard his footsteps, turned sharply and swung the heavy bag of coins hard, striking the priest's temple. Joaquin's face showed astonishment before he collapsed, flaccid, to the floor. He was bleeding from the ear as the Black Knight leaned over him, checked the pulse in the throat and sighed when he could find no sign of life. Very well, he thought, best to make this one's crimes clear to all and he bent to his work after locking the door. When Warren came down to the friar's quarters later, he found Joaquin prone on the floor, stomach down. He nearly vomited with shock when he saw that the man's member had been neatly severed and inserted into his anal orifice. The Black Knight's token and scroll lay beside him, Warren bent and carefully unrolled the fine parchment. A neat, meticulous hand clearly spelled out his crimes, under the declaration had been added, with the Black Knight's token under;

"This man was punished for crimes against the Goddess Ceridwen. Beware, Warren ap Daffyd, yer crimes are known to Her as well. She watches, She waits, She punishes."

Justine entered and her gasp of horror surprised Warren. He whirled, sword at the ready, relaxing when he saw his wife's white face.

"What has happened, Warren?" she whispered, trying to get past him for a better look.

"Ye do not want to know, Justine. We should get both Sean and he buried. Send his things back to the Church at Londinium, and once 'tis done, we will have no more of his kind at Westerland. I need a drink!" he said heatedly and stalked from the room, Justine in tow. The Black Knight watched them go then took his leave as well. Once he was well away from Westerland, he removed his hood and took several breaths of Ceridwen's clean, forest-scented air. The Black Knight then laughed 'till he nearly fell from his horse, recalling Warren's pale and frightened face when he regarded Joaquin's displayed body. Perhaps this would finally end Westerland's illicit activities, once and for all. Three days later, the Bishop of Londinium, Patricius, appeared at Camelot in a religious fervor. He complained bitterly about the friar's death under the blade of the Black Knight and demanded justice.

"Justice, Bishop?" Arthur inquired tightly. "What of justice for dozens of young frightened young boys, violated horribly by this man? Yer friar was a sodomite as these letters will attest; here are the copies I am sending on to the Church at Rome. Ceridwen's man took him for his crimes. I do not know what ye teach, but our Goddess regards forced sex with such a young boy as against natural law, a sickness of the soul. Perhaps yer Church, in its haste to convert the world, is too lax in recruiting priests?" he suggested acidly. "Now go away, I have more important things to do than to listen to yer tirades," he said in dismissal and Bedwyr opened the door.

The Bishop took the hint and left, returning in haste to Londinium to plan a tour of each and every parish in Britain. "The stain of sodomites wearing the vestments of priests must be removed from the Holy Church!"

he told his staff and the good men among them agreed heartily. It took the Bishop all that winter and into the spring, he began with his own parish, but come summer more than a dozen priests had been defrocked and excommunicated. Most left Britain willingly, those who would not perished under mysterious circumstances, the Black Knight's token always found nearby.

That Spring and Summer were otherwise unremarkable, the Knights and King blessed the Goddess' name that it was so. Tournament time came and went, but only four men were found worthy to join the Outer Circle and were accepted among the junior Knights in hearty companionship. Harvests were again huge, the Knights all rode out to assist in gathering the abundant foods, joining with the common folk until all was stored, dried and put away by Samhain. The Harvest Festival at Camelot was a merry affair and Maegwyn ap Uriens took a wife at the height of the festivities. The woman was of Avalon; Gwenhyfar put up a fight before allowing Camelot's great room to be used for the joining ceremony. She refused to attend, however and all duly noted her absence.

After Samhain, a breathless farm boy arrived at Camelot from the Severn Valley, aboard a rickety horse. He told a tale of Saxons raiding his family's farm, driving off their few cattle and emptying their storehouses. Arthur sighed, realizing that this was probably the work of a few hotbloods, and sent Lancelot with a division of Knights to deal with the matter. Two weeks later, the patrol returned to Camelot with nine scruffy men in tow.

"Who are they?" the King asked, surprised.

"They appear to be subchiefs of Cerdic's, tired of leading the quiet life, or so I gather from hearing them talk. Do we ransom them back, or kill them now?" Lancelot answered and Arthur could hear his weariness clearly.

"We will try the peaceful way first, Lance. Send the ransom demand to Cerdic; if he pays he can deal with 'em. If no payment comes, then we'll deal with it the only way we can, swiftly and surely!" Arthur told him, handing him a cup of strong ale. "Now, come in, all of ye. Make generous use of the baths, gentlemen, ye all smell like rusty horses," he laughed and led the patrol inside.

With the last boat of the shipping season came a small shipment of silk threads and spices, as well as mighty fighting men from all over wanting to serve at Camelot. The castle was full of Germanic tribesmen, as well as Gauls, Arabs, Romans, and even the occasional Oriental for that entire winter. After the holidays were over and the guests firmly ensconced at Camelot and other noble households all over Britain, Arthur and the Inner Circle took a men's holiday at the hunting lodge to relax, away from wives and children. It was a pleasurable two weeks, when they returned they found all still calm. Gwenhyfar's latest pregnancy was progressing well enough, although at four months she was still ill in the morning. The Queen greeted Arthur over the mound of correspondence she was answering; he sat and took over his share of the mail as usual. The pair laughed and talked all morning, when the work was finished Gwenhyfar returned to her bed for a short nap.

Arthur took advantage of the free time to work with Lancelot at swords. He had felt the need to sharpen his skills of late, what with the nine "guests" in Camelot's detention area. Cerdic had not yet responded to the ransom demand, the time was running short. Arthur had given the Saxons six months to come up with the ransom payment; two of those months had already passed. He hoped that Cerdic would pay up rather than fight, but it never hurt to be prepared either he reasoned. He worked himself into a full sweat, afterwards indulging himself in a long bath with his sword-brothers before meeting with Lord Merin and his allies in an attempt to break the deadlocked negotiations. The realm required the proposed guardtowers along the eastern border to stop the raids altogether, Arthur told himself grimly, and Merin's group must understand the need. If this set of negotiations resolved nothing, Arthur determined mentally to call upon the Black Knight's aid to remove the obstacles preventing it permanently.

That night, Lord Merin's lands received a fatal visit from the Black Knight. Entering one home after another, Merin's bullyboys were in the process of gathering "servers" for their master's next feast. Seizing only the comeliest of females, married or not, the cruel men forced them from their beds and hearths, killing any man who stood in the way. One grandfather who had already lost two daughters to the slave trade tried to pitchfork the leader from behind, he was cuffed hard to the ground, blood trickling from his mouth.

"Now, stay out of the way old man!" the leader laughed with an evil leer. "She'll be returned to ye in the morning, only slightly used. Ye won't have to provide such a large dowry for her after tonight!"

"Nay, 'tis ye who will pay the price!" a voice answered from the shadows. The leader collapsed suddenly without further comment, a knife hilt protruding from his throat.

"'Tis the Black Knight!" shrieked one of the others. "Leave the wenches and run for it, boyos!"

"I think not, Tomas of Darkensdale!" the Black Knight chuckled coolly as the knives flew like early snowflakes, each finding its intended target in a man's body. When none of them stood, the Black Knight retrieved his knives, turning to the group of frightened and white-faced women.

"Are any of ye hurt?"

"Nay, the Goddess be praised," the least frightened one of them answered.

"We stand in thy debt, Sir Black Knight," another added.

"Soon, Merin will be called by the Goddess to answer for his crimes. Sleep ye sound, ladies," he told them, blew them all a collective kiss and disappeared into the night. More than one longing sigh was heard among them as the women dispersed throughout the town, back to their homes. The Black Knight went directly to Darkensdale and hid outside the guardhouse where Merin's bullyboys slept and took their meals. He slipped the heavy oaken bar across the outside of the door and set the building alight. He waited till he could hear the screams for help, then he ran across the courtyard shouting; "Fire, fire in the guardhouse!"

In the confusion, he was easily able to slip into the castle proper and find his way to Merin's private treasury. Pushing open the heavy, iron-reinforced door, his eyes beheld box upon box of silver and gold coins, bags of rough gemstones littered the floor and the Black Knight noted that among them were many good sized rare diamonds, sapphires and rubies among the closest bags at his feet. Rare furs also were stockpiled on the shelves, ermine, tiger, and lion were amongst those the Black Knight recognized. His rage was kindled at the vast amount of wealth this room alone held, he knew that even if Merin paid his three years of back taxes, it would still hardly make a dent. He could not help stuffing a handful or two of beautiful, fiery cut diamonds into his booty bag before creeping from the room. He knew that Merin often spent time in his treasure room; he guessed that the discrepancy would soon be noted and raged over. Ceridwen's man was sure to leave his token behind, so that none of the servants or staff would be blamed, boldly pinning it to Merin's own banner that hung threateningly over the hoard. It was quite late when Ceridwen's man returned to Camelot, stowed Eclipse in his stall, wiping the soot away from the animal's white ring and blanketed him, leaving him to a good rest after leaving plenty of water and grain.

Removing his hood, Aaronn entered Camelot's kitchens by way of the scullery door. He found Cai loading a plate of food to set beside the foamy tankard already on the table. Washing his hands, Aaronn sat and drained the whole cool cup of mellow apple ale, then dug into the plate of crackling bacon, eggs, and toasted bread. Quickly devouring it all, Aaronn asked for more, Cai smiled to see him still packing it away as he had when he was young. When finally finished, Aaronn took his plate and flatware to the washing area and placed them in the sink of soapy water that always stood at hand.

"My thanks, Sir Cai, 'twas delicious." he said, embracing the seneschal warmly.

"Ye are most welcome, Aaronn," Cai smiled. "Ye can call me brother, ye know."

"Very well, brother Cai," he smiled.

"Now get yerself to bed, boyo. Today is Gaheris' wedding and the King has a celebration all planned, as well ye know. Already this morning, I have had a pigeon message from Land's End that Orkney's royal ship has been sighted and those two royal pains in the arse are expected here by mid-morning. We will need every available eye to watch over Morgause plus everyone else," Cai told him seriously.

"Aye, we agree on that!" Aaronn laughed. "Know where I can get my best price for these?" he asked, pulling two of the cut stones from his bag. They flashed their brilliant fire into Cai's eyes, causing them to widen with surprise. Cai pulled the candle lamp closer for a better examination.

"Great bountiful Goddess, where did ye get these?" he breathed after a few moments when he saw their high quality. "They are worth a fortune!"

"Ye do not want to know where I got them, but I would like ye to have these beauties, my friend," Aaronn pressed them into the seneschal's hands. "They are a gift from Ceridwen the White, in thanks for all yer help and yer silence in Her Cause."

"I accept them with thanks, Aaronn, and gladly. I can put them to good purpose, I assure ye," he chuckled, stowing them in an inner pocket. "I shall tell no one where they came from."

"Of course ye will not," Aaronn grinned wearily. "Please, brother, let me sleep as long as possible?"

"Of course I shall!" Cai returned, laughing a bit as he mimicked Aaronn's inflection exactly, then pushed him to the doors. "Good rest to ye, Sir Aaronn." Olran was just staggering from his bed, headed to the necessity when Aaronn came through the door. The latter was concerned immediately at his friend's decidedly unwell appearance.

"Olran, what is amiss?" he asked.

"We held Gaheris' bachelor party last night, remember?" Olran replied painfully. "He insisted that since I am yer friend and ye were absent, I had to drink yer share as well as my own," he added, reappearing and holding his head. Olran went to the hearth, swung the kettle over the fire and tried to grind the last of the caffe beans, but the pain in his head prevented any further actions.

"Here, let me do it for once," Aaronn laughed softly and ground the beans as quietly as possible out of consideration for his friend's aching head. He finished the brewing process, then poured and honeyed the brew to Olran's preference.

"Thanks, brother," Olran smiled painfully, sipping of the delicious beverage. "Ahhh, I feel better already."

"Wake me when Morgause arrives, please brother?" Aaronn yawned as he lay down on his huge four-poster bed. As soon as he was asleep, Olran began picking up the clothes that were scattered everywhere, finding the booty bag in the process. When he picked it up, a few of the uncut diamonds rolled out, the meticulous Olran picked up the biggest of them, holding it up in front of the firelight. He gasped silently as he beheld the rough gem, seeing that they were of rare, high quality, he wondered mentally what these little beauties would be good for as his head and body aches began to fade rapidly. By the time his second up of caffe was consumed, he was fully groomed and dressed for the day's activities, reserving his formals for the wedding and feast afterwards. Leaving the room quietly, he went downstairs for breakfast. After he had fully sated his hunger, he offered any help that might be needed, Cai took him at once to the kitchen, handed him an apron and asked that he tend the roasting meats.

"Please, Sir Olran. I am suddenly so very short-handed. When the staff heard that Queen Morgause would be here, they quit flat and left, saying that they would not cook or serve the likes of an evil witch like her," Cai practically begged.

"No fears, Sir Cai. Of course, I shall be glad to help," Olran chuckled, taking the apron and basting tools from his hands. "Ye will be sure to send a comely girl around with something cool to drink in a while, aye?" he added and Cai just had to laugh, so earnest was his tone. The tension broken, Camelot's seneschal returned to his proper duties, assured that the meats would be done to a hunter's perfection under Olran's watchful eye.

Done they were, and just in time too, for as they were taking the meat off the spit, Lot and Morgause arrived in a carriage, dressed as the proud parents and pulling another cart loaded with gifts behind them. After Gaheris greeted them Morgause went to the bride's chambers to assist, while Lot remained with his son and the rest of the male wedding participants.

The day went off well enough, no major disturbances for arguments, at least until Lord Merin arrived alone from Darkensdale, his usual aplomb evaporated by the Black Knight's nocturnal visitation. He dared say nothing about the whole event, but he was enraged by the thorough arson job on the guard's quarters. Those who had not perished or been burnt severely in the fire had quit at first light this morning, leaving Merin without so much as an honor guard as escort to Sir Gaheris' wedding. There must be a way to find out who the Black Knight was and destroy him, Merin's devious mind reasoned, the thought consuming and distracting him all day and for many a day afterward.

Gaheris and his bride were given the run of the hunting lodge for their honeymoon, as so many of the other Inner Circle had. Upon their departure, the feasting began anew. Cai thanked Olran for his all day assistance with everything from the meats to the final clean up, shooing from the kitchen after first sharing a welcome and relaxing cup of wine with the thin, wiry man. On the way out, Olran spied the lovely, shapely and hardworking Brianne, who had worked all day beside him, bringing him many cups of cooling ale or wine to quench the thirst brought on by working so closely with the hot fires.

"Brianne, are ye also excused for the day?" he asked, invitation in his voice.

"Aye, Sir Olran, that I am," the girl from Lesser Britain answered in the odd accent from that kingdom, her voice warm and pleasing to the ears.

"Would ye care to come with me to the dance?" he asked.

The girl's face fell in disappointment and she shook her head.

"I've nothing fine to wear, Sir Olran. Perhaps ye should ask one of the noble ladies," she answered sadly.

"Come with me," he invited. "I wager there's something in the stores 'twill fit yer figure," he chuckled and took her hand. In the storage closets of Camelot were stored outgrown or unwanted gowns from many a noble woman, together the two found a lovely, sapphire-blue gown that matched her eyes exactly. Hose, unders and petticoats were also found for her before Olran took her up to his room to change. He sent a royal page to wake Aaronn much earlier, but they found him within the quarters, just finishing a cup of wine in the quiet of his quarters. Olran went to change into his own formals, leaving Brianne to change into her finery behind the privacy screen. She and Aaronn sat and talked while they waited for Olran to emerge, but he made no appearance. Finally, Aaronn peeked into the room to find Olran half-dressed in his formals and snoring softly on top of his coverlet. Smiling fondly, Aaronn tucked him in, blew out the lamp, banked the small heath for the night and closed the door quietly.

"Yer escort seems to have fallen asleep due to exhaustion," Aaronn chuckled softly. Brianne's face fell and she made to leave. "Perhaps I would do in his place?" Aaronn asked invitingly.

"Ye are most kind to offer, Sir Aaronn. If ye are willing and have no one else to partner ye, I would like to go, very much," Brianne answered shyly. "I shall be the envy of every girl in the castle, noble or common! To have the honor of being escorted to the dance by, 'the Knightly Knife', the handsomest man among the Outer Circle of Camelot!" she giggled and took his proffered arm. The two danced awhile, only to disappear back to Aaronn's quarters to share the Mother's blessing. Sleeping together comfortably late into the day, they had breakfast with Olran before Brianne made her good-byes to both men before returning to her duties. Once she was gone, the two men spoke of Merin's attitude, Aaronn explained what had happened at Darkensdale.

"Ye should have heard the talk once Merin left," Aaronn chuckled, delighted that the traitor was finally beginning to feel the heat. "The tale was that his whole brigade, at least those still alive or able to walk, quit him flat."

"He said nothing to Arthur, nothing at all?" Olran asked.

"Not a bloody word, my friend. What could he say, after all?" Aaronn answered with a wide grin. "That the Black Knight destroyed his private army of bullyboys, who were gathering unwilling women for his next orgy? Not likely. We have finally got him where we want him, my brother," he chuckled.

"Where did ye get those diamonds in yer booty bag?" Olran asked.

"From Darkensdale's treasure room. Merin's got so much stuff stockpiled in that vault, Arthur could fund Britain for years on what is there," Aaronn told him, his rage at Merin's greed not yet abated.

"When his treachery is finally proven and he's dead, the Crown will have its share!" Olran said with finality.

"Aye!" Aaronn added, smacking his fist into his palm.

Camelot relaxed after the wedding and soon the winter holiday season was upon them. It all went smoothly until the day of the Winter Solstice when suddenly, inexplicably, Gwenhyfar's labor pains began four months too early. The child was delivered stillborn some twenty hours later, much to everyone's grief. Gwenhyfar's sobs could not be silenced, no matter what anyone did to assist. She moved out of the royal suite again in mid-winter, vowing privately never to return. Arthur understood her reasons, but could hardly be expected to wait forever for her to return to his bed. After the Spring Solstice, he confided miserably to Cai that he was randy as a tomcat.

"What shall I do, Caius?" he asked plaintively. "She now says she will never again share my bed. I cannot be celibate, 'tis not in me to be a monk!"

"Artos, she needs this time. My God, ye could see the child was a male! If only she had been able to carry it another few weeks, Britain would have an heir. She thinks 'tis her fault, somehow, I suppose," Cai tried to comfort his foster-brother. "Try waiting a bit longer, brother. If she is not back in yer bed by Beltane, then we will find another solution," he grinned, lopsidedly.

Arthur tried to laugh it off, but inside he was divided. The nobles, Christian and other, were screaming for an heir to the throne. Gwenhyfar seemed unable to hold a child in her womb long enough to deliver it alive. He now loved her deeply, as did all the people, how could he divorce her without shaming her? He sighed, told himself it was all in the Goddess' hands and mentally girt his loins for the duration.

That night, in the dark of the moon, a silent ship tied up at Land's End. A single passenger and two horses disembarked, the animals' wrapped feet making only dull thuds on the boards of the dock. A chink of coins could be heard, the ship pulled away from the dock just as silently as it had tied up. The rider mounted up on the giant black warsteed and rode away slowly to avoid excessive noise, then turned the stallion's head northward. Trotting off purposefully up to the signposts, they stopped for a moment. After the rider read it carefully, they went on their way up the coast road, headed for the crossroads of Londinium, disappearing into the dense fog.

Three days after the dark of the moon, King Warren of Westerland Keep strode drunkenly out of the tavern in Daffydsdale and towards the castle gate. He was singing raucous and bawdy songs as he wove and stumbled on his way, but as he walked along the tone of his songs began to reflect the anger he felt towards his situation. Who would be there to stop him from singing the traitorous and vengeful words anyway, he thought through the mist of his drink-clouded mind? Arthur Pendragon was a weakling, a usurper of the throne of Britain, he thought on, so he deserved anything bad that happened to him. Warren staggered on, unaware that two separate sets of eyes watched him from opposite parapets, one pair gray, and one pair dragon-green.

"His time has come, O Black Hunter. Obey the commands of Ceridwen and slay the traitor Warren of Westerland, lest he plot new evil against the Pendragon!" the Black Hunter heard in the depths of his mind.

Unaware that he was being observed, the ebon-clad archer sighed softly; he had not heard Ceridwen's voice for some time. He drew the black arrow and sighted down its length at the staggering Warren. The man wove so it was difficult for Ceridwen's archer to keep his target in focus. Warren fell to his knees suddenly, calling out for Marcus to come and help him. Those were the King of Westerland's last words, for the black arrow whistled out of the night and into the base of his throat, severing the great veins in the neck. One single gurgle was all that could Warren manage before he fell over into the ever-widening pool of his own life-blood.

"Take him, Mother, his blood is forfeit to thee," the Black Hunter whispered, then gathered up his gear and quickly made his way down from the heights. He was completely oblivious to the fact that other eyes had seen it all. Those eyes now crinkled discerningly as the Black Hunter retrieved his precious arrowhead, leaving the shaft in Warren's throat and a token pinned to his cloak. A smile creased the observer's face before the figure departed into the night. The Black Hunter, however, waited until Prince Marcus made his belated appearance at the scullery door of Westerland, a candle lamp in one hand, a sword in the other.

"Da? Da, are ye out there?" he called out in a quavering voice.

"Nay, Marcus of Westerland. Ye are the last son of Warren, that makes ye the inheritor of Westerland Keep. See that ye live by the King's Law from now on and that ye rule justly and fairly, otherwise, his fate will be yers!" the Black Hunter's voice echoed from somewhere. Marcus' lamp finally lit upon Warren's sprawled body and the blood around him.

"Mother, come quickly, 'tis Da!" Marcus screamed in panic.

The young man dropped his lamp and weapon in his haste to return to the safety of the castle walls. The Black Hunter made his escape, returning to Camelot just as false dawn broke. He went right to the King's quarters with his report, sounding his signature knock on the door.

"Aye, just a moment." the King's voice answered alertly.

His footsteps could be heard crossing the room before the door opened, just a bit. "Good morning, My Lord Pendragon," the Black Hunter greeted, still in hooded mask. "I have something very important to discuss with you, alone," he stressed the last word meaningfully.

"Come in, I am quite alone, I assure ye," Arthur invited, sighing. "I was just pouring caffe, would ye care for some?" he added, opening the door a bit wider to admit the man. Arthur locked the door immediately as the Black Hunter crossed the room and poured a cup for himself, adding enough honey to suit his taste.

"Ye should expect a messenger from Westerland Keep today, My Lord. He will be carrying the news that King Warren ap Daffyd of Westerland Keep is dead. Demands for an investigation will surely follow. I tell ye straight, My Lord, the Goddess Herself called for his death by the black arrow," he went on.

"Are ye certain, Black Hunter?" Arthur asked, wanting to be sure.

"Aye, My Lord Pendragon. On my oath to Ceridwen, I vow that I did not take personal revenge on Warren."

"Very well then, one does not question the Goddess Ceridwen's commands, I know," Arthur replied reassuringly.

"I am sorry to have distressed ye so early in the morning My Lord Pendragon, but Warren's death was by the Goddess' command," the Black Hunter said.

"I believe ye, Sir Knight," answered Arthur. "Thank ye for coming to me directly and immediately. I shall exonerate the Black Knight, of course, after an appropriate investigation."

"Thank ye, My Lord, and good morning," the Black Hunter said as he put down his empty cup and left the room.

Arthur shut the oak door, crossed to his liquor cabinet and withdrew the crock of Orkney whiskey. He poured a generous glug into his cup and drank it straight down. Dressing carefully, he washed out his mouth with a special herb mixture that sweetened the breath before calling for Sir Cai, Sir Bedwyr and Sir Lancelot to attend him. When Marcus arrived from Westerland, he found the King in council with the three most senior Knights presently in residence at Camelot.

"Of course, the matter will be investigated thoroughly, Prince Marcus," Arthur assured the distraught young man. "But I tell ye straight, the Black Knight has not yet once dispatched anyone who was not a traitor of some kind. Are ye sure ye wish for a full Crown investigation of the situation?"

"We have naught to hide from an impartial tribunal, Sire," Marcus snuffled noisily.

"Very well then Prince Marcus, or should I say, King Marcus of Westerland?" Arthur nodded thoughtfully. "Sir Bedwyr, will ye head up this tribunal?"

"Of course, Sire." Bedwyr agreed readily, already anticipating delving into Westerland's dirty laundry.

The tribunal wrapped up in a month, with the testimony offered by long lines of former farmers and other common folk being the most damaging of all offered during the inquest. In the end, the Black Knight's actions were defended and Ceridwen's justice was proven. Reparation was ordered by the Crown to those who suffered under Warren's lustful appetite, much to the despair of Justine and Marcus, who moaned for months that they were ruined.

A week before the royal couple's wedding anniversary, the Queen paid Sir Cai a surprise visit, begging his assistance to help plan a huge celebration. A shocked, but pleased Sir Cai was delighted, for he had been thinking along the same lines as the Queen. Also, he had made certain inquiries among the Knights as for a suitable lady to relieve Arthur's stress at being parted from the Queen. When she came to him, he forgot all the arrangements he was making for Arthur's bed, instead plunging full steam into planning the party with Gwenhyfar, which included moving her back into the royal suite. Arthur came back from hunting with Aaronn and Olran to find a radiant but hesitant Gwenhyfar awaiting him, an apology on her lips.

"I thank ye, my husband, for yer patience," she finished at length. "Again, I have acted the fool and still ye keep me to wife."

"I am glad to have ye again at my side in all things, Gwen," Arthur told her gently and took her into his arms, inwardly thanking the Goddess for his wife's change of heart.

"And here, gentle people, ends this tale of the Black Knight of Avalon. There are many tales yet to tell of his deeds, but not tonight," the storyteller yawned hugely. "I must rest, as ye should also. Tomorrow night, there will be more stories of the Black Knight and the Knights of Camelot, if ye wish for me to continue the tale. Sleep ye sound, my children," he blessed them.

The village leader invited the man to a bed in his home. Gratefully the old man thanked him and went with him to the humble and cozy home. Soon, the village slept under the Goddess' watchful, loving eyes.

Made in the USA
Monee, IL
11 November 2020